GW01605639

THE ESCHATON SEQUENCE

Other Books by Frederik Pohl

BIPOHL
The Age of the Pussyfoot
Drunkard's Walk
Black Star Rising
The Cool War

THE HEECHEE SAGA
Gateway
Beyond the Blue Event Horizon
Heechee Rendezvous
The Annals of the Heechee
The Gateway Trip

With Jack Williamson:
The Starchild Trilogy
Undersea City
Undersea Quest
Undersea Fleet
Wall Around a Star
The Farthest Star
Land's End
The Singers of Time

With Lester del Rey:
Preferred Risk

With C. M. Kornbluth:
The Space Merchants

Homegoing
Mining the Oort
Narabedla, Ltd.
Pohlstars
Starburst
The Way the Future Was (memoir)
The World at the End of Time
Jem
Midas World
The Merchants' War
The Coming of the Quantum Cats
Man Plus
Chernobyl
The Day the Martians Came
Stopping at Slowyear
The Voices of Heaven
O Pioneer!

The Best of Frederik Pohl (edited by Lester del Rey)

The Best of C. M. Kornbluth (editor)

N SEQUENCE

.nd of Time

of Eternity

ore of Time

K POHL

A TOM DOHERTY ASSOCIATES BOOK

New York

Publishing History: Tor hardcover, October 1996
Tor paperback, July 1997

Publishing History: Tor hardcover, November 1997
Tor paperback, October 1998

Publishing History: Tor hardcover, June 1999

First SFBC Science Fiction Printing: July 1999

Published by arrangement with:
Tor Books
Tom Doherty Associates
175 Fifth Avenue
New York, NY 10010

Visit The SFBC online at *http://www.sfbc.com*
Visit Tor's online at *http://www.tor.com*

ISBN: 0-7394-0506-3

PRINTED IN THE UNITED STATES OF AMERICA

Contents

THE ESCHATON SEQUENCE

THE OTHER END OF TIME

Before

When the first message from space arrived on Earth, five people who were on their way to the eschaton were busy at their own affairs. For one, Dr. Pat Adcock was having a really bad day with her accountant in New York. For another, Commander (or, actually, by then already ex-Commander) Jimmy Peng-tsu Lin was on the lanai of his mother's estate on Maui, glumly running up his mother's telephone bill with fruitless begging calls to every influential person he knew. Major General Martín Delasquez had just been given his second star by the high governor of the sovereign state of Florida. Doctorat-nauk *(emeritus) Rosaleen Artzybachova was discontentedly trying to make the time pass with chess-by-fax games against a variety of opponents from her boring retirement dacha outside of Kiev. And Dan Dannerman was holed up in a seedy pension in Linz, Province of Austria. He was hiding from the* Bundes Kriminalamt *with a woman named Ilse, who was by profession an enforcer for the terrorist Free Bavaria Bund, more commonly referred to as the Mad King Ludwigs. (Dannerman himself was a mere courier in the same group.) Most of these five people had not even met each other yet. Pat Adcock, being an astronomer by profession, might conceivably have had some rough idea of how the message would affect all their lives—though even she couldn't have known just how, or how very much. None of the others could have had a clue.*

All the same, all five of them were, in varying degrees, startled, thrilled or frightened by the message, because nearly everybody in the world was. What would you expect? It was a major historical event. It was definitely the very first time that the patient astronomers who tended the SETI telescopes, or for that matter anybody else, had received an authentic, guaranteed alien message from an extraterrestrial source.

Of course, that left a lot of large questions. Not even the few dogged hangers-on in the nearly extinct SETI program had been able to interpret what the message said, either, except for a few fragments. The dits and dahs of the radio signal were not Morse code. They were certainly not in English, either—were not, in fact, in any recognizable language of any variety; unless pictures are considered to be a language of sorts. When the signals had been painstakingly massaged by some of the world's biggest and fastest computers, which they naturally were very quickly, it turned out that at least one chunk of the message wasn't in words at all. It was in pictures. When the bits were properly arranged, what they displayed was an animated diagram.

In their hideout on the Bonnerstrasse, Dannerman and his girl watched it over and over on their wall screen, Dannerman with curiosity, Ilse with only cursory attention. She was one of the very few who didn't give a hoot in hell what the stars had to say. Even her cursory interest didn't last, since whatever this bit of drek from space was meant to convey, she declared, it certainly had nothing whatever to do with the unswerving determination of the Mad King Ludwigs to free Bavaria from the cruel Prussian grip—to which liberation at any cost, she reminded him, they had both agreed to dedicate their lives.

As a matter of fact, the diagram really wasn't much to look at. That didn't keep the channels from repeating it endlessly, usually with some voice-over commentary provided by somebody who possessed several scientific degrees and a passion for seeing himself on TV. The commentaries varied, but the diagram was always the same. First the screen was dark, except for one tiny brilliant spot in the middle of it. Then an explosion sent a myriad smaller, less bright spots flying in all directions. The expansion slowed, followed by a general contraction as all the specks slowly, then more rapidly, fell back to the center of the screen. Then the central bright spot reappeared . . . and then the commentators took over.

"Unquestionably there is much more to the message," one said—this one an elderly Herr Doktor *from the astronomy department of the University of Vienna, "but we cannot decipher the remainder as yet. That is a great pity, since as you see the diagram by itself is quite uninformative in the absence of the rest of the message. This segment, by itself, is no more than perhaps five per cent of the total transmission, merely the first few seconds. We have not been able to decode the rest. Still, I believe I can interpret what that fragment is intended to show. It is nothing less than a description of the history of our universe, compressing to a few*

seconds a process which in fact will require many tens of billions of years. The model begins by showing the tiny and—I must confess, even to those of us who have given our lives to the subject—the quite incomprehensible quantal-realm object that preceded the birth of the universe. Then the object explodes, in what is called the Big Bang, and the universe as we know it begins. It expands—as we actually do see the universe doing now, when we measure the red-shifts with our telescopes. Finally it contracts again in what the Americans call the 'Big Crunch.' "

"Big Crunch! What nonsense. Come to bed now," Ilse said crossly. "You have seen all that a hundred times at least, Walter."

"You don't have to call me by my party name here," Dannerman said absently, watching the screen. The Herr Doktor *had begun talking about Stephen Hawking's theory of repetitive universes, just as he had the last three times Dannerman had watched that particular interview.*

"Do not tell me what to do. You are a dilettante," she said severely, "or you would not say a thing like that. It is basic doctrine, which you have not adequately studied: There is no security ever unless there is security always."

"I suppose so," he said, his attention still on the screen. He switched channels until he found the diagram on another newscast.

"You are impossible," she told him. "At least turn down that totally useless sound. I am going to sleep."

"Fine," he said, but he did as she asked. He didn't look away from the wall screen, however, in spite of the fact that he was beginning to be as tired of the damn thing as she. What Dannerman wanted was something different. He wanted her to go to sleep without him; and when at last her gentle, ladylike snores assured him that that had happened he moved silently to the door, collecting his down jacket on the way, and slipped out.

He wasn't gone long, but when he came back Ilse was sitting on the edge of the bed, arms crossed, wide awake, greeting him with a glare. She was quite a pretty woman most of the time, but, in this mood, not. "Where were you?" she demanded.

He said apologetically, "I just wanted some fresh air."

"Fresh air? In Linz?"

"Well, a change of scene, anyway. And, all right, I stopped in the bierstube *for a drink. What do you want from me, Ilse—I mean, Brunnhilde? I get tired of being jailed twenty-four hours a day in this dump."*

"Dump! Your words show your class origins, Walter. In any case, what I want from you is proper dedication to our cause. Also, if you

were seen you would become far more tired, because in five minutes they would have you in a real jail."

"Hell, uh, Brunnhilde. The Bay-Kahs aren't looking for us in Austria, are they? Anyway, that was part of the reason I went out. I wanted to see if anybody was watching the pension. Nobody is."

"And how would you know if they were, dilettante? Security is my task, not yours, Walter. Did you telephone anyone?"

"Why would I go outside to telephone?" he asked reasonably. It wasn't a lie; Dan Dannerman preferred not to lie when a simple deception would do.

"So." She studied him for a moment; then, "All the same," she said, softening slightly, "you are not entirely wrong. I too would like to leave this place. It is in Bavaria that we are needed, not here."

"We'll be there soon," he said, trying to make her feel better. The funny part was that he did want her to feel better. All right, the woman was a criminal terrorist, a known killer with blood on her hands, but he had to admit to himself that he was—almost—fond of her anyway. He had noticed that about himself before. He often came to like the people he put in prison, though that didn't keep him from putting them there anyway.

He reached for the control for the wall screen, and Ilse moaned. "Oh, my God, you are not going to turn that on again? It is not of any importance to us."

"It's just interesting," he said apologetically.

"Interesting! We have no room in our lives for what is only 'interesting'! Walter, Walter. Sometimes I think you are not a true revolutionary at all."

Of course, she did not know then just how right she was about that, and by the time she found out much had happened. For one thing, the second message from space had arrived. That was the one that showed the furry, Hallowe'en-grinning scarecrow creature with the twelve sharp talons on each fist crushing the Big Crunch in his paw, and, one after another, the seven other aliens, picture-in-picture like little cameos surrounding a central figure, that went with it.

No one knew quite what to make of it, though there were plenty of speculations. In their nightclub routines the world's standup comics had a wonderful time with this brand-new material. It was one of them who christened the seven peripheral aliens the "Seven Dwarfs," and another who claimed that the whole message was either an alien polit-

ical broadcast or part of some ET children's horror animation film, inadvertently transmitted to all the billions of nonpaying viewers on Earth. The more easily frightened scientists—plus every buck-hustling guru of every bizarre religious cult in the world—thought it was more likely to be some kind of a warning.

They didn't know just how astonishingly right they were, either.

For all of the persons involved, by that time a great deal had changed in their personal lives as well. Dan Dannerman, having finished his assignment with the Mad King Ludwigs, was busily infiltrating a dope ring in New York City. And Ilse, glumly marching around the exercise yard of the maximum-security prison at Darmstadt, was cursing the day she'd ever met the man.

1
Dan

When Jim Daniel Dannerman heard the WHEEP-*wawp* of the police sirens, he was on the way from his family lawyer's office to his cousin's observatory to beg for a job. The sirens gave him a moment's confusion, so that for the blink of an eye he could not remember which one he was going to see, the autocratic career woman who was the head of the Dannerman Astrophysical Observatory or the five-year-old girl who had peed her pants in the tree house on his uncle's estate. He was also already en route to the eschaton, though, to be sure, with a weary long way still to go. He didn't know that was true yet, of course. He had never heard of the eschaton then, and after the first moment he didn't pay much attention to the sirens, either. City people didn't. Cop chases were a normal part of the urban acoustic environment, and anyway Dannerman was busy accessing information that might come in handy on his new assignment. He had been listening to the specs of the Starcophagus, the abandoned astronomical satellite that had suddenly seemed to become important to the Bureau, when the shriek of the stop-all-traffic alarm drowned everything else out. Every light turned red, and he was thrown forward as the taxi driver slammed on the brakes.

Every other vehicle at that intersection was doing the same thing, because the ugly stop-all enforcer spikes were already thrusting up out of the roadway. In the front of the cab his driver cursed and pounded the wheel. "Goddam cops! Goddam spikes! Listen, they blow one more set of tires on me and I swear to God I'm gonna get rid of this crappy little peashooter I been carrying and get me a *real* gun. And then I'm gonna take that gun and—"

Dannerman stopped listening before she got to the ways in which she was going to take the city's police system on single-handed. He was watching the drama being played out at the intersection. The car that was being pursued had tried to make it through the intersection in spite of the spikes, and naturally every tire had been stabbed flat; the three youths inside had spilled out and tried to get away on foot, dodging among the jam of stalled vehicles. They weren't going to make it, though. Police were coming at them on foot from all directions. The running cops were weighed down by radio, sting-stick, crowd-control tear-gas gun, assault gun and body armor, but there were too many of them for the criminals. The police had the kids well surrounded. Dannerman watched the fugitives being captured with mild professional interest—after all, he was in the law-enforcement business himself, sort of.

His driver perked up a little. "Looks like they got 'em. Listen, mister, I'm sorry about the delay, but they'll have the spikes down again any minute now—"

Dannerman said, "No problem. I've got time before my appointment."

It didn't placate her. "Sure, you've got time, but what about me? I'm stuck trying to make a goddam living in this goddam town—"

The thing was, she had one of those Seven Stupid Alien figures hanging from her rearview mirror and it was singing out of its picochip the whole time she was talking, a shrill obbligato behind her hoarse complaints. That wasn't particularly odd. There were pictures of the aliens all over the place. On the kids being arrested, belly-down on the pavement: the backs of their jackets displayed little cartoon figures of the alien they called Sneezy—gang colors, those were; but even his lawyer's secretary had had a coffee mug in the shape of another on her desk. The taxi driver's singing good-luck piece was the fat one named Sleepy, for its half-closed eyes—well, there were three of the eyes, actually, on a head that was maned like a lion's. It wasn't much like the ancient Disney original, but then neither were the secretary's Doc or the gangbangers' Sneezy.

It was an odd thing, when you thought about it, that the hideous space aliens had become children's toys and everybody's knickknacks. Colonel Hilda had had an explanation for it. It was like the dinosaurs of a generation or two earlier, she told him on the phone: something so horrible and dangerous that people had to translate it into something cuddly, because otherwise it was too frightening. Then she had gone on to tell him that the space message might, or might not, be relevant to his new assignment, but it wasn't his job to ask questions about it, it was his job only to close out his assignment to the Carpezzios' drug ring and get cracking on the new job.

It wasn't the first time she'd explained all that to him, either, because that was the way it was in the NBI.

That, of course, Dannerman didn't need to be told. After thirteen years in the National Bureau of Investigation, he knew the drill.

The funny thing was that Dannerman had never set out to be a spook. When the college freshman Jim Daniel Dannerman signed up for the Police Reserve Officers Training Corps he was nineteen years old, and the last thing in his mind was the choice of a career. What he was after was a couple of easy credit hours, while he went about the business of preparing himself for a career in live theater. He hadn't read the fine print. All the way through his undergraduate program and even in graduate school it had meant nothing but a couple of hours a week in his reserve uniform, plus a few weekends; By the time he did read it—very carefully, this time—it was his last day of graduate school, and he had just received his orders to report for active duty.

By then, of course, it was a lot too late to change his mind. But it hadn't been a bad life. When you worked for the Bureau you went to interesting places and you got to meet a lot of interesting people. The downside was that sometimes you had a pretty good chance of getting killed by some of those interesting people, but so far he'd been lucky about that.

The other downside was that when you had to go under cover there was always the problem of remembering all the lies about who you were and where you'd been all your life. That was one of the things that made the new assignment look pretty good. As the colonel had explained, the only identity he had to assume was his own. Indeed, the fact that he was a sort of relative of the person under investigation was what made him the best choice for the job.

Dannerman snapped off the portable and leaned back, closing his eyes. He hardly noticed when the traffic jam began to dissolve, because he was working out just what he wanted to say in the interview with his cousin. There wasn't much doubt that he would get the job he was going to apply for—the lawyer had all but promised that. Dannerman was pretty sure the old man meant it, if only because he had a little bit of a guilty conscience over Dannerman's lost inheritance. But it would be embarrassing if he was turned down. He was surprised when the taxi stopped. "Here you are, mister," the driver said, friendlier now when tipping time was near. She pulled the slip with the ten-o'clock fare update out of the meter and handed it to him, peering over his shoulder at the plaque over the building door. "Hey. What's this T. Cuthbert Dannerman Astrophysical Observatory business? I thought telescopes were, you know, like on the top of a mountain someplace."

Dannerman glanced at the midtown skyscraper that housed the observatory and grinned at the woman. "Actually," he said as he paid the bill, "until this morning, so did I."

Time was, indeed, when astronomers shared the night with the bats and the burglars, huddling their freezing buns in drafty domes on the tops of snow-clad mountains. If they wanted to peer far into space, they had no choice. That was where the telescopes were. That was time past. In time present the camera had made the all-night vigils unnecessary. The spread of electronic communication and control exempted the astronomers from having even to show up anywhere near their telescopes—and the best of the world's telescopes, or at least the ones of that kind that were still working, weren't where they were easy to visit anyway. Like the Starcophagus, they were in orbit. But wherever the data came from, they arrived—processed, enhanced, computerized, digitalized—at an observatory comfortably located in some civilized place.

Uncle Cubby's final gift to the world of astronomy occupied the top floors of the building, but of course there were turnstiles and guards between the street door and the elevators. Dannerman presented himself at the lobby desk and announced his name. That drew interest from the guard. "You a relative?" he asked.

"Nephew," Dannerman admitted. "Mr. Dixler made an appointment for me to see Dr. Adcock."

"Yes, sir," the guard said, suddenly deferential. "I'll have to ask you to wait over there until someone can show you to Dr. Adcock's office. It'll just be a moment."

It wasn't just a moment, though. Dannerman hadn't expected that it would be. The observatory's private elevator doors opened and closed a dozen times before a large, sullen man came out and lumbered over to the holding pen. He was not deferential at all. "You the guy from Dixler, J. D. Dannerman? Show me some ID." He didn't offer to shake hands. When he had checked the card he passed Dannerman through the turnstiles and into an elevator, and only then introduced himself. "I'm Mick Jarvas, Dr. Adcock's personal assistant. Give me your gun."

Dannerman took his twenty-shot from his shoulder holster and passed it over. "Do I get a receipt?"

The man looked at the weapon with contempt. “I’ll remember where I got it, don’t worry. Who’s this Dixler?”

“Family lawyer.”

“Huh. Okay. Wait here. Janice’ll tell you when you can go in.” That ended the conversation, and Dannerman was left to sit in the waiting room. It didn’t bother him. It gave him a chance to see what a modern astrophysical observatory was like. This one wasn’t like the mountain-top domes he remembered from his childhood. It was full of people glimpsed down corridors, elderly men talking to young dark-skinned women in saris, groups drinking Cokes or herbal tea out of the machines, a couple of people sharing the waiting room with him and improving their waiting time by talking business on their pocket phones. What interested him most was the big liquid-crystal screen behind the receptionist’s desk. It was showing a great pearly mural that he recognized as a picture of a galaxy, some galaxy or other; switched to a picture of what he took to be an exploding star; switched again to a huge photograph of an orbiting observatory. He had no trouble recognizing that. It was the one he had been studying on the way over; it was also, he was aware, the gift that had eaten up half of Uncle Cubby’s fortune before he died. The observatory was Starlab—sometime uncharitably called Starcophagus, for the dead astronomer who was still orbiting inside it. Starlab was the ancient, biggest and best—but unfortunately no longer operational—astronomical orbiter of them all.

Dan Dannerman’s only previous experience of an astronomical facility had been when he was four years old and his father had taken him to visit Uncle Cubby in the old optical observatory in Arizona. Starlab was quite different, and all the engineering specs he’d been able to dig out of the databank didn’t make it real for him. Getting up, he strolled over to the reception desk and cleared his throat. “Janice? I mean, I don’t know your last name—”

“Janice is good enough,” she said agreeably. “And you’re Mr. Dannerman.”

“Dan. I noticed you were showing the Starcophagus on the wall a minute ago—” She had begun shaking her head. “Is something wrong?”

“Dr. Adcock doesn’t like us ever to use that word here. It’s the Dannerman Astrophysical Starlab. Mostly we just call it Starlab.”

“Thanks,” he said, meaning it; it was a useful bit of information for someone who was about to ask the boss for a favor.

“It used to be the Dannerman Orbiting Astrolab,” she went on, looking him over, “but Dr. Adcock changed that. Because of, you know, the initials.”

"Oh, right," he said, nodding. "DOA. I see what you mean. I guess nobody wants to be reminded about the dead guy up there. Anyway, I was wondering if you could fill me in a little bit. I understand, uh, Dr. Adcock's trying to get a mission flown to reactivate it."

"There's talk," she admitted cautiously.

"Well, when's that going to happen, do you know?"

"No idea," she said cheerfully. "You'd have to ask Dr. Adcock about that—wait a minute." She paused, squinting as she listened to the voice in her earpiece, and paid no further attention to him.

He went back and sat down. Evidently he was to be kept waiting for a while, as was appropriate for someone who wanted to ask a favor. He didn't mind. It was what he had expected from a cousin-by-marriage he hadn't seen for years, and wouldn't be seeing now if the Bureau had not taken a sudden and serious interest in just what the woman was up to.

2
Pat

Dr. Pat Adcock's morning was pure hell—crises in the money problem and the Starlab problem, not to mention all the usual flurry of regular observatory problems—but she took the long way from the bursar's office to Rosaleen Artzybachova's anyhow. That way passed by the reception room, and that let her get a quick look at her waiting cousin Dan.

She let him wait. She was impatient to hear what Rosaleen had to tell her about Starlab's instrumentation. Then the bursar had had no good news for her, and she needed to do a little thinking about that. She needed, too, to think about whether she wanted to go out of her way, at this particularly hectic time, to find some kind of spot on the staff for her job-seeking cousin. It was not a good time to be adding to the payroll. On the other hand—

On the other hand, family was family, and Pat wasn't displeased to have one of her few remaining relatives ask for a favor. Especially when the relative was Dan Dannerman. So she rushed through her meeting with Rosaleen Artzybachova, door closed and electronics off; the woman might be old but she was still sharp, and she was doing a good job of tracing the history of all the additions and retrofits Starlab had suffered in its observing career. "And there's nothing that would account for the radiation?" Pat demanded. "You're sure?"

The old lady looked up at her thoughtfully. "Are you getting enough exercise?" she asked. "You look like you could use some fresh air. Yes, I'm sure."

"Thanks," Pat said, not answering her question. But when she got back to her own office the first thing she did, even before she closed the door, was to study herself in the wall mirror. It wasn't really exercise she needed, she told herself. It was rest. A good night's sleep, for a start, and no worries. But what were the chances of that?

While Pat's office door was open the walls were displaying a selection of the major current projects of the observatory: the Lesser Magellanic Cloud, with its new gamma-ray bursters; the huge mass of neutral gas in Capricorn that Warren Krepps was investigating; and, just for the sake of prettiness, some particularly nice shots of nearby objects like Saturn, Phobos and the Moon. Those weren't really high-priority projects. The Dannerman Observatory didn't do much planetary astronomy, but the pictures were the kind of thing that impressed possible donors when, after leading them through the grand tour of the observatory, Pat took them into her office for the glass of wine and the kill.

When Pat closed her privacy door the display changed. Then what the walls showed was Starlab, and, on either side of it, like a portrait gallery, the images of the aliens from the space message. Pat didn't look at the freaks as she settled herself at her desk. She didn't need to; but she wanted them there, to remind her.

Time for Cousin Dan? She decided not; it wouldn't hurt him to sit a while longer, and there was still the business of the observatory to run. It took more than science to keep an enterprise like the Dannerman Observatory going.

After her name Patrice Dannerman Bly Metcalf Adcock was entitled to put the initials B.S., M.A., Ph.D., D.H.L. and Sc.D. Considering that she was still a young woman, not very much more than thirty (and looking younger still when she got enough sleep), that was quite a lot. To be sure, the last two degrees were honorary, being the kind of thing you got from small and hungry universities when you happened to be the head of an institution that might offer useful fellowships to underemployed faculty members, but she had truly earned all the rest.

The trouble was, they weren't enough. Why hadn't someone told her to slip a couple of economics and business-management classes in among the cosmologies and the histories of science? Her skills at reading a spectrogram were all very well, but what she really needed to understand was a spreadsheet.

And this morning, like most mornings, the problems were mostly money. Kit Papathanassiou was requesting twenty hours of observing time on the big Keck telescopes in Hawaii. Pat knew that Papathanassiou would make good use of the time, but the Kecks were a big-ticket item; she cut it to five hours. Gwen Morisaki wanted to hire another postdoc to help out with the Cepheid census in NGC 3821; but that job only amounted to counting, after all, and why did you need a doctoral degree for that? Cousin Dan? Probably not, Pat thought, and decided to offer Gwen an undergraduate intern from one of the local schools. That wouldn't save much money. You could hardly hire anybody for less than the average postdoc would gladly accept, but a dollar saved, plus its cost-of-living adjustment, was a dollar plus COLA earned. This month's communications bills were higher than ever; Pat reluctantly came to the conclusion that it was time for her to get on everybody's back again about keeping the phone bills down. She didn't look forward to it. Hassling the staff to watch pennies was not what she had earned all those degrees for. Maybe, if things got better—the way she dreamed they might, if the Starlab thing worked out . . .

But it was all taking so *long*.

That was a big disappointment. Pat had hoped that once the judge decreed that the feds were obliged to honor the contract Uncle Cubby had made with them—had to provide a Clipper spacecraft to take a repair mission to Starlab and, what's more, had to pay for putting the old spacecraft into working order—why, then, the whole thing should have been automatic. It wasn't. The feds and the Floridians were dragging their feet. Somehow somebody somewhere in their bureaucracies had begun to suspect that she knew something they didn't.

Well, she did. And it was none of their damn business.

She leaned back and studied the pictures on the wall. Not the Starlab itself. She didn't need to look at that again; with Rosaleen Artzybachova's help she had already memorized every centimeter of that. What she was looking at was the freak show from the space messages. There were eight of the aliens, starting with the universe-crushing scarecrow, and every one of them was ugly. One looked like Pat's idea of a golem, huge bipedal body with some arms like elephant limbs and some like limp spaghetti, and the bearded head with its glaring eyes; that was the one the comics called "Doc." Another—the "Grumpy"—looked a little like a sea horse with legs; a third, the "Dopey," had a whiskered kitten's head on a chicken's body; another might have been a huge-eyed lemur if it weren't for its own extra pairs of limbs, and she couldn't recall what nonsensical name it had been given.

Pat closed her eyes and sighed. She wished, as half the world wished, that she knew why the unidentified transmitter of these unpleasing pictures had wanted humans to see them. What were these creatures? Not a zoo; these were not animals; most of them wore clothing, some carried artifacts of one kind or another—some that looked unpleasantly like weapons.

Of course, the fact that they had weapons didn't mean they were killers. Everybody carried weapons. Pat kept one on her person whenever she left her office or her home—not counting whatever additional firepower her bodyguard carried—and she certainly wasn't intending to shoot anybody. Unless, of course, she absolutely had to.

Which raised the question of under what circumstances the freaks might think they absolutely had to; but she didn't want to think about that. Pat Adcock had considered the possibility that some of those alien creatures might be hanging around somewhere in Earth orbit, where the mission to Starlab might encounter them, and decided that the odds were strongly against. There wasn't any reason to reconsider that question now—most likely.

She opened her eyes and looked at her watch.

Actually, she had kept Cousin Dan waiting long enough. She pushed the button that transformed her desk screen to a mirror, checked her hair and her face—yes, still not bad, in spite of what Rosaleen had said—then sighed, pushed the control that unlocked her door and restored her wall display to the one she was willing to let the world see and called the receptionist. "My cousin still out there, Janice? All right, then send him on in."

3
Dan

When Dannerman entered his cousin's office they didn't kiss. Nor did they shake hands, and she didn't even look up at him. Her attention was on her desk screen, displaying the resumé he had given Mr. Dixler to send over. "Says here you've got a Ph.D.—but it's in English literature, for Christ's sake? What the hell does Dixler think we're going to do with an English major here? Do you know anything at all about astronomy?"

"Not a thing," he said cheerfully, studying her: blue eyes, rusty brown hair, yes, that was the cousin he remembered, though now physically well matured. She was wearing a white lab coat, but it hung open. Under it was a one-piece skorts outfit, thermally dilated to adjust to room temperatures. She kept her office warm, so a lot of Pat Adcock showed through the mesh. At thirty-something she was almost as good-looking as pretty little Patty D. Bly had been when they were children; two marriages and a career had just made her taller and even more sure of herself. "I just happen to need a job pretty badly," he added.

She finally looked up to regard him thoughtfully, then smiled. "Anyway, hello. It's been a long time, Dan-Dan."

"It's just Dan now that I've grown up, Cousin Pat."

"And it's just *Doctor* Adcock if you're going to work here," she reminded him, a touch of steel peeking through the velvet. "I don't know about hiring you, though, Dan. It says here you got your doctorate at Harvard and your dissertation was called 'Between Two Worlds: Freud and Marx in the Plays of Elmer Rice.' Who the hell was he?"

"Early-twentieth-century American playwright. Very seminal for Broadway theater. Some people called him the American Pirandello."

"Huh." She studied his face. "Are you still stagestruck?"

"Not really. Oh, there's a little theater group in Brooklyn I help out now and then—"

"Christ."

"It wouldn't interfere with my work," he promised.

She gave him an unconvinced look, but changed the subject. "So Dixler wants me to give you a job here. I was surprised when he called; I thought you weren't speaking to him."

Dannerman shifted uncomfortably. "You mean about Uncle Cubby's estate. Well, I wasn't, but I thought the least he could do was put in a word for me with you."

She was gazing at the screen again. "What happened to the job you had with, it says here, Victor Carpezzio and Sons, Importers of Foods and Fragrances?"

"Personal problems. I didn't get along with the Carpezzios."

"And you've had—" She paused to count up. "Jesus, Dan, you've had four other jobs in the past few years. Are you going to quit here too because you don't like somebody?" He didn't answer that. "And you've been dicking around with little theater groups all over the place, not just in Brooklyn. I thought you were the kind of guy who went for the macho kind of thing."

"There's enough macho in the world already, Pat."

"Hum," she said again. Then, "All right, our mutual uncle gave a lot of money to found this observatory, that's a fact. But it doesn't mean we have to support the whole damn family."

"Of course not."

"If we decided to take a chance and we did give you a job for Uncle Cubby's sake, don't expect it would be anything big. You'd be getting minimum wage, daily COLA, no fringe benefits. This is a *scientific* establishment. We're all highly trained people. You just don't have the skills for anything better than scutwork."

"I understand, Dr. Adcock."

That made her laugh. "Oh, hell, Dan, I guess Pat's good enough. Considering we've known each other since we were in diapers. You don't bear any grudges, do you? About the money, I mean?" He shook his head. "I mean, you got as much as I did under Uncle Cubby's will."

"Not exactly."

"Well, you would have if you'd been around when the will was probated. Then the whole thing wouldn't've been eaten up by inflation by the time you collected it and you wouldn't be looking for a scutwork job now, would you? What were you doing in Europe anyway?"

"I guess you'd call it postdoctoral research," he said, coming reasonably close to an honest answer. The statement was technically true, at least; he really had had his doctorate by then and what he had been doing in Europe surely was research of a kind.

"And maybe there was a girl?"

"You could say a woman was involved," he admitted, again skirting the truth—Ilse was indeed female, and so was the colonel. "I guess I made a mistake, not keeping in touch."

"I guess you did. All right, I don't see why we shouldn't do old Dixler a favor—and you too, of course. We'll find you something to do. Go down to Security and get your badge and passes from Mick Jarvas. You can start tomorrow—but remember, you get no medical benefits, no tenure. You'll be a temp, hired on a week-to-week basis, and how long you stay depends on you. Or, actually, it will depend on me, because I'm the director here. Is that going to give you a problem?"

"No problem."

"It better not be a problem. I don't mix family loyalty and science. We've got a lot to do here right now, trying to get Starlab back on line and all. I don't want you thinking that the fact that we played together when we were babies is going to get you any special privileges."

Dannerman grinned, thinking about the kinds of games they'd played. "You're the boss, Pat," he said. But of course she'd been the boss then, too.

As soon as he was out of the building he paused before the window of a betting parlor to lift his commset to his lips and make his call. He didn't give a name. He didn't have to. All he said was, "Mission accomplished. I got the job."

"That's nice," the voice on the other end said chattily. "Congratulations. You've still got one thing to do with the other guys, though."

"I know. I'll phone it in when I get home."

"Make sure you do, Danno. Talk to you later."

On the subway ride home Dannerman pretended to watch the news on his communicator—the hot new story was that the President's press secretary had been kidnapped—but he wasn't paying it much attention. He was content with the day's work. To be sure, he didn't know exactly why he was going to work for his cousin, but he was reasonably sure he would be told in time. What he had to take care of with the Carpezzios wouldn't take long. And of course the eschaton, that ultimate transcendence, had never yet even crossed his mind.

4
Dan

The process of getting photographed and fingerprinted for the job had made Dannerman late leaving the observatory. It got even later; he got caught in the rush hour and the subways were running even slower than usual because of a bomb scare at the Seventy-second Street station. That meant the trains weren't allowed to stop there until the security police finished checking out whatever suspicious object was worrying them, so Dan Dannerman had to travel an extra stop north and make his way back on foot through the jammed sidewalk vendors along Broadway. The peddlers did their best to slow him down—"Hey, mon, here we have got tomorrow's top collectibles, get them today while the price is right!"—but Dannerman was interested only in food just then. By the time he'd picked up some groceries for his dinner and got home, all the other tenants had finished their meals. He had the condo's kitchen to himself.

He dumped his purchases on the kitchen table and began to cut up the vegetables for his stir-fry. While he was waiting for the rice to steam he tried to get some news on his landlady's old screen. All the stories looked very familiar. The only additions to the ones he'd heard on the subway were that a new serial killer seemed to be at large in the city, two senators were under indictment for embezzlement, the heavyweight boxing champion of the world had announced his plans to enter the priesthood, the President had received a ransom demand for his kidnapped press secretary and the time for the free-fire zone that the Law'n'Order Enforcers had announced for the Wall Street area had just expired, with only seven persons wounded. Nothing very interesting. Nothing about the possible bomb in the subway, even on the local menu; but then the services hardly bothered reporting that sort of thing anymore.

Stirring up the fry didn't take more than five minutes, but Rita Gammidge must have smelled it cooking from her room. "Evening, Danny," she said, appearing at the door as Dannerman was ladling it into his plate. "Um. Do I smell chorro sausages in there?"

Rita Gammidge was his landlady. Tiny, old, white-haired, quick and inquisitive, she owned the duplex condo where Dan rented his room—well, his half a room, if you went by the original layout. The condo was a valuable piece of property, originally eight big rooms and three baths; but Dannerman knew that the condo was also about the only thing Rita had saved out of what must once have been a considerable fortune before she, and a lot of others, were wiped out in the Big Devaluation. Dannerman did what was expected of him. "Join me," he invited. "There's plenty for two."

She hesitated. "If you're sure—?"

"I'm sure." There was. There always was; the rents Rita collected were barely enough to keep her ahead of the taxes and the maintenance charges, and so he made a point of cooking enough for both of them. He knew that the other thing she wanted from him was his day's rent, so they settled that before they began to eat.

"The good news," she said, ringing up her deposit, "is today's inflation adjustment was only two per cent."

He nodded, and remembered to tell her, "There's other good news. I've got a new job."

"Well, wonderful! Calls for a drink—let me supply the beer." She had unlocked the fridge and brought out a bottle from her private stock—one half-liter bottle for the two of them to share—before she thought to ask, "What was wrong with the job in import-export?"

"No future," he said. As was usual with most of the things he told people about himself, the statement was true enough; whatever future there had been with the importers had vanished when the colonel ordered him to drop it and try to hook on with his cousin. "The place I'm working for now is an astronomical observatory."

"Oh, boy! What, do you think there's money in looking for Martians?"

"There aren't any Martians, Rita, and anyway that isn't what we do." He explained to her, from his small and very recently acquired store of astronomical knowledge, that the Dannerman Observatory spent its time analyzing data about distant gas clouds and quasars, trying to puzzle out the origins of the universe. Then he had to explain why the observatory was called "Dannerman."

Rita approved of that. "It's good to have family, these days," she said, chewing wistfully. "You're close, you and your cousin?"

"Not really. She's not a blood relative. She was Uncle Cubby's wife's sister's daughter, and I was his younger brother's son."

"Even so," she said vaguely, and then commented: "You could have put a little more sausage in the fry."

"Nobody's making you eat it."

She didn't take offense. She didn't even seem to notice what he'd said. She went on dreamily, "We used to eat really well while Jonathan was alive—truffles, guinea hen, steaks you could cut with a fork. Oh, and roast beef, and rack of lamb, and three or four different wines at almost every meal. Dan, do you know we used to have as many as twenty-four at dinner some nights? We'd eat in the main dining hall—that's where the Rosenkrantzes and the Blairs live now—and we had the butler and the maids to hand everything around. If anybody wanted seconds, why, they could have as much as they wanted. There was plenty, and we didn't even mind when the servants took the leftovers home. And then, if the weather was nice, we'd go out on the terrace for coffee and brandy afterward."

"I don't have any coffee," Dannerman said, to keep her from getting her hopes up.

"Neither do I," she said, swallowing the last of her beer. "Thanks for dinner. I'll clean up—and, Dan? It's nice about your cousin, but this city's no place for a young man like you. You ought to get out of it while you can."

"And go where?" he asked. She didn't have any answer for that. She didn't even try.

Before Dannerman unlocked the door to his own room he checked the telltales. They were clear. No one had entered while he was out; his stock of collectibles was still intact, and so were the more important items concealed among them. He locked the door behind him and began his evening chores.

After Rita finished partitioning the condo for lodgers, her original eight rooms had become fourteen. Dan Dannerman had a windowless chamber that had once been a kind of dressing room to the condo's master bedroom, now occupied by the Halverson family of four. His part got the huge marble fireplace, but it was the Halversons who got the direct entrance to the bath; when Dan wanted to use it he had to go down the hall.

All in all, Dannerman would gladly have traded with the Halversons. He couldn't use the fireplace, because of pollution regulations, so it was just an annoyance that took up wall space he could have used for his personal stock of inflation hedges.

Those were the goods that people with jobs bought from the pitiful sidewalk vendors, the fixed-income people or the no-income people who were reduced to selling off their possessions to stay alive. It didn't matter what you bought. With daily inflation running at two or three per cent, sometimes more, anything you bought was bound to be worth more than you paid for it if you just held it for a while. It was part of Dannerman's cover to be just like everybody else who had a little spare cash, but not enough to put it into the good inflation hedges like option futures. He spent his surplus on collectibles as fast as he could. In Dannerman's personal store he had glass paperweights, small items of furniture—all he had room for in the tiny chamber—a Barbie doll from the 1988 issue in nearly mint condition, old flatscreen computers, bits of costume jewelry, CDs, optical disks and even magnetic tapes of music of all kinds. Of course, the stock in his room didn't represent all of his *real* capital, but since he couldn't admit what his real capital was he couldn't draw on it; the Bureau would hand it over to him, fully inflated with whatever the then-current cost-of-living adjustment might be, when he retired. Meanwhile, in times of unemployment Dannerman, too, had had to protect his cover by setting up a booth along Broadway and selling off goods.

He checked his watch and noted that it was time to take care of his last bit of business with the Carpezzios. He dialed the number, let it ring once; dialed again for two rings; then dialed again and waited for an answer. "Nobody's here but me," said the voice of their main shooter and watchman, Gene Martin.

"Shit," Dannerman said. He wasn't particularly disappointed, and not at all surprised—he had timed it for when none of the bosses would be in—but that was just the way you started most sentences around Carpezzio & Sons Flavors and Fragrances. "So take a message. I can't come in, I have to go to the dentist, but tell Wally he'll have to do the meet tonight himself."

"He'll be pissed," sighed Martin. "You got a toothache?"

"No, I just like to go to the dentist. See you later." And he would see him later, Dannerman thought, but not until it was time to testify at their arraignment, and they wouldn't be very sociable then.

That taken care of, he had chores to do. From behind a print-book set of *Lee's Lieutenants*—not a very good investment, really, but one of these days he intended actually to read the books—he pulled out his rods and cloths, turned on his room screen and switched his pocket phone over to the screen to check the day's messages while he cleaned his guns.

The messages were almost all junk, of course. That was what he expected; his pocket phone was set to record everything that came in as voicemail except for the ones from Hilda. He reminded himself to add calls from the observatory to the priority list, now that he had a job, and set himself to review the day's garbage accumulation. People wanted to cast his horoscope or sell him weapons. A men's-clothing store was inviting him to a private advance sale of the season's newest sportswear and impact-resistant undergarments. A real-estate office had forced-sale condos in Uptown to offer. A couple of news services urged him to subscribe; a finance company offered to lend him money at just one per cent over the COLA; in short, the usual. There were just two real calls. One was from the theater group in Brooklyn, and, although the caller didn't give a name, he recognized the voice: Anita Berman. The other was from the lawyer, Mr. Dixler. Both wanted him to return their calls, but he thought for a moment and decided against it. Dixler could wait. And Anita Berman—

Well, Anita was a separate problem, and Dannerman wasn't quite ready to deal with it. Thoughtfully he left the phone live, while he began cleaning his twenty-shot, considering the case of Anita Berman. She was a sweet lady, there was no doubt of that. She liked him very well, and that was for sure, too. But Hilda thought she was a security risk, and now with the new job Hilda was bound to think Anita was excess baggage.

That was going to be a pain, he thought, and then remembered that he still had homework to do. He put the cleaning materials back, coded the room screen for library access and, automatically wiping the sales messages as they came in in their little window at the corner of the screen, cued in the search he had begun in the taxi for data on *astronomy, orbital instruments.*

It took him only a moment to access once more the entries for the Dannerman Observatory's wholly owned satellite, Starlab.

There was a lot about Starlab that Dannerman had no need to retrieve from the databanks, because he clearly remembered when it had been launched. He had been only nine at the time, but his mother had taken him to Uncle Cubby's grand compound on the Jersey shore for the launch party. The whole family was there to watch the launch on television, Cousin Pat and her parents included, as well as a dozen famous astronomers and politicians, but while the astronomers and the politicians were thoroughly enjoying the party, Dannerman's mother had been a lot less thrilled. It was Uncle Cubby's fortune that paid for the satellite, as it was also Uncle Cubby's fortune that endowed the Dannerman Astrophysical Observatory a little later; and, while Starlab and the observatory were undoubtedly great contributions to astronomical science, what they represented to Uncle Cubby's heirs was a considerable depletion of the remaining fortunes they might someday expect to inherit.

Still, there was no doubt that Starlab had done great things for astronomy in its time. When it was built there was still money around to spend on pure science. It was designed to house a few actual living astronomers for weeks at a time as they took their spectra and their shift measurements. That part had been abandoned early, when it became too expensive to ship human beings up to orbit; the last of the visiting astronomers had died up there, and was still there. No one had been willing to spend the money to reclaim his body. But Starlab's instruments had gone on working for more than twenty years—

Until, three years earlier, they stopped. Just stopped. The transmissions ceased in the middle of a Cepheid count, and the satellite did not respond to commands from its surface controllers.

Dannerman put the screen on hold and got up to get a beer of his own from his private cooler. It all seemed pretty straightforward: satellites went out of commission every day, and the money to fix them got scarcer. Why was this one particularly interesting?

He meditated over that for a moment, sipping the beer and wiping the new messages as they arrived—until one came in, voice only but definitely the voice of a female, that said flirtatiously, "Hey, Danno! I hear you got a new job. Give me a call and let's see if we want to celebrate."

There wasn't any name on that one, either, but there didn't need to be. No one called him by the code name "Danno" but Colonel Hilda Morrisey.

A call from the colonel was not one he could answer on the open lines. Dannerman pulled down an old flatscreen converter from its place on his shelf and jacked it into his modem. Then he dialed the number he knew by heart. His screen instantly showed a bewildering fractal pattern of wedges and wriggling lines, until he cut in the 300-digit-prime synchronized-chaos decoder.

Then Colonel Hilda Morrisey was looking out at him, plump, dark, bright-eyed—just like always.

"Evening, Colonel honey," he said.

She didn't acknowledge the greeting. She didn't waste time on congratulating him on getting the job, either. "All right," she said, "cut the crap. Have you done your homework?"

"I sure have, Colonel honey, all you gave me, anyway. Starlab went out a few years ago so the observatory applied for a repair mission to fix it. Naturally nothing happened. The red tape—"

"Don't tell me about the red tape."

"Anyway, the application wasn't moving. There's no public support for space missions. Let's see, I think the latest polls show about seventy-four percent opposed to spending another dollar on it anywhere. How much of that is Bureau dirty tricks, do you suppose?"

"Never mind."

"Anyway, now, all of a sudden, my cousin Pat got hot. She took the government to court, and she won, but it still don't move. So now she's doing a lot of wheeling and dealing on her own."

"And spending serious money, right. Okay, look. I had hoped to have background checks for you on the people you'll be working with but, right now, with this President's press secretary thing, it's hard to get any action out of Washington. So far it looks like two of them are dirty—not counting your cousin. One's a bruiser named Mick Jarvas—"

"I've met the man."

"He's a doper; that might be useful. He used to be a professional kick-boxer, now he's your cousin's bodyguard; he stays with her wherever she goes, so he knows what she does outside the office. The other one's a Chink named Jimmy Peng-tsu Lin. He's an astronaut, or was until the People's Republic privatized its space program and he went freelance. He got in some political trouble in the People's Republic, too, but I don't know exactly what yet. That's all I've got so far. Any questions?"

"Matter of fact I do have one, Hilda. Mind if I ask how the Carpezzio case is going?"

"You're not on the Carpezzio case anymore, Dannerman. That's just a routine drug bust and we'll handle that."

"You shouldn't do it yet," he said, as he'd said before—knowing that it was useless. "If you'd just wait two weeks till the major guys from Winnipeg and Saginaw get in—"

"Can't do it. You're needed on this one."

"But you'll just be getting low-level dummies—"

"Danno," she sighed, "are you empathizing again? You damn near blew the Mad King Ludwig operation because you didn't want to get your girlfriend Ilse in trouble."

"She wasn't my girlfriend," he protested. "Exactly. I just thought she was basically a decent human being." And, for that matter, the

Carpezzios weren't that awful, either; sure, they sold drugs, but they were loyal to their people and he was going to miss some of those all-night parties in the loft with its constant aroma of room freshener and oregano that they hoped would keep any stray police dog from detecting the more interesting scents from their merchandise.

"Your kind heart does you credit, but forget it. What you're on now is a number-one priority from the director himself. Don't screw around with anything else, you hear? Check it out; see what you can get. And I want you to report in every night about this time."

"You're not making it easy for me. Do you want to tell me what I'm looking for, exactly?"

"No."

"Come on, Colonel! How the hell can I do my job?"

She hesitated. "You might see if you can find out anything about gamma-ray emissions from the Starlab," she said reluctantly.

"Gamma rays?"

"That's what I said. Don't use that term unless someone else uses it first."

"Aw, Colonel, you don't give me much to go on."

"I give you all I can. Tell you what, I'll see if they want to give me permission to tell you more. Now, get some sleep. You want to be fresh and pretty for your cousin tomorrow—and that reminds me, have you ditched that actress from Brooklyn yet? Well, do it. Your cousin likes men, and we want you concentrating on making her like you."

5
Dan

With Starlab out of action the Dannerman Astrophysical Observatory didn't have a telescope of its own anymore; what it had was people. A lot of people. More than a hundred full-time scientific and clerical people worked there, with another twenty or thirty visiting astronomers, postdocs and slave-labor graduate students on and off the premises. That was good, for Dannerman's purposes; tradecraft said that the first thing you did in a new assignment was to let yourself be seen by as many people as possible so that they would get used to you, think of you as part of the furniture and accordingly pay no attention to you. On his first day in the new job he covered all the floors the observatory occupied, and was pleased to be generally ignored.

Most of the staff had no time to chat with a new low-ranking employee, at least until they discovered he happened to be a Dannerman. Then they became more cordial, but were still busy. If the observatory didn't have any instruments of its own, it did have shared-time arrangements with ground-based and radio telescopes in New Mexico and Hawaii and the Canary Islands, not to mention neutrino instruments in Canada and Italy and even odder observatories everywhere in the world. The scientists made their observations, and then they, and all the other specialists at Dannerman, massaged, enhanced and interpreted the data and added it to the general store of human knowledge.

Of course, Dan Dannerman wasn't qualified for any of that. If you didn't count Janice DuPage, the receptionist who doubled as payroll manager, or old Walt Lowenfeld, who ran the stockroom, Dannerman was pretty nearly the least professionally qualified human being on the payroll of the observatory. He hadn't been granted the dignity of a title, but if he had it would have been "office boy." Exploring the observatory was made easy for him, because his work took him everywhere. It included carrying things from the stockroom to the people who needed them, making coffee, killing, for Janice DuPage, a wasp that had somehow made it into the reception room, fetching doughnuts from the shop in the lobby for Harry Chesweiler, the senior planetary astronomer on the staff . . . taking messages, in fractured English, from the Greek friends of Christo Papathanassiou, the quantum cosmologist from the island of Cyprus . . . getting Cousin Pat's jewelry out of the safe for her when she was going out socially . . . bringing tea with a measured twenty cc of clover-blossom honey, no more and no less, for old Rosaleen Artzybachova, well past ninety and still spry but crotchety, as she pored over her instrument schematics. What he did, in short, was whatever they told him to do. "They" could be anybody, because he took orders from any of the fifteen or twenty principal astronomers and physicists and computer nerds and mathematicians who made up the major science staff of the observatory, and from any of their assistants as well. But he especially took orders from Cousin Pat Adcock, because she was the one who ran it all.

Cousin Pat wasn't a bad boss, as bosses went. She wasn't really a good boss, either, though. She seemed to have little patience and no interest in whether any of her employees might have lives of their own. She snapped her orders out—not only to her low-man-on-the-totem-pole cousin but even to people like Pete Schneyman, the mathematician-astrophysicist who, it was said, was high on the list for some future Nobel laurel (and had been everybody's logical best bet for becoming the next director until Pat Adcock came along) and to old, honored Rosaleen Artzybachova. Maybe part of the reason for the impatience, Dannerman thought, was that everybody knew that the only reason Cousin Pat was the director was Uncle Cubby's money. But she seemed tense and preoccupied most of the time. Janice DuPage whispered that Pat hadn't always been like that and probably one reason was that, having gone through two husbands, she didn't currently have even a steady boyfriend. "Maybe so," Dannerman told the receptionist. "But she was a bossy little kid, too."

He didn't believe that was the explanation, anyway. There had to be something else, something most probably to do with the Starlab; or else what was he doing there?

What he was doing there, of course, was following Colonel Hilda Morrisey's orders. As ordered, he kept his eyes and ears open, and if he didn't find much that interested her in his nightly reports it wasn't for lack of trying. It wasn't because the people he worked with weren't willing to talk, either. They were a sociable lot—particularly with somebody who, however lowly his present status, was a definite relative of their great benefactor. "But all they want to talk about is their jobs, Colonel," he complained to her on the coded line. "Dr. Schneyman kept me after work for an hour talking about stuff like something he called isospin and how proton-rich nuclei were created in novae and neutron stars."

"Screw that stuff, Danno. That's not what you're there for. What about the gamma-ray item?"

"Nobody brought it up, so I didn't either. You told me—"

"I know what I told you. Have you at least made contact with Mick Jarvas and the Chink astronaut?"

"I haven't seen Commander Lin yet at all. He's been out of the office; they say he's in Houston, doing something about getting ready for the repair flight."

"I've got one other name for you. Christo Papa—Papathana—"

"The Greek fellow, right. From Cyprus."

"Well, there's a file on him, only I haven't accessed it yet. It's been crazy here." She hesitated, then said, "The thing is, they found the President's press secretary, only he was dead."

Dannerman was scandalized. "Dead? Cripes, Hilda! That was supposed to be a strictly commercial snatch!"

"So something went sour. The word isn't out yet; the President's going to announce it at a news conference in the morning. Meanwhile, everything's pretty screwed up, so it'll be a while before I can get more. And keep after Jarvas."

"He isn't exactly a sociable type."

"*Make* him sociable, Danno. Didn't I tell you this assignment is *priority*? Do I have to teach you all over again how to do your job? And, look, see if you can get into some of the technical part of the work there. You're not going to find much out while you're running the coffee machine."

Dannerman followed orders as best he could. He didn't achieve much with Cousin Pat's bodyguard, though he tried getting Jarvas to go with him for lunch or a beer. He got a frosty turndown. Jarvas didn't socialize outside the office. At lunchtime he went out only with Dr. Pat Adcock, and on the rare occasions when she lunched on sandwiches in her office he preferred to go out and eat alone.

Dannerman did better with the other instruction. It occurred to him that the databanks for astrophysics were reached in just about the same ways as the ones for critical studies on American playwrights. When he pointed out to Pat Adcock that he could be more use in research than fixing squeaky drawers, she reluctantly agreed to allow him to do an occasional literature search.

That was useful. It gave him a good reason to talk shop with his coworkers, and, when Harry Chesweiler found out he spoke good German and at least halting French, the planetary astronomer was delighted. "Hell, boy," he boomed, his mouth full of a bagel, "you can do something for me right now. Pat's been after me to check out some little CLO she's interested in—"

"A what?"

"A CLO. A comet-like object. I don't know why she's getting interested in it now—it came through a couple years ago—but it does have some unusual characteristics. She wants to know its orbital elements for some reason, and I've got all this Ganymede stuff to work up. We don't have any data for the sectors and times she's interested in, so you'll need to check some of the other observatories. Use my screen if you want to; I'd like to get out early for lunch, anyway."

The good part of checking up on the CLO was that it was more interesting than making coffee, and it didn't really require any knowledge of astronomy. With the information Chesweiler left for him Dan Dannerman began calling up other observatories to beg for copies of any plates they might have.

The main sources, Chesweiler had explained, were out of the country: the German Max-Planck Institut für Extraterristrische Physik, which had both an optical and a gamma-ray observatory still more or less functioning in orbit—gamma rays!—and Cerro Toledo in South America, which had one that observed in the extreme ultraviolet. The woman at Cerro Toledo refused his attempts at French—he knew no more of her own language than the taxi-driver Spanish any American needed—but had good enough English to make clear that, while she was perfectly willing to transmit the plates he asked for, she wanted to be paid; Dannerman took a chance and agreed to the price she asked.

The man at Max-Planck was a cheerful youngster named Gerd Hausewitz. He was considerably more cooperative, especially because Dannerman's German was what he'd acquired in his four years in the Democratische Neuereich. Hausewitz was about to go home for the day, he mentioned—it was nearly six o'clock in Europe—but he promised to get the plates, and Dannerman, feeling cheerful, went back to replacing the wilting flowers on the desk of Janice DuPage.

Talking German again had reminded him of the good times in Europe—of the parts of those times that were good, anyway: the cakes with mountains of *schlag* on the ring boulevards of Vienna, the beer in Frankfurt, the girl named Ilse who had invited him into her bed and then into the secret society called the Mad King Ludwig. It was the Mads he had been working on, but Ilse was a definitely valuable fringe benefit. Undoubtedly she was a terrorist, and almost certainly she had been involved in the group that had tried to spread cholera in the drinking water of the UN in New York, but she was also about the most beautiful woman he'd ever shared a mattress with.

Dannerman took a short lunch hour, and when he came back it was Janice DuPage, the receptionist, who checked his carry gun for him.

"How come?" he asked.

"Checking weapons is my job when Mick's out bodyguarding Pat Adcock."

"Huh. What does she need a bodyguard for, anyway?"

Janice looked at him unbelievingly. "Daniel, what galaxy do you come from? Pat's a good-looking woman. She needs some kind of muscle to protect her from rapists and kidnappers and general scum—not counting sometimes she likes to wear some pretty high-priced rocks when she goes out. Why do you carry a gun?"

He shrugged. "Everybody does."

"And everybody knows why."

He persisted, "So why does she hire a retired kick-boxer who never won a fight that wasn't fixed?"

"Ask him yourself. And some Kraut's been calling you, it's in your voicemail."

Gerd Hausewitz was as good as his word, but before he transmitted the plates he wanted to talk to Dannerman again. "Anything wrong?" Dannerman asked.

The broad face on the screen looked troubled. "Just that it's a funny thing, Dr. Dannerman. You said you were looking for a comet-like object, both in EUV and our gammas? But comets do not radiate in such frequencies."

"I guess that's what makes it only comet-*like*," Dannerman said equably.

"To be sure, yes. But my superiors were interested that you should ask, and interested also in your Starlab satellite. We understand there is to be a flight to repair it, is that correct?"

Dannerman's expression didn't change, but he was suddenly more interested. "Yes?"

"That would be splendid, naturally. It is a fine instrument. However, we have found nothing in the literature to describe the plans for repair. Could you perhaps send us a copy of the mission plan, if it is not too much trouble?"

"I'll have to ask the boss."

"Of course. But please do. We would greatly appreciate. Is there anything else I can do for you?"

Dannerman hesitated, then took the plunge. "Your gamma-ray observer—"

"Yes?"

"I was just wondering, have there been any unusual gamma observations lately? In the last couple of years, that is?"

The German looked puzzled. "Unusual? There are of course the bursters, but those occur all the time. Nothing *unusual,* however. Why do you ask?"

Dannerman backtracked swiftly. "It was just something someone said. It's not important. Anyway, thanks for the plates."

After Dannerman passed the plates on to Harry Chesweiler, the German's question stuck in his mind. He wished he knew a little more about astronomy. Did this CLO have anything to do with Starlab? Did the fact that it wasn't a normal comet mean anything? Why was the man from Max-Planck asking about the satellite in the first place?

Colonel Hilda would want the answer to that, too, so Dannerman got into conversations on the subject as much as he could manage. He didn't get much. No one seemed to have access to the Starlab flight plan; Dr. Adcock was handling that directly with Commander Jimmy Peng-tsu Lin. No one really knew just what had happened to Starlab, not even Dr. Artzybachova, though she gave him a frosty look when he asked.

At the end of working hours, when all the employees were lining up at Janice DuPage's desk to collect their day's pay before inflation knocked another two or three per cent off it, he dawdled to ask more questions, with little more success. It wasn't that the people in line with him were unwilling to talk, but what they wanted to talk about was their own special programs—black holes, galaxy counts, red-giant stars, red-shift measurements.

When Dannerman got the conversation onto the prospective repair mission for Starlab they were happy to discuss that, too, or at least to discuss what a newly functioning Starlab would mean to their hunt for organic molecules in interstellar gas clouds, or for the "missing mass" that seemed to concern some of them. Whatever that was. By the time the line carried Dannerman to Janice DuPage's desk he decided he didn't even know what questions to ask until he got more information from Colonel Hilda.

Then, as he was handing his cash card over to Janice DuPage for his pay, she said, "Oh, there you are, Dan. Dr. Adcock wants to talk to you before you leave."

And when he got to his cousin's office she glared at him. "What's this I'm hearing about you? Why are you asking for the Starlab flight plan?"

He wasn't surprised that she asked the question; he had no doubt that Pat Adcock kept an ear to everything that went on in the observatory. "I wasn't asking for myself, Pat. I got some data for Dr. Chesweiler from the Max-Planck people, and they were the ones who wanted to know. I thought it would be, you know, professional courtesy to give it to them."

"Professional courtesy isn't your department. You aren't a professional here, and it's none of their damn business. You don't pass out any information to anyone outside the observatory without my personal approval. Ever. Do you understand that? And, another thing, Janice tells me that you've made a payment commitment to Cerro Toledo for their data; we'll have to pay it, but you ought to know you don't have any authority to do that, either. Dan, this just isn't satisfactory. I don't want to have to warn you again, but— Hold it a minute."

Her screen was buzzing. Dannerman couldn't see the face on it, but he recognized Harry Chesweiler's voice. It sounded excited. "I've got your orbital elements for the CLO, and they're damn funny. There's definite deceleration, and—"

"Wait, Harry," she ordered, turning back to her cousin. "That's all, Dan. You can go. Just be more careful in the future."

He shared the elevator going down with two of the scientists, arguing over what the search for WIMPs really signified. They seemed close to coming to blows, so he interrupted. "What's a WIMP?"

They paused to stare at him. "Weakly interactive massive particle," the postdoc who'd been talking to him about the missing mass said.

"Oh, thanks. And, say, long as I've got you, there's something else I've been wondering about. If there's a comet that radiates in gamma and EUV, and it is slowing down as it comes toward the Sun, what does that mean?"

The other man laughed. "Means it isn't a comet, that's all. Maybe it's one of your fucking WIMPs, Will."

"Jesus," the postdoc said, "what are you telling him that for? You know it couldn't be a WIMP. Maybe some old spacecraft?"

"You know of any old spacecraft that would be coming in toward the Sun, Will?"

"So it's probably just a screwed-up observation. Anyway," the man said, getting back to his own subject, "believe me, WIMPs are definitely out there, and they make the difference; they're why the universe isn't going to expand indefinitely."

Dannerman gave up. He was glad enough when they came to the ground floor and he could get out. This debate about whether the universe would continually expand, or rebound to a point again, was sort of interesting, but not, as far as he could see, in any way relevant to any of the questions he was working on.

And, as far as he could know, it wasn't, of course. Because, of course, at that point Dan Dannerman had still never heard of the eschaton.

That night there was a call waiting from the lawyer, Dixler, begging him to have lunch with him the next day. That was a puzzle. Dannerman could think of no reason the lawyer would want to talk to him, and even fewer reasons why he would want to spend an hour with the man. But when he had reported in to Colonel Hilda she said, "Do it. See what he wants."

"It sounds like a waste of time to me."

"So? We're the ones who're paying for your time, if we want you to waste it then you do it. Maybe he knows what your cousin is spending her money on."

"What's that about her money?"

"She's liquidating assets, and it isn't just to pay off her lawyers. I'd like to know why. Something else, Danno. You didn't mention the query from Max-Planck about Starlab in your report."

He stared at her. "Oh, Christ, you've put a tap on the observatory lines."

"No tap is allowed without a court order, you know that, and we can't apply for one without taking the chance that she'll find out about it," the colonel lectured him. "Of *course* we put a tap on their lines. I don't like this questioning by the Krauts, though. What do you suppose their interest is?"

"You could ask the Bay-Kahs," he suggested.

"No, I couldn't, even if everybody wasn't going ape about the press secretary. But I did get some data for you, like on that old lady, Rosaleen—uh—"

"Artzybachova."

"Sure. I think you ought to cultivate her. She's an instrument specialist; it says in her file that she helped design the original Starlab project. Is Starlab what she's working on there now?"

"I don't know what she's working on. She always blanks her screen before she lets me bring her tea in."

"You need to get into their system, Danno. Your cousin's keeping secrets, and that's where she's keeping them, I bet."

"Are you telling me you can't break her code?"

"It's a closed circuit. Get in. And, listen, Danno, I've been checking your file and you haven't been on the range for nearly two weeks."

"I'll fit it in."

"Damn right you'll fit it in. You want to keep your skills up. Martial arts, too, Dan, because you know what occurs to me? It occurs to me you'd make a pretty good bodyguard for your cousin."

He protested, "Mick Jarvas already has that job."

"Maybe something can be arranged; I'll work on it. Any questions, outside of the usual one?"

"You mean the usual one that asks you what this is all about?"

She sighed. "Yes, that's the usual one, all right, and the usual answer is still no."

That was it. She wasn't going to tell until somebody higher up authorized it. That didn't surprise Dannerman; but what did surprise him was that, when he finally did get a clue, it came from that old fart of a family lawyer, Jerome Dixler.

The place the lawyer had chosen for lunch was a small private club way downtown on Gramercy Park. The place appeared to have a theatrical history. When Dannerman checked his twenty-shot and carryphone at the cloakroom—the gun was no surprise, but he was a little astonished that the club did not allow phones to ring in their dining room—he was informed that Mr. Dixler hadn't arrived yet. He spent ten minutes in the lounge, studying full-length oil paintings of famous members, all actors of a century or more ago whose names were familiar to him only from long-ago courses at Harvard. When the lawyer showed up he was out of breath. "Real apologies, Dan," he panted. "The traffic gets worse every day and that driver of mine— Well, I did make it. Here, let's get to our table and order something to drink."

Dannerman was mildly flattered, more intrigued, by the fact that Dixler had put himself out to try to be on time. Still, he didn't get to business right away, whatever his business was going to turn out to be. While the waiter was bringing cocktails the lawyer went over every item on the menu, discussing the provenance of the basic foods that went into it and the way the club's chef prepared it. Dannerman knew he was meant to feel courted. Clearly Dixler had taken him to a pretty expensive place, although Dannerman's own menu was bereft of prices for anything. He wondered just what it was that the lawyer wanted from him that justified this kind of entertainment.

Dixler was in no hurry to get to it. As soon as the orders had been placed he said brightly, "Well, then, Dan. How're you getting along with dear little Pat?"

"Well enough. I don't see much of her in the office."

Dixler clucked. "That's a pity. You know Cuthbert always hoped you two kids would get together someday."

"Him, too."

"I beg your pardon?"

"Nothing. Someone else said the same thing, just the other night, but I don't think it's going to happen. For one thing, Pat never got in touch with me after Uncle Cubby died."

Dixler gave him a wounded look. "You never called me, either, Dan. I hope you're not holding a grudge about that problem with your inheritance."

"There wasn't any problem. There just wasn't any inheritance by the time it got to me. You explained it all when I got back from Europe. As executor you liquidated the estate."

"Had to, Dan. It's the law. I'm sorry it worked out the way it did, but I put the whole bequest into government bonds the way I was supposed to; it's not my fault inflation was so bad there wasn't much there when you got home. If you'd kept in touch while you were in Europe—"

"Yes, everybody's in agreement about me, aren't they? Pat told me I should have kept in touch, too. Well, I'm not blaming anybody." Dannerman wasn't, either, not really; there wasn't any point since there wasn't anything that could be done about it now. He changed the subject. "Anyway, it didn't work all that well for Pat, either, did it? I hear she's having her own money troubles."

Dixler looked startled. "How'd you hear that?" Dannerman

shrugged. "Well, I suppose offices gossip. It's true enough. I don't think I'm violating lawyer-client confidentiality if I say that divorcing two husbands cost her a lot."

"Ah," Dannerman said, nodding. "I guess you handled the divorces for her."

The lawyer winced. "Really, Dan, that's unkind. I did the best I could for her. No attorney can do more than his client lets him, and she—well, she didn't provide me with the best cases, you know. That's about all I can say with propriety. Wouldn't say that much, you know, if you weren't family." He worked on his salad in silence for a moment, then came to the point. "Let me take you into my confidence, Dan. I guess you wondered why I asked you to come down here."

"I suppose it's because the club is sort of historic, and the food's good," Dannerman offered politely.

"Historic, sure; they say John Wilkes Booth used to eat in this very room. If you like history. I don't; and there's good food in plenty of places that are a lot more convenient. There's only one reason I keep my membership in this place and that's because nobody I know ever comes here. It's private. What I wanted to talk to you about is confidential, and in a way it does have to do with Pat's financial situation. You see—" He hesitated, then put his fork down and got it out. "There are some funny rumors going around about what your cousin's up to. I mean this repair mission on that Starlab orbiter. It's not just that the observatory wants its telescopes working again. People seem to think there's more to it. In fact, some people say there's some kind of technology in Starlab that isn't supposed to be there. The kind that might be worth a lot of money to whoever got his hands on it."

Dannerman kept his expression blank, but his level of interest suddenly elevated. "How can that be? Starlab's just an old astronomical satellite."

The lawyer shrugged. "Whether the rumor is true or not, it appears that your cousin thinks it is. She's spending pretty heavily out of what's left of her personal fortune to get what she calls the repair mission going."

That was a good deal more puzzling than enlightening. "Why does she have to spend her own money? You read me Uncle Cubby's will. Unless I heard wrong, it seems to me he left the observatory pretty well financed."

Dixler shook his head. "She has to account to the board for anything she spends out of the endowment. If she wants that mission to fly she's got a lot of off-the-books expenses to deal with. I wouldn't call them bribes, exactly. But not exactly legitimate, either, if you know what I mean. She doesn't want to have to explain them to the board, so she's been dipping into her capital to pay them out of her own pocket. She's been buying uncut diamonds, too."

For the first time Dannerman was startled. "Uncut *diamonds*?"

The lawyer shrugged. "For what purpose I do not know. She certainly doesn't plan to wear them, and she's got better inflation hedges than diamonds already." He shook his head. "Dan, I don't have to tell you, that's not like her. So she must have some pretty powerful reason—and there are these rumors."

"What do the rumors say, exactly?"

The lawyer said shrewdly, "That's what I'm asking you to find out. You work there; you should be able to get the facts on it."

Dannerman quelled a sudden impulse to laugh in the man's face. "You're not asking me to be a *spy,* are you?"

"Oh, no! Nothing like that! I wouldn't ask you to *pry* into your cousin's affairs. All I want you to do is keep your ears open . . . and, of course, give me a call when you find anything out."

"So you can figure out some way to cut yourself in on the profits—if there are any?"

Dixler flushed, but he controlled his temper. "My reasons," he said, "aren't actually any of your business. If you want to take a guess about them, you're welcome, but I don't choose to discuss the subject."

"Let me think about it," Dannerman said. The lawyer waved graceful permission with one hand, and began to talk about what a fine man Cuthbert Dannerman had been and how charming Dan and his cousin had been as children. Dannerman listened but didn't need to say much; Dixler was conducting the conversation by himself. Only when the meal was finished and they were getting their checked belongings at the cloakroom did the lawyer say:

"What about it, Dan?"

Dannerman was listening to a message that had come with his carryphone and gun. He looked up. "What?"

Dixler lowered his voice. "I said, will you do what I'm asking for me? I can make it worth your while, Dan."

"*How* worth my while?" Dixler shrugged and was mute. "Well, I'll do what I can," Dannerman said ambiguously. "Now, if you'll excuse me, I have to run. Looks like I've got an appointment I hadn't expected."

"Fine," said Dixler. "I'll be waiting to hear from you."

As Dixler got into his limousine Dannerman waited for the doorman to produce a cab. He was thinking hard, but not about the lawyer's offer. He was listening again to the message that had been on his phone. What it said was:

"Dr. Adcock will be returning to the observatory some time after two-thirty. You should be waiting at the street entrance before she gets there."

There wasn't any signature, but there didn't need to be: the message had been addressed to him as "Danno."

He made it by two-thirty, but with only moments to spare; but it didn't seem he had needed to hurry. The sidewalk outside the building was as crowded as always, but there was no sign of his cousin. Not at two-thirty, not at two-forty, not at almost three.

Dannerman leaned against the side of the building between two storefronts to keep his back covered; he had no doubt there were pickpockets among the horde of pedestrians. There was a policeman moving methodically down the block, making the sidewalk vendors pack up their wares and move on. He gave Dannerman a searching look, as he did the four or five other idlers who were standing around, doing their best to look as though they were waiting for someone. Some probably were. One at least wasn't, because as soon as the cop was ten meters away the man strolled over to Dannerman. Out of the side of his mouth, not looking at him, he muttered, "Smoke? Get high? Want to have a good time?"

"Get lost," Dannerman said. He looked at his watch. He had stretched his lunch hour a good deal longer than Cousin Pat would approve; if it happened she had come back a little earlier than expected, and was up in her office wondering where he was—

She wasn't. He saw a taxi roll up before the building entrance, and Pat Adcock and her bodyguard got out.

Dannerman wondered just what he was supposed to do, but not for long. Two of the idlers had moved quickly toward the curb. As the cab was pulling away one of them jumped Mick Jarvas from behind, the two of them falling to the ground; Dannerman heard a sickening crunch that sounded like a bone breaking. The other grabbed his cousin, snatched her necklace, knocked her down too and began to run—straight at Dan Dannerman.

Dannerman's reflexes were fast. "Hai!" he shouted, and stopped the man with a full body block. The mugger squawked, and then lost his voice as Dannerman spun him around and got an arm around his throat. The other mugger got up from where he had left Jarvas writhing on the sidewalk and started over to him; then, as Dannerman turned to face him, releasing the man he had captured, the two turned and ran, disappearing into the crowd.

As Dannerman helped his cousin to her feet and handed back her necklace she looked at him with shaky wonder. "Well, thanks, Dan," she gasped. "You're pretty handy in a street fight, aren't you? And you even got my beads back."

"Just glad I was here, Pat," he said modestly.

"So am I." She turned to the policeman who was trotting toward them at last, sweaty in his body armor and looking annoyed. It was only when she had finished reprimanding the officer for not being present when needed and ordering him to call in for an ambulance for groaning Mick Jarvas that Cousin Pat finally remembered to revert to type. "One thing, though, Dan. I'm glad you happened to be here, of course. But you do know, don't you, that you're supposed to be back from lunch no later than two. And it's a pity you let those muggers get away."

He didn't answer that. He especially didn't tell her the reason, because he didn't want to mention that while he had the "mugger" in a choke hold the man had gasped aggrievedly, "Come on, Danno! Don't be so fucking rough!"

6
Dan

On the way home that night, Dannerman stopped to do what he should have done days earlier—put in his once-a-month hour's practice on the firing range at the YMCA. As long as he was there he put in another hour on the exercise machines to keep his muscle tone up. When he got home he was hot and sweaty, but the guns had to be cleaned.

His practiced fingers knew how to do that without much direction from his brain, so he put something on the screen to watch while he cleaned the weapons. He hesitated over the choice. One of his store of Elmer Rice plays, for the fun of it? Some of the briefing tapes Hilda had downloaded for him, for the sake of duty? He compromised on looping the two messages from space again; maybe they had something to do with his assignment, as the colonel had hinted, but anyway she'd stirred his curiosity.

He did the easiest weapon first, the registered twenty-shot, his eyes on the screen. Even slowed down to catch details, the first space message gave no more information than it had the first time he saw it, in the Neuereich. The universe expanded and collapsed; and that was that.

He paused before running the second message, because the stink of his bomb-bugger was getting to him. Once the chemicals in a bomb-bugger mixed they produced not only thrust for the bullets but a god-awful smell; he rinsed the whole weapon, firing chamber and all, in water with neutralizer added, then carefully added enough of each chemical to top them off from the canisters hidden under his bed. Then he turned on the second message and began to clean his ankle gun.

He didn't get far. There were angry voices just outside his door.

One was his landlady, Rita, in a bad mood; the other, whining and apologetic, belonged to one of the upstairs lodgers, Bert Germaine. When he opened the door, Rita diverted her attention from the lodger to Dannerman. "I didn't see you in the kitchen," she said accusingly. Then, wrinkling her nose, "What's that smell?"

"I guess it's the low-power loads they make you use on the YMCA range. Sorry about that."

She shrugged, turning back to look for the other lodger. But that conversation with the other lodger was over, because Germaine had taken advantage of her distraction to sneak away. "Little bastard," she said morosely. "I ought to kick his ass right out of my condo. Can't pay the rent, oh, no, but he always has a couple dollars for lottery tickets every day."

Dannerman took the hint. "Let me settle up."

"Oh, honey," she sighed, "I wasn't talking about *you.* You're the best goddam tenant I have, you know that. Only how can I make ends meet when I have to put up with deadbeats like Germaine?"

"Look at the bright side, Rita. Maybe he'll win his hundred million dollars, then he'll pay everything he owes all at once."

"Maybe pigs will fly. Dan," she said, looking him over, "when was the last time you got a haircut?" He shrugged. "You really ought to take more pride in your appearance, a good-looking young fellow like you. Which reminds me," she added. "There was a girl here looking for you."

"Oh?" he said, wondering: Colonel Hilda? Somebody from the office?

"Said her name was Anita. Said to tell you they missed you at the theater. Is she the one I used to see here sometimes, like a month or two ago? Not that I'm complaining about your having guests," she added hastily. "You pay your rent on time. I'm not going to worry if you have somebody visit you now and then, and one thing I will say for you, Dan, the ones I've seen have always looked pretty respectable. Not like the hookers that little bastard Germaine tries to sneak in. He's always got the money to pay them, you bet; and still he says he can't pay his rent!"

When he was safely locked in his room again Dannerman didn't start the tape again. He was thinking about Anita Berman.

That was not an enjoyable subject—not meaning Anita herself, who was about as enjoyable a female as he had ever dated, but the fact that he would soon have to do something about her. The troubling question was, do what? He didn't really want to break off their relationship. But she was beginning to sound serious, and that was something he couldn't afford.

Then Hilda's call came in on the coded line and he put Anita Berman out of his mind for the moment. He started in right away with the colonel. "Thanks a lot for setting me up this afternoon. You could've told me about it first."

"What for? I knew you could handle it. Now Jarvas is out of the way for a while, right?"

"I guess so. They were still at the hospital when I left."

"He's out," she said positively. "His arm's broken. So tomorrow morning you go in to your cousin and see if you can get his job."

"You broke his arm on purpose."

"Damn straight we did. So now his job's open, because what's the use of a bodyguard with a broken arm? Get it. Her bodyguard goes wherever she goes, so you can keep tabs on her when she's out of the observatory. Now, let's hear your report."

There wasn't much to say, until he got to his lunch with the lawyer. She scowled at that. "Him, too. Maybe we should sell tickets."

"You don't act surprised at what he said," he pointed out.

"You mean because this Dixler thinks your cousin's trying to make some money out of the Starlab? But we already knew all that, of course."

"Hell, Hilda, I didn't! So now that I know that much, how about telling me the rest?"

She shook her head. "Don't hassle me about that. What else?"

He hesitated. "One thing. I want to go back and visit at the theater. They're opening *The Subway* tomorrow night and I want to be there."

She frowned again. "Is that wise? The only reason we let you do that theater crap was because it made good cover on the Carpezzio job, and that's over for you. Don't get the two things mixed up."

"It's personal, Hilda."

She sighed and surrendered. "That goddam Berman woman, right? Well, I won't say no, but if there's any fallout it's your ass, Danno. All right, I've got some orders for you. We can't get through your cousin's encoding; we need a key. That Greek fellow—"

"Papathanassiou."

"That one. He probably has it, and I've got his data packet; I'll pass it on to you. Couple of others, too, but the Greek's is the one that looks good. You ought to be able to get something out of him."

"Blackmail him, you mean?"

"Whatever. And that Chinaman we were interested in, Jimmy Lin.

He's coming back tomorrow morning, so you want to get on him, too." She reflected for a moment, peering past him. "Did you clean your clothes after firing your bomb-bugger? Once you fire one of those things the stink stays, so everybody's going to know you've got a hide-out gun."

"I will," he promised; then, "Hey! You've had me followed!"

"Well, sure. If we didn't do that how would we know if anybody else was following you? You're clean, so far—and, don't forget, the first thing you do in the morning is see if you can go for Jarvas's job."

But, as it turned out, that wasn't an option. Somebody had forgotten to tell the bureau's armbreakers that Jarvas was left-handed; and when Dannerman put his card in the turnstile at the observatory entrance the next morning his cousin Pat was ahead of him, and beside her, punching out the combination to summon an elevator, was Mick Jarvas, a translucent cast on his right arm.

"Morning," Dannerman said, trying not to grin.

"And good morning to you," his cousin said, smiling. She reached over to touch him on the shoulder—not affectionately, exactly, but a lot more amiably than before. "You surprised me yesterday, old Dan. For an English major, I mean," she said. "Listen, come see me this afternoon. I've got an errand for you to run."

"Sure thing, Pat." He might have asked what kind of an errand, but he didn't get the chance. As they stepped out of the car at their floor she almost bumped into a large, sand-colored man with short black hair who was waiting there.

"Why, Jimmy," she said. "I didn't expect you so early."

"I just dropped off some of my stuff. I have an appointment downtown to check in at the embassy in half an hour," the man said, holding the elevator door open.

"Well, I won't keep you," Pat said. "You know Mick Jarvas, of course? And this is my cousin, Dan Dannerman. Commander Jimmy Lin."

Dannerman hadn't had any clear idea of what he expected a Chinese astronaut to be like, but Jimmy Lin wasn't it. The man was taller than he had imagined, and a lot huskier; he wore a flowered Hawaiian shirt, and shoes that, Dannerman was pretty sure, would have cost him a month of his observatory pay. "Glad to know you, Commander," Dannerman said, automatically extending his hand.

But the People's Republic astronaut obviously didn't share the pleasure. He didn't accept Dannerman's hand. He didn't even speak to him. He gave him a long, hard look, then turned to Pat Adcock. "I'll be back before lunch," he said. "We can talk then."

"I've got a lunch date; make it this afternoon," she said, gazing after Lin as he let the elevator door close behind him. Then she turned to Dannerman with a mildly puzzled look. "He's usually chummier than that. You didn't forget to shower this morning, did you?" He shrugged. "Well, let's get to work; you can sort that out later."

Dannerman would have to sort that out, somehow, if he was going to carry out the colonel's orders, but it was going to be harder than he'd thought. He hadn't expected that kind of unprovoked hostility from Lin; and he was going to have to come up with something better than a broken wrong arm to get Jarvas out of the way. And then, as he checked his weapon with Jarvas, there was another curious thing. The bodyguard gave him a long look, partly abashed, partly pugnacious, but, though he seemed to want to say something, he didn't get it out.

There was one thing Dannerman could do, though. Hilda had kept her promise and transmitted the background packets on the observatory employees who had turned up in the sin file. Two of them were unlikely to help: the astrophysics grad student three weeks past her period and frantically sending faxes to her boyfriend, now in Sierra Leone; Harry Chesweiler, identified as a former member of the Man-Boy Love Association. But the packet on Christo Papathanassiou did look good. The old man had got himself picked up for questioning about a terrorist assassination back in the old country. That, Dannerman thought judiciously, could be made to work—whether or not Papathanassiou was actually guilty of anything.

Dannerman couldn't do anything about it for the first couple of hours that morning, because he was kept busy with his nominal observatory duties. And then, when he went looking for the Cypriot, Papathanassiou was nowhere to be found. He wasn't in his office. He wasn't in with Pat, or in the room of number-crunchers all the scientists used to set up their mathematical models. When Dannerman looked into Rosaleen Artzybachova's cubicle he wasn't there, either, and the old lady herself was, incredibly, doing push-ups on the floor. "You want me?" she called, looking up at Dannerman.

"Actually I was looking for Dr. Papathanassiou."

"Try the canteen," she said; and that was where Dannerman found him, attacking a wedge of some unfamiliar kind of pastry smothered in heavy cream.

He looked defensive. "One has to keep one's blood sugar up," he said.

"Good idea," said Dannerman. "Mind if I join you?" And when he had a dish of sherbet for himself he said, "I was kind of hoping I'd run into you, Dr. Papathanassiou. I was looking at those tapes from space again last night—"

"Those odd-looking alien creatures? Yes?"

"And I just didn't understand about this Big Crunch."

"Ah," Papathanassiou said, gratified, "but really, it's very simple. The universe is expanding; in the future it will collapse again; that's all of it. Of course," he went on, "the mathematics is, yes, rather complex. Actually it was the subject of my dissertation in graduate school, did you know that?" Dannerman did, but saw no reason to say so. "It was necessary to use symplectic integrators to predict the next fifty quadrillion years of motion in only our own galaxy. You've heard of the three-body problem? What I had to solve was the two-hundred-billion-body problem."

He tittered. Dannerman pressed on. "But what I don't understand is, when the universe collapses again, what does it collapse *to*?"

"Ah." The astronomer ruminated for a moment, licking cream off his upper lip. "Well, you see, when everything has come together again great velocities and pressures are involved. First all matter is compressed. Then the atomic nuclei themselves are compressed. They become a new form of very dense matter which is stable—well, temporarily stable. Are you following me so far?"

Dannerman nodded, not entirely truthfully.

"Excellent. Interestingly, some workers once thought that sort of thing might happen in a particle accelerator. They called that state 'Lee-Wick matter,' and they feared it would be so dense that it would accrete everything else into it. Perhaps, do you see?, even turning the whole Earth into Lee-Wick matter." He wiped his lips with a napkin, grinning. "They were incorrect. No accelerator can reach those forces, though at the Crunch—"

"Yes?"

"Why, then," Papathanassiou said, nodding, "yes, perhaps it could be possible. Not in the form of Lee-Wick matter, no; one is pretty confident now that that doesn't exist after all. Rather it would be in the form of strange matter. That's to say, matter made from quarks—do you know what a quark is? Well, never mind; but strange matter would be very dense indeed, and it would keep on getting denser and denser. You cannot imagine how dense, Mr. Dannerman."

"Like a black hole?" he hazarded.

"Far denser than even a black hole. It would encompass the entire universe, you see, for as soon as it began to form it would transform everything around it into strange matter. Do you know our story of King Midas and his touch of gold? Like that. But only for a tiny fraction of a second, because such matter has a net positive charge—no electrons, you see—and so it tries to fly apart, like a bomb. Have I answered your question?"

"Well, yes." Dannerman cleared his throat. "That part of it, anyway. But it's funny you should mention a bomb."

Papathanassiou's cheerful expression faltered. "I beg your pardon?"

"Someone was asking about you," Dannerman lied. "He mentioned bombs? And a brother?"

The astronomer's smile was gone. "I don't understand. Who was this person?"

"I don't know. Greek, I think. You know that bar downstairs? I was having a cup of coffee, and he sat down next to me and asked if I knew you. Do you think I should mention it to Dr. Adcock?"

"Dear God, no!"

"I mean, so she can find this man and make him stop. He said some very unkind things about you, Dr. Papathanassiou."

"No! Please, no," the astronomer begged.

"Well," Dannerman began, then paused as his communicator beeped at him; there was an incoming call on the observatory system. In any case, he thought, that was a good place to stop; the hook had been planted, and it would be worthwhile to let Papathanassiou worry for a while. "I'd better take my call," he said. "Anyway, I won't say anything to her today. But I need to think this over; maybe you and I can talk again tomorrow? Here? I think that would be a good idea—and, oh, yes, thank you for explaining to me about the Big Crunch."

The call turned out to be Gerd Hausewitz from the Max-Planck Institut again, and he was looking aggrieved. "You promised to supply the specs for the Starlab mission," he reminded Dannerman.

"I know, Gerd. I've requested them."

"It is only that we supplied the data you asked for at once."

"I know you did. What can I tell you? I don't know how it is in your place, but here it takes time to get people to move."

"Yes, of course, Dannerman, but—" He looked over his shoulder and spoke more softly. "—my superiors are quite interested in this matter. They were not pleased that I delivered your material without at once receiving what we asked in return. This could be difficult for me here."

"I'll do what I can."

"Please, Dannerman."

"Yes, I promise," Dannerman said, half turning as he cut the contact. Someone was at his door and, surprisingly, it was the Chinese astronaut, PRC Space Corps Commander James Peng-tsu Lin.

He was wearing a propitiatory smile. "Hey, Dan," he said. "I owe you an apology."

"I beg your pardon?"

"No, really. I was pretty rude this morning, and I didn't mean to be—had to get down to the embassy and all that red tape, had a lot on my mind. So let's start over, okay?"

"Glad to, Commander Lin—"

"Just Jimmy, all right? Listen, what I was thinking, are you free for lunch? Looks like we're going to be working together for a while, and I like to get to know new people when they come to work here. Especially if they're Pat's cousin. They tell me there's some pretty fine ethnic food just around the corner—?"

"That'd be fine," Dannerman said, with pleasure. Whatever had turned Lin around was a mystery, but it was also a break: you didn't often get a subject volunteering to let you interrogate him. "I'll get my stuff and meet you at the elevator."

And then, as he picked up his twenty-shot weapon from Mick Jarvas, another little mystery solved itself. Jarvas was in the men's room, but when he came out he looked almost cheerful until he saw Dannerman waiting for him. Then he gave Dannerman that peculiar look again as he handed over the gun. He didn't let go of it.

"Is there something you want to say to me?" Dannerman asked, holding the barrel while Jarvas held the butt—he was glad to see the safety was firmly on.

Jarvas's eyes were on the ground, but Dannerman thought he muttered something. "What did you say?"

Jarvas looked up angrily. As he let go of the gun at last, he managed to get it out. "About that business in the street yesterday? I just said thanks."

Jimmy Lin was in the waiting room, busily chatting up the receptionist. In the elevator he said appreciatively, "I have to say your cousin Pat doesn't mind hiring other good-lookers. How'd you like to do the Twin Dragons Teasing the Phoenix with that Janice lady?"

"The what?"

The astronaut guffawed. "The Twin Dragons Teasing the Phoenix. It's an old Chinese expression. It's like, well, like when a lady has two gentlemen paying attention to her at once." He grinned sidelong at Dannerman. "Just a joke, you know. Phew, what a mob." He led the way along the block to turn the corner, moving rapidly. When he noticed that Dannerman was lengthening his stride to keep up with him he said apologetically, "Sorry, I guess I'm always in a hurry. It's a genetic fault; my dad was the same way—except with the ladies, of course. Anyway, here's the place."

To the surprise of Dannerman, who had been preparing himself for Chinese food, the ethnic restaurant was not Oriental at all. What it was was Tex-Mex. The place was almost as crowded as the sidewalk, but Lin had a whispered conversation with the waiter and money must have changed hands; they got an immediate table. "I hope you like this stuff, Dan. I guess I got an appetite for it in Houston. First time I was there this lady from El Paso introduced me to it, then I introduced her to the Jade Girl Playing the Flute. Aw," he said, grinning, lowering his voice as he glanced at the waitress who was hovering just out of earshot, "that doesn't mean anything to you, does it? It's another of those old Chinese expressions. One of these days I'll show you some books that were written by my great-great-I-don't-know-how-many-greats granddaddy, Peng-tsu. I got my middle name after him; the old man's kind of famous, in some circles, anyway. He was a Taoist sage two thousand years ago—I'd have to say, a pretty *horny* Taoist sage—and he wrote some dandy books on what he called 'healthful life.' His idea of health, though, was to prong the ladies as often as he could and make up a list of all the ways there are of doing it. Well, enough of my sordid family history. Let's go ahead and order, we don't want to keep that good-looking little cowgal over there waiting, and then you can tell me all about Dan Dannerman."

And that was the way it went. It didn't take Dannerman long to realize that the astronaut was as interested in pumping him as he was in finding out about the astronaut. They didn't talk shop. They talked the way long-lost friends talk when they catch up on each other's lives after years of separation. Jimmy Lin wasn't reticent about himself. Garrulous would've been more accurate; in the first half hour Dannerman learned that the Lins were a wealthy old Hong Kong family who moved to Beijing after the reunification and got even richer there, as the People's Republic discovered the wonders of entrepreneurialism.

Jimmy Lin himself had been educated in America, of course. That, along with the fact that he spent a lot of his spare time in his father's place on Maui, accounted for his accent-free American English. Then, instead of going into the family business, he'd been accepted for astronaut training. "But," he said, sighing, "I'm no credit to my ancestors. The top brass fired me out of the astronaut corps a year ago—they had some damn political charge." He looked ruefully embarrassed. "What they called it was 'left-wing, right-wing zigzag deviationism,' if you can imagine that. But actually about half the corps got dumped at the same time for one pretext or another. My opinion, they just decided there wasn't any money to be made in space anymore, so they cut back. So now I have to scratch for work." But after every little datum he supplied about himself he paused inquiringly to give Dannerman a chance to supply a little quid for his quo. He was fascinated by Dannerman's interest in the little theater in Brooklyn. ("Coney Island! Wow! That's really what you call Off-Off-Off Broadway, isn't it? I didn't think *anybody* went to Coney Island anymore!") He was searching about Dannerman's years in Europe—Dannerman was glad he'd been thorough about covering his tracks with the Mad King Ludwigs—and sympathetic about the fact that, although Dannerman and Pat Adcock had inherited the same amount from Uncle Cubby, Pat had actually got hers and Dannerman's had shrunk to invisibility through inflation before he collected it.

But of the repair mission to Starlab he would say nothing at all. "The thing is, Dan," he said, all good-natured candor, "I'm in line to fly that bird. Provided I don't screw up with your cousin and, well, she just doesn't want it talked about yet." He glanced at his watch. "Well, this's been great, but we better get back to the office. I hear Pat's got a job for you to do this afternoon."

When Dannerman was summoned to his cousin's office, though, the first thing she said wasn't about the errand. It was "What the hell did you promise the Germans?"

He shrugged, less interested in the question than in the fact that Mick Jarvas was standing there beside her desk, looking truculent again. "They asked for information about the Starlab repair mission."

"They can't have it."

"All right," he said agreeably, "but can I give them a reason?"

"No. Well, hell, I guess you have to say something. Tell them we've got a problem, you don't know exactly what it is, but it'll all be cleared up in a week or so."

It seemed to Dannerman that his cousin had a lot in common with the colonel. He ventured, "Meaning when you get back from your Starlab trip?"

She glared at him. "Who told you I was going to Starlab? Just do your job," she ordered. "No, wait a minute, I didn't mean for you to go. I need something delivered to the Florida embassy. You're going to take it, and it's important. I'm sending Mick along with you, just in case."

Jarvas stirred. "I can handle it all by myself," he muttered.

She ignored him. To Dannerman she said, "Give me your belly bag." When he unsnapped it and handed it over, puzzled, she dumped the entire contents on her desk.

"Hey!" he said. There was personal stuff there, his cash card, his ID, the key cards for the office and the condo.

"Shut up," she said. She unlocked a drawer of her desk and took out a small, soft-sided leather satchel. She stuffed it into his belly bag; it fit, but just barely. She thought for a moment, then put his ID back.

"You can pick up the rest of your stuff when you get back, Dan. What I want you to do, take this bag to the Floridian embassy and give the bag to General Martín Delasquez personally. Nobody else, understand? No matter what they say. It's to be hand-delivered, and he's expecting it. Wait for him while he checks it out, and when he says it's okay you can come back here. Mick, give him his gun."

"Right, Pa—Dr. Adcock," the bodyguard rumbled, pulling the weapon out of his pocket. "Come on, Dannerman."

In the elevator he was fidgety, glaring at Dannerman. Just before they reached the ground floor he asked, "Do you know what this is about?"

"Don't have a clue."

"Neither do I. Listen. Maybe you're not as big a prick as I thought you were, but my orders are that that package *stays* in your belly bag until you hand it over to the guy it's meant for. No peeking. I don't want to have any trouble with you."

"You won't," Dannerman said, meaning it. He didn't want to cross Jarvas just when the man was being nearly human. In any case, he was hoping that the subway ride would give him a chance to engage Jarvas in conversation.

But that didn't happen. Jarvas was working at the business of being a bodyguard. He stayed close to Dannerman, keeping anyone else from touching him even on the subway, his good hand always near his own weapon, and he wasn't talkative. When the train speeded up to pass what some terrorist had done to the Fourteenth Street station, all lightless and covered in dark green radiation-proof foam, Jarvas crossed himself awkwardly with the arm that was in a cast. Dannerman considered mentioning to him, as a conversation opener, that he really had nothing to worry about, the residue from the terrorists' nuclear satchel bomb was no more dangerous than the general atmospheric levels—as long as you didn't linger there, of course. But as soon as he opened his mouth Jarvas gave him a warning scowl.

He closed his mouth again, and followed Jarvas meekly as they got out at Chambers Street.

The Floridians had their place on Embassy Row, just like the rich foreign countries. Theirs wasn't one of the big-money establishments—it wasn't anything like the Swedish embassy on the corner, twelve stories high and immaculately kept, and of course not a patch on the embassy of the United Koreas across the street. But then Florida was stretching a point to have an "embassy" at all, since it wasn't really an independent nation. At least not in name.

The Floridians took themselves as seriously as one, though. Both Jarvas and Dannerman had to turn over their guns even before they got to the scanners in the vestibule, and then Dannerman had to turn over his ankle gun as well. Jarvas gave him a scowl for that; at least, Dannerman thought with resignation, the scanners hadn't picked up the bomb-bugger. Then they had to sit for half an hour in a sort of barred quarantine chamber before a guard was available to escort them to the office of Major General Martín Delasquez Moreno. Jarvas sat like a stone, a scowl on his face. After a moment Dannerman decided to improve the time; he checked his mail, wiped it all, then accessed a news broadcast. But he had time only for a couple of items before the door guard leaned in and ordered no electronics.

Then they just sat.

When the armed guard came for Dannerman he pointed to Jarvas and said, "You stay."

"Hey! I've got my job—"

"Your job is stay here. Come on, you."

Leaving the fuming Jarvas behind was a surprise for Dannerman, but not altogether unwelcome. It occurred to him that, without Jarvas by his side, it was a chance to sneak a quick look into the leather bag; but it really wasn't, with the armed embassy guard watching every move.

When he got to the office of General Delasquez the man seemed surprisingly young—probably a relative of somebody high in Florida's government, Dannerman supposed. He was wearing the full dress uniform of a general of the Florida State Air Guard, and when he shooed the guard out with an offhand gesture the man was meek to obey. Delasquez closed the door. "Hand it over," he ordered; and then, when he had the leather bag in his hands, "Turn around. This is not your concern."

But by then what was in the satchel was no longer much of a secret to Dannerman, because he'd felt its contents as he took it out of his belly bag. It felt like a few dozen pebbles. It wasn't pebbles, though. When the general had finished his inspection and had locked the bag in a drawer and told him he could turn around again, he forgot to put the jeweler's loupe away, but by then Dannerman had figured out that they were gemstones, almost certainly the diamonds Jerry Dixler had mentioned Pat was buying.

"Wait," the general ordered, and keyed on his phone. Dannerman couldn't see the picture, but he knew his cousin's voice when she answered. "Your application has been received and is satisfactory, Dr. Adcock," the general said. "The documents will be processed immediately." And then, to Dannerman, "You can go."

With their errand completed, Jarvas loosened up a little. He listened almost politely as Dannerman answered his questions about what had happened in the general's office, then actually managed a grin. "Got that done, anyway; your cousin'll be happy about that." Then he stopped short in front of the Swedish embassy, eyeing the curbside vendors. "Hey, Dannerman, how about some candy? I've got kind of a sweet tooth."

"Not me, but go ahead." As he watched Jarvas haggling with the woman at the pushcart he wondered how Jarvas got away with his drug habit; the candy addiction was a tipoff, and so was the fact of his mood swings. In some ways Cousin Pat didn't seem to be as sharp as he'd thought. But it was good that Jarvas was mellower; maybe on the way back he would be more talkative.

The other good thing in his future, he thought, was that that night he could go back to the theater. He must have smiled, because the guard outside the Swedish embassy gave him a suspicious look before going back to eyeing the vendors and loafers along the crowded sidewalk. Dannerman kept getting nudged as people bumped against him, but if any of them were pickpockets, as they likely were, he had nothing left in his belly bag worth picking.

He felt droplets of cold water hitting the back of his neck and looked up; the meticulous Swedes had permanent crews at work in hoists overhead, to keep the building washed down. Even so, they were just barely keeping ahead of the pollution. As he moved away he felt someone touch his arm. It was a young boy, no more than fifteen. *"Vill herrn växla? Vägvisare?"* he hissed. Dannerman shook his head, but the boy persisted. *"Vill ni knulla min syster? Ren flicka, mycket vacker."*

Dannerman realized the boy had taken him for a Swedish tourist. "Asshole," Dannerman said cheerfully. "I don't want your sister, and besides I'm an American."

The boy changed gears without a blink. "Okay, sport, how about a little American happy time? Sticks, ampoules, mellow patches, I can get you anything you want."

"No sale." And then, as Jarvas came toward them, munching on caramel popcorn, he said, "You can try my buddy there. He might be in the market for some dope."

It was a light impulse, and he regretted it. The boy took one look at the expression on Jarvas's face, and then dodged across the street to try his luck with the Koreans. And all the way back in the subway Jarvas stood cold and angry beside Dannerman, and wouldn't say a word.

7
Dan

There was one job remaining for Dannerman to do that day. It was a fairly nasty one, and not one he looked forward to, but it was best to get it over with. So at quitting time Dannerman went looking for the Cypriot astronomer, Christo Papathanassiou. The man was standing over the screens in his office, preparing to shut them down for the day. When he saw Dannerman in the doorway he gave him a quick, apprehensive look. "Sorry to bother you, but I need to talk to you for a minute," Dannerman said. "I've got a problem."

Papathanassiou sat down again, stiffly waiting. "See, Dr. Papathanassiou, I'm in a little trouble with my cousin, and I don't want to make it worse. When I went down to the lobby to get something for Dr. Chesweiler that man was there and he started up again."

The astronomer still didn't speak. He didn't look surprised at what Dannerman was saying, only sadly resigned.

"And now," Dannerman went on, "I'm really worrying about not telling my cousin about it. You see, what the man says—well, he says you've been mixed up with some bad business. You have a brother—I think he said the name was Aristide? Yes. And this Aristide was implicated in an assassination on Cyprus. A Turkish tax collector, I think he said. Shot in the back as he was opening his own front door."

Papathanassiou stirred. "I know of this case, yes. A very sad business. But it was long ago, more than five years, and Aristide is only my half-brother. My father's youngest son, by his third wife. We were never close, so what has that to do with me?"

"Well, Aristide's on Interpol's wanted list, and it seems they have some idea you helped him get away."

Papathanassiou nodded somberly. "I was aware they had that idea.

I was questioned at the time, of course. That is all. Never since. But how does it happen, Mr. Dannerman, that you know so much about Interpol?"

"Who, me? Oh, I don't know anything about Interpol," Dannerman said quickly. "That's just what the man said. But if Pat finds out I knew about this and didn't tell her she'll be even madder."

"Madder about what?" Papathanassiou inquired.

"Well, that's where I have this problem. She wanted me to get some data for her, and I said I'd already done it. Actually I hadn't. And now I can't remember the specs for what she wanted, and I can't ask her, because I'd have to admit I lied about doing it already, and I can't look them up because they're in her secure file. So what I wanted to ask you, Dr. Papathanassiou—"

The old man held up his hand. "Permit me to guess," he said. He didn't seem angry or surprised, only sorrowful. "I imagine what you want is for me to give you the access code for the secure file. Simply so you can carry out Dr. Adcock's orders, of course. And then, I imagine, you will no longer feel it necessary to tell her about this other matter."

"Well . . . yes. That's about it," Dannerman agreed, and did not enjoy the expression on the astronomer's face.

It was a long subway ride to Coney Island, and at rush hour the trains were packed. It hadn't taken long, after Papathanassiou left—without saying good-bye, Dannerman remembered—to access the secure file and dump it all into a coded transmission for the National Bureau of Investigation office. But it hadn't left time for anything like a leisurely dinner—at least, not if he wanted to get to the theater early. The best Dannerman could do was to pick up some falafel and a juice box, figuring he could stave off starvation on the way, and then there just wasn't enough elbow room in the standing-room-only subway car to eat them. They were at lower Manhattan before he was able to squirm his way to the corner of the car. He managed to eat his dinner there on the long stretch under the East River, doing his best to avoid spilling hummus on the luckier seated passengers around him, but he took no pleasure in it. For one thing, all that congested body heat had caused all the high-tech micropores in the garments of his fellow passengers to open, and the collective odor was not appetizing. More than that, there was the depressing business with Christo Papathanassiou. Dannerman could not help empathizing with what the old man must be feeling. Hilda was right about one thing anyway, Dannerman admitted to himself. He had the bad habit of letting himself feel what his victims went through. In a way, it was an asset for a professional spook. It had certainly made it easier for him to get along with, for instance, Ilse of the Mad King Ludwigs, not to mention even the Carpezzios. But sometimes it made him feel, well, guilty.

By the time the train had come out of the ground and begun to run on the old elevated tracks, Dannerman even found a seat. He took advantage of the time to run through his messages, none of which mattered to him, and then did what most of his fellow passengers were doing: stared blankly into space, or watched the advertisements as they circled around the display panels just under the ceiling of the car. What caught his eye was a commercial for a soft drink with a mild tetrahydrocannabinol content—the obligatory surgeon general's warning ran in inconspicuous type under the prancing cartoon figures, along with the legend "Not to be sold to anyone under 14." The figures, comically struggling with each other for the soda, were the seven aliens: the Sleepy with its red-shot eyes and pursy little three-cornered mouth, the Happy with its ominous shark-toothed grin, the Bashful, the Doc—all of them, in their sanitized and anthropomorphized Disney-like forms. As cartoons, the creatures were funny and not at all threatening. But suppose, Dannerman thought, suppose the real creatures were somewhere not far away, possibly as close as Starcophagus. Suppose the messages from space had in fact been warnings. Suppose the creatures were actually a clear and present danger that the world really needed to be warned about. Dannerman remembered the little song the taxi driver's Grumpy doll had sung—"Hi-ho, hi-ho, to conquer Earth we go, we'll steal your pearls and all your girls, hi-ho, hi-ho." But it might not be a joking matter.

Dannerman dismissed the notion; it was simply too fanciful, and, besides, he had nearer concerns. He leaned back, closed his eyes, and thought about just what it was that he was going to say to Anita Berman.

There were a million ways of breaking off a relationship. The trouble was that they all started from the same point: you had to *want* the relationship to be broken off, and Dannerman was a long way from being certain of that. It was the job that mandated the break, not his personal wishes. Although the life of an NBI agent was surely full of interesting incidents, there was a part of Dan Dannerman that sometimes thought wistfully about what it would be like to live a more settled existence. To have a home of his own, for instance. In something like a four-room apartment somewhere in the outer suburbs, with a regular job that didn't require him to move somewhere else on short notice. A home that he could share with someone else on a more or less permanent basis. With someone, for example, who was a lot like Anita Berman. . . .

That wasn't a useful speculation, either. He wasn't going to resign from the Bureau, for what else would he do with his time? By the time he got to the stop for Theater Aristophanes Two he had managed to bury that line of thought along with imaginings about the aliens and the memory of his conversation with Christo Papathanassiou, and was only looking forward to an evening that was all his own.

The people who got out with him were a mixed lot; Coney Island wasn't the worst neighborhood in Brooklyn, but it wasn't the best either. It was not what you would consider a natural place for a theater, but the old Ukrainian Orthodox church they had converted into Theater Aristophanes Two had one great advantage. It was cheap. It was a sound building, too, because the Ukrainians had done their best to make the area livable—built a church, tore down the worst of the burned-out tenements, turned some of the vacant lots into vegetable gardens. But when the Ukrainians moved out and the immigrating Palestinians, Biafrans and Kurds moved in, the neighborhood went sour again. The new people apparently didn't go in for farming—maybe there weren't any farms in Palestine or Iraq? Anyway, now there was little behind the chain-link fences but burdock and trash, and the church had lost its congregation. The theater group had been able to pick it up for a nominal rental and a lot of sweat equity—it needed the sweat work, because it had been looted twice and flooded three times in Atlantic hurricanes. On warm evenings it still smelled a little like low tide at the beach. It wasn't very big, either. Maximum seating capacity was not quite two hundred. That had its good aspects; it was easier to fill than a bigger house, and most of all it kept the theatrical unions from bothering the group . . . even though it also meant that Theater Aristophanes Two had no chance at all of ever turning a profit.

But that, of course, wasn't what they were there for. The members of the group were there because theater was in their blood—or because it was what they were trained for and nothing better offered itself.

Dannerman arrived early. The lobby doors were locked; but when he knocked the "manager," Timmi Trout, peered out of the ticket window and came out to let him in. "Dan," she said, pleased, "hey, we thought we'd lost you. I should've known you'd be here for the opening, anyway. They're still rehearsing—it's a mess, because we open in an hour, and that idiot Bucky Korngold's out of the cast because he got himself arrested yesterday on some damn drug charge. Can you imagine?"

Dannerman could imagine very easily. Practically everybody in the group had a day job, of course. Bucky Korngold's had been dealing drugs; he was one of the people Dannerman had been investigating in the Carpezzio matter. He said, "Mind if I go in and watch?"

"Of course not." She hesitated. "Anita's going to be real glad to see you, you know. She's been kind of worried about you . . . but, hey, you'll talk to her yourself. Go on in."

He did, and took his seat in a back row as inconspicuously as possible. The cast wasn't so much rehearsing as shouting at each other for missing cues and stepping on each other's lines—normal enough for a final rehearsal at Aristophanes Two—and he saw Anita Berman at once. For one thing, she was the prettiest woman on the stage: slim, tall, red-haired, with a deep, carrying voice that was perfect for unmiked theater (and of no use at all in the heavily enhanced productions on Broadway).

She saw him right away, too. When she caught sight of him at the back of the theater she looked startled, then perplexed, then gave him a tentative, not quite forgiving, see-you-in-a-minute wave. And it wasn't much more than a minute before the director abandoned his attempts to get the performance running like clockwork. "Go back for makeup, all of you," he ordered. "A bad dress rehearsal means a good show, they say. Maybe you can take comfort in that. I know I will."

And Anita Berman jumped down from the stage and ran up the aisle to meet Dannerman. It was clear she'd made up her mind for forgiveness. "I'm real glad you're here," she said, putting up her face to be kissed.

She clung to him for a moment, then pulled back to look at his face. "I guess we've kind of been playing telephone tag."

"I'm sorry about that," he said, meaning it—meaning at least the "sorry" part. "I've got this new job and it keeps me really on the jump."

"I figured it was something like that. I guess you're making a lot more money there—?"

"Maybe soon, anyway," he said vaguely. "But it takes all my time. Matter of fact, I'll have to be going out of town pretty soon."

"Ah," she said. "For very long?"

"I don't know that yet."

She was silent for a moment, then said, "Dan, dear, listen. I've been thinking about us. I know some men still like to be in control, and maybe—well, if you think I was rushing things, talking about moving in together—"

"That's not it," he said uncomfortably. "Look, you need to get ready for the performance and we've got a lot to talk about. How about if I meet you after the play?"

She gave him a sudden smile. "That'll be fine, Dan. Come backstage and we'll go to the cast party. You can tell me all about the new job and your trip. I'll be waiting for you."

So Dannerman had the whole duration of the play to decide on a story about where he was going on the trip he had invented on the spur of the moment, and how long he would be away.

There was a funny thing about that, if only he had known it. It was part of Dannerman's tradecraft as an NBI agent to tell selected fragments of truth in order to deceive. For a change, this time it was the other way around. Although he didn't know it yet, the deception was truth. He was indeed going away, in fact very much farther away than he could ever have imagined.

Fidgeting in his seat while waiting for the curtain to go up, Dannerman was trying to decide what to do about Anita Berman. He didn't *have* to break up with her. Well, not just yet, anyway. Sometime, yes, because a permanent, committed relationship was out of the question for anybody in Dannerman's line of work. The worrisome part was that, he was pretty sure, the longer he waited the worse it would be for her when the break did come; and how bad was he willing to make it for sweet, pretty Anita Berman?

When the play began, he was glad to put that question out of his mind; what was happening on the stage held his interest. Maybe the old adage was right; the blunders of the rehearsal had disappeared and the cast was flawless in the first act of *The Subway.* Anita was beautiful even in her 1920s bargain-basement flapper costume, and whoever the actor was who had taken over for poor Bucky Korngold, he didn't miss a beat.

Even the play itself was going well with the audience. *The Subway* was definitely one of Elmer Rice's more squirrelly works, and Dannerman was the one who had first urged it on the group. It was ideal for them. It was short. It used a large cast—always an asset for an Off-Off-*Off*-Broadway theater, when everybody involved wanted to get on stage where some slumming big-time media critic might just possibly think their performance worth a few seconds' commendation in a review. The play was cheap to produce, since it only required one impressionistic—and therefore inexpensive—set. Most important of all, *The Subway* was just about totally forgotten. No major company had given it a production in close to a hundred years, and so the troupe didn't have a million library tapes floating around out there to compete with.

He had also vowed to the group that *some* critics, at least, would be sufficiently intrigued by a long-lost classic of "modern" American theater to make the long run out to Coney Island to see its revival. He was happy to see that he had been right about that. He was pretty sure that at least six or eight of the audience members were actual critics. None of them were smiling, but he didn't expect that. Critics didn't smile. The important thing was that they weren't walking out, either.

Then, when the first act ended, at least two of them were actually clapping. Well, the whole audience was enthusiastic in its applause—not surprising, since a good half of its members were in some way related to one of the actors—but it was a good sign. In the intermission crowd that packed the lobby—once the vestry, when the place had been a church—Dannerman attached himself, as inconspicuously as possible, to a woman he was nearly sure was a TV talk-show host, trying to overhear what she was saying to her companion. But she was only commenting on the buskers on the sidewalk outside: two Arab kids tap-dancing while a third, in an "I ♥ Allah" T-shirt, worked the intermission crowd for cash. He started for another potential critic and was annoyed when someone touched his arm. He turned to face a short, plump woman who was placidly gazing up at him. "Why, Danno," she said, "it really is you, isn't it? Nice to run into you like this. Why don't we step outside for a little air?"

"Damn it, Hilda," he said. "What the hell are you doing here?"

She didn't answer that, but then she didn't need to. She simply steered him firmly out of the doors and around the corner to where a large truck was parked at the curb. The liquid-crystal display on its side glittered with the words NIITAKE BROS. MOVING & STORAGE, but Dannerman knew it was not going to be any ordinary moving van.

It wasn't. It turned out to be a complete mobile NBI surveillance station, with a Police Corps master sergeant saluting smartly as Colonel Hilda Morrisey brought him in.

"It's time for us to do a little business," she said cheerfully. "Take a pew, Danno. Want some coffee? A beer? We're pretty well stocked here, and Horace'll get you anything you want."

"What I wanted was to be left alone for one damn evening with my friends."

"Another time, Danno. How's it going?"

"As well as can be expected, considering you picked Korngold up the day before the opening."

"Not me. *They,*" she corrected. "They picked everybody in the operation up, but I wasn't involved. I've been off the Carpezzio business as long as you have, because your cousin's is more important. Let's have your report."

She absorbed the news about the Floridian general and the diamonds without comment, but winced when he told her that the "muggers" had broken Mick Jarvas's wrong arm. "We'll have to do that another way," she said resignedly. "You've got to get his job, because she's going out to Starlab and you're going to have to go with her."

He goggled at the woman. "Into *space?* Nobody goes into *space* anymore!"

"She does; that's what she was bribing the general for. And she would've taken Jarvas along for muscle, but we'll have to change that."

"You want me to go into *space*?" he said again.

"Why are you making such a big deal out of this? Lots of people have gone into space."

"Not the Bureau! And not recently for almost anybody."

"Well, until recently the Bureau didn't have a reason."

He looked at her more carefully. "Something's happened," he said.

"That data from your cousin's file happened, Danno," the colonel said triumphantly. "I knew there'd be something there. You know what it was? Synchrotron radiation!"

He said impatiently, "Cut the crap, Hilda. I don't know what that is."

"Well, neither do I, exactly. But that's what started your cousin off. Seven or eight months ago the observatory was trying one more time to reactivate the satellite, and they detected a burst of this synchrotron radiation coming from it."

"But you said to check into *gamma* radiation."

"I know what I said. The agent who passed the word along must've gotten it wrong; anyway, the word is it's definitely synchrotron, not gamma. There wasn't much of it. It lasted just for a few seconds. But it was definite, according to your cousin's analysis, and the thing is, there isn't supposed to be anything on Starlab that could cause it." She paused, studying his face. "So you know what that means? Something's been added to Starlab."

"Are you going to tell me what that is?"

"I'll show you, as much as we know. Horace? Will you start the simulation now, please?"

The sergeant touched one button, and the inside of the truck body went dark; touched another, and the simulation tank at the front of the body lit up with a picture of Starlab, sailing along in its perpetual fall toward Earth, with its ruff of solar panels soaking up photovoltaic power to run the instruments that were no longer responding, and its huge collector eyes staring unseeingly out at the universe.

"As you can see," Hilda instructed, "it's big. That's because it was designed to let astronomers live there for weeks at—"

"I've seen all this, Hilda. It's no secret. Christ, they've got a model of the thing in the observatory waiting room."

"Don't rush me, Danno. We're coming to what you haven't seen. This is stuff we got from your cousin's observatory records. She had this whole segment deleted from the public bank—decided to keep it a secret, I guess—but once our technicians knew what to look for they had no trouble retrieving it. This is enhanced imaging, otherwise you couldn't see anything at all. Watch that little thing coming in from the upper right."

"I see it." It was a nearly featureless lump, by comparison with the huge Starlab no bigger than a football. It slipped past the great solar vanes and gently caressed the sheathing of the main body of the satellite. It didn't bounce away. It stuck where it touched. Then, while Dannerman watched, the object draped itself to the curvature of the shell. In a moment it was almost invisible again, except as a nearly imperceptible swelling of the hull.

"So what the hell is it?" Dannerman demanded. "Space junk?"

"Did that look like junk? It didn't crash into the satellite, did it? Looks to me like it *docked* with the son of a bitch."

"What then?" As the idea struck him: "Does it have any connection with the CLO?"

"Good question," she said approvingly. "I ran that past the experts as soon as they dug out the clip on the object. They said no. They said this thing was way too small to be taken for a comet, although they couldn't turn up any later observations of the object; lost it somewhere, I guess. But they didn't exclude the possibility that this thing had come in on the CLO and been dropped off."

"Like a probe?"

"I guess. Anyway, they're pretty sure it is some kind of an artifact."

"Well," he said reasonably, "if it's an artifact somebody would have to put it in orbit. Who's been launching spacecraft lately?"

"Nobody. Not openly, anyway."

"Some terrorist bunch?"

"God, I hope not. If there's some kind of technology that can launch an artifact without anybody detecting it we need to know about it. If terrorists got hold of it . . . well, can you imagine what it would mean if the Mads or the Irish or the goddam Basques could put up their own satellites?" She shrugged expressively, then added, "But maybe that would be better than the other possibility, at that. Your cousin seems to think it's extraterrestrial."

"But that doesn't make any sense, Hilda! If she thought that, why would she keep it a secret?"

"Money," she said shortly.

"From what, damn it?"

"Oh, Danno," she sighed, "you know what your trouble is? You just don't think like a normal human being. You aren't greedy enough. Think about it: some kind of technology that can produce synchrotron radiation where there isn't supposed to be any. The brains tell me that it can't be done without a big particle accelerator—those things that run out of subway-tunnel kind of things, fifteen or twenty miles long. So that means there has to be some pretty hot hardware up there. If it's alien, it's worth money to whoever finds it. For us, on the other hand, it doesn't matter whether it's from some weirdo ET or somebody on Earth; we want it."

"So let the Bureau send a mission up to get it," Dannerman said reasonably.

She shook her head. "That's one option, sure. But maybe we can't. It's tricky. Starlab's private property; your uncle paid for it out of his own pocket. Maybe we could get around that—that's what we've got lawyers for, for God's sake—but then there's the other problem. We don't want to alert other people to what's going on. The goddam Europeans might send up a mission of their own if they knew we were after something; they can move faster than NASA, and you know there's no security there. And anyway the goddam Floridians still control the launch facilities."

"So?"

"So—*probably*—the final decision hasn't been made, because too many of the top people are all tied up with the press-secretary thing—so probably we want to let her go ahead, but send one of our own along to make sure we get first crack at whatever's there."

"Ah," said Dannerman glumly. "Like me, you mean."

"Exactly like you, Danno, so you have to take Jarvas's place. I've got an idea about that. Sergeant? Kill the display and let's have some light again while we brief Agent Dannerman on what he's going to do for us."

As she turned to get something out of a locker, Dannerman tardily remembered the other thing that had been on his mind. He sneaked a look at his watch.

It was late. The play would be long over before he got away from the colonel. And so he wouldn't be keeping his promise to meet Anita backstage; which meant that probably that particular problem had already settled itself.

8
Dan

When Danny Dannerman was eight years old, spaceflight was still a going business. Young Danny was a pretty normal American kid, too, so naturally he did a lot of daydreaming, picturing his grown-up self as one of those grand spacefaring adventurers with sharp uniforms, rows of ribbons, the look of eagles on their faces and all. But that was then. Then he was a child. As he was growing to become a man, the space program was dwindling at almost the same rate of speed—few human heroes but a lot of machines; then, as money began to run short, fewer machines, too. Even instrument launches got rarer and rarer, and the dream dried up.

Until now.

Now it had become not only real but *personal,* and Dannerman had never reckoned on anything like this. When he joined the National Bureau of Investigation he knew, as every rookie knew, that the work could take you anywhere in the world; but it had never occurred to him that it might someday take him right out of it. All the way home from Coney Island, in the subway train sparsely occupied by drunks and sleeping homeless people, he thought about what he had let himself in for. Climb into a giant kind of sardine can and let them lock it shut behind you. Lie there, strapped in and helpless, while a few dozen exploding tons of fireworks blasted you, hard as a hammer blow, right off the surface of the Earth. Oh, the idea was exciting, all right; but it kept him awake for an hour after, very late, he finally got to his narrow bed in Rita's condo, and then he dreamed all night of spaceships and hideous, sharp-toothed aliens and a long, terrifying fall out of orbit. He didn't know what final smashup he was falling to. The dreams never got that far. But all night long he was falling, falling; and when the speaker clock woke him at 6:45 (the only time he could expect to beat his neighbors to the shower) he was edgy and unrested.

And then, as he was getting ready to leave, Hilda called. "You're awake. Good. You've got a busy day ahead of you, Danno. I should've told you there wasn't much time. Now there's no time at all."

"What are you talking about?"

"I'm talking about your cousin, what do you think? She got all her papers signed last night. She's planning to launch tomorrow."

The news beat Dannerman to the office. By the time he arrived, half the observatory staff was clustered in the reception room, all chattering. "What's going on?" he demanded, as Janice DuPage checked his sidearm. "Where's Jarvas?"

"In Dr. Adcock's office. So're Dr. Artzybachova and Commander Lin. They're going up to the orbiter, Dan!"

"Up to the Starcophagus?" he asked, hoping to learn more than the colonel had been able to tell him.

Even in the excitement of the morning she took time to give him a reproving look. "To the *Starlab,* right. We don't use that other word, remember? Anyway," she went on, the spirit of the morning taking over again, "she's going to make an announcement as soon as everyone's here—that'll be any minute now—but that's what it is, all right. I saw the documents myself when they came in. Isn't that wonderful, Dr. Papathanassiou?" she added, as the old man came up to hand her his ancient Uzi.

"Yes, quite wonderful," he said, managing to avoid noticing that Dannerman was standing right beside him.

"It calls for a celebration," said one of the postdocs. "Is there any money in petty cash, Janice? Maybe Dan could go out and get some supplies—"

"I'll ask Dr. Adcock as soon as she's made the announcement," Janice promised, and someone else predicted:

"She won't want to spend the money."

"So what the hell," the postdoc said happily. "We'll take up a collection. God! To have observing time on Starlab! You don't know what that's going to do for my T-Tauri count!"

But they did know; they all did know, because almost all of them had observations they wanted to make, and only the skimpiest budget of hours Pat Adcock had been willing to buy for them on the Keck, or the big twin instruments in Arizona, or even the ancient radio dish at Arecibo. They didn't need party "supplies." They were all partying already, and when the interoffice channel lighted up and Pat Adcock's flushed face appeared on all the screens there was a cheer from everywhere in the observatory.

Pat had to have heard it, even locked in her private office; she looked startled, then grinned. "I guess you all know what I'm going to say already," she said. "Well, it's true. The mission is on. We're taking off tomorrow; in seventy-two hours we'll be on Starlab. Dr. Schneyman will be in charge while I'm gone—and—and wish me luck, all of you!"

But she hadn't said what kind of luck she wanted. Dannerman wondered what she was going to tell them all if she got back with a fortune in new technology, but the old orbiter still out of commission . . . but it wouldn't matter, of course. If she was right—

If she was right, the whole world was going to change, and Dannerman himself would be part of it . . . provided, that is, he reminded himself, he did what the colonel wanted him to do and won the chance to go along.

He patted his belly bag, where the pouch Hilda had given him was packed away. What he needed now was a chance to use it.

Pat had firmly vetoed the notion of a party, but not much work got done at the observatory that morning anyway. Word of the mission had got out. Janice was kept busy on the phone, fending off calls from well-wishers, listening to complaints from the downstairs security guards, besieged by reporters with their tinycams who wanted statements from Dr. Adcock. When Pat took her crew out to an early lunch most of the staff took off, too, determined to celebrate even if they had to do it at some nearby restaurant. The observatory finally began to quiet down.

It was time for Dannerman to do his job; all he needed was for Janice DuPage to cooperate. He lurked around the reception room, waiting for her to leave her desk for a moment. It didn't happen for a long time. She seemed fixed at her desk, making him wonder what sort of bladder the woman had. But finally, with hardly a quarter of an hour before Mick Jarvas would be back with his charges, Janice stood up, put the elevator door entrance on lock, picked up her purse and moved toward the washrooms.

Dannerman didn't wait. As soon as she was out of sight he was in the gun locker. A coded computer file might defeat the skills the Bureau had taught him, but a simple locker was not a serious challenge. In thirty seconds he had the locker open, peering past the gun racks until he found Jarvas's private cubbyhole. And when he had it open, there, in among the candy bars and the anti-inflation trade goods and the porno disks, was a package, unmarked, with three sealed medical-looking patches that, he knew, did not contain any physician-prescribed medications.

Bingo. Dannerman pulled the patches out, stuffed them in his belly bag and replaced them with three of the ones Hilda had given him the night before. By the time Janice returned from the ladies' room he was innocently watering the reception-room plants and realizing that he had not left himself enough time to eat lunch. No matter. A missed meal was a small enough price to pay for the mission.

Jarvas was predictable. As soon as he had escorted his charges back from lunch he made a beeline for the gun locker, then for a cubicle in the men's room.

Ten minutes later Dannerman knocked on the lintel of the office where Jimmy Peng-tsu Lin was conferring with Pat Adcock. "Excuse me," he said. "Jimmy?—Commander Lin, I mean? I hate to bother you, but Mick Jarvas is acting kind of funny out here. He's a pretty big guy, and I wonder if you could give me a hand with him."

That brought them both to the doorway, where they gazed incredulously at Jarvas. Who was dreamily waltzing up and down the corridor, pinching the ass of Rosaleen Artzybachova in passing, grabbing unsuccessfully at the breast of Janice DuPage. Rosaleen was laughing; Janice was only annoyed. As he neared Pat Adcock's office she found her voice. "Come in here, Jarvas!" she commanded.

"Sure thing, sweet buns," he said amiably. "Hi, Danny. How's it going, China boy?"

Pat looked bewilderedly at Dannerman as he was closing the door behind them. "What happened?"

Dannerman shrugged. "My guess, he must've got his hands on some extra-powerful dope. You never know what they're going to be selling you on the street."

The bewildered expression changed to anger. "Crap! Mick promised me he doesn't do drugs anymore. I couldn't have a doper for a bodyguard."

"Oh? Well, why don't we just ask him to take his shirt off?"

"Aw, Dan," Jarvas said, suddenly pouting. "I thought you and me were friends."

Pat looked from one to the other, then made her decision. "Do what he says, Mick."

"I don't have to. I got pers'nal privacy rights, don't I?"

She turned to Dannerman. "Take it off him, Dan."

Dannerman looked at Jimmy Lin, who spread his hands; evidently personal combat wasn't one of his specialties. It wasn't something Dannerman would have sought with somebody like Mick Jarvas, either; but the former kick-boxer was giggling. Apart from good-naturedly pushing at Dannerman's hands he hardly resisted as Dannerman pulled the tabs of his shirt loose, *zip,* and slid it down over his back.

On Jarvas's rib cage, just under his right armpit, there was one of Hilda's inconspicuous, flesh-colored patches.

Jimmy Lin chuckled. "Well, what do you know? He really is mellowed out."

"Oh, shit," said Pat, too disappointed to be furious. "What am I going to do now? He can't escort me in that condition."

Jarvas gave her a happy grin. "Course I can, hon. Little joy never hurt me. Just makes my reflexes sharper and all."

He might as well not have been in the room; Pat, biting her lip, didn't even look at him. "I was counting on him," she told the air.

It was the cue Dannerman had been waiting for, but Jimmy Lin forestalled him. "If you need a new bodyguard, Pat," he offered, "what's the matter with your cousin? He's handy enough with his fists, you tell me."

"Danny? For a *bodyguard*?" Pat Adcock stared at him, then at Dannerman. "I guess you're big enough," she said thoughtfully. "What kind of gun do you carry?"

"Twenty-shot spray with quick-change clips. Same as always."

"Are you sure you know how to use it? Oh, right, you were rotsy in college, weren't you?"

"Protsy, actually."

She sighed and made up her mind. "I don't really have much of a choice, do I? All right, Dan-Dan, I guess you're about due for a promotion. How would you like be an astronaut for a while?"

Not much work got done in the observatory that afternoon, either. At least not by Pat Adcock and her spacefarers. As soon as they'd sent Jarvas, sniveling, back to his home in the company of one of the larger postdocs, Pat declared herself through for the day. "Take me home, Dan. I've got to pack. You better take an overnight bag, too."

"Sure thing, Pat. I'm new at this, though. What sort of stuff do you pack to go into space?"

"How do I know? I've never done it before either. I guess they'll give us all the space stuff we need at the Cape, but we'll be gone five days, according to the mission plan, so take whatever personal things you think you'll need. And, oh, yes, don't forget your gun."

"You're expecting trouble?"

She didn't answer. Just, "Don't forget, I want you back at six A.M. to get us to the airport."

Six o'clock, Dannerman thought dismally on the ride up to Pat's Yorktown condo. That meant getting up not much after four; it was a long way from Rita's Riverside Drive place to Yorktown. But at least he could make it an early night.

As soon as he had reported his success to Colonel Hilda Morrisey he went looking for his landlady. "I'm taking your advice and getting out of town for a while, Rita," he told her.

"Hey, great! Where are you going?"

"Florida," he said, and stopped her lecture on how nasty the Floridians were since they got their own government by taking out his payment machine. "I'm not sure how long I'll be gone, so I'd better pay a week or so in advance. I don't want you throwing my stuff out into the street."

"Oh, Dan! I wouldn't do that," she protested, "not even if you were away for even a month."

"It won't be that long," he assured her. "I'm sure of that."

9
Dan

The captain's voice woke Dannerman as the plane was making its approach to the José Martí airport outside the Cape. He hadn't intended to sleep. He hadn't realized he actually was sleeping until he woke up, saw the red light on the seat back before him to show that the airbag had just been armed and saw Pat Adcock stirring beside him. "Look there," she said, yawning as she gazed out the window. "That's our Clipper." There it was, gleaming ceramic white, forty meters tall, with work trucks and people busy around it.

So it wasn't a dream. It was real. That was the ship that was going to lift Dannerman and the others right off the solid planet they had been born to, and all those childish fantasies would become fact.

"Are you scared?" his cousin asked him, giving him a searching look.

"Oh, no. Well, not really *scared.* Are you?"

"Certainly not," she said. "Going into space isn't what worries me. Uncle Cubby brainwashed me pretty well, you know; it was his dream, only he never could pass the physical to make it on his own, and I guess he infected me. That's not what's bothering me."

He looked at her with new interest. "But something else is?"

"Well, yes." She squirmed around to look back at Jimmy Lin and Rosaleen Artzybachova, in their own seats a few rows back. "For one thing, I don't know if I can trust Lin," she said moodily as she straightened again. "Delasquez, either. That's why I want you along, Dan. Keep an eye on those guys while we're up there."

"But they're the pilots you picked," he said reasonably.

She shrugged. "I had to take what I could get. Just be careful about them, okay?" She peered up and down the length of the plane. "Do you suppose it's too late to go to the can?" she asked.

It was. The stews were cruising the aisle, checking seat belts and picking up empty glasses. He said consolingly, "We'll be on the ground in a moment."

"Yes? And then what?"

He said, surprised, "Then there'll be a chance to get to the ladies' room right away."

She gave him a pursed-lips look. "That's right, you've never been in Florida before, have you?"

He hadn't understood what Pat had meant by that, but as soon as they were off the plane it became clear. The passengers were not permitted to step off the plane and go freely about their business. The passengers were immediately herded into long lines for customs inspection—well, it wasn't called "customs," exactly, since Florida wasn't really an exactly independent country, however determinedly they insisted on their own laws and practices. The processing was just as thorough, though, and the first step was that one of the agents collected everybody's carry weapons. Dannerman hated to give up his twenty-shot, but all the more seasoned Florida travelers seemed to take it as a matter of course. The agent tagged each gun and gave the owner a claim check—"So you can redeem it, señor, when you leave our beautiful Free State." Then another set of agents searched methodically through everyone's bags and pockets. For a moment Dannerman thought they might even insist on a body-cavity search as well, but it didn't come to that. It was bad enough, though; the inspector gasped in outrage when she patted him down and found his ankle weapon.

She held the gun in her hand and gave him a severe look. "This is contraband weapon," she announced. "It is conceal. This is not permit in the Free State of Florida. It must be confiscate." She beckoned to a state policeman, who patted his own gun to make sure it hadn't fallen out of its holster as he strolled toward them.

The cop waved all four of the party over to a little quarantine ghetto while the customs agent and her supervisor debated the matter in Spanish. Pat was irate. Rosaleen Artzybachova waited patiently for a resolution to the problem. Jimmy Lin showed amusement. "Danny, Danny," he said reproachfully, "don't you know any better than that? When you go to Florida you leave your own gun at home. Nobody brings a gun to Florida. You don't need it. You can always pick up another on the street—there's not a block in the state where you can't buy anything you want."

Dannerman didn't answer. He did know better; he just hadn't wanted to part with his service special.

"It's all right," Pat announced, waving in relief to a tall man who had appeared at the customs desk. Although he was wearing a different uniform this time, gleaming dress whites with clusters of ribbons at his chest, Dannerman recognized General Martín Delasquez. He spoke rapidly to the customs agents, then approached them, looking grave.

"What a pity, Dr. Adcock," he said to Pat, ignoring Dannerman. "Your man has attempted to break our law. Therefore he is forbidden admission to our state. However, I believe that we can avoid the legal penalties. I have arranged that he will be placed on the first return flight to New York, and the rest of you may proceed to the staging area."

"Oh, no!" Pat Adcock exclaimed. "I want him with me."

Delasquez shook his head politely. "But it is impossible, you see?" he said reasonably.

"Maybe not," Dannerman said. He had been watching Delasquez carefully. The general looked at him for the first time.

"You spoke?" he asked, his tone frosty.

"Yes, I did, General. You know what I bet? I bet you have enough authority to get us all through these bureaucrats, don't you, General?"

Delasquez said coldly, "It is apparent that you do not understand the gravity of your situation."

"I bet I do. For instance, I bet I know what would happen next. I bet while I was waiting for the next plane the cops would ask me a lot of questions. I wouldn't want to lie to them, either. And if the subject of our first meeting came up I'd have to tell them anything they wanted to know—you know, like the articles I delivered to you in New York?"

Delasquez did not respond for a moment. He studied Dannerman in silence, then turned to Pat Adcock. "Who is this man?" he demanded.

She shrugged. "He's my cousin."

"And do you know what trouble this could cause?" She didn't answer, only shrugged again. Then Delasquez smiled. "Well, what harm can it do? It is only a technical violation, after all. I think I can persuade the authorities to let you pass."

"And get our guns back for us, too, please," Dannerman added.

10
Dan

The flight started tamely. The takeoff thrust was not much worse than some of the high-speed scramjets Dannerman had taken to cross an ocean, but the Clipper was still being an airplane then.

He hardly noticed when the takeoff jets switched over to the higher-speed contoured flow, but then the time came when the scram cut over to rocket thrust, and he noticed that, all right. That was *real* acceleration. He was squashed into his seat for four long minutes. His belly sagged, his head drooped, he realized for the first time that even his eyeballs had weight on their sockets. Then he fell forward against his chest straps as the thrust cut; he was suddenly weightless, and they were on their way.

It was about then that Dannerman realized that space travel took a long time to happen . . . and that while it was happening there was nothing much to do. What he wanted to do was to get out of his seat and roam around the Clipper, but he had been warned against that. He quickly saw why. Every course correction brought another jolt, not nearly as violent as the first but unpredictable for either time or direction. Then the gimbaled seats tilted, the motors roared, and you were lucky if you didn't bite your tongue or bash your head.

A window, at least, would have been nice. He didn't have one. All he had was the tiny TV screen on his armrest, but all it showed was black, empty space. By his side Rosaleen Artzybachova sat with her eyes placidly closed, maybe even napping; well, spaceflight was nothing new to her. She could not have been comfortable; her feet rested on a pair of gray metal boxes, lashed to the seat supports, and so her knees were squeezed almost into her belly. Just ahead, but out of his sight, Pat was in the third-pilot seat, trying to talk to Delasquez and

Lin at the controls; Dannerman couldn't make out the words, and if the pilots answered he couldn't hear.

In the seat next to him Artzybachova opened her eyes and gazed at him. "Are you all right?" When he nodded, she asked politely, "And how are you enjoying spaceflight? Is it what you expected?"

"Well, no. Not exactly. I thought we'd have to go through more training—"

She laughed. "Like high-G conditioning in those awful old centrifuges? Drills for emergency actions? Thank heaven, we don't do that anymore. We don't wear spacesuits, either."

"I noticed that." What Dannerman himself had on was the slacks and jacket he had put on that morning. Dr. Artzybachova and Jimmy Lin were wearing one-piece coveralls, General Delasquez the combat fatigues of the Florida Air Guard.

Dr. Artzybachova was still being grandmotherly. "Are you hungry? I brought some apples and I believe there are other things on board."

"Hungry? No."

"And you don't have to pee or anything? You should've gone before we took off."

"I don't," he said shortly, but she had put the idea in his mind. He quelled it, for there was an opportunity here to be taken. "Dr. Artzybachova? Can I ask you something? Is there something, well, peculiar about what we're doing?"

She gave him an amused look, pale eyebrows raised. "Define 'peculiar.' "

He chose his words with care. "This is supposed to be a simple repair mission, right? But there are all these rumors—"

"What kind of rumors?"

He spread his hands. "Something about some kind of radiation from Starlab that wasn't supposed to be there? I don't understand that very well, Dr. Artzybachova; I was an English major. And something about those messages with the Seven Ugly Space Dwarfs?"

"You are very skilled at listening to rumors, Mr. Dannerman." It wasn't a compliment.

He pressed on. "I get the idea that that's really what this mission is about. Something *alien* on Starlab? Something that might be worth a lot of money. Pat wouldn't talk to me about it—"

"That is not surprising," the old lady observed.

"I guess not. Will you?"

Dr. Artzybachova studied his face for a moment, considering, while the Clipper rolled itself into a new position. "I suppose it could do no harm now. In a little while you will see what we all see—whatever that turns out to be. Or it will turn out that there is nothing worth seeing, and then we will simply try to determine what repairs might make Starlab function as originally designed again. So," she said, sighing, "yes, the rumors are true. Fifteen months ago your cousin's observatory detected a burst of synchrotron radiation from Starlab. No one else appeared to observe it, but then no one else was actively trying to reestablish communications with the orbiter. So she called me at my dacha. I flew at once to New York. We examined all the logs of instrumentation changes and, no, there simply was nothing on Starlab that could have produced that emission. So we performed a data check."

Dannerman pricked up his ears; this was new. "What kind of data check?"

"A fortunate coincidence: the Japanese were getting ready to replace one of their old weather satellites, so they did a census of everything in orbit—to select a safe slot for their satellite, you see. One of their instrument people was a former student of mine. From her I got all their obs of astronomical satellites—including Starlab. When we massaged the data it became clear that there was a steady flux of very low-level radiation coming from it, in several bands—none of it compatible with the presumed dead-board status of the satellite. In addition, optically, there was a blister on the side of the satellite that didn't belong there. Finally, just recently we got another indication. There was a comet-like object—"

"Yes, I know about the comet-like object."

She regarded him thoughtfully. "Yes, I suppose you do."

"And what all this adds up to?"

"Oh, Mr. Dannerman," she said, sounding less patient, "I have no doubt that you know that, too. All the evidence taken together, there is strong reason to believe that something extraterrestrial has established itself on Starlab."

"An *alien*?"

She looked pensive. "Probably not a living one, no. At least I hope not. More likely some sort of automated probe. But definitely some sort of technology that is not terrestrial in origin."

A quick course correction spun their chairs around; the old lady grimaced and closed her eyes. Evidently she had finished her story.

But Dannerman hadn't finished thinking about it. It sounded wholly preposterous, but this apparently sane woman seemed to give it credence. He cleared his throat. "Dr. Artzybachova?" And when she opened her eyes again, "I can see that new technology might be worth a lot of money. But what do you do with it when we find it?"

"*If* we find it. But that I cannot say until we see it, of course. That is what I am along for, me and my instruments." She tapped one of the boxes with a toe.

"I was wondering about them," he said.

She smiled. "Of course. Did you think I could examine what we find—whatever we find—by smell, perhaps? Although it may be that none of these instruments will be of any use, since we have no data on what might be there."

"But you must have some idea—"

She raised her hand amiably. "But, Mr. Dannerman—Dan, may I? And please call me Rosaleen; it was a notion of my mother's when I was born. She was much taken with the wife of your American president and gave me a name as close to hers as she dared." She paused, then finished her thought. "But, Dan, I really don't know what will be on Starlab, you see. I only have hopes. I hope that there will be some useful-looking devices which I can remove and bring back for analysis. Do you know the term 'reverse engineering'? For that, so that perhaps they can be copied in some way. Will that happen? I don't know. Will there be anything alien in Starlab at all? I don't know even that much, either; it is all hopes. It is quite possible that, even if there is something there, it will be so unfamiliar that I will not dare to try to remove it. Or there may be nothing at all. In either case, we will have done all this for nothing."

He looked at her. "Seems like a pretty long shot, the way you describe it."

"Ah," she said softly, "but think of the payoff. If we win our bet there will be unimaginable benefits, and not just in money. I would not have left my comfortable summer place in Ukraine just for the money, only for the chance to learn." She looked pensive for a moment, then smiled. "Whatever it is, we'll find out for sure when we get aboard. Now, Dan, if you'll excuse me, we should be coming around toward North America again and I'd like to check the uplinks for news."

Dannerman must have drifted off to sleep again, in spite of everything, because the next thing he remembered was Jimmy Lin's cheery hail. The astronaut was swinging weightlessly toward them, hand over hand, pausing to float in space upside down by Dannerman. "So how do you like micrograv?" he asked amiably; then, glancing at Artzybachova and lowering his voice: "Tell you one thing, if my great-great had ever gone into orbit he would've had to write three or four new books. You don't know what screwing is until you try it weightless."

Rosaleen turned to him, her arms still waving in the graceful flow of tai chi. Ignoring the astronaut's remarks, she asked, "Are we getting close to Starlab?"

"Not too far. That's why I'm going to the head now; if we have to wear those damn suits I won't want to need to pee. I recommend the same to you two, soon's I'm through. But don't stay out of your seats any longer than you have to, okay? And sing out when you're both strapped in again. The general claims he ranks me, so he's doing most of the piloting, and he has a heavy hand with the delta-vees."

Dannerman's bladder was signaling to him with increasing urgency, but he didn't get his turn for a while. He deferred to Rosaleen Artzybachova out of politeness, and then to General Delasquez because he wasn't given much choice when the pilot came back and pushed his way past; then to his cousin out of politeness again. By then his fidgeting was becoming conspicuous. Dr. Artzybachova, observing it, did her best to distract him. "Have you seen?" she inquired, reaching over to adjust his screen. It was displaying something tiny and oddly shaped, but when she turned up the magnification it became a satellite with antennae and solar collectors poking out in all directions.

"Starlab?" he ventured.

That amused her. "No, of course not. It is simply a dead old orbiter, I think a military one, and probably Russian; but it is interesting, is it not?"

Oh, it was interesting enough, as a souvenir of the days when wars were actually fought between nations, instead of between legions of police on one side, and on the other a horde of criminals and a few squads of slippery terrorists. He cast a longing look at the toilet, but Pat was still locked inside. "Well," he said to the Ukrainian woman, forcing jolliness into his tone, "was there any interesting news in the uplinks?" Dutifully she rehearsed the principal items for him: England's MI-5 had caught a dozen Welsh freedom fighters redhanded in possession of nuclear materials; some Sikhs at the Marseilles airport had machine-gunned Moslem pilgrims en route to Mecca; and in Washington the President had finally announced the death of his kidnapped press secretary. Hilda would be going crazy, he thought; but he didn't think it long. The door to the toilet was opening, and he was already unbuckling himself to go there.

Pat was looking baffled when she finally came out, and when Dannerman got his chance at the toilet he saw why. The writing on the cubicle wall wasn't graffiti. It was instructions, a complete tech manual to the use of a micrograv toilet, and it took a bit of doing. As he was finishing up with the complex flush maneuver he heard squawking from outside. He hurried back to his seat, Rosaleen waving him on; and there, spinning slowly on the screen, was an orbiter that he recognized because he had spent so much time studying its pictures. There was no doubt about it. Just disappearing from view between the solar-collector struts and a communications dish was the blister that might, or might not, have come from outer space. The construction was *immense.*

"So that's Starlab," he said.

"Of course it is," Rosaleen said fretfully. "And, look, the optical mirror has been left uncovered all this time—who knows how much damage it's taken from microjunk impacts?"

"There's a little ship attached to the side," Dannerman observed.

"Yes, the ACRV—the Assured Crew Rescue Vehicle. It was supposed to take crew back to the Earth in an emergency, but poor Manny Lefrik never got a chance to use it."

"Manny Lefrik?" Memory clicked the name into place: the astronomer who had died on Starlab. "Did you know him?"

She sighed. "Of course I knew him. Very well, in fact, and on this very satellite; Jimmy was quite right about making love in microgravity." And then, noting the expression on his face, "Oh, Dan! Can you not believe that I was not always a million years old? But buckle yourself in quickly; there will be much maneuvering now. Hurry!"

She was right about the maneuvering. Docking was tricky, with a lot of swearing in three languages from the pilots up ahead as they jockeyed the spacecraft to its port. But then there was a faint metallic crunch and a shudder, and a cry of satisfaction from Pat Adcock. The Clipper had mated with Starlab.

Beside him, Rosaleen Artzybachova was busily removing the containment straps from her instrument cases. "Let me help you," Dannerman offered.

She hesitated. "Yes, perhaps it would be better if you took one. But do be careful with it!"

"Stay put, you people," Delasquez called from up front. "We're checking the life support."

But Starlab's systems were apparently working, even after all these years; the internal pressure and temperature were all right—a bit chilly, maybe, Jimmy Lin suggested, but they wouldn't need the suits.

("Thank God," Rosaleen muttered gratefully. "I hate trying to get in and out of those things.") Even the lights were working—some of them, anyway. Enough.

Then the arguments started. Pat wanted somebody to stay behind in the Clipper, preferably one of the pilots. "For Christ's sake, why?" Jimmy Lin snarled.

"Just in case."

"Just in case, screw that. Nothing's going to happen here, and anyway Dannerman can stay on board if you want him to. I'm going in."

And he did, Pat right behind him; even encumbered with one of the instrument boxes Rosaleen Artzybachova squirmed ahead of Delasquez, who was angrily stuck with going through the shutdown checklist. In spite of Lin's suggestion, Dannerman was not far behind. As he squeezed through the docking port, tugging his own massive toolbox, he heard Rosaleen's shocked voice—"Do your mother! Everything's all *different*!"

11
Dan

It wasn't what he had expected. He hadn't expected Starlab to be so warm, but it was. That was passive heating, Rosaleen said, only sunlight. He certainly hadn't expected it to stink. But it did, a rancid, pervasive odor, part chemical, part almost like cinnamon. Was it the decaying body of the abandoned astronomer? Not likely. It wasn't really a spoiled-meat smell, and besides the mortal remains of the lost Manny Lefrik must have long since finished all the decay that was possible to him.

But that was not the greatest shock. Rosaleen Artzybachova had been right. It was all different. The views of the Starlab interior he had studied displayed gray metal cabinets, sunshine-yellow and warm red walls, patterned wall hammocks. Those things were still here, most of them, but to them had been added objects that the schematics had never displayed: green-flecked lumps of transparent matter, like lime Jell-O, with glittering sparks of gold and diamond light flickering within it; a great copper-colored pillar, six-sided, that gave out perceptible warmth; a huge cupboard sort of thing with a door that slowly swung closed when Dannerman tried to peer into it—things for which he had no easy name. There had been structural changes, too. Even some of the walls were gone. The partitioned space of the original had been opened up, and here and there, all about, stuck at crazy angles from the remaining walls, were the machines that were like nothing Dannerman had ever seen before. The more he looked the stranger they got. He saw some that were palely luminous, some velvet black; they were rounded or jagged-edged, some with brightly glowing dots on the surface that flickered and changed as he watched, some faintly crackling or humming. None of them looked *normal.*

"Jesus," he said. "I guess you were right, Pat. That's not any human stuff."

Pat's face was glowing in triumph. "Effing well right it isn't, Dan-Dan! It's *alien.* And it's *ours*!"

"But what do those things *do*?"

"What's the difference? My God, Dan," she said happily, reaching out to caress the pinkly glowing surface of one of the machines, "once we get this stuff back and figure out how it works—can you *imagine* what it'll be worth? We'll make a bundle out of this."

"If we can move it," Rosaleen Artzybachova muttered, trying to fasten her instrument box to a handhold on the wall while, like everyone else, she was distractedly staring at everything around her. "Pat, I recommend you do not touch anything until I have had a chance to study it. The rest of you, too."

Pat pulled her hand back; beside her, Jimmy Lin was doing the same thing. "What's the problem?" he asked.

"How do I know what problem there is? Perhaps there is no problem at all, or perhaps if you touch it it will fry you to a crisp. If you want to experiment I suppose it is your right, but I would prefer that you help me."

"Me, too?" Dannerman asked, trying to keep his own instrument box from bumping into anything; in the micrograv environment it weighed nothing, but its mass made it hard to handle.

"Oh, Dan," Rosaleen sighed, "what help could you be? At least the others have some experience with instrumentation. No. Go and explore."

"I'll go with him," Pat said suddenly.

"You also want to be a tourist? And, General Delasquez, is that what you are indicating, too, with that scowl? Well, why not? If there are too many unskilled helpers here it will be worse than none at all, so go. Look for old Manny's body; perhaps we can give it a decent burial in space while we are here."

"And maybe get rid of some of the stench," Martín Delasquez growled.

The old woman ignored him. "Or perhaps you will meet some interesting stranger, and then you will come back and tell us. If you can."

A few meters down the main transverse Pat stopped and consulted a scrap of paper from her pocket. The general gave her a suspicious look, but brushed past her to go off on his own. "Let him go," Pat muttered without looking up. "Maybe he'll see something we don't. Let's see, we follow this transverse to the second junction—"

Dannerman drew the obvious inference. "You're looking for something specific."

She glanced after Delasquez's disappearing form and lowered her voice. "Right you are, Dan-Dan. I want to see where that blister was attached, from the inside. Come on, I think I know where I'm going."

The way you got around in the effectively gravitationless Starlab was by pulling yourself along by the handholds spaced along the walls, or by hurling yourself like a slow-moving projectile from point to point. Neither Dannerman nor Pat was up to projectile standards, so progress was slow.

They didn't speak. Pat was concentrating on the chart in her hand, Dannerman thinking about the implications of Rosaleen's final remark. If artifacts had been added to Starlab, as they had, someone had to have put them there. And it was at least a reasonable possibility that that someone was still there.

Dannerman kept his eyes peeled as they drifted along the passages. Ears, too, but there wasn't much to hear. Even the chatter between Rosaleen and Jimmy Lin became inaudible after the first few turns. Apart from the cryptic noises that came from the alien machines, the only sounds Dannerman heard came from Pat and himself.

When Starlab's designers planned the satellite they allowed for weeks or months of occupancy by its observers. That meant they had to make arrangements for living quarters. So they did, but they were not lavish. The residents weren't given rooms. What they had—Dannerman perceived as he pulled himself through the square-sided passages of the observatory—was no more than coffinlike cubicles. The things were doorless, though fitted with stiff fabric panels to provide at least the illusion of privacy, and they were small—smaller than any broom closet Dannerman had ever seen, and not much more elaborate.

There was more of Starlab than he had expected. For Pat, too, it seemed—when, twice, she paused to look uncertainly around and when, once, she had to retrace her steps for half a dozen meters. Dannerman assumed she was lost, and the way she muttered to herself made that assumption plausible. "But it ought . . . ought to be . . . right *here,*" she murmured, touching a bare spot on the corridor wall; and then, "Hell! It *is*!"

Is what? Dannerman asked, but only silently. He didn't have to say it out loud because Pat was already demonstrating the answer. Her fingers traced the lines that made up a hexagonal shape on the wall; the lines were new, bright metal. "They cut a patch out here. Then they entered. Then they welded it up again."

"Who 'they'?" Dannerman asked.

She gave him a look of mild surprise. "The people who brought this new stuff aboard, of course."

"Then *where* they?"

There was less surprise this time, but more visible worry. "Yes, that's the question all right, isn't it? Probably there wasn't a living 'they' at all, Dan, just some robot probe machinery."

Dannerman made a neutral sound. In his view, the word "robot" did not exclude some mean-tempered clanking thing that could be quite as unpleasant to meet as any of the Seven Ugly Space Dwarfs. "One thing, though," he said.

"What?"

"If all the machinery we've seen came on the thing that looks like a blister—probably from the CLO, I guess—how did it all fit?"

Pat opened her mouth to answer, and then closed it again. Obviously it was a hard question. The amount of unfamiliar gadgetry in Starlab could easily have filled a dozen objects the size of the blister. Some of them were far too large to have been squeezed through the space traced on the wall, as well.

"I don't know," she said at last. "Maybe—"

But whatever the "maybe" was going to be, Dannerman never heard it. She stopped in midsentence, turning toward a sound that came from one of the corridor openings; and so did Dannerman, his hand on his twenty-shot.

What appeared in the corridor wasn't an alien. It was General Martín Delasquez—who also had his hand on his gun, and a look of alarm on his face.

His expression cleared. "Oh, it's only you," he said. "I thought it might be whatever's been eating the corpse."

"The corpse?" Dannerman repeated.

"The dead astronomer, Manny something? I found his body."

"Well, that's not so surprising; we knew that he died here, so his body had to be somewhere around."

"Sure you did. But did you also know that his head was missing?"

"Rats," Rosaleen Artzybachova informed them. "A headless corpse? Of course it is rats. They go wherever human beings go. It is not surprising that some managed to get aboard Starlab somewhere along the line, or that they would mutilate a corpse."

"And then disappear," Jimmy Lin suggested sardonically.

"And then die of starvation," she corrected him, "or of plague, or whatever. Or possibly they have not disappeared at all but are still aboard. Rats are excellent at avoiding attention."

"But—" Pat began, unconvinced.

"But," Rosaleen overrode her, "in any case they are not our problem. Our problem is merely to detach some of these artifacts and stow them on the Clipper."

Pat nibbled her lower lip in silence. Martín Delasquez, looking at the single cobalt-colored metal lever that Rosaleen had so far detached, said, "You aren't doing very well at that, are you?"

Rosaleen Artzybachova swung around to confront him. "You have some criticism? Would you like to do this yourself? No? That does not surprise me. It is much easier for someone like you to complain than to try to understand how these things are interconnected, or what will happen if we separate them."

"But someone like me," Delasquez said, "does not claim to be an expert on instrumentation. You do, do you not? Isn't that why you are here?"

"I'm earning my way," Rosaleen said grimly. "And I'm not getting paid for my services twice."

Delasquez looked insulted. "Are you referring to the gems I was given? But those were not for me! They were to make it possible to get clearance on such short notice for this flight."

The quarrel distracted Pat Adcock from her thoughts of corpse-eating creatures. "Oh, hell," she said, "what are you fighting about? There's plenty to go around, just as we agreed."

Jimmy Lin cleared his throat. "I think not," he said politely. "You know what I think, Pat? I think we're going to have to refigure all that."

"The hell with that!" she said sharply. "We made a deal, and we're sticking to it. Remember, Starlab's my satellite! Well, the observatory's," she qualified, "but as far as you're concerned that's the same thing. Starlab was built and launched with my uncle's money, so it's private property. Mine."

Lin gave her a long, bland look. Then he shrugged—not in the manner of someone who is convinced, only in the manner of someone who has decided not to pursue the question for the moment.

However, Dannerman decided as he watched the squabble, Lin was not going to put it off forever. Then there was General Delasquez, silently listening. He was another who was presumably looking forward to renegotiating their arrangements.

Pat Adcock was taking charge. "Right, then. Rosaleen, what do you think? How long will it take you to get this stuff detached?"

"First I have to figure out what it is, Pat."

"Well, damn it, do it!"

The old lady pursed her lips. "I kind of agree with Jimmy," she said. "Why don't we talk about how we're going to split it up?"

"Rosaleen! Not you, too!" Pat bit her lip, then surrendered. "All right. We can settle this after we land. What we have to do now is pick out the likeliest items and shift them to the Clipper. When we land in California I've got a crew—"

Rosaleen interrupted her sharply. "California?"

Pat said apologetically, "I'm sorry I didn't tell you before, Rosie. We couldn't go back to the Cape, though, could we? The vultures would be waiting to snatch it all away. Anyway, it's all arranged. I've got a crew and a chopper waiting in California. We'll offload as fast as we can and get the stuff to a safe place, and then—"

"We're not landing in California," General Delasquez said.

"Damn it, Martín! You agreed!"

"I have reconsidered the question. We will return to the Cape."

Dannerman sighed softly, because he knew what was coming. The four of them were regarding each other like stray tomcats, paying no attention at all to him.

Pat gave the general a sour look. "Don't be foolish. The arrangements are all made," she said crossly.

Delasquez shook his head. "No. I have also made arrangements. The State of Florida can make good use of this technology. We have suffered under Yanqui tyranny long enough; with this we can have full independence at last."

With the gun in his hand Dannerman spoke up. "And a little something extra for you personally, Martín?" he inquired politely.

That was when it all got rough. Delasquez fumbled for his own gun, tangled in the incongruous gilt-leather holster. Jimmy Lin was also reaching for something, no doubt a weapon of his own, but he didn't get very far. Rosaleen was perched just behind him, still holding the rod of blue metal; she didn't stop to speak but swung it and caught Lin on the side of the head.

"Oh, no, you must not," said a new voice.

Dannerman barely registered the fact that the voice was unfamiliar; he had Delasquez in the sights of his twenty-shot.

Then there was something like a flash—a tingle—a sudden sense of falling, and the weapon never did get fired.

12
Dan

A while later—he had no idea quite how long it had been—Dannerman blinked and opened his eyes. The other four were stirring around him, and they all looked bewildered. They were in the Clipper, though Dannerman didn't remember going there. He had a recollection of his gun being in his hand, though he wasn't sure why. He glanced hastily around, in case it was floating in the nearby air. It wasn't. He observed General Delasquez looking around in the same befuddled way, and, beyond him, Jimmy Lin, looking perturbed as he rubbed the side of his head. "What the hell happened?" he asked.

Rosaleen Artzybachova said shakily, "I think I must have had a touch of micro-G vertigo."

It looked to Dannerman as though they all had. Everyone seemed dazed, and Pat was weeping softly. "All for nothing," she whimpered. "Hell."

Jimmy Lin said pensively, "Bad enough there wasn't any of that alien technology; even Starlab's own equipment is ruined."

"Ruined," Rosaleen Artzybachova echoed. She sounded more than dazed, Dannerman thought; in fact, really ill. It was her age, most likely, he decided. But she kept on doggedly with the litany of loss: "Electronics fused, power supply ruined—there must've been a plasma arc. A big one. There's nothing left worth salvaging. Might as well start back. We can't do any good here."

Dannerman was scratching the back of his neck—as, for some reason, so were the others—as he was peering into the pilots' screen at Starlab's hull. He pointed at the bulge that had no business being there. "I really thought that was going to be something interesting," he said.

"Just some kind of sticky space glop, I guess," Jimmy Lin said. "All right, get strapped in. We're ready to undock."

Despondently, the five of them took their places, ready for the long return flight to Earth. . . .

13
Dan

And at the same time, but a very long way away, Dannerman blinked and opened his eyes . . . and squawked in unbelieving outrage. In a place he had never seen before, he was being held firmly by two people in Hallowe'en trick-or-treat dress—big ones, with a froth of white concealing their faces and an astonishing number of arms—while a smaller one in a different costume was interestedly, but inexpertly, undoing the flaps of his clothing to undress him. Shouting around him made him look about; all four of his companions were similarly held and two of them, Jimmy Lin and Pat, were already naked. He bellowed, "What the hell *happened*?"

He wasn't asking anyone in particular, but the goblin who was taking his clothes off gave him an answer—sort of an answer. It seemed to have the body of a large chicken; it gazed up at him out of mournful huge kitten's eyes and worked its slack jaw for a moment, and then it spoke. "Do not struggle. The handlers may damage you."

And Pat Adcock cried, half laughing, "My God, Dan! It's Dopey!"

14
Pat

Yes, the chicken with the cat's face did look like the Dopey the transmission from space had warned against; and the pale, bearded giant that never spoke was likely enough the Doc; and that was a subject for wonder; but Pat had other things on her mind. Pat Adcock had had fondly held hopes blighted before. Never like this. She had been so *close*! After all those interminable, exhausting weeks of court battles and conspiracy there had been that one great, exultant moment when it looked as though all her dreams were paying off. . . .

And then, *bam,* reality hit her right between the eyes and these bizarre creatures from a nightmare had snatched all the triumphs away.

But it wasn't a nightmare. Even that consolation was denied her. Improbable as it was, the Dopey was real, the whiskered Doc was real, the space aliens truly did exist and they had taken Pat Adcock prisoner. It was almost more than she could take in—the astonishment, the incredible strangeness of it all—but the wonder was diluted by fear. And diluted again by discomforts of several kinds, including her increasingly urgent need to go to the bathroom.

It was all more than she could handle, because nothing like this captivity had ever happened to Pat before. She had never been in jail. She had never in her life been restrained against her will in any way at all, unless you counted the times her nanny had made her sit in a corner for some five-year-old's wickedness. She wasn't prepared for it, and she didn't like it at all. She didn't like the six-sided chamber that was their prison, like a scaled-up honeycomb cell the size of a backyard swimming pool, or the bright mirrored surfaces that reflected their own naked bodies whichever way they looked. She didn't like being naked, for that matter—at least, not under these circumstances.

Pat was not a prude about her body, but she had always been selective about whom she displayed it to. She especially didn't like the fact that there were no private spaces inside the cell, not even a toilet. About that she was, indeed, quite prudish.

She was not the only one suffering from affronted modesty. That dedicated sexual athlete, Jimmy Peng-tsu Lin, sat with his back against a wall, his bloodied head down in shame, hugging his knees to his chest to conceal as much of his privacy as possible. Dannerman and the general were less obvious in their discomfort, though the general, she saw, had a lot to be discomforted about. Lacking the built-in corsets of his uniform, his body sagged and bulged in unexpected ways. Both men, she observed, did their best to turn away from whomever they were talking to. Only Rosaleen Artzybachova seemed unaffected—very likely, Pat thought with interest, because she stripped down pretty well, for a woman of that age. All that exercise appeared to have paid off. Pat resolved to try a bit more of it for herself when she was back in her real life. . . .

If she ever was.

There did not seem to be a very high probability of that. They were well and truly captured, all five of them.

They were all responding in the same way, too. All five of them—well, all but Jimmy Lin, who was fully occupied in nursing his bashed head and his embarrassed nudity—had immediately begun to check the mirrored wall, centimeter by centimeter, looking for a doorway, perhaps, or at least some sort of gap. There wasn't any. "I guess we're stuck here," Dannerman said at last, and no one disagreed. All they could do was ask each other unanswerable questions and complain—"pissing and moaning" was the term Dannerman had used. It wasn't a good choice of words. Pat was uncomfortably aware that they had so far really done only the moaning part.

From all the questions a few facts were established early. They certainly were not on Starlab anymore, because gravity pressed them down as it had on Earth. They almost certainly were not on their own Earth, either, because of that same gravity. It was Rosaleen Artzybachova who noticed it first, but then they all agreed. They seemed to weigh a little less, pressed a little less heavily on the soles of their feet when they stood, perhaps could even jump just a bit higher, than they had for all their previous lives.

"Also," Rosaleen went on, "you will notice that we are breathing quite normally."

Pat frowned. "Yes?"

"Which means that the atmosphere here contains approximately an Earth-normal partial pressure of oxygen. I imagine the rest is probably nitrogen. Some inert gas, at any rate; and not helium or carbon dioxide, because we would know it if so, from the effects on our voices or our alertness. All the other inert gases are comparatively rare, so I believe," she said thoughtfully, "that it must be nitrogen." She reflected for a moment, then added, "The temperature is a bit warm—more like North Africa than New York, I would say—but still in a livable range."

Jimmy Lin looked up at her to make a face. "So, Dr. Artzybachova, put it all together and tell us what we need to know. Where are we?"

"Not on Earth, of course," she said at once. "Perhaps we are on a planet, I am not sure of that, but in any case not a planet of our own solar system—too much gravity for Mars or Mercury, not enough for any of the gas giants. And, of course, not on Venus, because the heat would have killed us at once. There are other possibilities. Perhaps we could be on a spaceship undergoing constant acceleration, but I doubt that also—I believe we would hear the rockets."

"If they use rockets," Dannerman offered.

"A good point," Rosaleen agreed. "But I think I do hear something. Perhaps motors somewhere? It doesn't sound like rocket engines. So we come back to the one clear fact: we are not on Earth."

Of course, that question was not seriously asked in the first place. They didn't really need much proof that they weren't on Earth, because the proof was right before their eyes. Nothing on Earth was like their cell, and nothing on Earth looked like the creatures who had disrobed them here.

There was argument about that, too: What were the creatures? Were they really the Seven Ugly Dwarfs from the space message? Rosaleen polled the group. Jimmy Lin had no opinion on that, partly because he was distancing himself from the others with his embarrassment and his sore head, and mostly because, he said, he had spent much of his recent time in a place where they did not pay a great deal of attention to such cartoons, namely at the Jiuquan space center in the People's Republic of China. Martín Delasquez didn't think their captors really resembled the figures from space, either, but there was no doubt in Pat's mind at all. It was simply statistically unlikely, she was sure, that two unrelated sets of such bizarre creatures could turn up at once.

She noticed that Dannerman took little part in the discussion. He was restlessly checking the cell out, not saying much, until abruptly he announced: "I'm hungry."

So, Pat realized once he mentioned it, was she. And wanting other creature comforts, too. "And I wish I had something to drink," she said wistfully, thinking of the silver decanter of ice-water always on her desk.

Rosaleen said, "I'm sure we all feel the same way, but the less fluid you take in the less you will have to discharge. Which we all must do." She looked around at the others, almost smiling. "We do not have a choice, you know. Shall I be the first?"

She paused for a moment, but no one answered; no one had a useful answer to give. "Very well," she said, and walked purposefully over to one wall, where she squatted down without further remark.

"Oh, hell," Pat said unhappily. "Hey, guys. At least you could all turn your backs." Jimmy Lin raised his head long enough to laugh sourly, glancing at the mirrored walls. Dannerman paid no attention—very conspicuously and politely paid no attention. He redoubled his study of the mirror wall, but by the sense of touch only, his eyes half closed against any impolite reflection. Martín stood by him, watching.

"There's nothing to see in the wall," the general pointed out.

"Nothing I can find so far, anyway," Dannerman said obstinately. "But those goddam bug-eyed monsters walked right through it, so there has to be something."

Rosaleen finished her task matter-of-factly and stood up. "That wasn't the wall where they came in, anyway. They came through the one next to it, where Pat's standing."

Which started another argument, even more pointless. Which wall? How could you possibly tell which wall, anyway, when they all were identical? There was no mark of any kind on any of them, not even a seam where two panels joined. Pat ran her fingers wonderingly over the smooth, warm surface herself. It looked as though it should be glass-hard. It wasn't. As she pressed her fingers against it the tips actually entered the wall, faintly dimpling it as they might a surface of modeling clay, but they penetrated no more than, perhaps, a millimeter or so. She tried harder, finally pressing with all her weight. No good. She could get fingernail-deep into the surface and no farther. And she could find no sign at all that it had ever opened up to let the extraterrestrials through. If she hadn't seen the creatures walk right through it she would not have believed it possible.

Jimmy looked up unhappily. "Tell me something. Suppose you did find a way to get through that thing, even got all the way out of here?" he said. "I don't think you ever will, but what if you did? What would you do then?"

"Then," Dannerman said, "I'd figure out what to do next, but we'd be that much ahead. As long as we're stuck in here we can't do anything at all."

Jimmy shrugged, but said nothing. Neither did anyone else; some truths were too obvious to be argued.

Then, "But this is interesting," Rosaleen called from her place at a far wall, gazing at the floor.

"What is?"

Rosaleen gestured to where she had relieved herself. "The urine is disappearing. Look, there is only a trace now, and it is getting less."

Even Jimmy Lin got up to see that. It was true. The tiny pool of pale liquid was dwindling, and a moment later it was gone. Martín Delasquez hesitated, then stopped to touch the floor where it had been. "Dry," he reported. He didn't need to. They could all see for themselves that there was no trace of urine, not even a faint stain on the milky-white, slightly resilient flooring.

"Well," Rosaleen said encouragingly. "At least we seem to have a sewage system."

Martín scowled at her. "But still no food and nothing to drink."

She shrugged. "And nothing we can do about it, either, is there? Meanwhile I am quite tired. I think I will try to sleep."

Pat watched, incredulous and almost admiring, as the old woman lay down on her side, curled in the fetal position, folded her hands under her cheek and closed her eyes. "You know," Pat said, "I could use some sleep myself."

"We all could," Dannerman said. "But one of us ought to stay awake."

Jimmy giggled. "Are you talking about setting sentries? To guard against what?"

"Against I don't know what," Dannerman said, "but that's the exact reason why I think one of us should stay up. I'll take the first turn, if you like."

Martín Delasquez said heavily, "Yes, I agree we should set a guard and, yes, we might as well sleep, since we have nothing better to do. Perhaps we will think more clearly when we are refreshed, so, very well, let us— Wait! What is that?"

He didn't have to ask; they all saw what was happening at the same time. A patch of one wall clouded momentarily, then bulged into a pair of figures as the Dopey and a Doc came through. The Doc was carrying small parcels in several of its arms; the Dopey gestured, and the Doc began setting the parcels on the floor as the wall closed seamlessly behind them.

Dannerman wrinkled up his nose. "That's what I was smelling on Starlab!" he said, staring at the Doc. "It was that thing!"

* * *

All the captives were standing in a defensive clump now, even Rosaleen, watching warily. Pat Adcock sniffed. Yes, there was a queer odor, not entirely unpleasant—part of it like something from a spice rack, part something sour and distasteful. There was no doubt that it came from the extraterrestrials. She stared at them, realizing for the first time just how unhuman they were. The Dopey was not at all human in form—torso like a Thanksgiving turkey's, but a big one; its prissy little feline face at the level of Pat's chest. It wore clothing—a sort of pastel-mauve muumuu—and it carried a kind of muff made of coppery metal mesh. After it had signed an order to the Doc it put its hands back in the muff before Pat could get a good look at its fingers. There was something odd about them, but she wasn't sure what. Then, as it turned slightly, she saw that the muumuu had an opening in the back from which protruded a scaly, iridescent, spreading tail as colorful as a peacock's.

Pat felt at least a hint of reassurance from the fact that the Dopey was wearing a garment. Clothing implied civilization; civilization implied some possible, however remote, hope that there could be some sort of meeting of the minds between them. The one they called the "Doc," on the other hand, was almost naked except for a sort of cache-sexe over where she supposed it kept its genitals. It was also very big. More than two meters tall, Pat guessed, at least twice as tall as the Dopey—of course, the snapshots in the message from space had given no indication of scale. And it was not in the least human. The word that crossed Pat's mind was "golem." The thing stood on short, bent legs, like the Greek version of a satyr, but no satyr had ever had six arms, two huge, thick ones at the top, four lesser ones spaced along its torso, and all tipped with sharptaloned paws. Now that she had a better look at the creature she saw that the white beard was not a real beard: the strands feathered out, more like fern fronds than any kind of animal hair. A cluster of the same sort of growth peeped out from the jockstrap garment.

The Dopey worked its slack little mouth for a moment and spoke. "You stated that you required food. These are food, I think."

That took Pat by surprise. "You speak English," she said. It sounded like an accusation; the alien didn't reply.

"Stupid question," Martín reproved her. "He just did speak English. You, then. Will you tell us why we are here?"

"You are here," the creature said, "so that you may be learned." Its voice was shrill and grating, as much like the cawing of a parrot as any human speech, but the words were clear enough.

"Learned what?" the general demanded. The Dopey didn't reply. "For whom?" No answer for that, either, and Rosaleen tried her luck:

"Can you say how we got here?"

The Dopey considered. "Not at present. Perhaps later," it said at last. Pat thought it seemed to be waiting for something, but didn't pursue the thought; she had other things on her mind. Food, for one thing, and she wasn't the only one. Jimmy Lin was rooting around in the sparse collection: mints, apples, corn chips—she recognized the provenance; it was what they had had on their persons in the Clipper. It wasn't much. It was welcome, though; she selected an apple, carefully excavated a bruised spot with a thumbnail, then bit into it. It was as moist as she had hoped.

Jimmy was less pleased. He was muttering dissatisfiedly to himself in Chinese, then looked up at the Dopey and snarled, *"Wo zen mo nen chi zhe zhong dong xi!"*

The alien didn't miss a beat. *"Ni bao li zhi you zhe xie,"* it replied. Every human jaw dropped at once, and Pat cried:

"You speak Chinese, too!"

"Of course. Also Cuban-Floridian Spanish and Dr. Artzybachova's Galician dialect of Ukrainian, as well as a number of other human languages. This was necessary for my work on your orbiter. One moment."

It turned to the wall. Almost at once the mirror bulged and admitted a pair of Docs, carrying a large metal object. They set it down and stood waiting. The Dopey said, "You now have all you need. Now you are simply to go about your affairs in the normal way. You may breed if you wish."

That appeared to be all it had to say. It turned and left through the wall, the Docs silently trooping after. Dannerman sprang to the wall as soon as they were through, but, as before, the wall flowed like mercury around the departing aliens, and re-formed as solid as ever.

"Well," Dannerman said encouragingly, "at least now we have something to eat. Jimmy? What was that you and the BEM were talking about?"

Lin was looking amused—at least an improvement, Pat thought, over his sullen withdrawal of before. "I was just complaining about the food. I didn't expect an answer, but then he said—in perfectly good Mandarin—that it was all there was among our possessions. But what about the other thing he said, Pat? Are you ready to start doing the breeding bit?"

She said simply, "Shut up." She was watching Rosaleen Artzybachova, who was examining the metal object the Docs had carried in. It seemed to be a rectangular, fauceted tank, with pipes dangling from it that led nowhere. Rosaleen cupped one hand and held it under the faucet; when she twisted the lever, water came out. She sipped it and nodded.

"I think it's the portable-water recycler from Starlab," she reported. "It appears there is some water in the tank, and it tastes all right. However, I suggest we use it carefully. There's nothing here to replenish it; in Starlab it had a condenser to collect moisture from the air and a still for wastewater from the toilets but, as you can see, those have been disconnected and left behind."

"And, of course, we don't even have regular toilets anyway," Jimmy smirked. Pat scowled at him. But that was not all bad, she thought; she was not enthusiastic about drinking water that had come from a toilet, no matter how meticulously it was treated and distilled. But when she said as much, Dannerman laughed.

"And where do you think that water came from in the first place? Anyway, it looks like they're going to take care of us. Maybe the Seven Ugly Dwarfs aren't so bad after all."

"But they are still the ones the broadcast warned us against," Rosaleen reminded him, and no one had any answer for that.

15
Pat

Of all the things Pat Adcock missed, the ones she would least have expected were clocks. They had none. There wasn't any day or night in their cell; the white glow came always unvarying from the ceiling. She felt time dragging for her, with nothing to do, but the only clues the prisoners had to measure how much of it was passing were their own internal ones—the number of times they (unenthusiastically) ate some of the scraps the Dopey had given them, or slept (uncomfortably stretched on the bare cell floor), or, when the remorseless demands of their metabolisms made it necessary, did their best to come somewhere near the impossible wish to urinate and move their bowels in private.

It was not a kind of existence Pat Adcock had ever expected for herself. Not Patrice Dannerman Bly Metcalf Adcock, who had never in her life gone hungry, except in the occasional struggle to get rid of a few extra pounds, who had, from tiniest childhood, always lived a life of privileged security—well, reasonable security, if you didn't count the natural hazards everyone faced from street violence or random terrorist acts. Pat was accustomed to being a person of position. She was entitled to give orders to nearly two hundred people, as the operating head of a reasonably prestigious scientific enterprise. She was also used to all the perquisites that went with being more or less rich.

What Pat Adcock was used to was being an organism efficiently adapted to the ecological niche she occupied. She had all the skills necessary for that life; knew how to juggle budgets even in runaway inflation; how to discourage a date who wanted more intimacy than she cared to give—and how to motivate one who didn't; how to find a clean and comfortable ladies' room at need, wherever she was; how much to tip a headwaiter and when it was best just to give him a smile; how to—

Well, how to *live,* in the particular world she was designed to live in.

But not in this new world, which seemed to call for skills she didn't have and didn't know how to acquire. So nothing in Pat's previous life had prepared her for the present confinement and privation, not to mention the humiliating aspects of their captivity. Naked, weaponless, surrounded by the mirrored walls—wherever she looked six Pats, or sixty times six Pats, looked back at her, dwindling as the reflections became more distant. They were penned like abandoned dogs in an animal shelter, waiting to be adopted—or to be put to death. Nor did they have any more control than a stray dog over their future. They could tell time only by events. Only in their case the events weren't inspections by possible new owners, they were occasions like the time when they got the food from Starlab, and the time when they were at last given back their clothes, and the frightening time when they killed the Dopey.

No circumstances were ever so bad that a little human effort couldn't make them worse. As their tempers grew short they became quarrelsome. Pat snapped at Martín Delasquez for snoring, Dannerman and Rosie Artzybachova withdrew from the others, each busy at some not discussed thoughts of their own, while Martín and Jimmy Lin argued fiercely over whether the lack of blankets to sleep on was worse than the lacks in their limited larder, and whether mints, apples and corn chips represented a diet they could survive on. For Pat, who was trying to force herself to down one more meal of that sort of trash, it was the last straw. "Oh, shut up, you two, for God's sake. Dan, what's the matter with everybody?"

It was a rhetorical question, but she could see him making the effort to give her an answer. "It's prisoner neurosis," he said. "You see a lot of it in jails; that's why you have so many murders in prisons. Actually, it's the policeman's best friend, because when people are hiding out from the cops, after a while they just can't stand each other. That's when they do something foolish and get caught."

Jimmy was listening with a half smile. "You know all about that, don't you, Dannerman?" he said.

Dan gave him an opaque look. "It's common knowledge. Psych 101, or don't they teach that in Chinese colleges?"

Lin met him stare for stare, then shrugged. "Actually, I got my bachelor's at the University of Hawaii," he said, and dropped the subject. Pat frowned, chopping a bruised part out of the apple she had just picked up; there was something going on between the two of them, but she couldn't guess what. Jimmy was being his usual irritating self, of course, but Dannerman—well, what was Dannerman up to, exactly? He prowled their cell for hours at a time, then sat silently, seeming to be trying to work something out, though she couldn't imagine what.

Rosaleen was talking to her. "Do you notice anything about the apples?"

Pat looked at the fruit, puzzled. "Well, I think that's the second or third I've had with a bruise in the same spot."

"Really," Rosaleen said thoughtfully. "That I hadn't noticed. What I was talking about was how many are there. I never packed that many."

"And actually I only had one package of corn chips," Pat said. "I don't understand. Are they raiding a supermarket somewhere?"

"If they are, they could give us a little more variety," Martín said sourly.

Dannerman speculated, "Maybe they figure that's all we need, since that was all they found on us."

"Or maybe they have some way of multiplying the food—you know, loaves and fishes," Rosaleen said. "But they could find something better to multiply. There's stored food in Starlab. If Dopey—" She hesitated before she said it, but they did need a name for the creature. "If Dopey can bring the potable water still from the orbiter he can bring us some of the food, too."

"Or," Jimmy Lin said, "he could bring us a bed, maybe one of those four-posters with curtains that come down? So we could get on with that breeding he was talking about?"

Pat gave him a freezing look. It was nice that Jimmy seemed to be coming out of his funk, but she didn't want him starting anything that could not be properly finished. As a matter of fact, the subject had been on her mind from time to time. This enforced intimacy was stimulating glands that she didn't really want stimulated just then. She thought almost wistfully of ex-husband Ferdie Adcock—not of that son of a bitch of another ex-husband, Jerry Metcalf, who had been a disappointment in all areas, including the bed. Ferdie, on the other hand, had been a truly rewarding lover, in almost every way a fine choice for a mate . . . if only she had been able to overlook his unfortunate habit of keeping his amatory skills current by constant practice—on two of their maids, on the assistant cook, on an occasional picked-up professional and, most troublesome of all, on several of her (formerly) best friends.

But Ferdie was far in the past and even farther away in space. As to the nearer candidates—well, she thought, simply as a speculation; there was no intention to do anything about it, of course—there was General Delasquez. Not counting the flab, he was a powerfully proportioned man, though too bossy in his disposition to be a really first-rate choice. Jimmy Lin himself? Yes, she admitted to herself, under some circumstances the Chinanaut might have been a definite possibility. Even on Earth it had once in a while crossed her mind to wonder just how much of the know-how of Jimmy Lin's great-great he might have inherited. Of course, there were problems with Jimmy, too, one of the most annoying of them being the prospect of becoming just one more scalp on his boastfully long list. That wasn't necessarily a total disqualification. Pat Adcock was not a jealous woman, except with husbands. In the case of a casual lover that sort of thing might have been bearable—under normal conditions. However, under normal conditions they wouldn't be stuck with an audience of three interested onlookers while they got it on.

Which left only one—still purely theoretical—contender. Dan.

Actually, she conceded to herself, watching Dannerman move about the enclosure out of the corner of her eye, there wasn't really much wrong with her cousin, if you overlooked his habit of thinking private thoughts he didn't choose to share with anyone. Dan wasn't a bad-looking man. He wasn't a stranger, either. They had been pretty close at one time, and if they hadn't gone off to separate schools the two of them might sooner or later have decided to become a lot closer. Dan was a definite possibility, she thought—still purely theoretically, of course.

But, under the circumstances, she was determined that it had to be theoretical. Without privacy, making love with him or with anyone at all was simply out of the question—at the moment, anyway, she added to herself . . . and then noticed Jimmy Lin's knowing grin as he watched her covertly eyeing Dannerman.

They kept making small, but inexplicable, discoveries about their cell. Rosaleen pointed out a curious thing about the floor. It not only soaked up and removed their biological wastes, it did the same for trash of all kinds—their apple cores, for instance. Throw them on the floor, and an hour or so later they were gone. Yet the floor was selective about what it caused to disappear. Their food supplies were scattered on the floor, for lack of any better place to put them, and they were never touched. "It discriminates," the old lady said, sounding pleased—well, the cell was, after all, an interesting machine. "Also we must have used all the water the tank could hold by now, but if you notice it's not empty. Somehow the water is being replenished."

"Have you noticed that we don't stink very much, either?" Jimmy Lin put in. That was also true, Pat realized. Add the open "toilet" to the fact that bathing was impossible, and the air of their cell should have been pretty ripe. It wasn't. Their air was constantly being changed. The shadowless light that came from the ceiling was less of a puzzle—even on Earth there were such wall installations that glowed in much the same way—but the greater mystery of the walls resisted all explanation. "Talk about making money from alien technology," Martín said bitterly. "Do you have any idea what that kind of hardware would be worth for prisons? Let the guards walk in and out, but keep the convicts secure?"

Rosaleen, doing leg lifts with her hands pressed against the wall in lieu of a barre, gave him a look. "It would be worth a great deal for many things far more useful than prisons, actually."

Jimmy Lin laughed. "You have something against prisons, Rosie?"

"Yes," she said. "Now more than ever, but always. We had enough experience of prisons in Ukraine. My mother's uncle was taken away to one when he was fourteen years old; he didn't come back until he was sixty-two, and dying. Also my mother's father, my grandfather, who died there. We learned much about prisons in my family from my great-uncle, because he had many stories to tell."

"Did he have any good advice to give?"

"About escaping? No. About how to survive, yes; my great-uncle said the important thing was to go on doing what you should be doing if you were free—as much as you possibly can, that is. Some things would naturally be impossible."

Pat made the connection. "That's why you do your exercises every day?"

Rosaleen hesitated. "That is one reason, yes. The other reason—Well, that is not important. What is important is to keep a sense of purpose. In my great-uncle's case he constantly continued his education; he had been taken right out of school when they arrested him. He organized classes with the other prisoners and at night, instead of sleeping, they taught each other what they knew. Before he died he could speak French, German, Georgian, some English and Japanese and even a little bit of Hebrew. He was pretty nearly in Dopey's class as a linguist, almost, and that wasn't all. He could recite poetry for hours—Mandelstam, Okujawa, Shakespeare, Petrarch—and he knew the names of all the kings of England and France, in order. And much more. But he didn't spend much time thinking about escaping. There would have been no point in running away from the camps, you see, when the whole country was a prison."

"Much like our own situation," Jimmy Lin said sourly; and no one had anything to say to that.

When Dopey came again the three men were sleeping restlessly on one side of the cage, and Rosaleen was teaching Pat tai chi. They were trying to be as quiet as possible, but when Pat saw one of the wall panels begin to cloud she called out at once. By the time Dopey was inside the men were getting up, bleary-eyed but curious.

"You asked for the food from Starlab," Dopey said. "Also blankets so that you may sleep in more comfort." The parade of Docs that followed him began setting down racks and cases of objects.

"Hey," said Jimmy Lin, for the first time in their captivity looking almost pleased. He began sorting through the new rations even before the Docs had set their burdens down and trooped out. Besides the blankets, the Starlab ones hemmed with metal rings to keep them from floating away, there were scores of food packets of all kinds. Some were in pop-open cans, some sealed in plastic. Freeze-dried, radiated or canned, they needed no refrigeration, and they came in many varieties. Pat saw packages labeled "omelette" and "fried tomatoes" and any number of vegetables: green beans, white beans, red beans, pickled cabbage, raw cabbage, beets. There were soups, stews and quiches; there were powders that were dehydrated fruit juices or coffee, and Pat was suddenly aware of just how hungry she was. She wasn't the only one. Martín held up one opaque plastic sack, reading the label wonderingly: "What is 'hassenpfeffer'?" he demanded, and Jimmy Lin exulted: "Look! There must have been some Chinese on Starlab; there's bok choy! And rice, and I think these other things are dim sum!"

The only one not poring over the larder was Dannerman. He was gazing at Dopey. "What's the matter, Dan?" Pat asked, but he didn't answer her. He said to the alien:

"You heard what we said about the larder on Starlab. You can hear everything we say in here, can't you?"

The creature inclined its mournful head, the equivalent, Pat thought, of a nod. "Of course. That is my assignment. I am tasked to monitor you. Also to provide you with everything you need so the observation can continue as long as possible."

Pat looked up from the canned ham in her hand. "You aren't

doing a very good job of that. Why don't you give us back our clothes?"

"To provide you with what you *need*," Dopey said firmly.

"Well, we need clothes. Tell him, Dan," she said, but Dannerman was looking thoughtfully at the alien. It was Rosaleen who picked up on the question.

"Clothing is a definite need for us," she declared. "We are not animals. We will be definitely harmed by prolonged exposure. Also there are items that we carried in our clothing which are essential to our survival—medications, for instance."

Dopey hesitated, then did a curious thing. He jammed his little paws deep into the copper-colored muff; his eyes closed, he seemed to be listening to voices unheard by the others. Then his eyes opened and he declared, "The clothing will be brought."

"That's more like it," Jimmy Lin said, his mouth full of something he had seized from the food supplies. "How about answering some questions for us, too? Where are we?"

"You are in this pen. You do not require more information than that."

"Well, then," Martín Delasquez tried, "at least tell us what you're monitoring? What do you want us to do?"

"Simply to continue as you are," Dopey said, as though that should have been obvious. Then, as the walls opened and three burdened Docs came back in, he added sharply, "Do not touch your clothing yet!" It was not really a necessary order. They couldn't have, anyway; the three Docs had formed in a line between the captives and the pile of clothing. Dopey paid them no further attention, but began carefully examining each garment. As he finished with one he tossed it past the Docs to be claimed—a brassiere for Rosaleen Artzybachova, a single sock, a pair of men's undershorts claimed by Dannerman. The underwear came first, because, Pat thought, it was the easiest to check out. As Dopey came to the outer garments he was more thorough, investigating pockets, running his long, tapering fingers over seams to see if anything was concealed inside them. He was looking for weapons, it seemed. He found them, too: two guns and a bomb-bugger in Dannerman's effects, a gun and a knife in Martín's, more guns from the others, even two little switchblade knives from the garments of Rosaleen Artzybachova. "Christ," Pat said. "We were all ready to fight a war!"

"I simply took routine precautions," Jimmy Lin said defensively, watching as Dopey pulled a sixty-shot sidearm out of his jacket.

Rosaleen spoke up, to the Dopey: "That's just a pen! Please let me have it."

The Dopey didn't respond, except to turn the pen over a few times, then take it apart. Evidently he decided it would not make a good stabbing weapon; he tossed it over and turned to everyone's shoes. That took longer. He ran his fingers inside each shoe, apparently measuring to see if there was enough thickness anywhere to conceal a weapon. On one of Jimmy's shoes he hit pay dirt: the heel unscrewed, and inside it was a coil of razor wire.

"Hell," Jimmy said, and resignedly went back to getting dressed. They were all doing it, now. It was surprising, Pat thought, how much more formidable Martín Delasquez looked once he had his military camouflage jacket on again, gold braid with its embroidered general's stars. For Pat herself getting dressed again after so long bare was less pleasant than she had imagined. The waistband of the slacks was uncomfortably tight; the pantyhose unpleasingly constricting; and her feet seemed to have swelled, because it was an effort to get them into the shoes.

The three Docs abruptly turned as one and left, carrying the confiscated weaponry; and it was only then that Pat realized that while they were dressing Dopey had slipped through the wall and was gone.

"Damn it," Dannerman said. "I was hoping we could ask him some more questions."

"Which he probably wouldn't have answered anyway," Pat said. "So let's eat!"

The canned ham had been cold and greasy, the pita bread Pat ate with it dry and leathery, but her belly was full. Eating made a difference. Being clothed made a difference, too; Pat couldn't help feeling that things were taking a turn for the better. Maybe only a very small improvement, with a very long way still to go, but everybody seemed cheerier. Martín in uniform stood taller than before, and what they had received was not merely food and clothing. Dopey had returned all their pouches and belly bags. Pat was pleased to get her watch back and her rings, less pleased to have the packet of tampons that she always carried in case of emergency; it reminded her that her period would be coming along sometime soon, and that one pair of tampons would not be adequate to her needs.

Rosaleen held aloft a small bottle. "My painkillers," she said exultantly.

"Were you in pain?" Pat asked wonderingly.

"Dear girl, at my age one is always in pain; exercise helps a little, but these are better—though they do not solve the real problem. May we not discuss it, please? I have a suggestion."

There was something in Rosaleen's tone that made Pat anxious to hear more, but she didn't press the point. "Yes?"

"Let us make an inventory of all our possessions. Dan, since you still have your screen, perhaps you can keep the tally."

Her tone made Pat curious. "Dopey didn't return yours?"

Rosaleen pursed her lips. "He probably thought it contained a weapon."

Delasquez laughed. "And, of course, it did. What, simply a sharp little blade, for emergencies? He took mine too, for the same reason."

"And left us no weapons at all," Jimmy Lin said. Something in his tone made Pat give him a closer look. But when she started to ask him, Dannerman cut in.

"Hold it," he commanded. "Of *course* none of us have any weapons—but if we did"—he glanced meaningfully at the wall—"we had probably better not mention them out loud. Let's get on with the inventory, shall we?"

It didn't take long. There was Rosaleen's multicolor pen (but nothing to write on with it but some coarse wrapping paper from the food larder) and a reading glass; a collection of key cards and IDs from all of them; a nail clipper; two pocket combs; some loose coins—very few, because hardly anyone carried cash. That was it. Most of them had left their more interesting gadgets in the lockers at the Cape. "No weapons there, anyway," Jimmy said ruefully. "I guess if we put all our coins and stuff in a sock we could make a cosh." Dannerman gave him a warning look, prompting him to add quickly, "Although there's not enough mass there to do any real harm to anybody anyway."

Pat could restrain her curiosity no longer. "Rosie? What's this 'real problem' you're talking about?"

Rosaleen shrugged. "I don't suppose there's any need to keep it secret; it is simply that there is nothing that can be done about it. Painkillers are not the only medication I need. I have a good many other troublesome conditions. They are well controlled by implants, but the implants need to be refreshed from time to time—beta blockers, polyestrogens, most of all the implant that helps to ward off Alzheimer's. I don't suppose any of you have anything like that on you?"

General shaking of heads. Jimmy Lin, his mouth full of rice, offered, "I have allergy medicine. I don't suppose that would help?"

Rosaleen shook her head, unsurprised. "Not at all. I doubt you'll need it, either; there may be allergens around here, but not the ones you've needed it for. So," she added, "I have some weeks at least, conceivably even some months, before the implants wear off, then—Well, let's look on the bright side. By then we may all be dead anyway."

16
Pat

What Pat Adcock discovered—what millions of jailed men and women had discovered before her—was that prison reduced life to fundamentals. There were no decisions to make or crises to meet; the high spot of the day was eating.

Their larder was a mixed bag. The fruit juices were good, once you mixed them with water—she could have wished for an ice cube or two, but they were certainly drinkable without. There was even real wine. It wasn't very *good* wine, but it came in little plastic cups, which could be rinsed out and used for other things. No beer, though, which annoyed Jimmy Lin, and the coffee was a disappointment. Not only was it at the same temperature as everything else they had, but it was the European kind of coffee, heavy on chicory and made from beans burned black. Only Martín and Rosaleen seemed to enjoy drinking it.

Still, things were looking up a little. Not counting the fact that she was tired of seeing herself reflected in the cell's walls no matter where she looked; if anything could make her crazy, she thought, it was those mirrors. Not counting the fact that Jimmy Lin had formed the annoying habit of following her around, brushing against her in a pretty unmistakable way; but at least now she had clothing.

But none of it was good enough.

Time was passing, and it was all *wasted* time. Pat Adcock had little practice in time-wasting. She was used to a world in which she always had something to do, usually more to do than she had time to do it in: work to get done, plans to make, social obligations to fulfill, amusements to seek. Here she had nothing. She even missed the annoying everyday flow of sales messages on her comscreen and the solicitations of street panhandlers. Pictures from her childhood flashed through her mind, the images of pacing polar bears and sullenly squatting gorillas from Sunday zoo trips with Uncle Cubby or her parents. The parallels hurt. "We're zoo animals. We have nothing to *do*," she complained. "It doesn't make sense."

Dannerman shook his head. "No, you're wrong there. Everything makes sense to somebody."

"Even this?"

"Even anything. People used to talk about senseless crimes—like murdering some eighty-year-old guy on welfare to steal his shoes; they think it makes no sense to kill somebody for so little. But to the guy who did it, it made perfect sense. He wanted the shoes."

"Thank you for the lecture, Dr. Dannerman," Jimmy Lin said.

Dannerman said stubbornly, "I'm only saying that all this must make some kind of sense to Dopey and the others, from their point of view. All we have to do is figure out what their point of view is."

"It sounds like you're taking their side, Dannerman," Martín rumbled.

"Oh, hell, why are people always telling me that I'm taking the bad guys' side?"

"What people?" Martín asked, puzzled.

"Different people." He didn't elaborate. There was something there he didn't want to discuss, Pat was sure, though she couldn't imagine what. "Anyway," he said, "I'm just trying to understand what's happening. Probably they want to know more about us before they reveal themselves."

Pat asked, "How much do they have to know? Isn't that why Dopey was hanging out in Starlab all that time, eavesdropping on Earth?"

Martín said heavily, "Maybe that is not enough for them. I am remembering what the old sailing-ship explorers used to do when they encountered new indigenes. They would kidnap a few and take them aboard their ships to look them over. Your Christopher Columbus—" he began, and then stopped, scowling. They all heard it: a distant sound, almost like a shriek, faint and far away. "What the hell was that?" he demanded.

No one answered until Rosaleen shrugged. "If this is a zoo," she said, "we may not be the only animals on exhibit."

"It sounded human to me," Jimmy said uneasily. Dannerman said nothing, but he was frowning. Pat thought she knew why. The scream had sounded human to her, too. In fact, it had sounded a lot like the voice of Dan Dannerman.

The scream didn't come again. They listened; they tried to be as quiet as possible so that they might hear, but there wasn't much to hear. Dannerman reported that he had heard, might have heard, a faint hum that could have been distant machinery. Pat herself thought she caught a whisper of speech—of a voice of some kind, anyway. When she reported it Dannerman shook his head. "I didn't hear anything like that. Did it sound human?"

"How can I tell? I thought it sounded as though it were asking for something."

To her displeasure, Jimmy Lin took that to be a cue. He moved closer to her. "Perhaps it was asking for something which I too would like," he said, one hand casually resting on her shoulder.

The man was making her uncomfortable. She shrugged herself free. "Knock it off, Lin."

"But why?" he asked reasonably. "I am aware that such things are better conducted in privacy. I would prefer it so myself, but what can we do? Modesty is pointless here."

"The point," she said, "is that I don't want to make love with you, Jimmy. If you're looking for a comfort woman, look somewhere else."

"Hey!" Rosaleen said good-naturedly. "Where do you want him to look, exactly? I've been out of the comfort business for forty years."

"But what else is there to do?" Jimmy Lin asked in a tone of reasonableness. "It is a perfectly natural thing, and also good for you. My honored ancestor said it all in his book. He said it was unhealthful to go for very long without sex, and all my life I have done my best to follow his advice."

Rosaleen said pleasantly, "If you need to masturbate no one will prevent you. If not, perhaps you won't mind if we change the subject."

He glowered at her. "To what?"

She hesitated before she spoke. "I've been thinking about those messages from space. You see, I think most of us took those pictures of aliens as some kind of a joke, perhaps some satellite controller with time hanging heavy on his hands. Very well, that was a mistake. Now we know better about that, but what about the rest of the message?"

"What rest?"

"The original pictures. The scarecrow creature crushing the universe at the time of the Big Crunch. What do you suppose that means?"

Dannerman said, "I asked one of the astronomers the same thing.

He thought it meant that we were being warned against something that was supposed to happen after the universe has finished expanding, and fallen back and contracted again."

At least, Pat thought, they were on a subject she knew something about. But she frowned. "That kind of speculation doesn't make any sense. Nothing could happen after the Big Crunch. It's like wondering what the universe was like before the Big Bang. The answer is there wasn't any. That sort of thing isn't science, it's metaphysics."

Rosaleen shook her head. "You know more about that than I do, Pat, but even I know that some quite good scientists have speculated about the subject."

"Arm-waving. Smoke and mirrors," Pat said dismissively.

"But perhaps for the aliens it isn't."

Pat shrugged. It was true that cosmologists had built any number of pretty speculations about the origins and end of the universe—she had spent many boring hours learning about them in graduate school—but they had always seemed idle daydreaming to her.

Martín shared that opinion. He said impatiently, "There is no point in thinking about such things. The trouble is simply this: We have been kidnapped. That is not a speculation, it is a fact. Governments have considered such things an act of war."

Jimmy said, "Fine. Now, if you'll just let them know about it at the Pentagon, I'm sure they'll have a rescue fleet here right away."

Martín glared at him. "You are very good at sarcasm, Lin. Less good at taking action. We should do *something*."

Rosaleen attempted to defuse the antagonism. "Very well," she said, "since no one else seems interested in trying to interpret the meaning of those messages, I agree that Martín is right. We should do something else. What is available to us? When we were discussing what people in prison on Earth do I am afraid I distracted us with my reminiscences of life in the old Soviet Union. So let us try again. Is there some action that is possible for us to take?"

Jimmy said sourly, glancing at Dannerman, "Why don't you ask the expert?"

Pat frowned. "What do you mean, expert?" But Dannerman seemed unsurprised. He was already answering the Chinanaut.

"First thing," he said, "if I had any specific ideas, I don't think I'd say them out loud. Remember Dopey hears everything that goes on. But if you want general principles I don't see any harm in discussing them—just in the abstract, of course."

"Of course," Rosaleen said impatiently. "Well?"

"What prisoners do depends on what they want to accomplish. If their primary goal is to escape, they do things like digging tunnels, they hide themselves in bags of waste, they get weapons, or make them, and force a guard to take them outside. Or they take hostages for the same purpose. Or they go on a hunger strike—of course that only works if the people on the outside care whether they live or die."

Martín demanded, "Which would you recommend?"

"What I would recommend," Dannerman said, "is that we don't talk about this any more."

"Fine," said Jimmy Lin caustically. "Your advice is that we do nothing, then. Is that why you spooks couldn't even catch the guys who kidnapped the press secretary?"

Dannerman opened his mouth angrily, then glanced at Pat and closed it again. He didn't answer. He simply turned his back and walked over to survey the food store.

There was an undertone here that Pat couldn't identify. She wasn't enjoying it. "What's going on here, Jimmy?" she demanded.

He jerked a thumb at Dannerman. "Ask him."

"Hell," she said, and marched over to Dannerman's side. "Dan, what's Jimmy talking about."

He stood up and popped a cup of wine before he answered. "How do I know?"

"I think you do know. Why does he call you a spook?"

Dannerman shrugged. "Maybe because I was in protsy in college—you know, the Police Reserve Officers Training Corps."

"Not good enough, Dan. That was a long time ago. What about now?"

He took a long pull of the beer before he answered. Then he sighed. "All right, Pat. I don't suppose it matters anymore, and it's the truth. I work for the National Bureau of Investigation."

It was no more than she had guessed, but she felt adrenaline shock flood through her body. "You're a *spy*!"

"I'm an agent of the Bureau, yes. I was ordered to find out what was going on with you and Starlab—"

"Dan!"

He looked remorseful—no, not remorseful; stubborn and sullen. "Well, Jesus, Pat, what did you expect? This was major stuff. As soon as the rumors got out, the Bureau had to find out what you were doing."

"Bastard!" she said, scandalized. "I wouldn't have believed it of you! You come to me with a hard-luck story about needing a job, and all the time you're a goddam spy. Honestly, Dan, what did I ever do to you? Are you still pissed off because you didn't get your share of Uncle Cubby's money?"

"It wasn't a personal matter. I had orders."

"Orders to do what? To steal whatever there was on Starlab for the damn Feds?"

He said uncomfortably, "Well, I suppose that's one way you could put it."

"Is there some other way? So tell me, just how far were you prepared to go for the good old Bureau, Dan? Liquidating me if necessary, for instance?"

"Oh, hell, no, Pat. What kind of a person do you think I am? I've only, uh, shot two people in my life, and I couldn't help that; both of them were doing their best to kill me at the time. Nobody ordered you liquidated."

"And if they had?"

"They wouldn't," he said stubbornly, and that was all he would say.

When Pat curled up on the floor with her face to the wall and her eyes shut tight, she didn't go to sleep. She wasn't planning to. She just wanted to be alone for a bit, as alone as you could get in this place. The National Bureau of Investigation! Everybody knew what that was all about—cloak-and-dagger stuff, with all too much emphasis on the dagger. Now her own cousin turned out to be one of them.

It wasn't just Dan Dannerman, she told herself, feeling abused. Every last one of her comrades had in some way betrayed her trust—Delasquez and Jimmy Lin trying to hijack the goodies on Starlab for another country, even Rosaleen Artzybachova hitting her up for a bigger share of the pie. If Pat Adcock had been a weeping woman she would have allowed herself a few tears of self-pity. As she wasn't, she simply went to sleep.

When raised voices woke her, nothing had improved. She lay with her back to the room, unwilling to turn around and join the others, while Martín and Jimmy Lin were arguing about the food. "But it is nothing but party leftovers," Jimmy Lin was complaining. "It's the stuff nobody wants to eat. What kind of people would have ordered all this stuff?"

Then there was Rosaleen's voice, patiently trying to keep the peace: "There were astronomers from a dozen different countries on Starlab in the early days. I imagine each chose the sort of menu they preferred."

"And ate all the good stuff, and left the remainders for us."

Then Martín's voice, deeper but equally irritated: "I am tired of breaking my teeth on bricks of filthy, uncooked Russian stew."

Rosaleen offered, "I've told you, if you do what I do and soak it for an hour or so it gets softer. A little."

"And then it is cold grease."

She didn't try to deny it. "Try the fruit compote, at least."

"I've had enough of the fruit compote," Jimmy Lin said. "Who knows how long this stuff has been in storage, anyway?" Pat turned away from the familiar bitch session. She had her own feelings about the dehydrated beef (or was it goat?) Stroganoff. She found herself thinking wistfully of a fried-egg sandwich, perhaps with a couple strips of crisp bacon, on whole-grain toast. Or a fresh salad, lettuce with the dew still on it, perhaps some slices of avocado, maybe even a few curls of green pepper. . . .

There wasn't any help for it. She got up and headed for the food, ignoring her companions. That wasn't hard to do. Rosaleen had begun quietly exercising, off by herself, and Martín and Jimmy had moved away to whisper together over the water tank. Only Dannerman was by the larder, and he looked apologetically at her but didn't speak.

Neither did she. She was not yet ready to talk to the duplicitous spy, Dan Dannerman. Ignoring him, she took her time studying the available choices, reading labels, peering at the foods that were visible through glass or plastic. None of them looked attractive, but there were many she hadn't yet tried. She settled on a packet of irradiated chili; at least it would not require soaking to be chewable.

Martín had been right; cold, it was fairly nasty. She had turned her back on Dannerman as she ate, but was not surprised to hear his voice. "Are you still mad?"

She didn't answer. "Because," he said, "I'll apologize if you want me to."

She didn't answer that, either, and apparently he gave up. When she finally peeped around he was over with Rosaleen, doing his best to learn some of her exercises. That was another annoyance for Pat. It had been on her mind to do the same thing, because she could feel herself gaining fat on their preposterously unbalanced diet, but how could she do that while he was there?

The worst part was that it seemed all four of them had decided that Pat was in a bad mood and better left alone. As long as they were ignoring her how could she effectively shun them? She went back to the larder, for lack of anything better to do . . . and was glad when, while she had almost decided to try some more of the damned fruit compote, the patch on the wall suddenly fuzzed and bulged and Dopey came in, oddly without Docs. He was pushing ahead of him a thing that looked like a portable top-loading washing machine. It moved easily on spherical bearings. "This device is to heat your food, as you wish," he said. "If you put things into it they will become hot. This is not the device from your Starlab, however. That object was far too primitive to be of any use here."

They all clustered around while he demonstrated the use of the cooker. Pat hadn't forgotten that she wasn't speaking to any of the others, but put that matter on hold for a while. Operating the cooker looked simple enough. You put things in from the top and left them for a while, and in a minute or two they were hot. When Rosaleen reached to take the container of spaghetti and meatballs out Dopey stopped her. "No, be careful! You will do yourself harm if you put a part of your body into the device. Use these." He plucked a pair of sticks from under one arm and showed them how to lift the packets out without putting their hands in the cooker. Rosaleen eagerly popped the packet open and sniffed the steam that was coming out of it. "I think it's actually too hot to eat!" she said happily.

"It will cool if you wait for a moment," Dopey informed her. "In any case, this instrument will be useful when you have renewable food supplies in the next phase."

Dannerman was suddenly alert. "What next phase? What's going to happen?" Silence. "Well, when will it happen?"

Dopey looked evasive—or simply uncertain; how could you tell with a kitten-faced chicken? "That is unclear. That sequencing is not my decision to make. There are also—" He hesitated. "—some technical problems which have hampered communications."

Pat asked the question for all of them. "What technical problems are you talking about?"

Dopey turned his large kitten eyes on her, then did again the thing with the muff: jammed his hands into it, gazed vacantly into space for a moment, then said, "There are bad people who would harm our project. I may not say more at this time."

"What kind of bad people?" No answer; only that continued stare. Pat bit her lip. The alien was at least answering some questions now, but she was running out of the right questions to ask and Dopey was volunteering little. Nor was she getting much help from her fellow prisoners. Out of the corner of her eye she noticed that Delasquez and Jimmy Lin, though they seemed to be listening intently, were strolling slowly around behind the alien. It crossed her mind that they were up to something.

Not in time.

By the time she began to guess what that something was, and long before she had even begun to decide what, if anything, to do about it, Dopey was turning to leave. The wall began to cloud, preparatory to letting him through.

He didn't get that far. "Grab him!" Delasquez shouted, hurling his weight against the milky place in the wall. Lin did as ordered—threw himself on the alien, who squawked once in astonishment and then was still.

If Delasquez was trying to escape, he failed. The wall was not deceived. He struck against it and was hurled violently back into the cell, as the wall turned mirror-bright again against him. Delasquez didn't walk away; he was catapulted backward, staggering into the pile of Dopey and Jimmy Lin on the floor. He sat down heavily on top of them and gasped dismally, "Mother of God, that hurt!"

From beneath him Lin, breathless and equally dismal, begged, "Get off me." He struggled to his feet and backed away, Delasquez at his side, the two of them looking apprehensively at the alien.

Dannerman gave them both a hard look, but said nothing as he knelt by Dopey's side. "Is he breathing?" Martín asked.

"I don't know. It didn't feel like it," Jimmy Lin said uneasily.

"Maybe he just had the breath knocked out of him," Martín offered, but Dannerman looked up and shook his head.

"Knocked out of him for good, I'm afraid. I don't know much about his anatomy, but there isn't much doubt about it. He's really dead."

Ever since they had been taken captive there had been no times for Pat Adcock that she could think of as really good, but there had never before been one quite as bad as this. She had a pretty good idea of what was done to zoo animals who murdered their keeper. Was it going to be done to them?

Dannerman was saying, "Well, that was stupid," and even Rosaleen was looking reproachfully at the two, Jimmy Lin shamefaced, Martín belligerent but—crossing himself? Pat couldn't be sure. The general's right hand was fingering the left shoulderboard of his uniform jacket as he answered.

"It was your suggestion, Dannerman," Delasquez said.

"Bullshit! I never said anything about attacking Dopey!"

"You spoke of taking hostages. Well, we decided to try it. The other part, trying to crash out, that was my own idea, I just thought of it at the last minute."

"Obviously it wasn't a real good idea," Dannerman said. "Taking a hostage wasn't much better. That only works if you don't kill the hostage."

"His death was simply an accident. How could we know the thing was so delicate? In any case, it's done. And we have an opportunity." The general reached down to the corpse—but with his left hand, Pat saw in puzzlement; his right hand was still close to his lapel. He was trying to pick the coppery metal-mesh muff from Dopey's slack hands.

"Wait!" Dannerman cried warningly, but too late. As soon as Martín's hands touched the metal he screamed, jolted erect and fell unconscious to the floor.

"Damn fool," Dannerman snarled, leaping to his side. But ancient Rosaleen was there before him, her ear pressed to the general's chest.

"No breath. No pulse," she reported. "Electrical shock, I think. Dan, do you know CPR?" She didn't wait for an answer, simply bent her mouth to the general's for artificial respiration. Dannerman didn't speak, either, as he dropped to his knees and began pounding a fist rhythmically on Martín's chest. Beside Pat Jimmy Lin was muttering to himself, but it was Pat who caught the first flicker of a reflection in the mirror wall. "Watch out!" she cried as a pair of the great, ungainly Docs came lumbering in. But the creatures paid no attention to their prisoners. If there was any expression on their white-bearded faces Pat could not identify it; they were strictly businesslike. They bent down to Dopey's body, disentangled his fingers from the coppery muff and bore it away through the wall without a sound, leaving the corpse abandoned behind.

Rosaleen had paid no attention, continuing to breathe for the general. Pat watched, nervous, unsure of what to do; she knew what CPR was, of course, but she had never seen it done before, had not expected it to be so violent. Beside her Jimmy Lin was glumly watching. "What do you guess they'll do to us now?" he asked the room in general. No one answered.

It was a good question, Pat thought dismally, shifting from one foot to another. The two Docs had shown no punitive intention, but then the Docs never spoke, never seemed to show any independent thought or emotion at all.

Then Dannerman sat back on his heels, regarding the patient. He placed one finger at the base of Martín's neck and held it for a moment. "It's irregular, but it's beating," he informed Rosaleen; and then, as she lifted her head for a moment, Martín gasped and coughed and opened his eyes, staring wildly about. He struggled to sit up, but Dannerman pushed him back. "Stay put," he ordered.

"What— What—" Martín tried.

"You got yourself killed, Martín," Dannerman informed him, "Lie still for a while. I think you'll live, but don't push it." He tested the pulse with a finger again; then, Pat was puzzled to observe, Dannerman's fingers moved to the lapel of Martín's uniform jacket, as though feeling for something. When he stood up he looked almost amused, but all he said was "Keep an eye on the walls for me while I see if Dopey had anything we can use." He walked over to the corpse of the alien and looked down at it. The slack mouth was open, so were the eyes; the peacock tail, half erected, seemed to have lost some of its scales.

"Are you going to search the body?" Pat asked.

He gazed at her for a moment. "Unless you'd rather do it yourself? Don't worry. I've done it before, though of course the others were at least human."

"Be careful," she begged. He nodded and knelt beside Dopey's corpse. The creature had worn only the one garment, and, though Dannerman poked at it—diffidently at first, then with more assurance as there was no punishing electrical shock—it seemed to have no pockets. It did have some sort of decoration, things like glassy buttons sewn on it; Dannerman tugged at them experimentally. The Dopey had also worn a bangle over the base of its tail, and a wristlet of the coppery metal, but Pat caught only a glimpse of them as Dannerman completed his search of the corpse.

He sat up and shrugged. "I guess he carried everything he had in that muff," he said. "At least, I can't find anything."

"Maybe he carried some stuff internally," Jimmy Lin offered.

"Good thinking, Jimmy. Do you want to give him a body-cavity search? Because I don't think I'd like to."

"I wonder why the Docs didn't take his body away?" Rosaleen mused, squatting beside the semiconscious Martín.

Dannerman shrugged. "Maybe they'll come back for it. Maybe we'll wish they would, because I imagine it's going to decay pretty rapidly."

Rosaleen nodded, then checked herself, staring at the body. "Perhaps not," she said. "Look at that!"

Pat peered at the dead alien, and saw what Rosaleen meant. Something was happening to the corpse. The bottom of it, where it touched the floor, was soaked with a dark brown liquid, and Pat noticed a sharp, nasty smell, as of some foul brew cooking on a stove.

Dannerman knelt for a closer look. "The floor's dissolving it away," he announced incredulously.

"Please, Dan, don't get too close to it," Pat pleaded.

"Don't worry," he said dryly. "Although it's kind of interesting. That's a great waste removal system; I bet if I lay down right next to Dopey the floor would leave me alone—but, no, I'm not going to try it." He stood up and looked around. "How's the patient doing?"

Rosaleen was supporting Martín's head while holding a cup of water to his lips. "Seems to be improving. He opened his eyes and looked at me."

Dannerman nodded. "So the question now," he said, "is what we do when, and if, somebody takes a dim view of this. Do we just take our punishment, whatever it is? Or do we try to fight back?"

"What have we got to fight with?" Pat demanded.

He looked at her quizzically. "Whatever we can find," he said.

From her post by the patient Rosaleen called, "I do not think that fighting back would be advisable. Not now, anyway."

"I think you're right," Dannerman agreed. "After all, if they want to hurt us they wouldn't have to get into hand-to-hand combat. They wouldn't even need weapons. The easiest thing would be just to leave us here until we run out of food and starve. Speaking of which," he said, "why don't we see what cooking can do for some of those rations?"

Pat stared at him unbelievingly. "You want to *eat* now?" she demanded. "With this dead body turning into mush right here?"

"Well," he conceded, "maybe we might as well wait until it's gone. It seems to be going pretty fast right now, anyway."

Indeed it was, Pat saw, as she gazed down on it, holding Dannerman's arm for reassurance; more than half of Dopey had already turned liquid and been sucked away. The smell was still there, but no worse than before; and actually, Pat admitted to herself, Dannerman was right. The process was kind of interesting to watch, not to mention that it implied a kind of technology she had never before imagined. "Just one more damn thing," she murmured to Dannerman, "that would have been worth a fortune if we could have taken it back to Earth."

Dannerman looked down at her, seeming almost amused; tardily she remembered that she wasn't speaking to him. She looked away. Dopey's body was nearly gone, one of the little arms sticking up and then collapsing into the general mulch. Pat frowned. Something was missing. What had happened to the wristlet? "Dan?" she asked. "Did you notice—"

But he was giving her a scowl and a quick headshake. Puzzled, she opened her mouth to complete her question . . . just as the wall turned milky again.

They all spun around to face it as another Dopey walked in—this time not alone. Two of the golem-like Docs followed him and stood silently protective behind him as the Dopey glanced incuriously at the almost disappeared remains of his own body, and then said in reproach, "You should not have done that."

17
Pat

"But they *killed* you," Pat gasped; and, "Yes, they did," Dopey confirmed, sounding impatient. "Please. One moment." It did not seem to be a subject that interested him greatly. He turned his great eyes on the two Docs, who instantly moved forward to pluck Martín out of Rosaleen's hands. Naturally the general squawked and protested; naturally it did no good. One of the things picked the general up from behind, the two great upper arms holding him, the other four restraining his arms and legs; the other golem methodically stroked and patted Martín all over, each touch lingering for a moment and then moving on. The whole process took no more than a minute or two. Then, without warning, the Docs dropped Martín sprawling. They retreated to stand, silent and impassive, with their backs to the wall, apparently no longer interested in their environment.

"Yes," Dopey said, as though one of the Docs had reported to him—but Pat hadn't heard a sound, "the examination shows that General Delasquez is not seriously injured. It will not be necessary to replace him, as it was me due to your ill-advised action."

"About that," Jimmy Lin said at once, swallowing hard. "You know that was just an accident, don't you? I mean, we didn't want to *hurt* you. . . ."

Dopey gave him a severe look. "Whatever your intentions, your action caused the loss of some data, which I must restore for this copy. Please inform me of the nature of our discussion just prior to my death."

They all looked at him blankly. "You want to know what we were talking about?" Jimmy ventured.

"Yes. That is what I said."

"Well," Jimmy said, trying to remember, "actually, I don't think it was anything much—"

"Except," Rosaleen cut in swiftly, with a hard stare at Jimmy Lin, "that you were explaining this whole matter of 'copies' to us."

"I was?"

"Oh, yes, absolutely," Pat said, picking up her cue. "Is that why you aren't angrier about getting killed by those idiots? Because you're just a copy?"

Dopey looked almost offended. "I do not understand the term 'just' in that context. Of course I am a copy. We are all copies, are we not? How else could we have been transmitted here from your Starlab?"

"Transmitted?" Rosaleen repeated, fumbling in the dark. "Then—well, then that means we didn't come here in a spaceship?"

Dopey seemed amused. "Indeed not. That is a strange notion, Dr. Artzybachova. Persons do not travel on spaceships. That would be impossible for almost any person, yourselves included, since the transit times would be greater than your life span, due to the limitation imposed by the speed of light. As an astronomer, you at least must know that, Dr. Adcock."

"Oh, right," Pat said, nodding vigorously, trying to help the process on. "That's what you were explaining to us. Please go on."

The funny thing was that he did go on. Pat did her best to keep an expression of pure exultation from her face: it was, after all, the very first time they had been able to trick their captor, and that in itself promised at least some hope for the future. The other prisoners listened in silence: Rosaleen concentratedly frowning; Martín frowning also, but probably about something else; Jimmy Lin merely curious; and Dan Dannerman—well, something was going on with Dan, too, Pat thought, because the man seemed abstracted, and he appeared to be turning something over and over in his pocket as he listened.

She postponed the question of Dan Dannerman, because what Dopey was saying was certainly fascinating. It seemed there was some sort of great search going on, all through the universe, for intelligent races. Automated probes had been sent out on the quest in uncounted numbers; they traveled slower than light, because there was no way for ordinary matter to go faster. But then, when some sort of civilization was detected, a "terminal" was set up and observers like Dopey were "transmitted" to a listening post; and when "specimens" like themselves were obtained they too were "transmitted" for further study—

"Hold it!" Pat commanded. "What do you mean, 'transmitted'? Not even photons can exceed light speed."

Dopey said patiently, "I did not use the word 'photons.' The transmissions are carried by a different particle, the name of which—" He hesitated, while his fingers moved rapidly in the muff. "—is 'tachyons' in your language."

"Oh, my God," Pat breathed, remembering her days in graduate school. "Tachyons! Yes, I've heard of tachyons. They were, what's his name, Gerald Feinberg's theory, right? Particles for which the speed of light was a limiting velocity, yes, but a *lower* limiting velocity, so that they could travel only *faster* than light."

"Precisely," Dopey confirmed. "It is the nature of tachyons that the lower the energy the faster they move. The carriers used in this case are quite low in energy and thus have a virtual velocity of—" He hesitated, the long fingers moving inside the muff. "—of somewhat more than one hundred thousand of your light-years per second."

Pat gasped. "Good God! But I'm pretty sure scientists looked for the things, and they were never found."

"Indeed," Dopey said politely. "Perhaps your scientists should have looked harder."

Rosaleen was shaking her head. "But how could you transmit *objects* on these carriers?"

"Not objects. The object is analyzed, so that a sort of—I believe you would call it a 'blueprint' is made, and that is what is transmitted. And, of course, once the blueprint exists copies may be made as desired."

"Like you," someone said.

"Precisely," said Dopey, seeming gratified; the class was beginning to understand its lesson. "Such occurrences are quite common in my situation. In fact, in my time on your orbiter it was necessary to discard and reconstitute me—" He paused to think for a moment. "—at least twenty-five times. You realize I was there for six years four months, observing, and there is damaging radiation in the environment."

"But," said Rosaleen, reasoning it out, "if it was that important, why have you stopped?"

"Stopped? Why do you think the monitoring has stopped? There are automatic machines still in place to carry out the assignment, of course." He seemed to be tiring of the conversation. He shoved his paws into the copper muff and his eyes went vacant again, and then he said, "If there are no other questions—"

"Wait," Martín said thickly, pushing himself up. "Don't go yet. I have something else to ask about your, ah, your purposes in kidnapping us." He hesitated, glancing at his fellow captive. Pat instantly thought he looked suspicious . . . a suspicion that was confirmed when Delasquez rattled off a couple of high-speed sentences in Spanish: *"Si ustedes están interesados en establecer relaciones, no pierdan su tempo con esta gente. Mi gobierno en Florida les ofrecerá mejores condiciones."*

"Hey!" Jimmy Lin yelled. "None of that! Talk so we can all understand you!"

Martín gave him a frosty look. "Why? I was merely asking if they were checking us out as a precaution, before proceeding to make contact with the rest of the human race."

Dopey said politely, "Actually that is not an accurate translation, General Delasquez. Your precise message was, 'If you are going to want to establish relations, don't waste your time with these people. My government in Florida will give you a better deal.' However, that contains an incorrect assumption as to the purpose of this operation."

Dannerman glared at Martín, who glared defiantly back, but then closed his eyes and went to sleep. Or pretended to, Pat thought angrily. Dannerman turned to Dopey. "Then what is the purpose?"

Dopey was silent for a long moment. "I do not think I may discuss that. Moreover," he added, sounding sorrowful, "I believe that you have not been candid with me about our discussions before General Delasquez and Commander Lin leaped on me and crushed me to death. That is not fair. Please do not attempt to deceive me again. Also," he added, turning toward the wall, but looking over his plume at Dannerman, "please also learn that you must not attempt to steal things which do not belong to you and you do not understand."

It sounded as though the message was meant for Martín Delasquez—but then why was he looking at Dannerman? Before Pat could ask, Dopey was gone through the opening wall. A moment later the Docs followed.

"I guess the conversation's over," Dannerman said wryly.

Pat sighed. "You know what would be nice? It would be nice if he would, just once, say good-bye when he goes." And then she turned to the unfinished business of Martín Delasquez. "Bastard," she said. "What were you trying to do?"

Delasquez would have had a harder time of it—Pat would have seen to it herself—if he hadn't abruptly pressed his hand to his forehead, staggered and sat down. "Pardon," he said. "Perhaps I am not entirely recovered. In any case I was merely attempting to establish contact in another way, in the hope that something could be gained for all of us."

"Sure you were," Jimmy Lin sneered. Pat opened her mouth to tell the general a few more home truths about himself, but then closed it again. What was the point? Dannerman seemed to have lost interest in the subject; his hands were still turning something over in his pocket, and his expression continued to be abstracted.

For a while the others pressed Pat for all she could remember about these "tachyons," but it wasn't much; she had said just about all she retained from those long-ago courses, and after a few minutes Rosaleen turned to something more useful. She had been experimenting with the cooker Dopey had brought, and ten minutes later there were heavenly smells of decent meals coming out of the thing.

The reality was as good as the aroma. Pat had forgotten how fine a cup of hot Irish stew could taste. Even Martín recovered swiftly enough to cook up and devour some sort of fried-banana thing. It wasn't until they were all on their seconds that Rosaleen cleared her throat. "Patrice?" she said. "Were there not some studies, long ago, about how to produce these tachyon things Dopey was talking about?"

Pat swallowed and thought for a moment. "Studies? But the tachyons were never found."

"Yes, you said that," the old lady said patiently. "But I do recall some speculations on the subject. It was while I was studying at the high-energy institute in Kiev; we were analyzing the instrumentation of the synchrotron, and the instructor mentioned, purely for our entertainment, I am sure, that someone had once suggested faster-than-light particles could be generated with a sufficiently powerful instrument."

"With a synchrotron?" Pat said, and then, "Oh! That radiation from Starlab!"

Rosaleen nodded. "Exactly."

Then Pat had to explain what they were talking about to Martín and Jimmy Lin, who had heard nothing about synchrotron radiation being observed from the orbiter. Dannerman, on the other hand, listened for only a moment, then said, "I think I'll take a little nap."

He wasn't the only one. Martín was losing interest in the discussion; he lingered only for a few moments, then silently removed himself to a side of the cell and lay down, closing his eyes. Rosaleen yawned. "A full belly makes a sleepy brain," she said. "Do you think one of us should stay awake?"

"Not me," said Jimmy Lin; so Pat volunteered. It wasn't that she wasn't drowsy herself; it was that she had something else on her mind. Not Martín's treachery; not what Dopey had told them, astonishing though that was; the thing that was preoccupying her thoughts was the delicious fact that, at last, she had her comb back. It was what she had yearned for—well, one of the things, anyway—and while most of the captives had stretched out to nap away their full bellies Pat knelt before the mirror wall, carefully drawing it through the tangles of her hair.

That was one good thing about the place, she thought. You never had to hunt for a mirror. The bad thing was what the mirror revealed. Pat gazed discontentedly at the dark roots on her hair, the smudges of unidentified filth on her blouse, the circles under her eyes. What was even worse was that she was uncomfortably aware that she didn't smell very good, either. The hoarded drops of perfume from her carryall were running low, her little deodorant stick was long gone—and in any case the deodorant paste had left her unwelcome thatch of armpit hair sticky and tangled.

What she needed was a bath. She thought longingly of a slow soak in a hot tub, with scented bubble-bath foam rising high over the steamy water . . . and, yes, then also a wardrobe of clean clothes to put on afterward. Even a bar of soap would be fine. She thought of all the million little soap chips she had thrown away over her lifetime because they got to be too small to bother with. She would have paid a high price for any one of them right now.

A stirring a few steps away from her attracted her attention. It was where Dan had settled himself to sleep, but he didn't appear to be sleeping. He had taken off his jacket to wrap it over his head—well, that was a sensible enough thing to do, to keep the light out—but she saw that he had one hand up inside the garment, right in front of his face, and the hand was moving as though he were doing something with it inside the jacket.

Pat informed herself that whatever he was doing, it was none of her business. Picking his nose? Something equally distasteful and private? Not to mention that she wasn't really speaking to the man. . . . But it went on for a surprisingly long time, and curiosity overcame her scruples. "Dan?" Softly, so as not to wake the others. "What are you doing?"

The motion stopped. A moment later Dan's head popped out, regarding her. "It's nothing," he said.

"Well, sorry. I just thought—"

But he was shaking his head as though to tell her not to pursue the subject. Baffled, she watched as he wrapped the jacket around his hand and stood up. He looked as though he were pondering something. When she opened her mouth he shook his head at her again, then seemed to come to a decision. He touched the wall with one hand, then raised the other, wrapped in the jacket, to press against it. He held it there for a bit, frowning, then slowly moved it up and down.

He seemed to be expecting something. Whatever it was, it didn't happen. He shrugged and sighed. . . .

And then something did happen. The wall puckered and opened just where his hand was. A moment later a great fist—a Doc fist, taloned and immense—poked through and snatched the garment from his hand. "Shit!" he said, jumping back.

"What—?" Pat began, but almost at once the wall puckered again, the fist reappeared, it dropped the jacket on the floor and was gone again.

Dannerman looked angry. He picked up the jacket and shook it free. "The bastards," he muttered. "I guess they saw what I did after all, and now they've taken it away from me."

18
Pat

Pat didn't think she had screamed when that fist poked through the wall, but she must have—must have made some sort of noise, anyway, enough so that a sleeper or two woke and saw something going on. Then their questions woke the rest. "It was the wristlet, wasn't it?" she demanded. "You took it off Dopey's body!"

He admitted it with a nod. "I had one of those glass buttons, too," he said. "Did you know they glow in the dark? Under my coat I could see it easily; and the bracelet looked like metal, but it was soft. Rubbery. It slipped right off when I pulled at it."

Rosaleen was looking at him curiously. "What did you think you were going to do with them?" She had wakened totally and quickly, as though there were no difference between sleeping and waking for her; Pat wondered if that was what it was like to be old.

Dannerman shrugged. "I didn't know. It occurred to me that maybe they were a sort of key to the wall, so I tried that out—"

"Didn't work, did it?" Jimmy Lin growled. "Now you've got them even madder at us."

That was more than Pat could stand—this from one of the men who had actually killed the first Dopey! But, surprisingly, it was Martín who came to Dannerman's defense.

"You are wrong, Lin," Martín said heavily. "He was quite correct. It is the duty of a prisoner of war to try to escape, by any means possible." He hesitated, then added, "I beg your pardon, Dannerman. You are not as useless as I thought. Now I think I will go back to sleep."

* * *

The entertainment was obviously over, so, more slowly, Jimmy and Rosaleen Artzybachova followed his example. Dannerman sat awake, leaning against the wall with his eyes half closed. After an indecisive moment Pat sat down next to him. He raised his head to look at her. "Are we friends again?" he asked hopefully.

Pat considered. "Well," she said, "not active enemies, anyway. Right now I'm a lot madder at Martín than I am at you."

"So is it all right if I say something?" When she nodded he cleared his throat and added, "I want to apologize. I'm sorry about lying to you and all. Will you believe me when I say I never wanted to do anything to harm you?"

She thought about that for a moment, then shrugged. "We'd have to get into a definition of what 'harm' means, wouldn't we?"

"Well, I mean *personal* harm. I admit what I was doing might have kept you from making a lot of money, maybe—"

"Damn straight it might. Important money. Money I needed, as a matter of fact; my second divorce came pretty close to cleaning me out." She thought about that might-have-been money, then relented. "Let's let it drop. Tell me, though. How'd you get into the spy business in the first place?"

"You mean, how did a nice guy like me get into a racket like that?" He grinned. "It just happened. I was in protsy in college, I told you that. I didn't think it would last past graduation, but they called me up."

"Into the army?"

"Not the army," he said wearily. "I keep telling you; it was the *Police* Reserve Officers Training Corps. I guess I was a natural for them, with my background—well, you know how we grew up. Golden kids, private schools, all of Uncle Cubby's rich power-broker friends hanging around when we spent our summers at his place. So I made a lot of contacts, and then when I grew up I had entry into all kinds of places. Sometimes that was pretty useful for the Bureau."

"I suppose," she said thoughtfully. "What the hell were you doing in protsy in the first place?"

"Easy credits . . . and, well, yes, there was also a girl. . . ."

She laughed out loud. A couple of the sleepers stirred, and she lowered her voice. "That's the story of your life, isn't it? Was she the one you brought to Uncle Cubby's for Christmas just before your father died?"

"No, that was a different one," he admitted. "You had a guy there, too. Was he the one you ran off and married?"

She gave him a sharp look, then smiled. "No. Actually not even close. Well, maybe neither of us is that much different from Jimmy

Lin, just a little less outspoken about it." She nestled against him comfortably, then remembered to pull away.

He turned to look into her face. "What's the matter?"

She said uncomfortably, "I don't think I smell very good right now."

"So join the club."

"Damn it, Dan, I don't want to be in that club! I'd give anything for a bath—or at least for a little more water and somebody to chain Jimmy Lin up while I sponged myself off." She paused to smother a yawn. "Hell. Tell me something, Dan. Do you see any way of ever getting out of here?"

He gave her a warning look, but only said, "Did you notice how that thing reached right in to where I was standing to grab the stuff?"

"Meaning they're watching us?" She shuddered involuntarily, looking about. Well, she hadn't really ever doubted that they were being observed, but still—

On the other hand, getting out of this place was definitely the central concern in her mind, and she couldn't let it go. "So the walls have ears. Right. But do you have any ideas?"

He considered the question for a moment, then picked his words with care. "I hope so, Pat. There has to be something."

His tone struck Pat as somber. "But you have thought of what that is?"

"If you mean something that could help us escape," he said, glancing at the ceiling, "no. Not really. What I'm thinking is that there are all these people back home who don't have any idea they've been watched all this time."

There was an expression on his face that Pat couldn't identify—stubbornness, worry, concern? Something of all of them, plus a kind of determination she had never before associated with Cousin Dan-Dan. "I have a duty," he said, and stopped there.

In the silence she leaned back against him, wondering. It had never occurred to her that a cloak-and-dagger spook might be driven by conscience and concern as much as by—well, by whatever misguided adolescent yearning for colorful action might make a person get into that line of work. It was a new feeling for Pat. Not a bad one. It made him a lot easier to be comfortable with. . . .

Which she was. Comfortable. In spite of everything; comfortable enough to be definitely drowsy. When she yawned, he did, too. "We'll figure something out," he said. "Right now I'm sleepy."

And so, Pat realized, was she. It occurred to her that it would be nice for them to untangle themselves so they could stretch out, but by the time she had got that far in her thinking she was already asleep with her head on Dannerman's shoulder.

What woke Pat up was someone talking. The person was intruding on her dream, and she didn't want to let go of it, especially not because of the green-skinned woman playing a musical instrument who was intruding into it. When she opened her eyes she discovered her head was in Dannerman's lap and Jimmy Lin was grinning down at them. She sat up abruptly. "What did you say?" she demanded fuzzily.

"I was asking Dan what you were doing. Looked like the Jade Woman and Flute bit to me. Of course, Dan claims it didn't happen, but then old Dan's a real gentleman about a lady's honor, isn't he?"

"Damn you," she said. "Can't you turn off your testosterone for a while now and then? What is it, do you get a kick out of making trouble?"

His expression changed to belligerency. "Are you talking about the accident? Well, you know what? I'm not sorry we killed the little son of a bitch, even if it didn't take. Sooner or later I'm going to find some way to make him give us straight answers, and if he won't do it I wouldn't mind killing him all over again."

Dannerman was sitting up straight now, glaring at Lin. Pat was pleased to see that he was getting angry, too, but a little disappointed, too, when she realized that the anger wasn't at Lin's smarmy remarks. "You're an idiot," he said flatly. "If you really wanted to do something like that you're sure making it hard by advertising it ahead of time."

Lin shrugged and stalked away. Dannerman hesitated, then patted Pat on the head, easing it off his lap. "I've got an idea," he said, and got up without saying what the idea was. What he did was only to head for the stack of miscellaneous supplies Dopey's golems had brought.

Pat gazed after him, her back propped against the wall, knees hugged to her body. She was thinking about the connotations of being patted on the head. "Pat on the head" was a metaphor for tolerant dismissal and there had been a time, in her rad-fem undergraduate days, when any male who ventured such an act did so at his own peril. But she didn't feel tolerated, and certainly she didn't feel dismissed. What that casual touch had felt like was affection. Maybe even *sexual* affection. Tentative, yes, but under the circumstances about as forthright as was feasible. Under other circumstances . . .

Under other circumstances, Pat told herself wistfully, something nice might come of that; but not under these.

She shook herself and stood up, curious about what Dannerman was doing. He had borrowed Rosaleen's multicolor pen and was busily printing something out on a scrap of wrapping paper from the Starlab booty, shading what he was writing with his other hand. Rosaleen Artzybachova was sitting cross-legged nearby, watching him curiously. When Dannerman saw Pat standing over him he complained, "The damn ink smears on this stuff."

"That's what wrapping paper is like," she agreed. "What are you writing?"

He paused to add a word, then covered the sheet with his hand. "You could call it a diary," he said. "We don't have much privacy here, and there are some things I'd just as soon not advertise to the world."

She frowned. There was something odd about his tone. "So we can't see it?"

"Oh," he said. "I didn't say that. I guess a few friends could take a look."

"Like me?" Rosaleen offered. "It's my pen."

"Why not?" Dannerman said. "Only do it like this, please." He cupped the scrap in two hands and lifted it to his eyes, opening the hands at the thumbs just enough to peer inside. "Can you do that?"

Rosaleen gave him a baffled look, but did as instructed. "Thank God for radial keratomy," she muttered. And then, "Oh."

She closed her hands again over the scrap, looking at Dannerman with interest before she passed it to Pat. "You know the drill," she said. "I hope your near vision's in good shape."

It wasn't, particularly, but when Pat had done as ordered, opening narrow slits between fingers for light, she managed to make out the blurry scrawl:

If anybody has any useful ideas for escape etc let's share them like this.

"Oh," Pat said, too. "I see what you mean." By then Martín and Jimmy Lin were clamoring for their own turns, and Dannerman was already writing something else. When he passed it to Pat it said:

Concealed weapons? I have flex. glass knife in belt. Martín, what's in lapel? Anybody else?

By then they were all industriously writing little messages of their own, squabbling over their turns at Rosaleen's pen. "Hold it," Rosaleen ordered. "Let's make sure everybody sees everything. How about if we pass them around in alphabetical order—Adcock, Artzybachova, Dannerman, Delasquez, Lin. Then you can dispose of the messages when you're finished with them, Jimmy."

"How?"

"I don't know, swallow them, maybe?"

Lin looked rebellious, but Dannerman said, "Maybe we can burn them up in the cooker?" And when they had all seen the first message he gave it a try; it worked. The crumpled scrap of paper became ash, and he teased it out and ground it into powder with his heel for the floor to remove.

By the time they had finished taking inventory they had discovered they possessed a remarkable little armory: Dannerman's glass blade, Martín's plastic stiletto, a garroting cord from Jimmy Lin. Even Rosaleen had a pair of knitting-sized needles in her boots; apologetically Pat admitted to being the only one who had entered the Clipper without fallback arms.

But when they had exchanged all the information they had to offer, secure from the prying outside eyes, the temporary euphoria subsided and she felt let down. It was nice to know that they had some weapons. But what was the good of weapons when they had no plan to use them?

Passing secret messages around was a kind of pleasure Pat hadn't experienced since high school, but it palled. There was really nothing for them to say, and besides they were all getting hungry again.

While they were cooking their individual meals Rosaleen was investigating the cooker. "There must be a power source for this thing somewhere," she said puzzledly. "I can't find it. Maybe it's in the base? The rest of it's nothing much but sheet metal."

"Funny sheet metal," Martín rumbled. "It isn't even warm on the outside."

"Like a microwave," Pat offered.

Rosaleen shook her head. "It's not a microwave. Those vegetables Jimmy put in were foil-wrapped, and it didn't spark. I don't exactly know what—oh, hell!" Tardily they all smelled the scorching as the container of beef stew inside began to burn.

"Damn," Dannerman said. "I had my mouth all set for that stew." But it was powdery ashes before they could lever it out, and in the long run Martín simply picked the cooker up and shook them out of it for the floor to dispose of.

It was Martín, then, who noticed another curiosity. "Look here," he said, pushing at the device. "The wheels don't roll anymore."

Pat looked and discovered that they weren't actual wheels, anyway; they were just metal balls. When she pushed at the gadget hard enough it slid sluggishly over the rubbery floor, but the wheels weren't turning. "But it rolled easily enough when Dopey pushed it in," she said, perplexed.

"Maybe," Rosaleen said thoughtfully. "Or maybe they never did turn. I think we've got another piece of that far-out technology we were looking for here."

"For all the good it will do us," Martín said grumpily.

Dannerman and Pat took their food over to sit against the wall. Dannerman was deep in thought—probably, Pat supposed, about ways of getting them out of their prison cell. She hoped so, anyway. She was just getting used to the fact that her own cousin was a gumshoe; the annoyance was fading, curiosity was beginning to assert itself. She said, "Feeling talkative, Dan?"

He blinked at her. "What? Oh, sure. What's on your mind?"

"Well, you told me that after college protsy they drafted you into the army—all right, the protsy—"

"Had to be the protsy, Pat. They had snappier uniforms and no thirty-kilometer hikes."

"Then what?"

He chewed reflectively for a moment. "Well, when they called me up it turned out they didn't need any more people in uniforms. They needed undercover ops. They thought I'd do just fine mingling with the white-collar criminals and the yuppy terrorists. I objected. I said I didn't want to spy on my old friends, so they said, sure, we can give you something else. And they did." He shook his head wryly. "They ordered me to infiltrate one of the ultralight plane gangs in Orange County—you know, like the Deadly Force and the Scuzzhawks? The gangs that had been taking over little towns and scaring the hell out of the citizens? It meant wearing the same leathers for three or four weeks at a time and never taking a bath—not all that different from here, you know? Except that there were occupational hazards. The reason they needed gang infiltrators so badly was that they were having a pretty high attrition rate with the agents that managed to get in at all. All kinds of casualties: one plane crash, two ODs—and one guy who was found washing up with the surf. It didn't take me long to call in and say that, after all, I thought investigating tax frauds and radical-chic terrorists was more along my line of work."

Jimmy Lin had settled down nearby, listening intently. Pat gave him a glance, then grinned at Dannerman. "I think you made the right pick. I can't really imagine you as a Scuzzhawk. But, look, that was eight or ten years ago, at least? And you didn't quit when your hitch ran out?"

He said simply, "I found out I kind of liked it."

Fascinated, Pat persisted. "What else did you do?"

"Whatever they told me to do, pretty much. That outfit I used to work for in New York before I came to you—that was drugs. And I did a lot of antiterrorist stuff, too: the Free Bavarian movement, the Spanish guys that blew up Nelson's column in London, all that."

"And you'd go in and make friends with them, and then the end result of all these adventures was you put somebody in jail."

Dannerman gave her an injured look. "Only the bad guys."

Pat looked at him wonderingly. "Dan-Dan," she said, "you know what I think about you? I think you didn't keep on being a spook for the money. I think you did it because you want to protect people. You're a kindergarten teacher, you know that? José pees on Elvira's milk and cookies, so you give José a good swat—but you're doing it for his sake as much as for hers."

Dannerman looked as though he was getting hot under the collar. "Somebody has to keep the peace. Do you have any better way of doing it?"

"No," she said, studying him analytically. "I don't. Actually, I think it's kind of sweet." He shrugged. "You weren't that kindly a kid, you know. What happened? Do they teach compassion in the spy school?"

"Not exactly. We did take a course in sensitivity training, but basically it was to teach us how to manipulate people." He looked at Jimmy. "Of course," Dannerman said, "I'm not the only one with experience in this area, am I?" Lin was silent, waiting, watching Dannerman's face while the bowl of goulash was cooling on his outstretched thighs. "I mean," Dannerman went on, "you knew I was an agent. You had to find out from somewhere."

Lin sighed. "If you're asking if I'm a professional spook like you, the answer's no. But, yes, I did know. They told me at the consulate, first thing, as soon as I got back from Houston. That's why I started cozying up to you." He glanced penitently at Pat. "See, Pat," he said, almost pleading, "I want to go home, I mean without getting arrested. They've got a warrant out for me at Jiuquan. It's a chickenshit political charge, but they're serious about it; jail's involved, and, trust me, you don't want to be in a Chinese jail. They told me I could square it by performing a little service for the state. So, I ask you, what could I do?"

Pat didn't answer that. Instead, she asked, "What's this Jew-choon place you're talking about?"

"Jiuquan," Dannerman corrected. "It's the Chinese space center, like our Cape and Huntsville and Houston all rolled into one." Then, to Lin, "Tell you what. Let's change the subject, all right? No hard feelings. We all did what we had to do . . . and look how much good it's done any of us."

Time passed. Pat was interested to discover that time kept right on passing, even when there really weren't any events to mark the passage. Oh, there were a few slow, but visible, processes of change. All three of the men were developing tacky-looking beards, and Pat's own axillary growth was no longer scratchy stubble.

But very little *happened.* Once or twice Dopey put in a brief appearance, not talkative, seeming harried. Sporadically someone would have a notion and commit it to paper to be passed around, but none of the ideas seemed to go anywhere. Sleeping, eating, defecating took up just so much of their time, and the rest hung heavy. Pat was mildly pleased to discover that she could beat any of the others but Rosaleen at chess, once Rosaleen had made a wrapping-paper board, and while she and Dannerman were playing their hundredth game Jimmy Lin was attempting to fabricate a deck of playing cards out of more scraps of the paper towels. "At least I might have a chance to win something at poker now and then," he said sulkily.

Pat rocked back on her heels as a thought struck her. "It's your move," Dannerman said.

"Wait a minute. Give me the pen and a piece of paper, will you, Jimmy? Something just occurred to me."

And she began to print: *Would it do any good if we tried to get Dopey into a game of something?* She was just about to hand it to Dannerman when Jimmy called: "Hey, looks like Dopey's coming back!"

Indeed the mirror wall was turning milky again. Caught with the scrap of paper in her hand, Pat stared about, looking for a place to hide it. There wasn't any. Desperately she popped it in her mouth and began to chew.

She forgot to swallow when she saw what was happening. Dopey was indeed entering through the wall, but he wasn't alone. He was leading two other human beings through the wall.

"Hey!" Jimmy Lin shouted in delight. "Naked women!"

So they were, being shepherded into the cell by a pair of Docs, looking terrified and angry at the same time. Each of them was rubbing the back of her neck with one hand as she clutched her bundle of clothing with the other. "You said," Dopey explained, "that you required additional breeding stock."

They looked very familiar to Pat Adcock. She swallowed the lump of paper as she stared at them, clutching Dannerman's arm. "Sweet Jesus," she gasped. "They're both *me!*"

19
Pat

It was frightening, it was unbelievable, but Pat had to face up to the fact that it was true. These two women were indeed herself. They were two precisely identical copies of Dr. Patrice Adcock—oh, a lot cleaner, yes, and a lot less frayed-looking, but in every other way exactly herself. Their voices were the same. Their appearance was the same. The way they were hurrying into their clothes—Dannerman politely looking away, Martín impolitely observing, Jimmy Lin frankly ogling—was just the way she had done it when she first got clothing again. And when she asked, "Where the hell did you two come from?" what they answered was just what she would have said:

"Starlab." They said it in chorus, too, and then stopped short to stare at each other—to stare at everything around them. "Jesus," one of them began, a half-second before the other, who paused to let the first one finish with the flip side of Pat's question. It wasn't "Where did you come from?" but "Where in God's name are we?"

That got several answers; the habit of talking in chorus was contagious, Pat thought. Jimmy Lin, giggling, said, "You've been abducted by space aliens," and Rosaleen said compassionately, "That's a long story," and Dannerman proposed, "You go first, please? Tell us everything that happened. It might be important. Then we'll tell you everything we know."

As Pat Adcock listened to her duplicates talk she discovered a strange feeling in herself. It was pride. She was proud of herself—of her two new selves. They were less than an hour in this bizarre and terrifying new place, and yet they were managing to tell a coherent story. Oh, with repetitions and interruptions, of course—many interruptions—but it showed, she was gratified to think, some real strength of character.

The first thing her two duplicates remembered was waking up; they had been lying on what the first new Pat described as a kind of army cot and the other as a morgue slab. There were aliens all around them, and they weren't just the Dopey and the Docs that stripped them and convoyed them to the cell. "I saw one of the ones they call 'Bashful,' " the other said. "You know, the ones with the big eyes and the dewlaps that cover their faces? He was doing something with a big machine that looked kind of like a refrigerator. What? Oh, I don't know what, but he was making lights go on and off—the lights were in that green jelly stuff, you know? Like we saw on Starlab. A *lot* of it was like on Starlab." They hadn't observed their surroundings very closely, because as soon as they were awakened they were unceremoniously stripped by the Docs. And their necks hurt, they said, rubbing them reminiscently. "Let me see," Rosaleen ordered, and Jimmy Lin chimed in, "Me, too!"

"Knock it off," Pat said wearily, elbowing him out of the way. She and Rosaleen bent to inspect the nape of the women's necks. "Here?" Pat asked, touching a vertebra.

"Up a little higher. There." Pat and Rosaleen studied the hairline—how neatly trimmed, Pat thought with a twinge of jealousy—but there was nothing to see.

"Maybe you bumped yourselves," Jimmy offered, crowding in to look. But they denied that.

Then, yes, the Dopey and the Docs had gone through their clothing and handed it back to them. "There was a whole pile of other clothes there," one remembered, and the other confirmed it.

"I saw something with a lot of braid on it—it looked like that jacket you're wearing, Martín. All in a heap, with a lot of other stuff. No, they weren't doing anything with it; it looked like they just tossed it there."

"Maybe they're making clean clothes for us," Pat said hopefully.

"Maybe." And then they were marched down a long, busy passage, lined with bizarre things that probably were machines, they thought, to the point where they saw all the rest of the captives. "Wall? No. I didn't see any wall. Not from the outside, not until we were inside here. No, it didn't look like glass. It didn't look like anything at all. All I saw was the bunch of you, playing cards or something, but it didn't look like you saw us . . . and then we were here and there were these big damn mirrors all around us."

"And those machines?" Rosaleen asked. "What did they look like?"

But she didn't get much of an answer. They had been too full of other questions for close study. One of the devices they passed was making a kind of coffee-percolator sound, one of the new Pats remembered, and the other said another one was giving off heat; but, "Just weird, you know? Like the stuff on Starlab." Then she pleaded, "Our turn now. What *is* this place?"

Pat took over. "Come over and sit down," she offered. "Want something to eat? Jimmy, make us some of that lousy coffee, anyway."

Pat Adcock, who had been an only child, had never had any experience with this sort of thing. She had never had sisters before, much less identical triplets. She was astonished to discover how much she liked it. There was something warmly pleasing about sitting with the two new versions of herself, the repulsive coffee cooling untasted in their hands, while she took over the job of briefing them.

There was a lot to be told. Pat had not realized just how much she and the other captives had had to learn in all those long days in the cell until she had to summarize it all for the two new Pats: their capture, their imprisonment, their futile attempts at escape—the whole disheartening story. It was bad enough for the original five captives, even worse for the new arrivals . . . who, Pat thought, not only had the shock of finding themselves in this bizarre new predicament, but also of suddenly being inexplicably part of a perfectly matched set of three.

They took it well, increasing Pat's pride in them. Took it well most of the time, anyway; not counting their outrage when she explained the toilet arrangements to them. They were almost (though not quite) as repelled when she told them that everything they did, all the time, was watched from outside the cell. "They have no right!" one of them exclaimed—barely before the other.

Pat sighed, sparing a quick look at Dannerman, who had written something on a scrap of paper and was holding it covered, impatiently waiting. "They have the power," she said. "I don't know about 'rights.' Except that we don't have any at all." And to Dannerman: "Is that what I think it is?"

"For the new ones," he said, handing it to Pat. She glanced at it: it was what she had expected, a synopsis of the parts of the briefing that were not to be spoken out loud.

She showed the newcomers the technique of managing to read it without ever letting it be exposed to hostile eyes. When the first one read it she said nothing, just looked affronted and unhappy when she passed it to the other. When the other finished she giggled wanly. "Passing notes back and forth," she said, "it's like being in school again."

"Only school was never like this," the other one agreed, and Pat marveled: they were thinking the same thoughts she had thought. Well, they would, wouldn't they? Being the same person . . . except for being a lot cleaner.

Which made her think of something. She glanced at the other captives, all of whom had edged close to listen in, and lowered her voice. "Listen," she said. "They left you your perfume, didn't they? Could one of you spare me a couple of drops?"

They could, and Jimmy Lin stepped closer, inhaling. "Ah," he said, "that's really fine. I'd almost forgotten what a woman was supposed to smell like."

Pat gave him a look of disgust. "Shoo," she ordered, and then, more politely, "All the rest of you, could you just leave us alone for a bit? So we can get used to this?"

The other three considerately took themselves over to the cooker, but Lin looked rebellious. "Who are you to give me orders, Ice Queen? Maybe these other ladies appreciate a little male attention."

"We don't," one of the others said briefly. "Get lost." When he moved sulkily away she stared after him. "What's the matter with him?"

"He's horny."

"Well, sure he's horny. He's always been horny, but he didn't use to act like that."

"Ah, no," Pat said, remembering. "Not quite as forthright, anyway. But that was then. You were his boss then. Now that doesn't matter anymore."

The other Pat was staring after Jimmy, who was now sulkily demanding his share of what was coming out of the cooker. "Speaking of that kind of thing . . . well," she said, now almost whispering, "excuse me for asking, but I don't suppose anybody's actually getting any, are they?"

"In this goldfish bowl? I wish."

"Because," the other went on, "I couldn't help seeing the way Dan-Dan looks at you, you know? Is something new going on with you two?"

Pat had to think about that one. "I wouldn't be surprised," she said finally, surprising herself. "He's not really a bad guy when you get to know him . . . I mean, not counting that he's a goddamn spy."

That took explanation, too. Everything did, not helped by the fact that the new arrivals not only looked the same but talked at the same time, with the same words, and then stopped and stared at each other. "Hell," Rosaleen said at last. "We've got to do something about telling you apart. Let's start by naming you. You"—the original—"you're Pat. And you"—the one nearest her—"you can be Patricia—"

"It's Patrice, actually," the two new ones said together.

"All right, Patrice. And you're Patsy."

The third one looked rebellious. "The hell you say! Nobody ever calls me Patsy!"

"Oh, come on," the Patrice said soothingly. "It's not so bad and Rosie's right about needing names."

The Patsy scowled. "So why don't you be Patsy, then?" Then she surrendered: "Oh, well, I guess it makes no difference, but you owe me."

"Fine," Rosaleen said, smiling for the first time. "That's settled: Pat, Patrice and Patsy. Now, hold still." She was pulling out her multicolor pen. "Just so the rest of us can know which of you is which I'm going to put a little beauty spot on your foreheads."

"Hey!" both of them protested at once.

Rosaleen overruled them. "It's just for now; it'll wear off by the time we think of something better. Let's see. We'll do blue for you, Pat, just to be fair. Red for Patrice; and I'll do green for Patsy." And then, mimicking Dopey: "Are there any questions?"

She was talking to the Pats, but it was Jimmy Lin who spoke up. "I have one. Which of you is going to be the lucky girl who gets me?"

Pat opened her mouth to chastise him, and then closed it again. What was the point? Better just to ignore him, she thought, and, hostesslike, was about to ask her new best friends if they were ready to eat again when something happened. It sounded like a distant *crump* of a blast—thunder? an explosion?—and a moment later that constant, featureless white light from overhead dimmed and reddened. It only lasted for a second. Then it was bright again.

"What the hell was that?" Patsy asked.

Nobody had an answer. Patrice asked, "Does that happen a lot?" and Pat shook her head.

"Never before," she said. "It sounded like something blew up."

Rosaleen Artzybachova said, "Did you feel the floor shake?" Dannerman thought he had; none of the others were sure. But there wasn't any doubt that something had happened, and, though they chewed the subject over the next half hour or so, all they could agree on was that they didn't like it.

Except for Jimmy Lin. Who said, grinning weakly, "How about that? Just *talking* about sex I can make the earth move for you."

Whatever it was, it didn't happen again. By their second day—well, by the time they woke up from their second sleep after their arrival—the two new Pat Adcocks were at least no longer speaking in chorus. Nurture had triumphed over nature. There hadn't been many differences in their experience, and those only small ones. Patsy had burned her hand trying to learn how to use the cooker; Jimmy Lin had been a little too forthright when he managed to get Patrice alone—well, not "alone," but at least a couple of meters from any of the others, enough for him to deem the privacy adequate—and it had wound up in a screaming match. Things like that. But however little the differences had been, they were enough to set each of them off on somewhat different trains of thought.

What all the Pats had, and kept, was a preference for each other's company. They ate together. When one of them had to use the toilet the other two stood protectively before her, glaring the three males down. They slept nestled next to each other, woke at the same time, whispered to each other. Within the small group of captives they had become a separate subunit. It was, Pat thought, a little reassuring to have two companions whom she could trust absolutely, since they were herself.

The other four were not as pleased. Dannerman and Rosaleen embarked on a chess marathon, doggedly ignoring the three Pat Adcocks. Martín Delasquez hardly spoke to anyone, retreating into sleep, or pretended sleep, for hour upon hour, while Jimmy Lin went the other way. He was hyperactive, Pat thought. He seemed hardly to sleep at all. He kibitzed the chess players, tried unsuccessfully to get Martín to play some other game with him and, of course, did his best to talk sex with any or all of the three Pats. If they were worried about getting pregnant, he offered, the revered ancient Peng-tsu had the answers for that, too. "We could do Approaching the Fragrant Bamboo, for instance," he said. "That's doing it standing up, you know? And Peng-tsu says you can't get pregnant that way. You don't believe that? All right, then there's always the Jade Girl and the Flute, or The White Tiger Leaps—that one," he said, with a wink, "I don't want to tell you about, but any time you like I could show you."

All that sort of talk had long since become pretty stale for Pat, but the two new ones were more tolerant. They let him talk. Anyway, Pat thought, that was better than Jimmy's other main occupation, which was feverishly writing out notes with ideas for doing something—going on a hunger strike, capturing Dopey and torturing him until he did whatever they wanted—maybe using some of the concealed weapons they still possessed, maybe by dunking his limbs or tail into the cooker. Pat wondered if the man was going insane. When he passed around the suggestion for cooking Dopey's plume, on the grounds that that was bound to hurt but unlikely to kill the creature, he was almost trembling with excitement; but then, a few hours later, he was talking enthusiastically about some of his ancestor's other sexual proposals . . . when the wall clouded and Dopey came in.

As always, he was bombarded with questions as soon as he appeared: "Why were you gone so long?" from Jimmy Lin; "What was that explosion?" from Dannerman.

One answer did for both of them. "There was an incident," Dopey admitted, his fingers working nervously, his bright tail dimmed and still. "It caused some problems for a time, but it has been dealt with. Now I have some news for you—"

Pat wasn't letting him get away with that. "What kind of incident?" she insisted.

He hesitated, staring around at them with those great eyes. Then he spoke to Dannerman. "In your previous life you were assigned to dealing with 'terrorists,' is that not correct? That is, with criminal persons who performed violent and destructive acts? Yes. Well, it is something of that sort here. I can say no more about it, except that the criminals have been, ah, neutralized."

"Neutralized how?" Jimmy asked suspiciously, but Rosaleen overrode him—probably, Pat thought, because she didn't think they would like to hear the answer.

"Never mind that," she said. "What he means is, are these the same 'criminals' who were interfering with your communications?"

"Yes, precisely. The terrorists."

"I see. And perhaps the same ones who transmitted the message that described you people as destroying the universe?"

For a moment Pat thought that Dopey was going to relapse into his trance state again; it seemed to be a troubling question. But then he made a breathy sound—almost a sigh—and said, "Yes. They are the same. Through trickery and violence they managed to infiltrate the link to your Starlab for a brief time. Of course, I observed their transmission at once and was able to jam the rest of it."

"But then they did it again," Dannerman offered.

Dopey said mournfully, "Indeed. This time I failed to observe it, as they had caused the death of one of me. But my replacement dealt with them. No," he added, waggling his head against the next burst of questions, "that is all I may say on that subject. But I have received new instructions for you. I am instructed to accelerate your program, and so a device is being prepared which will give you more complete information—"

"Device? What kind of device?" Rosaleen demanded.

"It will be explained when it is ready," he said severely. "Please do not interrupt. I have further instructions. I am directed to provide you with whatever additional matériel from your Starlab you require—except, of course, anything that can be used as a weapon."

"Why are you being nice to us?" Martín asked suspiciously.

"I do not make these decisions. I simply carry out instructions. If there is anything in particular you wish, simply inform me, now or later. Otherwise I will use my own discretion."

"We don't have room for anything else in here!" Pat put in.

"Yes. That has been anticipated. Other accommodations are being prepared for you." He paused, eyes closed, fingers busy in the muff. It looked to Pat as though he was getting ready to leave, with a million questions unanswered; Rosaleen evidently thought the same, because she spoke up.

"Tell me one more thing. Are you going to bring any more of us here?"

"More copies of you here? I know of no such plans. It is possible, however, that there will be other human beings. Two additional human missions to Starlab are currently being proposed, and of course if they reach the orbiter they, too, will be copied for study. Now I must go."

He turned, then paused to look back at Jimmy Lin. "One more thing. Please do not give any more thought to the plan of capturing and torturing me. I do not think you could succeed, but if you did it would be very unpleasant for me, and it would do you no good at all."

20
Pat

Pat Adcock was deep in sleep when the sound of her own voice yelling jerked her awake. It didn't come from her own throat; it had to be one of the new Pats, and she jumped to a conclusion. "Is that damn Jimmy trying something?" she demanded, sitting up and rubbing her eyes.

But it wasn't Jimmy Lin. It was one of the Docs, and the person shouting was Patsy, hanging by one arm from the Doc's grasp. "Damn you," she cried, shaking herself free. "Don't grab a person like that!"

The Doc hesitated, glancing at a second Doc standing stolidly by. "Where's Dopey?" Pat demanded; no one answered, and he wasn't there. The second Doc, which was holding some sort of metallic object, didn't speak, of course: They never did, as far as Pat knew; perhaps couldn't. Or simply had no reason to. What it did was make a gesture, and at once the first one abandoned Patsy and casually reached out for the arm of the nearest other human—it happened to be Jimmy Lin—holding him firmly while the other jammed the object down on Lin's head.

"Hey!" Jimmy squawked in alarm, reaching up with both hands to tug it free. In vain; the Doc's grip was firm. Pat thought for a moment of trying to rescue the Chinanaut from whatever new torture the Docs had devised. She could see the thing plainly now: a sort of helmet, made of the same coppery mesh as Dopey's muff. On Jimmy's head it looked almost like a garish wig, cut along the lines of one of those flapper hairdos of the early twentieth century, what they called a "French bob," she thought. And while she waited Jimmy stopped struggling.

"Hey," he said again, sounding startled but now—astonishingly—

almost pleased. "There's a Frenchman talking to me. He's saying—no, just wait a minute, I'll translate for you when he's done."

"I speak French," Rosaleen said eagerly—only the first to make the claim; she was quickly followed by all three Pats and both other men.

Jimmy waved impatiently for silence. "He isn't speaking French. He's speaking Chinese. Shut up so I can hear."

"Chinese!" Martín muttered angrily, as the two Docs left as wordlessly as they had come in. One of the Pats—Pat thought it was Patrice—complained:

"That is *so* inconsiderate!" Both of them were echoing Pat's own thoughts. Chinese, for God's sake! Dopey was showing even worse judgment than usual. But there was nothing to do about it but wait until Jimmy Lin was willing to talk to them.

Evidently the Frenchman's message was short. After a moment Jimmy took the helmet off and gazed at them. "Well," he said, "that was interesting. It didn't actually tell much, but—hey!" Martín had grabbed the helmet from him. Jimmy reached to take it back, but Martín fended him off and settled the thing on his own head. "Now, what's the use of doing that?" Jimmy demanded pettishly. "You aren't going to understand Chinese, Martín."

Martín said triumphantly, "He isn't speaking Chinese! He's speaking Spanish."

"But that's impossible," Jimmy protested. "He was speaking quite excellent PRC Chinese, with a well-educated accent, though there was a trace of the Beijing tones—"

"Be quiet!" Martín thundered. "I can't hear while you're making all that racket! Also, I know who this man is. I will tell you all about it if you will simply let me listen."

Looking petulant, Jimmy Lin did as ordered, but the others didn't. Under the dark eye-patches of the helmet Martín was scowling at the noise, but he said nothing more until it was over. Then he took the helmet off and held it in his hand for a moment.

"The man speaking, he is Hugues duValier. He's a navigator with Eurospace; I met him once at Kourou. What he is saying is a communication meant for everybody in the world. It sounds as though they finally got their own Starlab mission off."

"What did he say?" Dannerman demanded.

Martín shook his head. "Try it for yourself. Since he is so unexpectedly versatile, I am curious to see if perhaps this time he will speak in some language you can understand."

"Hey!" Pat cried as Martín handed the helmet to Dannerman. "What happened to alphabetical order? Who said all the men go first?"

"What happened to women's rights?" Patrice chimed in, and Patsy added:

"Oink, oink, you sexist pigs."

But Rosaleen said, "It's faster if we don't argue. Let him go; we'll all get a turn." And Dannerman placed the helmet on his head.

21
Dan

Dannerman settled the thing on his head as rapidly as he could; he wanted to see this linguistic marvel, wanted even more to find out just what the Frenchman had to say. The helmet didn't fit particularly well and it was heavy. The goggles—opaque eye-shields, actually—dug into his flesh over the cheekbones, but they did their job. He could see nothing but blackness, could hear the sounds from his companions only faintly through the thickness of the helmet.

Then the blackness dissolved. Dannerman was looking at a man dressed in an astronaut's EVA spacesuit, helmet tucked under one arm, and the man was looking directly back at him. It didn't look like a broadcast. It seemed that the man was standing before him, solid in three dimensions, seeming almost near enough to touch. When the man spoke he sounded as though the conversation was one-on-one. He said:

"Hello, ladies and gentlemen. You may recognize me. I am Colonel Hugues duValier, and I am speaking to you from the astronomical observatory called Starlab. I am not alone here. I am in the company of a person who has a message of great importance for everyone on Earth. I cannot show him to you at this time. However, he is a friend, and he has given me the responsibilty—and the privilege—of delivering his message to you.

"You will remember that some time ago these two broadcasts of alien origin were received all over the world." A screen appeared beside the figure, displaying the two old space messages one after another. "Some people thought these were some sort of a joke. Others came closer to the truth, imagining that they were warnings of an extraterrestrial invasion. That is both true and false. There is a threat of invasion by evil people, that is true. What is false is that the evil ones are not the ones shown in the messages. The evil ones—the people who are even now planning to attack our planet and do us all great harm—are the ones who sent those first false messages in order to deceive you. These brutal creatures are called by a name which is difficult for me to say; it sounds like the 'Horch.' They possess a very high technology, particularly in weaponry. They have fought many wars, over long ages of time, and in them they have succeeded in destroying many other civilizations in other solar systems. Only a few races have been able to defend themselves against the Horch. Some of them are the people whose pictures the Horch sent to you—pretending they were enemies—but they are in fact the ones who can help you defend yourself against these attackers. Their name is even more difficult to pronounce; my friends here call them 'Beloved Leaders.' You already know what they look like, from the deceitful transmissions the Horch sent. What I will show you now is a picture of a Horch."

The image of the astronaut flicked out of sight and another being appeared. It didn't look like a picture. To Dannerman the creature looked as though it were actually standing there, no more than a yard or so away from him. It was taller than Dannerman himself, and gazing threateningly at him. It was certainly not from the gallery that had already been displayed, though equally ugly. Stocky body, wearing metallic armor. Long lizard head on a long and supple neck, with a lipless mouth filled with sharp teeth. Instead of arms it had two boneless limbs, like an elephant's trunk, fraying into half a dozen digits at the ends. In one "hand" it carried an axe, in the other a spiked club. It was, in fact, the very model of the kind of alien invader you would never want to see appearing out of your skies.

The image shrank to a picture inset on the screen and the colonel appeared again, looking grave. "I have been shown the evidence, which is indisputable, and so I now know what terrible things the Horch can do," he said somberly. "They will do such things to us, too, if we let them, and we have no defenses of our own that could withstand them. Still, we have been offered strong allies. With the help of the Beloved Leaders—as these friends are called—we can defend ourselves.

"Without them we are doomed.

"That is all I can say now. In twenty-four hours I will speak to you again, and then I will give you more details about the choices before us. Until then . . . please. Be warned."

The picture went to black. The message was over.

Thoughtfully Dannerman removed the helmet. "He spoke to me in

English," he announced. "Rosie? Why don't you take a shot and see what he does for you?"

"Thanks a lot, Dan," Pat said with annoyance.

He shook his head. "You'll get your turn. Wait till we've all seen it." He settled himself on the floor and waited, staring into space.

Then Patsy, last to have her turn, took the helmet off and shakily, "Wow. That was an ugly one, all right."

Dannerman had been thinking. He said, "Something strikes me as peculiar. The astronaut spoke to me in English; was it the same for you Pats? Yes, I thought so. Rosaleen?"

"Why, yes. He spoke in Ukrainian. With a few Russian words, actually, but his accent was good. Why do you say that's peculiar? Clearly this is an announcement transmitted to everyone on Earth, like the others; naturally they would want it to be in languages everyone can understand."

"That's not the peculiar part. Did you see duValier's lips move?"

"His lips?" She looked puzzled, but Jimmy Lin was quicker.

"You're thinking it was lip-synched for each of us?" he demanded. "No. Forget lip-synching. Maybe you could get away with that for European languages. Mandarin Chinese, no. DuValier was actually speaking those words, Dan."

Dannerman nodded. "But that wasn't exactly what I was thinking. What I'm thinking is that it *wasn't* lip-synched, and that's the part that's hard to understand. Martín? Did this Colonel duValier know all those languages?"

Delasquez looked indignant. "That ass? No! I was astonished to hear him even speak Spanish. I do not even know how he succeeded in getting a spacecraft on course to Starlab, he is such a notorious fool."

Pat was looking at Dannerman expectantly. When he didn't speak she prodded. "What's your point, Dan?"

"I wish I knew. The whole thing sounds funny."

Patrice nodded. "I know what you mean. If I saw that on TV at home I'd turn it right off. 'Beloved Leaders,' for Christ's sake! Only—well, if what he says is the truth . . ."

Jimmy Lin finished the sentence for her. "Then," he said, "the world is really in the deep shit."

22
Dan

Dannerman didn't have to be told that the world was in trouble. It always was. That was the reason it hired him and others like him, to do their best to protect it against itself.

Now here was the biggest threat of all, and shouldn't—he asked himself—shouldn't he be doing something about it? There was only one answer to that for Jim Daniel Dannerman. The question wasn't *whether.* It was *what.*

And to that he had no answer. Every other time he had found himself in harm's way he had known exactly what he wanted to accomplish. If he'd been in any doubt, Colonel Hilda Morrisey or someone like her would have spelled it out for him at the briefing. There was always a hierarchy of defined objectives. First, you stayed alive. Second, you got the evidence. Third, you called in the strike force and watched the malefactors being led away.

Here there was no briefing to tell him what to do. There was also no evidence to get, no way to get out and no strike force waiting to be called. And here the stakes were higher than they had ever been before. It was the entire population of Earth who were at risk now—Hilda herself, and sweet Anita Berman from Theater Aristophanes Two, and his landlady Rita, as well as everyone at the Dannerman Observatory . . . as well as everyone else he'd ever known in all his life, villains and colleagues and civilians alike. He wondered what they were doing now. He wondered how much comfort they could take in the promise of help from the "Beloved Leaders."

And he wondered, too, just how much help those Beloved Leaders had any real intention of giving. There just wasn't enough data! He knew nothing useful of those shadowy figures, had no idea what sort of bizarre alien personality traits motivated them. And had little reason to believe that benevolence was among them.

He opened his eyes when he heard Pat raising her voice. She was saying something harsh to Jimmy Lin, who was grinning as he held her by one arm. She wrenched herself free, saw Dannerman looking at her and came over to sit beside him. "Bastard," she said.

He didn't take it personally, but, "You mean Jimmy?" he asked, just to make sure.

"Who else? You'd think he'd have enough decency to give it a rest, the way things are."

"I take it he was hitting on you."

"Me, and Patsy, and Patrice—he doesn't care. He just wants to get laid. He said—" She hesitated, then shook her head. "He said what he always says, so what's the use of talking about it? Forget him." Then she looked apologetic. "Did I interrupt something?"

"Nothing that was going anywhere," he admitted.

"Well, if you're sure . . . Listen, I've been wanting to ask you something, Dan. What did you mean about it's being funny?"

"Funny? Oh, right. I almost forgot. Well, it is funny. Why would Dopey show us that message?"

"Why? Hum." She thought for a moment, then said, "Yeah, I see what you mean. Dopey doesn't do anything that doesn't do him some good, so what good can that do him?"

"That's the question, all right. I don't suppose you happen to have an answer?"

"I wish I did. I wish I knew how much of it to believe, too."

"So do I." Dannerman thought about telling her some of his own doubts, but there wasn't much point; they weren't clear in his own mind. Anyway, he saw that Pat was glaring again at Jimmy. Who was standing over the cooker, waiting for his next meal to heat, and leering at them.

"Bastard," she said again. "Not that I don't understand how he feels. It's been a long time—but here? With everybody watching? Although I have to say he thought about that part, too."

"Oh?" said Dannerman, surprised to find a sudden interest growing.

She looked at him, her expression unreadable. "Well, yes. Like in an airplane, you know, when you get a couple of blankets from the stew. There are all those blankets from Starlab. Then—well, did Jimmy ever explain the Rabbit Nibbles the Hare to you?"

"Frequently," he said—surprised again to find that he was feeling just a tiny bit of unexpected jealousy. "Is that what you and Jimmy talk about?"

"It's what Jimmy talks about," she corrected. "All the time." She was still studying his face as she added, "But, listen, Dan, just for the record—I mean, in case you're interested—Jimmy and I never actually did anything. Not now, or ever. The only thing I ever wanted from Jimmy Lin was for him to help me make a lot of money."

One more surprise: the feeling of relief. But, "Always thinking of the big bucks, aren't you?" he chided. He meant it lightly, but her expression changed.

"I don't want to be poor," she said.

"I'm sorry—"

"No, you were right. I wanted the bucks. That's why I wanted Starlab so badly."

"Our dear old family lawyer told me you had made some bad investments," Dannerman said, remembering.

"Did he now? Our dear old family lawyer has a big mouth, but that wasn't it. Well," she said, reconsidering, "I did make one real bad investment, maybe. That was Ferdie. My ex-husband—the sweet one. He'd spend the whole day lying naked by the pool, communing with nature, when he wasn't writing poetry. Ferdie was very Zen; made me learn my mantra and everything. But after a while I got tired of having this big, healthy man around the house who couldn't even remember to flush his own toilet, but I couldn't let him starve, could I? So before the divorce I endowed this lectureship for poetry and got him put in charge of it. I figured that would keep him eating for the rest of his life."

"And your generosity bankrupted you?"

"Well, not directly. It cost me a bundle, but I had plenty left . . . but, on the other hand, yes, I guess it did, because after I'd laid out the cash to finance the lectureship—and, believe me, Dan-Dan, I was generous—the next thing that happened was Ferdie's lawyers came to see my lawyers and said, 'Okay, now that we've got that out of the way, let's talk about how we're going to divide up the community property.' "

"Skunks," he said. The diffuse light that came from nowhere made her unkempt hair radiant.

"Lawyers," she corrected. "He got some really good ones working for him, I'll say that much. They had every last thing I owned on their database. I had to give him half—which meant I had to sell off a lot of stuff that I didn't really want to sell, to keep the house and the personal stuff. But Ferdie really was a sweet man." She stretched and yawned. "Now you," she ordered.

He considered. "What do you want to know?"

"Everything. Especially about the women. Start with whoever it was who kept you from collecting Uncle Cubby's inheritance."

He leaned forward and lifted her hand to kiss, and the hell with who might be watching. It was the first time in a long time—maybe, he reflected, the first time ever—that he'd had this kind of boy-girl talk without having to lie through at least some parts of it, to cover up what he was really doing. But now there was nothing to lie about. "That would be Ilse, I guess. In a way, anyway. She was in the Mads—"

"The what?"

"The Mad King Ludwigs. The Bavarian secessionist movement. Well, the terrorists; that's what they really were. I was undercover, investigating them, when Uncle Cubby died, and I'd cut all my links with home. We were on the run, Ilse and I, although I always kept my team leader informed. And Ilse finally must've rumbled me. Or someone else did, and tipped her off."

"Who were you running from?"

"The Bay-Kahs—the Bundes Kriminalamt. The cops. They were after us because we'd tried to blow up the Kunstmuseum as a protest. I made sure the bomb didn't actually go off—maybe that's what made the Mads suspicious—but we had to get out of there. Anyway, one night Ilse and I had a lot to drink in this pension in the Alps. Now that I think of it, I was the one doing most of the drinking. Then I just went to sleep, not a care in the world, and when something woke me up an hour or so later, in the middle of the night, Ilse was gone and four big bastards with hockey sticks were crashing through the door after my blood. I knew them all. They were *aktion*—the organization's muscle men. I'd seen them doing their stuff at demonstrations, but I hadn't expected them to be coming after me just then."

He leaned back, meditating. "You know how you're never prepared for the really big challenges? If you knew something like that was coming up you'd get a good night's sleep first and make sure your reflexes were all tuned. . . . Mine weren't. I was still half in the bag and all tangled up in the bedclothes, and there I was."

"But you overpowered them anyway."

"Oh, no. I did break the arm of one of them, but the other three beat the shit out of me, until Hilda got there."

"Another of your women?"

That made him laugh. "Jesus, no. My team leader. She'd been surveilling the building. When she saw Ilse come out and the leg-breakers go in she decided she'd better make sure I was all right. Which I was, after I healed up for a while, though I had to stay out of sight for a month or so—the Mads had planted a couple people in the police, and they had to be collected first." He scratched himself. "Hilda had intercepted the lawyer's notice about the estate," he added, "but she didn't pass it on, because she didn't want to blow my cover."

"Poor bastard."

She was yawning as she said it, which made him yawn too. "Dirt poor," he agreed drowsily. Well, except for what the Bureau had been putting away for him, but he couldn't collect that until he retired . . . which didn't seem like a very early probability . . . unless, he corrected himself, you considered that in a way he was, perforce, pretty much retired already. . . .

His thoughts were going in circles again. He abandoned them and let himself drift off. It was getting to be a habit to fall asleep with Pat Adcock on his shoulder, he thought, and couldn't decide whether it was a good one or not.

His body had its own opinions. When Dopey appeared again and roused the whole cell Pat's proximity had started a few glands flowing; and Dannerman woke with a major erection and the rapidly dissipating recollection of some more than normally erotic dreams. Beside him Pat was scrambling to her feet. "Come on, Dan!" she urged him.

"In a minute," he said, waving her away. By the time he felt fit to stand up everyone else was clustered around Dopey and his two Docs as they dispensed more largesse.

"I have brought you more blankets and food," Dopey said unnecessarily. "You do not presently need them, I am aware, but there is always the risk that supplies may be temporarily interrupted. Meanwhile, I have some urgent business."

"What kind of business?" Patsy asked, but was outweighed by two or three others demanding to know what kind of "temporary interruptions" Dopey was talking about.

"Merely more of the difficulties we have already experienced," he explained. "They will be dealt with. Now, as to the more important matters—"

But Rosaleen, poking around in the mounting heap of supplies the Docs were lugging in, had more important matters of her own. Arms akimbo, she faced Dopey angrily. "We need more than food and blankets," she said. "We need medical supplies. We need—"

"We need to know what's going on on Earth, too," Patsy put in.

Dopey said defensively, "I cannot promise that. I do not have authority to make such promises. I have in fact asked those who decide for permission to provide you with additional data, but I have not received an answer. You do not understand how difficult things have become."

"I don't *care* how difficult things have become."

"But, you see, at present I am unable to reach the ones who could give permission. Just at present, that is to say."

"Everything's 'just at present,' " Jimmy Lin sneered, and Dannerman, looking at the stack of food packages, had a comment of his own:

"You must expect us to be here for a long time."

"That is also not for me to decide, but the reason for the large quantity is that I do not know when I will be able to get more. I have said this. Now we must deal with the urgent matters. Do you have any questions about the announcement made by your Colonel duValier?"

Dannerman was surprised that that was the "urgent" business, but it was Pat who spoke up. "We've got plenty of questions, but they're not about Colonel duValier. For instance, these 'Horch' the colonel talks about in what you transmitted to the Earth. Are they related to the problems you're having?"

Dopey didn't answer immediately. Dannerman expected him to thrust his paws into the muff and go again into the thinking-it-over trance, but he merely looked pained—as much as a kitten face can look pained. Finally he announced, "There is a disjunction here. You are correct in one respect. The Horch are indeed responsible for our problems, because they are evil. They have performed acts of terrorism which have caused great hardship for us. You will understand what terrorists are like, Agent Dannerman, from your own experiences with Colonel Hilda Morrisey. The Horch are criminals in much the same way as your human terrorists, but far more dangerous than any you can imagine. However, you have made a false assumption."

"Which is?" Dannerman demanded.

"That message has not been transmitted. The reason for that is that Colonel duValier has not yet arrived on Starlab."

"Hah!" Jimmy Lin shouted. "I knew it! It was a damn simulation."

"The problem was not understood," Dopey admitted. "It will be corrected."

Something was bothering Dannerman. He asked, "Why bother with simulating somebody who isn't there? If you wanted to send a message that seemed to come from a human being, why not use one of us?"

Dopey hesitated again. "That would not be effective," he said, and would not say why. The only subject that he seemed willing to discuss was what their reactions had been to the message, and when they began asking questions in return—what would be in the second message? What other languages would it be delivered in?—he did not respond at all.

Not until, at a venture, Pat asked, "Are we in personal danger from these Horch?"

That made Dopey pause to think once more. "At this time, no," he said at length.

"Oh, fine," Patrice muttered. "You're making me feel all cuddly warm and protected."

"I understand you. That is sarcasm, meaning the opposite," Dopey said. "You will, however, be protected."

"By you?"

"I? No, of course not I. That protection will come from a far more advanced race than my own."

"Meaning," Dannerman asked, "those odd-looking scarecrows we saw on TV?"

Dopey winced. "That was an unfair picture our enemies transmitted. The Beloved Leaders come from a light-gravity planet and thus are rather frail in physique."

He paused as Jimmy Lin made a sound of disgust. " 'Beloved Leaders,' " Lin sneered.

Dopey looked inquiring. "Your tone of voice indicates disapproval," he said.

"You damn bet it does! 'Beloved Leaders' is what the old Koreans called their dictators. That's not a good name, Dopey."

"Thank you," the alien said. "That too is useful, although I am not sure that a change will be permitted. At any rate, because of their evolutionary heritage the Be—the persons in charge, that is, would not be on a planet of this mass."

"So they're not really going to be around to save us?" Jimmy Lin demanded in alarm.

But that was one question too many. Dopey evidently had what he had come for. Without farewell, he turned and disappeared into the mirror, which re-formed seamlessly behind him, like a puddle of mercury closing over a stone.

Dannerman stared after him for a long minute, though there was nothing to see but his own reflection in the wall. He was puzzling over something, and it showed. "What's the matter?" Pat demanded. "You still wondering why he showed us that message?"

"Actually no," Dannerman said. "I think that's pretty obvious now, isn't it? He's using us to be his sneak-preview film critics, getting our reactions before he puts the thing on the air. No, it's something else."

He hesitated for a moment. Then, "Tell me something, Pat. When we were talking I mentioned Hilda to you, didn't I?"

"Sure. Your boss in the Bureau. I remember."

"But did I ever say her last name? No, I didn't think so. So how did Dopey know that it was Morrisey?"

23
Dan

So Dannerman had one more puzzle to add to his collection. He was certain he'd never mentioned Hilda Morrisey's last name, and the Bureau did not advertise the names of its personnel. And it was not information that could be picked up from the monitored broadcasts.

But Dopey had known it.

In fact, Dopey seemed to know quite a few of the things they had never spoken aloud. How? There was one easy answer to that: Someone might have been sloppy in concealing some of the notes as they read them or passed them around. But that didn't explain Hilda Morrisey, and Dannerman didn't believe it anyway. What he believed was that Dopey possessed sources of information they didn't know about.

Whatever those sources might be.

He snorted in disgust—muffled quickly, because he didn't want Pat, or any one of the Pats, to come over to see what was bothering him. That had happened twice already, and he had waved them away. He wished he didn't have to. He wanted badly to talk it over with the others, because someone else, Rosaleen maybe—well, any of them—might have a clarifying insight he had missed. But if even the eyes-only note-passing was compromised, they would simply be giving more information to Dopey, or Dopey's masters.

Would that matter? Would that sort of information be useful to them? Dannerman could form no satisfactory answer to that, either, but it was simple basic tradecraft to deny as much information as possible to the enemy, and—

His thoughts were interrupted by a new sound. Something had begun squealing shrilly, somewhere. When Dannerman raised his head he saw Patrice holding the helmet in her hand, looking puzzled. "I think it wants something," she said.

"It wants one of us to put it on, of course," Rosaleen said crossly. "Give it to me."

Evidently she was right. As soon as she had it settled on her head the beeping stopped. By then most of the others had converged around her, clamoring to know what she was hearing. Rosaleen didn't take the helmet off, only held up her hand and said, "Relax. It's basically the same message, but with a few—improvements. Give me a moment."

"Then this time we do it in alphabetical order, remember?" Pat reminded them. "Pat comes before Patrice or Patsy, so I get the first look."

Jimmy Lin emitted a long, exasperated sigh, Martín muttered something that sounded obscene. Dannerman only waited; he was as impatient as anyone, but he accepted the fact that it would go faster if they didn't argue. When all four women had had a look—each looking puzzled, even faintly disappointed, when they were finished—his turn came. As soon as the helmet was on his head and the eyepieces in place the figure of the French astronaut popped into being and began to speak. *"Messieurs et mesdames,"* it began, *"je m'appelle Colonel Hugues duValier, peut-être vous me connaissez, et je suis—"* And then the French language was drowned out by another voice, overriding the colonel with unaccented American English:

"Ladies and gentlemen, I'm Colonel Hugues duValier. Maybe you know me; I am an astronaut at present in orbit on the astronomical satellite known as Starlab. I have a message of the greatest importance for everyone on Earth—"

It was the same message as before, but reworked to remove their objections. The colonel wasn't risking any distractions to his audience by speaking in many tongues; there was a simple voice-over, the same thing viewers heard on any newscast anywhere in the world. The phrase "Beloved Leaders" was still there, but modified to: "they are called 'Beloved Leaders,' but we can know them simply as the forces which have so far—and very successfully!—born the brunt of the attack." When Delasquez and Jimmy Lin had had their turns Dannerman asked about languages, just to clear up one final point. The answers were the same as before, Ukrainian for Rosaleen, American English for Dannerman and the Pats, Spanish for Delasquez and Chinese for Jimmy. "But this time," Rosaleen said, "the Ukrainian was all Ukrainian. They corrected some of the Russian words."

Dannerman nodded thoughtfully, but said only, "Fast work. Dopey must have real good production facilities."

When he stopped there, Pat gave him a perplexed, maybe even an unfriendly, look. "Is that all you have to say about it?"

He shrugged; Jimmy Lin answered for him. "What's to say? We're just Dopey's damn test audience, aren't we? And we did our job for him. He listened to everything we criticized, and he changed the message around to suit. Now—" He turned and faced the wall, cupping his hands around his mouth. "—are you listening, Dopey? Okay, then listen to this. You got it right this time. It's fine the way it is, so don't bother us with any more revisions; just keep the food coming." He turned to Dannerman, grinning. "Does that about cover it? Because if it doesn't we could—"

He didn't get a chance to finish the sentence, because he was interrupted. Abruptly the ground began to tremble. Everyone who was standing suddenly began to reel; Jimmy grabbed Martín Delasquez's shoulder to steady himself, nearly bringing them both down. "Oh, hell," Jimmy grunted, his voice as shaky as the floor. "They're doing it again."

The odd thing, Dannerman thought, was that this time he hadn't heard any explosion, just the sudden uneasy twist and slide in the floor beneath him. But the tremor was a big one. Some cans of something or other on top of their stacks of supplies were jarred loose and clattered to the ground. Rosaleen sat down abruptly. There were yips of surprise from at least two of the Pats. Then it was over.

No. Not quite over. Just as everyone opened their mouths to tell each other that this one had been an unusually bad one, all right, something else happened. The mirror walls flickered and changed color. Jagged streaks of bright red danced around them like slow lightning flashes; that permanent diffuse pale glow from overhead darkened and their only light came from the radiant walls as they turned lurid orange in one spot, blotchy bright red in another. For a moment they seemed to go almost transparent, and through the nearest one Dannerman saw, or thought he saw, a shadowy ziggurat of bright metal. A Doc was standing there transfixed, all of its arms raised toward the sky in what looked like abject terror.

Then the colors faded. The faint visions from outside clouded and disappeared. The steady overhead glow returned, the walls became featureless mirrors again and everything was as it had been before. Everything but the prisoners, at least; but they were all shaken and bewildered. "What in the name of God was that?" Martín Delasquez angrily demanded of the room at large.

Rosaleen was the one who tried to answer. She was getting back to her feet, wincing, with one of the Pats helping her on either side. "I think it must have been some kind of a power failure," she said soberly. "I do not think that is a good sign."

At least they had a new topic of conversation to keep them busy for a while. In fact, they had two of them. One was the debate on what caused the tremor, why the power had seemed to fail and make the walls go all weird—some new questions, some just repetitions of the familiar ones about just what the hell was going on here, anyway. Whatever it was, it clearly was something that mattered to them. It made Dopey jittery and, no doubt, it threatened their own fragile security as well. But that particular discussion had nowhere to go; all anyone had to contribute was unanswerable questions and speculations, none of them very satisfactory.

The other area of discussion, Dannerman thought, was more productive. During that momentary lifting of the veil some of the captives had caught glimpses of what lay beyond the wall. None had had time for a clear view, but most had seen something. What they saw depended mostly on which way they happened to be facing. Patrice and Jimmy Lin were out of it, because they had been looking the wrong way and hadn't seen anything at all, but each of the others had at least a hazy impression to report.

It was Rosaleen Artzybachova who interrupted the hubbub with a suggestion. "Listen, please. Each of us should do his or her best to draw what we saw before we forget. Then we can compare notes."

Patsy bobbed her head at once. "Good idea," she said, reaching for Rosaleen's pen, and then paused long enough to give Dannerman a questioning look. "Is it all right for us to do it this way? Or should we be trying to keep the drawings covered?" she asked.

Before Dannerman could respond Martín answered for him. "Why do you ask Dannerman for permission?" he asked, giving Dannerman an unfriendly look. "It is obvious that there is no point in hiding such drawings. Who can doubt that Dopey knows what is outside the wall far better than we do, so what information could he gain?"

Patsy was still looking expectantly at Dannerman. He shrugged. "I guess that's true," he said, though his own reasons had little to do with what Dopey already knew, and a lot with whether all their secretive note-passing had served any useful purpose.

When they began drawing it turned out that Martín had seen the same metallic tower as Dannerman, though it was hard to recognize the thing in the man's crude, kindergarten-style drawings. Rosaleen, on the other hand, produced a workmanlike engineer's view of what looked as much like a row of file cabinets as anything else Dannerman had ever seen. ("They were tall, though," she said. "At least three meters, and there was something fuzzy that I couldn't make out on top of them.") Pat and Patsy had had the benefit of a year of art in college, and both provided neat sketches—an elongated, two-domed metal object for Pat, looking a little like a steel camel hunkered down to the ground; for Patsy a broad corridor between more rows of the file-cabinet objects, with something that might have been a vehicle a score of meters away. "It wasn't moving," she said, "but I'm pretty sure it was some kind of a car. And there was somebody, well, something, standing outside of it."

Patrice, looking on enviously, commented, "You know, it looks a little like the way Dopey brought us in here."

"I thought so too. And the person, or whatever, that was standing there—it could have been a Doc. Like the one you saw, Dan."

He nodded abstractedly, his attention on the handful of drawings. Patsy was still watching him, her expression quizzical. "Dan?" she said. "Are you all right?"

He looked up. "What? Oh, sure."

"You're not talking much."

That was the simple truth, not to be denied; but he wasn't yet prepared to say why. "I've got something on my mind," he said, truthfully enough; and then, when Patsy suggested maybe he should write it down, he could think of nothing better to say than "Not yet."

All three of the Pats were looking at him, the expressions on their faces less friendly than they had been. They thought he was being hostile, he knew, but could think of nothing useful to do about it. Rosaleen, who had been watching silently, felt the tension. She coughed. "If I can propose something we ought to do?" she suggested. "Each of you, which way were you looking when the wall went transparent? If we compare notes maybe we can make a kind of map of what's around us."

It was a sensible proposal. As they all began trying to recall just which way they had been facing, they included Dannerman in the conversation civilly enough; but that was as far as it went. And when, some time later, Pat began to yawn, she didn't look toward Dannerman. All three of the Pats curled up close together, and Dannerman did not sleep that time with any warm and pleasing head on his shoulder.

* * *

By the time he woke up Rosaleen had completed making a fair copy of the map their collective glimpses had produced. Of course it wasn't complete. In the center Rosaleen had drawn the hexagonal cell they were in, with each side numbered counting clockwise from their main point of reference, the area they had set aside as latrine. Dannerman's tall tower was at Side Two. There was nothing at One or Three except Rosaleen's small, neat question mark; Four was the cabinet things she herself had observed, next to them at Five Patsy's broad corridor and at Six Pat's angular steel camel.

He handed the chart back to Rosaleen with gratitude. "Good work," he said.

She nodded, and forbore to ask any questions. She turned away—not hostile; simply accommodating his desire to be silent—and limped back to show it again to the others. Dannerman watched her go with a frown. How long had Rosaleen been limping? And how long would it be before this very old lady began to show other signs of distress? If a chance ever came for them to escape, would she be able to take it?

And if she couldn't, would they be able to leave her here?

They were not pleasant thoughts. It was a relief to be distracted from them when the helmet began its plaintive beeping cry once more.

By the time it was Dannerman's turn all four of the women had already heard the message, and in each case their expressions ranged from shock to incredulity. Pat, who went first, ordered everyone who followed to hold all comments until they'd all seen it; they grumbled, but they obeyed.

Then Rosaleen handed it to Dannerman, her face bleak, and when he put it on the colonel appeared at once.

"Mesdames et messieurs," Colonel duValier began, and once again the voice-over took up the message in unaccented American English:

"Ladies and gentlemen, this is the most important message you will ever hear. Some of it will startle you even more than what you know already. Some of it you will find very difficult to believe. I found it so myself; but I was given proof that I could not deny, and our friends from space stand ready to give those same proofs to you.

"What it concerns is Heaven.

"That startles you at once, doesn't it? I'm sure that many of you believe in God and His Heaven, just as I do; and I'm equally sure that, like me, you consider that that sort of thing is a religious matter, not a scientific one. But what I now know is that it is both.

"What our friends from space have discovered in their scientific investigations—which are far more advanced than our own—is that at a time in the far future, a very long time from now, something very strange will happen. At that time every intelligent being who ever existed in the universe will come to life again, and then will live forever. In scientific terms that is called the 'eschaton.'

"There is also another name for it. It is what we ordinary people have been used to calling 'Heaven.' "

He paused, staring seriously at Dannerman. "Yes," he said, "you heard me correctly. We are talking about Heaven. The very Heaven that priests and religious leaders of all kinds have told us about. You see, it's real, and our new allies have discovered definite scientific proof of this fact.

"I cannot explain all this to you now. I am not qualified, and there is no time. For our eternal life in Heaven is threatened, and the people who are threatening it are the ones I told you about earlier, the Horch. I warned that they intended to conquer the Earth. I did not say that their reason for doing so—just as it has been their reason for conquering, and often for wiping out, countless other intelligent races in the past—is so that when the eschaton arrives they, and they alone, can be the dominant race, who will be able to rule everyone else . . . forever."

The colonel smiled sorrowfully, then waved a hand. A screen appeared, showing the second message from space: the expanding and contracting universe, with the scarecrow and the Seven Ugly Dwarfs. "Do you remember this picture?" he asked. "Probably you didn't understand it when you first saw it. Neither did I, but now it has been explained to me. The diagram shows the universe expanding, then contracting again as it reaches its maximum growth and then falls back. It is at that point at the end of the final contraction, when the Big Bang has been replaced by the Big Crunch, that the eschaton will occur.

"You see, the message that picture tried to convey is true—that part of it, at least. But one part of it was a lie. It was sent to you by the Horch, in order to deceive you. It is the Horch, not our friends from space, who want to dominate the eschaton. And they are ruthless enough to subjugate or destroy every living thing that stands in their way.

"That is all I have to say to you at this time, except for one thing.

It is now up to you, the people of Earth, to decide whether you want to invite our friends to come to Earth. If you do, they will display for you all the proofs I have mentioned. They will do more than that for you if you wish; they will give you freely of their immense store of knowledge.

"However, first you must, of course, have time to think all this over. Then I will speak to you again, and tell you what they propose. Until then, au revoir."

The figure went to black. Slowly Dannerman removed the helmet. "Wow," he said, and handed the helmet to Delasquez. Obviously everyone who had already seen the new message was burning to have something to say about it, but they managed to keep quiet until Jimmy Lin, at the bottom of the list, had his turn.

Then they all began to talk at once. "What a load of bullshit," Jimmy Lin said scornfully. "Heaven, for Christ's sake!" And Martín complained:

"It is blasphemous to talk of Heaven in that way!" And Patsy began:

"Yes, sure, but—listen, Dan-Dan, ever since I heard it there's something I've been trying to remember. Pat? Patrice? Didn't we have something in college about—"

But by then Dannerman knew what he had to do. "Hold it!" he ordered. "All of you! Don't say another word."

That was more than Martín Delasquez could stand. He said angrily, "Who are you to be giving us orders, Dannerman? I have had enough of being bossed around by you!"

But Rosaleen put her hand placatingly on his arm. He was fuming, but he listened to her. "Please, Martín," she said. "I'm sure Dan has a reason for this. Let's listen to what he has to say."

Martín looked darkly suspicious, Jimmy Lin looked only hostile, but both of them kept quiet. So did the Pats, waiting while Dannerman thought out what to do.

After a moment he nodded, satisfied. "Here's the point," he said. "Evidently Dopey wants information again. He must think we have some, or he wouldn't go to this trouble, and I guess we do. But let's not give it away."

He raised a hand to prevent questions, then turned and faced the mirror wall, just as Jimmy Lin had done earlier. "Dopey," he called. "You hear us. None of us is going to say or write another word about that message until you agree to our terms. If you want us to tell you everything we know or think—I mean tell you out loud; no more secrets; we'll talk it over in your presence, and you can ask as many questions as you like—if that's what you want, then come here and let's talk. But it's going to cost you, because this time we aren't going to do it for nothing!"

24
Patsy

The Dr. Patrice Adcock they were calling "Patsy" (she was willing to answer to that name, because she didn't have any choice about it, but she never *ever* thought of herself that way) was angry. She sat Buddha-like, her legs tucked into the lotus position, glowering at the world. She knew she shouldn't be angry. She conceded to herself that Dan-Dan had some reason for ordering them to be quiet, and she supposed those orders might make sense. Why should you give away what you might be able to sell? All the same, she wasn't used to being told what she could or could not talk about.

What she was bursting to talk about was that whole "eschaton" business. It was right on the tip of her tongue, if only she could compare notes with Pat and Patrice to goose her memory along. That ancient and ill-recalled episode had been a very minor item in her education, no more than a grace note in some course she had taken for easy credits. She could almost see the face of the professor who had talked about it. It was the young dark one with the bedroom eyes—what was his name?—and he hadn't called it the eschaton. Something like—oh, yes. The "Omega Point." Whatever that was supposed to be. But she was pretty sure that it was precisely the thing that Colonel duValier had been blathering about in the message on the helmet.

Farther than that, however, her unaided memory would not take her.

It was perfectly obvious to her that everybody else was dying to talk it out, too. Well, of course they were. Was it even remotely possible that this notion of eternal life ten-to-the-zillionth years in the future could be *real*? Or that some hideous creatures from outer space might be doing their best to turn that eternal heaven into some kind of perpetual hell?

The whole thing was ridiculous.

The other thing about it was that it was also, just possibly, quite true.

In any case, she couldn't help thinking about it, and neither could any of the other six captives. It put a damper on all other subjects for conversation. The seven of them did their chores, completing Rosaleen's inventory, cooking and eating their meals, using the "latrine" when there was no way to avoid it; but what they were thinking about was this eschaton thing. If only Dopey would show up! Then maybe Dan could work out some kind of deal with him and then they could all talk freely, and maybe scratch that burning itch to hash the subject out.

But Dopey didn't show; and time wore on.

As she was beginning to get sleepy she said something about Dopey's absence to Pat, who had nothing useful to say in return. "How would I know why he doesn't come? Maybe that power glitch is screwing things up for him."

"Well, sure, but there must be something else going on. It couldn't be just the glitch; he got that new duValier message out to us after that happened, didn't he?"

"Beats the hell out of me," Pat said irritably. "Anyway, maybe we're not supposed to talk about that, either."

Pat wasn't the only one who was short-tempered. Everybody was getting antsy under the burden of Dan's rule of custody of the mouth. Then, when they were all getting sleepy, Pat didn't join Patrice and herself. Instead she nestled up next to Dannerman again, just as before; evidently his silence was now understood and thus forgiven. And as Patrice was settling herself down she glanced at the two of them, and then whispered to Patsy, "What's *she* got to be pissed off about?"

It was a fair enough question. Pat had Dan-Dan, and what did the other two of them have?

There was certainly some jealousy there. There was also quite a lot of sisterly (or sort-of-sisterly) loyalty. To be fair about it, Patsy thought justly as she drifted off to sleep, you couldn't really say that Pat actually *had* Dan-Dan. Not in the total lack of personal seclusion that was their present condition. Patsy wondered drowsily if they could talk Dopey into giving them a few more of the helmets, because if everybody but Pat and Dan were wearing a helmet there would be at least the illusion of privacy while they got each other, as they were obviously yearning to do. Or maybe she and Patrice could patch together some of the blankets from Starlab and make a kind of a screen to hide the lovers as they went to it. Or—

Or maybe somehow, miraculously, the U.S. cavalry would come charging over the hill with bugles blowing and pennons flying, and wonderfully carry them back home; and then the two of them could do whatever they damn pleased . . . and so could she, with whoever was handy . . . and . . .

And then the world would be fine again, but none of that was actually going to happen. The cavalry wasn't really coming to rescue them, was it? Their future was very uncertain but definitely dark—if the seven of them turned out to have any real future at all—and when Patsy finally did succeed in falling asleep there were tears on her cheeks.

They slept, and they woke up, and they spent most of another long day of trying to keep from talking about the things that really *had* to be talked about. And when finally Dopey did appear, without warning, simply walking in through the mirror, he said only, "I was delayed."

"We understand that you were having problems," Rosaleen said courteously. "You needn't apologize."

He looked flustered, Patsy thought; his peacock tail was rippling in dark colors and the expression on his furry little face was troubled. But he said firmly, "I did not apologize. I simply stated an explanation. I am now prepared to transact business with you on the basis you proposed."

Everyone was listening intently, and Patsy thought they all looked delighted—well, so did she. But Dannerman was making sure of the terms. "No holds barred?"

Dopey looked faintly puzzled. "I assume that what you mean is without reservation. I agree to that. However, I must tell you that there are things I cannot do, because at present they are physically impossible to me. The Horch terrorists have caused serious interruptions in our communications with the Beloved Leaders, and even certain of the resources of this base are temporarily not available to me. But please, you must help me to evaluate the message for Earth."

It was what Patsy had been waiting for; she opened her mouth eagerly, but Dannerman raised a hand. "Wait one," he said. "If your communications are down, what's the point?"

"They will be restored," Dopey said doggedly. "Please. Do not argue. Remember that you are not indispensable."

"Sure we are," Jimmy Lin said, his face angry. "You need our input."

"But not necessarily from your particular specimens, Commander Lin. Do you not realize that it would be possible to produce new copies of all of you, copies who would remember nothing after being taken from Starlab, and extract the information from them?"

"What I realize," Dannerman said firmly, "is that if that were what you wanted to do you wouldn't be talking, you'd be doing it."

Dopey looked irresolute. "It is true that there are at present some difficulties in this respect," he admitted. "Very well. I agree. Now tell me—"

"No, no! You first!"

The creature didn't like that. The lips on the little kitten face were drawn back—almost, Patsy thought, as though he were going to hiss at them. Then he relaxed. "I will agree," he capitulated. "What do you want from me?"

"Information!"

The little paws drummed impatiently on the muff—not inside it, Patsy observed, and realized that in this interview, unlike any other, Dopey was not keeping his hands in the muff. Was there something wrong with the thing? "Be more—" Dopey stopped as there was another ground tremor. A mild one, this time, Patsy observed gratefully, but was surprised to see the way Dopey reacted: his tail went all dark, his eyes were fastened on the wall, there was something like fear on the little feline face.

But nothing happened to the wall. Dopey's fan slowly began to regain its color. "Be more specific," he ordered. "And hurry."

"All right," Dannerman said. "What's wrong with the wall?"

Dopey paused to think. "The terrorists have done some damage to our systems," he said at length.

"The whole truth!" Pat snapped. "You promised!"

"But that is the whole truth," Dopey said, seeming surprised. "Do you wish to know details? Very well. Approximately, ah, nineteen of your days ago the Horch succeeded in transporting some of their weaponry into our base; since then there has been fighting. Each time their attack has been defeated, and each time they succeeded in transmitting new forces and attacked again. Much damage has been done, and communication with the Leaders has been interrupted."

"Who's winning?"

More hesitation. "I do not know," Dopey confessed. "I have no doubt that in the long run our Beloved Leaders will prevail, but as your sage John Maynard Keynes once said to your president Franklin Delano Roosevelt—it was on a documentary broadcast while I was still on your Starlab—the trouble with the long run is that in the long run we are all dead."

"I'm glad to see you've kept your sense of humor," Dannerman said caustically. "I'm only surprised to discover that you have one. More details!"

"But I do not know any more details," Dopey said in surprise. "I know nothing of weaponry. Many of our people are dead now and much has been destroyed; that is all I can tell you. In any case, now it is your turn. Are there errors in the second broadcast?"

Dannerman looked rebellious, but gave in. "Not as far as I know. Nothing significant. Did any of the rest of you notice anything?"

No one had. "That is good," Dopey said gravely. "Now, about your comments on the eschaton—"

If Patsy had been prudent—if all the Pats had—they might have held out for more information from Dopey. They weren't. Pat and Patrice were as eager to talk as Patsy, and it was Pat who got in first. "We heard about it in a history-of-science class in graduate school. The professor—"

"Dr. Mukarjee," Patrice supplied eagerly.

"Yes, that's the one. He told us about some scientist a long time ago, just before the turn of the century, I think it was, who claimed the same thing. Only he didn't call it the eschaton—"

Patsy raised her hand, excited and impatient. "The Omega Point! That's what he called it."

Pat gave her a grateful look. "How smart of you to remember that! Anyway, it was the same thing—universe expands, universe contracts, Big Crunch, everybody reborn in heaven."

Then they stopped, having run out of recollections. "His name," Dopey insisted. "Who was this scientist?"

The Pats looked at each other. "Tinker?" Patrice hazarded.

Pat frowned thoughtfully. "I was going to say maybe Doppler. Something like that." Patsy just shook her head.

"That is not satisfactory," Dopey complained. "Now I must try to have a data search conducted through that primitive equipment on Starlab. Have you nothing else to add?"

They looked at each other again. "Nothing," Pat said, and Patrice said:

"Only something Dr. Mukarjee said. He said that was just another example of the ways most cosmologists went kind of loopy after a while."

"That is not a useful datum," Dopey declared, but Dannerman cut in.

"Sure it is. Now you know he was a cosmologist; that ought to help identify him. Anyway, that's all we've got, so now let's talk about—"

But what it was Dannerman wanted to talk about he didn't get a chance to say. The ground shook, the wall flared again, the sound of distant thunder drowned out his words.

This time the display lasted for many seconds. No one spoke, though Dopey was whimpering softly. Patsy, eager to take advantage of any new visions that might come through the wall if it happened to go transparent again, faced it unblinking through all its swirling changes of color. It didn't. It cycled rapidly through the entire spectrum, then resumed its milky mirror sheen. She turned just in time to see Dopey's plume vanishing through the mirror as the creature sped away.

"Oh, damn the thing," Pat said feelingly. Rosaleen was more tolerant.

"He's frightened," she observed. "I don't blame him. If we knew everything he knows we might be terrified, too."

"I'm already terrified as much as I can handle, Rosie," Pat said. "Well. What do we know that we didn't know before?"

The answer to that, Patsy thought, was "damn little." She listened as the others tried to piece meaning together from what Dopey had told them, but there wasn't a lot of meaning there. All right, things were even worse than they had expected; but what kind of news was that?

She scowled at her own reflection in the mirror wall, half listening to what the others were saying, mostly filling with resentment. For just a moment there she had been reminded that she had another life, a life in which she was not a helpless pawn stranded in a demeaning captivity, but a responsible human being who held an important job. She was, for God's sake, a highly trained *scientist.* It was time for her to act like one, she told herself. It was time to stop being so damn *passive* and start to take *action. . . .*

The problem was, she could not think of any productive action to take.

She looked at the others. Dannerman, at least, seemed to be actually doing something, even if only going over everybody's recollections, repetitively, demandingly. Maybe, she thought, that was the way he had learned to interrogate witnesses in spook school. Was there any point in it? Did it matter how much they learned, when there was nothing they could do about it, anyway?

A snarling, buzzing sound interrupted her. It interrupted everyone else, too. It was not a sound any of them had heard before, and so it took them a moment to realize that it came from the helmet.

"What the hell," Dannerman said.

"I think it wants to be picked up again," Patrice said.

Jimmy Lin said nervously, "You sure? It sounds like it's broken to me. Could be dangerous."

"Oh, for God's sake," Pat said in exasperation, snatched the thing from the floor and pulled it on over her head. . . .

And then a moment later, she gasped, "Hey! It's a damn *Horch* and it's trying to tell me something!"

25
Patsy

Whatever it was that Pat was seeing, it was brief. Hardly more than a minute or two; and when she pulled the helmet off her head, her expression both astonished and bewildered, and handed it to Patrice, it was without a word. Not without a struggle, though. Martín was already grabbing for it, but Pat pushed him away. As was right and proper, Patsy told herself, even in that moment; at least now they were doing alphabetical order again. And was quick to take the helmet when Patrice, as startled and uncertain as Pat herself, handed it to her.

The most astonishing thing Pat had said was true. It was a Horch that faced her in the simulation space. It was not at all the same Horch that Colonel duValier had displayed, either. This one carried no vicious-looking weapons, wore no armor, seemed much less evil. But it was certainly a Horch, all the same; and how such a thing could manage to use the device of the Beloved Leaders she could not guess.

Nor had time to.

The Horch didn't speak. It gestured—with both its boneless arms and with its sinuous, long neck as well—toward a corner of the field of view, and immediately a picture appeared there. Patsy was looking at a street scene in what, she knew, had to be a city, though not any kind of city she had ever seen before. The street itself was not a mere strip of hard surface. It was a moving ribbon of what looked like liquid metal, on which what looked like great, multicolored dragonflies danced, and now and then launched themselves into the air to fly into doorways set into tall buildings, high in the air. The buildings were alabaster and goldenrod and fleshy pink, some of them (it seemed to Patsy) a dozen stories tall. All this was what she saw in the first eyeblink, and she had no time to study details. Almost at once the view pulled back, as though the camera were rising to the sky. *Through* the sky; accelerating, it flew higher and higher until it was out of the planet's atmosphere entirely, looking down on the whole planet, pale blue and tainted white, as from orbit.

Then a spacecraft came into view, coppery-red and glittering, and the point of view approached it, entered it as though the ship's hull were only mist, showed the inside. A Beloved Leader swam languidly in zero-gravity there, the very scarecrow of the original message from space. It waved a fragile arm at its viewscreen, and something—*something,* something huge and dark and craggy—came plunging from nowhere at the planet. It blazed an eye-searing meteor trail through the atmosphere, and when it struck the surface it exploded with the power of a billion nuclear bombs.

And that planet died before Patsy's eyes.

No time to think about that now, either; immediately she was looking at another street scene (different street, dense with fast-moving vehicles; different buildings; different beings, these looking like wraiths with heads like sunflowers), but the story was the same. Pull back into space, see a Beloved Leader negligently take aim on the world, observe that world destroyed. And instantly there was another. And another, and another—the pace speeding up, the planets all different, the end always the same. And then—

And then the velocity slowed. A world appeared in the field of view that she recognized at once. It was the world Patsy had always known: their own Earth, northern hemisphere. Down toward the fringes that approached the equator she could see the hook of Italy, the wedge of India with Sri Lanka hanging like a teardrop from its tip, the narrow Red Sea. And when the view went inside the object in orbit this time it was not an alien spacecraft. It was an orbiter she recognized: their own Starlab! And there was no giant asteroid plunging toward the planet—not yet—but what was happening inside was even more frightening. There was no Beloved Leader present. What there was was Dopey, clinging to a wall while a pair of Docs worked over a human figure spread-eagled against a bulkhead. The Docs were doing something to the back of the man's head. Then they drew back. The human figure turned itself—it was Martín!—and silently pulled itself to a lineup, joining Dannerman, Jimmy Lin, Rosaleen and Patsy herself. The Docs herded the humans, who moved like zombies, into the Clipper, and it dropped away en route to the planet.

That was it. The picture went black.

* * *

They had all seen the same thing. They had all had the same reaction. "So the Horch want us to believe that the Beloved Leaders are mass murderers," Dannerman said meditatively. "Which, of course, is what the Beloved Leaders want us to believe about the Horch."

"So where does that leave us?" Jimmy Lin demanded. No one answered, but of course the answer was obvious, Patsy thought. They were left right where they had been all along: in their cell.

"But, if the Horch are telling the truth, Dopey also sent copies of us back to Earth," Rosaleen said. "Why would he do that, do you suppose?"

"We will damn well ask him that," Martín said, his face grim.

"If we see him again," Dannerman said.

That alarmed Patsy. "Why? Do you think he's going to abandon us?"

"I think he may not have much to say about it," Dannerman told her. "If things are as bad as he says— *Now* what does the thing want?" he added, as the helmet snarled at them again.

Martín was the nearest; he picked it up. "There's only one way to find out," he said.

Pat was outraged. "You're doing it again! It's my turn first!"

Martín looked at her contemptuously and, without replying, jammed the helmet down on his own head.

"Damn the man," Pat snapped in Patsy's general direction. Patsy didn't answer. All these things that were happening were coming a lot too fast for her comfort—yes, and a hell of a lot too weird, too. She couldn't sort them out. Beloved Leaders killing planets: all right, she was perfectly willing to believe that that was what the Beloved Leaders did. It wasn't good news, but at least it was comprehensible; they were being warned. But what was the meaning of sending copies of themselves to Earth! That was *scary.*

Then everybody fell silent as Martín Delasquez slowly lifted the helmet off his head. He stared at them blankly until Jimmy Lin snapped, "Well?"

"Yes," Delasquez said, organizing his thoughts. Then he took a deep breath and delivered his report. "What I was seeing—it was, I think, the VIP dining area at Kourou."

"Kourou? in South America?"

"The European launch center," Delasquez confirmed. "That's what it looked like, anyway—I did a six-month exchange mission there once. But what is astonishing—I was seeing it out of my own eyes."

Rosaleen was the first to react. "Your *own* eyes? But how do you know it was you?"

"It was. I saw my Academy ring on my hand—and I know my own hand. And there were all kinds of European Space Agency people there too—at other tables—I think I even saw Colonel duValier—but I wasn't with them. I was at a table by myself, except for one other man. He was in uniform, and he carried a sidearm, and he wasn't eating. Didn't even have a plate in front of him. He was just watching me. It was—" He hesitated, trying to think of the right word. "It was—It was very *unpleasant.*"

"Let me have that," snarled Jimmy Lin, reaching for the helmet. Pat was ahead of him. She snatched the thing from Martín's slack grip.

"My turn!" she snapped, and put it on.

Martín was paying no attention. "I could taste the food," he said wonderingly. "I was eating an omelette, one of the kind with vegetables in it? And there was the shell of a papaya on the table—I could still taste it—and a brioche. Quite good coffee, too. And hot; it almost burned my tongue."

Rosaleen was listening intently. "You could taste and feel? So it wasn't just a television picture?"

"It was just as though I were there," Martín insisted. But by then Patsy wasn't listening anymore, because Pat had claimed her attention. She was making sounds of distress, and Patrice was standing anxiously beside her, begging to know what was wrong.

Then Pat moaned, gasped and pulled the helmet off as though it burned her. "It was all woogly!" she cried, suddenly white-faced and shaking. Patrice put her arm around her; if Patrice hadn't, Patsy would have, because she had never seen Pat look so shaken. "I guess I was on Earth, all right—partly, anyway. But I was in jail!"

And of course there were about a million questions about that, but Patsy didn't wait to hear the answers, didn't even wait to find out what Pat meant by being "partly" on Earth. She went right to the source. Snatched the helmet out of Pat's hand, pulled it over her head, snapped the goggles into place—

It was a good thing that Pat's complaints had prepared her, at least a little bit. Even so, the shock was almost paralyzing as she found out what Pat had meant by "woogly."

She wasn't seeing one scene. She was seeing two of them—no, not merely seeing; she was *present* in two different places. Feeling, seeing, hearing, smelling; all the senses were involved. And everything was doubled. In one scene she was seeing herself with the helmet over her head, saw Pat—right up close, as though she were holding her in her arms; no, she *was* holding Pat in her arms, because she could feel Pat's body shaking. And at the same time, in the other scene, she was looking at a bare room with bright lights, a small table with nothing on it, a straight-backed plastic chair, dun-painted walls without any pictures or ornamentation of any kind. She saw all this second scene from a recumbent position, because she was lying on a hard, narrow cot, curled up on her side with her open hand under her cheek, but wide awake. She was staring into space. And she could see the door to the room, all right, and, yes, Pat had been perfectly right.

There were steel bars on the door. She was definitely in some kind of a jail.

When Patrice took her turn—no argument about who was next this time, not even from Jimmy Lin; everyone wanted to know what the "woogliness" was all about—she reported seeing the same thing. Two separate scenes. Both wholly real, in every sensory way. The only difference was that in the scene that corresponded to their cell, she saw Patsy there instead of herself.

"Dopey said they were monitoring our copies," Rosaleen said meditatively.

"But like this? Seeing with our eyes?" Pat was still shaken. "It gave me a damn *migraine!* Only—" She hesitated, remembering. "Only what I saw was three different scenes, not two. Two of them were here, from different angles; it was the other one that looked like a jail."

"Damn well *was* a jail," Patrice said feelingly.

Rosaleen sighed. "Yes," she said, following out some private thought process of her own. "It must be so."

"*What* must be so?" Patsy demanded, and Rosaleen looked at her with compassion.

"It explains much," she said. "These copies of us that the Horch showed us, the ones the Beloved Leaders made and returned to Earth? They were fitted with some sort of transmitters to pass on everything they saw and felt—"

"How?" Jimmy Lin asked.

"Oh, Jimmy, what foolish questions you ask. How do I know how? With a magical incantation, perhaps, or perhaps they implanted a tiny broadcasting station in the left nostril—who knows what kind of technology is here?"

"Damn," Dannerman said feelingly. "I see what you mean, Rosaleen. That's how Dopey knew the name of my boss, Colonel Morrisey."

"Yes. And much more," Rosaleen said. She turned back to Patsy and Patrice. "And when, in kindness, Dopey provided us with you two, he first turned you into observing devices—"

"Hey!" both of them said at once.

"Yes. And so now, at least, we know just how Dopey was able to read all our little secret messages that we passed around with such care. You two read them for him. Whatever you saw he saw too."

In these last two days Patsy's life had been violated in more ways than she could count—the violation of the nudity taboo when she was first brought in, the endless privacy violations that came with everyone being huddled together in the one common pen for everything—for sleeping, for eating, even for going to the damn *toilet.*

But this latest violation was something new. Until now she had had the illusion that at least her private central self was intact. Now that illusion was destroyed. Some weird creature somewhere—not just Dopey; who knew what other bizarre beasts were eavesdropping as well?—some*body* was seeing and feeling everything she did.

And beyond doubt was still doing it. It was, she told herself, an intolerable situation . . . except, of course, that she had no choice but to go right on tolerating it.

26
Patsy

If the others had taken the news as hard as Patsy, they didn't show it. They were all clustered around whoever was wearing the helmet at that moment, every one of them demanding another turn. It was like Christmas at Uncle Cubby's, with every child demanding the one best toy at once. Even Dannerman and Rosaleen, though Dannerman had reported resentfully that his turn had been a washout, since as far as he could tell he was simply in bed asleep. (Which, Patsy thought, supported her own feeling that it was the middle of the night—assuming they were in the same time zone.) And Rosaleen had seen nothing at all, didn't even share Dannerman's conviction that the reason was that she had been asleep.

But then there was Jimmy Lin.

His turn lasted longer than any of the others were willing to tolerate. He clung to the helmet, trying to wave them off with his arms; and when at last he took it off he was beaming. "You guys had me worried," he said. "You know, armed guards, and jail cells, and all that? But I was just fine. I'm pretty sure I was in Jiuquan—the Chinese space center? And I was in my old Fiat electric? Driving somewhere from the base? I know that road; it hadn't changed much since the last time I was there. I could see the launchpads way off by the hills—oh, there's no doubt about it; that's where I was. And I was in uniform; I could see the sleeve of my tunic. It looks like I got a promotion, too, because I was wearing full commander's stripes."

"I thought you got kicked out of the astronaut corps," Dannerman objected.

Jimmy scowled at him. "Well, I did. But I know what I saw, so I guess they reinstated me. Anyway, I wasn't alone in the car, and I don't know for sure where the two of us were going, but I think we were planning on having a pretty good time. Oh, and the language we were talking in was *Chinese*."

"What were you talking about?" Dannerman demanded.

Jimmy gave him the ghost of a smile. "What do you think we were talking about? It was a *date,* man!"

"Old reliable Lin," Martín groaned. "Always right there with his gonads blazing."

"Don't be so envious," Jimmy said, enjoying himself. "Let's see, what else? It was maybe late afternoon, I think. Probably we were just coming from a shift at the base. I was kind of hungry, but I was also—well, Martín, yeah, I have to admit that I was feeling kind of horny, too."

Rosaleen had been listening intently, but now she frowned. "What I don't understand," she said, "is—assuming it's true that they've planted bugs in our copies—how come we're receiving anything from them? Dopey said they'd lost their communications."

"Maybe only with the Beloved Leaders at their headquarters, wherever that is?" Patrice put in.

Dannerman nodded. "That could be it. Remember, Dopey also said something about using the Starlab equipment to track down the Omega Point man? He may not have contact with his Beloved Leaders, but apparently he still does with Starlab."

Rosaleen considered that. "It sounds plausible," she said, and hesitated. Then she reached for the helmet. "I think I would like to try another turn for myself."

That made everyone quiet down. Jimmy handed her the helmet without a word. Rosaleen carefully settled it around her head and fumbled with the opaque goggles until they locked in position.

She was silent for a moment, while everyone waited. Then she removed the helmet again. "Yes," she said in a colorless, conversational tone, "there is nothing there but blackness for me." She handed the helmet to the person standing beside her, who happened to be Martín, and added, "I can think of only one explanation. There is no copy of me on Earth."

"But we saw you being sent there in the Horch message!" Pat said worriedly.

Rosaleen did not respond to that, except to say, "I think I would like to rest for a while."

Then a most surprising thing happened. Martín took the helmet from Rosaleen's hand, but he didn't put it back on. He laid it on the floor and, instead, took Rosaleen Artzybachova's arm and helped her over to a position by one wall. He settled blankets around her until he was sure she was comfortable.

Patsy stared. Could this be *Martín*? For a moment she almost toyed with the thought that when they weren't looking Dopey had somehow slipped a doppelgänger general in among them in Delasquez's place. Well, that was fantasy, sure; but to find General Delasquez caring for somebody else was almost as fantastic.

By the time he came back the others were gathered around the cooker—all but Jimmy Lin, who had seized the chance to get back in the helmet. Martín didn't speak. He stood over the pile of rations, staring down at it, but making no move to take anything for himself.

Impulsively, Patsy spoke to him, keeping her voice low so that the others might not hear. "That was nice of you, Martín."

For a moment she thought he wasn't going to answer. He reached down and selected a ration packet at random. Then he said, "My mother was like that. Quite old, but active, alert, in fact a very brilliant woman . . . until her sister died."

"Her sister died?" Patsy repeated. The man was being even more difficult than usual.

He studied the packet for a moment, then slit it open with a thumbnail. "They were quite close," he said. "Then afterward it was quite different for my mother. Her condition deteriorated very fast."

He looked up at Patsy for the first time. "I see you don't understand," he commented.

"No. You're right. I don't."

"But this must be very similar for Rosaleen. You see, there is no copy of Rosaleen on Earth, although we saw her being sent there. How can that be? Because, of course, the Rosaleen who returned to Earth has died."

Died.

Patsy stole a look at Rosaleen, lying with her eyes closed and only a part of her face visible among the blankets. What could that feel like, losing one of yourself? Patsy tried to imagine how she would feel if Pat died, or Patrice, but she didn't try for long. The thought hurt, with kinds of pain Patsy had never felt before.

Something else was troubling her, too. It felt like guilt. Rosaleen's exposed face was gray. Although she had stood as erect as ever while they were talking, Patsy remembered that Rosaleen had been biting her lip, and when she turned away she had limped worse than ever.

That was where the guilt lived. It was her fault, after all—that is, it was Dr. Patrice Adcock's fault—that the old woman was here in this place, a place that certainly was not a good environment for an ailing woman in her—what were they?—at least her nineties. Maybe more. Rosaleen had been comfortably retired to the leisure of her Ukrainian dacha, as at her age she had every right to be, until Pat called her in for this mad venture, with its even madder consequences. If she died as a result of all this—

Patsy finished her meal and lay down to sleep, hoping to blot out some of the things that were on her mind. She did not want to think of Rosaleen's dying, and she was glad when at last she seemed to be drifting off to sleep.

The sleep didn't last long; what woke her was another groundshake—not big, but enough to rouse her. She opened her eyes in time to see the wall doing its magic trick. The bright mirror was streaked with glowing pink and red, the colors shimmering over the surface like oil on a pool of water. The display lasted for a dozen seconds; then the swirls of color disappeared. It didn't turn transparent this time, and a moment later the wall was a bright and unflawed mirror again, and nothing had changed.

The others were all awake, Martín and Rosaleen standing by the cooker; Patsy covertly studied Rosaleen's face, but it showed nothing but fatigue. Jimmy Lin was holding the helmet in his hand, his expression thunderous. "What a time to lose contact!" he cried; and, as soon as things had settled down again, hastily jammed the thing back on his head.

Patrice gave him an unfriendly look, then turned to Patsy. "I think the son of a bitch is getting laid in China," she muttered. "Did you get enough sleep? I took another turn while you were out and I was—we were—still in that jail, and nothing was happening. Except that I was dressed and sitting in the chair. Just sitting there, with, I guess, nothing to do. Martín did a little better, though."

"I will tell her," Martín said. He fished a ration packet out of the cooker, juggled it a moment in his hands before passing it on to Rosaleen and made sure that the old lady was able to handle it before he told Patsy what he had observed. He had been standing at a lectern at the front of a briefing room, while some other astronaut at another lectern was going over a 3-D virtual of the interior of Starlab. "It didn't look the way we saw it when we were there. It was, I imagine, the way it had been before Dopey's people rearranged it. And every once in a while someone would ask me if that was how I remembered it, and I said yes." He hesitated. "That isn't the truth, of course. I must have been lying to them. But I didn't *feel* like I was lying. And that guard with the gun was sitting right behind me."

That was interesting, but Patsy had nearer concerns. She drew some water from the tank and rubbed it over her face, then used the space they had set aside as the latrine, leaving the others to argue with Martín as to how he could tell whether or not his copy was lying. She didn't listen. She was thinking about Rosaleen—and thinking, too, at the same time, that splashing a few drops of water on her face was all well enough, but, God, what she would give for a real *bath.* Not to mention some clean clothes. Not to mention—well, everything that made civilization worth having.

By the time she was as presentable as she had any way of getting Jimmy Lin was out of the helmet and his face wore a broad grin. "That," he announced, "was *great.* Listen, I'm not one to kiss and tell, but—"

"Do not tell, then," Martín said savagely.

"Yes, but honestly—"

"Shut up," Pat ordered.

"Ah," said Jimmy, understanding at last. "I'd just be rubbing salt in the wounds, eh? Well, I can see how you feel, but I have to say—no," he corrected himself, catching Pat's glare at him. "I guess I don't have to say. But you know what I'm thinking."

And he turned and headed for the cooker. Over his shoulder he called, "The dinner was great, too. Gave me an appetite."

"Son of a bitch," Patrice said moodily, and changed the subject. "Patsy? Did you hear about Dan-Dan?"

"What about Dan-Dan?"—looking at him.

Dannerman said reluctantly, "I guess it's important enough to tell. All right. About half an hour ago I took a turn in the helmet. I was awake, all right. I was getting dressed. And I had a hell of a hangover."

"What were you celebrating, do you know?" Patsy asked curiously.

"I don't think I was celebrating anything at all. I think my duplicate is in the deep shit. I was wearing a collar, you see."

"Collar?"

"The tracker kind," he said impatiently. "The kind they put on you so they always know where you are. So they can hear everything you say, and everything anybody says to you."

"Oh, hell," Patsy said, suddenly sympathetic. She wanted to put her arm around him, checked the impulse with Pat standing right there. "So you're in trouble, too?"

"House arrest, I guess. Pretty much the same as Martín and you."

Pat turned to Patsy. "Any ideas? Can you figure out why we're all in trouble back home—all but Jimmy, anyway?"

"Maybe," Dannerman offered, "it has something to do with what Martín is saying about lying to them."

"But why would we all be lying?" Patrice asked reasonably. "I mean, all but Jimmy, I guess. What reason could we have?"

Dannerman shrugged. No one said anything for a while, and Patsy looked around the cell. Martín and Rosaleen were talking quietly over by the cooker. Jimmy Lin was sitting with his back to the wall, hands locked behind his head, a broad, reminiscent grin on his face.

Pat was looking at him, too. "Bastard," she said. "But, hey, think about it. Suppose we could get this little piece of technology back to Earth! Suppose we put these bugs into, I don't know, maybe a couple of vid stars, boy and girl—or boy and boy, or whatever; listen, any kind of preference anybody had. And then we could rent out helmets while they were getting it on. Can you imagine what kind of money people would pay? Mad sex, any kind of sex, without all that trouble of actually having to find Mr. Right and then getting a motel room and all . . . and no worry about catching something or getting pregnant or— Well," she said hastily, aware of Dannerman's eyes on her, "I mean, simply as a commercial venture."

"I know what you mean," he said kindly. Then he added, "I was thinking of something, too. I was thinking, what if the Bureau had this technology? Then they wouldn't have to get people like me to infiltrate terrorist groups or criminal gangs or whatever. Just catch one of the gang, stick a bug into him, set him loose. From that moment on everything he saw or did would go right to the Bureau."

"Oh, Dan!" Patrice said in dismay. "Do you know what you're saying? It wouldn't have to be just criminals! What if some government used that to keep track of everybody, all the time? Talk about your police states!"

And Pat said meditatively, "Maybe that isn't a kind of technology we would want to bring back, after all."

Silence for a moment, and then Dan said, "I wonder if we have a choice. I wonder if that might not be some of this wonderful stuff that the Beloved Leaders are going to give the human race if they're let in."

Then there was more silence, a lot of it, as everybody thought about that. Until Patsy sighed and shook herself. "Maybe I should take another turn in the helmet," she said, and accepted the device as Dannerman handed it to her.

As soon as she was locked in the pictures flashed before her, just as before—the same doubled images: herself in the helmet as seen through Patrice's eyes, and at the same time the bare cell on Earth. There, she discovered, she seemed to be eating breakfast. Some machine-scrambled eggs, far overcooked for her taste, some dry toast, a cup of weak coffee. She didn't much like the taste of the food. Even less liked the dizzying duplication of images, which threatened to give her a headache. She closed her eyes to shut them out for a moment, and discovered that made no difference; she could feel that her eyelids were clamped shut, but she was still seeing both scenes.

Maybe, she thought, there was a way to ease that particular problem, at least. If Patrice were simply to keep her eyes closed and sit as still as possible while she herself was in the helmet, wouldn't that cut down on the "spillover"? It might be worth a try, she thought. And was on the point of taking the helmet off to tell her so, when the floor shook again under her feet. She staggered. The helmet images blurred and distorted, but through Patrice's eyes she could see that the wall was flaring again.

By the time she got the helmet off it was a kaleidoscope of color and the ground was still shaking, slow, remorseless swings back and forth. Patsy sat down abruptly to keep from falling—as everyone else was doing—and they watched the light show on the wall in fascination and fear. It flickered through the spectrum, settling on a dull red that felt as though it were actually radiating heat. . . .

Then—it disappeared.

There was no color at all where the wall had been. The smooth, resilient floor had turned into a pattern of closely woven metal strands. The ceiling, too, had changed; the even white glow was gone. Where it had been there was now a mesh that looked like bleached burlap, through which a pale light filtered from somewhere else. The same light illuminated the scene beyond the walls: Rosaleen's "file cabinets," the broad corridor along which Dopey had brought them to the cell, the two-domed metal object and all sorts of other things, too many and too strange to take in at once. Nothing obstructed her view.

Everybody was up and staring now. And Jimmy Lin, standing at the urinal, reached out with one hand to where the wall had been. He pulled his arm back slowly and turned, blinking, to the others. "There's nothing there," he said. "There isn't any wall at all anymore."

27
Patsy

There was a story Patsy remembered about a lion in a zoo. For ten years that lion had paced restlessly back and forth in his cage, snarling at the bars. Then, one day, the keeper was careless. He went away and left the door open. When the keeper was gone, the lion padded over to the door, and sniffed at the air of freedom for a moment . . . and then turned and lay down in the farthest corner of his cage, his head on his paws, his eyes squeezed shut, until at last the keeper came back and closed the door.

That's you, Dr. Pat-known-as-Patsy Adcock, she told herself. You've been pissing and moaning about wanting to get out of here ever since you arrived. Now you've got your big chance. There's nothing to stop you walking out of here whenever you like. Well?

But she hesitated.

So did everyone else, all of them staring apprehensively at the vista around them, strange machines and distant gleams of light and, from somewhere, a pall of smoke drifting over them. No one moved . . . until Jimmy Lin, glancing wildly back at the rest of them, took a deep breath, then carefully stepped over the little puddle of his own recent urine and walked through the space where the wall had been. Not far. Just a step or two, actually, before he stopped to stare around. But he was definitely *outside.*

That did it for Patsy Adcock. If Jimmy Lin could do it she certainly could. She turned and marched resolutely out into the space she had never seen before. Behind her Pat called worriedly, "Hey, watch it, hon! What're you going to do if the power comes back on and you're stuck out there?"

That stopped Patsy, frozen on one foot, until she remembered.

"No, it isn't like that," she called back. What she remembered was how it had been when Dopey brought them to the cell. It was a one-way wall. They hadn't even seen the thing as they approached from outside, had simply walked into the space where the others were clustered, and had then been astonished to see the wall of mirrors bright and impenetrable behind them.

Everyone was staring after her. She saw Rosaleen, her face still gray, crossing herself, and Martín standing with his mouth open, and Dannerman experimentally poking his own arm through the space where the wall had been. And she took a deep breath, looking at the bizarre structures around her, and said to herself, Okay, sweetie, now you've got your freedom. Use it!

Or (the echo sounded in her mind) lose it.

Things were happening in that outside world, now revealed to them. Patsy sniffed acrid smoke, heard distant, and sometimes not so very distant at all, crashes and pops from whatever it was that was going on just out of sight. Jimmy Lin, greatly daring, had ventured, a step at a time, five or six meters down the broadest of the passages, Patrice close behind him and Martín and Rosaleen peering after them. Dannerman and Pat were on their knees at the margin of their cell, poking at something on the floor. When Patsy drew close she saw that where the base of the mirror wall had been there was now only a shiny line of alternating coppery and colorless segments, each less than a centimeter long. "It wasn't real," Pat marveled, looking up at Patsy. "The wall, I mean. It wasn't *solid.* It was just some kind of projection, and when the power went off it just disappeared."

"And so did the floor," Dannerman added. "Not just our floor. Look outside here." The floor on the other side of the boundary was the same metal mesh as inside, or most of it was. But a few meters away there was a section that looked as though it had been repaired with ordinary cement—not recently, either; the patch was stained and potholed. Actually, everything looked pretty helter-skelter to Patsy. Some of the machines looked naked, as though they had been meant to have some sort of case or cover. (The mirror walls they'd seen on the way in? Maybe so, Patsy thought, because she could see the same buried hexagonal lines as surrounded their cell.) Some looked very old, corroded with time.

"It's a mess," Jimmy Lin reported, returning. "There's a machine out there that looks as though it ran itself to destruction—bearings scorched, housing popped off—like a car engine that ran out of oil."

"I don't think they used oil," Patrice said.

Rosaleen said thoughtfully, "I wouldn't be surprised if they used some kind of energy to reduce friction—like maglev, you know? Or something like the balls the cooker moved on, and when the power went off—"

"The cooker!" Jimmy Lin interrupted, looking stricken. And when they put it to the test it was what they had feared. The packet of chili Pat dropped in sat there at the bottom of the well, unwarmed.

"Oh, hell," Jimmy said, contemplating another period of uncooked food. And of worse; at a sudden thought he picked up the helmet and tried it on, then morosely set it down again. "No power there, either," he said. "What do we do now?"

Dannerman had a prompt answer. "I think," he said, "that somebody ought to go out and see what's going on."

"Are you volunteering?" Pat asked. "Because if you are, I'll go along."

Dannerman looked pleased, then frowned. "Better not," he said reluctantly. "I won't go far, and it's easier if I do it alone."

"Don't you want to eat something first?" Rosaleen asked.

"Put some in to soak," he ordered. "I'll eat it when I get back." And turned and left without looking at Pat again.

When Dannerman was out of sight Pat stared after him for a moment, then sulkily took over the job of opening packets and filling them with cold water to soften. Patsy looked at her with compassion. She was pretty sure that exploration hadn't been the only thing on Pat's mind, or on Dannerman's, either; if ever she had seen two people with a strong compulsion to get off by themselves it was they. But Dannerman, Patsy thought, had been right; he had the skills of his Bureau training and Dr. Pat Adcock did not. Score one for responsibility in the face of temptation.

She joined Pat at the task of preparing food. It wasn't a job she really enjoyed, but it had one great advantage: it was a task she was confident she could handle. And confidence in dealing with everything else in this challenging new environment was absent from her frame of mind. Were the others as stunned—well, say the word: as *frightened*—as she was? She couldn't tell. They didn't seem to show it if they were . . . but on the other hand, she told herself, probably she wasn't showing that total interior terror either.

By the time her job was done the others were clustered at the base of the things that looked like file cabinets (though if they had drawers, nothing any of the captives could do had managed to open one). As she joined them she heard Rosaleen say, as she stood with one hand on Martín's shoulder, "Listen. Am I wrong or have the explosions mostly stopped?"

"There aren't very many now, anyway," Martín agreed, looking up at the top of the cabinets. "I wish I could get up there. I might be able to see something useful."

"You can't," Pat said positively. "You're too big to lift. But I'm not. If you guys give me a hand I think I can make it to the top."

It turned out that, indeed, she could—not easily, and not without a couple of near misses that threatened to drop her to the floor. But she did it. Stepped from Jimmy Lin's crouching back to Martín's hunkered-down shoulders. Braced herself with her palms against the cabinets as the general slowly rose. Got her arms across the top of the cabinets and, with both men pushing from beneath, scrambled on.

Patsy heard a faint sound of crunching as Pat got to her feet, examining the legs of her slacks. "It's a mess up here," she reported, panting. "There's scratchy stuff all over, like spun glass, but not that hard; there are big balls of it on some of the tops, but a lot is just broken into powder."

"I think that might be what I saw before," Rosaleen called. "Is it orange? And luminous?"

"Orange, yes. Luminous, no." Pat raised herself on tiptoe, shading her eyes to gaze in the direction the others had gone. "No sign of Dan. I can see where the smoke's coming from, though; it's a fire—I can see the flames—but not very big, and a long way off. And around in the other direction"—as she turned—"there's—hey! There's sunlight! Real sunlight, I'd bet a million dollars on it, and—oh, my God—*trees*!"

"Trees?"

Patsy couldn't say which of them had incredulously repeated the word—maybe it was all of them—but Pat was positive. "You damn bet they're trees, and not too far away, either. Closer than the fire." She appeared at the edge of the cabinet, peering down. "Do you think some of us should go take a look?"

"No," said Rosaleen firmly. "Not now. Wait till Dan comes back." Because, she didn't say, Dan was the only one of them who seemed to have an actual plan—or, Patsy thought, if not a real *plan,* at least the determination to keep trying to find things that would be useful to them.

And then she thought what it would be like if Dan didn't get back, and shuddered.

28
Patsy

It was foolishness, Patsy scolded herself—yes, and it was gender treason as well—to allow herself to feel so lost simply because Dan Dannerman was away.

It was also embarrassing, because the other women in the party were clearly not as troubled about it as she. All three of them were asleep, even Pat, while Jimmy was morosely poking at the machine that looked like a two-humped camel, just outside the cell boundaries. (Poor Jimmy, she thought, almost sympathetically; he was taking the loss of the helmet hard. But of course it had had more to offer him than anyone else.) Martín was flat on his back, hands locked behind his head, open eyes regarding their tattered ceiling with incurious distaste. Once more he had positioned himself next to the sleeping Rosaleen. At least, Patsy was grateful to him for that; if freedom was an unexpected challenge for all of them, it was a challenge that could hardly be met for Rosaleen Artzybachova. The old lady couldn't move without wincing. Taking part in any exploration was out of the question for her; the ancient body wasn't up to it.

But Patsy's body was, and she was too restless to sit still. "I'm going to look around," she called to Martín, keeping her voice low.

But not low enough. Martín didn't answer but Rosaleen did. "Be careful," she said, not opening her eyes. "Yell if you need us."

Yell if you need us. And what, Patsy asked herself, could a couple of unarmed men and three equally unarmed women, one of them frail and old, do if she should really need help? As well she might, in this baffling combat zone.

That was a thought that should have been frightening. Oddly, she wasn't particularly frightened. Oh, there was a lot of fear, even something not too remote from panic, that sat there at the back of her mind, ready to appear if something startled her, but curiosity outweighed the fear. Everything she saw was a new mystery—not one that she could hope to solve, no, but something to wonder at. That smoke that drifted overhead, sometimes pale, sometimes inky black and stinking with some foul chemical odor. The machines all around—all silent, some in ruin. When she looked up, crane her neck as she would, she could get no glimpse of anything that looked like sky, only layers and layers of construction and mechanical puzzles.

The first time she saw a Doc standing motionless before her she yelped out loud. She couldn't help it.

But the creature didn't move. Its eyes were open behind the fuzzy beard, but unfocused; the half-dozen limbs were hanging loose and still. So it was with the next one she saw, a moment later. It was alive, all right. She could see an artery pulsing in the Doc's throat and it seemed to be breathing.

Patsy couldn't resist. She passed a hand before the creature's eyes, the way they said tourists used to do for the guards at places like Buckingham Palace. It didn't blink.

Patsy was almost smiling as she turned away, and that was when she saw the dead Dopey.

Oh, Jesus, she whispered to herself, staring. The body had been roughly handled. It lay in a pool of sticky dark fluid and its head had been crushed.

But it was smaller than Dopey—smaller than *their* Dopey, at least—and the peacock plume was far more modest: matted and discolored now, but nothing like the great fan that Dopey had worn.

That was enough for Patsy. She turned on her heel and headed back to the company of the others. Rosaleen was standing at the perimeter of the cell, leaning on the useless cooker, Martín close behind. They were both watching for her. "Yes?" Rosaleen said, and Patsy poured out everything she had seen.

"I was frightened," she finished. "I'm sorry."

"But why should you be sorry? Of course you were—" Rosaleen didn't say "scared shitless"; she was kind, and only said "startled."

"Thank you," Patsy said, and then was immediately startled again. They heard a faint chittering sound, and when she turned something very strange was coming slowly toward them. It was a round . . . well . . . a round *thing,* turtle-shaped, beach-ball-size. Possibly it was an animal, possibly not. Feathery fronds extended upward from the short-legged body, and clinging to the tip of each frond was a tiny creature, no bigger than a mouse. The little creatures were all peering worriedly behind them, chittering softly to each other; and Patsy was almost certain she had seen them before. That shark-toothed grin on the tiny faces surely belonged to the variety of the Seven Ugly Dwarfs called "Happy." "But I didn't think they would be so small," she said stupidly.

She had spoken softly, but the little things heard. One of the creatures turned and saw the humans staring at them. It squeaked in shrill alarm. All dozen of them turned, toothy mouths wide in fear. There was a chorus of chittering, and they turned their mount toward another corridor and galloped away out of sight in obvious panic.

"My God," Rosaleen remarked behind Patsy, crossing herself. "Patsy? Did it not seem to you that they were running away from something?"

And so it had; but it was Martín who saw what that something was and called, "It's all right. It's only Dan coming back."

In spite of everything, some little part inside of Patsy had been hoping that when Dan returned he would be bringing good news. She couldn't imagine what the good news might be. Certainly not like—like—well, like finding that Colonel duValier's expedition had got to Starlab, and found the transmitter there, and used it to ship themselves and a brigade or two of commandos here to rescue them. She hadn't really expected anything like that, but there had still been a hope that Dan would have *something* to report that might make things look better for the captives.

He didn't. What he had was a bundle of metal rods tucked under one arm, and a discouraging report. "Looks like somebody's dismantling this whole enterprise," he said. "I went about two or three hundred meters down one of the corridors, heading toward where the smoke was coming from. I didn't want to get too close—"

"Thank God," Pat put in.

Dan gave her a glum look. "I figured I had to be cautious," he said, defending himself although Pat obviously hadn't intended an attack. "There was a lot of destruction, some of it still going on. I saw a big damn thing that looked like a school bus—"

"A *bus*?"

"Well, it was all yellow, and it had wheels, or anyway those big ball-bearing things, and it was on fire. I could see it melting, liquid metal flowing out onto the ground like water, and a stink you wouldn't believe. And then there was this other thing right next to it, kind of a pyramid, and it began to burn, too."

"I hope you had the sense to get out of there," Pat said.

Dan gave her a somewhat mollified look. "You bet I did. But wherever I went there was all this wreckage. Oh, and bodies. I saw a couple dead Dopeys and a bunch of others I couldn't recognize—maybe like that thing you said you saw, Patrice? That looked like the Bashful? But these were too burned to tell, and some of them were pretty ripe, too. I think they'd been lying there for days, some of them."

That seemed to conclude the report. No one spoke until Rosaleen said philosophically, "Your food is ready. Me, I think I will get some sleep."

Martín was frowning over the pile of metal rods Dan had dropped. "And what are these things?"

"I picked them up," Dan said, selecting one of them and hefting it. "I thought they might do for clubs. Or spears, maybe. And who knows? We might be needing some kind of weapons before long."

There was another unwelcome thought for Patsy. Weapons. To defend themselves, that was, against some invisible enemy that could melt metal objects without even being seen. Perhaps some of her fellow prisoners could take comfort in having a club to bash somebody with—if they ever came across somebody who could be dealt with by simple bashing—but all the rods meant to Patsy was one more wholly inadequate response to problems they could not really hope to solve.

For lack of something better to do, Patsy picked out a couple of packets of food and carried them over to where Rosaleen lay huddled in silence, next to the water tank. Although the old lady wasn't moving, Patsy didn't think she was asleep. Still, she tried to be quiet as she juggled the food packets, but she dropped one.

It made hardly any noise as it bounced from the mesh flooring, but Rosaleen opened her eyes and looked at her. "Oh, sorry," Patsy said. "I didn't want to disturb you. I thought you might be, ah—"

"Yes? You thought I might be what?"

"Well, praying, I guess."

"Praying?" Rosaleen looked surprised, then comprehending. "Ah. You saw me crossing myself."

"Well, yes." Patsy was embarrassed to have brought the subject up; conversations about religion, with religious people, always embarrassed her. She said, "It's just that— Well, how long have we known each other, Rosie? And I never knew you were religious before."

"Am I?" Rosaleen pondered the question. "I don't think I am, exactly. You might say I'm just stubborn. It's a kind of a family tradition. My mother's grandfather was the metropolitan of Rostov, back in Soviet times. He died in the camps, like a lot of our family, so I kind of go to church every now and then just to spite the memory of Joe Stalin. On the other hand—" She looked wistful, then smiled. "You know, my mother didn't want me to take science courses in school, she thought it would ruin me as a believer. Now, if there's really some scientific proof of Heaven, I'd really like to have had a chance to show it to her."

Patsy suddenly shivered. "You know—maybe you will."

But really, you had to face up to this eschaton thing, she told herself. You can't just go on ignoring the whole subject. Suppose what the French colonel said is real. Suppose it doesn't matter all that much what happens to you here, even if maybe you die. No, she amended herself, that's not a maybe; you damn near certainly will die here, and probably before very long. Okay. Fine. For if the colonel was telling the truth then all that happens is you go to sleep, and next thing you know you're wide awake and healthy and happy and, hey, *immortal*! That wasn't too shabby, was it? Living forever in Heaven . . .

But it wasn't really a very comforting thought. Future immortality was a theory; dying was a *fact.* Not to mention the other thing. Even if the theory was right, what about these damn mysterious Horch? Or, for that matter, about the equally damn mysterious Beloved Leaders?

She shuddered again, and began picking over the stored foods. They were as discouraging to her as ever, but she settled on something that called itself potato soup and set it to soak in cold water; maybe it would turn itself into vichyssoise, she thought optimistically. Then, on second thought, sighing, she picked out a couple of others and set them to soak for when the others woke up.

Rosaleen was giving her a questioning look. Patsy said sorrowfully: "I wish I hadn't got you into this, Rosie."

Rosaleen looked surprised, then gave her a little never-mind headshake. "Oh, don't blame yourself, Patsy. Look at the bright side. I'm not dead yet—here, I mean. Whereas actually, if I understand what has happened, the one of me on Earth isn't that lucky. So perhaps accepting your invitation to come along has produced a net gain for me after all." Then she smiled. "What foolish things we think of. Shall I tell you what has been on my mind for hours now? I have been wondering who might have taken over my old office at the observatory."

Nearby, Patrice confided, "You know, so am I, Patsy. Who do you suppose has taken over ours?"

"I hope nobody," Patsy said with indignation. "This jail thing must be some kind of misunderstanding; when it gets cleared up we'll be back in charge."

"*We* will?"

Patsy looked at her in surprise, then nodded. "Oh, yeah, I see what you mean. That would make a problem, wouldn't it? I mean if we all got back. Anyway," she said, stretching her arms, "I wonder how old Papathanassiou's getting along with his gamma-burster counts. And poor dumb Mick, and all the rest of the guys. . . ."

"And—" Patrice began, and stopped, frowning. Something was moving toward them through the maze of machinery. Everyone was suddenly standing, half of them with metal rods already in their hands.

They they saw what it was: a Doc, walking slowly and gazing from side to side. When it saw them it stopped, immobile, waiting.

And what it was waiting for . . .

That appeared a moment later. It was Dopey, bedraggled, limping along, hurrying fearfully toward them.

"Please!" he begged. "Help me! They'll kill me if they find me!"

29
Patsy

There was the world turned upside down for you, Patsy thought, their arrogant little jailer now pleading hysterically for their protection. "It is not safe here," he sobbed, wringing his fussy little hands. "They go about looking for the Leaders' people and they *butcher* us. Also they're destroying everything in the base!"

"The Horch?" Pat asked, moved to sympathy.

"No, not the Horch themselves! What would the Horch be doing in a place like this? It is the machines they've sent, the killing ones . . . and I am very hungry."

Dannerman gave a quick look at Pat—how kindly did she feel to the little freak?—before he said, "I'm afraid we really don't have enough even for ourselves—"

Dopey looked astonished, then indignant. "But I cannot eat your food! No, there is plenty of good food for me in the base, but I dare not go near it—the whole area is swarming with the surrogates of the Horch. You must help me! I have thought this out carefully; what you must do is very clear. You are a very violent race. I am well informed in this respect; remember, I monitored your whole planet for some years. You can fight them, drive them out—"

"With this?" Dannerman demanded, brandishing his spear. "You took our guns away from us."

"But you can have them back," Dopey said eagerly. "I can get them for you. There are better weapons as well. Beloved Leader weapons! Very powerful! As powerful as those of the Horch surrogates, and I will show you where they are."

"If you've got weapons like that, why don't you fight them yourself?"

Dopey looked sorrowful. "The Beloved Leaders' weapons require a great deal of energy."

Dannerman laughed sharply. "And the power's out, so this is all bullshit."

"Bullshit?" Dopey looked trances for a moment, then indignant. "No, certainly what I ask of you is not 'bullshit.' There is a standby power source which is quite adequate, but I dare not activate it by myself. The Horch surrogates would be sure to detect it and then—" The creature shuddered, and added, "Also fighting is not a characteristic of my race. Those others who were fighters were of a different kind, and they are already dead. As I will be if you do not help me now."

Pat gave him a curious look. "You seem to be really scared of dying all of a sudden."

"No," Dopey said. "You have misjudged this matter. I am not afraid of dying. The death of one copy is of little importance when new copies can easily be made. But afraid of failing to carry out the tasks of the Beloved Leaders? Oh, yes, I am very much afraid of that."

"So you'd rather die than fail to carry out your task?"

"No, no! How can you misunderstand me so? To die is no excuse! Do not forget the eschaton!"

Ah, thought Patsy, her curiosity satisfied at last. The eschaton! The eternity of immortal bliss in heaven that waited for them all—assuming the Beloved Leaders were right—but less blissful by a good deal, it seemed, for anyone the Beloved Leaders found wanting in his duties to them.

If it was a fantasy, it was clearly very real to Dopey. He showed it in his look and demeanor: the plume draggled and gray, the little kitten face wrinkled in worry. Then, impatiently: "Must we stay here and argue? It is not safe here. The Horch surrogate machines may detect us at any time. You must leave the base for a place of safety and wait there; my bearer and I will secure your weapons and bring them to you. It will take some time, as we must go very cautiously and by a roundabout route, but I believe we can accomplish this, and then, once you are armed, I will lead you to the power generator—"

"Hold it," Dannerman ordered. "Go back a bit. What's this about a place of safety?"

"A place of *relative* safety, perhaps I should say," Dopey qualified. "Outside the bounds of the base there is a habitat area which has been prepared for you—it was to have been in a later stage of your experiment, but it is available now. I promise you you will find it quite pleasant, not unlike certain portions of your own planet. Also there are dwellings already prepared. There is clean water in a stream. There are trees and flowers—"

"I knew it!" Pat shouted triumphantly. "I saw them! And they were in the open, with real sunshine!"

Dopey squinted at her in reproof. "There is no sunshine at present," he corrected her, "as it is presently night in this portion of the planet. But you will be safe there, relatively, and I will have the bearer prepare a map to guide you."

"If it's nighttime, how will we find our way?" Rosaleen objected.

"I said it was night. I did not say it was *dark,*" Dopey told her, glancing at the Doc. He didn't say a word, or even make a gesture that Patsy could see, but at once the golem stirred itself, pulled out a pen like Rosaleen's—hell, no, Patsy realized; it wasn't *like* Rosaleen's, it *was* Rosaleen's, a copy no doubt made as they copied anything else they chose—and swiftly began to sketch a diagram on a scrap of wrapping paper. "It is not far," Dopey reassured them. "Perhaps, ah, two kilometers. See here"—snatching the completed map from the Doc—"you go that way, past that large orange object, do you see? Then you will see the open space just ahead. Go across this meadow, here, and around this lake, here, and there will be a path. It will lead you to the encampment, and you will wait there until the bearer and I return with your weapons. Then—"

"Stop right there," Dannerman ordered. "Why should we do what you tell us?"

"Why, because that is what the Beloved Leaders would wish," Dopey said in surprise. "Also to save your own lives, since it can be only a very short time before the Horch surrogates arrive here."

"That's what you say," Dannerman said. "We have no reason to trust you. We've seen what you people do."

Dopey looked perplexed. "You have *seen*?"

"On the helmet," Dannerman told him. "Your Beloved Leaders have blown up dozens of planets—"

Dopey looked stricken. "I did not realize the Horch had taken over that circuit," he moaned. "But the people of those planets were enemies! They refused to cooperate with the Beloved Leaders—"

"So you killed them all?" Pat asked in horror.

Dopey said earnestly, "It was not an evil act! Do you not understand? In effect, we merely transported them all, instantly, to their immortality at the eschaton."

Dannerman was staring at him. "Jesus," he said, shaking his head. Then, obstinately: "But you yourself sent copies of us back to Earth from Starlab."

Dopey recovered himself quickly. "So much argument for so little purpose, when time is passing by!" he said in indignation. "But of course we sent copies to Earth, how else could we obtain primary-source data? The observation units we installed did the copies no harm."

That was too much for Patsy. "Then why the hell are our copies in jail?" she demanded.

"Ah," Dopey said, "yes, I see why you are concerned. But it was necessary to alter the memories of those copies, since we did not wish to prematurely reveal our presence. And then they became suspicious after they discovered the device in Dr. Artzybachova at the autopsy—"

He stopped there, suddenly aware of the way Rosaleen was staring at him. "The autopsy," she repeated, as though she had to say it out loud to make it real.

"Unfortunately, yes," he said sadly. "I am sorry to say that your copy was the first living human subject in which we implanted the device. Of course, we had experimented on the head of the corpse in Starlab. But that was in a very poor state of preservation and we were not well experienced in the procedure when we did your copy, Dr. Artzybachova. I regret it, but your copy did not survive."

By the time Dopey had left with his zombie—urging haste at every breath—all the captives had had a chance to study the map. It impressed Patsy: the Doc had sketched as quickly as it could move the pen, but the result was as carefully drawn as any Geodetic Survey chart. Who would have thought that speechless golem capable of such detail? But the important thing was that everyone agreed that they could follow it. Rosaleen, who had been very quiet, not to say subdued—well, Patsy thought, why wouldn't she be, now that her fears were confirmed?—spoke up at last. "It is all quite clear," she said, her voice colorless, her expression blank. "We should have no problem."

"*If* we go to this place," Dannerman said argumentatively.

Martín scowled at him. "Do we have a choice? You yourself have seen what damage these 'surrogate' things can do."

"Maybe we don't," Dannerman conceded, but his tone was reluctant.

Patsy was studying his face. "What's the matter?" she asked. "Don't you want to leave here?"

He shrugged. "Martín's right about that, we probably can't stay here. It's the part that comes after that that I don't like. The son of a bitch wants us to fight his battles for him! Christ! We don't owe him a thing. It's his fault we're here in the first place."

"But we are here," she said reasonably, "and those Horch surrogates do look as though they're killing everything they can catch. Maybe he's right. Maybe we need to fight them just to stay alive."

He grunted. "You're pretty warlike, all of a sudden."

"I don't want to die any sooner than necessary, is that so strange?" She gave him a disapproving look. "I thought you were the trained killer here. What happened?"

He shook his head. "What happened," he said, "is that I'm well enough trained to stay out of other people's fights, especially against superior forces."

Martín rumbled, "I understand your concern, Dannerman, but we can deal with what comes later later. The question is, what do we take with us when we leave? Food, of course; remember what Dopey said. He cannot eat our food, so we probably cannot eat anything we find there, either."

"How the hell are we going to carry all these things?" Jimmy Lin said, staring at the mound of food containers.

"Well, that I can answer for you," Dannerman said. "We can use the rods I brought back and the blankets from Starlab to make travoises."

Martín kicked at the rods contemptuously. "Most of those rods are too thick to fit through the blanket loops," he pointed out.

"So we use the others. Let's get on with it."

"Hey," said Patsy and Pat at once, and Patrice added, "It's not that easy. What did Dopey say, two kilometers? Rosaleen can't walk that far."

"Fine," Dannerman said. "She won't have to. We'll make a travois for her, too."

Martín said with disdain, "Using those toothpicks? The thing will come apart in ten minutes, and then you will drop the old lady on her ass. It's simpler for me to carry her."

30
Patsy

When they started on their trek to their new home, Patsy was filled with worries. What was waiting for them there? Would they be able to follow the Doc's hastily drawn map without getting lost? Would they be able to see where they were going at all, since Dopey had told them it was night outside? But when they reached the edge of the Beloved Leader base—cut as cleanly as with a knife, one moment surrounded by the hulking dead machinery, the next looking out on a sprawl of meadow and woods—at least one of those worries disappeared. They all stopped dead in their tracks, looking up. "Oh, my God," Patsy breathed. "Will you *look* at that sky?"

They all were looking. They couldn't help it. Overhead there were a zillion stars, far brighter than anything she had ever seen on Earth, and far more of them. There were red stars and blue ones, yellow ones, white ones. On Earth star colors were so muted that you had to stare at even, say, Betelgeuse to be sure that it was really ruddy instead of featureless white. Here there was no doubt. The colors were as unmistakable as traffic lights, and nearly as brilliant. There seemed to be at least a thousand stars up there that were brighter than Venus at its maximum from Earth. There were a dozen or more that seemed even brighter than the Moon. Patsy had heard of, but had never seen, starlight you could read a book by. This was starlight you could do brain surgery by.

Next to her Pat sighed. "You know what, friends?" she murmured. "We're definitely not in Kansas anymore."

Two kilometers wasn't much; Patsy had jogged more than that some mornings before breakfast, along the bridle path in the park . . . in the days when Patsy was still Dr. Pat Adcock, who not only jogged but worked out in the gym once a week—most weeks, anyway.

Those days were past. Confinement in that tiny cell had left them all out of shape, and a two-kilometer hike was now a *lot.* They took turns dragging the travoises that were loaded with most of their Starlab food, three of them at a time with Rosaleen limping painfully along when she could and riding on Martín's back when she couldn't, and the other two following behind to pick up whatever rations fell from a travois and toss them back onto the pile.

But there was so much to see! When she was dragging a travois Patsy's eyes were on the sky as much as on where she was going; when Jimmy Lin relieved her to drop back and do pickup she was glad to see who was there with her. "Patrice!" she hissed, trying to keep her voice low enough that the others might not hear. "Do you know what I think? I think we're in the middle of a globular cluster!"

Patrice bent to pick up a pair of soft-plastic packs and tossed them into Jimmy Lin's travois. "So does Pat," she whispered. "We were talking about it before. At first I thought maybe we were at the core of the galaxy, you know? The star density might be about the same. But we'd know that, all right, and—"

"Hey, back there!" Dannerman called. "Pay attention to what you're doing, we can't afford to lose any food." But he had stopped at the edge of a dark lake, setting down the handles of his own travois to consult over the map with Rosaleen and the general.

Patsy would have supposed that Jimmy Lin would be right up there to take part in the debate, but he lingered when everyone had stopped. "What were you guys saying about a globular cluster?"

Patrice frowned. "Sorry, we were trying to keep it quiet. What about it?"

"Well, to start with, what is it?"

"It's what it says it is. It's a tight cluster of thousands of stars, more or less shaped like a ball. But if that's what we're in, then we're *really* pretty far from home; most of them are in the galactic halo, none of them closer than several thousand light-years."

"Wherever they are, their stars are really jammed close together," Patsy added. "Thousands of them might fit into the space between Earth and Alpha Centauri . . . a lot like what you see up there."

Jimmy craned his neck, then had an objection. "So how do you know we're not in the core of our own galaxy? Christo Papathanassiou told me once—"

"That there were a lot of stars crowded together there, too? Sure there are. But there's something else at the core, and that's a hell of a big black hole. If we were anywhere near that we'd know, because we'd all be dead now from the radiation."

From up ahead, Dannerman was trying to get their attention. "Quiet!" he ordered. "Do you hear that?"

And as soon as they stopped talking, Patsy did. It was a thick slobbering noise, not quite a roar, definitely not friendly.

In a moment Patsy saw what it was. Something was crossing from a patch of shrubbery toward the lake, off to their right, no more than thirty or forty meters away. There were two somethings, one larger than the other. Patsy couldn't make out details, but the heads looked as huge-mouthed and wide-nostriled as a hippopotamus—though wearing something puzzlingly like a mustache. Not really a mustache, she corrected herself; the strands weren't hair; more like the tentacles of an octopus. The bodies, though, were streamlined as a seal's, and they flopped along the ground on their fins like any pinniped. As she watched, the smaller of the two slipped into the water; the other planted itself on the shore and gargled at them again before following the other.

"Christ," Pat breathed from up ahead. "Was I wrong, or were those things wearing some kind of collars?"

"Perhaps they are pets," Rosaleen said dryly. "I don't think I want to try to return them to their owners just now, though. Please, can we proceed?"

They did. They gave the lakeside a wide berth, all of them watching worriedly to see what might come up at them out of the water. But nothing did.

Once past the lake the distance was short. They crossed a meadow—delightfully speckled with patches of phosphorescent grasses, smelling peculiarly of mown wild onions and mint. Once or twice Patsy thought she heard a distant whickering from the woods, and Jimmy Lin startled everybody when he declared he'd seen something flying there. But then they crossed a little ridge, and there before them, laid out in the brilliant starshine, was a valley with a bright stream running through it, and some sort of structures beside the stream.

"They look like tents," Patrice said in awe.

"Yes," said Rosaleen, summoning up the strength to stand for the last little bit. "Dopey said there would be dwellings for us."

"Tents aren't 'dwellings,' " Jimmy Lin complained; and then, when they were closer: "My God, they aren't even tents! They're what you call 'yurts.' Like the things the Uighur ethnics live in, up in Xinjiang Province, you know? And they *stink*."

So they did; as soon as Patsy came within range she smelled it, a long-ago aroma of spice and decay. On the other hand, she was well aware that she herself was far from fragrant, and she eyed the stream water longingly.

She wasn't the only one, though not for the same reason. Behind her Dannerman asked, "Think we can drink that river water?"

Rosaleen was limping after him. "What choice do we have?" she asked, painfully crouching over the stream for a closer look. Most of the others followed. At that point in its course the stream ran over a pebbly bottom, and, in the glory of starlight from that blazing sky, it looked crystal-clear. It also looked empty. If the stream held any population of fish or insects—or of whatever would pass for either in this place—Patsy couldn't see them.

She put a finger in the water and quickly revised her thoughts of a quick bath; that water was *cold*. Next to her Dannerman hesitated, then dipped his cupped hands into the stream. He lifted the water to his nose to smell, then tasted it.

"It seems all right," he said judiciously. "Tastes good, in fact."

That was enough for Patsy. She cupped her hands in the stream, drank; and then realized how thirsty she was and drank more, and then more still. She wasn't the only one, either. Most of the others were following Dannerman's example, until Rosaleen said thoughtfully, "I wonder if we shouldn't have boiled it first."

"Boiled it how?" Pat asked, but Patsy wasn't listening. She was remembering what a case of violent diarrhea was like, learned well from some heavy-drinking and poorly sanitized picnics in her college days. What would that be like here, without any pink medicine waiting in the dorm dispensary to calm the outraged bowels down?

But it was a little late to think of that, and now everybody—no, she corrected herself: every one of the men; the women seemed less bossy—had a plan to offer. "We need to make a fire," Jimmy Lin was saying, and Martín was arguing, "First we must fix up some sleeping accommodations for Rosaleen," and Dannerman was urging that they check the woods out, in case there were surprises there.

"Fire first," Jimmy insisted. "To keep vermin away, and so we can cook some of this crap instead of eating it cold."

"Cook it in what?" Pat asked. It was a reasonable question. Patsy thought wistfully of the score or so of pots and kettles and asparagus cookers and omelette pans in her (seldom-used) kitchen in New York. Would they have to reinvent pottery? Dig out clay? Throw bowls on a wheel, the way she vaguely remembered from one of the less enjoyable courses she'd taken in high school? But Jimmy dismissed all questions. "Get me firewood," he ordered. "Preferably dead stuff that's fallen to the ground; let me worry about the rest of it." And, when there still were arguments, grandly: "Don't forget, I was an Eagle Scout at Kamehameha High."

It was Dannerman who lost out. Exploration, they decreed, would have to wait for daylight; meanwhile Martín and Jimmy Lin had their way. Patsy found herself carting wood from the edge of the forest—ears alert for any sound, eyes searching the dimness—while Dannerman cut it into quarter-meter lengths with the serrated blade from his belt, and Martín drafted Pat and Patrice to drag everything out of the yurts for inspection. Everything the yurts contained was old, fragile and decayed; but there had been things that could only have been pallets that still seemed useful. Well, *maybe* useful. Certainly not comfortable. They were sacks filled with powder that had once been leaves and grasses, along with brittle sticks that still had sharp edges; and they were more than three meters long and less than a meter wide.

They would do. Martín ordered four of them returned to the largest and cleanest of the yurts, three to another—why, Patsy thought, amused, they were doing sex-segregated dormitories! And when he had made sure Rosaleen was comfortable, or as comfortable as she could hope for, he emerged to help Jimmy Lin rasp deadwood into a kind of powder with the little files from Rosaleen's hair sticks. And then Jimmy did his Eagle Scout thing, spinning a stick between his palms against a rock, finally getting a smoldering glow from the friction. And ten minutes later he had his campfire going, throwing out orders in all directions. "Only put in small sticks," he commanded. "Not too much wood. What we want is an Indian campfire—small, so it won't use up our fuel too fast. And now—who's for a real home-cooked meal?"

But no one was. What they wanted was sleep. Exploration could wait, eating could wait—it had been a long day for everyone. For Patsy, too, but somehow she found herself volunteering to take the first watch to keep the fire fed. She had had some idea that, once everyone else was well and truly asleep, she might just dip herself into that brook and try to get at least the surface layers of grime and stench off her long-unwashed body. That notion didn't last; when she tried the water with one toe it was even colder than she had remembered.

Replenishing the fire was about the easiest job Patsy had ever had. Jimmy's orders had been explicit: no more than four or five sticks at a time, none at all until there were no more flames, just glowing coals, because you didn't want actual flames. Patsy debated what to do with the longest sticks, too long to fit in the tiny fire. She didn't want to try to break them for fear of waking the others up, wasn't sure she had the strength to do it, anyhow, and had no idea where Dannerman had left his glassy blade; but then she worked out a simple solution. She laid them across the fire until the middle sections had burned through, then picked up the ends and tossed them in. Nothing to it.

The hard part was staying awake. For the first hour or so little pin-pricks of fear kept the adrenaline flowing. Distant whickerings in the wood, the gentle plop of something falling from a tree, a nearby growl (which turned out only to be Martín snoring)—every sound was an alarm. Almost anything, Patsy thought, could leap raging at her out of the trees; but then time passed and nothing did, and the fears, while not going away, changed character. Were they really going to try to take on the might of the Horch killing machines with a handful of popguns? Should they be doing that, anyhow? (Or was Dannerman right about the dangers of taking sides?) And, that biggest question of all, how much truth was there in the promise of eternal bliss (or otherwise) in this improbable eschaton? The questions revolved themselves through her tired brain—with, of course, no answers. She was fed up with the endless supply of unanswerable questions.

But then she had only to lift her eyes to the sky to see the kind of marvel she had never expected to behold. It was—there was only one word for it—*magnificent.* She noticed, as time went on, that the stars were appropriately wheeling across the heaven, just as they should do; that pair of blue-white beacons that had been low on the horizon when they arrived was now gone from view, and on the other side of the sky—she supposed she should call it the "east"—there was a whole new puzzle to gape at. Streamers of pale light stretched among the newly risen stars, some of them almost as bright as the stars themselves, almost enough to make her squint. She realized with a sudden shiver—part excitement, part wonder at being privileged to see such a thing with her own unaided eyes—that she was looking at stars in the very act of stealing gas from one another, a spectacle she had never before beheld except in plates from Starlab or the old Kecks.

She was so absorbed in the sight overhead that she wasn't aware

Dannerman was coming up to her until he called her name, and then she jumped. "Jesus, Dan-Dan! What are you doing up?"

"Time to relieve you," he said, following her example and staring toward the east. "What the hell's that? It looks like something you'd see under a microscope?"

Well, it did; all filamentary and webby. But she was glad to be able to explain something at least, when so little was explainable. "They're exchanging matter. Stars can do that when they're close, and some of those are probably nearer each other than Pluto is to the Sun. So you're looking at the naked hearts of stars, Dan. If our models of star evolution are right," she went on, warming to the subject, "some of those stars used to be red giants, but when the gas was stripped away they were rejuvenated. They became what we call 'blue stragglers,' with surface temperatures five or six times as hot as our own Sun. The bad part of that," she began, but Dannerman held up his hand.

"Please, Patsy. Don't tell me any bad parts right now, okay? You better get some sleep while you can. It's almost daylight."

And he was right about that, too, of course. Past the cobwebby gas streamers the far horizon was beginning to lighten; and Patsy felt the sudden weight of her fatigue. Gratefully enough she climbed onto the pallet that had been set aside for her, Pat stirring gently as she came in, Rosaleen moaning faintly in her sleep. It was not a comfortable bed. Whoever made it must have had skins like armor plate, she thought, and closed her eyes.

But she hadn't told him what the bad part was.

The bad part was that some of those cannibal stars would sooner or later glut themselves on the mass they had stolen from the others. And then there would be a nova, maybe even a supernova, flooding the space around it with radiation of all kinds . . . at the congested distances of the globular cluster.

When might that happen? The astronomical time scale was far slower than the human. Such things might take centuries to occur, but when they did—

When they did, this would not be a good place to be, and the life expectancy of anyone out in the open under that suddenly lethal sky would be short indeed.

31
Patsy

Patsy woke up with bright sunlight outside the opening of the yurt and the sound of somebody yelling at somebody, not very near, but not all that far away, either. When she peered out she saw that it was Dannerman who was doing the yelling. The person he was yelling at was Pat, placidly hanging her underwear on a tree branch to dry. "It's just damn *foolish* for you to go wandering off by yourself," he scolded. "Who knows what's out there?"

"But you said yourself we needed to check out our surroundings," Pat said reasonably, adjusting the bra to catch the sun.

"Not alone!"

"No," she said, acknowledging the justice of what he said—but not, Patsy thought, particularly penitent about it, either. "I should have waited till the others woke up. But, Dan, I found this lovely pond just a little way down the stream, and I got a *bath.* Well, sort of a bath—no soap, of course, and it was really cold—but I can't tell you how much better I feel. Maybe the two of us can go out later?" And then, looking past him, "Well, good morning, Patsy. Did you have a nice sleep?"

Damn the woman, Patsy thought. Damn the man, too; they might as well be married if they were going to squabble like that. She didn't answer, simply turned and headed for the bushes. Then, delighting in the luxury of being able at last to pee without an audience, she relented. She was just jealous, she admitted to herself. Not merely jealous of the Dan-Pat relationship, although she was certainly envious of that, but *extremely* jealous of the bath.

On the way back she paused to peer down the stream and, yes, she was nearly sure that, just past where the brook made a bend around a grove of tall, emerald-leaved trees, there was a definite widening. That went right to the top of her list of priorities. Not to be taken advantage of just yet, maybe; she hadn't missed Pat's complaint about the cold, but as soon as the air warmed up a little . . .

It was astonishing how that thought elevated her mood. She glanced up, and there was the sky. The blue sky, with fleecy little muffins of fair-weather clouds scattered around, and the sun. The sun! Of course, it wasn't their familiar sun of Earth; too large, too orangey. But it was a great deal better than that unending featureless white glow they had lived under in their cell, and she was interested to observe that, even in daylight, a scattering of those incredible stars were bright enough to be visible in the sky. This was not an *awful* place, she told herself. It was even sort of pretty: the grove of trees behind her was hung with clusters of things like bright-yellow berries; the spiky ground-cover stuff underfoot that was like grass (but wasn't any grass Patsy had ever seen) was spotted with wildflower dots of color. Most important of all, she was *outside*. Things might be heading for something even worse than what had gone before, but at this moment, Patsy thought, they didn't seem bad at all. So she had a cheery smile for Pat and Dan as she rejoined the group, and another for Rosaleen and Martín Delasquez, doing something with the stack of ration containers. The only ones missing were Patrice and Jimmy Lin, and about as soon as the thought crossed her mind they both appeared out of their respective yurts, Patrice heading toward the bushes without a word, Jimmy yawning, barely glancing at the others, making a beeline to check the condition of his pet campfire.

To Patsy's eyes the fire was behaving just as it was supposed to behave. It was a neat bed of glowing coals, sixty or seventy centimeters across, with only a couple of lately added sticks palely flaming on top. Clearly, however, it did not meet Jimmy Lin's expectations. He pushed the burning sticks together and carefully added two more, just so, muttering to himself. Then he caught sight of Rosaleen. "What are you doing?" he demanded.

She didn't take offense. "We're counting our rations," she said, "and at the same time looking for containers that won't burn if we boil water in them."

"Thought so," he said, patiently superior. "I told you to leave that sort of thing to me, didn't I? What you should do now is find a big empty container and fill it with water, while I get some rocks from the brook."

He made a production out of it, selecting golf-ball-sized pebbles, which he carried back and painstakingly placed on the coals. "Give them ten minutes," he said, wise old expert showing the tenderfeet how to get along in the wild. "Then the rocks will be hot enough; we drop them in the water and they'll have it hot in no time."

"Hey," Pat said, admiring against her will. "More Boy Scout stuff?"

He didn't deign to answer, merely walked off to the shelter of the trees to relieve himself.

"Bastard," Dannerman said, but his tone was tolerant. He glanced at Pat. "Shall we eat something? And then go explore?"

"If Rosaleen's through with her count?" Pat said, looking toward the stack of rations.

"In a minute," Rosaleen called. "Martín's found a couple of other packets—I guess we dropped them."

But Martín was standing a good three or four meters away—how could we have dropped any of the packets over there? Patsy wondered—and his expression was forbidding. He was holding two of what looked like dehydrated stew packets, and staring at the ground.

"Something's been nibbling at these things," he called. "And I think I see what was doing it. Only they're dead."

Jimmy Lin's hot-water scheme worked fine—to be sure, at the cost of some burned fingers, transferring the hot pebbles to the container of water, but in a few minutes the container was gently simmering and meals were coming along. When Patsy got her stew, though, it was lukewarm and only partially softened. It didn't matter. She'd lost most of her appetite when she saw the three little dead creatures—looking a little like lizards, maybe, though densely furred—with their mouths wide open in the rictus of death.

"Different chemistry," Rosaleen said soberly. "I guess I can forget that idea." And when someone asked what idea she was talking about, she explained, "I was thinking we might try some of the fruits from those trees when our rations run out, but if our food kills them, I doubt their food will be any better for us."

Patsy stopped eating to look at the heap of rations. It had not occurred to her to think of it as a nonrenewable resource. She didn't like the conclusions that thought led to. "Rosaleen? With seven of us eating, how long do you think the food will last?"

Rosaleen looked at the tally in her hand. "Let's see, three meals per day per person, that's twenty-one portions a day, divided into, according to this, two hundred and seventy-three portions . . . say, thirteen days. A bit more, maybe."

"And then?"

"And by then," Rosaleen said firmly, "I presume Dopey will have come back with the guns, and we'll have taken over the base and there'll be all the food we want from Starlab."

"Or not," Patrice said.

Rosaleen nodded. "Or else we will probably have been killed in the attempt, so it's not a problem."

"So then why were you counting the food?"

She hesitated. "I suppose because there is always the chance that Dopey won't come back."

It was what Patsy had known she would hear, but that didn't make it any nicer. She pressed the point. "And if Dopey doesn't come back, and that's all there is, how long before we starve to death?"

Rosaleen didn't answer at first; while she was thinking Dannerman spoke up. "Did you ever hear of a man named William Bligh?"

"I don't think so."

"He was the captain of an old sailing ship, the *Bounty,* hundreds of years ago. I guess he was a pretty mean son of a bitch, even for those days; anyway, his crew mutinied. Somebody made a book out of it. I never read the book, but one summer in graduate school I worked for a local theater, and they put on a musical based on it. I sang the first mate, the guy who led the mutiny. He was a man named Fletcher Christian."

"I didn't know you were a singer."

"Who said I was a singer? They weren't fussy about that kind of thing at the theater. Neither was I; they didn't pay anything, but you got to meet a lot of girls there. Anyway, Christian made the mutineers put the captain and some of his loyal crew over the side in a longboat instead of hanging them out of hand. The mutineers gave them two days' rations or so, and Captain Bligh managed to get every man in the boat safely to a British port a couple of thousand miles away. They rowed six or eight weeks before they reached land, and all that time they lived on the little bit of water they could catch when there were rainstorms, and the food that was only supposed to be rations for a couple of days."

She thought that over. Another month or two in this place, with nothing to eat at all? And no realistic hope of rescue? "That's not particularly good news," she said.

Dannerman nodded. "We don't really need three meals a day, though. Two would be enough, I think. That ought to give us another couple of weeks, anyway."

But that wasn't really great news either.

32
Patsy

When everyone had eaten, Pat and Dan took off on their mission of exploration. It surprised no one to see that they were walking hand in hand as they left. No one said anything, though—well, no one but Jimmy Lin. "Hey, guess what?" he said, grinning, pointing to where Pat's laundry still hung on the tree. "The lady left her underwear behind. Probably figured it would just get in the way?"

Nobody responded but Patsy, and she said only, "Shut your mouth." She turned her back on him and walked over to where Patrice was sitting cross-legged on the ground, studying some carved wooden objects pulled out of the yurts. "It's none of his damn business what they do," she said—then, lowering her voice, "Although, you know?, he's probably right. How about that bath?"

"In a while," Patrice said absently, looking at a piece of age-darkened wood as long as her forearm, one end flattened and rounded. "Rosaleen wants to go along, but she's resting. Patsy? What do you think this thing is?"

Patsy considered the question. Although the object was worn and chipped at the edges, she was pretty sure of its identity. "I'd say a snow shovel—if they ever had snow here," she hazarded. "Some kind of a shovel, anyway." She squatted beside the other woman, poking through the little pile of artifacts. Most were wood—the shovel, a rod with a pointed, fire-hardened end (too thick to be a spear; maybe a digging stick?), something that looked like a salad fork, several things that didn't look like anything Patsy recognized at all. What wasn't wood was glassy rock—one pretty obviously a sharp-edged knife, the others harder to identify. "They didn't have any metal, did they?" Patsy discovered. "Sort of like the Stone Age?"

"More like pre-Columbian America," Patrice said thoughtfully. "Those yurts are pretty well built . . . and doesn't this look like writing?" She flipped over an oval chunk of wood, and it was true, there were things that looked like wobbly characters incized on the wood. "Makes you wonder who these people were."

But Patsy didn't want to wonder about these unknown people. They were tall and skinny; they lived in tents; they farmed—there was the remains of an overgrown produce plot along the stream—and they were gone. That much they knew, and the only important fact in the lot was the last one. The Skinnies were gone. There was no chance they would ever know anything more about them; but when Patsy said as much, Patrice got a funny expression. "You're sure of that? You don't think we'll all meet up again at the eschaton?"

Patsy gave her a hard look, and got up to put some new pebbles in the fire to heat. That was another thing she didn't want to think about.

Then, when Rosaleen woke up and announced it was time for the adventure of the bath, there was another one. Patrice helped Rosaleen to the "ladies' room" in the bushes; Martín, gathering wood for the fire, decorously diverted himself to a part of the grove they hadn't investigated, and a moment later appeared again, looking perturbed. "There's something odd here," he called. "Come look."

As the others straggled over, Patsy saw what he was talking about. "It just stops," she said, looking in wonderment at the vegetation. It did. The gnarly trees they had used for firewood stopped short, in a mathematically precise straight line; the branches on the near side swooped and dangled in all directions, but on the side away from them the branches were bent at sharp angles. Past them was a growth of quite different vegetation, equally dense, but thick shrubbery rather than trees. There was no point where a shrub crossed into tree territory or a tree branch into the shrubs'.

Rosaleen studied the line of demarcation for a moment, then painfully lowered herself to grub at the ground. A moment later she had revealed the same sort of line that had surrounded their cell, metal and glassy segments alternating. "Do you know what I think?" she said wonderingly. "I believe there used to be one of those walls here."

"I think so, too," Martín confirmed. "And it had to be here for a long time—long enough for the trees to grow up against it."

Patsy was craning her neck to see what was past the shrubbery, and what she saw made her catch her breath. "Look at that," she called.

There was open ground there, but planted—planted in regular rows of tall stalks.

"It looks like farmland," Patrice said, staring. "And there's a path—and, hey, what's that thing over there on the ground?"

The thing along the path was definitely a machine. It had three wheels, bicycle-size, though the spokes were wood—the whole thing was wood, as far as Patsy could see, and it had a sort of basketwork thing in the middle. A farm cart? But if there was a farm, where was the farmer?

That was the next shock. There was a stirring among the tall, ruddy-leafed stalks, and a creature appeared, holding half a dozen banana-shaped fruits (or husks, or *something*) and staring at them.

It was nothing Patsy had ever encountered before, though even at first glimpse there was something about it that looked vaguely familiar. What it looked like was a scale model of one of the ancient big-bodied, long-necked dinosaurs, maybe the kind that was called apatosaurus—though in this case an apatosaurus that was covered with curly hair all over its body, strands poking out from the colorful embroidered shirt and kilt it wore on its tubby, watermelon-size body, and curly bangs that hung over its tiny, lashed eyes—and a very small apatosaurus, at most a couple of meters from the end of the tail that rose behind it to the little head on the end of its sinuous, long neck. It stood on its hind legs, and its front legs—no, Patsy decided, you'd definitely have to call them arms and hands—were holding what it had just collected.

If the watchers were startled, the creature was petrified with fear. It made a sharp mewing sound, dropping its harvest, and flopped itself onto the machine in the path. Patsy saw what the basket was for. It supported the creature's belly as it lay flat, its legs pumping reciprocating levers that turned the rear wheels, its hands on a tiller that evidently guided the wheel in front. As the vehicle rolled away the long neck swayed around so that the fear-filled eyes could stare back at them.

When he was out of sight Patrice shook herself. "He doesn't look like one of the Seven Ugly Dwarfs," she said thoughtfully, "and he's definitely not a Beloved Leader. But I could swear I've seen somebody like him before."

Patsy had the same feeling. She said, "Maybe he's a prisoner like us. Maybe there are other intelligent races of captives around—even those things in the water last night, maybe?"

"Oh, hell, no," Patrice said positively. "This thing had a velocipede and it wore clothes; they didn't."

Rosaleen sighed and turned, automatically reaching for Martín's arm. "Think about it, Patrice. If you live in the water, what do you need with a velocipede? Or clothes, for that matter. People like us wear clothes to protect us against the weather, but there isn't any weather underwater. In any case, it's time for my bath."

Martín looked alarmed. "That's risky. Maybe that thing went to get help."

"Yes, perhaps so," Rosaleen said, "but it's time for me to clean myself up a bit. You've all been very polite, but I really need a bath."

"We'll take a couple of spears along," Patsy promised.

"You'll take me, too!" Martín insisted.

"We will *not*," Patrice said indignantly.

But in the long run prudence won over modesty—what was left of modesty, after those long nude days in their first pen. The compromise they finally reached was that Martín would come along to carry Rosaleen to the bathing pond, while Jimmy Lin stayed behind to keep an eye on the place where they had seen the dinosaur with the velocipede. Then Martín would stay nearby as long as they were in the water; but he would concede enough to their modesty to sit with his back to them. "And no peeking," Rosaleen called good-naturedly as they began to undress.

Patsy was the first to be naked, but she paused before getting into the water, appalled at the sight of Rosaleen's nude body. The woman was *skeletal.* Her breasts, never ample, were mere flaps of flesh; her ribs showed; her hip joints protruded, and so did her knees and elbows.

Patrice had begun helping Rosaleen toward the water; Patsy turned away in embarrassment and splashed in. The water was still cold, but bearable. After the first shock Patsy began to swim. She couldn't help glancing around at the woods every few moments, but, really, there wasn't much to fear. Was there? And it was so wonderful, so *fine,* to be free in the cleansing water after all that time of filth and deprivation. . . .

She rolled over on her back to look back at where Patrice was helping Rosaleen in the shallows. She noticed that Patrice was holding one of Dan's metal spears, and wondered if she shouldn't have one, too—wondered a moment later whether she wasn't being reckless in swimming out so far from the others. Treading water, she looked around.

That was when she saw the tiny pairs of eyes on the surface of the pond, three or four sets of them, nearer to the other bathers than to herself.

She screamed a warning and didn't wait to see if they would respond. She began to swim as fast as she could toward the shore. Yells and screams spurred her on; when she reached the bank she stood up to look. Martín was there already, splashing fully dressed in the shallows, furiously stabbing at something in the water with his own spear. She didn't see the eyes; she did see the water swirling there as though something large were moving under the surface. Patrice was hurrying Rosaleen out of the water, peering back over her shoulder in panic.

Patsy began to run along the bank toward them, pausing to catch up another spear from the stack beside their clothes. Martín might need help. . . .

Martín did need help. Something huge and slate gray erupted from the water behind him; he screamed something—in Spanish, Patsy thought, though she could not make out the words—and fell back into the water. "Oh, God!" Patrice cried. "It got him!"

Patsy didn't hesitate. She splashed into the shallows to where Martín was half floating, half resting on the muddy bottom of the lake. She didn't see the creature that had attacked him. There was a stain in the water—blood? From Martín? But it was some distance away, and the surface was swirling there; something was there and bleeding. When she reached Martín's body it was motionless. Dead? Patsy tried to imagine what it was like to be killed, to die suddenly, without warning. . . .

But maybe he wasn't dead. The spear in one hand, she wrapped her fingers in his long, coarse hair, trying to pull him ashore. The man weighed twice as much as she. She was barely able to move him, and his face was underwater, time passing; if he hadn't been killed by the amphibian he might drown. When Patrice splashed in to join her she let her take over with the task of pulling the general toward dry land, while she remained in the water, on guard with the spear, watching the swirl of bloody water. Across the pond something was heaving itself out of the water; a good sign, Patsy thought hopefully. They were running away. The thing didn't really look like a hippo, more like a walrus; and it galumphed across the ground in its pinniped fashion. It stopped, turning to look at her with those protuberant eyes, then leaned forward, scooped up some mud, formed it into a ball and threw it at her with its finlike paws.

The mud fell far short, splashing in the middle of the pool. Patsy almost laughed at that pitiful display of hostility. Why, they're as frightened as we are, she thought. It did not occur to her that there had been several of the creatures.

She didn't even see the one that was coming up behind her.

She never saw it at all, only felt the sudden touch of something cold on her back, and then the sharp agony of an electric shock; and then Patsy Adcock's question was answered, and she knew at last what it was like to die.

33
Dan

Before Dannerman and Pat had gone a hundred meters they weren't walking hand in hand anymore. They were arm in arm. Very soon thereafter their arms were around each other's waists, and their pace had slowed—no longer a march, now an affectionate stroll. They weren't so wrapped up in each other that they didn't take note of what was around them. That was what they were there for: to explore their surroundings. Dannerman observed that the path they were on had once been trodden hard by some creature's feet—but not recently, since it was now broken here and there with clumps of the wiry grass spikes. It was Pat who first saw the trees that looked so much like cherries (though the bright red fruits that hung from their branches were segmented with hard scales like tiny, ruby-colored pineapples), and it was Dannerman who pointed out the hill that rose off to their left, looming a good hundred meters over the surrounding terrain. ("We could climb that and see everything for kilometers around. Maybe next time.") But they both knew that the thing they were most interested in exploring was not geography; and when Pat looked up at Dannerman, he naturally kissed her; and when they moved their faces away the only question was which of them could first get out of their clothes. They wasted no time. The weeks of enforced abstinence and excessive intimacy were all the foreplay they needed.

When they were done Dannerman propped himself up on one elbow to take some of his weight off her body and gazed reminiscently at her face. "You know, I thought about doing this a lot when we were kids."

"Well, so did I," she said, taking his ears gently in two hands and pulling his head down for a kiss. "But right now it's a little uncomfortable. Oh, don't let go of me—let's hug for a while, okay? Only next time," she added as they shifted position, "we ought to bring a blanket. This mossy stuff has some pretty sharp stickers."

After a while they walked a little farther down the path, remembering that they were supposed to be checking out the area for points of interest. They didn't find many. They had their clothes back on, but Dannerman was comfortably aware that they could get them off again quickly enough if they chose. He rather expected they would choose.

It crossed his mind that probably they shouldn't stay away from the others too long—Dopey might come back and then they would have to think seriously about this mad plan of his to reconquer the base for the Beloved Leaders. Or, alternatively, Dopey might not come back at all. Then they would have to think even more seriously about simple survival. But he didn't want to think about such matters just then, because he was too busy feeling good. It was, he decided, about the best he had felt in a long time—certainly since they had boarded the Clipper for the trip to Starlab. Maybe for a good deal longer than that.

Finally it was Pat who had to say, "Maybe we ought to start back."

Dannerman blinked down at her. "Oh, do you think so? I was sort of thinking that maybe we could—"

"Of course we can," she said, patting his shoulder. "It doesn't have to be here. There's plenty of nice secluded spots right near the yurts, so whenever we like we can just excuse ourselves for a bit and—" She paused, looking curiously at his face. "What's the matter?"

"It just seems so, well, obvious," he said.

Then she did laugh out loud. "Oh, Dan-Dan. Do you think there's one soul back there who isn't absolutely sure of what we were doing here? Come on. Let's see if we can get back without getting lost."

But of course they didn't get lost, because they'd never got that far off the well-marked old path, and of course what Pat said was right. Dannerman switched gears without difficulty. He didn't forget the pleasant feeling in his loins, but he remembered to pick a few of the bright red fruits to carry back, just in case, and even before that he was testing strategies in his mind in the event that Dopey really did bring them their weapons.

That was the part of the Dannerman mind that the Bureau training and experience had honed to a sharp edge. He considered the prospects. If, in spite of everything, they were going to get involved in combat with the Horch machines the first thing they would need was more information. They would need to know, from Dopey, just what parts of the Horch machines were vulnerable to a projectile weapon; and they would have to decide how to allocate the available weapons. He had no doubt that Jimmy Lin and the general could handle a gun; the females were iffier. "Pat?" he asked. "Have you ever been checked out on that little gun you used to carry?"

But she wasn't listening. She was suddenly straining to hear something. "What's that?" she asked, her face suddenly worried.

But by then he had heard the sudden distant screaming, too, and he was already beginning to run.

When they reached the bathing pool there was Martín Delasquez, lying on his face by the side of the pond, his feet still in the water, with Rosaleen, naked, struggling to try to turn him over; and just meters away a clothed Jimmy Lin and a naked Pat were frantically trying to pull the limp form of the other Pat, also naked, to dry land.

What he couldn't see was what it was that they were trying to flee from, but the women were shouting the answer to that. The amphibians? How could that be? What were they doing here, so far from their own pond? But then he saw the little eyes, only a few meters from shore, and then there was no doubt. He didn't waste time wondering. He and Jimmy got the inert hulk of Martín Delasquez pulled away from the water, while the two Pats did the same for the third. "Let me," Jimmy panted, taking over from the Pats; once again his Boy Scout training was useful. Dannerman stood guard, knee deep in the muddy shallows at the water's edge, spear ready. When he stole glances over his shoulder he saw Jimmy bending over the motionless woman, doing the mouth-to-mouth and the rhythmic chest-hammering of CPR, while Rosaleen and the other Pats copied his actions on the form of Martín. Which Pat was which? Hard enough to tell them apart at any time, it was impossible when they were naked.

If the amphibians had any intention of attacking on dry land they kept it in check. Dannerman knew they were there, saw water swirling, caught a glimpse or two of gray flesh; but they seemed more interested in getting their own wounded member to the safety of deep water than in the creatures that had stabbed him. Slowly Dannerman retreated to the high ground, spear still ready, but beginning to feel a little safer.

When he looked around Martín was stirring at last, coughing, looking dazedly around, trying to sit up. But the other Pat . . .

Jimmy was still working on her. He kept it up for long minutes, kept it up long past the time when Dannerman could still feel hope. Then Lin sat somberly back on his haunches.

"She's dead," he said. He thought for a moment. "If we had adrenaline, or shock paddles," he began, and then shook his head and repeated, "She's dead."

Dead?

Dannerman felt the word like a physical blow. *Dead.* It did not seem possible. Yes, sure, they had all faced the strong probability that they might all be dead before long, starvation most likely, possibly some other assault from this hostile place. But not now. Not so *soon.*

"Dan?" It was Rosaleen, drawing on her clothes and looking at him. "Don't you think we ought to get out of here?"

He roused himself. "Yes, of course. But—" He hesitated, looking at the two living Pats and the one that lay motionless on the ground. "But *which*?"

The nearest Pat glared at him angrily. "It's Patsy, you fool," she said, and began to cry.

34
Dan

They didn't walk back to the yurts. They fled. As rapidly as they could, all of them craning their necks to watch for pursuit—but Dannerman knew that if the amphibians attacked again there was very little they could do about it. He had organized them as best he could, but under the circumstances his best was not a lot. Martín had turned out to be able to walk, more or less. He was staggering, confused, seeming tranced and bewildered, with little strength in his limbs. But Jimmy Lin supported him on one side and Patrice on the other, and he managed. Rosaleen Artzybachova was making it on her own—not very well, either, but limping after the others with Pat's help; Pat was carrying Patsy's bundled-up clothing, too, and she had a spear to handle as well, since she was all they had in the way of a rear guard against the amphibians.

Dannerman was carrying the body of Patsy. Jimmy Lin had offered, but Dannerman could not let the man touch her damp, cooling and naked body. Dannerman had her cradled in his two hands, each one also holding a spear. Part of the time he walked backward, scanning the path behind them for possible attackers; there were none. One of Patsy's lax arms hung toward the ground. The other lay across her body, as though trying to preserve modesty. But she had no modesty left to preserve. Though her head hung down Dannerman could see that her eyes were open and so was her mouth. Patsy Adcock would never have let herself be seen in so unflattering a pose. She didn't look pretty. She barely looked like herself; she looked only dead.

Dannerman looked away. They had other things to think of. They would have to bury Patsy, which meant somehow digging a grave. He would have to organize some sort of guard duty to watch for a possible attack. What he would do if that happened he did not know; the yurts were simply not defensible. But there would have to be some sort of plan. Useless or not, it would have to be tried.

There was another thought swelling inside him, bursting to come out—well, no, he corrected himself; not a thought exactly. A pain. A deep hurt that he had never experienced before and did not know how to deal with. Sooner or later he would have to let it come to the surface—

But not yet.

As soon as they had crossed the little stream he put Patsy's body down, as gently as he could, and began giving orders. Martín was to be put to bed in one of the yurts, Rosaleen in the other. Jimmy Lin would be the first to stand guard, while Pat searched the yurts for something to dig a grave with. The others listened attentively. They didn't offer objections to his seizure of command. They moved. But they did not, exactly, obey. Jimmy Lin's first care was for his precious little fire, and only when that was fed did he, not Pat, begin looking for digging tools. Rosaleen flatly refused to be shut away from the others, so Patrice hauled a pallet out of a yurt for the old lady to lie on. Then Jimmy returned with a couple of flat-bladed wooden things that would do as scoops, and he and Dannerman began using their metal spears to loosen clods of dirt, while Pat and Patrice silently dressed Patsy's body. They didn't talk much. There wasn't much to say.

Digging a grave took a long time with crude tools, even though Pat and Patrice pitched in, scooping the clods of earth away when Dannerman and Jimmy had loosened them. Dannerman didn't notice the passage of time. He was glad for something to do, because that interior ache was rising willy-nilly to the surface of his thoughts. When the grave got too deep for both of them to be able to dig, he hopped out and let Jimmy stab and scoop while he confronted it.

The problem was this: How did you mourn the death of one-third of a lover?

This stiffening corpse by the side of the deepening grave was *Pat.* True, it was not *the* Pat, with whom he had made love just hours before, but certainly *a* Pat, indistinguishable from the very *alive* woman with whom he had talked and played and shared so much of a life, from childhood on. No, there was no doubt of it. When someone you "loved"—it was the first time he had used that word, even to himself—when someone you *loved* died you had to feel pain. Dannerman did feel pain, a lot of pain. But how baffling it was to see two copies of that beloved woman alive and well and helping to dig the grave.

To be sure, those other two were definitely mourning. There was no confusion in the tears and self-reproach. "If I hadn't panicked and stabbed the thing," Patrice kept muttering to Pat, even while she was scooping away the loose dirt into a pile. "Maybe they wouldn't have done anything. Maybe—"

The maybes were not helpful. Dannerman stood up. "My turn, Jimmy," he called, and replaced the astronaut in the pit. He had barely begun to dig when Jimmy Lin yelled and grabbed for a spear, and when Dannerman turned to look he saw a regular circus parade approaching: four or five of the great Docs, marching toward them, with Dopey perched in the arms of one of them.

"What is going on?" Dopey called fretfully. "Why are you digging holes? I have brought you your guns—it took a very long time to secure them, with much danger. Now there is no time for the digging of holes, since we must hurry and reclaim our base from the Horch!"

Dopey didn't take kindly to being told that the conquest of the Horch machines would have to wait. But then, when someone had explained to him what had happened, he was disgusted but surprisingly helpful. "General Delasquez," he remarked, "is forming a habit of electrocution. Fortunately one of these bearers is medically trained; I will have him treat the general."

"The hell you will," Patrice snapped, surprised and angered. "What does that thing know about human medicine?"

"Why, a great deal," Dopey assured her. "It was he who implanted the devices on your Starlab. He will know what to do for General Delasquez—also for Dr. Artzybachova, who, I observe, is also quite unwell."

Patrice started to reject the offer with indignation, but Rosaleen overrode her. She raised herself on one elbow and said, "Let's see what he can do, Patrice. I'm not much use to you this way."

That was all the consent Dopey needed. He didn't speak, but one of his golems bent over Rosaleen, picked her up with surprising gentleness and bore her away to the yurt where Delasquez was raucously snoring. Dopey didn't bother to look after them. He waddled toward the grave, where Dannerman had replaced Lin at the bottom, gazing disapprovingly at Dannerman's digging. "What are you doing? Is this some form of human death ritual? If you wish a hole dug to dispose of the cadaver one of my bearers can do this far more quickly."

Dannerman didn't look up. "We'll do it ourselves," he said shortly.

Dopey clucked in annoyance. "How you waste time," he complained. "I am very near to the limit of my endurance. We must act at once, or I must rest for a bit."

"Rest, then," Jimmy Lin says. "If the amphibians attack we'll let you know."

"Attack? Why would they attack? Although," he added meditatively, "it is unfortunately the case that they are not truly civilized anymore. They subdue their prey with electric shocks. You have seen such animals on your own planet? I believe they are called electric eels? But it was foolish of you to get so near them. They have no recent experience of land dwellers, you see; they have been isolated in their own pen for many generations. Now that the walls are down they are no longer confined, and who knows where they may wander to?"

No one responded but Jimmy Lin, turning his head to glare somberly at the alien, and all he said was "Shut up."

Dopey looked surprised, but obeyed the command; perhaps he was getting used to it. "Very well," he said after a moment. "It is foolish to delay, but I will rest for a few minutes. Wake me when you are ready for the reconquest of the base."

Dannerman glanced up long enough to see Dopey climb into the huge arms of a Doc. He didn't bother to watch as the huge golem carried him away, another Doc waddling irritably after. He was concentrating on carving out a straight, flat base for the grave.

He lost track of time. He was surprised when Patrice called down to him, "That's good enough, Dan."

He looked up in confusion. All five of his fellow prisoners were standing there, looking down on him, even Rosaleen and Martín. He had not even noticed that they had left the yurt. He peered up at Rosaleen. She was standing straighter, and there even seemed to be color in her face. "What did he do to you?" he asked wonderingly.

Rosaleen gave him the ghost of a smile. "God knows. As soon as the Doc touched me I was asleep. When I woke up, Dopey was there, lying on the ground—he's exhausted, you know—and the Doc was doing something to Martín. And then Martín woke up and we came out here."

"Dopey's still in the yurt?"

"Oh, yes. Sound asleep. Funny," she added. "I didn't even know he *could* sleep. He snores."

"Yes, yes," Pat interrupted, single-minded and impatient. "Dan? Do you need help getting Patsy down there?"

"Of course not." He took Patsy's body from Pat and Patrice and, gently, clumsily, stretched it out at the bottom of the pit. As he climbed out, Pat jumped in to straighten Patsy's corpse.

At the graveside, Patrice fretted, "I wish we had a coffin. I wish—do you think we should say some words over her?"

"My mother taught me some of the funeral prayers my grandfather used to say," Rosaleen offered. "I learned them in Ukrainian, but I could try to translate."

But Pat was shaking her head as Dannerman helped her out of the grave. "I'll say what needs to be said," she said firmly. "Patsy, we loved you. Good-bye."

35
Patrice

Once you've dug a grave you need to fill it back up again. Patrice knew that. But, as the first scoops of dirt plopped onto Patsy's body, she could hardly bear to look, much less to take part in the work. For the first time she understood why people bothered to box their dead in coffins before they laid them away. The coffins weren't to protect the deceased. They were there for the sake of the witnesses, to spare them the sight and sound of clods falling on a face that was once as alive as their own.

But as each successive shovelful of dirt fell on Patsy's body the shape at the bottom of the hole looked less like a human person and more like some random lump of anonymous earth; and, grimly, Patrice picked up a scoop and took her place with the others.

That earned her a grateful look from Jimmy Lin. "Thanks," he said, and then paused to look back at where Martín and Rosaleen were sorting over the guns. Dopey was returning in the arms of one of the Docs. Jimmy looked at Patrice again, this time pleading. "Listen, you can finish without me, can't you? Because I'd really like to check those weapons out—"

"Go ahead," she said. And beside her, Pat saw the expression on Dannerman's face and added:

"You too, Dan. We'll be all right."

The funny thing was, Patrice thought as the men hurried to join the others, that Pat actually did seem to be all right. She wasn't weeping. She didn't even look particularly unhappy. She was frowning slightly in concentration as she dealt with the task at hand, efficiently sliding her ancient scoop into the dwindling pile of dirt, methodically dropping the clods in place to fill the lowest parts of the rising layers of dirt.

It was a good example to follow. Patrice followed it. It was easier refilling the grave than digging it had been, and then, when it was all in, and they had scraped all the loose dirt possible off the ground, there was a small mound to mark the burial place. Patrice knelt to pat it smooth. She was so absorbed in her task it was a surprise to hear Pat's voice. "Patrice? That's good enough. I'm going to clean up a little."

Another good example to follow, and Patrice followed it. But then, as they knelt beside the stream, she looked over at the others. "Then we'd better see what's going on," she offered.

"Sure," Pat said absently, scrubbing at her hands. The water was cold, and the clayey soil sticky; the dirt didn't want to come off. Then she paused, looking over at Patrice. "Listen. You're not sore at me, are you?"

"About what?" Patrice was honestly baffled for a moment, then clarity came. "Oh, you mean about you making out with Dan-Dan? No, of course not."

Pat didn't seem satisfied with the answer. She was looking at the gravesite. She sighed. "Easy for you to say, maybe," she said. "It might not be so easy for Patsy. She was the one that got killed." Then, just before she plunged her face into the water, she added, "You know what I'm wondering? I wonder if there's any truth to this idea of everybody meeting everybody again at the eschaton. Because if there is Dan and I might have some explaining to do."

As Patrice rinsed the tearstains off her own face she considered what Pat had said. Could it be true that some sort of high-tech heaven was waiting for all of them? For herself, for Patsy—for all of the Pats, including the one on Earth? And for Husbands One and Two (and what would that reunion be like?), and for feckless, ill-tempered Mick Jarvas and all the other people at the observatory, and even for Uncle Cubby, finally getting to see what his heirs had done with his money? Not to mention Hitler and Stalin and Napoleon and everybody else, all the way back to Tiglath-Pilesar and Nebuchadnezzar . . . and Dopey, too, in fact all the Dopeys there had ever been, as well as all the other myriad extraterrestrials in this astonishingly populated universe, wherever found.

She couldn't imagine it. Would Patsy in fact be ticked off at being allowed to get killed? Would it be like the wronged dead of the old superstitions, coming back as ghosts to haunt those who had harmed them in life? Only these wouldn't be the sort of ghosts that contented themselves with dripping blood from an unseen wound, or shrieking pitifully in the night. These would be *real*—at least as real as she would be herself, in this fantastic rising-up time in the remote future.

She lifted her face from the water and stopped herself short. No! It wouldn't be like that at all. If they did see Patsy again, it would be that same Patsy who was themselves. Who knew everything about them and forgave all, just as they forgave themselves—and, for the things that weren't really forgivable, simply accepted them and got on with it.

She laughed out loud and stood up, startling Pat who was drying her face with the hem of her shirt. "No," she said, "if it's all true you won't have to explain. It'll be all right."

36
Patrice

The others were gathered around the guns that lay on the ground, spilled out of the coppery-mesh sack Dopey had brought them in. There were far more than Patrice had expected, and as they approached Rosaleen smiled at them. "Pick a couple for yourselves," she invited. "All the guns are duplicated, so there's plenty to go around."

"But what's going on?" Patrice asked. Dannerman and Dopey were confronting each other; still in the Doc's arms, Dopey's face was at a level with Dannerman's, and they both looked angry.

"Oh, what do you think?" Rosaleen said, sounding exasperated. "Much argumentation. Simply listen and you will hear it all for yourself."

Her voice carried to Dannerman, who twitched slightly but stood his ground. "You stay out of this," he ordered Dopey. "We have to consider our options."

"But you have no options!" Dopey squawked.

"Of course we do! Fighting your damn Horch machines for you is only one of them. We can stay here—"

"You cannot!"

"Why not? You've supplied us with guns. We can defend ourselves in case the amphibians come back . . . or who knows what other wild animals might be around?"

Dopey said plaintively, "You speak such nonsense, Agent Dannerman. There aren't any wild animals on this planet."

"Not even the ones that killed Patsy?" Jimmy asked.

"Not even them. They are simply control groups—exactly like yourselves, you see! There are eight different species out here, kept in separate reservations, and they're all intelligent. Some of them have been here for many, many generations. They're all that's left of races that have become extinct in their home planets—it is," he added boastfully, "in a sense, a kind of ecological thing. But no wild animals."

"What about the furry lizards?" Patrice demanded.

"I know nothing of lizards. Perhaps they were food animals for one of the species. No. The reason you have the guns is to deal with the Horch machines. They are quite large. They have high-powered torches and cutting instruments, and their job is to destroy this whole base."

"So let them," Martín growled. "I vote with Dannerman. We stay here."

The little alien squealed in irritation. "But you cannot! You will die if we stay here?"

Dannerman said soberly, "Maybe we should take that chance. We may be able to find something growing that we can eat so we won't starve—"

"Not starve!" Dopey said impatiently. "Fry. Here, ask your own astronomers, now that they have finished with this foolish ritual. You should understand the problem, Drs. Adcock. Have you not observed the stars?"

Patrice had a sinking feeling, but it was Pat who spoke up. "Are you talking about dangerous radiation, from black holes, supernovas, all that? But there hasn't been any, or we'd all be dead already."

"Of course there has not been any! That is because the Beloved Leaders long ago established a screen around this entire planet so that all lethal radiation was filtered out. But when the power went down, so did the screen."

That stopped them all. Dopey seized his advantage. "So you see," he said, "you have no other option. No. You must help me. I have given you weapons. I have also provided all these bearers, to carry the excess weaponry and whatever else we need for our task. And, of course, to help with Dr. Artzybachova," he added politely. "Now we must restore power and wipe out the remaining Horch surrogates before they finish destroying so much that took so long to build!"

Jimmy Lin emitted a sarcastic yelp. "What, the six of us? Against machines that defeated your own fighters?"

"But your numbers are not a problem," Dopey said in surprise. "Once the standby power is restored we can make many copies of you, all you need—a whole army if you want them, Commander Lin!"

Lin looked flustered, but Dannerman was the one who responded. "The hell you will! We've had enough of making copies!"

Dopey looked astonished. "You object to this? But why? We need not keep the extra copies forever; once the machines are gone we can simply delete the unwanted ones."

"No!" Pat cried.

Dopey stared at her. "Is this some taboo for your people? Well, perhaps we need not make more copies. It is possible that some of your experimental copies may still be alive."

And there was another conversation stopper. Dopey paused, surprised by the sudden silence as everyone was staring at him.

It was Patrice who asked the question, once more angry and startled—and very nearly fed up with Dopey's habit of dropping unexpected surprises on them. "What experimental copies are you talking about?"

Dopey looked uneasy. "Perhaps I neglected to tell you of them," he said apologetically. "There were only a few. Actually, I do not think many will have survived. There was quite heavy fighting in the laboratory area."

It was Rosaleen's turn to be indignant. *"Laboratory?"*

"To investigate your anatomy and biochemistry, of course. How else could the Beloved Leaders know how best to help your people?" And then, when he saw the expressions on their faces, "I was not personally involved in these studies," he added hastily. "Some of the copies may still be quite fit. Please do not argue anymore! Do you want me to take you to look for these other copies or not?"

37
Patrice

One thing you could say about Dan Dannerman—Patrice thought as they approached the stark metal structures of the compound—was that he reacted fast. Conquering the wilderness was out; rescuing their other "copies"—if any—was in.

Dopey would not allow them to enter near their old cell; too far to travel in Horch territory, too dangerous. So they traveled a quarter of the way around the compound perimeter before he paused and pointed to a passage. "There," he said. "This way will be safest—though we must be alert and ready for attack at every moment!"

Everyone stopped, while Dannerman conferred with the little creature. Patrice was glad enough for the chance to sit down. All this activity after all those weeks of confinement was tiring. She glanced up at the sky and shivered. That alien sun was setting; those enemy stars were popping out in all their incredible number, and the breeze had turned cold. She touched the butt of the thirty-shot weapon in its holster under her arm and wondered what it would be like to fire at something that would probably be doing its best to kill her. She was not ready for this kind of adventure—

But, ready or not, it was time to move on. Dannerman finished his conversation with Dopey and turned to give his orders. "Two of the Docs will go first. Then the rest of us, spread out, all but Rosaleen—"

"I can walk!" she protested.

"Sure. When you have to you will, but for now one of the Docs will carry you at the back. And, everybody, *quiet.* Dopey says the Horch machines are not particularly sensitive to sound, but we'll take no chances. All clear? Then let's go."

Patrice shivered again. This time it was excitement, not cold. The last time she had taken part in an invasion of enemy territory she had been ten years old, playing Good Guys and Bad Guys with the Abwyth kids from next door. She was out of practice. She hadn't had a real gun in her hand then, either; probably wouldn't be holding one, ready for action, now, if it weren't for the fact that right in front of her Dan and Jimmy Lin had their guns out. So did Pat, by her side; for them it seemed to be deadly serious.

It didn't seem that way to Patrice. It seemed like just another children's game. Behind the two Docs in single file at the head of the procession and the five humans who were capable—well, more or less capable—of firing their guns were the other Docs. One carried their spare weapons. Then there was another Doc that carried Rosaleen in one of its assorted arms, and the last one carrying Dopey himself. It was a regular circus parade. And why were they in it? Because Dan Dannerman had said so, and what an exasperating man he was. First he warned them all against getting into other people's fights. Then he reversed himself without notice. Now he was—and all the others with him—suddenly a warrior on the side of the Beloved Leaders against the Horch. Patrice gazed darkly at the back of his neck. In a way, she didn't envy Pat for her lover; in some ways Dan was a most unsatisfactory man. Lovers were supposed to communicate. Not Dan Dannerman; you never knew what he was going to be doing next.

But in another way, of course, she envied Pat very much indeed.

She hoped the Doc who was striding ahead of them knew where he was going. Patrice didn't. Nothing looked familiar, except in the way that one patch of desolation looked pretty much like all the others. She had long since stopped wondering about the strange objects they were passing. There was one period, not long after they entered the compound, that she didn't like to think about. First there was a hint of something foul in the air. It became a definite stench—growing, then horribly intense, then gradually fading again—that could be nothing but dead things. She never quite saw the corpses, whatever species they were, but there was no doubt of what she was smelling, and no doubt that there had been a lot of killing somewhere nearby. But after that there was nothing but their slow march, and nothing happening. . . .

Then something did happen.

Between the time Patrice saw the first Doc suddenly turn and begin to run back, squeaking in a shrill soprano, and the time she saw the big silver-colored spidery thing appear from between the orange-colored crystal sphere and the jade pylons and they all began shooting at it, there was only a moment. It was time enough for her to be astonished that the Doc had spoken at all—before that she had never heard one of them make a sound—but then she saw that Dannerman had flung himself to the ground on one side of the corridor, his thirty-shot out and firing, and Jimmy Lin had done the same on the other, and she realized she had to follow their example. It all happened very fast. The Doc was able to run only a few steps before there was this sudden staccato sound, like shrill bees buzzing, *bzhit, bzhit, bzhit.* Patrice saw nothing that looked like either a projectile or a ray, but she saw the effects, all right, as at once the first Doc's head burst open—spray of orange-red blood and tissue flying out in all directions—and then the Horch machine was skating toward them, *fast,* on its spidery wheeled legs. The second Doc leaped forward to catch its fellow—too late—and there was more *bzhit, bzhit* and the whole right side of that one's body exploded, too. But by then everybody was shooting—even Patrice herself, startled at the unexpected recoil from the gun Dannerman had given her and her shots going wild, even Pat, next to her on the ground . . . even Martín Delasquez, standing wobbly but erect in the middle of the passage, but shooting his heavier gun with two hands. They didn't all miss. Pieces flew off the machine. Two of its legs collapsed and it clattered to the ground; a moment later something inside it flared and crackled and it lay still. And behind her, where he had hidden himself behind the massive trunk of the Doc that had been carrying him, Dopey was crying, "Stop firing! The machines do not respond quickly to sound, but it will attract them if you keep on shooting!"

In the sudden silence both Jimmy Lin and Dannerman jumped to their feet and ran to inspect the wrecked machine. Dannerman gave it only a glance, then turned back, leaving Jimmy to kick at the thing suspiciously; Dannerman ran straight to Patrice and dropped to his knees beside her. "Are you all right?" he demanded.

She rolled over to gaze up at him. "I'm fine," she said, "but I'm Patrice. That's your Pat"—who was already getting up and looking toward them—"over there."

The two Docs that had been given the point were both messily dead, but so was the Horch machine. Dopey was fretting. "I should not have used two of them to draw fire. I can only spare one now, but we must not delay. Have you all got loaded guns?"

Dannerman might or might not have been listening; his expression was unreadable. He was standing over the destroyed machine, his gun in one hand, the other arm around Pat's waist beside him. Patrice was standing nearby, somberly watching them. She did, after all, wish it was she that Dannerman was holding. It wasn't envy, exactly. She didn't feel any real jealousy of Pat—she definitely wanted Pat to have someone to hold her, too; she wanted nothing but good for Pat. But it would have been better, she thought, if Dopey had produced an extra Dan Dannerman or two along with the Pat Adcocks. She turned to look at the others. Rosaleen and Martín were fussing over each other, while Jimmy Lin checked the magazine of his gun, and the three remaining Docs were standing quietly, waiting for orders. That was reassuring, a little bit. They had all got through at least this first firefight—well, all but the two dead Docs.

Dannerman kicked at the dead machine, triangular body now blazing quietly, the long legs crumpled. He turned challengingly to Dopey. "If they're that easy to kill, why couldn't your people handle them?"

Dopey looked defensive. "Because there were so many of them! They kept coming. Every time we thought we had them cleaned up the Horch managed to capture another channel and they sent more of them in and it was all to do over again—and, finally, we had no fighters left to oppose them. Please, let us move on; we are very exposed here."

Dannerman shook his head. "Tell me first, how many more of those things are there?"

"How do I know? A few. Not very many, I think—but, please—"

Dannerman disregarded the urging. He had another question: "Are you sure you know where we're going?"

"Out of my own knowledge? No, of course not. How could I? There is so much destruction, I cannot recognize anything. But the bearers do, so please hurry."

Dannerman didn't answer right away. He stood there, with his arm around Pat's waist; he was thinking about something, but Patrice could not guess what. Whatever it was, he did not choose to share it.

Jimmy Lin was losing patience. "Are we going or not?" he demanded.

"Yes, sure," Dannerman said at last, then kissed Pat and took up his place in the procession as Dopey ordained it. With two Docs fewer to deploy, Dopey ordered the one with the weapons to take the point. Then came Dannerman and Jimmy, then Pat and Patrice and Martín; then the other Docs with their passengers, Rosaleen and Dopey himself.

Patrice's heart was still pounding from the excitement of the fight. She had seen shoot-outs on the television news, of course—just before they left there had been the one between the police and the subway terrorists, when the Lenni-Lenape Ghost Dance Revengers tried to blow up Grand Central Terminal, and there had been at least a dozen other battles over the years—but she had never expected to take part in a gunfight herself. She had never imagined someone (well, something) actually trying to kill her! And herself shooting back!

The funny thing was that she wasn't frightened. It had something to do with having a chance to do some shooting herself; it was certainly far better to be taking action, any kind of action, than just having things happen to her. She rehearsed every moment of the fight critically, looking for things she might have done wrong. She resolved to be ready for the weapon's recoil next time—if there was a next time. She wouldn't miss, she vowed . . .

And almost fired her gun in reflex when the lead Doc suddenly stopped, glanced around, then down at the ground.

Then it moved on a few more meters to an intersection and simply stood there, waiting.

Dannerman and Jimmy Lin were the first ones on the spot, and they both recoiled. "Oh, Christ," Jimmy moaned. "Makes me want to puke!" It did Patrice, too, as soon as she saw what they were looking at. It was a corpse—not human, not a Dopey or a Doc—or, more accurately, it was about half of a corpse.

"It's a Bashful," Patrice said, recognizing it: one of the ones she and Patsy had seen before being brought to the cell.

"It looks like that other Dopey did, after we killed him," Lin said in disgust. Apparently the built-in waste-disposal system in the flooring had been in the process of disposing of this bit of waste when the power went off.

"Yes," said Dopey, climbing down from his bearer and puffing toward them, "it is one of our fighters, mercilessly murdered by the abominable Horch machines. And, see, he has his weapon with him."

"This thing?" Dannerman asked, picking up the shiny object that lay next to the corpse. He handled it cautiously, Jimmy Lin and Martín fidgeting as close to him as they could stand, both obviously yearning to get their own hands on the thing. Patrice had no such desire. She didn't want to touch it at all; it looked deadly. Clearly it was not designed for a human being. It didn't have a stock; it had a belly plate of some dark red substance that looked rubbery; it didn't have a trigger, but a pair of metal loops, like the finger holes on a pair of scissors. And it didn't have sights.

When Jimmy Lin pointed that out Dopey said impatiently, "Sights? Why would it have sights? Such things are not necessary.

When it is aimed there is a beam of green radiation, like a pocket torch—"

"You mean a flashlight?"

"Yes, are they not the same thing? That green ray is not the particle flux itself, only a beam of light to help you guide it, but what you touch with the beam of light will be destroyed by the particle flux. To fire it? Nothing is easier. You put your fingers in those loops and draw them together; the closer they are drawn, the more energy the particle beam carries."

"Like this?" Jimmy Lin asked, experimenting.

Dopey closed his eyes in silent despair. "Yes, exactly like that," he said, obviously restraining himself, "and if there had been any power for the weapon you would have killed Dr. Artzybachova. Please, all of you! I know you are not experienced with this weapon, but you must take care!"

To Patsy's surprise, Dannerman had another of those off-the-main-point questions. "So why are you bothering with us amateurs? Why don't you make more of your trained fighters?"

Dopey looked evasive. "Yes, that would be better in some ways, perhaps," he agreed. "But—"

"But you can't do it, right?"

Dopey hesitated for a moment. "That is true," he said at last. "At this moment. Once we have restored the power—once we have access to the damaged terminals—then it is quite possible that we could do so. But please, let us not waste time—"

Dannerman held his ground. "That's the other thing. So we get the power on, and we kill the rest of the Horch machines for you—"

"For all of us, Agent Dannerman! Your lives are also at risk!"

"Whatever you say. Then what?"

"Why, then we attempt to restore the damaged terminals. If we cannot, we simply wait for the Beloved Leaders to restore communication. Is that not obvious? Now I must insist—"

"Which will be when?"

"Oh, Agent Dannerman, why do you choose this time to ask foolish questions? It will happen when it happens. First the Beloved Leaders must send another physical spacecraft with a new tachyon terminal dedicated to the proper channel. How long will that take to get here? I do not know how long. Since such a spacecraft cannot exceed the speed of light, perhaps very long. But, you see," he added reasonably, "the length of time does not matter. If we grow too old to be serviceable we will simply generate new copies of ourselves to replace us. That will be no problem."

"No problem?" Dannerman repeated, mildly enough.

"Not at all. And we can repeat it as often as necessary. In that way we can continue to carry on our duties here for centuries if that is necessary. Now no more questions! We must go!"

38
Patrice

Until, without warning, the lead Doc stopped short and stood motionless, waiting for the rest to catch up, Patrice hardly noticed where they were going. She could not get what Dopey had said out of her mind. *For centuries, if that is necessary.* But centuries of what? Of carrying out Dopey's plan? Growing old, in this miserable place? Never going home again? Manufacturing a new Pat Adcock and a new Dopey and a new everybody else when the present ones were too old or too enfeebled to carry on? And then what? Then quietly allowing themselves to die, with the next generation in place . . . and the next . . . and the next. . . .

Whatever joy that prospect might have for Dopey, it had none for Patrice. On the other hand—

On the other hand, she told herself, to test out the implications of it all, those replacements would likely include an allotment of new Dan Dannermans, so that there might be enough of him for Patrice to have one of her own. But then what? Make some more Pat Adcocks, too, so that Martín and Jimmy Lin might have mates as well? (And how would those new Pat Adcocks feel about that?) And what did you say to the new arrival, blinking and confused as he stepped out of the machine: "Hi, I'm Patrice, and we've copied you so that I can get laid now and then. Unfortunately there's not much else to do around here. But welcome."

The thought was comical enough to make Patrice laugh out loud. It wasn't a happy laugh, and it made Pat turn and frown at her. But none of the others heard, because Dopey was pounding his little fists on a machine that looked like a huge, green-enameled refrigerator and shrieking joyously, "That's it! That's the terminal."

Patrice looked around, bewildered. Everybody else seemed excited about it; even Rosaleen and Martín, supporting each other, tottered over to touch the thing, and Pat and Dannerman were hugging each other. "I've been here before," she whispered, so softly that no one heard. But it was true. It had been a different place then, everything working and intact, but it was where she and Patsy had first discovered themselves in this place.

It was different now, and what struck Patrice was the pervasive odor that hung in the air. It was the same decaying-meat stink she had smelled before. There definitely had been fighting around here, she thought. The terminal was intact, and so was everything on that side of the little square they were in. But on the other side ruined machinery and long-dead ashes showed that somebody had been doing something violent not long before. Dannerman turned to Dopey. "You said you were going to bring us to the experimental copies!" he said accusingly.

Dopey looked away from the Doc he was talking to. "The copies? Yes. Their space was quite near here. I do not see them, so perhaps—" He shrugged and returned to the Doc, which silently listened, then moved away.

Dannerman advanced on the alien, his gun in his hand, his expression dangerous. "If there are any human beings here we want to see them. Now!"

Dopey looked up at him, the kitten whiskers trembling, the plume draggled. "Certainly you can look around, Agent Dannerman. If any survive I do not think they would have gone far; this is where their food was kept. But please, remain on guard! The Horch machines were careful not to destroy this terminal, so it is quite likely one or more will be somewhere near this area to watch over it. And—"

He stopped, gazing toward the second Doc. Which had abruptly moved swiftly toward the wreckage and begun to pull away one of the metal plates. There was movement behind it. At once everybody turned, guns ready—

A face peered out of the space behind the plate. It was looking directly at Patrice. And, "Oh, God," said yet another Dr. Patrice Adcock, "you're more of *me*!"

39
Patrice

It all evened out in the long run, Patrice thought to herself—wondering if she were going out of her mind: You lose one Pat, you get another to fill the gap. This particular Pat, though, was something special; she had clearly been through hell, even more hell than the rest of them. Her face was haggard, her bearing twitchy. Patrice longed to comfort her.

But reunions had to wait. Dopey had no particular interest in one Pat more or less—his main concern was dispatching one of the Docs to find the standby generator and start it up—and the only interest the new Pat showed in Dopey and his Docs was to stay as far away from them as she could. "First things first," Dannerman ordered. "I want somebody with a gun at every entrance in case one of those things shows up."

Nobody argued, though Patrice would have preferred to fuss over the new Pat, as Rosaleen alone could be spared to do, instead of standing guard, weapon out and ready, where she could see a few dozen meters down a passage. She wasn't doing a very good job of guarding. She couldn't help peering worriedly over her shoulder at the new Pat Adcock. The woman looked really terrible. Extreme fatigue, yes; that figured. Marks of pain and stress on her face, why not? She'd obviously been through a tough time; but there was something else that was nagging at Patrice while her new copy was doing her best to answer questions. And there were lots of questions. "Are there any others?" "Not anymore." "Do you mean the others are dead?" "Christ, yes! Can't you smell them? But listen, do you guys have anything to eat?"

Well, they didn't; Dopey had promised there would be all the food they wanted, once the terminal was working again, so why encumber themselves? (But Pat had observed he'd taken food for himself; probably that didn't count as an encumbrance.) He was fidgeting about, doing his best to ignore the petty human concerns. "Please," he begged in agitation. "It will be some time before the bearer can have the power on line, perhaps as much as an hour. Then all will be well, but now we are still in great danger. Be vigilant! We must not be stopped now, when we are so close— What?" Dannerman was saying something to him, pointing to the new Pat. "Oh, very well," Dopey said impatiently, and glanced at the two remaining Docs. Who at once moved toward the new Pat. . . .

Who shrieked "Keep them away from me!" and turned as though about to run, but Dannerman stopped her.

"It's all right," he soothed. "Honest! I just want you checked over. This one's done it for us before, with Martín and Rosaleen. He's a kind of medical specialist—"

"I know what kind of specialists they are!" But by then the one Doc had her firmly held and the other was gently tapping and probing with its smaller arms, just as they had done with Martín Delasquez. The new Pat whimpered softly throughout the examination, but she didn't resist. The procedure took only a few moments. Then the Docs released her and stepped back, once again motionless in that corpse-like standby mode.

"This transcription appears to be well enough," Dopey announced. "There is a certain amount of malnutrition, yes, but that will be mended when we have the terminal going. Otherwise her condition is normal, apart from some exhaustion—allowing, of course, for the fact that she is pregnant."

One conversation stopper after another, Patrice thought; the creature was full of them. She backed away from her sentry post—not so far that she couldn't still see down the short corridor, far enough so that she could look their new recruit in the face. "Are you, uh, all right?" she asked.

The woman stared at her, backing away from Dopey and the Docs. "*He* says so," she said shortly. And then, "Well, I guess I am. More or less." She was looking from Pat to Patrice; it seemed a time for introductions.

"I'm Patrice; this is Pat. There was another one—well," Patrice said, firmly closing that topic, "there was another one, but she died. What should we call you?"

The newcomer opened her eyes wide at that, but she answered civilly enough. "The others just called me Pat, mostly, because there was usually only one of us alive at a time. But Rosaleen said I was Pat Five, if that helps."

Dannerman swore. "Pat *Five?* They had that many of you?"

"They had at least that many of me," she corrected. "I don't guarantee the count. But you can call me Five if you want to. What's happening?" And when they had done their best to fill her in she scowled at the Dopey. "You mean the best we can hope for is to stay alive with the bird and the brutes in this wreckage—forever?"

The Dopey craned his neck to peer at her over his plume. "Wreckage? But it will not remain wreckage, Dr. Adcock Five. Once the Horch problem is eliminated we will build it all up again, better than ever, you will see. That will be a job for the bearers, that is what they are good at."

"They seem to be pretty handy gadgets to have around," Dannerman remarked, causing Patrice to give him a sharp look. What was the matter with the man? Was he losing his mind . . . or thinking about something he didn't want to discuss? She wondered which.

"Oh, yes, highly intelligent," Dopey was agreeing. "Unfortunately their people foolishly declined to cooperate with the Beloved Leaders. They resisted quite violently, in fact. Ultimately it was necessary to dispatch most of their race directly to the eschaton. These specimens have been preserved; they are quite tractable now, since they were amended to remove their violent natures. Of course, they are no longer capable of acting on their own very much, but they are very good at following orders." Dopey's mind didn't seem to be on what he was saying; he was twisting in all directions to peer down the various approaches. "You've all got your weapons ready? We could be attacked at any time."

Patrice exhaled softly. *Amended,* she repeated to herself. *Quite tractable.*

She looked around at the others to see if they were thinking what she was. She couldn't tell. Dannerman had gone off to talk to Martín and Rosaleen, the others simply looked grim. Whether it was because, like herself, they were considering the possibility that the Beloved Leaders might have some similar plans for the human race she did not know.

"Damn," Pat said ruefully. "You know, I was almost getting to like the little shit."

Pat Five looked at her curiously. "For God's sake, why?"

Lamely, "Well . . . he brought us food. And other things. We would have starved without him."

Pat Five said in disgust, "Oh, Pat, what's the matter with you? You don't really understand what kind of people they are, do you? Tell me something. When you see the supermarket fish clerk checking the pumps in the lobster tank, do you think she does it because she wants the lobsters to be happy?" She glared at Pat, then abruptly added, "Why didn't you ever ask me how I got pregnant?"

Uncomfortably, "I did wonder, I mean about the implants."

"Right, the implants," said Pat Five, nodding. "The implants made a real problem for the damn birds. When they found out about them they just took the things right out, and, honey, that was not fun. Not for me, even though I was the lucky one; I survived the operation. Dan Three told me that the first two of us they tried didn't. Of course, they didn't bother with anesthesia. . . . And then they killed Dan, too. I think it was something about studying how the human body reacted to pain; he was screaming so loud I bet he could be heard all over the compound."

Patrice shuddered, but there was something else she wanted to know. As delicately as possible, she began, "Who was the—ah—the—?"

"The father?" Pat Five shrugged morosely. "Rosaleen thought it was Jimmy, one of the Jimmys, but I don't know. I'm not sure I ever met the gent." She glanced casually at the surviving Jimmy, who was standing suddenly thunderstruck. "All I know for sure is they had sperm they'd collected—I don't know whose—and so they did it to me by artificial insemination, you see. Looked like they just didn't want us to have any fun at all."

"Hey!" said Jimmy Lin, finding his voice at last. "I mean—hey!"

Pat Five scowled at him. "What are you getting excited about? I'm not going to ask for child support."

"It isn't that," he protested. "I just—you know—I mean, I feel sort of responsible if it was my, uh, sperm—"

Pat Five looked at him thoughtfully, then softened. "Well, don't worry about it. Listen, I think being pregnant had its advantage. I'm pretty sure that's why they kept me alive when the Horch started shooting and the birds terminated all the others. They'd gone to a lot of trouble to knock me up; I guess they didn't want to waste all that work." She glanced at Dopey, nervously making his rounds of the guard posts. "There were two of those goddam birds arguing about it in the examining room," she said, nodding toward the shattered partitions at the far end of their space, "while a couple of the goons held me down. I was sure I'd had it. But then the birds walked off and the goons just dropped me and went away. And I've been here alone ever since."

* * *

Patrice couldn't stand still another minute. Pat Five's tale of horrors was more than she could handle. She moved toward the broken partitions. "Over here?" she asked. "Is that where they were doing it?"

"Don't go wandering away from your post!" Jimmy Lin ordered, and Pat Five chimed in:

"I wouldn't go there at all if I were you—"

But that came too late. Patrice had reached the partitions and peered through them. She couldn't see clearly in the minimal light that filtered in from outside, but that, Patrice thought, the contents of her stomach trying to rise up through her throat, was a good thing. There were bodies there. A Dannerman. A Jimmy Lin. Another of those half-absorbed corpses, caught incompletely flushed away when the power died, that was facedown but, she thought, probably had been another Jimmy Lin. The stench of decay was awful. She retreated to the others, holding her hand over her face.

Pat Five laughed—not unkindly. "I warned you," she said. "I've been living with that for days. The birds said it was all right, you know; they just sent them on early to the eschaton."

"So they told you about the eschaton?" Pat asked.

"That Tipler business, sure. They were asking a lot of questions about it just before they terminated the guys— Is something the matter?"

Pat and Patrice were exchanging glances. "You remembered the name!" Pat cried.

"Of course I remembered the name. Frank Tipler. Tulane University. He wrote a book. I also remembered that old what's-his-face told us it was a lot of crap, since the Hubble Constant showed that the universe wasn't ever going to collapse again anyway."

"I've been wondering about that myself," Patrice said, and Pat put in:

"Dan says it doesn't matter if it's true. What matters is that the Horch and the Beloved Leaders act as if they believe it's true, and—"

She stopped there, blinking; they were all blinking, as suddenly the lights were on. And from across the space Dopey chortled: "We have the power! Now we can serve the Beloved Leaders again!"

40
Patrice

The return of the lighting made things clearer but didn't make them better; the place was still a ruin. An eye-hurting flicker told Patrice that, in spite of damage, just beside her one of those magic mirror walls was trying to reconstitute itself near the "examining room": bright mirror surface leaping from floor to ceiling, then crackling and turning dark again, over and over. "Stand back, Patrice!" Rosaleen warned urgently, but there was no danger there; Patrice was already hastily backing away. At the tachyon terminal Dopey was babbling in excitement as a Doc was doing something to its controls. Patrice couldn't see what, exactly, but she couldn't even see the controls, for that matter. Whatever they were, they were invisible to her. But Dopey was in ecstasy—delight, certainly; fear, too. "This is our most dangerous time," he called, then, joyously: "See, here are some weapons! Take them! Be ready! The machines will surely detect this energy, and they—oh, hurry!" But he was talking to the Doc again, not to the humans, who were quick to seize the trombonelike things as the Doc lifted them out of the cavernous interior of the terminal, then closed the door for the next batch.

"What about our food?" Jimmy Lin demanded, hefting the weapon.

Dopey looked at him distractedly. "Please be careful with that, now there is power! Food? Of course we'll get food from your Starlab, as soon as we are prepared to deal with the Horch machines. First the weapons, then a few more fighters. I believe we should make more copies of you, Agent Dannerman, since it is probable that there will be some losses. Also General Delasquez and Commander Lin; I think it is best to copy the males first, don't you? Since, as I understand it, all of you males have had some weapons training, while the females have not. Or not very much. But of course," he added hastily, turning away to urge the Doc to greater speed, "if you wish we will copy more females as well, as soon as we have finished destroying the Horch machines—"

"Shut up," Dannerman said, pointing one of the weapons at Dopey. Who goggled at him uncomprehendingly.

"But I have asked you, Agent Dannerman, to be very careful with that weapon! It could easily accidentally go off—"

"Not accidentally," Dannerman said.

Patrice had never seen the alien look so bewildered. He stared, his plume agitatedly flickering, then turned to the nearest armed human, which happened to be Martín Delasquez. "I order you to shoot him," he said.

Martín glanced quizzically at Dannerman, then shifted his weapon as well to cover Dopey. "No," he said. "Do what Dannerman says."

Dopey was wringing his little hands again. "But what— But the Horch machines—"

Dannerman said, "It's simple. If you can get things from Starlab, you can send things to Starlab. Like us."

"That is true, yes," Dopey said, uncomprehending but reasonable. "However—"

"So do it. Tell that thing to transmit us, right away."

"No, no!" Dopey cried in panic. "We must fight them here! The Beloved Leaders would wish that!"

Rosaleen had been listening intently; now she took a hand. "Dopey," she said soothingly, "you just haven't thought it through. If we fight the machines here we might lose, don't you see? What Dan means, if we go to Starlab we'll be safe. There's only one terminal there; we can guard it day and night, until your Beloved Leaders get around to reestablishing the communication channel there. That's what you had in mind, isn't it, Dan? Wouldn't that work?"

Dannerman didn't bother to answer. Dopey looked bewildered. Then, pettishly, he said, "Yes, I suppose so, perhaps. But I absolutely forbid it. I—"

Dannerman put his fingers in the loops of the weapon. "Don't forbid," he said, the gun squarely pointing at Dopey. "You'll do it our way or you'll have failed your assignment because you're dead . . . and then what will you tell your bosses when your eschaton comes around?"

* * *

It wasn't that easy. Dopey hadn't stopped arguing. In fact, he never did stop his frantic arguing—or pleading—even after he had given in and allowed the Doc to start the transmissions. Dannerman had to singe a corner of the alien's plume with the weapon before he would go that far.

But it was happening.

They were going home! Patrice stared in wonder and unbelief as the first batch entered the chamber—Rosaleen and the two other Pats—and the door closed behind them. To take them *home*! Which meant that in a moment Patrice herself could go home! She could hardly believe it, could not take in the sudden change in her outlook—first a dreary and interminable existence in the ruins, then, in the blink of an eye, the sudden prospect of return to Starlab—to *Earth*—to her *life*! And it was all *happening*! The terminal door opened again and it was empty. "Now you!" Dannerman ordered, pointing to Jimmy Lin. "And take Dopey with you, but keep an eye on—"

He stopped, listening. Dopey squealed in terror, and then Patrice heard it, too: a heavy, rapid thudding, and the distant buzzing sound like a hive of bees. The Doc that had started the generator was running ponderously toward them—

And behind it, rapidly catching up, one of the spider-legged machines.

This time Patrice was ready. She had her gun in both hands, aiming it carefully. Whether she hit the thing or not she couldn't tell—both Martín and Jimmy Lin were firing at the same time, and she saw the pale beam from Dannerman's Beloved Leaders weapon wavering toward the thing as well. Someone did. The machine spun around crazily and burst into flame, just as the other had.

Dannerman didn't wait. "Do it, Lin!" he ordered. "You too, Dopey; there'll be more."

But Dopey was complaining, wringing his little hands. "I cannot function without the bearers!"

"Then take them, damn it! All but the one running the transmitter!" And as the alien started to object, simply picked him up and threw him inside. The two Docs followed stolidly, making a tight fit; but then the door closed and they were gone. As the door opened again, Dannerman looked around and saw Patrice standing there. "Now you," he ordered. "Martín, too. I'll hold them off—"

Patrice obeyed. . . .

But not Martín. He grunted, "Who elected you hero?" . . . and shoved Dannerman bodily inside, as the door closed.

All Patrice saw was a pale lavender flash that went right through her closed eyelids, and a sickening jolt. And then the door opened and they all fell in a heap out into the weightlessness of Starlab. "That son of a bitch Martín," Dannerman groaned. "We'll wait. Maybe he'll make it. . . ."

They did wait. For long minutes. But Martín didn't come.

41
Patrice

Never had the stale air of Starlab smelled so much like home. Never had the queasiness of microgravity felt so dear. Patrice couldn't stop grinning—nor either of the other Pats, nor Jimmy Lin, nor even Rosaleen, arms crossed over her belly to hold in some unannounced pain. Only Dopey and Dannerman seemed immune. Dopey, held in the arms of one of the Docs, was babbling: "Please, you must keep a weapon drawn and pointed at the terminal, in case one of the Horch machines follows. Why are you not listening to me? But it is *urgent*!"

And, though Dannerman had his gun in his hand—his own gun, not one of the now useless energy weapons—he was indeed not listening. He was looking around the Starlab corridor as though trying to get his bearings. "Jimmy," he snapped. "Do you think you can find the astronaut return capsule? Go check it out. I want to know if it's still workable . . . and if you think you can fly it."

"Sure," Lin said, "if that's what you want. But wouldn't it be easier to radio for a rescue ship?"

"Do you want to hang around here? Just do it. Go." And as Lin went off Dopey was frantically demanding to know what was happening.

"But you can't just leave the terminal unguarded, Agent Dannerman! Have you not heard me? If one of those machines follows—"

"It won't," Dannerman said grimly. "Stand back." He took aim at the closed door of the terminal and fired the whole clip.

"Now, that was foolish of you, Dan," Rosaleen said gravely. "How did you know they wouldn't ricochet around and kill us all?"

"I didn't," Dannerman admitted. "I guess I didn't think. But it looks like it worked." The high-speed loads had gone right through the door, and from inside there was a crackling and a smell of something electrical burning. "But let's make sure," he said. "Where's that bar you conked Jimmy with?"

Dopey gazed in horror as Dannerman methodically began to smash at the portal. "No!" he screamed over the crash of metal. "You mustn't! We'll be cut off from the Beloved Leaders until they send another drone, perhaps for many, many years!"

"So I hope," Dannerman agreed. "In fact I'm counting on it. The longer the better. If it's long enough, just maybe—the next time you guys come around to visit us—we'll know how to handle you."

After

Later . . . much later, and a very long distance away . . .

Dan Dannerman saw the pale lavender flash; the door of the tachyon terminal opened and he leaped triumphantly out, eager to join the others in the safety of Starlab.

Startlingly, the others weren't there.

Still more startlingly, he wasn't even in Starlab. He was in a place he'd never seen. A pair of the wheel-footed Horch machines were standing there, but they weren't shooting at him. Nor could he have fired back if they had; he had no gun in his hand. Behind him he heard the door cycle shut behind him, then open again. The disheveled figure of Dopey spilled out, catapulting into him. The little creature glared at him. Then, as he saw the quietly buzzing machines observing them, Dopey's plume turned woeful gray and he began to sob.

"What's happened?" Dannerman demanded. And, clutching at straws, "Did we die? Is this your damn eschaton?"

Dopey stared at him mournfully: "Eschaton? Oh, you are a great fool, Agent Dannerman! Of course we have not yet reached the eschaton. We simply have been copied once more . . . and now we are in the hands of the Horch."

THE SIEGE OF ETERNITY

With affection and gratitude this book is dedicated to my shipmates on the schooner Rembrandt van Ryjn, *who know why.*

Before

The world was going about its everyday business when something happened that was quite strange.

For one part of the world, that everyday business it was going about amounted to nothing more than watching its television screens. Some of the world's people gazed at a prizefight in Kenya, some watched cop shows and soap operas in the Americas, a tiny fraction sat somnolent before the finals of the English National snooker matches. When those programs were interrupted for a news bulletin that part of the world was seriously annoyed.

The bulletin that interrupted their programs quickly made the viewers forgive the annoyance—at least, it did for that fraction of those viewers who believed it was real. The bulletin said that a genuine message from space had been received on a seldom-used radio frequency. Most of the message was indecipherable. A small portion was easier to decode and it turned out to be a crude form of video. Before long the simple animated drawing it displayed filled all the world's screens.

The animated sequence started with a dark screen, except for one tiny pinpoint of intense brilliance. Then that spot exploded. Smaller, less brilliant spots of light flew in all directions. That runaway expansion gradually slowed. Then it stopped entirely and reversed itself as all the spots, first slowly, then at increasing velocity, fell back to the center of the screen.

That was it. That was all there was.

As entertainment, it was pretty poor stuff. But, after all, it did come from some off-Earth source. The people at the radio telescopes were sure of that; so the scientists and the newsmakers began to try to figure out what the cartoon meant. Their best guess was that it represented a condensed account of the life of the universe: beginning in the Big Bang, expanding as far as that original impetus would carry it, then recollapsing into the Big Crunch as everything fell back together again. So said the pundits. But not even they could think of any good reason why some extraterrestrials would want to tell the human world about it.

However, that wasn't the end of it. A few months later there was another of the same. This one was somewhat more interesting, too. It had people in it—well, sort of people, at least, though they were not in any way human ones.

This second message ran a little longer than the first. It started with that same old birth-and-death-of-the-universe bit, only this time a figure then appeared. The figure looked either comical or terrifying, depending on how seriously you took it. The creature depicted was as skinny as a scarecrow, and it had a head with a wide, toothed mouth that grinned like a Halloween pumpkin. Its "hands" were a forest of fingers, at least a dozen of them on each side; each digit ended in a menacingly sharp talon, and what the creature was doing with them was pitilessly crushing the bright coal that had been the universe. It wasn't alone, either. Around it appeared seven other, smaller figures, each one uglier than the next. One had a beard. One had a stupid smile. One had half-closed eyes. All were perfectly hideous, by the standards of any ethnic group on Earth.

That was it. A moment later the picture winked out. All that was left was the attempts of the world's savants (and some of the world's non-savants, who played it for laughs) to figure out what it was all about.

Some people, especially the people who made their living as the world's stand-up comics, took it to be a joke. It didn't take some of the comedians very long to identify the scarecrow as the one from Oz, and not much longer than that to give identities to the seven others. They mixed up their children's classics, to be sure. But the one with the beard they called Doc, the dumbly smiling one Dopey, the drowsy-eyed one Sleepy: why, they were the Seven Ugly Space Dwarfs, though there was no Snow White anywhere to be found.

Not everyone was amused. The world's terrorist crazies were getting particularly active around then, and some people thought the message might have something to do with that. Others took it to be a warning of some modern-day Armageddon about to happen, or perhaps an advance notice of the Second Coming of Christ.

It wasn't any of those things, though. As it turned out, it was a whole lot worse.

1

Uptown traffic was terrible and there was an abandoned vehicle on the Henry Hudson Elway at Sixty-first Street that everybody was afraid to approach until the bomb squad got there. Colonel Morrisey's driver had to detour all the way over to Broadway. It was snowing enough to slow everyone down, and the traffic went from terrible to worse.

Fortunately they wouldn't be coming back that way, because a plane would be waiting near the yacht basin on the river. But the woman who was on her way to arrest, or rearrest, her favorite agent was getting short-tempered. Her name was Hilda Jeanne Morrisey. She had kept that name unchanged all her life, even through her two marriages—both of them brief, ancient and (as she now thought) pretty damn stupid, since there were so many less troublesome ways of having sex. Hilda Morrisey stood a hundred and sixty centimeters tall and

10 A.M. Traffic Advisory

The New Jersey Turnpike is mined between Exits 14 and 15 southbound. One lane is open during mine-removal activities.

An abandoned car, presumed booby-trapped, is in the northbound Henry Hudson Elevated Highway at Sixty-first Street and traffic is diverted.

The Lenni-Lenape Ghost Dance Revengers have declared a free-fire zone within four hundred meters of the World Trade Center from 4:00 to 4:30 P.M. today.

No other warnings currently in effect.

weighed fifty kilograms, give or take a kilo or so. That weight also had not changed since her long-ago days as a police cadet, although it was true that it seemed to take more and more effort to keep it so. Her rank in the National Bureau of Investigation was full colonel. It had taken a lot of work on her part to keep that unchanged, too. Colonel Morrisey was long overdue for the promotion that the Bureau's higher brass kept trying to force on her.

The thing about that promotion wasn't that Hilda Morrisey objected to either the higher pay or the higher rank. What she minded was the consequences. Being promoted one step higher would automatically move her to a desk in the NBI headquarters in Arlington, Virginia, and Hilda hated desk jobs.

The place where she felt at home was in a communications truck in, say, Nebraska, commanding a raid on their rad-right religious militias, or flying high over the Sea of Marmara to listen to the furtive, coded reports of the agent she had run into the Kurdish command post somewhere on the slopes of Mt. Ararat. Or, for that matter, her present assignment in New York, which was recruiting bilingual Japanese-Americans to penetrate the car factories in Osaka, who were apparently violating the trade agreements by using New Guinea–made parts in their allegedly all-Japanese cars.

Anywhere, in short, but in a desk job. A brigadier's star was hers by right of seniority, but accepting it would cost her all those fun jobs. True, Bureau policy was "Up or Out," but not for Hilda. She had been beating that rule for years. When the personnel people got too antsy about her status they always had to buck the question up to the director himself. Who always said, "Hilda won't take Up, and she's just too damn good for Out. Give the silly bitch another waiver." And they always did.

The other thing about Colonel Hilda was that, even at never-mind-how-old, she was still a pretty neat-looking woman—which is to say one who had very little trouble in attracting any man who attracted her. Like, for instance, the man friend of the moment, Wilbur Carmichael, who—once this distasteful job was complete—she had every intention of giving a call that evening.

But the other thing about those jobs she liked so well was that every once in a while they had a bad spot. Like the present one, which required her to do something she really hated, namely to arrest—or rearrest—one of her own.

When they reached the corner of Jim Daniel Dannerman's block Sergeant McEvoy had to slam on the brakes to avoid hitting the overflow from a minor riot going on. Two sidewalk vendors were having an argument in the snow. It had got violent. Punches were being thrown, and one of them had overturned the other's tray of inflation-beating collectibles. Tarot cards and genuine guaranteed simulated Confederate currency were all over the sludgy, gray-black snow at the curb. The bystanders had joined in, and two street cops were doing their best to cool everybody down. When they caught sight of Master Sergeant McEvoy's uniform they hastily cleared a path for the Bureau van.

In front of Dannerman's apartment building Hilda unbuckled herself and looked over at the sergeant. "Target status?"

Sergeant McEvoy already had his head down over his instrument panel. "He's back in his room. He got himself one of those gyro sandwiches at the place on the corner and took it back to his room to eat."

"I hope he eats fast," Hilda said, stepping out into wet slush.

A little man was waddling hastily toward her. He wore a fleece jacket, a wool cap and an armband that said *Neighborhood Watch* and he was shaking, of all things, a golf club at her. A golf club! Obviously one of those nuts who had some sort of airy-fairy objection to carrying a gun like everybody else. He was belligerent enough for anybody, though. "Move it, lady!" he barked. "No double-parking today; you got to leave room for the plows to get through." Then, as he caught sight of the sergeant stepping out of the other side of the van—Sergeant Horace McEvoy, in full Federal Police Force uniform, big as a house and with his hand on the butt of his shotgun, the man added, "Oh." He didn't look impressed. He just looked surly, but he backed out of the way.

As Hilda got out of the elevator on Dannerman's floor she saw the landlady peeking at her out of one of the rooms. Clearly the woman recognized Hilda Morrisey. She didn't say anything, though she was looking surly, too.

The colonel let herself into Dannerman's room with her own key, and caught him in the act of taking off his wet socks. He was sober, if unshaved. He didn't look like the agent she had commanded through a dozen tough assignments, but then no one could look like an agent when he was wearing a house-arrest radio collar. "Oh, shit, Hilda," he said, wearily but unsurprised. "Don't you ever knock? I could've been doing something private."

"You don't have anything private anymore, Danno," she told him. "Did you sign that release yet?"

He touched his spy collar. "You know damn well that I didn't."

She nodded, since it was the truth, but only said, "Then put your socks back on. They want you in Arlington. You can eat your lunch on the plane."

* * *

Dannerman didn't ask any questions—not in his room, not in the car that took them to the VTOL pad by the river, not on the way to Arlington. He chewed away at his cold and congealing lamb sandwich with full attention. He didn't even ask for anything to drink with it. When the sandwich was all swallowed and its paper wrappings neatly stowed in the seat back, Dannerman closed his eyes. He kept them that way until the plane circled the Washington Monument, preparing to set down at the Bureau's pad across the Potomac. Colonel Morrisey approved. It was precisely the way she would have comported herself if, unimaginably, she had ever found herself in his position.

Hilda Morrisey was as fond of Dannerman as she ever let herself get of any of the field agents she was charged to run. She certainly didn't *spoil* them, but they were—well—family. As long as they remembered that she was the head of their family, with the power to punish or, occasionally, reward, Hilda gave them her unflinching support and even a little bit of as much as she had to give in the way of affection. Dannerman, now, had had quite a lot of both. The man was often a pain in the ass, and irritatingly likely to go off on tangents of his own, and at such times he needed to be brought back in line. But he generally got the job done.

Hilda's affection for Dan Dannerman wasn't sexual. At least it wasn't exactly sexual, though at rare times when she had nothing better to do she had let herself daydream a little about Danno as a stud. She certainly wasn't sexually jealous of him. She knew that he was currently banging some actress in that little theater group in Coney Island he played around with, plus God knew how many other previous women, now and then, when he was out in the field—well, God knew, but He wasn't the only one who knew. So did Hilda, because it was her business to know that sort of thing. She had sometimes even felt a little hostility toward the other women she knew Dannerman bedded, like that Kraut terrorist bimbo who had put him in the hospital. Hilda had to admit she'd enjoyed putting the cuffs on that one.

But it didn't pay to think that way about Dan Dannerman. Not only could she not afford to get sexually involved with anyone in that-much deep shit, but he was her property. The Bureau had strict rules about that. And so did she.

Dannerman opened his eyes at last when the sound of the plane's

Federal Reserve Inflation Bulletin

The morning recommended price adjustment for inflation is set at 0.37%, reflecting an annualized rate of 266%. Federal Reserve Chairman Walter C. Boettger predicts continuing moderation in the inflation rate for the next sixty days.

engines changed. They were switching to hover mode; they had arrived. While the plane was depositing itself on the landing pad by the three-story structure that was the visible part of the Bureau's headquarters Hilda peered outside. Three people were waiting in the cold drizzle. It wasn't until they were out of the aircraft and Sergeant McEvoy and the two headquarters guards were hustling Dannerman away that Hilda realized that the third of the waiting men, his face obscured by the rain hood, was Deputy Director Marcus Pell himself.

Pell didn't offer to shake hands, and Colonel Morrisey didn't bother to salute. "Good to see you again, sir," she said, electing to be a little more deferential than usual. "Now, unless you've got something you need me here for, I guess I'll just catch the return flight."

He gave her the smile she specially disliked, the one that said he was about to give her an order she didn't want to hear. "Not today, Hilda. I want you to sit in on the Ananias team briefing before we interrogate your boy again."

"Sir! I've got this Japanese car-parts thing—"

"Screw the Japanese car parts. Don't look so unhappy; we've got some lunch for you, if you haven't eaten yet? Fine. Let's go."

There was no use arguing, but she hesitated. "What about Dannerman?"

"Well, what about Dannerman? He can sweat for a while. Do him good."

The Operation Ananias team had expanded since the last time Hilda visited Arlington. A dozen people waited in the deputy director's private briefing room, half of them strangers. As promised there was a small salad and a plate of sandwiches at each place on the blond-oak table, and big ceramic coffee jugs scattered handily about. Some people were eating, and that was good enough for her. As soon as she was seated she began to follow their example.

The deputy director, in no hurry to get started, was thoughtfully sipping at a cup of coffee while keying through his notepad. The men and women around the table were murmuring to each other or staring into space—except for the woman across the table, who was signaling for Hilda's attention. It was Pell's vice deputy, Daisy Fennell. She was pretending to scribble with one hand on the palm of the other, looking at Hilda with a questioningly raised eyebrow. Hilda got the message. She shook her head: no, Dannerman hadn't signed. Fennell pantomimed a sigh of resignation and went back to her own notepad.

Hilda chewed methodically (lettuce crisp, good; but whoever had had the idea of putting fruit-flavored dressing on it needed reeducation) as she sorted out the people on the team. The screen ID'd the civilians at the table for her and the Bureau personnel were mostly easy: Daisy Fennel, two of the staff psychologists, the elderly Asian woman who was in charge of electronic operations. That left one she couldn't quite place; a Bureau man, she was sure, but what was his specialty?

She got no help from Marcus Pell, either. As he refilled his coffee cup, he said, "Might as well get going. All you Bureau people know each other, of course, and I guess the rest of you have introduced yourselves around already. The colonel here is Hilda Morrisey, who has been Agent Dannerman's keeper. Hilda, this is Dr. Xiang-li Hou, from the Naval Observatory—" And went around the table, repeating what the screen had already said. The stout black woman in the paisley dress turned out to be a cerebrospinal surgeon from Walter Reed; the two youngish women with the careworn looks were legislative liaison from, respectively, the Senate and the House, and one of them, surprisingly, had her senator sitting next to her: Alicia Piombero, the black woman from Georgia. (Not the worst of the senators, Hilda knew, but still the enemy: the damn Congress was always trying to mess around in Bureau business.) The aggressively trim-looking man with the obvious hair transplant was a brigadier general from the Pentagon; the one who looked like a prosperous corporation lawyer was. Was some kind of a lawyer, at least, though his specialty wasn't given. He wasn't a bad-looking man, though. He might almost have been a somewhat older edition of Wilbur Carmichael, whom—Hilda glanced at her watch—if this damn meeting ever got itself over with, she might still get a chance to see that evening.

She looked up at Pell as he finished. "So now we all knew each other, and I'd like to thank all of you from outside the Bureau for volunteering your time to—I beg your pardon, Dr. Evergood?"

The surgeon had raised her hand. "I said, 'Who volunteered?' It was put to me as an order."

"Which makes us even more grateful to you, Dr. Evergood," the deputy director said, smiling tolerantly. "What we're here for is a matter that urgently affects the national interest. You probably know some of the background, but I'm going to ask Vice Deputy Fennell to fill in some of the details. Daisy?"

Morning Report
To all National Bureau of Investigation units
Subject: Current terrorist alerts

Welsh Nationalist Dawid ap Llewellyn, sought in connection with the British Museum firebombing, has been reported in Mexico City, presumed en route to a United States destination. Scotland Yard requests Bureau assistance in apprehending this fugitive.

The Rocky Mountain Militia Command deadline for amnesty for convicted assassins in federal custody expired at midnight. The threatened release of anthrax agents in the Missoula, Montana, water supply has not occurred, but emergency measures are still in force.

All standing alerts remain in effect.

The vice deputy didn't miss a beat. "You all remember the messages from space that came in two years ago. Many people thought they were a hoax. A few did not. One of those was an astronomer named Dr. Patrice Adcock, head of the Dannerman Observatory in New York City, who believed they came from an abandoned astronomical satellite called Starlab. Dr. Adcock, by the way, is on the premises and you will be seeing her later."

Hilda suppressed a grin as she translated for herself: what "on the premises" meant, of course, was "in one of our confinement cells." Daisy Fennel was as slick as the deputy director himself; she had come a long way since she was Hilda's own field manager, back when Hilda was a junior agent and the quarry of the moment was the man who had placed a bomb in the Smithsonian. And Daisy hadn't aged very much in the process. She hadn't gained a gram, and, Hilda observed, hadn't touched her sandwiches, either.

"Dr. Adcock," the V.D. was going on, "discovered some astronomical evidence that an unidentified object had entered our solar system and conjectured that it had dropped a probe which attached itself to the Starlab satellite." She glanced at the man from the Naval Observatory. "Dr. Hou?"

The astronomer stirred himself. "Yes. At Mr. Pell's request I made a study of that comet-like object. The data are sparse but consistent with what you just described, although I saw no probe being dropped."

"Neither did Dr. Adcock," Daisy agreed, "but she came to believe that one had been, and that there might be some sort of extraterrestrial technology on Starlab. So she asked the space agency to provide her with a spacecraft to visit the satellite, ostensibly with the purpose of repairing it and putting it back in service; she believed she had the right, under the original contract when Starlab was launched. The space agency was unable to grant her request—"

The translation of that, Hilda knew, was *we leaned on them* to slow her down until we found out what the hell she was up to.

"—because, among other reasons, no American space pilots were available. However, Dr. Adcock recruited two other pilots: one was a Floridian, General Martín Delasquez, the other a Chinese national, Commander James Peng-tsu Lin. She obtained a court order requiring the agency to provide a Clipper spacecraft to carry out the mission. In addition to herself and the two pilots, she had obtained the services of a Ukrainian national, Dr. Rosaleen Artzybachova, an instrument specialist who had helped design Starlab in the first place; Dr. Artzybachova was to go along to study Starlab's present instrumentation."

The V.D. paused. "At this point," she said, "the Bureau had become aware that Dr. Adcock's purpose was not to repair the satellite, but to see if there was indeed some alien technology now present on it, which she conjectured might be worth a lot of money."

Marcus Pell held up his hand; now that they were coming to the good part he was taking over. "Which it damn well would be, of course. As well as being of great national interest to this country. So we took a hand. We arranged for one of our agents, James Daniel Dannerman, to go with her. This is not public information, and I caution you all not to discuss it with anyone outside this team. Go on, Daisy."

"So," she said, "the five of them—Adcock, the two pilots, Artzybachova and our agent—launched to the orbiter and came back. They reported that nothing had changed—no alien technology—and the satellite was not repairable. And that seemed to be the end of it."

She looked inquiringly at the deputy director, who nodded. "That's when it got hairy," he said. "Dr. Artzybachova was ill when they landed, I guess because of the stress of the trip—she was, actually, a very old lady. She returned to her home, near the city of Kiev, Ukraine, and died shortly thereafter."

He paused to look around the table. "I caution you again that what you are about to hear is highly classified, and not under any circumstances to be discussed except within this team.

Starlab, one of the largest and best of the world's astronomical satellites, was the property of the T. Cuthbert Dannerman Astrophysical Observatory. It was designed to house visiting astronomers for weeks or months at a time, in the days when passenger launches to Low Earth Orbit were merely very expensive, not preposterous. Then it was called the Dannerman Orbiting Astrolab—the DOA for short—until the last scientist to use the place, a condensed-matter physicist named Manfred Lefrik, had the bad judgment to die there. By the time the automatic monitors reported to Earth what had happened it was far too late to save his life and, in view of the declining interest in space exploration, not worth the trouble to send up a ship to rescue his body. What the Observatory did, however, was to rename the satellite "Starlab," because they thought "DOA" sounded too apt. Still, some people preferred to call it the Starcophagus.

"There is an organization of Ukrainian nationalists who think Ukraine should be ruling Russia, the way it used to like a thousand years ago, instead of the other way around, the way they claim it is now—I don't know enough about Russian-Ukrainian history to get the details straight. And don't want to, actually. Anyway, this group wants to take over Russia, and they're willing to use terrorist tactics to make it happen.

"Of course, that's a local matter. Normally the Bureau wouldn't consider it an American concern. But, like a lot of these cockamamie terrorist groups, they've got cells here and they get a lot of their financing from Ukrainian-Americans. So the Russians asked us to lend a hand. And one of our assets in place in the Chicago cell passed on a report that the Ukrainians had autopsied the old lady . . . and found something weird.

"Take a look at your screens."

It wasn't necessary to do anything to comply. The pop-up screens were rising again at every place, and what they displayed was a sort of X ray of a human skull. Where skull joined spine there was a fuzzy object the size of a hazelnut.

"This is a slice of a PET scan," Pell said. "It shows the thing the

Ukrainians found in Dr. Artzybachova's head. And this other one"—*click*—"comes from the head of our agent, Dan Dannerman. There's one just like it in Dr. Patrice Adcock's head—and, we think, though we can't get at them to check, in the heads of Commander Lin and General Delasquez as well. Nothing like it has ever been found in the heads of anybody else we've examined, just in the people that went to Starlab and came back."

He paused there, gazing amiably around the table, until Senator Piombero couldn't contain herself any longer. "Well, what is it, Marcus? Some kind of a tumor?"

The D.D. shook his head. "No, it's not a tumor. We have a copy of the Ukrainian report on the object they took from Dr. Artzybachova's body. It's metal. It does not resemble any human artifact. It appears to have been implanted in them while they were on the orbiter." He paused, giving the group a sort of half smile—not so much a smile as the grimace of somebody who had bitten into something really foul. "Now we come to Operation Ananias. There seems to be a lot of lying going on. Both Dannerman and Dr. Adcock deny that anything of the sort happened. The Floridians haven't been very cooperative, but we've established that General Delasquez denies it, too; we haven't been able to get much out of the Chinese about Commander Lin.

"But what it is, definitely, is a piece of that extraterrestrial technology that Dr. Adcock went looking for. We want to find out why one of our senior agents is lying to us, not to mention that we damn well need to know exactly what the implant thing is." He glanced at his watch, seemed about to add something but changed his mind. "There's more, but let's leave it at that for the moment. Now we should go to the interrogation theater so you can get a look at Dannerman and Dr. Adcock yourselves."

2

With all twelve of them in it at once the elevator was pretty crowded. Conversation wasn't easy, but that didn't stop Senator Piombero. "What I'm wondering, Marcus," she said, leaning past the man Hilda couldn't quite remember to get the D.D.'s attention, "is, why don't you just take the thing out of your agent's head? I mean surgically? I certainly wouldn't want anything like that in my own head."

> According to the flow charts, the National Bureau of Investigation is part of the nation's federalized police force, but it keeps itself clear of the street cops. Those are the thin blue line—though noticeably thickened since the passage of the police draft laws—that does its best to keep the peace-loving citizen from the muggers and murderers. The street cops share a headquarters with the Department of Defense in the old Pentagon. The NBI's headquarters is a few kilometers away, in suburban Arlington, and it has a different mission. Its quarry is the transnational crooks and druggers and terrorists. It has inherited its ID files from the old FBI, and its habits from the old CIA. Although it chooses its agents from the police draftees, the ones it picks are the cream of the crop, and they know it.
>
> —*Inside the Beltway:* "The NBI."

"That is one option, yes," he agreed. "Unfortunately— Well, that's your department, Dr. Evergood."

"It's not that easy," the surgeon said obstinately. "I've studied both subjects. Of course, the implants can be removed. But they are much more complex than they appear on your screens. Each of the implants has a large number of fine processes that do not show up well in those images but reach deeply into many areas of the brain. My opinion is that removing them might well kill the patients, and at the least would almost certainly cause severe loss of much brain function. I wouldn't like to take that kind of a risk if I didn't have to."

Watching Senator Piombero, Hilda suspected the woman wouldn't be satisfied with that. She wasn't. She gave the surgeon a narrow-eyed look, then turned to the deputy director. "Maybe we can get a second opinion," she suggested.

He looked surprised. "Of course, Senator. If that's what you wish. But Dr. Evergood is perhaps the best in the world at this kind of work. We've been grateful to her in the past for what she's been able to do for some of our own people. Truly amazing results."

Hilda repressed a shudder, because she'd seen some of those truly amazing results: mummified corpses in life-support capsules, looking at the world through electronic lenses and getting around in overgrown wheelchairs. She did not want to think of her Dan Dannerman like that.

"So you see," the deputy director said sunnily as the elevator door opened. "Now if you'll go to your right we'll go into the Pit of Pain."

The senator persisted. "Well, then, couldn't you, ah, secure the device the Ukrainians removed from the instrument person?"

Pell looked surprised. "Oh, didn't I say? They don't have it anymore. The silly buggers let somebody else steal it."

Hilda Morrisey knew the Pit of Pain well. She had watched many an interrogation from one of those seats, had often enough been the interrogator down in the pit herself, when the subjects were bombers, tax evaders, smugglers, all the kinds of nasties that the Bureau had to deal with. It had never been like this before, though. The problem had never concerned ridiculous alien creatures from Mars or some other preposterous place. More important still, the sweaty person being interrogated had never before been one of her own.

As the Ananias team took its seats in one corner of the stands Hilda saw that Senior Agent Dannerman was already sitting on one of the straight-backed chairs. He didn't seem to be doing much sweating. In fact, she noted with a faint, hidden grin of approval, he looked pretty much as though he were asleep.

Daisy Fennell said chattily, "It's all right to talk up here; they can't hear us. Now if you're all ready?" She looked at the D.D. He nodded; she spoke into the microphone at her place; down in the pit the door opened and the interrogator came in. Hilda didn't know the interrogator, who was female, young, good-looking in a severely no-nonsense kind of way—probably new to the Bureau headquarters. She placed a hand on Dannerman's shoulder and said, "Wake up. I need to ask you some questions."

If Dannerman had been asleep at all, he woke quickly and completely. He glanced knowingly toward the one-way mirror, yawning, before he said, "Is there any coffee around?"

"No," the interrogator said concisely, seating herself across the table from him. She plunged right in. "Agent Dannerman, you are accused of filing false reports to the Bureau."

"Yes, I know that; I didn't do it. By the way, I have to pee."

The interrogator ignored that. "When you returned from the Starlab orbiter you reported—"

"I know what I reported. Pee, remember? I have to do it."

For the first time the interrogator looked uncertain. "I think that can wait until we finish here. You reported—"

"Well, if you think it can wait," Dannerman said agreeably, "but it doesn't feel that way to me. I think it'd be better if you took me to the men's room. Or else I can just go in my pants."

The interrogator didn't scowl at him. Didn't look at the mirror, either, just got up, walked stiffly to the door and summoned a male guard to escort Dannerman to the toilet. The deputy director was frowning. Hilda wasn't; in fact, she was feeling a faint glow of pride; her agent, faithful to his training, was controlling the interrogation. He was a good boy. . . .

Except, she reminded herself glumly, that he wasn't.

When Dannerman was back in his chair he was more cooperative; he'd made his point. Yes, he'd gone to Starlab looking for traces of alien presence. No, there hadn't been any. Yes, he was sure of that; he'd said so about a hundred times now, hadn't he? Yes (as the interrogator activated the table's pop-up screen and he glanced at it), he had seen that X-ray before. He was willing to take the Bureau's word that it was of his own head, but what that object was he had no idea.

"And you're aware that one just like it was found in Dr. Rosaleen Artzybachova's skull on autopsy, and that it is definitely a piece of alien technology."

"So you tell me," he agreed.

"Do you think the Bureau's lying to you?"

Agent Dannerman has one personal trait that comes in useful to the NBI. He was born rich, grew up among rich people and thus had entry to circles the average NBI agent couldn't penetrate. The late T. Cuthbert Dannerman, who was his uncle on his father's side, not only endowed the Dannerman Astrophysical Observatory but had enough left over to bequeath a tidy little fortune to his two surviving relatives, one of whom was Dan. Unfortunately for Dan, he was in deep cover abroad when the will was probated. By the time he got his hands on the money the world's rampant inflation had shrunk it to chump change.

"I hope not, but you think I'm lying to you and I'm not. Hell, friend, you ought to know that by now; your shrinks have tested me a thousand times, and I always came up clean."

In the spectator seats Hilda, and most of the others, looked at the pair of Bureau shrinks, who shrugged and nodded reluctantly.

"I don't know why that is," the interrogator agreed. "What it looks like is that you've found some way of beating the tests."

"Now, how could I do that?" Dannerman asked. "They shot me so full of drugs I was out of my head for weeks."

The interrogator paused. Then she said, "There is a way of settling this once and for all."

"Yes, I know what that is. You want to cut my head open so you can get a good look at that thing."

"That's right. There's a release form right in front of you, if you'll just sign it—"

"No, I can't do that," Dannerman said apologetically. "I wish I could help. But I hear that the operation could turn me into a vegetable."

"Maybe could. No one knows for sure. Not until they open you up and get a look."

"I'm sorry. That's not good enough. I'm not signing."

"You don't have a choice," she said. "The deputy director is *ordering* you to sign the release."

"Well, that's different," Dannerman said cheerfully. "Let him give it to me in writing, and then let me give a copy of it to my lawyer . . . and then we'll see."

* * *

Dr. Patrice Dannerman Bly Metcalf Adcock attained her position as head of the Dannerman Astrophysical Observatory by virtue of her training as an astronomer, and also because she was the niece by marriage of the late T. Cuthbert Dannerman, whose money had funded the Observatory in the first place. Patrice Adcock was luckier in her inheritance than her cousin by marriage, Dan Dannerman; she was able to transfer her legacy to inflation-proof investments as soon as she received it. But two divorces depleted her cash . . . which was why she seized on the chance of riches from the Starlab orbiter.

That was enough for the deputy director. "I think we've heard enough from Agent Dannerman," he said to the room in general, then spoke into his microphone.

As the interrogator, hearing, terminated the interrogation and took Dannerman out of the Pit, Dr. Marsha Evergood raised her hand. "Mr. Pell, you understand I can't undertake the operation without his consent."

Pell said heartily, "Naturally. No one in the Bureau would ask you to, Dr. Evergood."

"But if he won't sign—"

"I give you my word that you won't have to pick up a scalpel until you have his signature on the release form. Now they'll be bringing Dr. Adcock in."

Signature, signature, Hilda thought, cudgeling her memory. There was something about signatures. . . .

Down in the pit they were bringing the Adcock woman in, but Hilda wasn't looking at her. She was looking at the other Bureau man, tardily remembering where she had seen him before. He was the man who'd replaced old Willy Godden when he retired as Chief of Documents: the branch of the Bureau which was in the business of providing you with any papers, and any signatures, you might happen to want.

3

As Senior Agent Dan Dannerman, currently on administrative leave, left the Pit of Pain his interrogator cozily took his arm. "I'm sorry about all this, Agent Dannerman," she said, looking up at him with large eyes and an apologetic smile, "but I guess you know how it is. Still want that coffee? Why don't you wait in the conference room here and I'll get it for you."

"Fine," he said. But he was already talking to the door she had closed behind him, and when he tried it it was locked.

He had expected no less. The conference room—call it the "holding cell," because that was what it was—offered him a choice of two backless benches to sit on, both bolted to the floor. He chose neither. He perched on the edge of the table between them, idly examining its surface. The thing was undoubtedly packed with electronics. Lacking a pass card there was no easy way for him to get at them, though, and in any case what would be the use? This wasn't some crime gang that was holding him. It was his own Bureau—what had been his own Bureau, anyway, until all this preposterous crap hit the fan.

That was what was very wrong with the way things were going for Dan Dannerman. Under other circumstances he would have known what to do—what to try to do, anyway: maybe try to get into the table's electronic resources, maybe position himself by the door to coldcock this young woman when she came back with the coffee, maybe try to rid himself of the collar that made any escape attempt useless, maybe— Well, he'd been trained for almost everything that could happen to a Bureau agent in the field. But never for this.

Sooner than he expected the interrogator was back, juggling a little tray in one hand, carefully closing the door again behind her.

There were two cups on the tray. When Dannerman had taken his and seated himself she sat down on the bench across from him with the other and became conversational. "Like I say, I'm sorry to meet you this way, Agent Dannerman. I do know who you are, and I only wish I had your record. I'm Merla Tepp."

He nodded, slightly amused. She was being the good cop. She wasn't bad at the job, either. Although she dressed for no-nonsense business, she'd allowed herself a hint of perfume and the makeup, and all in all she was quite an attractive young woman. "So," he said sociably, "can I go home now?"

"You mean back to New York? I don't know. I'm waiting for orders. Was I rough on you in there?"

"You were doing your job."

"Thanks for taking it that way, Agent Dannerman. This is my first week in headquarters, and I get the jobs nobody else wants. You know how it is."

That was too obvious to require a response, so he didn't try to make one. The woman sipped her coffee, gazing at him over the rim of the cup. She wasn't being flirtatious, exactly. Confiding, maybe. She said, "Do you mind if I ask you a question? Why don't you want to sign that release?"

That was pretty obvious, too. He said it anyway. "Because it might kill me."

"Well, yes," she admitted. "I can't blame you for that. But don't you want to know what that thing is? What does it feel like, anyway?"

What did it feel like? It felt like nothing at all. He hadn't felt it being put in, hadn't known it was there at all until, without warning, the damn Bureau pickup squad had scooped him up and hustled him in for examination. And ever since then they'd asked him the same damn questions over and over again, just like this little jumped-up cadet—

Who was, after all, young, and rather pretty, and would have been more so if she'd let herself look girly instead of efficient. And it had been a long time since he'd seen his own girl. So all he said was, "I can't feel it. What's this, they've detailed you to soften me up?"

She looked at him quizzically over her coffee cup. "Do you think I could? When Colonel Morrisey and Deputy Director Pell couldn't? But we won't talk about it if you don't want to." She leaned back against the wall, trying to get comfortable. "Sorry about these benches. Do you want to talk at all, or should I just shut up? Like you could tell me about some of your missions."

"Or you could tell me about yours," he suggested, beginning to feel amusement.

"Mine aren't very interesting. They had me infiltrating some of the radical religious-militia groups in the Southwest. We cleaned up one little bomb factory, but it was taking a long time and that wasn't getting me any promotions. So I applied for a tour here."

"So you're a career agent."

"I guess so," she said, finishing the last of her coffee. "I was in protsy in college, and they called me up for active duty."

The Police Reserve Officers Training Corps; Dannerman grinned in spite of himself. "Me too."

She said doubtfully, "Well, maybe it was a little different for me. See, my parents were very religious. I grew up in a fundamentalist group; and the Bureau needed somebody who could get inside some of them. So the machines kicked my name out. But I guess I'll stay in the Bureau. It isn't that bad—"

And so on, and so on. The woman seemed to like talking about her life in the Bureau. Dannerman let her talk. It was a new and relaxing experience for him, these days, to be closeted with another agent when the other agent did all the talking. "—so here I am," she finished. "Want some more coffee?"

> When human beings began to wonder if there were other intelligent races somewhere in the universe they began the SETI program—the "Search for Extraterrestrial Intelligence." That meant they listened for radio broadcasts from space, in the expectation that they might somehow establish peaceful communication with them. They did not take seriously the idea that some of those extraterrestrial intelligences might have similar programs of their own, with expectations a good deal less peaceful.

"Well, sure. And if you could find something to eat to go along with it?"

"I'll see what I can do," she promised, gathered up the cups and left, naturally locking him in again.

Dannerman yawned and stretched, wondering absently what the Bureau had in store for him next. Wondering what he would do if in fact the deputy director did give him a direct order, in writing, to sign the release. He didn't think that was likely. Marcus Pell was too sharp a bunny to put anything like that in writing, especially if he thought Dannerman would file it with his attorney.

Which, Dannerman reflected, wouldn't be all that easy, since he didn't really have an attorney. Unless you counted the old fart of a family lawyer who had screwed up his inheritance and helped him get the job with Cousin Pat's observatory that had led to his flight to the orbiting old Starlab and thus to all this other stuff. . . .

He turned as the door opened again, expecting Merla Tepp with the coffee refills.

It was Tepp, all right, but she wasn't alone. She had someone with her, and the someone was Dannerman's Cousin Pat. "I brought some company for you," Tepp said brightly, "and I've got to leave the two of you here for a bit. But I found something for you to snack on and the coffee's fresh."

Cousin Pat, aka Dr. Patrice Adcock, gave Dannerman a look that was part weary and mostly just hostile. As she took the bench across from him he ventured, "Hello, Pat."

Pat Adcock didn't answer. Dannerman hadn't really expected her to. She hadn't forgiven him, and in a way he didn't blame her. Nobody liked having a Bureau spook planted on them, especially when the spook was a cousin they had known since childhood.

He fingered his collar, studying her. It was the first time in many weeks that he had had a good look at his cousin. Apart from looking tired and cranky she looked smaller than usual, in her unornamented Bureau prison gown. Mostly she just looked mad.

He tried again. "So how've you been?" he asked sociably.

She gave him an eyes-narrowed look, but this time she answered. "Shitty," she said.

She didn't bounce the conversational ball back by asking how he was; she evidently didn't care. He sighed. "Pat, I know you're pissed at me, but what was I supposed to do? I work for the Bureau. The Bureau wanted to know what you were up to. If it hadn't been me, it would've been somebody else."

"Sure, Dan, but I wouldn't have trusted anybody else as much, would I?" She was silent for a moment, then said thoughtfully, "You just can't leave that thing alone, can you?"

He hadn't been aware that he was still fingering his collar. He took his hand away. "At least they didn't make you wear one."

"Sure not. Why would they? I've been in solitary confinement in this dump." Moodily she picked up her coffee cup, which reminded Dannerman to inspect the "food" Agent Tepp had brought. It was an opened box of cheese-flavored crackers, but still pretty full.

Pat Adcock watched him chew for a moment, then asked, "Dan? Do you know what's going on?" He shook his head, his mouth full of stale crackers. "What was the point of that business in the interrogation theater? They just asked the same questions they've asked a million times before."

He shrugged, chewing. Of course they had; it was pure theater, designed for the benefit of whoever was on the other side of that one-way mirror, but for what reason he could not guess.

She fidgeted, unsatisfied. "Listen, do you think the whole thing with the implants could be some kind of trick? Maybe there isn't really anything in our heads at all?"

He swallowed the crackers. "I wish. No, we've got them, all right. I saw the images come up on the screen the first time they examined me." And most of the other times, too, through all the tests—the X rays and the PET scans, the ionic-resonance tests when they bounced some kind of radiation off the back of his neck and tried to identify the chemical composition of whatever the damn thing was that had somehow, unbelievably, turned up in his skull. "Anyway," he said, "they'd have to go to a lot of trouble to fake it, and what would be the point?"

"You're the spook. If you don't know, who would?"

"Well, I don't know. I don't remember it ever being stuck into my head, either."

"Same here." She sighed. "They say we've all got one, Jimmy Lin and General Delasquez, too. They want me to sign some kind of release so they can take it out. I—I told them I would sign if you did, and if you didn't I wouldn't."

Dannerman blinked at her. That was an indication of some kind of trust, after all, and he hadn't expected it from her. He didn't know how to react to it, either.

He didn't have to, because Pat had decided to be conversational now. "Well, anyway, what've you been doing since I saw you last—I mean before they started all this nonsense about implants? How's that girl of yours?" she asked sociably. "The actress?"

That was a downer, because he'd spent a lot of time wondering the same thing. He confessed, "I don't know. I haven't talked to her in a while."

She nodded, looking at him thoughtfully. "I, uh, I hear you

weren't in real good condition to talk to her. I mean, they say you were drunk most of the time."

That touched Dannerman where he lived. "Just for the record," he said stiffly, "they shot me so full of their psychoactive chemicals that I was out of it. For weeks. I don't even remember what I was doing."

"I see. You're blaming somebody else for your behavior."

"I'm not blaming. I'm telling you what happened."

She didn't look convinced, but she didn't argue the point. He asked, "So, talking about love interest, have you got anybody special?"

"Now, how the hell could I? Anyway, I've got other things on my mind. Not just this crap here; I keep wondering what's happening at the Observatory. The way they came and took me away—God knows what they told the people."

Dannerman grinned. "They're very British about that. I imagine they told them you were 'assisting with inquiries.' "

"Yeah, well, they're not stupid there, you know. And I'm worried. You know I was having some money problems. I wish I knew what was going on with my funds—oh, what's this?"

What it was was Merla Tepp. Her face was as expressionless as she could make it, and what she said was, "Sorry to interrupt, people, but I've been ordered to take you for a little ride."

The ride wasn't that little. They were the better part of an hour speeding along the Beltway in one of the Bureau's unmarked electrovans, with two burly noncoms carrying stunsticks and riot guards sitting alertly behind them. At least they'd left the van windows transparent, so Dan and Pat could look out. He was a little surprised to see that it was dark; they'd spent the whole day stooging around. But the Beltway looked like the Beltway, wherever it was taking you, and Merla Tepp wasn't answering any questions. "Where are we heading?" No answer. "What's going on here?" No answer. "Who gave you the orders?" No real answer, but at least a kind of response: "Colonel Morrisey will meet us, and you can ask her when you see her."

But when the van at last turned into city streets one question answered itself. "Oh, shit," Dannerman said. "They're taking us to Walter Reed."

Pat blinked at him. "The hospital?"

"Damn straight it's the hospital. Listen, Tepp! If you think—"

But he never got to finish, and she didn't have to answer; one of the noncoms leaned forward and placed a huge hand on Dannerman's shoulder, while the other casually unlimbered his stunstick. Dannerman saw the light and shut up.

Anyway, they were pulling up to a back entrance, and Dannerman saw Hilda Morrisey moodily waiting in the damp cold. She wasn't answering any questions, either, or at least not right away. "No talking; these people aren't cleared," she said, nodding to the noncoms. "Wait till we get you settled." And then, when they got out of the elevator and were herded into a small room that was a close copy of the Bureau's cell, she said:

"What about it, Danno? Change your mind yet?"

He didn't answer that, and she didn't wait for him to. "All right," she said, her expression frank and open—the expression she wore when she was being most duplicitous, "I understand your problem. I admit there are certain risks. But have you ever thought of the fact that if one of you volunteered for the operation, we wouldn't have to ask the other one?"

"Hilda," he said dangerously, "cut the crap. What've you got us here for? Neither one of us signed the consent paper!"

"No," she agreed, "and that's too bad, because it would simplify things just to go in and pull one of the gadgets out. But I've got good news for both of you. There's another kind of test, something the lab guys have just figured out."

Hero Astronaut Returns Home.

Major General Martín Delasquez has unexpectedly returned to Florida after a tour of duty in Kourou, assisting the Eurospace Agency in preparation for a mission to the abandoned Starlab satellite. On arrival, the general scoffed at reports in the Anglo media that his tour was cut short for security reasons. "There is no truth to them," General Delasquez told reporters. "My task was completed, so I came home. That's all there is to it."

—*El Diario,* Miami

"Hilda!"

"Agent Dannerman," she said frostily, elevating herself to the height of her rank, "don't give me a hard time. Do you understand me?"

"I understand there's something I don't like here. Neither Pat nor I agree to any kind of surgery."

"Of course you don't, you've made that clear. And Dr. Evergood certainly won't perform any without a signed consent, so this isn't like that. There won't be any cutting into your heads. They think there's a chance they can get more dope on that thing in your skulls with some new X-ray thing—don't ask me what it is, all I know is it takes a long exposure and you can't wiggle. Have you eaten anything since you were in the Pit?"

"A couple of crackers, but—"

"That's too bad. It might slow things down."

Alarm bells went off in Dannerman's head. "Does that mean we get put to sleep?"

"Now, how would I know that? Sounds plausible, though, doesn't it? Some sort of tranquilizer, I think. Nothing big, I'm sure of that."

"Now, really, Hilda—"

"Really, Danno," she began, her voice suddenly harsher, "there's no sense arguing about it. I'm not asking for your consent. I'm just telling you what's going to happen because you don't have any ch—"

Then she stopped in mid-breath. She didn't even finish the word "choice." Her eyes went unfocused for a moment. Then she blinked and looked at them again. "You two stay here," she barked, and hurried out of the room.

Pat turned wonderingly to Dannerman. "What the hell was that all about?"

He gave her an abstracted look. "What? Oh, she got a message. In her private phone," he explained. "The little button in her ear; you probably didn't even notice it."

"What kind of message?" Pat demanded. He shook his head. "Dan! Tell me what's happening here! Do you think they're going to operate on us anyway? They can't do it without our signatures, can they?"

Dannerman considered the question. "That's what the law says," he said. And didn't add that the Bureau had its ways of getting around laws. And decided that if the next person through that door was carrying anything that looked like a hypodermic, then that would be the time to get physical.

The next person who entered wasn't carrying a needle. He wasn't even hospital personnel. It was Deputy Director Marcus Pell himself. He nodded to Dannerman and spoke to Pat. "We haven't officially met, Dr. Adcock, but I've seen a good deal of you."

He was being courtly. Dannerman had no patience with that just at that moment. "What's going on?" he demanded.

The deputy director sighed. "I'm not sure I know," he said. "There's been a rather surprising new development. There has just been a new transmission from that satellite of yours, Dr. Adcock."

"But there's nobody there!" Dannerman said.

Pat had a different reaction. She caught her breath. "Do you think it's one of those funny-looking extraterrestrials?"

"Not this time," Pell said somberly, studying his agent. "It was from a human being, Dannerman. He said there were a bunch of people up there in orbit. He said they were going to come back to Earth in the orbiter's Assured Crew Return Vehicle, the emergency vehicle that's supposed to—"

"I know what it's supposed to do," Dannerman snapped.

"Yes. Well. The funny thing about it, Dannerman, is this guy on Starlab said he was you."

That took Dan Dannerman back as nothing else had. He goggled at the D.D. "He says he's *me?"*

"That's what the man claims. We didn't believe him, of course. So we checked his voiceprint, and by God he was right. He is."

4

Colonel Hilda Morrisey liked orders that gave her some slack for interpretation, but this time she could have wished for a little less of it. The deputy director's parting order had been no more than, "Take care of those two and stick around." That was it. Nothing more specific. Especially nothing more informative, and then he was gone.

So when Dannerman demanded to know what was going on Hilda could only say, "I don't know any more than you do," wishing she did. She did turn on the screen in the van so he and Pat Adcock could hear the Bureau's recording of what the world had just heard. There was no secret about that! It had been a voice-only transmission, so the only picture on the screen was the legend *Transmission received from Starlab astronomical satellite, 2041 hours, 9 December.* Then the voice spoke, tinny, fuzzy, but definitely familiar:

"This is James Daniel Dannerman calling my associates in Arlington from orbit. Pat Adcock was right, except that it's a lot bigger than she thought. I'll try to bring some samples of the stuff we were talking about with me when I come back. That will be very soon, assuming Jimmy Lin can get this Assured Crew Return Vehicle thing working. And assuming that we can all fit in, because there are nine, ah"—the voice hesitated for a moment—"nine persons here, and we don't want to leave anybody aboard. Please acknowledge on this frequency."

That was it. Broadcast in *clear,* so every son of a bitch with a radio, all over the world, could have been listening in. And a lot of them had been. "Is that *me?*" Dannerman demanded, looking from Hilda to Pat; and, when they only shrugged, "Well, what does he—I—what do they mean, nine people? Only five of us went up there!"

"How would I know?" Hilda asked reasonably. "Maybe your friend Artzy-what's-her-name had quadruplets."

> **"Space Voice" May Belong to U.S. Intelligence Agent.**
>
> A retired member of the U.S. intelligence community has identified the "voice from space" as belonging to National Bureau of Investigation agent James Daniel Dannerman. Although the source declines to be identified, he states there "is no damn doubt at all" of the identification, adding that until recently Dannerman was reported to be under house arrest on unspecified charges. Officials of the NBI decline to comment on the report.
>
> —*The New York Times*

He gave her a dangerous look, but all he said was, "Play it again!"

So they played it again, and again, and then they switched to a news channel to hear all the things everybody had to say about this astounding report. Hilda gave that five minutes. Then she squirmed ahead to the front seat, phoning ahead to make arrangements at the headquarters. Then she just sat there, the dead phone to her ear, because she had nothing to say to either Pat or Dan and didn't want to hear any more of their questions. There was one good thing, she thought. There was at least a temporary hold to the D.D.'s little plan to anesthetize Dannerman and Adcock and then blandly hand Dr. Evergood the impeccably best "signed" release the skilled forgers of Documents could produce. Maybe that hold would be permanent. Maybe even this baffling new development was going to confirm what Hilda had always known in her heart. Her own Dan Dannerman simply could not possibly have been turned or subverted. Oh, sure, the evidence had looked pretty bad, but that just meant the evidence had to be wrong. There had to be some other explanation.

Now it appeared that there was one—well, sort of an explanation, anyway—but who was going to explain this wholly incomprehensible explanation?

At the headquarters she wasted no time. She hustled the two of them into an elevator, down to the accommodations she had arranged for them. "You can watch the news," she said, "or you can go to bed or you can do anything you like—except leave here. I'll see you in the morning."

"Have a heart, Hilda!" Dannerman begged. "I want to know what's happening!"

"So do I. Get some sleep. I've got work to do."

The truth, though, was that she didn't. Everyone else did. Every other person she saw in the Bureau's underground fortress seemed not only to have something to do, but to be about thirty minutes late in getting it done and desperately trying to make up lost time, but not Hilda Morrisey. The last time she had seen the joint jumping like this had been when the President's press secretary got himself kidnapped and murdered—no, she corrected herself, not even then. That was just an ordinary kill; the only reason the Bureau got involved in it at all was because the President demanded it. What was going on now was—was—well, what was it, exactly? Weirdness, that's what it was. Unthinkably preposterous weirdness. But it happened to be real.

She couldn't find Marcus Pell or the director herself. She couldn't even find Daisy Fennell. They were certainly somewhere, on some level of the subterranean headquarters. No one seemed to know just where. More likely, Hilda thought bitterly, the ones who did know simply weren't telling. The topmost of the top brass were holed up somewhere, dealing with this new crisis as best they could, and they didn't want to be bothered with peons who would only get in the way.

Hilda Morrisey did not like being one of the peons.

The obvious place for them to be was the Communications Center. That was the first place Hilda looked, but when she had looked in every other place she could think of she went back there. At least there she could get some idea of what was happening, although what was happening seemed to be only that half the population of the planet Earth was asking questions that nobody here could answer. There were plaintive coded queries from the Bureau's field managers by the score. There were begging—or pleading, or sometimes demanding—transmissions from fifty or sixty of the friendlies, the other national intelligence agencies with which the Bureau maintained some sort of cooperative relationship. Then there were the heavy hitters, the question from the Senate and the House, from State and Defense, from the White House itself . . . not to mention the endless flurry of concerned citizens who somehow had learned the Bureau's least classified call codes and wanted to be informed. These last were the least bothersome. The only answers they got didn't come from a human being; they were computer-generated and all they said was, *Regret have no further information at this time.*

Please watch your local newscasts. The other queries could not be brushed off so lightly. They took personal responses from some human being. Tending to them was what a large fraction of the Bureau personnel on duty were doing with their time, but though the responses were more elaborate, the information they contained was about the same.

But the little that was different about them was interesting. Hilda gleaned a fact here and a hint there and slowly pieced together a picture. Why had there been no further transmissions from this other Dan Dannerman? Because the Comm officer on duty had been bright enough and quick enough to send an instant narrow-beam order to this Dannerman on the satellite, telling him to shut up, do nothing, just wait there for further instructions. And a lucky thing that, for once, this other Dannerman had done exactly what he was told. . . .

There was a quick, breathy sound of surprise from the group clustered around one screen. They had heard something.

Half the Comm Center immediately dropped what they were doing to see what it was they had heard. "It was a blip," one of the technicians was saying excitedly. "No, nothing more. Just one quick pulse, but it definitely came from Starlab. Direct? No, I guess they're somewhere out of sight in their orbit; it was relayed from Goldstone, but it was positively— Hey! There's another one!"

It wasn't one. It was two. Everyone heard them this time, and the screen showed them moving slowly across the field, two brightly jagged spikes. So Dannerman was communicating again, more or less.

That was enough for Hilda Morrisey. She stood up, stretched, yawned and walked out of the Communications Center.

She knew what had happened, because it was what she would have done in the same case. What the closeted big brass had been doing was trying to figure some way of arranging a two-way conversation that the rest of the world couldn't hear. Apparently Starlab wasn't rigged for narrowcasting—well, it wouldn't matter if it were. Reporters weren't stupid, and they had resources of their own; undoubtedly there were forests of mobile antennae deployed all over Arlington, and probably all around Goldstone and the station on Wake and every other place where the Bureau might receive a signal. So they had worked out a simple code. The Bureau could ask a question, and Dannerman could answer by blipping his transmitter—something like one blip *yes* and two blips *no*—and maybe three blips for *How the hell do you expect me to do THAT?* But you had no hope of deciphering what the answers meant unless you knew what the questions had been.

She glanced at her watch. 0544. It would be daybreak in an hour or two, and she hadn't had sleep, shower or a change of clothing since she got out of the bed in her New York City apartment nearly twenty-four hours ago. The lack of sleep wasn't a big problem; the Bureau's standard-issue wakeup pills took care of it. The problem was something else. Surreptitiously she bent her head for a quick sniff at her armpit, envious of the crisp cleanliness of everyone around her. She knew why that was. They had all been able to take enough time off to get cleaned and changed. That was the way it was when you were headquarters-based, you kept spares of everything on hand in case of emergency. If she were to give up the struggle and let them hand her that damned promotion—

But that was out of the question. Hilda Morrisey didn't belong in this place. She was a field manager. She could make herself at home wherever the job took her, San Diego or New York, Berlin or Karachi. In those places she was the boss, and as long as her teams produced results nobody got in her thinning but still bravely blond hair. Here she was just one of a mob of fifty or sixty people of equivalent rank, with the top-heavy Bureau executive staff over them all.

Here, as a matter of fact, if anything she was in the way. But she couldn't leave. Not only was this whole business a puzzle that Hilda Morrisey didn't trust anyone but herself to solve, but it was her own agent who was at the core of it.

If she couldn't leave, sleep or bathe, the next best thing was to eat. She sought out the field-grade mess, sat at a table in a corner, swallowed another wakeup pill and thought.

The mess was usually deserted this time of night—or morning. Not this one. There were half a dozen others at the tables, and the graveyard mess shift, looking aggrieved at their unusual workload, was clearing up the tables that still others had left. While she was waiting for someone to take her order she popped up the table's screen and coded for the news summaries.

When a waiter approached Hilda dumped the screen and turned to give her order, but what he said was, "Excuse me, Colonel, but there's a junior officer asking to speak to you."

Hilda turned; the person waiting at the door was the interrogator, the junior agent, Merla Tepp. "Send her in," she said. And then, when the woman had come to the table, "Sit down, Tepp. I didn't expect to see you here for another couple of hours."

"I came in early, Colonel. Colonel? I'm sorry to interrupt your meal but I wanted to apologize. I wouldn't have given Agent Dannerman those crackers, except I didn't know he was scheduled for surgery."

"No, you didn't," Hilda agreed. "In fact, you don't know it now. You especially don't want to say anything about it to Agent Dannerman."

"No, ma'am. Ma'am? I'm pretty sure he suspected it."

Hilda surveyed the woman. "I'm damn sure he did; Dannerman's a fine agent. Just don't confirm it for him." She was silent for a moment, studying Junior Agent Tepp while her fingers were absent-mindedly playing with the screen keys. After a moment, she said, "Actually, I would have done just what you did. Have you eaten?"

Tepp looked surprised. "No, but, Colonel, this dining room is for—"

Hilda overrode her. "What this dining room is for is for people like me and our guests. Waiter! We'll have a couple of sandwiches and salads—if it's that fruity dressing, put the dressing on the side." She waved him away and told the girl, "That stuff is too damn sweet. You might prefer to eat the salad plain. I forgot to ask if you had any special dietary needs?"

"No, ma'am."

"Because God knows what the sandwiches will be." She leaned back, studying the girl. Although she knew she had never seen Junior Agent Tepp before, there was something vaguely familiar about her. She couldn't place the thought and abandoned it. "Actually," she said, "apart from giving them the damn crackers, that wasn't a bad move, putting the two of them together."

Tepp looked rueful. "I was hoping that if they got to talking, they might say something useful."

"Did they?"

"Not really, Colonel. I have the recordings—"

Hilda waved away the notion of looking at the recordings. "I didn't think they would. Danno's too smart for that, but it was worth a try. Means you were using a little initiative. I see by your file that you've only been with the Bureau for a little over a year."

Merla Tepp did not show any surprise at finding that the colonel had called her file up on the table screen. "That's right, ma'am. Mostly in the field in New Mexico, after I finished training."

"Checking into the religious nut groups." Hilda nodded. "I get the impression that you've been pretty interested in religion all your life."

Tepp hesitated. "You could say I was a seeker, Colonel. I was born Pentecostal, then when that didn't seem to be giving me what I wanted I tried Catholic. Then I went to shul for a year—I guess that's why you asked about dietary requirements? Then I tried Buddhism—"

> The American radical religious right came in five main flavors. There were the *fundamentalists,* who believe in the "verbal inerrancy" of the Christian Bible; the *born-agains,* who claim a personal experience with Christ; the *evangelicals,* who are either of the above plus a drive to convert others; the *pentecostals,* who are any of the above plus public demonstrations of ecstasy; and the *charismatics,* who differ from the others only in that they retain communion in a conventional Protestant or Catholic denomination. Generally speaking, what the fundamentalists thought the government ought to do about the possible space aliens who might have occupied Starlab was, if possible, to kill them, because they were probably the Antichrist. While most of the others thought they were probably angels of some kind and what the government should be doing was arranging for them to be worshipped. What they all agreed on was that everything the government actually was doing was wholly and unforgivably wrong.

She broke off as the sandwiches and salads arrived. Colonel Hilda waved to her to eat, doing so herself. She hadn't realized quite how hungry she was. With her mouth full, she paused long enough to ask: "And now?"

The girl grinned. "I guess you'd say the Bureau's my religion now, ma'am."

Hilda nodded. It was a good answer. It was the kind of answer she might have given herself, and, as a matter of fact, she suddenly realized what that puzzling familiarity was all about. Agent Tepp was just about her height, just about her weight, just about her general build; taken all in all, she was not far from a copy of what Colonel Morrisey had been, long before she became a colonel.

She had nothing more to talk about, so she switched the screen over to repeats of the news digests and watched them as she ate her meal. Another good thing about Agent Tepp was that she took the hint and didn't speak, either. When the waiter brought their coffee, she said, "Thanks for keeping me company, Agent Tepp, but I imagine you have duties here—"

Agent Tepp touched a napkin to her lips. "Yes, ma'am. Can I ask you something? If you're going to be on permanent duty here, you'll probably need an aide—"

Hilda didn't let her finish. "What's that about permanent duty? Have you been hearing latrine talk?"

"No, ma'am. It's just logical, I thought. But if I was wrong—"

"I hope to God you were wrong." Hilda thought for a moment. "Still," she said, "I wouldn't mind thinking about having you in my command if you wanted to come to New York."

Tepp looked disappointed. "Thank you, ma'am, but I'd really like to stay at HQ for a while."

"Fine. Now if you'll excuse— Wait a minute."

It was the deputy director on her screen. "Hilda, we need that Adcock woman. Get her down to the pit galleries."

So that was where he'd been holed up! Pell didn't wait for an answer. Hilda started to get up just as Agent Tepp was doing the same, saying regretfully, "Thank you for the meal, ma'am. It was a pleasure to talk to you."

Hilda put her hand on the woman's arm. "Maybe you can do me a favor. You look like you're about my size. Do you keep a change of clothes here? Fine, then lend me some clean underwear and find me a shower I can use."

5

Dr. Patrice Adcock hadn't been taken back to her cell. Instead they put her in a quite comfortable bedroom in a little suite that apparently was kept for VIP visitors who couldn't, or didn't choose to, go home to sleep. It had a really comfortable bed, which was a nice change from the iron-hard cot in her old cell. For all the good it did her. First she lay awake, wondering just what the hell was going on *now?* Another Dannerman? Radioing to Earth from *Starlab?* When she did at last fall asleep it didn't last, because that Morrisey woman woke her to say the deputy director needed to talk to her. Right *now.*

So Pat climbed wearily back into her jail uniform. She let herself be conducted to where Marcus Pell and six or seven other people were huddled around screens and little tables littered with coffee cups and the remains of largely uneaten food, and then what was it he asked her? It was, Did Starlab have facilities for something called a 300-digit-prime coordinated-chaos encryption system? Of course she had no idea about that. Whatever it was. Well—less patiently—who would know the answer? Anyone at the Observatory? She thought about that, then shrugged. Maybe, but they would all be asleep now, for God's sake, and anyway the real expert was Rosaleen Artzybachova, who was dead.

And then, the funny thing, they all suddenly looked both surprised and relieved. The deputy director man—was his name Pell?—nodded to the Morrisey woman. That was the end of it. The woman took Pat back to her new home and left her to lie awake an hour or so longer, with all the old questions and a dozen new ones to keep her from sleep.

So when a uniform knocked at her door and opened it a crack she woke at once. "Good morning, ma'am," the woman said civilly. "It's oh-eight-hundred, and you might want to get ready to see the deputy director." Then she closed the door, without saying when the deputy director was likely to arrive. Or why.

But when Pat Adcock came out of her very own private bathroom—another touch of luxury, complete with a full array of toiletries in their original unopened wrappings—she made a pleasing discovery. The guard must have come back while she was in the shower. Pat's own clothes—the ones she had been arrested in—were draped over the foot of the bed, cleaned and ready to put on.

A few minutes later, dressed in something other than that jail uniform after all these long weeks and pleased about that much, anyway, she opened the door. It led into a little sitting room, with comfortable chairs and pictures on the wall and even a fireplace—fake, of course, but a nice touch. A moment later Dannerman came out of his own room to join her, just in time for the guard to roll in a cart loaded with breakfast.

Dannerman gave her an appreciative grin. "Hey, nice outfit. Did you have a good night's sleep?"

She didn't bother to answer that, and after an uncertain moment he turned his attention to their breakfast. Pat took a while longer to get to it, but when she tasted the fresh, ripe papaya and the cold, sweet juice she dug in as well. It was the best meal she'd had since the police had picked her up at her Observatory.

Her Observatory. She wondered if it was really still hers.

Well, probably the Observatory itself was still running, more or less normally; Uncle Cubby's money was still available to finance its operations, and no doubt Pete Schneyman, or one of the other senior scientists, had taken over as acting director in her absence. Gwen Morisaki would be going right on with her Cepheid counts and Kit Papathanassiou with his cosmological studies and all the rest of it, whether she was present or not. Things might even be going better without her because, Pat had to admit, her last few months at the Observatory she'd been a lot more interested in Starlab than in doing science.

The other question that entered her mind was to wonder if she herself were in bankruptcy yet.

The economic fact was that she had hocked just about everything she owned to raise the money for her flight to the orbiter. Money shouldn't have been any problem at all. The government should have financed or provided the whole thing. But the government hadn't. So she'd had to find the money herself. It came to serious money, too, enough to bribe the Floridian authorities who controlled the launchpads at the Cape, to hire pilots, to fight the Feds' lawyers through the courts until, reluctantly, they did give in and provide a launch vehicle for her.

And then she had managed to get that Clipper launched with the five of them in it. And then—

And then it all went to hell. "Dan-Dan?" she said tentatively.

He looked up warily from his eggs Benedict. "Yeah?"

She said slowly, trying to think it through as she spoke, "You know what's funny, Dan? I can remember the flight up to orbit, I can remember the flight back. But all I can remember of what we saw in Starlab was that everything was just the way it was left when the satellite was abandoned. There wasn't anything there that wasn't on the specs. Nothing had changed."

How "United" Are the United Nations?

The current imbroglio in the United Nations General Assembly reminds us once more of the worser consequences of the infamous Resolution 1822. Under this, you may recall, the General Assembly decreed that each signatory nation was to elect one delegate to the Assembly by means of popular vote. This well-meaning "reform" was intended to ensure that the people at large, rather than some junta or clique, represented each country in its deliberations; the models for this were the European Community's Council and, more appositely, the United States Senate.

But what has been the effect? Rather than achieving unity, the delegates now represent parochial issues and, worse, political parties. In this "Parliament of Man," with its lamentable tendency toward passing sweeping resolutions that are meant to micromanage purely internal matters throughout the world, our own delegate, Mr. Hiram Singh—who, it will be remembered, was until recently First Lord of the Admiralty in the New Labor Party government—is not least at fault.

Do we really want to import the tawdry political practices of the Americans to govern our planet? We think not. We think it is time for a thoroughgoing reconsideration of this ill-advised measure.

—*Financial Times,* London

"Nothing had."

"Well, I know that. I remember *remembering* that, when we were on our way back. But I don't remember *seeing* it. Do you know what I mean?"

He frowned. "Well, that's the way it was for me, too. It's funny, now that you mention it."

"Do you think your Bureau people know why that is?"

But he was shaking his head. "Not those turkeys. They don't know any more than we do."

When the door opened again, the man who came in was the deputy director, Marcus Pell. He was followed by one of the uniformed cops. "Coffee for you too, sir?" the cop suggested.

"Coffee my ass. It might be breakfast time for you, but for me it's just the tail end of a long, long night. Get us a bottle of Jim Beam and some glasses." He turned to Pat. "You were right, Dr. Adcock."

He caught her off-balance. "What was I right about?"

"Alien technology. The man said so himself. The orbiter's loaded with it . . . among other things. No"—he held up his hand—"I don't know exactly whose technology, or how it got there. We're having to be careful about communicating. You know all about that, Dr. Adcock; that's what we got you out of bed for."

"Was I actually any help?" she asked curiously. "It didn't look that way."

He gave her a judicious look, punctuated by a yawn "Sorry. Well, you were and you weren't. What you did was remind us of Dr. Artzybachova."

"But she's dead!"

He shook his head, looking amused. "Not anymore. She's alive and well on your Starlab. Or one of her is. There are a lot of duplicate people around, wouldn't you say? So we sent her a narrow-beam query. She didn't have anything that could make a really secure link, but we worked out a code."

Dannerman was asking the deputy director questions, but Pat hardly heard. She was trying to get used to the idea of Rosie Artzybachova alive again. Then she remembered to ask a question. "Why are you making such a big secret out of it?"

He grinned at her. "You're asking me that? The lady that bet the ranch on finding extraterrestrial technology? Because if any part of what this man is saying is true, then there's a lot of stuff there that we want, and maybe we want to keep it for ourselves—ah, about time," he finished, as the door opened, and two of the uniforms came in. Silently they set down the whiskey, some mixers, glasses, ice, even a tray of hastily slapped-together hors d'oeuvres, glanced at the deputy director for permission to leave again, and did.

Pell poured himself two fingers of whiskey, disdaining the ice and the mixers. "Help yourselves," he invited.

Pat shook her head. "I didn't know prisoners were allowed to have liquor," she said.

He gave her a friendly smile—no, she thought, not really a smile of any kind of friendship; it was the kind of smile you manufactured to make somebody think you were being friendly when you wanted to soften them up. This was a complex and totally controlled man. "You're thinking about those federal charges against you. Bribery, filing false flight plans—all chickenshit, of course. You can forget them. They're dropped. And as for you, Dannerman"—he shrugged—"your suspension is lifted, too. You're back on duty, with full pay restored."

Incoming dispatch.
Spanish Federal Police, Madrid.
To Director U.S. National Bureau of Investigation.
Most secret.

Humint indicates probable major action by Catalan separatist forces in connection with the Iberian games, to be held in Barcelona this spring. Internal source states a large shipment of weaponry and explosive devices is expected from American sympathizers, probably channeled through Basque underground. Urgently request cooperation in dealing with this terrorist threat, in particular in identifying and embargoing arms shipment.

Dannerman looked wary, fingering his collar. "What about this?"

"Well," the deputy director said, "that's a whole other thing, isn't it? Are you sure you want it taken off?"

Dannerman's expression changed, now mostly puzzled. "Why wouldn't I?"

Pell's glass was empty; he refilled it, but this time with soda and ice and just enough whiskey to tint it lightly. "You know what you two have inside your skulls," he said. "Did it ever occur to you that some people might want to get their hands on those things? Even if they had to kill you in the process?"

Pat Adcock felt a sudden chill. "What people?"

"Why, Dr. Adcock," the man said cozily, "I would say just about anybody. Including some of our own people right here in the Bureau, I wouldn't be surprised. But don't worry about that; the President himself forbade any surgical attempts. So maybe you'd like to keep enjoying our hospitality for a while, don't you think? Or, if you'd rather go out into the world again, we'll supply you with as much protection as we can, same as we've done with Danno here, but there would certainly be a risk."

"Damn it," Dannerman said with feeling. "I knew I was being followed."

"Of course you did," Pell said, smiling that warm-hearted, empty smile again. "One way of looking at it, you were bait. If someone wanted to snatch you, we'd pick him up before he could get very far."

Dannerman was looking at him with distaste. "That's assuming they wanted to kidnap me alive. But if they were going to have to kill me anyhow—"

"You're not thinking it through," Pell said reprovingly. He reached out and tapped Dannerman's collar. "That thing is tough plastic and metal. As long as you had that on your neck nobody could whack your head off and hustle it away before we got to them. So what would be the point of killing you on the street? No, we figured you were pretty safe . . . and, of course, there were other reasons for having you wear the collar. There was always the possibility that you were dirty after all, wasn't there? Colonel Morrisey was pretty sure you weren't. But some people had other opinions, and we had to cover all the bases."

Dannerman said doggedly, "I want it off."

"Yes, I thought you would. Well, when Hilda comes back I'll have her take you down to the shop and they'll remove it. . . . Excuse me." There had been an inaudible signal; Pell lifted his phone to his ear. He listened for quite a long time, spoke briefly—Pat couldn't make out a word—and listened again. When he was through he looked up at them.

"Well," he said, sounding pleasantly surprised, "sometimes you get lucky when you least expect it. The Cape's socked in—thunderstorms, high winds; the weather's going to persist for a couple of days at least. So they can't land there. That's good; the last thing we want is to get the Floridians involved in this."

"So where will they land?"

"That's the question, isn't it? They're working on it. Meanwhile, the President has warned everybody, especially the damn Europeans, that Starlab is U.S. property and anyone who attempts to board it risks being shot at."

Pat stared at him blankly. "*Shot* at? What with?"

Pell said comfortably, "I always knew some of those old Star Wars orbiters might come in useful someday. There are two of them that still have some navigation capacity. They're in the wrong part of the orbit, but the guys in Houston are working on moving them into position even as we speak. Of course the Europeans and the Chinese and so on know that. So we can leave it alone for a while, and right now the first thing we're going to do is to get that party of nine down—and there are some surprises there. They're not all human, you see."

"Not all *human?*"

"That's what Dannerman says, yes. He said a lot of other stuff, too—until we told him to shut up, even in code, and report in full once he's landed." He hesitated. "One thing, though. You're an astronomer, Dr. Adcock. Have you ever heard of somebody named Frank Tipler?"

"Tipler?" She frowned. "I think I might've heard the name—"

"He was some kind of astronomer, too. Late twentieth century. We retrieved all we could find about him from the bank, but the only interesting thing was that he wrote a book once about how Heaven was astronomically real."

"Oh, right," Pat said, tracking down a faint recollection. "I remember hearing something about him—maybe in grad school? It sounded pretty silly to me. What does Tipler have to do with all this?"

"That's what I'd like to know. Dannerman—the other Dannerman, I mean—said we should look him up. If I get you access to the network, can you do the Bureau a favor and see what you can find?"

For Dr. Patrice Adcock the worst thing about jail was having nothing to do—this woman who had never before in her life found herself with nothing to do. Now things were looking up. She wasn't in jail anymore and, better still, she had a job to do that she was good at.

It took Pat an impatient half hour's waiting to get access to Bureau's databank—no, not the *classified* databank, of course, but to the one that accessed most of the country's libraries. Then it took a while longer to get used to the Bureau's procedures. She found the *American Men of Science* entry for Dr. Frank Tipler quickly and began sorting through some of the sources cited. She hardly noticed when Dannerman was back, collarless and occasionally touching his now bare neck to remind himself of the change. That Colonel Hilda Morrisey came in with him.

"New orders, Dr. Adcock," Morrisey said cheerfully. "We're all going for a little ride tonight. The people from Starlab are coming down, and we're going to meet them."

6

Dan Dannerman had never been in the deputy director's plane before. In spite of himself, he was impressed. It wasn't one of those custom-converted thousand-seat leviathans, like the President's Air Force One, but those few who had experienced both reported that it was just as luxurious. Dannerman and Pat Adcock were even given a private compartment of their own. Their little cubicle wasn't as fancy as the room Colonel Hilda had appropriated for her own use, and certainly it was nothing like the four-room private suite belonging to the D.D. himself, but it definitely was not shabby. It had full electronics. It had cut flowers floating in a sort of fishbowl, a pair of screens, a call button for one of the police-cadet flight attendants, even two pullout beds neatly made up in case they wanted to sleep on the way—on the way to wherever they were going, because neither Pat nor Dannerman had been given the word on where that might be.

Dannerman had lost his sense of time. Somehow a whole day had got away from him, all spent on waiting. After the long wait time while the deputy director got his ducks in order there was the waiting for the Bureau's sniffer squads to finish their routine inspections—you never knew where someone might sneak in a bomb. It was full dark again by the time they took off.

Dannerman saw Pat cast one yearning look at the beds, but then she resolutely turned her back on them. She had no time to sleep because she was busy at one of the screens, checking databases for information on the Tipler person for the deputy director. Dannerman wasn't sleeping, either, but the reason was different. The prospect of seeing this man who claimed to use his own name and spoke with his own voice had pumped him full of adrenaline. He used his screen on and off, sometimes to kill time by watching news summaries, sometimes to try to find answers to some of the questions that inflamed his thoughts. Perhaps some of the answers were there, but Dannerman didn't have enough clearance to penetrate these particular systems.

He was seriously considering trying out one of the beds after all when Pat made a small grunt of conditional satisfaction. She sat back, watching the printer squirt out hard copy.

"Did you find what you wanted?" Dannerman asked.

"I hope," she said, standing up, evidently getting ready to take the printout to Marcus Pell. "It's weird. You can read it for yourself on the screen."

"Weird how?"

But she was gone. He shifted to her seat and scrolled the screen, beginning to read.

> Dr. Frank Tipler was a highly respected cosmologist until he published the book called *The Physics of Immortality.* In it Tipler predicted that the universe, currently expanding, sooner or later would fall back to what is called "the Big Crunch," reproducing the conditions of the Big Bang, but in reverse. At that time, Tipler said, everyone who had ever lived anywhere in the universe would be reborn to live again as an immortal. Most of Tipler's colleagues laughed at his idea, but there were two significant groups who shared his opinion, though Tipler had never heard of either.

"Weird" was the right word. This Frank Tipler had published a book, back in the closing years of the twentieth century. It was called *The Physics of Immortality,* and what it was about was Tipler's theory—only he didn't call it a theory; he claimed it was fact, and offered a hundred pages of equations to prove it—that the universe, after expanding as far as it could, would contract again into what he called "the Omega Point" . . . and then some very strange things would happen.

The first part of it wasn't surprising. That was what the messages from space had described, years before: the Big Bang and the universe's expansion, the recollapse into the Big Crunch. The surprising part was the consequence that was predicted in Tipler's book. According to Tipler, at that Omega Point or Big Crunch, whichever you chose to call it, everybody who had ever lived would inevitably be brought to life again—in perfect health, at the peak of their powers—and would go on living forever.

It was, Tipler said, the scientific reality that underlay all the ancient human yearnings for a Heaven after death.

Dannerman scrolled the report again, just to make sure he hadn't missed something—like the reason why this alleged other Dan Dannerman wanted the Bureau to know about this Tipler person. He hadn't. That was all there was.

That was typical of the way the Bureau was run. Nobody told any inferior anything until they absolutely had to. Dannerman had a cynical theory about that. It was turf protection. The more information the higher-ups hung on to for themselves, the harder it was for some lower-down to leapfrog above them in the chain of command. Of course, that kind of secrecy never worked for long. Sooner or later some one person in the know would see a tactical advantage for himself in telling Dannerman what was up. . . .

Might, for instance, at least tell him where they were going. When they boarded the plane Pell had said they were going to meet the people from Starlab, and that was all. Dannerman craned his neck to peer out the window, but that didn't help. It was starry dark out there, no Sun or Moon to give him at least a clue about their direction of travel. The only thing he could be sure of was that they had to be heading generally west or north. Had to be; because otherwise they'd be out over ocean by now, and they weren't. He could catch glimpses of lights on the ground far below.

Resigned, he decided to get a little sleep.

As it turned out, it was very little. He had hardly closed his eyes when Pat Adcock returned from Pell's private quarters forward in the plane. She was holding a partly full cup of coffee, trying not to spill any, and she looked annoyed. "Oh, listen," she said, setting the cup down, "I got this from one of the stews, but I didn't stop to think about whether you might want some."

"I'd rather sleep. What's all this Omega Point stuff?"

She gestured toward the screen, which still displayed her report. "All I know is what it says there. I think somebody once mentioned Tipler and his idea in one of my seminars, but nobody took it very seriously, and I don't remember anything else about it."

"And you gave the report to the D.D.? What'd he say?"

She grinned. "He was asleep. I woke him up when I came in and what he said was, 'Shit.' That was all. Then he waved at me to get out, but I didn't go."

> Eschatology, which is the study of last things, is a fundamental part of nearly all of Earth's religions. Buddhism speaks of the eternal bliss called Nirvana, while the Biblical Book of Revelations describes the eschaton in more specific and concrete terms: "And death shall be no more, neither shall there be mourning nor crying nor pain any more." It is what some religions call "Heaven." As it turned out, there were other parties who didn't think of that state as religious. For them it was a strategic objective, and they were prepared to fight for it.
>
> —NBI briefing document

"You didn't?"

"Well, I had some questions I wanted answered—like what I was doing on this plane. So I asked him. I said I knew they wanted you along to confront this other Dannerman, but what did they want from me?"

Dannerman, who had been wondering the same thing, asked, "So why did they?"

"He didn't exactly say. He just said he'd rather I saw for myself."

"Saw what?"

She shrugged. "He didn't say that, either. Then when I stopped for coffee on the way back the stew told me that we were going to start coming down for a landing pretty soon, so we better strap ourselves in. Oh," she added, fumbling for her seat belt, "there was one other thing. You want to know where we're going? It's Canada. They ordered the escape vehicle from Starlab to come down at someplace called Calgary."

Calgary turned out to be really cold, and when Dannerman left the warm plane for the freezing dark outside an unexpected memory struck him. He had been there before. It had been a summer when the girl he was involved with at the time had made up her mind to go off on a fossil dig in the Alberta bone beds. Somewhere or other among his scattered possessions—most likely in one of the Bureau's warehouses for storing the things an agent couldn't carry around with him—he probably still had a souvenir of her. It was a pair of neckbones of some terrier-sized hundred-million-year-old dinosaur. She had had them made into cuff links for him, just before she told him she was marrying her paleontology professor.

Dannerman didn't remember Calgary very well, but something he had been told about its airport had stuck in his mind. It possessed a hellish long runway, because at one time it had been designated as an alternate emergency landing site for the old Space Shuttle.

Which, of course, was just what was needed for Starlab's Assured Crew Return Vehicle.

Another plane was coming in, also a big one. It looked to Dannerman like a troop transport. He strolled over to where Colonel Morrisey was watching it land, close enough to the deputy director so he could find her if he had orders for her, far enough away not to intrude. "Okay, Hilda," Dannerman said, keeping his voice down, "explain something to me. I understand the return ship from Starlab probably needs a lot of landing strip, but why in Canada, for God's sake?"

She didn't look at him. "Security, what do you think? Everybody in the world is watching Starlab now, and they've seen the ACRV detach itself to come down. There'll be people waiting at every possible airport in the States." She gave him a sidelong glance, almost affectionate. "Don't worry. It's all worked out with the Canadians; the President himself flew to Ottawa to make a deal with the Prime Minister. Where's your cuz?"

"Pat went into the terminal to get warm." Actually Dannerman was thinking of doing the same thing. There was a freezing wind coming across the bare space of the airport; he'd been lucky enough to have the anorak he was taken to the headquarters in, but even so his face was hurting from the cold. Pat hadn't been that fortunate. When she was arrested they picked her up indoors and she hadn't been out in the open air ever since. At the last minute one of the stews had found her a spare jacket that belonged to one of the pilots, but it was meters too big and did nothing for her bare legs.

What kept Dannerman out in the cold was the spectacle overhead. There were more stars than he had seen in years, and what looked like a handsome aurora borealis display off toward the horizon. But when he pointed it out to Hilda she said mildly, "Asshole, that's the Sun getting ready to rise." She paused to listen to the button in her ear, and then said, "They've got through reentry all right. They say ETA in thirty-five minutes."

Dannerman felt a sudden chill of a different kind. He was that close to seeing this person who claimed to be himself. He tried not to speculate—some bizarre alien creature that had duplicated his voice as a disguise?—but it was a queasy, unpleasant feeling all the same.

Hilda was squinting at the horizon. "It ought to be broad daylight by then, and that's what they wanted—they didn't want to risk a night landing, but they wanted them to get down as fast as possible. But I dunno. I hope this Chinaman knows what he's doing. Isn't he going to be landing right into the Sun?"

"That's not how it works," Dannerman said, out of the superior experience of somebody who had actually once made a return flight from orbit. "They swing around to land from the east—it's to take advantage of Earth's rotation." He looked to see if she was impressed. She wasn't. "I think I'll go use the men's room while I can."

When he was inside the warmth of the terminal seduced him into lingering. He spotted Pat, wanly hunched over a cup of coffee by one of the vast glass windows with her junior-agent minder alertly sitting just behind. He located the place where the coffee was coming from and, supplied, sat down next to her; she glanced up at him, fretfully curious. "What are all the soldiers for?"

Looking out at the floodlit runway, he could see what she was talking about. The troop transport had nosed up to the hardstand next to the terminal. Its clamshell bow had opened and three personnel carriers, each filled with armed infantrymen, eased themselves down the ramp, followed by a company or more of commandos on foot. The newcomers were all in U.S. combat uniforms, but a pair of RCMPs were glumly watching the spectacle. "I guess the Mounties don't want anybody interfering," he said.

The minder cleared her throat to attract his attention. "Can I get you anything, Agent Dannerman?"

When he took a closer look at her he recognized the woman: Merla Tepp, the one who had interrogated him. "Since when are you a stewardess?"

"Since I volunteered for the flight, sir. You know how it is. You want to be promoted, you stay where the big brass can see you."

"You'll go a long way," Dannerman said absently, glancing toward the huge window. Something was moving. As it rushed past he identified it as another plane dropping toward the runway, and turned to the minder. "Hey, is that—"

She shook her head. "No, sir, it isn't the Starlab ACRV. That plane's from Ottawa; it's expected."

"Maybe I should get back outside."

Junior Agent Tepp touched her right ear, the one with the communications button. "They'll let me know when it's time," she offered. "If you want to stay in the warm, there'll be a while yet."

"Thanks," he said gratefully, and then realized that it wasn't all generosity on her part. As long as he and Pat stayed inside she could, too. He yawned and sat down, suddenly aware that the warmth had made him sleepy. Drowsily he watched as the new plane slowed, turned off the landing strip and trundled toward the terminal; it had a familiar look to Dannerman, though he couldn't see its markings. Airport crews were already rolling a flight of steps toward it, and the door was opening almost before the plane stopped. Three or four people got out and hustled toward the group with the deputy director. At least one of them also looked vaguely familiar to Dannerman, but he couldn't make out the face. He yawned and closed his eyes. . . .

He didn't realize he had fallen asleep until he felt Merla Tepp shaking his shoulder.

"Show time, sir," she was saying. "They want us out there now."

It was full daylight now, though not a whit less cold. But at least the bosses weren't standing out in the freezing winds anymore; someone had got smart enough to collect an airport bus, and they were all inside it, its heater going full blast, at the end of the runway. A squad of the commandos was deployed around it in full winter gear, all of them carrying weapons; but the soldiers waved them in when they saw the uniformed minder.

That was when Dannerman saw who it was who had just come from Ottawa. It was the Bureau director herself. The Cabinet officer. The woman whose pictures showed her always superbly coiffed, wearing what the latest fashion decreed, and perpetually busy on the highest of high-level affairs. Dannerman had not been physically in the director's presence since she addressed his graduating class.

He could hear only fragments of what the director and the D.D. were talking about. "Yes, Marcus," the director was saying to her deputy, now suddenly deferential, "the Prez squared it all. I wrote the Prime Minister's order to the Calgary people myself." An unheard question from Marcus Pell, then an answer from the director almost as hard to hear, because she looked around and lowered her voice. She seemed to be saying that they'd promised something to the Canadians. Probably a share of whatever they got out of Starlab, Dannerman speculated, and amused himself by thinking about how much the Canadians would ever collect on that promise. If he knew the director, not a great deal.

> When the American Congress got tired of passing laws that instructed their successors of a few generations later—but not themselves—to balance the damn budget once and for all, they took a different tack. They simply decided not to bother anymore. It was simpler just to borrow more money. Of course, that led to the problem of paying the interest on the money they borrowed. That was a cost of government they could not escape, nor could they avoid paying for more and more police. So everything else had to be cut—notably the space program.
>
> —*Ad Astra*

"Here it comes," somebody said.

Dannerman caught a glint of metal over the mountains to the west. As predicted, the ACVR sailed past them, far overhead but descending as it banked and turned. It grew larger, settling down toward the ground, wobbling slightly . . . and then it was touching down at the far end of the runway. Plumes of smoke erupted from its tires as they squealed against the runway. Then suddenly the thing was screeching past them, still going a hundred kilometers an hour or better on its stilty landing gear. Behind it ground vehicles began to give chase: two of the personnel carriers filled with troops, a fire truck, an ambulance. "Get this thing moving!" the deputy director roared, and the bus driver obeyed.

The spacecraft was well ahead of them, still speeding. For a moment Dannerman feared that even the endless Calgary runway wasn't going to be long enough for this job. But it was—barely. By the time they reached the end of the runway the clumsy old antique was sitting there, its ancient ceramic tiles cracked and smoking, and two squads of riflemen had surrounded it—to protect it from any of those expected interlopers, Dannerman assumed, until he noticed that the ring of soldiers was facing in.

As they all piled out of the bus he could hear cracking sounds coming from it as it began to cool. "Get those people out of that thing," the director snapped.

One of the men with him cleared his throat. "It's risky," he said. "The lander's still too hot to touch; we have to wait a minute—"

"So cool it off!"

The airport fire chief rubbed his chin. "We could foam it, I guess," he said, "but I don't know if that would make much difference. And of course we can't use water."

"*Why* can't you use water?"

The fireman looked surprised. "It would crack the tiles. It might ruin the vehicle permanently."

"Now, what difference do you think that would make? Listen, half the radars in the world have followed that thing down. We're going to have visitors in the next hour. *Ruin* the son of a bitch!"

When the pumpers started to pour water on the spacecraft everybody jumped back. Even so, they were splashed. The water from the hoses flashed into steam as soon as it touched the skin of the spaceship. Droplets of boiling hot water that almost instantly turned into icy cold water flew in all directions, and the ceramic tiles snapped and popped loudly.

But it worked. Within no more than a minute or two the pumpers stopped, and the airport crews trundled the wheeled steps up to the cabin door.

It opened.

The first person out of it was a real surprise to Dannerman and a far greater one to Pat Adcock. It was *another* Pat Adcock, grimy, worn, hunching one arm around her chest against the cold as she cautiously made her way down the steps.

The second person was a greater surprise still, because it was yet an additional Pat Adcock; with her arm around the frail and limping figure of a new Rosaleen Artzybachova. Who was alive! Dannerman had gone to Artzybachova's memorial service himself, after she died on the way back from their trip to Starlab. But here she was, suddenly possessing a new life.

The third figure was still another Pat Adcock. That made three of them to go with the fourth Pat Adcock who was standing beside Dannerman, who moaned to herself, "Oh, *Jesus!* What is happening here?"

Then a chunkier, male figure appeared. It had an unfamiliar skimpy beard, but it was definitely Jimmy Lin, the Chinese pilot, sulkily staring around him and shivering in the chill. He was almost immediately followed by someone who—though also bearded, and definitely somewhat beat-up and exhausted—looked exactly like Dan Dannerman.

It *was* Dan Dannerman. The watching Dannerman couldn't doubt it any longer. That was the face he had seen in his shaving mirror—less bearded then, of course—every morning of his life.

How that was possible he could not imagine; but that it was real was no longer in doubt. Those clear memories of what had happened in his trip to Starlab? They had somehow been falsified. His head had been implanted with that damn gadget the X rays showed, and his mind had been tampered with. And he hadn't been aware of a thing.

He shook himself and turned back to the gangplank. That had been six persons; but the Dannerman on the radio had spoken of a party of nine. Who were the other three? More Dannermans? A couple of Martín Delasquezes, the Floridian copilot on the expedition? Maybe even some more Pats?

It wasn't any of those. It was something a good deal more strange. The figure that appeared in the doorway was huge, pale, and not in any way human. It looked to Dannerman like a multiarmed golem, and it carried another creature stranger still—a dwarfish being that looked like a turkey with a cat's head, incongruously wearing a gold-mesh belly bag.

But he had seen those things before, Dannerman realized. Drawings of them, at least; they were two of the weird aliens whose pictures had appeared in the mysterious messages from space, long before.

As that first alien made his way down the steps a second of the same species appeared. By then the ring of soldiers had instinctively dropped to their knees, their rifles zeroed in on the aliens. "Don't shoot!" wailed a thin, high voice Dannerman had never heard before; and it was only one more surprise to realize that it came from the kitten-faced turkey that was cradled in the first golem's arms.

7

For once in her life Hilda Morrisey wasn't sorry to be in the presence of the Bureau's highest brass. There were decisions now to be made that had never come up in any field operation. The procession of improbables that had come out of the old spacecraft had simply paralyzed her decision-making faculties.

Fortunately for the people who had to make those decisions, some of the problems solved themselves. What to do about the old lady from Ukraine? The first medics to arrive took one look at her and didn't wait for orders. In half a minute they had her on a wheeled stretcher and one of the medics was pushing it toward the open ambulance door while the other two palped and poked her from alongside.

The other human beings were all lightly dressed and clearly freezing in the cutting Canadian prairie wind—like Hilda herself. The director and her D.D. were softly debating high policy considerations, frowning, pausing to make hurried calls on their coded carryphones. They seemed impervious to cold. Hilda wasn't. She caught the eye of one of the Mounties, the one that looked to be the most senior officer around. "Any reason we can't get back in that bus?"

"Reckon not," he said, then took matters into his own hands. He hustled everyone into the bus—the Pat who had flown up from the Bureau's flight strip plus three (Hilda counted) additional Pat Adcocks, Dannerman and the bearded second Dannerman (apart from the beard quite indistinguishable to Hilda's eyes; if he was not the very Agent James Daniel Dannerman she had run in a dozen operations over the years, he was certainly so close that she couldn't tell the difference); the hired pilot from China named James Peng-tsu Lin, looking grouchy and, for some reason, upset. . . .

U.S. President Reported in Ottawa Airport.

Police sources confirm that the President of the United States arrived at the Ottawa airport early this morning for a top-secret meeting with the Prime Minister. The meeting is said to be related to the broadcast from the U.S. astronomical satellite, Starlab. No further information available at this time.

—*Toronto Star*

And three others.

It was the three others that made a peculiar situation totally bizarre. The little one that looked like a turkey didn't actually look that much like a turkey, after all. The face didn't belong to any kind of poultry. It was more like that of some ill-tempered tiger cub, Hilda thought. The plume that decorated its tail was almost peacock in its colorful splendor, but it wasn't made of feathers at all. It was a display of something more like fish scales that changed color from moment to moment as its owner gazed around in displeasure.

"Colonel Morrisey?" Hilda turned swiftly when she heard her name called, and wasn't surprised to find it was that ubiquitous junior agent, Tepp. The woman was pointing at the turkey, and her finger was shaking. "It's *Dopey!*"

And, Hilda saw, yes, it was. Its picture had been part of the zoo of weirdos that had been displayed in one of those unexplained—or now beginning to be explained—lunatic messages that had arrived from space a year or two before. This was the one they called "Dopey," all right. It was not really comical in appearance, but it wasn't particularly scary, either . . . unlike the other two.

Those were definitely frightening to look at. They were *big*. The bus sagged perceptibly on its springs as they entered. And they were sure-hell ugly: fish-belly skin, multiple arms, with a white-fluff beard over the lower part of their faces that was more like foam plastic than hair. Hilda decided they were the ones called "Doc." The Dopey-creature seemed quite at ease at being carried by one of the pale monsters. Even the six humans who had come out of the spaceship seemed to pay them little attention. The Earthbound ones in the welcoming party, though, kept a wary distance. One of the Mounties had dutifully interposed himself between the Docs and the humans, presumably in case these space monsters suddenly began ravaging and murdering, but he did not seem happy about it. And when the Dopey hopped down from the arms of his bearer and began to investigate the interior of the bus the Mounty said sharply, "Scoot! Get back there, you!"

The man was waving his arms as though at an unfamiliar, but probably not really dangerous, stray animal. Dopey peered up at him.

"But why?" he asked reasonably, and, to Hilda's surprise, in impeccable English. "I am simply curious about this crude vehicle."

"Get back," the Mounty said, his tone still firm although his expression was distinctly uneasy. The little alien flicked its great spread of tail and sulkily obeyed.

All this Colonel Hilda Morrisey was observing and trying to remember in every detail. She wasn't pleased. There should have been recording devices in place to catch every word and every movement for analysis later on. Those first few minutes after you got a suspect in custody were the most important; that was when some unguarded remark might slip out that you could pounce on later. She fretted over wasting opportunities. The sooner they got these—people—into Bureau custody, the sooner interrogation could begin.

But she couldn't do it here. All she could do at this point was listen.

There wasn't much to listen to. The human arrivals were obviously on the ragged edge of exhaustion. Dannerman and Dr. Pat Adcock—the *real* Dannerman and Pat Adcock—were trying to engage the new ones in conversation, but they were too wasted to respond much.

Except for one of the new Pats, who was looking thoughtfully from one Dannerman to another. When she caught the "real" Dannerman's eye she smiled, got up and sat down again beside him and began a low-voiced conversation. Eavesdropping, Hilda was startled to hear the woman begin a cozy conversation— "They call me Patrice—saves confusion. Well, it saves a *little* of the confusion, anyway. Listen, I'm sorry about the way I look. . . ."

Hilda raised an eyebrow. That was pickup-bar talk! The woman was actually, incongruously, making a move on Dannerman! While the other Dannerman and one of the other Pats were already sound asleep in a shared seat, the man's arm lovingly around the woman.

Horny little devils, Hilda thought wonderingly, and looked outside. The firemen were slowly trundling their trucks away, no longer necessary and a bit disappointed, while a tractor was nuzzling up to the spacecraft to haul it somewhere. The director was standing by the little ship, talking to a man in the doorway with a Bureau tag hanging from his jacket. Not far away the three ambulances were parked, with all the medics clustered around the vehicle where the old lady had been taken. As Hilda watched, that one moved off, siren blasting. A pair of the other medics came trotting over to the bus and climbed in, asking, "Anyone here need medical attention?"

The other Dannerman, roused by the sound of the sirens, looked up. Yawning, he pointed to one of the other Pats. "Better check Pat Five over. She's pregnant."

The real Pat Adcock gasped. Hilda stared at the new Dannerman. "You dog," she said, half-admiringly.

He gave her a weary shake of the head. "It wasn't me that done it, Hilda," he said. "But that's a really long story."

8

The situation wasn't that Pat Adcock—the *real* Pat Adcock, or so she couldn't help thinking of herself—had nothing to say to these three new selves. It was the other way around. She had too much. She had so many questions to ask and so many things she needed to express that she didn't know where to begin.

The real shocker was that one of her was actually getting ready to have a *baby.* That took a lot of getting used to. Pat Adcock had never been pregnant, had never really wanted to be—oh, sure, maybe now and then there had been a fleeting wistful notion, quickly gone away. Who had the time for bringing up a child? So now she sat mute in the bus while they waited to be told what to do, then stood mute in the doorway of the deputy director's plane while the D.D. and five or six others wrangled over Jimmy Lin. *This* Jimmy Lin. The one who had just returned from somewhere in space. The one who now was adamantly refusing to go anywhere at all until he had a chance to talk to the Chinese consul in Vancouver. The one, most amazingly of all, who turned out to be the father of this other Pat's child.

That was really hard to believe.

Down on the ground voices were raised in anger. The argument seemed to be between the deputy director and the RCMP officer, and the deputy director was losing. The Mountie was shaking his head firmly. Significantly, a dozen other Mounties were standing silently behind him.

Clearly the deputy director didn't want a major confrontation. He turned and stormed up the steps. "Canadian bastards," he was muttering. "First they take the old lady away from us, now it's the Chinese.

Well, it isn't worth a war." More loudly, to the people in the doorway: "Get your asses on board. We're going home."

As soon as they were airborne it started. The agents unstrapped themselves, heedless of the fact that the "Fasten Seat Belts" lights were still on. Colonel Morrisey reseated herself at a little desk by a window and pulled out a keypad. She tapped swiftly, then nodded to the other spook. "Recording has commenced," she said.

"Right," said the other female spook. "I'm Vice Deputy Director Daisy Fennell. I don't think we met before, because I flew in on the director's plane, but now I need to ask you some questions. You first, Agent Dannerman—" turning to the Dannerman with the beard. "I want you to begin at the beginning, starting with your launch to the Starlab satellite—"

But the new Dannerman was shaking his head. "First we have to eat," he said.

The vice deputy raised her voice and lowered its temperature. "Agent Dannerman," she began frostily, "you will do as I—"

He stood his ground. "Have a heart! You don't know how it is with us. We've been eating crap for months and we are damn *starved.*"

The vice deputy opened her mouth to speak again, but Colonel Morrisey stood up quickly. She murmured something to the other woman, then said, "I'll take care of that. But you start talking while you're waiting for the food, Danno."

"That'll be fine," he said, "if it's not too long." The look Hilda Morrisey gave him as she left was reproachful, but also amused, Pat thought.

"Begin," the older woman commanded. "You approached the satellite in orbit."

Dannerman nodded. "The first thing we saw was that there was some kind of blister on the side of the satellite that didn't belong there, and—"

Pat couldn't help herself. "But we *didn't!* I was looking for it; I'd seen it on the remote, and it just wasn't there."

"That'll do," Vice Deputy Fennell cut in. "You'll get your chance to talk later; now I'm taking Agent Dannerman's statement."

The new Dannerman looked at Pat quizzically, then went on. As soon as they entered Starlab, he said, they'd seen at once that it had been changed radically. New machines. Big ones. *Strange* ones. "The orbiter was full of them," he said, "and all the time we were there I had the feeling we were being watched. . . ."

* * *

It went on and on, Dannerman telling these incredible stories—these *untrue* stories, by Pat's own recollection!—while the three other Pats nodded agreement. But it hadn't happened that way!

Or had it? Had something gone really wrong with her own memory?

She hardly noticed when the food began to arrive, but all four of the returned people leaped at it.

And, as a matter of fact, when she absentmindedly took some for herself she discovered that it was an impressive meal, a tribute to the deputy director's airborne kitchen. There was a huge salad, the lettuce crisp enough to crackle, the cucumber slices neatly trimmed of skin, a few curls of a red onion and five different kinds of dressing in silver boats. It didn't go to waste. Before the steaks came—half-kilo steaks, beautifully marbled, still sizzling as the stew set them down—the three Pats and the recently arrived Dannerman (the other one had taken off for the deputy director's private office as soon as they were in the air) had finished the salad, every scrap, as well as the quarter-liter glasses of milk she kept refilling for them. The debriefing paused briefly for eating, and Pat took advantage of the chance. "Dan?" she asked. "I don't remember any of that!"

"No, of course not," he said kindly. "Dopey blanked out your memories."

"Who did *what?"*

Dannerman started to grin, but the Pat next to him tugged at his arm. He suppressed the smile. "It isn't your fault, Pat. They have all kinds of tricks—oh, what's this?"

What the stews were offering was fruit salad, and all four of the returnees cried a unanimous, "No!"

"Surprise us," one of them added. "Something that can't be freeze-dried or canned or irradiated, okay?" And then, looking at Pat, "We've been living on old stores from Starlab for months, so this is pure heaven—or would be, anyway, if this plane had a spare bathtub."

The Pat next to the real, or beardless, Dannerman apologized. "We've been a little short of that kind of thing for a long time, too. Especially poor Pat Five over there. At least Patrice and I managed to get a swim in a few days ago—oh, you want to know about the names? They were Rosaleen's idea. I'm Pat One. This is Patrice. Our pregnant one is Pat Five. What shall we call you?"

"Call me?" It was a problem Pat had not expected to face. What she was called was Pat or Dr. Adcock; that was an immutable given in her life, and there had never been a reason to think about it at all. Until now, when there were three others entitled to the same name.

"Anything but Patsy, please," said Patrice. "We had a Patsy, but— she died."

The Pat bit her lip; some interior struggle was going on. "Oh, hell," she said unhappily, "we'll talk about that later. Anyway, maybe I'll be big about this. You stay with Pat. I'll be Pat One."

"Well, thanks," Pat said, a little bit grateful, still a lot puzzled, just as a pair of stews made their entrance, carrying plates of hot apple pie with ice cream.

"Sorry we took so long," one of them apologized, "but those weirdos are in the galley, trying to find something they can eat. Christ but they take up a lot of room!"

"And they stink," said the other one, just as the *real* Dannerman came in from the front of the plane.

He seemed cheerful. "Hey, I'll take a piece of that, too. And some coffee. And then maybe a beer."

"A beer!" the other Dannerman said reverently.

The real one was grinning. "We're missing all the fun," he said. "The whole world's arriving in Calgary now. The Ukrainians are after Dr. Artzybachova, the Chinese are taking Jimmy Lin off in a hell of a hurry. Even the Floridians are complaining that you didn't bring their General Delasquez back."

"Martín's dead," Dannerman-with-a-beard said between bites. "We think he is, anyway."

"Yeah, well, I hate to second-guess the boss, but maybe moving the landing site to Canada wasn't the best idea he ever had."

Pat shushed him and turned to Pat One. "What do you mean, Martín's dead?"

It was a short question, but it had a long answer and not a cheery one. The Floridian pilot Pat had hired for her mission, General Martín Delasquez, had stayed behind to cover the rest of them while they escaped. Escaped from what? Well, there was sort of a war going on. A *big* one. How big? Well, as far as they could tell, it seemed to involve the whole damn universe.

Vice Deputy Fennell sighed. "How weird is this going to get? Let's get back to the beginning, from where you all entered Starlab."

If what these people were saying was true—and Pat realized that she didn't have any choice anymore about believing them—they had been through a hell of an ordeal. Taken captive on Starlab by the creature they called Dopey and his Docs—by them, but not *for* them; they were only subject races, doing their masters' bidding.

Backgrounder
NBI contacts file
LIN, James Peng-tsu, Cdr, PRC Spaceforce

Commander Lin has a somewhat shadowy background. A full commander in the People's Republic Spaceforce, he was dismissed from the service for reasons variously given as "political unreliability" and "sexual misconduct"; research has not definitively established which. If the misconduct was sexual, one account has it that Lin is given to reenacting the exploits of his remote ancestor, an ancient Chinese sage named Peng-tsu, who wrote a book extolling the necessity and varieties of frequent sexual experience. An alternative report, however, suggests that Lin is homosexual and the alleged heterosexual activity is a cover for what, in PRC eyes, is a serious crime.

Lin was hired as pilot by Dr. Patrice Adcock (see backgrounder file) in her mission to Starlab. There are now two of him, one who came back with the first batch of returnees from Starlab (this one bugged); the other with Agent J.D. Dannerman and the extraterrestrials. The second one is said to be the artificial-insemination father of the unborn child of the Dr. Adcock known as "Pat Five" (see backgrounder file).

And who were these masters? Why, all the newcomers agreed, the whole thing had been organized by that scarecrow creature from the space messages, a race of superbeings who chose to be called "Beloved Leaders," though why anyone should love them Pat could not imagine. Certainly their human captives had no reason to. They had been kept penned for weeks in a cell no larger than the airborne drawing room they were in, but without any of its amenities—without any amenities at all, even toilets!

That struck Pat as nasty. Then she heard a good deal nastier.

At least the original band of captives had been allowed to live intact, as a sort of control group of humans to be studied. But the aliens had other studies in mind as well, and those had been far worse. The aliens had made additional copies of their captives for anatomical research. Nearly all of those unfortunates had died during the experimentation, generally, Pat Five said, in considerable pain. She herself had been lucky. She had been the one who was chosen, pretty much at random, to become pregnant so the aliens could discover how human beings produced their young. Romance was not involved, nor even actual sexual intercourse. She had been artificially inseminated with sperm—from, she thought, one of the Jimmy Lins, though she couldn't be positive even of that—and so she alone of that group had survived.

Backgrounder
NBI contacts file
DELASQUEZ, Martín, Maj. Gen. Florida Air Guard

General Delasquez qualified for astronaut training in the U.S. NASA program, but never went into space due to the defunding of the program. When the State of Florida declared itself sovereign in its own territory, Delasquez became part of its Air Guard, rising to the rank of major general. He was attached to the Florida mission to the United Nations, stationed in New York City, when Dr. Patrice Adcock (see backgrounder file) hired him as copilot on her mission to Starlab. He returned with the others and was subsequently found to be bugged.

He was then hired by Eurospace as a consultant on Starlab when they proposed to fly their own mission to the satellite, in which capacity he served for some months at the Eurospace facility in Kourou, Guyana.

Delasquez is said to be well connected politically in Florida's Cuban-American circles. A second Delasquez is said to have died while with the others in captivity by the Scarecrows.

It did not seem to Pat that Pat Five had been all that lucky.

She tried to imagine what it might be like to be a laboratory specimen, with an unwanted new life growing inside her. Then she stopped trying to imagine it. It was more painful than she could bear.

9

Hilda Morrisey had a good imagination, too. She needed it in her work, but she also needed to be able to turn it off when it was troublesome. Which Vice Deputy Daisy Fennell evidently could not; the woman, listening with openmouthed horror, had completely lost control of the debriefing. Hilda quelled the uneasy stirrings in her own belly and spoke up. "Let's get back to business. One at a time, now. Go back to when you woke up in this place with the mirrors all around you. What happened next?"—pointing to the one who called herself Patrice.

Who shook her head. "I wasn't there. Patsy and I came along later—"

And then there was a whole confusing other story about this "Patsy"—still another copy of Dr. Adcock—and how she'd been electrocuted by some still other kind of alien monster that looked like a hippopotamus but delivered lethal electrical shocks. Only that didn't happen in the mirrored cell, it happened later on, after they'd all been taken out of the city—or the base, or the encampment or whatever you chose to call it—where they'd first arrived, and then been dumped out in the woods somewhere, because the other guys, the *other* variety of would-be universe-conquerors they called the "Horch," were fighting against the ones they called the Beloved Leaders—

Well, it went on like that. Hilda couldn't keep them from interrupting and correcting each other, not even with the help of the recovered Daisy Fennell. The two of them were trying to untangle the question of Horch *vs.* Beloved Leaders when the deputy director came in. He waved them to go on and listened for a moment, frowning silently. He didn't stay silent. That lasted only until one of the Pats said, "—so the Horch took over the helmets, you know, the things we could see things in, they showed us the Beloved Leaders destroying planets—"

"Hold it," the deputy director said. "Beloved what? Who loves them?"

"It's what the slave races call those scarecrow things," Daisy Fennell explained. "Remember? In the first transmission from space?"

"Beloved Leaders, my ass! Can't we just call them aliens?"

Hilda coughed. "There are a whole bunch of different aliens, sir."

He scowled and thought for a moment. "Scarecrows, then. That's what they look like, right? So who's fighting who in this war?"

"Basically it's those two, the Horch and the, ah, Scarecrows," Hilda said. "What they want is control of this eschaton thing."

"Which is what?"

Hilda gamely opened her mouth to try to respond, but one of the Pats saved her. "Remember what you asked us to look up, Mr. Pell? About this man Tipler? He wrote a book, back around 1995. It seems he thought at the end of the universe we'd all be born again and live forever."

The deputy director was staring at her. "You mean the Scarecrows got hold of the book by this guy Tipler?"

"Oh, no," one of the other Pats put in. "They thought it up by themselves. It wasn't until Dopey told us about it that we thought of Tipler."

"The little turkey told you?" Marcus Pell scratched his chin. "Well," he said, "maybe we should get it from the horse's mouth. Let's get them in here."

The first people in the room were a pair of armed guards. Not just armed, as everyone was these days—especially if they were in the Police Corps. These tough-looking individuals carried serious rapid-fire carbines. They took up stations beside the door just as the creatures they were guarding against came in.

Hilda smelled them before she saw them, but she wasn't prepared for what she saw. One of the big, pale creatures was carrying a selection of bowls and pitchers in various arms. The other was carrying the turkey-creature, Dopey. Who was spooning granulated sugar out of a bowl and complaining about the quality of it between mouthfuls. He was addressing the guards as they herded the golems into one corner of the salon. "Why do you treat the bearers as though they were dangerous animals?" he demanded, hopping down to the floor. "They are entirely obedient; it is their natures. Make them understand, please, Dr. Adcock, Agent Dannerman." He took one more spoonful of sugar, then handed the bowl to the Doc, dusting his hands on his belly bag. "Also make them understand that this simple sugar is not adequate for my diet. The bearer indicates it will not poison us, but why can we not have the proper food we brought from your Starlab?"

Astonishing Event!
Second Doktor-nauk R. V. Artzybachova Arrives in Kiev.

Hundreds of Ukrainians who mourned the death of the honored scientist of the Republic R. V. Artzybachova gathered outside Hospital No. 14 before dawn to welcome the return of their beloved technologist. The State Information Agency offered no explanation of how Dr. Artzybachova returned to life but stated, "There is no question. This is Dr. Artzybachova." Although the scientist was too weak to be interviewed, the Agency released a statement from her which said: "I am gratified to return to my beloved Ukraine. I wish to thank the president of the Republic and the leaders of the Democratic Duma, who have unfailingly striven to care for every citizen."

—*Vremya,* Kiev, Ukraine

The deputy director looked at him with dislike, then turned to the Pats. "Please ask this, ah, person—"

"You may call me Dopey. I do not take offense."

"—Dopey, then. Ask him about this war that's going on."

The tiger-faced little turkey made a sound of protest. "Address me directly, please. Please answer my question about the food as well."

Hilda repressed a smile. She didn't mind seeing the damn Bureau bureaucrats embarrassed, and the expression on the face of the deputy director was enough to make a cat laugh—well, not the particular cat (or cat-faced turkey) who was telling him all this. Certainly not the Docs who were simply standing where they were put, holding on to chairbacks and swaying slightly in the motion of the plane. And it wasn't making anyone else laugh.

The deputy director collected himself. "All the artifacts that came from Starlab are under seal in the cargo hold. They can't be reached until we land, and then they'll go directly to the Bureau technicians for analysis. Now tell us about this goddam war."

Dopey flirted his bright-hued tail in irritation, but complied. Hilda listened, doubting every word. Eternal life. Two great races, the Scarecrows and the Horch, each determined to rule it—forever. And willing to kill or enslave every other race in the universe to make sure they were the ones who won out. And not one word of it believable to as hardheaded a woman as Hilda Morrisey . . . if it hadn't been for the bizarre creature who was doing the talking.

When Dopey ran dry Pell had a question. "So how did this man Tipler get onto it?"

"Yes," the little alien acknowledged, "it is interesting that even a primitive like yourselves had some suspicion of the eschaton. Most races do not."

The deputy director sighed. "And you expect us to believe this crap?"

Dopey looked surprised. "Expect? No. I do not care what you believe. However, it is so. We know this, because we have been told so by our Beloved Leaders."

"Beloved Leaders," the deputy director began, his tone derisory; but then his expression changed. As he broke off, all the others turned to look at what he was seeing. One of the golems had surprisingly moved from his statuelike stance. Startled, the guards turned toward him, weapons at the ready; but all the creature did was to squat suddenly.

There was a noise as of a fountain, and a stain seeped out across the rug around him. Hilda stared in revulsion. The damn thing had pulled a little cuplike thing off its surprisingly tiny genitals, and now it was urinating on the floor! And when it had finished it stood up again, looking at the puddle in surprise.

Patrice glanced up at Dannerman with a little laugh. "You'll have to forgive our friend, Dan-Dan. They've got better floors where he comes from. They just, uh, absorb waste. I guess he never heard of flush toilets."

The deputy director stood up in disgust. "Christ," he said. "I'm getting out of here. Corporal, clean that mess up." And then, as he turned to leave, he took another look at the pouch Dopey wore on his belly. "And we'll want that thing for analysis, so take it away from him."

"No!" cried one of the Pats—no, at least two of them, and Dan Dannerman shouting something as well; but the nearest guard did as he was ordered. Or tried to. The little alien did his best to scuttle away, but the guard reached out for the reddish metal muff. And screamed. And fell back, or was thrown back, and fell to the floor.

10

Whatever the little alien's belly bag had done to the guard, the man hadn't died of it. *More's the pity,* Hilda told herself. If the damn fool had been dead, that would have been the end of it. His corpse could have been off-loaded and transported at leisure to the Bureau's autopsy facilities, where something useful might have been learned. Alive, he was a lot more trouble. He had to be personally escorted to the nearest emergency room, with a senior officer going along to make sure he didn't blab anything he shouldn't, and who was the lucky senior officer to get the job? Why, naturally it was Colonel Hilda Morrisey.

Infuriatingly the man was wide-awake and apologetic long before Hilda got him to the emergency room. The duty doctors were annoyed. "There isn't anything seriously wrong with this man," one said to Hilda. "He could stand to lose a few kilos, and I'd watch that liver, but he doesn't belong here. You say he had some kind of electric shock? Has he had medical treatment already?"

"No. Well, yes," she added, remembering that one of the golems had forced his way over to fiddle with the unconscious guard for several minutes. For all the good that could have done. "I guess you could say he had some first aid. But our plane was just landing, so we brought him right here."

When the doctor said it would probably be best to keep him overnight Hilda agreed, but required the privilege of saying a word or two in the patient's ear. When she was confident that he understood the importance of keeping his mouth shut about anything that had happened on the plane she left him. She hurried to the headquarters and one of the suites for visiting VIPs, and the first real sleep she had had in more hours than she wanted to count.

Hilda slept dreamlessly and woke herself early. She didn't need an alarm; it was a matter of will, and as soon as her eyes were open she knew where she was and what she had to do. First thing was to peek out into the suite's living room to make sure her uniform was back, cleaned and pressed overnight. It was. She retrieved it and headed for the bathroom, scooping up the underwear she'd washed and left to dry on the little line. While she was pulling her stockings on she called the Bureau's New York office on the secure line, voice only, and got the night duty officer. "Colonel Morrisey here," she told him. "I'm going to be stuck at HQ for a while. Any problems your end?" There weren't. All the ongoing operations were proceeding smoothly without her, the man said, and accepted her instructions to turn all her Studebaker files over to Major Geltmann. Then she made herself a cup of coffee from the little machine in the bathroom while she checked the situation reports.

As she expected, all four of the Pat Adcocks and both Dannermans had been stowed away in a safe house, with plenty of Bureau security surrounding them. What was more surprising was that the aliens were squirreled away with them. That couldn't be permanent, if only, Hilda reflected, because the woman agent who ostensibly lived there would have a lot to say about the damage to her carpets.

The only other item that concerned her was that a meeting of the Ananias team was scheduled for 0900. Vice Deputy Director Daisy Fennell was to be in the chair, and Hilda herself was listed as one of the participants. But Marcus Pell was not, and when Hilda checked a little farther it turned out that he, too, was logged as remaining overnight in the safe house.

Well, that made sense. If there was anything important for the National Bureau of Investigation to investigate, the place to do it was where the Starlab people were. Hilda felt a brief sense of resentment. She should have been there herself. Would have been, if she hadn't been stuck with that damn guard.

But she wasn't there, and meanwhile she had time for some errands of her own. She checked her makeup, swallowed the last of the coffee and took the elevator up to the motor pool, because she did not intend to sleep another night in that borrowed T-shirt from the Bureau's women's bowling team.

Twenty minutes later she was parking at one of Arlington's shopping malls. She did not miss the fact that the valet who took her two-seater gave her one of those oh-you're-a-cop looks—not hostile exactly, and certainly not deferential, just wary. She got the same look from the half dozen sidewalk vendors who were peddling inflation-hedge knickknacks just outside the mall entrance. Even the two city cops who were interrogating a young woman against a wall—shoplifter? someone with a cause who had, perhaps, tried to plant a stink bomb in the food department?—paused to salute her, but their expressions were as stony as the perpetrator's herself.

It was the uniform, of course.

Yanqui Bureaucrats Refuse to Release Delasquez Alleged Death Data.

Once again the Anglo politicians in Washington have denied the official demands of the sovereign State of Florida for a full and complete account of the so-called "death" of the "other" General Martín Delasquez.

—*El Diario,* Miami

Hilda Morrisey was proud of the uniform. It marked her, and everyone who wore it, as part of that group that was charged with protecting all these people—from themselves, often enough. But there were times when she didn't want to advertise what she did for a living. If she were going to stay in this area for a few days, away from the closets of her little New York City flat . . .

So once she had picked up the necessities she spent another half hour picking out things she could wear off duty. Some of them *nice* things. The sorts of things that made her look like the kind of woman a man, some man, might want to know better. Some man to replace Wilbur, who evidently wasn't going to be handy for a while.

On her way back with her acquisitions Hilda allowed herself a pleasant little reverie about that some man she had not yet met, idly switching on the news, half-listening to the garbled stories and wild speculations over the amazing reports from Calgary.

The message light flashed on the car screen.

She hit the display button. What turned up was an extract from the orders of the day. It said: *Col. MORRISEY, Hilda J. Reassigned Arlington HQ. Promoted brigadier.*

That took care of news, Wilbur and idle speculations. "You *bastard,*" she said to the air, switched over to manual drive and whipped the car around in the direction of the safe house and Deputy Director Marcus Pell.

* * *

The safe house had sixteen rooms and seven baths, not counting the Jacuzzi and the pool in the backyard. It needed them all. It was crowded, with four Pats, two Dannermans, two Docs, the Dopey, the deputy director and a couple of his interrogators—and eleven, count 'em, eleven guards in and outside the house, plus about half a dozen maids, cooks and cleaners. Who were, of course, also guards, even if they didn't flaunt their weapons quite as conspicuously as the ones in uniform.

The guard at the gate wasn't uniformed; he was dressed in overalls, and he held what looked like a leaf blower. (Bad cover, Hilda noted. The thing wasn't a real leaf blower, of course; it was something a lot more effective against any possible trespasser—but a *leaf blower?* In *December,* with patchy snow still on the ground?) He looked briefly at Hilda's uniform and the ID she flashed at him, then waved her on to the next guard. Or, actually, guards. There were two of them here, this time in uniform and standing at a checkpoint with stop-'em-dead spikes in the driveway just past their post. Hilda's rank wasn't enough to get her past them. She had to sit in the car, fuming, until the deputy director himself came strolling down from the safe house. He gave the guards a nod of the head, and waited until they had taken themselves out of earshot before he spoke. "Morning, Hilda," he said pleasantly. "I bet I know why you're here."

"I bet you damn well do, Marcus," she snarled. "I'm here to tell you that I'm quitting, and as soon as I get to a secure terminal you'll have it in writing."

He shook his head patiently. "No," he said, "I won't. Calm down, Hilda. You know this business is too big for you to sit out. Jesus!" he went on, his expression changing. "You wouldn't *believe* what kind of technology these people have! I was up half the night with that Dopey creature, and he talked straight through. My God, how he talked! Matter transmitters. Jail walls the keepers can walk through but the inmates can't pass. Weapons—oh, Hilda, the weapons they've got! You're not going to want to miss all this—"

"The hell I'm not!"

"—but," he finished, not missing a beat, "even if you did, you don't have the choice. The President has declared a national emergency, so no resignations are going to be accepted." He gave her a tolerant pat on the shoulder. "So you'll be with us for the duration, Hilda, and as long as you're here you might as well come in and get in on the fun. And by the way—congratulations on your promotion!"

* * *

Colonel—now Brigadier—Hilda Morrisey never allowed herself to waste time on resentment. That didn't mean she wasn't capable of carrying a grudge; sooner or later, she thought darkly, she would find a way to pay Marcus Pell back for all this. But that could wait.

Meanwhile, she had to admit that, yes, she really did want to be in on this bizarre affair. Pell led the way to a large room where most of the people from Starlab were gathered, the human ones, anyway. The room appeared to be the mansion's library, since the walls were lined solidly with cases of books, but no one was reading. A screen was displaying the Dopey creature, sulkily describing some other weird creatures who were involved with his "Beloved Leaders" in one way or another, but no one in the library was paying much attention to that, either. They were mostly eating. The room smelled of recent bacon and eggs, and there were pitchers of coffee and juice and remnants of toast and fresh fruits on the low tables. It looked to Hilda like the sort of breakfast pigout you might find the morning after a high-school-girl sleepover.

There was a Bureau interrogator sitting alertly in a straight-backed chair, but he wasn't interrogating. Sensibly enough, Hilda thought, he was simply listening as they talked among themselves, while his recorders were capturing everything that was said.

They all looked a lot cleaner than they had on the aircraft, and the ones from Starlab were wearing fresh clothes from the safe house's stores. They looked as though they'd had some sleep, too—not necessarily alone, Hilda thought, noting the way the Dannerman with the beard and the Pat who seemed to be affixed to him were cozily sharing a bowl of strawberries in one corner of the room.

> Tipler's thesis was that when the expansion of the universe finally ran out of steam and the whole thing fell back into that bizarre point in space that had exploded into the Big Bang—the "Big Crunch," as they called that ultimate collapse—everybody who had ever lived would live again. Tipler called it "the Omega Point." That even more bizarre creature, Dopey, called it "the eschaton." But it was the same basic idea.

When she checked around they seemed to be one Pat short. "A couple of doctors are checking Pat Five over," the one called Patrice explained. "Want some coffee? There are clean cups over there."

She took some. So did the deputy director, looking pleased with the way things were going. Dopey, who was in the next room, had been telling his interrogators all kinds of things about the mass of high-tech matériel on Starlab. Pell nodded. "We're going to have to go back up there to get it. The director's getting that set up now."

Hilda looked skeptical. "How are you going to know how to make it work?"

But that wasn't a problem, Patrice explained. Dopey himself didn't know how to operate most of it—he had admitted as much, evidently somewhat amused at the thought—but he didn't have to. One of the creatures Dopey called his "bearers" was a specialist in that sort of thing. He could operate any of it, and show the Bureau's people how.

Hilda looked incredulous. "The golem can do that?"

"One of them can. The other's a kind of biological-medical handyman; he's the one who fixed up the guard last night."

"And he fixed Rosaleen up, too," Dannerman-beard called from across the room. "Between the two of them they can do all kinds of things, if Dopey tells them to."

They sounded like pretty handy gadgets to Hilda. She opened her mouth to say as much to the deputy director, but he wasn't paying any attention to the conversation. He was scowling at the screen, on which Dopey was complaining one more time to his interrogators about how desperately they needed their real food. It clearly was not what Pell wanted to hear from the alien; he got up and headed for the door to the other room.

But as he opened it Dopey caught sight of Hilda just behind Marcus Pell. "Stop now," Dopey said peremptorily, waggling his plumed tail in reproof. "I do not require much rest, but I must have *some.* I will answer no further questions for the next—" he twiddled his little paws in his belly bag—"twenty-five minutes." He didn't wait for a reply but hopped off his perch on a coffee table and brushed past the deputy director as he entered the library room.

He advanced on Hilda. "My dear Brigadier Morrisey, I appeal to you as a woman. Please relieve our distress! See that the foodstuffs are delivered to us at once!"

Hilda Morrisey was not used to being appealed to as a woman. Actually, she thought it rather quaint, but she shook her head. "I have nothing to say about that, Dopey."

The little alien sighed. "In that event I will sleep for the remainder of the twenty-five minutes." And he squatted down on the floor, under a dictionary stand. As he closed his eyes the great fan of his tail bent forward, covering him from the light, and he was still.

The deputy director glared around the room, looking for someone to blame. Then he shrugged. "You're in charge," he snapped at Hilda, and hurried out of the room—on his way, Hilda supposed, to find a secure screen so he could check in with headquarters.

Being in charge was nice, Hilda thought, but it would have been even nicer if she knew what she was supposed to do. For starters she nodded at the guards and interrogators. "You can all take ten," she said. As they left gratefully she peered at Dopey. "Is that the way the thing sleeps?"

Patrice answered for all of them. "I don't know. We never saw him sleep before."

"Um," Hilda said, and then got down to business. "All right. Tell me what you've found out so far," she ordered, looking at her own Dannerman.

He looked rebellious. "Christ, Hilda! They've been talking for hours! It's all on the tapes, anyway."

It was a reasonable answer, so she tried a different tack. "Then let's get to something they *haven't* talked about. Don't you have any questions that haven't been answered yet?"

Pat spoke up for him. "Well, I do," she said, sounding tentative, turning to the other Pats. "You said something about another one of us who died?"

The two other Pats looked at each other. Patrice sighed. "Yes, that was Patsy. We were swimming and these other creatures—they looked sort of like seals—"

"More like a hippopotamus," Pat One corrected.

"Anyway, they had some kind of electric shockers. Like electric eels, I guess. And they lived in the water and— Well, things went sour, and one of them killed Patsy. Do we have to talk about this now? It was bad."

"I'm afraid you do," Hilda informed her—not cruelly, but not particularly sympathetically, either. Making people talk about things they didn't want to talk about was basic to her job description. "You have to talk about everything. Now, these animals with the electric shockers—"

"They weren't animals," Dannerman-beard corrected her. "They were fellow prisoners, just like us."

"Anyway, all that's on the tapes already," Patrice said. "There were lots of different kinds of—people—from different planets there and—Oh, hi!" she said, turning to greet Pat Five as she entered.

"Hi," Pat Five said, looking belligerent. She spotted the table with the coffee cups and headed toward it.

"Come on," Pat One coaxed. "Don't keep us in suspense. What did the doctors find out?"

"They found out I was pregnant," Pat Five said, pouring a cup and adding four or five spoonfuls of sugar. "They wanted me to go into a hospital here for observation. I told them screw that. There are plenty of hospitals in New York and I want to go home. And then I want to get back to work."

"So do I," said Patrice eagerly. "I was thinking about it all the time we were in that damn cell. . . ." Then her face fell. "Oh, hell," she said. "I didn't think. How in the world are we ever going to sort that out?"

"Sort what out?" Hilda demanded.

Canada's Rights in "Starlab" Technology Unquestionable.

We must not forget that Canada has a special interest in the Starlab venture, since it was on Canadian soil that the first returnees from Scarecrow captivity reached the Earth.

—*Globe and Mail,* Toronto

Pat—the real Pat—answered for them all. "Sort out which of us is going to run the Observatory, of course." They were all silent for a moment, then she added gloomily, "I don't think it'll be me, anyway."

Patrice gave her a curious look. "Why not you?"

She glanced bitterly at Hilda. "Because these people tell me I'm goddam *prey,* that's why. I've got this damn lump of something in my head, and according to them somebody's likely to grab me and saw my head off to get at it."

"Oh," Patrice said, nodding, "you mean the bug. I've got one, too."

Hilda snapped to attention. "You do?"

"Sure. So did Patsy—the one of us who died. And, of course, all the ones who went back to Earth—you two"—nodding at the Earthly Pat and Dannerman—"and Jimmy Lin, and Martín, and Rosie. It's a spy thing."

Dannerman, frowning, opened his mouth, but Hilda was in command. "Tell me exactly what you mean, 'spy thing,' " she demanded.

And was astonished to hear the answer. The bugs in the head were little transmitters—well, no surprise there; everyone had guessed that much. But these weren't simple sound-only bugs. You put on a kind of helmet that acted as a receiver, Patrice said, "And then you *were* the other person. The other you. I saw that jail cell you were in, Pat. Through your eyes. Just like I was there."

The bearded Dannerman confirmed what she said. "I was in your head once when you were waking up with a hangover, Dan. And Martín said he was at Kourou, and Jimmy Lin was back in the Chinese space center; in fact I think one time when our Jimmy was listening in the one of him that was in China was getting laid. He said it was just like being there. You could see, hear, taste, smell, feel—it was virtual-reality stuff, only better than anything I've ever seen."

Then they were all talking at once, waking Dopey. "You people are very noisy," he complained, peering out from under his great plume, but no one paid attention to him.

"You mean," Pat said shakily, "you could feel and see everything I did? *Everything?*"

"Well, just when we had the helmet on," Pat One said consolingly. "And we could only receive ourselves—Patrice and Patsy and I could tune in on you, Dan-Dan on the other Dan and so on. Dopey had a way of tuning in on everybody—that's why they put the bugs in your heads in the first place. But he never let us do that."

Pat was shaking her head. "Thank God I wasn't doing anything very interesting," she said. "But now I really do want to get this damn thing out."

"Even if it kills you?" Dannerman asked.

Dopey yawned a little cat yawn. "You people concern yourselves over such trivial things," he complained. "Why should that procedure kill you? The device no longer serves any useful purpose, since you have destroyed the relay channel on your Starlab. My medically trained bearer can remove it without harm to you."

Pat sat up, openmouthed. "You're sure?"

"Of course I am sure. Was it not he who installed the devices in the first place?"

11

Dannerman knew what going to hospital was all about, because he'd done it. More than once. You went to hospitals when, for instance, the knee-breakers of the Mad King Ludwigs or the Scuzzhawk enforcers had found out you were a narc, and consequently had beaten the pee out of you. Then, when you got to the hospital, the basic thing you felt was just gratitude that you'd made it there. All you hoped for was that maybe these people could make everything stop hurting.

This time was different. Dannerman had never before gone into a hospital when there was actually nothing wrong with him at all, and when the reason he was there was to let somebody chop holes into parts of his head where neurosurgeons hesitated to cut. Where, if they made one little slip, *pow!,* your brain was tapioca.

What made it worse—not that Dannerman required that it be made worse—was that the somebody who was about to stab him in the spinal cord wasn't even a human being. It was a two-meter-tall golem, with a lot more arms than seemed reasonable, from some preposterous part of outer space. The damn thing wasn't even looking at Dannerman as it stood impassive in the lurching Bureau van. It wasn't looking at anything. It seemed to be in a standing-up coma. And it smelled terrible.

The party had waited until after dark to make the trip to Walter Reed. Darkness wasn't perfect security. It wouldn't stop any professional snoop from switching on his IR scanner that turned any scene into broad, full-color daylight. But it might save them from being observed by some chance-met news reporter or simple civilian gawker who might just happen to be passing by the freight entrance when their little procession of cars slid through the door to the loading dock, and the door descended behind them.

> Walter Reed was meant as a veterans' hospital, but it happened to be really handy to the nation's capital. Presidents and congressmen noticed that right away, and so it became the sort of general all-purpose low-cost medical facility for the nation's top brass. What it didn't have many of anymore was military veterans, because there hadn't been that many wars lately. Now it was mainly the Federal Police Corps which supplied the bodies to fill those ready beds. The Bureau's casualties didn't mingle with shot-up street cops. The Bureau had its own little section, where security was easy to maintain.

Dr. Marsha Evergood was waiting for them on the dock. She glanced at the pair of aliens, the Doc and the Dopey, with a mixture of skepticism and dislike but said nothing as she led them into an elevator. They made a considerable procession, with the aliens, the three bugged humans and Colonel Hilda Morrisey. The Bureau's advance party had done its job. No one else was in sight. Not in the halls behind the freight dock, not in the elevator, which was manually operated by a uniformed Bureau cadet, not in the short stretch of hallway that led them to an operating theater.

It was a real operating theater this time, Dannerman saw. The difference between it and the Bureau's Pit of Pain were that this one had actual surgical machinery, some of the pieces faintly whispering and chuckling to themselves, and the glass wall to the gallery was ordinary glass. There was nobody watching in those seats, either.

Dr. Evergood planted herself at the head of the operating table and peered at the Doc. "How do you want to do this?" she asked the room in general.

The Doc didn't answer. It simply stood impassively, while Dopey methodically picked up surgical instruments and put them down again in disdain. "So very primitive." He sighed. "Still, we will do the best we can."

The best we can. That didn't really sound good enough to Dannerman. Involuntary little choking sounds that came from Patrice and Pat showed that they felt the same way.

There were four or five operating-room attendants in the room, meticulously scrubbed and masked. Though all Dannerman could see of them was their eyes, he was pretty sure that what he saw in those eyes was horror, as the weird little being from space touched their sterile racks with his unwashed fingers. What had become of asepsis? Why, for that matter, were Dannerman and Hilda and the two Pats allowed to enter in their inevitably germ-laden clothes, exhaling their germ-laden breaths, maskless, into the pure air of the operating room?

Dr. Evergood and Dopey talked for a moment in low tones. Then Dopey raised his voice. "Anesthesia?" he said. "No, of course not, we will have no need for your anesthesia."

"Hey," Pat said faintly.

Dopey turned to peer at her. "Have I alarmed you? But there is no reason to fear, this bearer is quite competent. You will experience little or no pain." He paused for a moment for some of that silent communion with the Doc. Then, "He is prepared to commence. Who wishes to be first?"

Dannerman glanced at Pat and Patrice. Both of them were gazing at him. "Me?" he said.

Dopey took it as an offer. "Then very well," he said. "If you will simply lie on that structure over there, Agent Dannerman? Facedown, if you please. Yes, that is fine. Do you Dr. Adcocks wish to watch? If not, you may wait outside, but I think you will find it interesting—oh, what are you doing to Agent Dannerman now?"

Dannerman felt something being draped over the back of his head as the nurses sprang to action. "They're masking the area," Dr. Evergood said.

"No, no, that is not necessary. One other thing, Agent Dannerman. Do you wish your actual memories restored in place of the simulations we imposed on you? That would take a bit longer, but if you wish—no? Very well. Then we can begin."

And they did. Or Dannerman supposed that they did, though all he experienced was the Doc's light touch at the base of his skull, then a sharp sting in the same place. . . .

And then Dopey was saying, "You may get up now, Agent Dannerman. Which of you Dr. Adcocks wishes to be next?" And next to the operating table Dr. Evergood was incredulously holding some coppery thing in the folds of a surgical cloth, and the two Pats were looking astonished and—well, yes, there was no other word for it—looking *terrified.*

One of the nurses took Dannerman's arm and led him away to the recovery room. Once outside the operating theater he pulled his mask off, gazing at Dannerman in wonder. But all he said was, "Holy shit."

* * *

The recovery room wasn't actually much of a recovery room, but then it didn't have to be. As far as Dannerman could tell, he didn't really have anything to recover from. What the room was in the normal course of events was an upper-floor solarium for the use of ambulatory patients. On this day the ambulatory patients were out of luck, because the deputy director had preempted the space.

Dannerman was surprised to see that there were two people in it already: the other Dannerman and the Pat from space—not the Patrice or the Pat who had just come from the Bureau's cells, who were still in the operating room; and not the pregnant Pat Five. It took Dannerman a moment to figure out that this had to be the one called Pat One; he was still having trouble keeping them all straight.

The nurse gazed from one to another of them unbelievingly, then shook his head. "We'll want you for tests and X rays," he said, "but you can just wait here now." And he left, still shaking his head, as Pat said:

"Are you all right?"

"I guess so," Dannerman said, rubbing the back of his neck. "Don't ask me what happened. I was asleep."

"Let me see," she ordered. Dannerman bowed his neck while the others studied the place where there should have been a wad of surgical packing, but wasn't.

They were still doing it when Patrice came in, rubbing the back of her own neck in the same way. She did have some answers, though. She had been watching while the Doc removed Dannerman's bug. "But I couldn't see much," she apologized. "It looked like the Doc used a couple of the scalpels to open up the back of your neck, Dannerman, but then he just reached in with the fingers of one of his little arms and fiddled around for a while. It didn't take long. Then he pulled this little metal thing out of you and handed it to Dr. Evergood. I didn't even see how he closed the incision up."

"Let me look," Dannerman pleaded. Obediently the Pat bent her head, but there was nothing much to see. A pair of faint pink lines surrounded her spinal cord just below the hairline. That was all there was, and even those were fading as he looked at them.

The door opened again. Dannerman looked up, but the Pat who came in wasn't the remaining one with the bug. It was the pregnant one, Pat Five, just back from an examination by the hospital's obstetrical staff and looking hostile.

The thought of Pat Adcock, any Pat Adcock, being pregnant was almost as bizarre for Dannerman as his own bug, or the freaks who had implanted it. It didn't seem to strike the other Pats that way. They were quick to find her a chair and perch on either side of it. "Tell," one of them demanded.

Pat Five shrugged. "They said I'm a healthy middle-aged primapara," she said. "They wanted to do ultrasound and all that stuff, but I wouldn't let them; I want to get back to my—our—own doctor."

"Right on," agreed Patrice. "But what about—" She glanced at the Dannermans, and lowered her voice before she asked her question.

Federal Reserve Inflation Bulletin

The morning recommended price adjustment for inflation is set at 0.74%, reflecting an annualized rate of 532%. Federal Reserve Chairman Walter C. Boettger expressed alarm at the increase, which, he said in a prepared statement, "is entirely due to public hysteria at recent events, does not fairly represent the nation's economic realities and which, if continued, will necessitate adjustments in the interest rate."

They had, Dannerman supposed, got into some of the more intimate aspects of pregnancy. He didn't listen in. What he did, though, was put on a pretense of eavesdropping, not because he particularly wanted to hear how the pregnant one was doing with such matters as morning sickness and bladder control, but so that he would not have to make conversation with that other Dan Dannerman sitting there, as uncomfortable as himself.

When he glanced at the other Dannerman he found the man looking at him in the same rueful and perplexed way. "Oh, hell, Dan," the other one said, coming over and sitting beside him, "I guess sooner or later you and I are going to have to talk."

"I guess so," Dannerman said stiffly. The question was what to talk about. He chose an innocuous subject to start: "Have they said anything to you about money?"

"Oh, sure. They said they had never had a situation like this before and they didn't know who was entitled to what."

"Same here." The bearded one was glancing at one of the Pats—*his* Pat—so Dannerman tried something a little more personal. "Are you two going to get married?"

That Dannerman looked resentful in his turn, but then he shrugged. "We never said so, but—yeah, I think we might. Funny, isn't it?"

It wasn't, exactly. Not really funny, but certainly, considering Dannerman's own experiences with Pat Adcock, pretty odd. There had been nothing like that between the two of them before they went to Starlab. Quite the opposite, in fact.

Jim Daniel was now looking a little bit embarrassed. "The thing is," he said diffidently, "Anita. The girl I, uh, we were dating. I thought about her a lot at first, when Pat and I were getting interested in each other, back in captivity. I think I had a kind of a guilty conscience, maybe; Anita deserved better than an occasional roll in the hay, and— Well, you know what I'm talking about. Have you seen her lately?"

It was a perfectly reasonable question, but Dannerman felt a sudden flash of warmth in his face, and knew it was anger. He was—yes, damn it, he was *jealous*. The unpleasant fact was that this other man who was not himself—never mind the fact that in some sense he actually was—had taken his very own Anita Berman to bed. Often. Knew all of her scents and habits as intimately as Dannerman himself. Nothing that had passed between them was secret from him, at least not up until the moment they had left for the Starlab . . . and there had been little enough happening since then.

Dannerman knew it was not a reasonable rage.

But what was there about the things that had been going on for all of them that was really reasonable? "Not lately," he said stiffly, and turned away. He knew perfectly well that sooner or later he and this other Dan would have to try to come to terms. Maybe they could. Maybe sometime they could be as close and amiable as the Pats. . . .

But not yet.

When Dr. Evergood arrived, looking baffled, she had two nurses in tow. It took them a while to sort out which three of the six persons involved had just come out of surgery, but after they did they got busy. The nurses began taking pulses and blood pressures and sticking tiny gadgets in the patients' ears to check their temperatures, while the doctor peered unbelievingly at the backs of the patients' necks. She didn't speak until she was quite through. Then she sighed in resignation. "*Nobody,*" she said, "heals from an incision that fast." She touched the back of Patrice's neck again wonderingly, then shook her head. "Anyway, they're waiting for you three in X ray, but Deputy Director Pell wants to show you something first."

She looked inquiringly at the nurse standing by the door, who nodded. A moment later Deputy Director Pell arrived. Not alone. Right behind him as he came in the door was Hilda Morrisey, carrying—

Dannerman noted with surprise—a lethal-looking carbine. She nodded impartially to the two Dannermans and stepped out of the way to let in four additional armed and uniformed Police Corps guards, two of them pushing what looked like an office safe on wheels.

"I thought you'd like to see what we took out of you," the deputy director said genially, nodding to Hilda. She took a pair of key-tabs out of her pocket, unlocked the safe and stood back as one of the guards lifted out a transparent box. Inside it was an almond-shaped coppery object not much bigger than the end of Dannerman's thumb.

"It's more complicated than it looks," the deputy director said happily, "and now we've got three of them. According to Dr. Evergood here, while it was in place in your heads it extruded little filaments that penetrated large sections of your brains, but your many-armed friend managed to get it to withdraw them again so it could be removed. Seen enough? All right, Hilda, take it away." And when Hilda had relocked the safe and the guards were rolling it away, he looked around at the Pats and added, "One thing. Which of you is the one that's pregnant?"

Pat Five raised her hand. "Me. Is something wrong?"

"You mean medically? No, nothing like that. You're fine, but I got a call from the State Department. The ambassador of the People's Republic paid them a call last night. They didn't waste much time; what he was there for was to serve them with a summons. The complainant is Commander James Peng-tsu Lin, and he's suing you and the government of the United States for custody of the child."

12

Unsurprisingly, Hilda Morrisey hadn't forgiven the deputy director. She wasn't very good at forgiving. She hadn't had much practice.

What she was good at was facing facts. In the present situation the deputy director held all the cards. She was stuck here with all these Headquarters cruds for the foreseeable future; therefore, she might as well make herself comfortable. For openers, that meant getting a place of her own—not too far away, but definitely not so near that she was under somebody's eye twenty-four hours a day.

Rank helped. The Bureau's housing office was eager to serve a brigadier. They quickly pulled three possible apartments for her out of the databank, and she signed herself out on personal time to look them over. The first was good. The second was better. The third was perfect. They called it a "studio," but it had a Jacuzzi and a balcony and, if you stood just right, even a view of the distant Potomac River. And it had a fine, strong bed, easily large enough for two persons who were on friendly terms. And, of course, when and if some other person might occasionally share it with her they would definitely be friendly indeed.

When she slipped in to take her seat at the team meeting the man from the Naval Observatory was talking about the comet-like object from space that might, or might not, have been the mother ship that delivered the pod that contained the equipment that let the Scarecrows take over Starlab. Hilda didn't listen very attentively. She was thinking of where one might best look for that suitable other person, and of whether the doorman would remember all the instructions she had given him about the personal stuff that would be coming from her New York pad by Bureau courier. She nudged the man next to her and pointed to the coffee pitcher. It wasn't until he had passed it to her with a wry look that she realized he was a new face on the team.

His name was Harold Ott. He was the Bureau's number two electronics nerd, and no friend of Hilda Morrisey's. It was Ott's disdainful opinion that flesh-and-blood agents were the hard way to obtain intelligence that could be got a lot more easily with one of his surveillance tools. Though wrong-headed, of course, the man did know his stuff. But what did his stuff have to do with the Ananias team?

He didn't seem any more interested in what the astronomer was saying than Hilda herself. Ott had his screen up and was idly playing with it. Doing what Hilda could not tell, because he had the privacy flaps up. He seemed to be waiting for something.

So was Daisy Fennell, in the chair. She was nodding absently as the astronomer complained that, although they had identified the object on its approach, no one had been paying much attention to it. Therefore, they had a very incomplete orbit and had not succeeded in tracking its subsequent course. Which would in any case be difficult, since it seemed to have been a powered, rather than a ballistic, flight. "Yes, well, thank you," Fennell said. "Now let's hear from Dr. ben Jayya—" And there was another new face at the table.

It might have been better, Hilda thought, to have done her apartment hunting on a different morning, since she'd missed all the introductions. As unobtrusively as she could she popped her own screen and did some hunting. Then she raised her eyebrows and looked at the doctor with more interest. Dr. Sidoni ben Jayya was a biochemist, and he had just been coopted to the team from his regular base of operations.

Which was Camp Smolley.

That made Hilda sit up. She had never visited Camp Smolley, but she knew what it was about. So did everybody in the Bureau, though not too many civilians did. Camp Smolley was biowar! And what the hell did *that* have to do with the Ananias team?

As it turned out, plenty. All three of the weird space creatures had been moved there. "For maximum security," he explained, "and for convenience in research. Our primary concern at the moment is feeding them, and so we have been analyzing some of the food canisters that they brought from Starlab."

> Camp Smolley began its existence as a top-secret research facility for the development of biological weapons. When the United States signed on to the treaty banning these, it continued its activities as a top-secret laboratory for developing defenses against biowar. When some busybodies in the Congress thought that was too close to actually making the things, it switched its efforts over to general biochemical research—most of them, anyway. In the change it was administratively reassigned to the NBI, and the Bureau found some uses for its skills it did not think necessary to report to Congress.

That made sense to Hilda. There weren't many biolaboratories better equipped than Camp Smolley's, and certainly none that was easier to keep private from the outside world. However, the problem of extraterrestrial nutrition was not a subject that interested Hilda a lot, and her attention began to wander again.

So did Daisy Fennell's. She was paying more attention to her own screen than to the speaker. Hilda studied the woman thoughtfully, because there was a lesson there for her. Time was when Fennell had been a field manager like herself. She had even once run Junior Agent Hilda Morrisey, when they were trying to infiltrate the religious-right groups that had been setting fire to schoolbook warehouses around the country. Daisy had been good at the work, too, until she had made the mistake of letting herself get promoted. As Hilda just had. And now here she was, stuck in administration, trying to keep people like this biochemist from telling the team more than it had any desire to know about the significance of chirality in organic molecules.

Across the table the man from the State Department did seem interested. He frowned and lifted one finger to signal he wanted to say something—it was as close as he ever came to raising his hand. "There would be serious international repercussions if we let them die," he pointed out. "Are you saying there isn't anything you can do?"

Dr. ben Jayya gave him a frosty look. "Of course I am not saying this. We have begun many lines of research. For instance, Dr. Appley has taken cell samples from each of the extraterrestrials. If we could grow the cells in sufficient quantity in a nutrient solution we might be able to feed these—creatures—on cells from their own bodies. There is, after all, one thing every animal can digest, and that is its own flesh. But we're having a difficult time finding the proper nutrients."

"And if that fails?"

Ben Jayya frowned. "But that is only one line of research, as I have just said! In addition we are making genetic studies. There is the possibility that we can immunize certain kinds of food animals against proteins from the aliens themselves, in which case the aliens might be capable of assimilating the meat from, let us say, a hamster or rabbit which has been made compatible—"

Statement of the Central Presidium.

The Central Presidium of the People's Republic of China has released this statement:

"Ever mindful of the vital concerns of its many people, the Central Presidium shares their just wrath at the latest provocation of the snarling dogs of global monopoly capitalism. They presume to kidnap the unborn child of our heroic People's Republic of China astronaut Commander James Peng-tsu Lin. Let these slavish tools of the multinationals keep their bloodstained claws off this heroic unborn Chinese citizen, or the consequences will strike terror to their hearts."

—*South China Morning Post,* Hong Kong, PRC

"I don't think," the State Department man said severely, "that that's good enough, Dr., ah, ben Jayya. They *must* be kept alive."

The biochemist shrugged. "Of course," he said, looking at Daisy Fennell, "there is also the fact that there are additional stores of food on the Starlab orbiter. The subject called Dopey has urged that a spacecraft be launched to obtain them—"

"That's being looked into," Daisy said quickly.

"—but even that, you must understand, is only an interim solution, while our researches must ultimately—"

But he didn't get a chance to finish saying what his researches must ultimately do. The door opened and the deputy director came in, quietly, but changing the climate of the room.

Everyone perked up. "Sorry I'm late. Hope I'm not interrupting," he apologized, knowing that he was, "but I think now it's time we gave everybody a look at the gadget we took out of our friends."

So that was what Harold Ott was doing in the room. The man was already on his feet, politely elbowing Daisy Fennell out of the way to get at the master controls. As he touched the keypad the room lights darkened and the projectors of a 3-D system arose from the tabletop. There was a brief polychromatic haze over the middle of the table, then it cleared and turned into an image of something that looked like a copper-covered almond, slowly rotating as they watched.

"I thought of bringing one of the actual gadgets in for you to look at," Marcus Pell said chattily, "but we're really not supposed to take them out of the secure lab."

One of the men raised a hand. "That's pretty big to go in somebody's head," he said doubtfully.

"It's enlarged so we can see it better," Pell explained. "The actual object is only a little over two centimeters long. It's a bug, all right, and we've got three of them. That's half the world's supply."

"Where's the other half?" the man asked.

"Scattered, I'm afraid. There's one in General Delasquez's head, and he's back in Florida. There's another in the Chinese pilot—not the one that just came back, the other one. We don't know where he is—somewhere in China, anyway. And there's the one the Ukrainians took out of the dead Dr. Artzybachova and they let get stolen. That one we're trying to locate; we have some leads."

The general said testily, "The people who stole it, they're terrorists, right? I don't like having that kind of thing in their hands. What if they take it apart and see what's inside?"

Pell looked courteously at the electronics man. "Harold?"

Ott pursed his lips. "It's not that easy. Here in the lab we've done about all the noninvasive studies we can, and they don't tell us much. Next step would be to use a can opener on one of them, but there's a considerable risk of destroying it if we do."

"So you're stymied?"

"Maybe not." He gave the deputy director an inquiring look and got a nod of permission. "It seems that one of the Doc creatures—the one that isn't a brain surgeon—is supposed to be an expert on that sort of thing. We think probably he could disassemble one for us, and then we could get a better look at it. It's a pretty impressive little gadget. Apparently it monitors full five-sense inputs and transmits them to at least orbital distance. We don't have any idea, really, what its range is. It uses some frequency that we haven't been able to detect. It isn't in any of the conventional radio bands. And it requires no external power source."

"Tissue and hair samples from the extraterrestrials give us clues as to the basic proteins, fats and other molecules that make up their bodies, but they are not enough; without invasive surgery we can't tell what less common compounds are required by their glands, nervous systems, etc. However, we have succeeded in isolating a number of their basic chemicals, and, through polymerase chain reaction and other techniques, are capable of manufacturing them in dietary quantities. The proteins are the most difficult. Proteins are basically composed of two parts, an alpha helix and a number of beta sheets. We have synthesized quantities of these. However, it isn't enough to put the right ingredients in a kettle and cook them up; the planar beta sheets, for example, must be folded in just the right way. Still, we have produced basic ration packs for each species, which should sustain life for a period. Whether it contains all the required vitamins and minerals is another question; we cannot guarantee that the ETs will not start developing something like scurvy or kwashiorkor over time."

—The Biowar Report

One of the men said thoughtfully, "I can see why you'd like to take it apart. If the alien can do it, what's holding you up?"

"Trouble is, we can't communicate with the Doc directly. He never speaks. The Dopey talks for him."

"But if he doesn't speak at all—"

"Well, that's another thing we'd like to know more about. Somehow the Dopey creature communicates with them."

Daisy turned to the neurosurgeon from Walter Reed: "Dr. Evergood?"

"Are you asking if the extraterrestrials are bugged, too? It doesn't look that way. Nothing shows up on X rays."

"Well, they've got something," Ott said stubbornly. "What about this little muff thing that the Dopey creature wears all the time? He won't let us investigate it. Of course, we could simply *take* it—" he added, looking at Marcus Pell.

"Not yet, anyway," the deputy director said. "Go on, Daisy."

The vice deputy turned to the State Department man, whose one finger was again elevated. Hilda resigned herself to five minutes of hearing about all the turmoil that was building up all around the world, but what he said was, "The Canadians are asking for one of those things, since we've got three now. They claim they're entitled to it under the Ottawa Agreement in return for letting us use the base at Calgary to get the people down. The President promised—"

Marcus Pell waved a hand negligently. "We know what the President promised. We'll certainly keep them informed, in due course. Is that all?"

"Well, no. There's also this Chinese custody suit."

Pell looked tolerantly amused. "Wouldn't you say that's a bit premature? The damn kid hasn't even been born yet."

"That's their point. They say the baby has a right to be born on the territory of the People's Republic so that he may enjoy full citizenship. What they want is for the mother to come to Beijing, not later than ninety days from now, and stay there for the delivery."

"Hmm." The deputy director considered for a moment, then shrugged. "Next time you see the ambassador, why don't you point out to him that unfortunately our domestic-relations courts are pretty well backed up with cases, so their suit might not get heard until the baby's getting ready for college." He gazed benevolently at the man from State, then said, "Now, I'm afraid, I've got some other matters to deal with. Brigadier Morrisey? If you can come to my office for a moment—"

Pell didn't speak to Hilda all the way to his private suite; he was listening intently to the messages coming from his earpiece, and she didn't interrupt.

When they got to the office a man was sitting there. He got up as they entered, and Hilda recognized him. Solly Garand. A field manager like herself—like she used to be, anyway. The deputy director said, "Colonel Garand, Brigadier Morrisey—you know each other."

"Sure do," said Garand, grinning and extending his hand to Hilda. "Congratulations on your promotion, Hilda."

Pell didn't give her time to respond. "Solly's been running some of our ethnics, including the Ukrainian group that's financing the irredentists. The ones that stole the bug from the authorities. You want to tell her where you stand now, Solly?"

"Right. I guess you know we've got assets in the expat group here in America, and now we've got one in Ukraine, too. That's courtesy of the Russians, because they don't want the Ukrainians getting anything they don't have—"

"Background her later, Solly. Cut to the chase."

"Well, we haven't located the device yet, but now we have a problem. It's this Dr. Artzybachova. The irredentists have tried to kidnap

Doktor-nauk Artzybachova Recovering

Administration officials at Hospital No. 14 confirm that Doktor-nauk R. V. Artzybachova has left the hospital for rest and recovery. Officials declined to speculate on her whereabouts or how long she would remain in seclusion, citing her advanced age and the exhausting experiences she has undergone.

State Information Agency, Ukraine

her. So she's left the hospital and now she's holed up in her dacha with a few bodyguards she trusts because they're from old zek families—"

Hilda interrupted. "From what?"

"Families of old concentration-camp people. From the Gulag. People who served time with Artzybachova's grandfather; she knows the irredentists are after her, and the zek children are the only ones she trusts. Only we think one of her guards is actually a terrorist."

Hilda mulled that over for a moment. Then she turned to the deputy director. "That's tough for the old lady, but why do we care? The woman looked pretty much past it in Calgary."

"Fooled me too," Pell said sourly. "That's why I let the Canadians have her, but it looks like what was wrong with her was mostly missing her medications for a few months. Anyway, we can't let the mob have her. Do you happen to remember what her specialty was?"

"Instrumentation—oh."

"Exactly. Oh. She knows more about the freaks' instruments than anybody else who's human. Does she know enough to get some use out of that bug? I don't know, but I can't afford to find out the hard way. That's where you come in, Hilda. I'm putting you in charge."

She blinked at him. "Back in the field?"

"In the field? Hell, no, Hilda. Solly'll be the field manager, but I want you right here supervising, and— Hold it a minute."

His screen was flashing urgency. He turned it away from his guests and took a message. Then he looked up, furious. "The goddam French!" he snarled. "That was a flash from State. That mission Eurospace was planning to Starlab—they're going through with it. The French sent this note"—he glanced at the screen—"blah-blah, Freedom of the Skies treaty, blah-blah, is an abandoned satellite, blah-blah-blah. So they intend to launch within ten days."

13

With the space freaks gone—gone somewhere or other, no one seemed to be willing to say where—the safe house changed character. The uniformed guards disappeared. So did most of the interrogators, a fact which carried an attractive fringe benefit: Now there was less back-and-forth calling between the safe house and the Bureau headquarters, and so the Starlab people had a chance at the one secure line.

Dannerman lucked out. He got the first crack at the phone, and the person he was calling answered on the first ring. "Hello, honey," he said. "Looks like they're going to let us out of here pretty soon. Any chance of dinner tonight, maybe—tomorrow at the latest?"

There turned out to be a very good chance. Anita Berman was a forgiving soul, and besides she had been watching the news like everybody else. "I've really missed you, Dan," she said, sounding as loving as ever.

"And I've missed you—I can't tell you how much," he said. Meaning it literally, too; because he was reluctant to say all the things he wanted to say to her with two of the Pats waiting impatiently for their turn at the phone.

Anita was saying, "Your voice sounds funny. Is everything all right?" Well, it undoubtedly did, and so did hers, but he couldn't tell her that it was because the secure line was chaos-encoded, and then decoded at the Bureau before being redirected to the open lines to New York. "Look, I have to get off the phone, but—" He looked over his shoulder, swallowed, said it anyway: "I love you."

He gave the nearest Pat a belligerent look as he hung up. She didn't return it. She had clearly been eavesdropping and the look she gave back to him was actually, well, affectionate; but as she took the phone all she said was, "Dan-Dan was calling you. It's about this French thing; he's in the library."

So he was, irritably switching channels. He looked up as Dannerman entered. "What French thing is Pat talking about?" Dannerman asked.

> The President: "The presiding officer of the United Nations Council recognizes the honorable representative of Democratic Agrarian Albania."
>
> Mr. T. Gabo: "Mr. Presiding Officer, what is the hurry? Why are we rushing to a judgment in this matter? The so-called Starlab satellite has remained in orbit for many years now. It will remain for many years more. Why must we proceed with such reckless haste to authorize a United Nations flight to secure and exploit this wonderful technological machinery which, we are told, will revolutionize our science?
>
> "I will answer that question. The haste is due to the desperate hunger a few large powers have to secure these secrets for their own use, a gain from which most of our great 188 independent nations will be excluded. I say, go slow! I say, wait until the vast majority of the world's nations have time to catch up, so that we may all benefit from this treasure trove. My little country of Democratic Agrarian Albania is not rich, but we have our pride! And we do not choose to be excluded from our rightful participation in this endeavor."
>
> —*Proceedings of the General Assembly,* Vol. XXVII, p 1122

His duplicate jerked a thumb at the screen. "See for yourself."

That was how Dannerman learned about the Eurospace intention. He peered at the news story, read the French communiqué and then shrugged. "I guess the Bureau isn't going to like that."

Dannerman-with-a-Beard looked at him. "The Bureau? Is that all you think?"

"Is there something more to think?"

"You just don't get it, do you? You haven't seen the kind of stuff they've got on Starlab. What if the French let the Scarecrows in again?"

Dannerman objected, "I thought you smashed the whatever-it-is."

"Sure I did, as much as I could. But what if the French luck out and get it going again?"

Dannerman confronted his copy amiably. "Too many ifs to worry about right now," he said. "Anyway, there's nothing you and I can do about it, is there? And I've got other things on my mind, like getting home."

The other Dannerman sighed, then shrugged. "Which brings us to another problem," he said. "Whose home are we talking about? Yours or mine?"

That was a stopper. "Oh, right. I didn't think of that. Rita's room isn't really big enough for the two of us, is it?" Then he brightened. "Anyway," he said, "I don't think we have to worry about that right now, either, because for the next couple of nights I hope to be sleeping somewhere else."

"Uh-huh," the other said, and Dannerman was pleased to see that he looked faintly jealous.

From the door a tentative voice—Pat's voice—said, "Dan-Dan?"

Dannerman turned around, but it was the other one she was talking to. She looked perturbed. "Rosaleen's left the hospital in Kiev and they won't tell us where we can call her. Can you find out?"

"I'll give it a try," he said, and left them together. It took Dannerman a moment to figure out which Pat it was. They had settled on different-colored outfits from the safe house's stores to tell them apart: blue for the "real" Pat, a red shorts suit for Pat One, a sparkly golden sweater for pregnant Pat Five. This one was wearing a gray tailored jacket—therefore Patrice—and she was lingering. She seemed to want to say something that embarrassed her.

"What?" he asked encouragingly.

She cleared her throat. "It's just— Dan, listen. If you thought I was coming on to you— Well, hell, I *was* coming on to you. Can I explain?"

"You don't have to. He told me."

She bristled. "Oh, really? So what did he tell you exactly? —Well, never mind, what he said was the truth. When we were all in the deep stuff up there and he was the only decent human male around—all right, I admit I got a kind of a crush on him. Well, on you, if you know what I mean, because when I came off the lander and saw you there I figured, hey, here's my chance to have a Dan-Dan of my own. But then I heard you talking to your girl—"

It was his turn to look embarrassed.

"Oh, don't get uptight. You sounded sweet. And it's okay. There's a whole world of men out there; I won't bother you again."

"Listen," he said gruffly, "it wasn't a bother. I was kind of flattered."

She looked him over approvingly. "You said the right thing, Dan. She's a lucky girl."

Surprisingly, she leaned forward and kissed him on the cheek just as the other Dan came back. He gave them both a surprised look, but what he said was, "I got a number in Ukraine, but there's something wrong with the line; I couldn't get through. But I got some news. Hilda's here! We're going home. She's got a van waiting outside to take us to the plane."

And right behind him was Hilda herself, in full uniform, with the brigadier's golden stars on her collar points. "Some of you," she corrected. "Not you, Danno. The deputy director wants to talk to you."

Hilda wasn't answering questions, either. Not while they were on their way to her little two-seat electro, not while she climbed in to the driver's side while she waved Dannerman to the other, not as she circled around the group loading themselves happily into the van and scooted past the saluting guards at the checkpoint. Only as they were turning into the road Dannerman caught sight of a determined little group of people, no more than half a dozen, waving hand-printed placards: *The Devils Are Among Us!* and *They Are the Antichrist!* and, succinctly, *Send Them Back!*

"Hey!" he said. "Those people are in the wrong place, aren't they? But how'd they even know about the safe house?"

"I wish I could tell you," she said grimly, out of the side of her mouth, and that was all she did say. She was driving fast and silent, with the car on manual so she could exceed the speed limit, and she wasn't talking. Dannerman squirmed around in the bucket seat to look at her face. It wasn't telling much; she was driving manually, and concentrating on it. He tried his luck. "Do you want to tell me what Pell wants with me?"

She obviously didn't. She didn't even look at him. "Come on, Hilda. This is a Bureau car, isn't it? So nobody's listening in. Is it about the damn European launch?"

She gave him a sidelong look. "He'll have to tell you himself."

"Well, if it's a job, don't you think I ought to get a little time off first? I want to go to New York!"

She didn't respond to that, either. He was silent for a moment, watching her. Her eyes were on the road and her face told nothing. Which told Dannerman a lot. She knew exactly what the deputy director wanted him for, and she didn't think he would like it.

Pacific States Ready to Share Defense Burden.

At an emergency meeting of SOPACTO heads in Papeete, Tahiti, all the states of the Pacific region reiterated their demand for complete sharing of all information received from the Starlab orbiter, and urged that the flight take place as soon as possible. Prime Minister Gribforth declared, "Australia will place all of its scientific and technical facilities at the disposal of the United Nations in the analysis of Scarecrow technology, but it must not be a European-American monopoly. The states of the Pacific region will not be excluded from this venture."

—*The Bulletin,* Sydney

He decided that it had to be the European space launch. He tried a different tack. "What I don't understand," he said chattily, "is how the French have the balls to try to take Starlab when they know we've got muscle up there. Do they think we're bluffing?"

Hilda sighed. "We just might be," she said moodily. "The D.D. checked it out. The Pentagon guys admitted that their best estimate for any of our military satellites was that it had a ten percent chance of still being operational. And we only have two that can be maneuvered into position."

"Hell," Dannerman said, startled.

"Exactly, Danno. That's not all of it, either. Ours aren't the only birds up there. The Russians have two. So do the Chinese. And NASA thinks theirs may be a little more reliable."

"Hell and damnation! What are you telling me, Hilda? Did those people build better war satellites than we did?"

"Better, no," she said judiciously. "The way I understand it, ours were a lot more sophisticated. They could deal with four or five more targets at once, and do it a lot faster. But that made them a lot more complicated, and those crude old Soviet jobs just had fewer things to go wrong with them as they aged."

She slowed down at the entrance to the Bureau's complex. While the guard was checking their vehicle for possible explosives someone might have planted in it, she said, "So we're trying a different tack. We're trying to get the UN in on the embargo; that would mean getting the Russians and the Chinese to join in."

She waved to the guard, who was signaling the all clear. As she started up again, Dannerman asked: "Are they doing it?"

"Well," she said, "not really. They're bargaining."

"So what you really need is time. Like having someone go to Kourou and kind of slow them down," he guessed. "Maybe someone like me?"

She didn't answer that. Unless a faint smile was an answer; but in Dannerman's opinion it was all the answer he needed.

But it turned out to be the wrong answer. When the deputy director at last saw Dannerman—half an hour after Hilda had gone in ahead, leaving Dannerman to sit in a tiny conference room to think about how he might handle the problem in Kourou—he discovered that Pell wasn't at all interested in discussing the French threat. "The Eurospace launch? No, that's being handled, Dannerman. You're not involved. What I want to talk to you about is Rosaleen Artzybachova."

Dannerman was actually startled. "But she's no problem, is she?"

"I'm afraid she is." Pell paused, looking at his screen, making a few changes. "I understand you want some time off, but that's all right. It'll take a day or two to get our ducks in order. Hilda will brief you, and then, Dannerman," he said, smiling pleasantly, "that's where you come in. You're going to Ukraine."

14

Back in her own familiar environment, and especially with that hideous spidery thing out of the base of her skull, the recently debugged Pat Adcock felt kilograms lighter and kilometers happier. If there was any little fly in the ointment, it was simply that there were too many of her.

That was a major management problem for the Dannerman Astrophysical Observatory. When the four of them finally presented themselves to the staff Pat expected an exciting time. The whole situation was totally bizarre even to herself, and at least she had had the time to try to get used to it. What the innocents at the Observatory might make of it she could not imagine, but certainly they would be baffled and confused and excited and—

They weren't. Well, they'd been glued to their screens, like everybody else in the world, and they knew all about how the bunch of them had been abducted to some galactically distant penal colony and what happened there. When Pat explained the dress code that they could use to tell them apart Janice, the receptionist, giggled. ("It's just that I never thought yellow was your color, uh, Patrice," she explained.) And Pete Schneyman, who had been in charge of the Observatory during her enforced absence, asked stiffly, "Which one is going to be the director?"

All four of them opened their mouths, but Pat was the first to speak. "We all are," she said. "We're going to take turns being physically present here, but there'll only be one of us at a time. We drew lots, and Pat One will go first."

"It sounds like a pretty lousy arrangement to me," the ex–temporary director observed.

It sounded that way to Pat, too. She thought about it all the way home—alone, for a change; Pat Five had an appointment with her doctor, and Patrice with a beauty parlor. Then, when she arrived in front of her apartment house and got out of her Bureau-supplied limo with its Bureau-supplied armed driver and its Bureau-supplied personal guard, she found two men waiting on the sidewalk, bundled up against the snow.

They didn't look to her as though they were there by accident. They didn't look that way to the bodyguard, either. "Wait a minute, please," the bodyguard said to her, even before the men moved toward the car.

The driver leaped out to join her, his hands on his gun. For a moment Pat thought there was going to be a firefight right before her eyes, but the shorter of the men was holding up some sort of document. The two Bureau agents studied it, asked a few questions and muttered among themselves. Then the bodyguard turned to Pat. "He's a diplomat," she said. "From China. He says he just needs to talk to you for a minute."

Pat hesitated, but the two Bureau operatives had their guns in their hands now, and the waiting men showed no signs of hostility. Indeed, they had no violent intentions. "Dr. Patrice Adcock?" the smaller one said. "My associate has a summons for you. Thank you. That's all."

They turned and walked away, leaving Pat holding a thick sheaf of folded paper. The man was a simple process server. And when Pat looked at the paper she discovered that she had been served with a suit. Commander James Peng-tsu Lin, plaintiff, was demanding of Dr. Patrice Adcock, defendant, that she proceed forthwith to the People's Republic of China so that the child she was carrying could be born as a citizen of his father's country.

She thought of telling them they had served the wrong, i.e., the nonpregnant, Dr. Pat Adcock, but what was the point? She sighed. "Thank you," she said politely to the Chinese. And to her bodyguards, "It's all right. Let's go upstairs."

There were too many of her for the apartment on the upper East Side, too. It had been comfortably roomy for Dr. Patrice Adcock, but with four Dr. Patrice Adcocks living there it was pretty damn cramped.

The Pats had done the best they could to resolve the difficulties. They'd drawn lots for sleeping quarters, and Pat considered she had done well on that draw. She hadn't got her "own" bedroom, no. That was the one with the canopied bed and the hot tub, and it had gone to

Pat Five as a courtesy to approaching motherhood. The two guest rooms had gone to Patrice and Pat One. Pat herself had the never-used maid's room. Small, yes; remote from the rest of the apartment, sure; but the maid's room not only had its own private little bath, it had a full-function screen monitor. The original purpose of that, Pat supposed, was so that the maid could do her meal planning and record-keeping without interfering with her employers.

But it worked.

So the fact that Pat couldn't be in the Observatory didn't mean that she couldn't do astronomy. As soon as she was out of the boots and heavy cold-weather slacks she made herself a cup of mint tea, sat down at her workspace and began digging into this crazy eschaton thing.

The Bureau had exerted pressure where it was needed. As a result some university library had messengered her its file copy of the Frank Tipler book, *The Physics of Immortality.* She opened it gingerly, for the book was packed in its own custom-built casing, with a note pasted to the front cover that said it was in delicate condition and should be handled with extreme care.

That was true enough. The old wood-pulp pages threatened to crack as she turned them, but she was able to read enough to remember the general argument of the book as prissy little Dr. Mukarjee had described it for his class in that ancient graduate-school seminar at Caltech. What Tipler called the "Omega Point" Dopey's people seemed to call the "eschaton." But it was the same thing.

And, of course, it was unbelievable. The only thing going for it was that some pretty powerful beings, somewhere in space, seemed to believe it very much.

On Earth there was still a lot of disbelief around, even about the reality of Dopey and the Docs. For Pat, who had seen—and touched, and even smelled—the aliens from Starlab, there was no question. These were real extraterrestrials, all right. But most of the world had seen only the news broadcasts the Bureau had allowed, and a considerable fraction of that audience skeptically supposed they were nothing but another set of TV morphs.

That didn't bother Pat. What bothered her was the skepticism from her colleagues, notably the fiercely combative arguments that were coming from the Max-Planck Institut für Extraterristriche Physik. The Germans weren't just skeptical. They were downright libelous.

Part of that particular fountain of hostility, Pat knew, was an old score being settled. The Germans had supplied some useful information which had helped to figure out what was going on on Starlab. They'd asked for information about her mission in return; she had refused to give it to them. Naturally they were going to piss all over anything connected with the Dannerman Astrophysical Observatory; whoever said that scientists were never motivated by petty angers?

Invasion Near? What We Must Do!

This latest alarming communiqué from the space aliens emphasizes the need for immediate and affirmative action on the proposals of the Albanians in the United Nations. As the Nigerian representative to the UN, Mr. Albert Ngoro, said this morning in New York, "The flight to the Starlab satellite must take place immediately so that we can begin to protect ourselves from a challenge that is sure to come." Mr. Ngoro also added that the flight must be multinational, and that one of our fine Nigerian weapons specialists should be a major member of the crew.

—*Daily Times,* Lagos, Nigeria

But they had, or seemed to have, a point. What the Germans claimed was that there couldn't possibly be any eschaton, or Omega Point, or grand resurrection, because there wasn't ever going to be a Big Crunch. Everyone knew, they said loftily, that the universe was never going to recollapse, but would simply go on expanding forever.

Well, there was no doubt about it. They did have a point.

Thinking of forever reminded Pat to look at her watch, and what she saw surprised her. It was midafternoon. She had forgotten to eat lunch.

While she was microwaving the handiest thing in the freezer Pat Five came in, looking harried. "Lunch? Yes, maybe so; what've you got there, meatballs? But I'll have to eat fast, because"—pausing to catch a glimpse of herself in the kitchen mirror and frowning—"I've got to go out again as soon as I change. Janice was right, damn her; this isn't my color, is it? I think I'll see what else we've got that might fit me now. Anyway, I've got an appointment with the lawyer the Bureau got me to respond to this suit—"

Tardily Pat remembered the summons. "Wait a minute," she said, in the middle of putting another carton into the microwave for herself. But when she displayed the document Pat Five shrugged it off. "We all got one. I guess they wanted to make sure it got to the right person. Aren't you going to ask me what the doctor said?"

"Of course I am," Pat said remorsefully.

"Well, brace yourself," Pat Five said, spooning Swedish meatballs into her mouth. "What she said was I'm going to have triplets."

"Triplets?"

Pat Five nodded. "That's right. Three of them. All girls, she thinks, but she wants to do another amniocentesis in a couple of weeks. And what've you been doing with your day?"

It took Pat a while to get back to her screen, because long after Pat Five had left she was still thinking about triplets. Three little girls. Genetically her own daughters!—although with the unfortunate genetic contribution of their presumed father, Jimmy Lin. But definitely her own flesh and blood. . . .

She couldn't handle that. It was a relief to turn back to the eschaton file.

If the Ugly Space Aliens were right, one of the Germans had posted, then the quantity astronomers called "omega"—the measure of how much mass the universe contained—had to be more than one. Okay, Pat thought. There was no argument about that; if the universe didn't contain enough mass, the force of gravity would not be strong enough to pull it all back together again. Of course.

Also of course, no one had any good way of measuring omega; you couldn't weigh every star and galaxy, not to mention all the dark and undetectable particles that might add vast amounts of mass to the total; so you had to try to estimate it from other values—values that you *could* measure. Sort of. Though with considerable difficulty, and with huge error bars. Values like analyzing the ratio between distance and rate of recession, to see if there was any evidence of slowing expansion.

For that investigations in a great many areas were under way—though what a pity it was, Pat thought, that they were so prone to giving contradictory results.

Taking one consideration with another, the consensus among Earthly astronomers was that the results that gave an omega of less than 1 were probably more trustworthy than the ones that didn't. That was what the Germans were contending, and for all of her professional career Pat had shared that view.

But not everyone did. And among those who did not were, apparently, those fantastic creatures whose images had appeared on the world's TV screens two years before: the monstrous "Horch," with their snaky long dinosaur necks and their brutal faces, and the even uglier scarecrow-bodied "Beloved Leaders." They could be wrong, too, Pat told herself. But they were obviously a lot more technically advanced than human beings. So maybe they knew. . . .

And maybe it was true that, at some unimaginable time in the future, she and everyone else she knew—and everyone she hadn't ever known or even heard of, as well—would be reborn in this improbable (but possibly real) eschatological Heaven.

Medical report
Gross morphology of extraterrestrials: "Docs."
Classified.

The physical measurements of "Doc A" are: Height, 246 cm, weight 185 kg, resting pulse 27, resting respiration 16.

For "Doc B:" Height 233 cm, weight 181 kg, resting pulse 25, resting respiration 16.

Both specimens are vertebrates and apparently mammalian. They possess the arms-legs-head primate architecture, except that they have two additional, smaller "arms" on each side. Instead of hair they possess a chitinous white growth on face, axillae and genitals. It has not been possible to obtain X rays or blood samples. However, stool, urine and saliva samples have been obtained which are currently under study. Curiously, few microorganisms have been observed even in the excreta.

It is desirable that additional studies be carried out, but the subjects do not respond to our efforts to secure their cooperation.

When the doorbell rang it was the live-in guard who responded, peered through the spyhole, opened the door. It was a permitted visitor. In fact, it was Dan Dannerman, escorted there by his own guard.

As the guards retired to wherever the guards went when they stayed out of the way, Pat looked him over. "Which one are you?" she asked.

He grinned wryly. "I'm the stay-at-home one. And you?"

"The same. That is," she added, "the one that still thinks you're a shit, Dan."

He didn't protest, and Pat felt quick sting of remorse. She tried to be more friendly. "I thought you were off with your girlfriend," she said, more sociably.

"I was, but now I've got a job to do. That's what I want to talk to you about." He hesitated, and then said without preamble, "It's about Rosaleen Artzybachova. She's in trouble. Her life is in danger." Then he noticed the expression on her face. "What's the matter?" he demanded.

"We buried Rosaleen months ago," she said.

"Christ, Pat, pay attention. I'm talking about the *other* Rosaleen."

"I know who you're talking about. But when you tell me her life is in danger it's just kind of funny."

He looked at her with disapproval. "I thought you and Artzybachova were friends."

Medical report
Gross morphology of extraterrestrial: "Dopey."
Classified.

The physical measurements of "Dopey" are: Height, 54 cm, weight (including clothing and metallic pouch, which he refused to remove), 17.6 kg, pulse ranging from 33 to 70, respiration ranging from 22 to 40. The cause of the variations in pulse and respiration are not known, and do not seem to relate to changes in stress or emotional state.

The subject, which speaks English, is extremely recalcitrant and states that it will not cooperate in further studies unless demands are met, which, it says, it has already communicated to relevant authorities.

Stool samples have been obtained and are currently under analysis. Preliminary reports have not yet been received.

"We were. Are. What about it?"

"She needs help. There are terrorists who are trying to kidnap her, for what she knows about that alien technology you were so hot for. Do you want to help her or not?"

"Help her how?"

He looked uneasy, but said, "I've been ordered to go to Kiev to take care of things there. It'd make it a lot easier if you came along."

"Why?"

"She's scared, Pat. She knows the terrorists want her, and she's not letting anybody near her that she doesn't know."

"She knows you," Pat said, stalling for time.

"Actually," Dannerman said, "she doesn't, or at least not very well. It's the other Dannerman she really knows, not me. But she and you have been friends for years. What's the matter? Are you afraid?"

And she naturally had to assure him that she certainly wasn't *afraid,* and in the process didn't notice that he hadn't said what "things" he was going to take care of.

15

When Hilda Morrisey met with the woman from the FZB, as the Russians had taken to calling their current successor to the Cheka, it wasn't in the gloomy old Russian embassy, and it certainly wasn't at Bureau headquarters. They met on neutral ground, a Steak 'n' Shake a few blocks from the embassy. When Hilda protested that they shouldn't be talking about secret matters in a public place the woman laughed at her. Her name, she said, was Grace. She was a lot younger than Hilda, and a lot prettier and better dressed, too: iridescent tank-top that made the most of her brassiereless breasts, and as mini a miniskirt as Hilda had ever seen—the latest thing from the ateliers on Nevsky Prospekt, no doubt. "Don't worry, dear colleague Hilda," she said. "It is quite safe here. All the busboys are friends. We call this place our commissary, since the food in the embassy is not great." And indeed there was never a moment in the whole time they sat there when a busboy or two wasn't nearby, rattling dishes at the tables of any other diners who might have overheard anything, dawdling over clearing the nearest tables so that no one could be seated too close.

The two of them confirmed their recognition signals with no problems. Only when they came to the specifics of the pickup Grace demurred. "You would prefer to use an American aircraft? Out of the question, dear colleague. It would certainly attract attention. No, we will supply a brand-new Russian MIG-90 VTOL; it is the same model we sell to the Ukrainians themselves, and it will have appropriate markings. I have already chosen the pilot, a very good man. He will whisk your people to Moscow—"

In the old Soviet days the country of Ukraine did not get the respect it deserved. Most of the world called it "the" Ukraine, as though it were some mere backwater province, while the country's Russian masters did worse. They *made* it a province. To patriotic Ukrainians this was an infamy. Wasn't Ukraine, as early as the tenth century, the first Christian kingdom in the area? Wasn't it, under the princes of the Rurik dynasty, an empire of its own, with the Russian hinterlands no more than a province itself? And wasn't it about time that glorious epoch was restored?

"Not Moscow. Vienna."

Grace put down her chiliburger. "But why Vienna? We can supply perfect security for you in Moscow. Your plane can be waiting at the airport to take them home, a quick transfer, no problem—"

"Vienna," Hilda said firmly.

Grace sulked for a moment, then gave in, and they spent the rest of the meal discussing why Moscow's Dynamo team could beat any Western footballers. And then, back in the Bureau headquarters, Hilda changed back into her uniform while talking on the secure lines to Frankfurt, going over the arrangements Solly had made with the assets in Ukraine. Everything was set for the mission.

But it was *wrong*. It was the first time one of Hilda's chicks had gone off on a mission without Hilda herself lurking somewhere near. Was there any chance that, even now, the deputy director could be persuaded to dump Solly and let Hilda go where she properly should go, near to the scene of action.

There wasn't. When she reported to the deputy director he scoffed at her. "Take field command? You? Not a chance, Hilda. I've got a job for you here; you're going to take over from Daisy Fennell."

Alarm bells went off in Hilda's head. "Running the damn team meetings?"

"Among other things, yes," Pell said, his tone suddenly frosty. "Things are heating up. I'm locked into all the negotiations with the UN, and that's turning into a full-time job. So I'm turning all the operational stuff over to Daisy for the time being, and you're the best choice to take over her assignments. I don't mean just the team meetings. I mean handling the freaks and keeping an eye on the Starlab bunch. You're the one who knows them best— What? Well, certainly you'll still be in charge of the Ukraine thing, too. If you need help, requisition it. Now, go talk to Daisy; she's got her hands full."

Daisy had her hands full, all right; she was in the middle of some problem with the Catalans and the Basques, and a field manager from Bangladesh was waiting to talk to her about Asian drug gangs. She waved Hilda to a seat while she finished dictating a note to the Spanish police, then leaned back and regarded her. "Congratulations, Hilda," she said. "Let's see, where do we start? You'll need to go out to Camp Smolley today, the freaks are bitching about their food and—well, everything; anyway, the one that looks like a parrot is. But the other two are having troubles, too."

"What kinds of troubles?"

Daisy waved a hand. "They'll tell you all about it when you get there. Then there's the team. Marcus doesn't want to lose momentum with the experts, so he wants a meeting every day—"

"All those people? *Every* day?"

"You can choose the participants yourself. You probably don't need the astronomer anymore—or do you? It's your call. And probably you can skip today if you have to; there won't be much time before you get back from Smolley. Then—wait a minute."

She frowned as her screen buzzed at her, listened for a moment, then said, "Apologize to him; I'll be with him in five minutes. Ten at the most."

She turned back to Hilda. "Sorry, where was I? Oh. The Starlab people in New York. Guards and surveillance are being handled by your old office; I've instructed them to report to you, but there haven't been any problems. The Chinese are still trying to get their hands on the pregnant one, and the damn Floridians are pissing and moaning about letting their General Delasquez get killed. Or abandoned. Or whatever happened to him up there."

She thought for a moment, then leaned back and smiled. "So what about it, Hilda? How do you like life in the fast track?"

The answer was "very little"; but all Hilda said was, "I'd rather be out in the field."

Daisy said sympathetically, "I felt that way, too, at first, but you get used to it. And there's a time to settle down, isn't there? Listen, while I think of it, my husband and I were wondering if you'd like to come over for dinner—"

Hilda goggled at her. Husband? When had that happened? And what did Daisy want one of those things for?

"—maybe tonight? You've never seen our house, have you? So, about eight? And there's somebody Frank and I would like you to meet."

All the way out to Camp Smolley Hilda was fuming to herself. Time to settle down? Time to turn into another Daisy Fennell? The worst part of it was that she hadn't ducked fast enough. Now she was committed to dinner with Daisy and Frank and Frank's really nice partner in the real-estate business, Richard, who had lost his wife to a mugger two years before and was just the kind of man Hilda ought to get to know.

She swore under her breath. Then, as she drove up to the entrance of the old biowar establishment, it got worse. There was a Police Corps lieutenant directing traffic at the turnoff, impatiently waving Hilda away with the other commuters until he saw her uniform. Then he saluted and allowed her to enter the public road that led to Smolley's access. But when she reached the gated drive to the labs there was half a company of police lining the far side of the road, across from the two-meter berm that surrounded Camp Smolley itself. Nearly a hundred picketers stood behind the police line, shouting and waving banners: *Beware the Antichrist from Space! God Is Not Mocked! There Is Only One True Word!* And one other small group, shooed away from the other by the police, who had a different crusade on their minds. Their placard read: *Free Dopey and the Docs!*

10 A.M. Traffic Advisory

No bomb or free-fire zones have been declared in the District or immediate environs.

There is unusual crowd activity at the White House and in the vicinity of the National Bureau of Investigation headquarters in Arlington. At present the situation is orderly, but alternate routes are advisable.

(Consult Maryland and Virginia notices for other areas involved.)

Damn these people! How did they know? The aliens had been moved here under the tightest security the Bureau could provide . . . but here were the protesters.

Naturally the protesters had no hope of getting into the biowar plant itself. Even Brigadier Hilda Morrisey couldn't pass until she parked her car and went through a metal detector, a patdown and a Bureau cadet with a sniffer like a portable vacuum cleaner to make sure there were no traces of banned chemicals on her person. Then they wouldn't let her take her car the remaining half kilometer to the building proper. "There'll be a shuttle van here in a moment, ma'am," the guard officer said. "You can wait inside if you like. Welcome to Camp Smelly."

She didn't like. She did it anyway, sitting with an unwatched news screen for entertainment. It wasn't entertaining; what was on at the moment was an interview with that Colonel What's-his-name Du-something, the French astronaut—or would-be astronaut, because as far as Hilda could tell he had never actually been in space. The interview was in French, but after the first few seconds an English voice-over translated his words. "We will be ready to launch to the so-called Starlab within the next few days," he said. "The American threat? It is pure braggadocio. I am not afraid. They dare not shoot us down; there are no national boundaries in space, and we have as much right to go there as they do."

"Son of a bitch," Hilda said out loud, startling the lieutenant, who had come in to get out of the damp chill. "Oh, not you," she said, waving at the screen. "That son of a bitch. And those sons of bitches across the road, too."

"Oh, don't worry about those people, ma'am," the lieutenant said earnestly. "Do you see that berm out there? Surrounds the whole base, and there isn't only full electronic surveillance, it's mined. Antipersonnel mines. Squirrels and birds won't trigger them—though we got a deer once—but I guarantee none of those creeps will get through. And here comes your van."

She never got a chance to tell the man that what she was worrying about wasn't the protestors breaking into Camp Smolley, it was how they had known enough to be there in the first place. When she got out of the van she was searched again before she was allowed to go through the ostensibly simple wooden door of the ostensible ancient mansion—neither of which had ever fooled anyone—and then had to be searched one more time before she was allowed to pass through the real door, bank-vault thick, ponderously opening on its huge hinges with a hiss of air being admitted to the lowered-pressure anteroom behind it.

None of that was really necessary, of course. No one thought there was any real need for Category Five containment for Dopey and the two Docs. If the things had brought any horrible alien plagues to Earth with them there had been plenty of opportunities to spread the disease before they ever saw Camp Smolley. But the director had decreed Category Five containment.

Hilda would have done the same. Not for any epidemiological need, but just to cover your butt for the congressional inquiry that sooner or later was sure to come.

Hilda's heavy uniform coat was taken away from her and then she was allowed into the wing where the aliens were housed. The warmth was wonderful, after the damp cold of outdoors, but suddenly Camp Smelly began to deserve its old nickname. The stench of alien metabolism was startling. In one room the two Docs were kept, one characteristically standing immobile, the other very uncharacteristically lying on a pallet on the floor, with two or three medics hovering around. The cadet who was guiding her explained, "It's diarrhea, Brigadier Morrisey. They were trying to get some minerals into their diet. They think it was the soluble calcium and iron that did it. Now Captain Terman's waiting for you in the laboratory."

Charity—at a Price!

When the High Governor's office announced that our brothers to the North were graciously willing to remove the "device" that was implanted in the brain of our brave astronaut, General Martín Delasquez, they were polite about it. They did not mention that the Yankee authorities have presented a rather large bill for the "costs" of these services.

If our information is correct, the only "services" the Washington government will contribute is the provision of a room for the operation to take place in. The actual surgery will not be done, in fact cannot be done, by any North American. It will be performed by the very "Doc" creature which General Delasquez himself did so much to bring to us. So once again we Floridians learn that "gifts" from the North are never without a price.

—*El Diario,* Miami

There were two more armed guards in front of the laboratory door, but they stepped aside to let Hilda and the cadet enter. The stink of the laboratory was different from the one that came from the sick Doc, but not a lot more pleasant; it seemed to come from an opened canister. Captain Terman stood there, watching a medic carefully measure out spoonsful of what looked like lavender slime. The stuff had orange-and-black lumps in it, and it smelled like a brewery.

The captain was an elderly man, even more past his proper age-in-grade than Hilda had been, and he waited until the canister had been capped before he turned to greet her. "Sorry I couldn't meet you myself, ma'am," he said, not really sounding very sorry at all, "but they're very strict about how much of this we can give them at a serving. Has the cadet told you what we do here?"

"I can see what you do here," Hilda said, looking around. "Show me what else you do, then I want to talk to Dopey."

What they were doing was a lot. Through a plate-glass window she got a look at a sterile-environment biology lab. Everyone inside wore clean suits and face masks; one woman was starting a centrifuge, two men were titrating drops of something into Petri dishes of something else; three other people, including Dr. ben Jayya, were clustered around a screen with dancing curves of red and blue and green—doing what Hilda could not guess. (But didn't think she needed to, since this was the sort of thing Camp Smolley was supposed to be best at.) In another room there was a long table that contained half a dozen objects, mostly metal. They were not any kind of objects Hilda had ever seen before; with a shock, she realized these were some of the things the rocket had brought back from Starlab. Inside a containment hood two technicians were carefully dismantling a six-sided gold-colored object the size of a hatbox. "Dopey says it's a recording unit," Captain Terman told her. "Wait a minute, I'll give you a better look."

He turned on a wall screen, and she was looking down into something that didn't look like any recording unit she had ever seen. No revolving spool, no drive heads; what was coming out of the machine, layer by layer, was a succession of flat, thin hexagonal things that looked more like filter paper than any mechanical device, but in half a dozen different colors, some of them faintly glowing. "We have three of these," Captain Terman said with satisfaction, "so we figured we could try to take one apart. That other stuff? Junk, mostly. That long green thing looks like a crowbar. If you ask me, that's what it is. There's no internal mechanism at all. Do you want to see Dopey now?"

"Probably. What's he doing?"

"Being debriefed, of course. Wait a minute, I'll show you." The captain touched the controls again, and Dopey appeared. The little alien was perched glumly on a chair, surrounded by his debriefers. His cat whiskers were drooping and his fan had turned leaden gray. He was talking in a low monotone, and when Hilda tried to make out what he was saying she frowned. "Is that Spanish he's talking? Why?"

The captain looked unhappy. "He said he was tired of speaking English, and both Herrera and Ortiz are bilingual. He was quite insistent. He's not easy to get along with, ma'am." He looked aggrieved. "You know that belly bag of his?"

It wasn't the most sensible question anyone could ask; Hilda was looking right at the thing. "What about it?"

"Well, the lab people want it for study. Only he won't let us take it."

"The last man to try that," Hilda said, remembering the flight back from Calgary, "nearly got electrocuted."

"Yes, ma'am. They know that, but they think they could use insulated tongs or something. Funny thing is, it doesn't seem to shock him, you know? I can't figure that part out. Anyway, he complains that our tests—they've been going over it with radiation counters and things—the tests are depleting its power reserve, and he can't live without it."

"Do we have any idea whether that's true?"

"No, ma'am. Only one way to find out, though—take it away from him and see if he dies. But I can't do that without orders."

Hilda nodded, eyeing the man. She wasn't going to be the one to get him off the hook; if someone ever gave that order, it wouldn't be Hilda Morrisey. "We'll let that go for a while. Let's go see him."

As soon as Dopey saw Hilda he pushed his way past his debriefers and scurried over to her. "Colonel Morrisey, you must help me!—what?" He paused to listen to something one of the debriefers said in Spanish. "Please make these people understand that we are starving! We must return to the Starlab and get more of our food."

"You have food," Captain Terman said quickly, glancing at Hilda.

"It is not food! It is certainly not *our* food—a teaspoon of that at a time, that's all you give us—and that other stuff will kill us. You see what happened to my poor bearer!"

"It is only diarrhea," the captain said. "The medics say he'll be better as soon as he gets it out of his system."

"And what if I get it, too?" Dopey bristled his whiskers at them. "I do not like to complain, Brigadier Morrisey, but these people simply do not know me. Can you not have one of the Dr. Adcocks come here? Or even an Agent Dannerman? Someone with whom I have been through adversity, who appreciates the sacrifices I have made?

Who would surely not allow these people to give us such foul food?"

Hilda was losing patience. "Shut up about the food for a while," she commanded.

"But I cannot! It is not as though I am asking you for something on my own behalf alone, Brigadier Morrisey! If you go to the Starlab orbiter, there is more than food there, there are wonderful things. Things that will be of great value to you! I have given Captain Terman a complete inventory—"

She turned to the captain, who looked defensive. "He gave us some kind of a list, sure, but it's gibberish. I didn't bother passing it along, because who can make sense out of 'quantum pseudo-rationalizer' and things like that?"

"It is not my fault that your language does not contain terms for truly advanced technology," Dopey said.

"I want that list," Hilda ordered crisply. "Do we at least know what the things look like? When we do go back to Starlab, we'll want to know what's what."

"I could ask him to describe them all," the captain said doubtfully.

"Describe? But why do I not have my bearer simply draw pictures of them for you?" Dopey said eagerly.

"I thought he was sick."

"It is the medical one who is sick. Do you see what your diet is doing to us? Oh, please, Brigadier Morrisey! Give us proper food! And arrange a flight to Starlab so that we can get more!" And added as an afterthought, "And, please, please, do instruct one of the Dr. Adcocks to come here so I will have the company of at least one person who understands me!"

Before Hilda left Camp Smolley the captain had managed to turn up drawing materials and she had the satisfaction of seeing the uninfected golem begin to turn out meticulous sketches of strange-looking machines. "I want these copied and couriered to me every day," she ordered. "This isn't satisfactory performance, Captain! Why haven't you done this before?"

He looked hangdog. "There's been so much to do," he complained. "You didn't even hear about the war stories he was telling—"

"War stories?"

"Stories you wouldn't believe, ma'am. We've got them all recorded if you want to hear them—"

Mr. Sanjit Rao: "Will the delegate from the Estonian Republic yield?"

Mme. P.T. Padrylys: "No, I will not yield to the delegate from Sri Lanka. The Estonian Republic cannot allow this inquiry by a few large powers to the exclusion of the smaller nations, whose right to the fruits of any technology arising from interplanetary activities is clearly delineated in General Assembly Resolutions 2357, 3102 and 3103, and on this subject I have a right to be heard."

The President: "The delegate from the Estonian Republic has indeed a right to be heard. However, her time has expired, and if we don't get on with this hearing, we will be here all day."

—*Proceedings of the General Assembly*

She did want to hear them. She was running late, would have to go directly home to change for Daisy's damn dinner party, but she waited an extra ten minutes while one of the techs produced the chip with the interrogation records on it, and then she got out of there. There would certainly have to be a lot of changes at Camp Smolley, she thought as she drove back onto the road.

When she could switch the car to automatic she popped the chip into the car's player. . . .

The man had been right. The stories were hard to believe. They weren't war as Hilda Morrisey knew war. They were stories of annihilation, of whole planets destroyed by dropping asteroids onto them, even of whole solar systems wiped out by making a sun go nova. The people of those planets weren't human, of course. But they were, so Dopey had said, quite intelligent, quite civilized, quite advanced cultures which had simply refused to accept the Scarecrows as their masters.

So there was an actual war going on, and it was universe wide.

She sighed and turned off the player. Not one word of it sounded plausible to her. It was the kind of children's fantasy you came across on the television when you were idly hunting for something worth watching . . . and immediately moved to the next channel. It couldn't be true. The astronomers had been definite about that. The universe was not going to recollapse in the first place. And if it did, it surely would not bring about the miraculous rebirth of everyone who had ever lived . . . a category which, for Hilda, included a fair number of people whose deaths she had personally helped to bring about, and certainly did not wish ever to meet again.

But if it *were* true . . .

Hilda Morrisey didn't spend much time thinking about her own death, and certainly not about some possible afterlife. If anything, she hoped there wouldn't be one. When Hilda thought about dying at all she thought of it as a sort of grant of executive clemency. Being dead meant you didn't have to face any more consequences of things you had done that someone, sometime, might want to hold you accountable for. She didn't want to think that she could have been quite wrong about that.

The next morning she woke early and with a great desire to get the taste of Daisy Fennell's quiche and ratatouille dinner and the chocolate-raspberry dessert that followed it out of her mouth. Her little apartment had a fully stocked kitchen, so Hilda was able to make herself some real oatmeal and pour herself some honest coffee, not flavored with Mexican chocolate or Florida limes. She had not expected so much domesticity from Daisy (though actually it had been Frank who did the cooking), and she especially had not expected the two teenage girls that Frank had brought to the marriage. *Jesus,* she thought, and put the dinner, and Frank's partner Richard, out of her mind.

Forintel sitrep
NBI Eyes Only

The Spanish police have asked us to investigate possible Stateside activities by members or sympathizers of the Basque nationalist organization, the Euskadi ta Askatasuna. It is thought that such persons, particularly in Southern California, are active in supplying funds and possible weapons to the Basque separatists in the Atlantic seaport towns of northern Spain.

No other new alerts are reported at this time. All current surveillance operations will continue.

The first thing she did in the office was recheck all the arrangements for Dannerman's mission. He was in Kiev, he hadn't yet made contact, it was now up to the locals to get him to Artzybachova's hideaway. The second thing was to report to the deputy director, who scowled ferociously at what she had to say. "Pickets? Around Camp Smelly? Now how the hell did they know where to go?" And it wasn't a rhetorical question, either: "Find out," he ordered. "And why haven't you convened a team meeting today? Don't give me you didn't have time, you have to make time, Hilda. And your man Dannerman—the other one—is being a real pain in the ass. Deal with him."

He did not say just how the Dannerman who wasn't in Ukraine was being a pain, but Hilda had a pretty good idea. When she got back to her little office she half expected to find him waiting there. He wasn't but there were five messages from him in her mail, increasingly hostile in tone, demanding she call him back.

She didn't. She was perfectly sure there would be a sixth call, and she would decide how to deal with him then. Meanwhile she had other things on her mind. She dialed the locator service and instructed it to find Junior Agent Merla Tepp and have her report.

Then she gritted her teeth and dropped in on Daisy Fennell to thank her for the perfectly lovely time. Fortunately Daisy was busy. They had at last located the last of the gang that had kidnaped and killed the President's press secretary and she was assembling a team to bring the man in. "Don't go away," she ordered Hilda, and finished giving orders on her screen. Then she turned and smiled. "How did you like Richard? Frank says he was really interested in you. He'll probably call you."

"That would be nice," Hilda said dismally. "Daisy, can't we do better than this Captain Terman who's running Camp Smolley?"

"Oh, Terman," Daisy said. "Yes, I suppose you're right. He lost a leg in the field and the director gave him that job himself—knew the family, I think. I guess he thought it didn't matter, because Terman was basically just a caretaker—who needed Camp Smolley? But if he can't hack it— Anyway, what I wanted to say about Richard—"

But Hilda was reprieved when Daisy's screen buzzed at her again. It only took a moment, then she turned and looked blankly at Hilda.

"Funny thing," she said. "It's that Spanish business. The police got an anonymous phone tip, and when they checked it out they found a munitions dump—all kinds of stuff. Even mininukes. The funny part is, our assets in the Basque community in California? They think it was the Basques themselves that phoned it in." She shook her head. "Listen, Hilda, it's crazy around here today, but how about you and I having lunch one of these days? You know, girl talk. I want to tell you more about dear Richard. . . ."

* * *

There wasn't going to be any way of avoiding a lunch and girl talk, but Hilda was firmly determined to avoid dear Richard. No friend of Daisy Fennell's would do, even for an occasional bed partner. But it would be nice to have *somebody,* Hilda thought. . . .

Back in her office, Cadet Merla Tepp was waiting. She stood up as Hilda came in. "You called for me, Brigadier. If it's about my application to be your aide—"

Hilda waved that aside. "What it's about," she said, "is the fact that there were born-again pickets at Camp Smolley yesterday. Looks like they came from the kind of groups you were investigating. How did they know?"

Tepp said promptly, "There was a rumor when I was investigating them that they had a lead into the Bureau."

"Did they?"

"I don't think so, Brigadier. I think they were just bragging. The woman who claimed to have it was picked up in the raids, and I'm pretty sure she's still serving time—that was for the arsons in the California schoolbook warehouses. I didn't interrogate her myself, but I've seen the transcripts. What the interrogators concluded was that she was lying. There probably wasn't a real body in place here, but there might have been a leak in the electronics."

"Thanks," Hilda said. "You can go."

The woman tarried. "Ma'am? About being your aide—"

"Go," Hilda ordered. "We'll talk about it later."

And perhaps they would, she thought; she was certainly going to need more help here. But there were things that had to be done first. She put through a call to the electronics man, to tell him that someone seemed to be able to tap into Bureau business. She called Personnel to produce a list of candidates to replace Captain Terman. What she needed, she thought, was a field-grade officer who knew enough about biology and technology to shake up the teams at Camp Smolley—or at least knew enough to know who to requisition as his operations officers. She was studying the personnel files of the first three candidates when Agent Dannerman appeared at her door.

She turned to scowl at him, and he was scowling back at her. "What's happening with the other one?" he demanded.

She elected not to bother with reprimanding him for walking uninvited into her office. "He's on a classified mission, out of the country."

"I know it's a classified mission, and I know it's out of the country. It's in goddam Ukraine, where Rosaleen Artzybachova is."

"And it's none of your business, Danno. How'd you even know about it?"

"Christ. Hilda, the Pats talk to each other, you know. He took one of them with him!"

She sighed and shook her head. "It's not your operation, and it's classified."

"Tell me one thing," he insisted. "What's he supposed to do with her when he finds her. Rescue her? Or cut her head off?"

16

It was the first time Pat Adcock had ever traveled on a passport—actually, on two different passports—that were not her own, and it was certainly the first time she had had to do any of that cloak-and-dagger *hsst!-here-are-the-papers!* stuff. It made her nervous. On the way to Frankfurt she slept as much as she could. She knew that, with the wig and a lot more makeup than she had ever worn before, she didn't really look a lot like herself; but she didn't want to test it by talking too much to her seatmates. She worried about making her connections, but when she walked into the lobby of the airport hotel there was Dannerman, smoking a large cigar and studying a German paper, just as he was supposed to be. *"Liebchen!"* he cried. *"Ma chérie!"* And as he flung his arms around her and gave her a surely unnecessarily big kiss—his stiff German beard scratched her cheek, and the son of a bitch tasted horribly of cigar smoke—he whispered in her ear, "Give me the passport and tickets."

She did—quite openly, because the Bureau spooks who briefed her had had no confidence in her ability to be surreptitious, and, although she watched carefully, she didn't see what he did with them. All she saw was that he picked up his briefcase from the armchair, tossed his newspaper down, put out his cigar and offered his arm. And as they left the lobby she looked back and saw that, yes, just as had been planned, somebody was casually picking up the paper, along with whatever Dannerman had slipped into it, as though simply to see what the day's soccer results were like.

On the Aeroflot flight to Kiev she hoped to feign sleep again, but Dannerman was having none of it. Probably it was the suppressed actor in the man, she thought irritably. He was playing his part to the hilt. Then it was champagne for the two of them, because the honey-blonde flight attendants were glad to make the flight as comfortable as possible for Herr Doktor Heinrich Sholtz, the statistician from the Gesellschaft für Mathematik und Datenverarbeitung mbH, who was combining business and honeymooning with his pretty (though surely a bit long in the tooth?) French bride, Yvette; and how charming it was that neither of them spoke the other's language, and so they could converse only in English. The second bottle of champagne (Georgian, of course, but still) came with the compliments of the captain, with his best wishes for the newlyweds. It went well with the pale pink caviar.

It wasn't such an awful assignment after all, Pat conceded to herself. In fact, the whole thing was turning into an adventure. Flushed with the wine, enjoying playing her cloak-and-dagger part, she thought of the three other Pats who had been passed over. She admitted to herself that she had been a little jealous of them. Sure, they had suffered privation and fear and even pain, but they were the ones who had had the *excitement,* too, had been to places where no other human had ever gone, had met alien creatures—all that—while all she herself had had to talk about was boredom and aggravation in the Bureau's jail. It was only fair that she get some of the thrilling stuff now, while they were condemned to stay at home because the Bureau didn't want to risk—

Didn't want to risk—

Abruptly Pat set the champagne glass down. Dannerman turned solicitously to her. "Is something wrong, Yvette?"

"Not really, Heinrich," she managed to say, but it was untrue. What was wrong was that she had suddenly realized what it was that the Bureau didn't want to risk. It was what the other Pats and the other Dannerman knew, those little facts about their captivity somewhere in space that the Bureau was not prepared to share, just yet, with the rest of the world. If these terrorists should capture them, they would surely find ways to make them tell everything they knew.

While if she and Dan were captured, even the most painful interrogation was bound to fail, because there wasn't anything of that sort that those two could tell. But that would not keep the terrorists from trying.

Pat had never been in Eastern Europe before. For that matter, she hadn't been in any part of Europe frequently enough to know it; her overseas traveling had been limited to the usual Grand Tour—Singapore, Japan, the PRC—that had been Uncle Cubby's graduation present, plus an occasional weekend seminar. For the seminars you flew in and you flew out, and there wasn't much sightseeing in between. You spent your time in colloquia and cocktail parties with your astronomical colleagues. If you found an hour or two for a quick peek at whatever the local attraction happened to be in whatever otherwise indistinguishable city that particular meeting chanced to be held in, you counted yourself a lucky tourist.

In Kiev she was a *very* lucky tourist. As long as she was able to keep the thought of what might happen if they were discovered out of her mind, there was a lot to enjoy. The Great Gate Hotel was surprisingly comfortable (Great Gate, Great Gate—oh, right, she tardily recalled. Mussorgsky. *Pictures at an Exhibition.* "The Great Gate at Kiev." Which explained the continuing low murmur of music in the elevators.) The food was good—well, interesting, at least: there seemed to be more garlic in the borscht than she had expected. The service was uneven, but always friendly, with a lot of, "What a pity you come in winter! Kiev is so beautiful in spring, the chestnut trees in bloom, everything fresh and lovely." The only thing that troubled her (not counting that one big worry at the back of her mind) was the bed.

What was wrong with the bed in their room was that there was only one of it. It was a big bed, with a comfortable mattress and a giant-sized duvet to keep them warm. But there was only the one. The Ukrainians evidently felt that a married couple, particularly a honeymooning married couple, had no need of separate-but-equal accommodations.

For a moment Pat had actually tried demanding that Dannerman sleep on the floor, but all that had got her was a warning finger to the lips and being dragged to the bathroom. There, with the shower running full tilt to cover his whispers, he pointed out that Slavs had a notorious habit of bugging foreigners and they were, after all, supposed to be newlyweds.

It wasn't until they were actually retiring that night that it occurred to Pat to wonder just how newlywed they were supposed to act. But he got chastely into his side of the bed, and, decorously pajamaed, she got into hers, and that night, at least, the unseen observers, if any, didn't have anything interesting to watch.

Meanwhile, there was sightseeing.

What they had to do (Dannerman had explained to her) was to wait until they were contacted. By whom? By the "zek children" who were supposed to be Rosaleen's bodyguards, but who, he explained, might also be members of the Ukrainian nationalist terror group, who were planning to kidnap Dr. Rosaleen Artzybachova for purposes of their own. Meanwhile they were to conduct themselves just as the newlyweds (but combining business with their honeymoon) Herr Doktor and Frau Doktor Heinrich Sholtz would.

And once they were contacted? What were they supposed to do then?

That was where Dannerman's explanations became vague and unsatisfying. Rescue Dr. Artzybachova, of course, he said; but when she asked him why they didn't simply turn the matter over to the local police all he could say was that some of the police were probably also members of the terrorist group themselves. The two of them would have to thwart the terrorists' plan on their own.

He didn't say how.

Meanwhile they acted their parts. Dannerman conscientiously reserved for their third day in Kiev a car with a German-speaking driver to take them into the evacuated zone around the ruined Chernobyl nuclear power plant. When Pat said plaintively that it was dangerous there he said, for the benefit of any possible eavesdroppers, "But we must, *ma pauvre petite,* otherwise how can I explain our visit here to the people who pay expense accounts?" (And then, in the bathroom that night with the shower going, "But maybe we'll be lucky. We won't have to go if they contact us first.") They visited the Ryemarket and the ancient catacombs by the banks of the Dnieper River—less extensive than the more famous ones in Rome, but ghoulish enough to give Pat pause. It wasn't that she found those narrow underground passages frightening. It was just that she found it obscene to stare at the mummified remains of ancient monks; when you were dead you were certainly entitled, at least, to privacy. They attended a folk-dance recital one evening (much leaping and parading, but the costumes were certainly beautiful) and an opera on another (*Boris Godounov,* of course). They told everyone they happened to meet just what the Herr Doktor Sholtz and his Parisian bride were doing in Kiev—engaged in a lengthy statistical analysis of health problems resulting from the Chernobyl disaster, and therefore desirous of getting a look at the territory to make the numbers come alive. And they looked at every cathedral and museum the city had to offer.

Pat found that she was enjoying herself. She was amused when a woman with a notepad in her hand urged them to sign a recall petition for the Ukrainian UN delegate—until the woman found out they didn't speak Ukrainian and obviously weren't eligible to sign. She was surprised to see how much Kiev resembled any American city—cops patrolling in pairs against possible urban violence; hawkers selling their inflation-proof merchandise just as though they were in New York (though in Kiev the knickknacks were heavily weighted toward old Soviet-style medals and decorations). It was, actually, kind of fun—provided you were careful not to think too much about what might go wrong.

> The area which suffered the worst fallout from the old Chernobyl nuclear explosion is called the "Zone of Alienation," and it was evacuated immediately after the accident. It didn't stay evacuated. Old people came back because they didn't want to change their ways, and they died there. Their families came to bury them. Some stayed. So did their descendants, some of them hunting mushrooms in the forests and selling them in Kiev, some simply scrabbling out a living for themselves on the old farms. Over time they were joined by hermit types and a few people hiding from the police. In all, a few hundred people still live in this area of nearly 20,000 square kilometers.

Surprisingly, Dannerman turned out to be an easy traveling companion. Well, she shouldn't have been surprised, Pat thought, remembering the long-ago days when they played together as children on Uncle Cubby's estate; but that had been years past and a world away. The two of them had changed. She had become a rather respectable astronomer, and he, damn him, had turned into a lousy gumshoe for the National Bureau of Investigation. What astonished her was how easily, living their roles as carefree sightseers, they had both turned back. They were even playing house again, just as they had when they were nine or ten years old—though, she reflected with an interior grin, without any of those you-show-me-yours-and-I'll-show-you-mine games they had graduated to a little later.

Of course, that sort of thing wasn't out of the question even now. Might actually enhance their cover as honeymooners, if indeed they were being watched.

Amused at herself, Pat brushed her teeth, and even picked up Dannerman's clothes where he had dropped them over the edge of the tub as he changed into his pajamas. As she was folding his pants she discovered something odd: there was an unexpected sort of interior pocket at the waistband, and what was in it was a peculiar little glass pistol. She sniffed it. There was a faint odor of vinegar. . . .

It was one of those strange little chemical steam guns they called bomb-buggers.

Hell, she thought glumly.

They were not children anymore, of course. And they weren't playing a game here in Ukraine.

So when they climbed into the big, welcoming bed, Pat turned away and stayed virtuously on her own side. So did Dannerman, and those unseen observers, if any, got nothing interesting to look at that night.

The next morning it was snowing again. Pat viewed it with mixed emotions. Maybe they wouldn't go into the evacuated zone after all?

But Dannerman was firm. The car was hired, the snow was only a light dusting; he was definitely going, she could stay in the hotel if she was that frightened of a little residual radiation, but that would make her whole presence here pointless, wouldn't it?

All through breakfast she considered that option, but who was Dannerman to tell her she was frightened?

Then, when they arrived in the lobby, complete with parkas and boots, the concierge was apologetic. Yes, he had arranged their picnic baskets, which the doorman would put in their car—there were no restaurant facilities in the evacuated zone—but it would be a different car. The German-speaking Stefan had had an unfortunate accident. He would not be able to take them after all. However, the concierge had arranged for another man, Vassili, very good, spoke little German but his English was excellent and he knew the zone very well. Besides, he was already committed to go to Chernobyl that morning, in order to drive an engineer who worked with the monitoring crew back from leave; he would drop the woman off at Far Rainbow, the town where the workers lived, and then simply take them on to the reactor itself. She would not be in the way. She would have her own food, as would the driver. Also, she knew the zone well, and perhaps could tell them things even Vassili didn't know.

At least the car was bigger than Pat had feared—the woman engineer sat in front with Vassili, and Dannerman and Pat had the fairly spacious backseat to themselves—and it had a good heater. Pat dozed on Dannerman's shoulder for the hour it took to get to the zone proper, and only woke when she heard the driver talking to him. They were passing a structure like a toll plaza on an American superhighway that sat on the other side of the road. The road wasn't any superhighway. It was paved, but it had a hard and potholed life. There were two or three cars going through the structure on the other side, and the driver explained: "Check wheels, cars, people for radioactivity, do you see? Us also when we come out." The woman rattled something, and the driver grinned and translated: "She says easy to get in, not so easy to get out. You step in wrong place, you pick up radioactive mud, then you have to take shower and wash clothes before you leave. No hot water, either. So please be careful where you step."

What Is Being Concealed?

Are there indeed intelligent creatures living on other stars in our universe? Yes, we are told there are, and some representatives of them are currently being held incommunicado in the chambers of the American spy agency. Do they possess priceless information which is being withheld from the great mass of peoples of the world? There can be no question of that, either. What must be done to rectify this wrong? There can be only one response. The General Assembly of the United Nations must convene its emergency session and seek, yea, demand, answers to all these questions.

—*El Ahram,* Cairo

Behind them was a little village of small houses; it was one of the purpose-built places where the people of the town of Pripyat had been rehoused, after the great explosion. Ahead was nothing. The dead zone didn't look particularly dead in its coating of snow, and when Pat said something the driver spoke briefly to the engineer and reported, "No, is not dead. She say you come back in two months in spring and you see everything wonderful green. Trees, meadows. Even crops still coming up in places, only nobody eat them. Too much cesium-137, you know what that is? You eat them, your children have two heads, unless you die first."

It seemed that the engineer did have a little English after all, because she wasn't letting Vassili get away with any of that. For the next twenty minutes, all the way to Far Rainbow, she spouted facts and statistics to the driver, who dutifully translated the flow of Ukrainian to Dannerman, who, in his incarnation as visiting research scientist, dutifully made notes. When they had dropped her in the company town the driver turned and made a face at Dannerman and Pat. "How she talks!

Amazing!" he said, and said nothing more until they were well clear of the town.

Then he stopped the car. He peered up and down the deserted road, then turned to his passengers. "You get out now. I must search you for weapons. Then we will meet a friend, and he will take us to Dr. Artzybachova."

17

Rosaleen Artzybachova stood as much as she could of the solicitous yammering from the three of them. Then she retired to the bathroom. She did not actually have to move her bowels, and when she did have to she managed the feat expeditiously enough. Still there she was, perched morosely on the pot for half an hour and more, because where else in her little dacha could she be alone?

Even so, she could hear them muttering to each other outside the bathroom door. They were getting impatient. They wanted decisions made and actions taken. Soon enough Marisa would be knocking in polite inquiry, or Yuri would, to ask if she were quite all right in there. Soon enough she would have to come out. Then she would have to face their tender, bossy concern again.

She didn't want to.

What Rosaleen Artzybachova wanted was to be left in the sort of peaceful solitude that had seemed so boring to her just a few months before all this began, and now seemed like heaven. She sighed, gloomily yearning for the tedium of those endless games of chess-by-fax. She stood up and flushed the toilet—not that there was anything there to flush apart from the sparkling (if faintly radioactive) water from the Dnieper River two kilometers away. She ran some more of that water in the sink and looked at herself in the mirror.

In just a few years she would be—God's sake!—a hundred. She observed herself critically. She was definitely more hunched over than she had been a few months before. That was osteoporosis, one of the side effects of those months in the captivity of the Beloved Leaders without her medications, and it would be with her for the rest of her life. Once the calcium was gone it didn't come back. But at least she had stopped losing it, and, taken all in all she looked no more than, well, perhaps seventy-five, eighty at the most.

But ninety-and-some was how old she truly was, and wasn't that enough of an age to content any reasonable human being? Was it worth the trouble to try to prolong it?

The zek children wanted her to prolong it. They wanted to save her from all the threats that were building up around her, and it would be impolite to refuse their kind, if unwanted, solicitude. When she opened the door Marisa was standing there. The girl had a couple of towels in her hand, not because she was carrying them anywhere but to provide an excuse for being in that place at that moment. "All right," Rosaleen Artzybachova said, roughly but fondly, "you see for yourself that I did not die in there. So please put those silly towels down and sit somewhere."

The dacha of Doktor-nauk Rosaleen Artzybachova had only four rooms, but that was because she only wanted four. It wasn't her father's dacha, though it was built on the same tenth of a hectare, on the same hillside fifty-two kilometers from Kiev, with the same pretty—if distant—view of the Dnieper River. Her father's dacha had also been four rooms, but those rooms were slapped together of rough-sawn boards from the trees at the top of the hill. It had not been anything like a luxurious country home. It was hardly heated at all, apart from one fireplace and the jawboned-together tangle of copper water pipes that was meant to, but seldom did, conduct some of the fireplace heat to the bedroom. Of course it was lacking electricity and running water. And, of course, it had been taken away from the family when the GehBehs carried her grandfather off to the camps.

When Rosaleen began to be distinguished in her field it had given her some satisfaction to buy the dacha back—cheaply enough, after that whole area had been contaminated by the explosion in the Chernobyl power plant—and then to tear it down and have the new one built in its place. Which had been not at all cheap, since the workmen demanded, and got, triple pay for the risks of working in the Zone of Alienation.

In the dacha's spacious living room Tamara and Yuri were somberly watching a news channel; the pictures on the wall screen were of Dopey and the two Docs, caught as they were being escorted from one place to another somewhere in America, but Rosaleen could not tell where because the sound was off. "Where's Bogdan?" she asked.

"He has gone to find an untapped phone," Tamara said. "He will be back very soon, I think. He says we may have to move tonight, tomorrow morning at the latest. Also there is another legal notice in the incoming."

"All right, fine," Rosaleen said, and gestured toward the samovar. While Marisa was getting her a glass of tea she sat down on the comfortable chaise, warmed to body temperature and thankfully free of the bedding her guests used, since there was no actual bed on the premises for anyone but Rosaleen herself. She didn't ask what the legal notice was about. She knew. Somebody somehow had persuaded the village clerk to make a fuss about her ownership of the dacha again. It was pure—pure—pure "chickenshit," she thought to herself, her America-acquired vocabulary always useful for such matters. No one contested that Dr. Rosaleen Artzybachova had owned the dacha in fee simple. What they were making trouble about was that it was clearly established in the official records that Dr. Rosaleen Artzybachova had unfortunately died, having left no will and therefore with her estate reverting to the government. Although this new Dr. Rosaleen Artzybachova certainly *seemed* to be in some sense the same person, there would have to be a hearing, and a court determination, and—

> Mr. L. Korovy: "And in our own country of Ukraine, what do we see? Our inflation rate has trebled, for no other reason than apprehension in our financial circles over the impact of these new technologies from space. And whose efforts are largely responsible for wresting these precious articles from their source and bringing them back to us? Why, none other than our own dear Doktor-nauk emeritus R. V. Artzybachova. Yet the Americans have usurped them from us and all the world!
>
> "This is clearly unsupportable. It is the evident duty of the United Nations General Assembly to, with immediate effect, begin a formal investigation into this matter, and then to ensure that the fruits of these discoveries are shared with all the world's people, particularly those who, like Ukraine, have done so much to obtain them."
>
> —*Proceedings of the General Assembly*

And, yes, it was chickenshit, all right. Rosaleen knew that the only thing those powerful unseen someones really wanted to accomplish was to get her out of the safety of her house. For what precise reason Rosaleen did not know, but was sure it was an unpleasant one.

She took a lump of sugar from the tray Tamara offered and placed it in her mouth. As she sucked the first scalding sip of the tea through it Tamara waved shyly to the picture on the wall screen. "Doctor? What was it like, to be a captive of those horrible creatures? Were you frightened?"

Yuri clucked angrily at her impudence, but Rosaleen shook her head at the man. She was grateful to all her companions in this new captivity, but small, young Tamara was the one who touched her heart. She expertly tucked the sugar in the corner of her mouth and said, "Yes, I was frightened, my dear. What was it like? Very much like it is here. Crowded. Frustrating. Worrying. Like being imprisoned anywhere, although you all smell better than the extraterrestrials did. Indeed," she said, smiling fondly at her three protectors, "no doubt better than I will in just a moment, since, as long as Bogdan is not here yet, I think I will do my exercises."

Tamara nodded, and began to set up the exercise machines. Marisa said fretfully, "But where is Bogdan?"

Where was he? Tugging at the weights of her exercise machine before the great picture window, Rosaleen asked herself the same question. It was curious that a short time ago she had been trying to postpone the discussion as long as she could, and now she was impatient to get it over with. All down the slope of the mountain the snow was still thick. The picture window's layered thicknesses of thermal glass and inert gases shut the outside cold away from the people in the dacha. But Rosaleen knew exactly how bitterly cold it would be out there if they had to leave. She did not look forward to being cold.

She didn't look forward to leaving her dacha at all, as a matter of fact, but Bogdan was firm. She could not stay here, he declared.

Well, she knew that. Apart from anything else, she could not allow her companions to remain in this place, where the ground was soaked with cesium-137 and all the residual radiation permeated even the house they were in. True, there was very little radiation left now. Not enough to kill. Not even enough to make one sick—had she not lived in it herself for the years of her "retirement," before Pat Adcock called her to the adventure of visiting Starlab? But in those pre-Starlab days no one had lived in the house but Rosaleen herself and her do-it-all housekeeper and companion, both too old to worry about the real dangers of the radiation. Those dangers were primarily to unborn children. So many had been born with incomplete hearts or brainless heads, with quick-growing cancers, with every sort of damage. Rosaleen would certainly never bear a child, but what about these young people who were protecting her?

Bogdan, of course, said that he was well aware of the problem and was monitoring their exposure. And he was the one who gave orders.

He was the doctor, in fact. That had been useful in getting her out of the Kiev hospital, where she had not been safe—Bogdan had said so himself. That was useful still, because he was the one who kept reporting to those who wanted to come and "interview" her that she simply was even now not well enough for that kind of stress. She trusted Bogdan. His grandfather had been the one who had tried to keep her own grandfather alive, in the camps of dreary memory. He had found the other zek children to guard her and wait on her—all descendants of men and women from the Gulag—Tamara, who was Bogdan's own niece, Yuri and Marisa from families his family and her own had known for generations. In the final analysis it was family that was important to Ukrainians—even to cosmopolitan Ukrainians like Rosaleen Artzybachova herself.

Except that to certain Ukrainians, the ones who wanted to regain for Ukraine the imperial status it had had under the Grand Duke Cyril, it was the nation that was important.

> When, in April of 1986, the controllers at the Chernobyl nuclear power plant managed to blow the thing up the resulting explosion spread a dusting of radioiodine, cesium-137 and hundreds of other radioactive isotopes over many thousands of square kilometers of the Ukraine and adjacent Belorussia. In much of that territory the human inhabitants stayed where they were, in spite of growing numbers of childhood cancers and shortened lives, because they had nowhere else to go. In the worst of it—the so-called "evacuated zone"—the people were moved out, but their livestock, and the wild creatures who shared the space, remained. The animals didn't disappear. They suffered their own cancers and mutations, but, without a human population to hunt or exterminate them, they multiplied.

Rosaleen could not understand those people. To be Ukrainian, yes, that was a good thing; she felt that herself. To have lasting angers against the Russians, yes, that, too. From Soviet times, from czarist times before that, the Russians had shown contempt for Ukrainian customs, language—and people. (Who but the Russians would have sited that terrible Chernobyl plant where it could do so much harm?) But to want to make Russia a mere province of a greater Ukraine, as in the long-forgotten (but evidently not by everyone) day of Cyril, that was simply insane.

Which did not mean that it wasn't real. If there was one thing about human nature that Rosaleen Artzybachova had learned in more than ninety years of life, it was that people frequently acted quite insane.

Rosaleen was just getting out of her after-exercise shower when she heard the excited voices from outside. She grabbed for a robe and was still tying the sash, dripping wet under the towelcloth, when she saw what was going on. Little Tamara was already in her fleece jacket, assault rifle in her hand, going out the door to take her post commanding the road; Yuri had turned the enabling switch for the mines buried under the pavement and had his hand hovering over the button.

What they were looking at, out the great picture window, was a little electric car whining up the grade. It was Bogdan's car, but there were more people than Bogdan in it. He had, Rosaleen observed without surprise, found more than an untapped phone. Marisa was scrutinizing it through her glasses. "It's Bogdan driving," she reported, "but there are two other men and a woman in it. I know one of the men: Vassili. I don't know the others."

"He's stopping," Yuri said.

Marisa took the glasses away from her eyes to give him a nervous look. "You're not detonating the mines, are you?"

Yuri didn't even look at her. He picked up the desk phone. "Tamara? They're supposed to get out of the car there. Keep them covered."

If Tamara answered, Rosaleen couldn't hear her; but what Yuri said was happening. The little car's doors opened and Bogdan and a woman got out, followed a moment later by the other two men, squeezing their way over the front seats to exit through the only doors the car had.

"I don't know them," Marisa reported, and Rosaleen clenched her teeth.

"Give me the damn binoculars," she ordered; and, when she had them to her eyes, studied the people carefully. Then she set the glasses down.

"I do," she said. "Two of them, anyway. Pat Adcock and Dan Dannerman. They were with me in captivity."

18

He was waiting for Hilda in her office when she got back from her five minutes with the deputy director: Lieutenant Colonel Priam Makalanos, fifty-five years old but looking no more than mid-thirties, tall, solid, reliable, pulled in from a dirty job in Hanford, Washington, (but one he had been doing well) to become Hilda's new chief at Camp Smolley. Makalanos hadn't been in the top three of the candidates Personnel had offered her, but he had one big advantage over the others. As a brand-new agent he had been part of the team that Hilda had run in El Paso, cleaning up some smugglers of fake antibiotics.

Although Makalanos had had no more sleep than you could catch on a red-eye across the continent, he had already been out to Smolley on his own initiative and was bright-eyed and bushy-tailed as he sat across from her. He'd done more than just visit, too. He'd brought back some samples. "I understand there's a team meeting this morning," he said, "so I thought you might like to show these around." He opened a duffel bag on the floor and pulled out a purplish metal object, hexagonal, the size of a hatbox, to put on Hilda's desk.

"It's one of the food containers," she said.

"Yes, ma'am. This one's empty, and it's been cleaned and sterilized. And these are some of the drawings the Doc made. The things that are on the Starlab orbiter," he added, pulling out a sheaf of papers.

Well, damn the man, Hilda thought, half-annoyed, half-proud of her choice; there was such a thing as almost *too* much initiative. But as she glanced through the papers pride won out over annoyance. They were wonderfully clear sketches of objects she didn't recognize but were clearly strange. "Do we know what the things are?" she asked.

Medical report
Food supplies of extraterrestrials
Classified

The food supplies consist of four items: a leafy vegetable, greenish yellow in color; a compressed bar, dark gray in appearance and with a high water content, apparently manufactured; another bar, greenish in color, circular in cross section and gelatinous in texture, also apparently manufactured; and a small quantity of brown powdery substance, perhaps used as a condiment. The two species of extraterrestrials apparently eat the same foods, though the "Docs" are not observed to consume the brown powdery substance and only infrequently the gelatinous bar.

Biochemical assays are under way, but are hampered by the fact that we have received only a gram or smaller quantities of each. Preliminary examination, following indications from the "Doc," show that the leafy vegetable and the gelatinous bar do contain several sugars, including small amounts of sucrose. More detailed analysis awaits further study. Elemental ash content of each substance, derived from mass-spectrometer analysis, is attached. This does not provide information as to the compounds contained, nor, of course, to the biochemistry. Data on these will be provided as available.

"Sort of, yes. I had the Dopey identify them, as much as he could."

"Well done," she said. "Now you'll need to familiarize yourself with the situation. When you get a chance, pull up the backgrounders on Camp Smolley and the whole Starlab business—"

"Already did, ma'am. I played them over on the flight."

"Well," she said, "good for you. All right. The team people should be getting together already, so you can take this stuff up there. I'll be there in a minute."

She gazed after him thoughtfully as he left. Makalanos was definitely a good man. A good *man,* as a matter of fact; and what a pity it was that he was working for her and thus off-limits for any other kind of relationship. She wondered absently what Wilbur was doing these days—would he maybe like to fly down to Washington one of these evenings?—and then turned to her screen. What she wanted those few minutes for was to try to check up on Danno's progress in Ukraine. There wasn't much to hear: contact had been made, there was no subsequent report.

And then, as she got up to leave, there was an annoying phone call. "Hilda? This is Wretched. I was wondering if you were doing anything for dinner tonight."

It took a while for her to realize that "Wretched" was just the man's Virginia Shore way of pronouncing Richard, and a while longer for her to figure out how he got her number at headquarters (Daisy. Had to be.), and even longer for her to get rid of the man without either making a date or hurting his feelings. So she was five minutes late for the meeting she herself had called.

But no one complained, because they were passing around the food container Makalanos had brought. They hardly even noticed her entrance. Senator Alicia Piombero was there in person today. She had the thing in her hand, and she was asking Makalanos, "What holds the lid on, magnets?"

"That's what I would have thought myself, ma'am, but it isn't. The two rims are so precisely flat that they stick to each other; you can't open it without pressing that little tab on the side. Now if you'll just look at your screens—"

And one by one he fed the Doc's sketches into the scanner, identifying them as he did. A stark white pillar—six-sided again—with vents like a fish's gills along the side: "According to Dopey that one's an environment modifier—like an air conditioner." An oddly shaped coppery object: "He says that has something to do with maintaining the orbiter's orientation in space; he didn't seem to know how. Maybe there's a kind of gyroscope inside?" Multichannel radio receivers, used for monitoring Earth's broadcasts. A different kind of receiver for the bugs they had implanted in the crew that was sent back to Earth. A large object with a door like a refrigerator. "Dopey says this is the transit terminal. Of course, this is the way it looks when it's in working condition. As I understand it, the actual one on Starlab was destroyed by Agent Dannerman as a precautionary measure. We do have some fragments from it in the lab, pieces that were knocked off."

"I've seen the pictures," Senator Piombero said testily. "Pieces of junk, a crowbar, two or three things we're told are recording devices, but we don't know how to make them work—and, what was it, twenty-three cans of food. How come we didn't get anything like the stuff you're showing us now?"

Makalanos glanced at Hilda Morrisey, throwing the ball to her. Alicia Piombero wasn't one of the senators Hilda actively disliked, like Eric Wintczak from Illinois, your damn archetypal liberal, not to mention old Tom Dixon from New Jersey and half a dozen others who were always a lot too curious about just what the Bureau was doing. All the same Hilda took her time to answer. "We got what we got, Senator. They tell me it was Dopey who picked the items to take back. I suppose he was naturally more interested in food for himself." She looked around the room. "I'm sure Colonel Makalanos wants to get back to Camp Smolley. Any more questions for him before he goes?"

"The question I have," the Senator said testily, "is when we're going to go up there and get those things."

"For that," Hilda said gratefully, "we need to hear from Delegate Krieg's associate here, Mr. Downey."

And while the staffer from the American delegation to the United Nations was telling them what complications the UN was giving them she nodded to Makalanos, who quietly departed. She'd have to get out to the biowar camp herself and see what he was doing, she told herself; maybe after lunch? Provided she could get this damn meeting over with.

It was about time, Hilda thought, that she got some personal help.

MOST SECRET
From Brig. Gen. Justin T. Carpenhow
To Joint Chiefs of Staff
Subject: Extraterrestrial weaponry

The full text of National Bureau of Investigation meetings on statements made by the extraterrestrial, "Dopey," in regard to weaponry employed by the so-called "Scarecrows" in subjugating or annihilating other extraterrestrial species, is submitted herewith.

Particular attention may be given to the weapons of mass destruction. These included destroying a planet by diverting a large asteroid or comet to strike it and triggering a release of bound underwater volumes of carbon dioxide from its sea bottoms. An even larger-scale effect is claimed by causing a star to go nova, this apparently in cases where the enemy species has bases on several planets or in orbiting habitats within a system.

Submit copies of this text be forwarded to Pentagon Long-Range Planning Section for analysis and determination of possible inclusion in research efforts.

MOST SECRET

She thought about the person who had volunteered for the job, Merla Tepp. Would she do? While the speaker was droning on Hilda furtively accessed Tepp's file.

It didn't take long to scan through it; there wasn't much to scan. High school grades, not startling but good. The same in college, with a degree in, of all things, agronomy. (But it was a state college and she'd said she came from farm folks.) No near relatives; "person to notify in case" was a widowed aunt by marriage who lived near Frederick, Maryland, also on a farm. Good scores in basic training, with special commendations in marksmanship and martial arts. Good efficiency rating in cadet school; and, in the field, two more commendations for the job with the radical-right godder groups. Her request for transfer to Arlington listed "to be near family" as the reason, and Hilda smiled at that. The reason was because Arlington was where the promotions were, of course, but Tepp knew enough not to say so. Tepp was, Hilda thought, an awful lot like the young Cadet Captain Hilda Morrisey herself, right out of the training corps and as determined as this one was to make a reputation for herself.

Which meant that Merla Tepp probably had a good chance of going a long way in the Bureau . . . and also that she would bear watching.

That was all right. Hilda had no doubt she could take care of herself against any ambitious junior. Quietly she put through a call to have Merla Tepp join her on the afternoon trip to Camp Smelly.

Hilda liked driving the little two-seater, but this time she let Tepp drive so she could both observe her and chat her up. There was no doubt in Hilda's mind that Tepp understood this was a kind of audition for the part. She was doing well. She drove competently and fast; stayed on manual even on the highway and expertly passed the vehicles on automatic, keeping up her end of the conversation civilly, respectfully, but not deferentially. Boyfriend? No, no boyfriend, at least not around here—though Aunt Billie was always wanting her to meet some of the young men from her church. What kind of church? Oh, Presbyterian; no, Aunt Billie wasn't from the fundamentalist part of the family. Friends? Yes, some; she was getting along well with the others in the general scutwork pool; one of the women had suggested the two of them take an apartment together, but she really liked being by herself. And when they pulled into the access road for Camp Smolley Tepp glared at the pickets, defying the chill and damp as they waved their posters, and shook her head. "They're everywhere, aren't they, ma'am? They're really good people, but it's about time they got a life."

And Tepp was clearly impressed, as she should have been, by Camp Smolley itself.

Smolley hadn't been quite mothballed once the United States signed the convention against biological warfare. It still did a little contract research—on phages, for the National Institutes of Health; on diseases that were affecting the Atlantic cod population, what was left of it, and the Nebraska cornfields. But it had kept its tradition of total security. If anything, it was even tighter since Colonel Makalanos had come aboard. He met them at the inner door, looking not at all like a man who had had essentially no sleep for more than twenty-four hours. "You're a tribute to the Bureau's wakeup pills," Hilda told him, "but I want you to get a night's sleep tonight. This is Cadet Tepp."

He shook hands, then said, "There's something I'd like you to look at before we go in to see Dopey. Him? He's fine. I let him sleep for a while, and now he's busy telling the debriefers about this universal war that's going on. Wait, I'll show you."

As they entered the workshop room he snapped on a screen, and there was Dopey, speaking in English again. Hilda paused to listen for a moment: "Yes, the Horch managed to penetrate our channel for that broadcast. Fortunately I was able to jam most of their message. What else was in the message? Nothing of importance. Only more of their vile libels against the Beloved Leaders. No, the Horch didn't come to Starlab in person; that is a foolish question. If they had, I wouldn't be alive to talk to you. They are utterly ruthless—"

Ruthless, Hilda thought. This from the creature who had cheerfully told them how his own people wiped out whole planets! She noticed a faint smile on Colonel Makalanos's face, and saw that he was looking at Tepp. The woman's expression was pure horror as she stared at Dopey.

Makalanos cleared his throat. "Over here, Brigadier," he said, pointing at a workbench. "You remember the recording device they were disassembling? Well, there was a problem."

There certainly was. The device was in a sealed cubicle now, glass-faced, with attached sleeves so that the workers could work on it from outside. "Dry pure nitrogen," Makalanos remarked. "Seems it was taking up moisture from the air—"

And that hadn't helped it a bit. Two of the dissected parts were on the table next to it, and they looked, well, *moldy.* Where mold had been scraped off so that the original material was visible the parts that had once looked like cardboard were now gelatinous and splotchy.

Whatever the gadget had done, it was clear that it would never do it again. "I've ordered a hold on opening the others," Makalanos reported. "The bio team has taken samples and they're working on them in their own lab; I haven't had Dr. ben Jayya's report yet. I was about to talk to Dopey about it, but perhaps you'd like to question him yourself?"

She would. She did. The creature gave her a lofty look. "But surely you understand that your primitive technology can't hope to deal with truly advanced devices."

"Can you deal with them for us?"

"No, of course not, not me personally." Dopey looked surprised at the question. "That is what bearers are for."

"Are you saying that one of your Docs could have taken the recorder apart without damaging it? Could he tell us how? He can't talk—"

"Yes, he can; and no, of course he does not talk. That is not necessary. He can draw schematics if that is necessary—that is, provided he hasn't been so starved on the inadequate diet you give us that his faculties have been impaired."

"I don't want to hear any more about your diet. We're doing the best we can," Hilda said grimly.

"But it is simply not good enough, Brigadier Morrisey. If you will go to Starlab—"

"I don't want to hear about that, either. I'm asking you about these gadgets."

Dopey's fan turned a sulky pale yellow. "And I am telling you that they are beyond your understanding. Why do you treat me this way? I have befriended your people at great risk to myself! I want you to bring one of my companions down here—one of the Dr. Adcocks, or even an Agent Dannerman. They can tell you—"

"You can tell us everything we need to know, Dopey," she said persuasively. "Now listen to me for a moment."

"I am listening, Brigadier Morrisey. What choice do I have?"

"No," she corrected, "you aren't listening. You're talking. What I want to say is that we have two sets of programs here. Your program is for us to send a flight to Starlab to get you more food. Our program is also to go to Starlab, because we want to learn from your people's machines. So we have a lot in common, do you see? But something prevents us from doing that."

"Yes, Brigadier Morrisey, something does: your bickering among yourselves."

> **Time for Change!**
>
> Although our delegate to the United Nations has continued his wise policy of restraint, the patience of the People's Republic of China is not inexhaustible. His call for an emergency meeting of the Security Council must be heeded. This newest provocation of the Americans in reassessing their inflation indices is the direct cause of the recent large losses in the Shanghai Stock Exchange. Their preposterous claim to "custodianship" of the artifacts from space is without justification, and we do not even mention their high-handed actions in regard to the child of our brave astronaut, Cdr. J. P. Lin.
>
> —Editorial, *New China Journal,* Taipei, Taiwan, PRC

"No, that's not it. We'll straighten out the bickering, trust me on that. What really prevents us is that we don't know what to do when we get there. How do we take the machines apart to bring them back for study? What's inside them? We don't want our people cutting into some piece of equipment the wrong way and ruining it, the way we did with your recorder. We particularly don't want one of our people touching the wrong thing and getting killed—or accidentally blowing up the whole Starlab. You don't want that either, do you? That would be no good for either of us. So what we need, you see, is for us to have really good, solid, detailed information about the machines before we leave—"

On the way to the room where the Docs were held, Dopey waddling sullenly ahead, Hilda reflected complacently that the skills of interrogation didn't change no matter who you were interrogating, eyewitness, felon, bizarre freak from interstellar space—all the same. Dopey had achieved a small concession from her: she had undertaken to get one of the Pat Adcocks drafted to keep him company. And now she had gained his cooperation in something that really mattered.

She hoped Merla Tepp had learned something from the exchange. The woman was clearly nervous, but that was not surprising in the presence of one of those bizarre freaks. Anyway, she controlled it well, at least until they reached the Docs' room. The great, pale golems were standing statuelike as usual, a medic attendant sitting quietly in a corner of the room taking notes on their behavior—not that there was any behavior to note, Hilda thought. Then, as Tepp got her first good look at them, a flash of pure horror escaped her control for a moment.

Even Dopey noticed it, as he was trying to get up on his platform. Panting, he piped up, "Do not fear, Cadet Tepp. They will not harm you. The bearers are—were—a highly civilized, intelligent race. It is a pity that it was necessary to modify them, but now they can do nothing without orders. Please, will you help me up there? I am very fatigued."

Tepp hesitated. Annoyed, Hilda picked the little turkey up herself. She was surprised to find how light he was, and how hot his body.

He didn't speak, merely gazed at the nearest Doc. Who touched his white-foam "beard" ruminatively for a moment, then moved swiftly to the side of the attendant. Gently, but irresistibly, he took the notepad from the man and began to draw.

Tepp made a small, worried sound, then said tightly, "Excuse me, please, Brigadier." She fled. Hilda was annoyed. The smell was getting to her, of course, but she was not going to let it interfere with her job. And neither should Tepp. Hilda crowded over beside the Doc, watching in satisfaction as the creature swiftly began to draw a recognizable diagram of the recorder.

Twenty minutes later Hilda, clutching the first batch of drawings, found Merla Tepp waiting for her in the cold outside air.

Hilda gave her a curious look. "Are you all right?"

"Certainly, Brigadier. I'm sorry. It's just I thought I was starting my period."

Hilda looked her over more carefully, with dawning suspicion. She leaned forward and sniffed Tepp's lips. The odor was definite. "Do you always vomit when you're having your period?"

"No, Brigadier. I'm in excellent health. I think I may have eaten something—"

"I think," Hilda said sharply, "that you just can't stand touching the little freak. Is that it?"

Tepp was clearly shamefaced. "I'm uncomfortable, yes. I'm sorry."

"Sorry isn't good enough," Hilda said, meditating.

"Oh, please, ma'am, no!" Tepp begged, fully aware of what might be coming next. "I do dislike them, yes, but it doesn't interfere with my duties."

"What do you call what just happened?"

"I give you my word it won't happen again. Please, Brigadier! It means so much to me to have the chance to work with you—"

"Get in and drive," Hilda said, cutting the conversation short.

In a way she wasn't displeased. It wasn't entirely a bad thing for an American to loathe and despise aliens of any kind. But to take this one on as her aide?

That was going to take further thought. On the way back to the Bureau Hilda devoted herself to catching up on the news on the car's screen. The UN was making trouble again; a speaker at a convention of police chiefs noted an encouraging drop in the number of terrorist actions in the past few weeks; nothing important, really. But she stayed with it, and did not speak again to Cadet Tepp.

19

"Come on," Dannerman said to Pat Adcock, half-pulling her out of the car. They stood silent in the packed snow, while the hooded figure in the parka kept them covered with an assault rifle. It was a weapon Dannerman knew well—well enough to suppress any thought of resistance. "Just stand still," Vassili was whispering nervously. "Do not startle her; she is quite young, and may do something foolish."

Her? She? But when the person with the rifle stood up and waved them forward Dannerman saw that it was a woman, all right, in fact no more than a girl, long hair spilling out from beneath the hood of her parka. And suddenly she was not alone. A larger figure, definitely a man, definitely also carrying a rifle, came out of the door to join her. He said something peremptory in Ukrainian. Beside Dannerman the man named Vassili groaned, objected, surrendered. "He says to you must immediately take off your outer garments."

"Here?" Pat cried in surprise. "We'll freeze!"

"But," said Bogdan, his English worsening with strain, "must do it, get weapons of you." And suddenly he had them covered with a gun of his own.

They didn't freeze, though Dannerman's teeth were chattering by the time he had been patted down and his carry gun and radio transmitter removed. Then they were allowed into the house that stood all by itself on the desolate hill.

It was warm there. In fact, the house was a pleasant and wholly unanticipated oasis of comfort. They came in through a kitchen, complete with every device modern domestic technology had to offer; they entered a living room with a huge picture window and a wall screen, as well as two or three expensive exercise machines scattered among the pieces of also expensive furniture. The furniture was not in the least modern. It was the sort of thing one might have found in a home of nobility in czarist times, with a huge samovar on a table and an icon of some tortured saint hanging above it. Another man and another woman were there, chattering worriedly in Ukrainian to Bogdan and Vassili. There also was Dr. Rosaleen Artzybachova, looking not a bit different than the way she had appeared when Dannerman first saw her, in the office of the T. Cuthbert Dannerman Astrophysical Observatory in New York City. She was smiling. She clapped her hands and spoke sharply in Ukrainian. Then she advanced on Pat and Dannerman, hands outstretched. "This is a pleasure I had not expected," she said, kissing Pat, hesitating only a moment, then kissing Dannerman as well. "This is better than our cell on that planet, isn't it? Wait—" as Pat opened her mouth to speak. "Before we talk, there is a custom I want to observe—when I am in my home, you see," she added, half-apologetically, "I become very Ukrainian."

She beamed at the woman who had resignedly hurried into the kitchen, and was returning with a tray. Which contained—

"Bread and salt," Rosaleen said proudly. "It is what we do to welcome friends. And who could be closer friends than we, who lived in such proximity for so long? Eat a little, please. Then we can talk."

"No," Pat said suddenly.

Rosaleen paused with the tray in her hand to look at her. "No?" she repeated.

Prison Cells from Space?

A source close to Sen. Eric Wintczak (D-IL) reports that the National Bureau of Investigation has identified a number of extraterrestrial technologies which it proposes to adapt for use in its own system. One is a sort of energy-field containment device to hold prisoners in an escape-proof cell while jailers and others can pass freely in and out, another is a way of using devices similar to the implants taken from the returnees to tap into the actual thoughts of the subject—a sort of mind control with unimaginable consequences for civil liberties.

—Washington (DC) Times-Post

"No, we are not the ones who were in captivity with you, Rosaleen. We're the ones who were returned to Earth. And Dan is still a spook for the Bureau."

"Yes," Rosaleen said placidly. "I am aware of that." She set the tray down before them and retired to sit down. "Excuse, please, the fact that I am quite old and still a bit tired."

"You don't understand!" Pat said. "We aren't here just because we're your friends! We're here because this man has been ordered—"

But Rosaleen raised her hand to stop her. "My friends have told me about his orders, Pat, dear. They were given to him by some higher-up spook by the name of Brigadier Hilda Morrisey in the National Bureau of Investigations headquarters in Arlington, Virginia. This Brigadier Morrisey is afraid that I will give information away that the United States wishes to keep for itself, and so she has ordered young Dannerman here to come to my home and kill me." She sighed, shaking her ancient head. "I was going to ask you about that. But won't you for God's sake please sit down and eat some of the damn bread and salt first?"

Pat Adcock did as she was told. She didn't do it right away. She had expected a lot more to happen after what she had said—something drastic, maybe. Certainly *something.* At least some kind of startled outburst from Rosaleen, perhaps some violent action from one of the zek children. What she had not expected was to discover that everyone present knew more about Dannerman's mission than she had.

"Eat," Rosaleen repeated testily, and so she ate. The bread was heavy, dark chunks cut from a round loaf; the salt wasn't the sort of thing you shook onto your french fries in America, but coarse crystals. It occurred to Pat that maybe there was something in the salt or the bread, some mood-altering chemical, maybe something like the date-rape stuff she had been warned against in college, something that would turn them into mere putty in the hands of these young Ukrainian zealots. But Dannerman seemed to have no such fears. He was chewing doggedly away on the tough bread, and she could read nothing from his expression. Nor did Rosaleen's guards reveal anything, except perhaps mild annoyance at the ritual. Then Rosaleen sighed.

"All right," she said, "now that we've all had a chance to settle down, would you like to explain yourself, Dan?"

He swallowed the last chunk of the bread. Then he said, "Sure. But

I want you to do something first. Will you ask your friends to put their guns down? Better still, give them all to you—you do know how to use them, don't you?"

"Why should we do that?" the one named Vassili demanded suspiciously.

Dannerman shrugged. Rosaleen studied him for a moment, then spoke. "Let's do as he says, Vass. Give me yours and pile the rest of them in front of me."

Vassili looked rebellious, then complied. Pat, trying to guess what Dannerman had in mind, had a sudden thought. "Be careful! He's got a bomb-bugger, too!"

Dannerman gave her a curious look, but slowly, carefully, tugged at the waistband of his trousers, revealing the little holster. "That's right. I want you to take this one, too, and give it to Rosaleen. Then we should all back away and give her a clear field of fire."

"And at whom should I fire, Dan?" Rosaleen asked, sounding amused.

"Why, that's up to you. You see, you're right. I did get orders from Hilda Morrisey, and they were to keep whatever information you have about Scarecrow technology from falling into the hands of the Greater Ukraine terrorists. The guys," he amplified, "who already stole the bug that was in the other Rosaleen. They think you can help them take it apart."

"Me? I can't."

Dannerman nodded. "I don't think you could, either. But they don't know that."

"So you were going to shoot me with that thing?"

"That was one of Hilda's options," Dannerman admitted. "It wasn't mine. I was pretty sure you'd agree to be rescued. That radio you took away from me? It's to call a plane to pick us up. Then the three of us, you and me and Pat, will fly to Vienna and then to the States. The Bureau can keep you safe there."

"Safer than I am here with my friends?" Rosaleen asked skeptically.

"Well, yes. A lot safer. You see, at least one of your friends is a terrorist."

Of course, that really hit the fan. All four of the zek children were shouting at once—mostly in Ukrainian, but Pat didn't need a translator to get the gist. The big one, Vassili, was standing up and pleading with Rosaleen.

But Rosaleen was shaking her head. "Stay where you are, Vass, please," she said. "I see now why Dan wanted me to have all the guns—assuming, of course, that he's telling the truth."

"Afraid so," Dannerman said. "Figure it out for yourself, Rosaleen. How did they know what my orders were?"

> *Steam gun.* This hand weapon, colloquially known as the "bomb-bugger," contains reservoirs for two hypergolic liquids which, when mixed, produce a rapid evolution of steam, propelling a droplet of liquid at a muzzle velocity high enough to wound or kill an opponent. Since the weapon contains no nitrogenous chemicals and no metal parts, it is a favored handgun for concealment. The colloquial name derives from the bombardier beetle, an Asian insect which uses a similar system to stun and capture its prey.

"You tell me."

"Because the damn terrorists have managed to get inside information from the Bureau. I don't know how. But they have, and that's how the Greater Ukraine guys knew."

"But these are my friends!" Rosaleen protested. "I trust them, and anyway that doesn't make sense. They've had all the time they need to kidnap me if they're terrorists."

"Oh, not all of them," Dannerman said. "I think only one. Which one? I don't know that, but probably you do. Which is the one who told you about my orders?"

And every eye in the room turned on little Marisa, who began to cry. "But we never would have *hurt* you," she managed to get out between sobs, and Rosaleen put down the gun to take the young woman in her arms.

"My dear," she said, patting her back. "I am sure that is what you intended, but can you speak for all the others? You must tell us all you know."

"They were coming for you tonight," Marisa said. "They waited until now because they wanted to take gospodin Dannerman as well, as a hostage. I was supposed to—well, I wouldn't actually have *shot* any of you, I swear that. But I was to make sure no one resisted."

20

Hilda Morrisey put the team meeting off as late as possible, because it had been one of those days. It wasn't just trying to deal with that temperamental freak, Dopey, or getting rid of the battalion of time-wasters who managed to track her down with one damn request or another. (The worst was the psychologist from Harvard who demanded—damn well *demanded*—that she give him access to the four Pats, or at least to the two Dannermans, because they were absolutely essential to his ongoing twin studies—and had both the Massachusetts senators insisting that she help the man any way she could.) There was still no word from Danno in Ukraine, either. And the deputy director was in a towering rage . . . and now each last member of the Ananias team was insisting on making demands of their own. Marsha Evergood: "You *must* let me borrow the medical Doc to see what he can do with some of our terminal cases." The astronomer: "If you want me to find the Scarecrow comet-thing you *must* make every large optical telescope in the country concentrate on checking for possible objects." The man from State: "We *must* know how to respond to this note from the Albanians by tonight—"

They all had one "must" after another, and, of course, they all had to take time to explain why their particular urgency was more urgent than anybody else's. Even the ones whose problems Hilda could do nothing about. The Albanian note was the deputy director's concern, not hers, but it wound up in her lap because the man from State hadn't been able to reach Marcus Pell.

That wasn't surprising. The note from Albania was one of the two things that were making Pell crazy because it was clearly the tip of the iceberg; every damn pip-squeak country in the United Nations was

Medical Report
For Bureau Eyes Only

Agents assigned to Walter Reed Hospital report that the "medical Doc" has effected a number of apparent remissions in terminally ill patients. (Copies of charts are appended.) Some patients resisted receiving this "therapy" as an apparent "laying on of hands," but blood work and gross physical studies indicate real changes. It is suggested that the "Doc" secretes some form of metabolically active biochemicals, administered through small penetrations from the talons in his smaller arms. Attempts to secure samples of these chemicals, if any, have been unsuccessful. The cure rate, however, is significant, especially in intractable cases of immune deficiency, carcinomas and most antibiotic-resistant infectious diseases. His major failures have been on patients who already have had surgical intervention, for example cardiac-bypass procedures.

demanding a share in whatever came out of Starlab, under threat of using their collective veto to make sure none of the big nations got any either.

Well, some good, old-fashioned political horse-trading would eventually settle that. It could probably be handled with a bunch of promises, which might or might not have to be kept. But what about the other thing that fed the deputy director's fury? It wasn't a thing, exactly; it was Senator Alicia Piombero, who had most injudiciously spoken off the record to somebody who had turned around and put it on the record; and so the day's crop of news stories. *NBI's New Spy Machine. Tomorrow's Prisons in the Bureau. How Scarecrow Machines Threaten American Liberties.*

It didn't surprise Hilda that Senator Piombero chose to miss that afternoon's meeting of the team. She wished they all had; and when at last she was able to adjourn it she breathed a sigh of relief. She checked herself out and headed for home; because this was the evening she had resolved to take for herself, in order to deal with something quite personal and not very far from urgent.

Brigadier Morrisey was not really off duty very often—she generally kept herself on call, and certainly kept informed of what was happening in her personal turf in the Bureau. But when she was off duty, she was all the way off. When she got out of her swirl tub she stood before the full-length mirror in her bath and studied herself critically for several minutes before beginning to dress. First came the underthings that no one in the Bureau would ever have imagined her wearing, the negligible panty-belt and the pushup half-bra that didn't really need to do much pushing. (But, at Hilda Morrisey's well-concealed age, she took all the help she could get.) The blouse was windowed silk, the kind that opened its mesh revealingly when the wearer was warm, as she had every hope she would be in the bar she had chosen for the evening. The skirt was mid-thigh length, not a practical choice for a Washington winter, but she had a long thermal coat to get her to and from her car.

The pickup bar she had selected was more than twenty kilometers from her little apartment. It was over the Maryland line, but conveniently close to the Outer Belt. Hilda was as careful about choosing a territory for hunting purposes as about dressing for the occasion. Most important, it had to be a place where she had never, or almost never, been before and where she thus was not known. And it had to have, in the background files of the local police, a reputation as a law-abiding and reasonably orderly singles bar. It didn't have to be fancy. Hilda had no prejudices about the economic status of her sexual partners. But it had to be fight-free and clean.

This one was at the fancy end of the spectrum. She parked and locked her car herself, ignoring the hostile looks of the valet parkers; she didn't begrudge them their tip, but she was not having any stranger poking around in her vehicle. She programmed her carryphone to store all messages lower in priority than Director-Urgent. At that point she was truly off duty; and she allowed herself to feel pleasingly expectant as she entered the bar.

It was a good feeling, and she liked what she saw. The bar possessed a two-person "band," an elderly woman on strings, a younger one on synthesizer. They were pumping out familiar tunes with a decent beat, and four or five couples were actually dancing on the tiny patch of hardwood. Hilda Morrisey was encouraged. The evening might well turn out successful, because she had almost always had good luck in bars where the customers actually danced. It was in just that sort of a place, for instance, that she had met Wilbur, the gentle (but not too gentle) and entertaining stockbroker assistant who was her most recent about-to-be ex-lover. Wilbur was a man she was going to miss. (But they'd had sex five times, and, under Hilda's self-imposed rules, that meant it was pretty near time to move on. If you carried on a relationship much longer than that you risked the kind of unacceptable complications that came along with habit.)

When she checked her coat the attendant made her check her carry gun and pass through a detector array. That, too, was a good thing, though no commercial detector was going to pick up her two emergency weapons.

Singles were three deep at the bar, busily hitting on each other. Hilda made no attempt to join any of them. Her practice was to check out the available talent before committing herself, so she walked slowly toward the ladies' room, inconspicuously noting which interesting-looking men seemed to be getting close to moving to one of the booths with the women they were talking to, and which were still searching. There were at least four possibilities, she thought, and her good luck was that three of them were fairly close together near the service corner of the bar. One of them was large, fair and amused as he chatted with the little blonde who was not getting anywhere with him. Hilda noted that he was also a good fifteen years younger than Hilda herself, but that wasn't really a problem, could even be an asset. Another was an older man—but not too old—and the third she hadn't really had a good look at, but the size of his shoulders was promising. In the ladies' room mirror she checked her hair—okay—and the little bleached-out circle around the ring finger of her left hand. (That was one of her best devices. When a man asked if she were married she could say, "Not now," and then when it was time to break it off she could confess that the husband was still around, and getting suspicious.) She esteemed herself ready for the encounter as she left the powder room—

But that was when she saw a familiar face gazing around the bar. It was that cadet agent—what was her name?—yes, Merla Tepp.

That spoiled things. Hilda didn't like to have Bureau people anywhere in sight on occasions of this sort. Reluctantly she decided it was time to cut her losses and try again on another night. Or perhaps simply in another place, she thought as she reclaimed her coat and gun; the night was still young, and there were other spots on her list.

Fortunately Tepp didn't seem to have seen her. But then, as she was heading for the parking lot her carryphone beeped.

That was bad news, too. It could only be something serious enough to get past her message block, and that meant that maybe there would be no prowling for her that night. She heard a car door gently close somewhere nearby, but paid no attention as she stepped into the shelter of a large van to take her call.

She never got the call, though. Just then someone hit her over the head from behind.

Hilda was knocked to the ground, half-stunned and cursing to herself. It was an unpleasant reminder of the fact that not all violence was political. Quite a lot was generated by people who wanted to own things without the trouble of working for them; and it was just her bad luck that a couple of them had chanced on her. She struggled to get at her gun, but one of the two attackers kicked her arm, sending the weapon flying, while the other had pulled out a knife. It was suddenly looking like a very bad evening indeed for Brigadier Hilda Morrisey.

And then there was rescue. She heard two muffled shots. The kicking stopped. The men fell away. She rolled over, getting to her knees, ready for whatever was going to happen; and when she looked up there was a figure with a gun standing there, and it was Junior Agent Merla Tepp.

Brigadier Morrisey tried to get up, got as far as a sitting position and thought better of it. She was woozy. Her arm hurt like hell where one of the bastards had kicked her, and her long coat was a filthy mess from the slush in the parking lot. She was vaguely aware of sirens coming into the lot and of Cadet Tepp standing over the prone figures of the attackers. Then Tepp let the cops take over and came back to Hilda, holstering her gun. "I called for backup," she said apologetically.

And she had got it, more than anyone could need for a simple mugging: there were three police cars there, and two ambulances. "One of the perps is dead," Tepp added. "And the other looks pretty bad." She didn't sound upset about having just killed another human being. She sounded as though she were making a routine report.

Hilda rubbed a hand over her face. "Good shooting," she said. "What— How—"

"I saw you going out," the cadet explained. "And I thought I better, uh, tell you what I was doing here. So I followed you and—"

Hilda said grudgingly, "A good thing you did. Thanks." Then she eyed Tepp more carefully. "You're pretty handy to have in a dustup. Didn't I see you got commendations in martial arts?"

"Yes, ma'am. Also in marksmanship."

> Mr. Shigasimu Yana: "I speak in support of the remarks of the gentleman from the Czech Republic. It is certainly essential to the well-being of our planet that we make maximum use of whatever technologies we may learn from extraterrestrial sources, but I would go beyond that. For many years Japan has urged the resumption of a full-scale international space program on scientific and humanitarian grounds. Now it is more urgent than ever. As the distinguished members of this body are aware, my country has languished in the grip of a great economic depression for some years. We have the skills and knowledge to participate in this needed space program; what we do not have is the capital. I submit that it is the duty of the countries which can afford it to provide funding for an enlarged space program, in which Japan stands ready to play a major role."
>
> —*Proceedings of the General Assembly*

Hilda sighed. Probably she owed the woman something, and in any case she did need an assistant. "All right. Do you still want to be my aide? Fine. You've got it. Report to my office by oh-seven-thirty in the morning; I'll be in by eight. And I'll clear it with the deputy director."

"Thank you, ma'am," Tepp said eagerly; and would have said more, but one of the medics had left the wounded mugger to the others and insisted on checking Hilda out.

The arm didn't seem to be broken, but Hilda was aware she was going to have a hell of a bruise. The blow to the head was something else. She really ought to let them take her to the emergency room, the medic was telling her; and while they were arguing the police sergeant was strolling thoughtfully toward them, rolling a little metal object in his fingers. He looked at Hilda with more interest than the incident seemed to warrant. "You the NBI woman who called it in?" he demanded.

"She's Brigadier—" Junior Agent Tepp began, but Hilda shushed her. She stood up shakily and let her ID holo do the talking for both of them.

"Oh," the cop said. He didn't sound impressed. He didn't sound particularly happy, either, but then local police hardly ever were really friendly to Bureau personnel. "Well, maybe that explains it."

"Explains what?"

"We searched their car," he said, "and found a locator radio. So we checked yours, Brigadier. This was stuck under your right front fender. You were bugged."

"Oh, shit," Hilda said. And didn't have to say what that meant: this was no simple mugging, these people had followed her from her apartment and what they were after was Brigadier Hilda Morrisey herself.

She would have none of the medic's desire to take her to the emergency room for a checkup, nor of Agent Tepp's to escort her home. She was perfectly capable of driving, and annoyed besides. This damn business would have to be reported. Which meant that people would know that Brigadier Hilda Morrisey was known to frequent make-out bars.

She was aware, as she was leaving the parking lot, that there was suddenly a lot of shouting going on from inside the bar—something on the news screen, odd enough to have distracted the clientele from the pursuits that had brought them there. But it wasn't her business and she had other things on her mind.

She was halfway around the Outer Belt when she remembered two things. The first was that Junior Agent Tepp hadn't finished explaining what she was doing in the place. The second was that she hadn't finished taking the call on her carryphone when the thugs attacked.

"Radio intercept received 2248 hours. Transmission follows."

And then, as she listened to the message, she learned what the commotion at the bar had been all about. She sat bolt upright behind the wheel. "Jesus," she said out loud. "*Now* we've got troubles."

21

Pat Adcock was the first to reach the old car, flinging the doors open, but Dannerman came slipping and sliding down the snowy hill after her, half-tugging old Rosaleen Artzybachova. "You drive," he ordered, hustling the old lady into the backseat, before trotting around the car to get in beside Pat. "Do you know how to drive this thing?" he asked as an afterthought, but she already had the motor going and was turning the car around. The car's screen had lighted up as soon as Pat turned the key, displaying some weird kind of creature that Dannerman didn't have time for. He slapped it off. "Hurry up," he ordered. "We have to get to the rendezvous before sundown, and we don't know if they have friends nearby— What?"

Artzybachova was pounding on his shoulder. "Turn that back on!" she demanded.

Dannerman craned his neck around in honest puzzlement. "What for? We can watch TV once we're in the VTOL—"

"Do it *now!* Didn't you see who was speaking?"

Pat resolved the dispute; as soon as she had the car heading downhill she reached forward and snapped the screen on again. "Oh, hell," Dannerman said sulkily. "What's the matter with you? What can be so important that we have to see it this minute?"

But then the picture showed an agitated-looking woman, with a sheet of fax flimsy in her hand. "—was received just minutes ago," she said. "We will repeat it now, and then we will go to the White House for comments on this astonishing new development. Stand by, please—"

She disappeared. There was a moment of white-screen silence. Then a picture appeared. It showed a bizarre creature with a pumpkin head and a spindly body and a mouthful of teeth, and Dannerman did not ask again what it was that was so important.

The Scarecrow didn't seem to be speaking; it stood stolid before the camera—whatever kind of camera it used—with its spindly arms crossed over its spindly chest, but there was a voice, and it spoke in English. "People of Earth, your difficulties are at an end. We have succeeded in establishing communication with you once again. Soon we will provide you with further information as to how you may join the legions of sentients who are proud to call us their Beloved Leaders."

The picture faded. "Oh, Christ," said Pat Adcock, almost going off the road. "It's starting all over again."

22

The Scarecrow message changed many things for Hilda Morrisey. Not just for her. For the whole damn world, of course . . . but all that she would have to think about later, when she found time. What it meant for her right now was another all-nighter, still wearing her makeout dress with no time to go home and change, up to her unsatisfied loins in things that had to be attended to *this instant,* if not before, loaded on wakeup pills, frazzled, harassed, overtaxed . . . and, yes, loving it, because it sure-hell beat doing nothing at all.

Lacking a specified job description, Hilda took a hand wherever she was needed. The entire Bureau headquarters staff had to be found and wakened and called in. The team had to be convened. Situation estimates had to be prepared. Current Bureau missions had to be prioritized. Some would go forward unchanged—the "clear and present danger" ones like imminent bombings, ongoing hijack plans, missions that involved serious loss of life or major property damage—though probably even some of them would be starved of manpower. Everything else had to go on hold. By 2 A.M. the headquarters was fully staffed and buzzing like a wasp nest, and Hilda had her own most urgent jobs under control. She had time, finally, to stop in at the clinic and get a pill for the head that was still pounding from the assault in the roadhouse parking lot.

That turned out to be a mistake. "About time you got here," said the duty doctor. "We buzzed you hours ago."

"For what?"

"For your post-trauma checkup, of course," the doctor said, picking up the phone to call in supporting staff. Then there was nearly three-quarters of an hour gone out of Hilda's life, just when she wanted the time most: X rays, blood tests, peeing into a bottle, having one or more medics stare, in relays, into the pupils of her eyes. Not to mention the infuriating business of having to count how many fingers were being held up before her.

It could not be helped. She'd hoped that no one would have reported the incident. That hope was doomed; Tepp, of course, had quite properly ratted her out.

At least no one was having quite enough gall to ask her what she had been doing in a pickup bar. Probably didn't have to, she thought gloomily as she finally made her escape. By now the rumors about Hilda Morrisey's sexual habits were no doubt already flying around the Bureau.

Just before she went through the door the head medic at last gave her the pill she'd asked for. "You really should get some sleep," the medic warned. "And you've been taking a lot of those wakeup pills; they're not advisable for more than seventy-two hours."

"Thanks for your concern," Hilda said, swallowing the pill and walking out on him. Sleep! Who wanted to sleep when the world was going insane? It wasn't just the Bureau, it was all of government. The President would be getting in an emergency meeting with his immediate staff, maybe the whole Cabinet; the Pentagon War Room would be filling up; all over the world, in every country, people in high places would be doing just what they were doing here.

Hilda reflected that headquarters duty might not be so bad, if it could always be like this. It was almost like one of those triumphantly glorious nights in the field when the net was spread and the evidence collected and it was time to spring the trap on the unsuspecting malefactors and open the celebratory bottle of champagne.

And then, as soon as convenient thereafter, to perform that other rite of celebration and get laid.

Unfortunately, neither one of those was going to happen very fast this time . . . but then, Hilda reminded herself philosophically, you couldn't have everything. For now, the rush was enough.

When Hilda entered the conference room Marcus Pell was already in the chair, conducting the meeting that, for a change, was unexpectedly dealing with matters of actual importance. He wasn't fooling around, either. The man the deputy director had in his sights was the astronomer from the Naval Observatory, and the man was sweating. "Yes, they did get a line on the broadcast, but it was too short for a real fix. The source is somewhere within about a five-degree area, but that's a lot of space to examine—"

"Examine it!" Pell snapped. "That message came from some kind of a spaceship, and I want to know exactly where it is. I thought you already had plates of the whole damn solar system."

"Not quite that much," the man said stubbornly. "And nobody was looking for this particular emission source. Unless it turns up serendipitously we're out of luck. So we'll need to organize a search—"

"Fine," said the deputy director. "See to it. What about you, General?"—looking at the man from the space agency. "If we find this thing, can we bring any of the space-based weaponry to bear on it?"

"Maybe yes, maybe no," the man said, and went into a lengthy explanation of why that would depend on where it was and, also, on whether or not the damn things would still fire after decades of neglect. "But the warsats aren't in optimum position for that purpose. You ordered us to redeploy them to protect Starlab, if you recall."

The Lessons of History

Our nation, which successively endured the tyranny of Spain, the United States, Japan and then the United States again for many years, is now said to be a free and equal state, with all the rights of every other member of the General Assembly. But do we have them? We have been denied a seat on the Security Council. We have been refused our request to make Tagalog one of the official languages of the United Nations. Our delegate has been given posts on only the most menial committees of the General Assembly, and no Filipino has ever been appointed to high office in the UN bureaucracy. And now we are told that our delegate will not even be permitted to take part in questioning the witnesses in the present emergency session.

It is time to make a stand. The forthcoming summit meetings on trade and human rights issues with the United States, Japan and the People's Republic will be the place to do this. If we are not to be given the status we deserve, we can retaliate. It is our right to do so, and it is our duty.

—*Manila Herald*

"And what position would be optimum?" the D.D. said fretfully—he too was paying the price for all those wakeup pills.

"Again, that depends on where it is. Those weapons were meant to be used primarily against other-nation assets and ground-launched missiles, not for targets that can be millions of kilometers away." The general coughed. "Excuse me, but I have to ask you this. Are you sure you're going to want us to fire on this extraterrestrial vessel?"

"That decision will be made when we have to make it; what I want now is to know what our options are." Pell checked the notes on his popup. "Let's talk about security," he said. "We assume the Scarecrows are monitoring all our broadcasts again, so we want to make sure nothing goes out to the public about using the orbital weaponry. God knows what kinds of armaments these people might have, so if it does come to pulling the trigger, we want to shoot first and we don't want them warned in advance." He paused, looking at Hilda, who had her hand up.

"It's the bugs, Deputy Director," she said. "I've been talking to Colonel Makalanos. There's another security problem there. Remember what the returned people told us? They said they knew everything the people on Earth wearing bugs knew."

The D.D. turned to the electronics man. He was calm. "We haven't detected any transmissions from them. Besides which, what would they be going to transmit anyway? The bugs don't have a chance to pick up much information while they're on a shelf in the lab."

"Then make damn sure nobody accidentally gives them any," the deputy director ordered. "No conversation inside the lab, especially gossiping about what goes on here. Is that what you wanted, Hilda?"

"Up to a point, sir. Colonel Makalanos called my attention to another possible problem. The one they call Dopey may be bugged, too—so as to communicate with the ones that don't talk, if nothing else."

"Ah," said Deputy Director Pell, sinking back in his chair. "Now, that's a problem." He looked around the table. "Recommendations?"

"Yank the damn things out of 'em," growled the man from the Pentagon.

Hilda spoke up. "I think not. If we did that, then Dopey couldn't communicate with the other two things. Besides, who would take the bug out of the one who knows how? If we have to make sure he isn't transmitting, it would be easier to kill him outright."

Pell stared at her. "Is that your recommendation?"

"No, sir! Only to take precautions. We can just keep them ignorant. But there are two bugs still in place—General Martín Delasquez in Florida and Commander James Lin in China."

The man from the State Department came alive. "Right! Can I pass this along to their embassies?"

"Just the fact that they may be broadcasting to the Scarecrows, yes. Make them an offer: if they bring the subjects here we'll have the bugs taken out; if not, they should at least take maximum precautions to keep either of them from knowing anything that might be useful to the Scarecrows."

The man from State made a note, and then looked up. "One other thing. Your agent in Ukraine has caused us a bit of trouble by—"

"I know what our agent in Ukraine did," Pell said irritably. "Can't we just apologize?"

"We already have, of course. They may want more."

"More what?"

The man from State looked ill at ease. "Well, they've suggested informally that we return him and the woman to Kiev for possible trial. . . ."

Hilda caught her breath, but before she could speak, Pell answered for her. "Not a chance."

"Well," said the man from State, "we may want to keep that option open, you know. There's all this trouble from the little countries in the UN. They're even talking about conducting hearings in the General Assembly."

"Since when do we give a damn what they do in the UN?" Hilda demanded, but the deputy director shook his head.

"Since we want them to support an exclusively American flight to Starlab," he said. "He's right. Let's keep our options open."

Turning her own agent over to some hanging judge in Kiev was not an option Brigadier Hilda Morrisey intended to keep open. If Dannerman had screwed up, he would get his lumps. But those lumps would be delivered by Hilda herself, not by some damn Ukrainian.

What she needed to do was to talk to him herself before anyone else did. Which meant she would have to arrange to see him first. She needed to find out when and where he would be arriving, and the place to do that was in her office. When she got there she found Lieutenant Colonel Makalanos waiting, and Merla Tepp sitting at a desk in the anteroom. "About those people from Kiev—" Hilda began, and Tepp nodded.

"Yes, ma'am. I checked. They'll be arriving in New York in two hours," she said. "I assumed you would want to interview Agent Dannerman, so I've booked you a place on the courier flight at 1400 hours."

"Hmm," Hilda said, eyeing her. Apart from her difficulties with the extraterrestrials, the woman wasn't bad at her job. Which reminded her to ask the question that had been on her mind. "Did you report what happened last night?"

"Yes, ma'am. As required by regulations. I—ah—I mentioned that the reason you and I were there was that we were looking into the question of electronic security leaks."

Was that a little presumptuous? But it wasn't a bad way to handle the present problem, so Hilda just said, "Fine. Get me a car to the courier plane, and send Colonel Makalanos in."

A doctor showed up uninvited to check her over again, and she allowed him to do it while she talked to the colonel. "Dopey's all right," he reassured her, pulling a sheaf of papers out of his bag. "When that message from space came in I didn't know if you'd want Dopey to know about it. So I told the people at Smolley to keep it under their hats until they got further orders from you."

Well. She hadn't lost her touch at picking good staff. She didn't comment, only asked, "What have you got there?"

"More of the Doc's drawings. According to Dopey, he's now given us pictures of everything on Starlab."

She nodded. "Give them to Tepp, tell her to make one copy for me and pass the others on to the deputy director. I'll look them over on the plane."

And she rose to shake his hand as he got up to leave. Priam Makalanos had a nice, firm grip, and a nice male aroma. What's more, he was damn good at his job. As she turned to collect her messages she reflected what a pity it was that he wasn't eligible for anything more personal.

A Father's Rights

Everyone is familiar with the high-handed actions of the Americans in the case of Commander J. P. Lin of the People's Republic of China and his solicitude for the welfare of his unborn child or children. The Delegate of the Mongolian People's Republic should support the demand of the People's Republic for the custody of this infant or infants, as well as the PRC's rights, and our own, to share in whatever benefits these space persons may bring.

—*Steppes Times,* Ulaanbaatar, MPR

But the first message on her screen was a note from the Maryland police, and it took her mind off Makalanos.

They had interrogated the survivor of the two who had attacked her. Apparently they had been told that she had been carrying big bucks, in *cash,* of all things. Why? Because she was planning to run off with somebody. Who had told them this crock of crap? The vindictive wife of the man she was supposed to be planning to run off with. But the only description they had of this woman was that she was kind of elderly and pleasant-faced, and how many thousand women like that were there in the District?

Hilda scowled at the screen. Was it remotely possible, she wondered, that maybe Wilbur's ex-wife had suddenly taken an interest in who her former husband was seeing, and decided to do something about it?

No. Not possible at all. The whole thing was nonsense. There was no ex-wife, only somebody who had wanted to get Hilda herself attacked or maimed. Very possibly somebody she had put away, sometime in the long course of her work for the Bureau.

So who was this individual who had gone to so much trouble to get her attacked? Hilda didn't know. She didn't care, either. She only cared that, regretfully, she would have to be somewhat more cautious the next time she went to a singles bar.

23

All the way from Vienna across the Atlantic, Pat Adcock was glued to the plane's passenger screen, trying to understand just what the message from space meant. She didn't get much satisfaction. From wherever on Earth the broadcasts came they were all the same: hysteria, everyone startled and frightened, everyone demanding reassurance and action. But there wasn't much of either to be had. News of any kind from the Scarecrows could not be good news. She was glad when the aircraft was settling down toward the airport in New York City and she could get back to the complications of her own personal life.

Which wasn't all that much better. The last thing Pat wanted was to be back in the clutches of the National Bureau of Investigation, but she wasn't given the choice. There they were, three of them. Two of the men had stunsticks in their hands; the other, standing by their waiting van, was an officer with a carbine slung over his shoulder. And that was not counting the two agents who had accompanied them across the Atlantic, now hustling them toward the exit.

Their jet hadn't gone to one of the passenger terminals. It had rolled to a stop on a bypass, far from the public parts of the airport, and there weren't even any steps for them to get down to the ground on. Instead someone had brought up one of the extensible gadgets ground crews used to lift the racks of packaged meals to the stewards' galley, accordion struts raising a wobbly platform up to the aircraft door. "Go," said one of the guards behind them, and Pat, Dannerman and Rosaleen Artzybachova stepped cautiously out onto the shuddery flat.

It was cold and wet outside, though nothing like the chill of Ukraine, and the interior of the van that was waiting for them was overheated. "Sit down, please," the officer said, the "please" contrasting with the hostile tone of his voice.

That was all he said. When Pat asked where he was taking them he didn't reply. She looked at Dannerman for support, but he was tugging absently at his false beard, his expression weary but resigned. Rosaleen Artzybachova, who had slept placidly through most of the flight, patted her arm.

"They're policemen," she explained. "It is their nature. Pay no attention. You did nothing wrong."

That was true enough, in Pat's own opinion, but whether the police were seeing it that way was an unresolved question. The van stopped in front of a doorway marked AIRPORT SECURITY, which did not seem like a good sign. As they were getting out another car raced up and parked a few meters away. Pat recognized the woman who got out of it: Hilda Morrisey, the Bureau agent who was Dannerman's boss. She was looking almost as tired as Pat herself was, and the dress she was wearing seemed to have been borrowed, for the way it failed to fit her.

Morrisey took charge. She shepherded the three of them into a conference room, vacated for her by the airport security people, and sat them down. "The Ukrainian government," she said, looking at Rosaleen Artzybachova, "is raising hell about all this, so I have to ask you a formal question. Do you want to go back to Kiev, Dr. Artzybachova?"

Rosaleen shrugged. "Not particularly, but I'd like to get out of this room. Am I under arrest?"

Hilda shook her head. "Of course not. Once you are debriefed you're free to go anywhere you like. You, too, Dr. Adcock."

Dannerman spoke up. "And me?"

Hilda gave him a chilly look. "You know better than that, Dannerman. The deputy director wants to talk to you himself."

"Well," Dannerman said in a placating tone, "I kind of thought he would. But there's someone I'd like to see here in New York, so how about if I come down tomorrow?"

"Not tomorrow. You'll go to Arlington with me on the return flight."

"Why?" Dannerman asked reasonably. "I did my mission; here's Dr. Artzybachova, where the Ukrainian terrorists can't get at her. I think I'm entitled—"

"No. Today. That's an order."

"But Hilda—" Dannerman began, his tone no longer reasonable; but Rosaleen interrupted him. She was smiling.

"Speaking of orders, I have a question. Do you know what I think? I think that the reporters will be after Pat and me to ask questions. Would you like to give me an idea of what we ought to tell them?"

Hilda transferred her chill gaze to Rosaleen. "Tell them nothing at all."

"But I don't think that would be possible," Rosaleen said reasonably. "They already know I was, ah, rescued—I do not use the word 'kidnapped,' as I believe my government does. So tell me what I should say about Dan's orders. Should I say that you instructed him to save my life? Or should I mention—as my friends told me—that that was only a secondary option, and in fact you authorized him to kill me to keep me from giving information to those foolish children?"

"Artzybachova," Hilda said harshly, "you're screwing around in places where you can get punished."

"Punished? But why do you speak of punishment, when we are all friends here? Friends do not say things that can cause their friends embarrassment. Just," she added, "as friends would not deny a friend a harmless few hours on his own. Would they?"

Hilda eyed her for a long, cold moment. Then she spoke to Dannerman. "First thing tomorrow morning, in my office, or your ass is chopped meat. Now. Let's start talking about just what happened in Ukraine."

24

Pat didn't mind the joyous clamor with which Pat Five and Patrice welcomed Rosaleen. Well, didn't really *mind* it. After all, the three of them had shared a whole harrowing existence as captives of the Scarecrows that she herself had missed. She didn't even mind that Patrice hospitably insisted that Rosaleen come and live with them—"There's plenty of room, now that Pat One isn't here, and I'm afraid the place where you used to live must be long gone by now." That was the first Pat heard that Pat One had been drafted to Camp Smolley to keep Dopey company, along with her own personal Dannerman. There wasn't really what you would call *plenty* of room, either. In fact, Pat gave up her own little bedroom to Rosaleen; old bones needed a real bed, and so Pat found that she would be sharing a bed with Patrice.

That wasn't the end of the housing problem. There also were the guards. When this Brigadier Morrisey said they would be set free she hadn't mentioned that they would have a Bureau agent keeping them company, three shifts of agents for each of the Pats and for Rosaleen as well, night and day. The agents did their best to stay out of the way, slept each night on futons in the dining room. But there were so *many* of them.

"On the other hand," Pat Five said, looking at the bright side, "now we don't have to pay a personal bodyguard anymore, do we?"

"Besides," Patrice added, "they're pretty good about lending a hand for the scut work in the Observatory. And we can use all the help we can get."

Pat blinked at her. "For what?"

"For the search for the Scarecrow ship, of course."

"But," Pat said reasonably, "now they know where it is, don't they?

I mean, they got a line on it from the transmission, so that's not our job anymore. The need is real telescopes and we don't have any—"

Patrice looked at Pat Five, then shook her head. "Oh, you don't know, do you? There's nothing there. The Scarecrows must've used some kind of relay to send their message, maybe a little drone too small to be picked up. The ship itself is somewhere else, so we're back to square one."

So, like every other observatory in the world, the Dannerman was officially commandeered for the Scarecrow hunt. The whole staff was put to work searching old plates—every plate every telescope in the world had taken, ever since that first observation of the comet-like object that was surely no comet, but the ship that had brought the Scarecrows to Earth's solar system.

Not all of the staff was happy about the new assignments. Gwen Morisaki didn't want to be taken off her Cepheid count, Christo Papathanassiou was, he said, on the very point of a breakthrough in his quantal approach to cosmology, and he absolutely must have computer time *now.* Pete Schneyman was worse. He was already glum about Pat coming back—about so *many* Pats coming back—and reducing him once more to second-in-command (or fifth!), which was probably why he was so irritable when he complained that checking stock images for some serendipitous observation of possible comet-like objects was the kind of thing you turned over to a machine, or, if you didn't want to waste valuable machine time on it, then to some two-for-a-nickel post-doc. The only one who didn't seem to mind was their planetary astronomer, Harry Chesweiler. The solar system was his turf anyway; his only request was that he be allowed to confine his own searching to the plane of the ecliptic, where he might get some useful data for his own studies. Even Janice DuPage, the receptionist, was drawing lines in the sand. She was willing to do what the Pats told her to, especially because it was what the government wanted, but she warned that it better not last longer than a week or so because her vacation was coming up and she wasn't going to miss out on her cruise to the Amazon and Rio de Janeiro . . . not to mention that it didn't make any sense to treat her like some irreplaceable astronomical expert when, geez, Dr. Adcock, she wasn't really any kind of a real scientist anyway, was she?

To all of them the Pats turned a deaf ear. There would be no exceptions. Everybody, and every computer, was to be totally immersed in the hunt for the Scarecrow scout ship. They even impressed into service the Bureau agents, because even an untrained cop could lend a hand now and then.

In principle, the hunt was simple enough. You looked at a recent picture of a section of the sky—recent being defined as anything in the past couple of years, since the Scarecrow scout had dropped its probe off to leech onto Starlab. You compared it with an older frame of the same area, and what you looked for was to see if there was a dot in the new frame that hadn't been there before. There was nothing to it. . . .

Except that there were some tens of millions of images that needed to be pulled up out of the world's astronomical archives and examined. Except that there were thousands and thousands of those little dots to be considered, since the space around Earth's Sun was crawling with comets and asteroids and bits of cosmic debris of every sort that were *not* the Scarecrow scout ship. Except that most of the plates had no precise equivalent and one had to be reconstructed.

Notes and Comment

Since the time of the Babylonians at least, probably since the days of the Neanderthals, human beings have scanned the night skies for points of light unaccountably moving among the fixed stars. The first of the wanderers—they were called *"planeten,"* in Greek—were the naked-eye planets, from Mercury to Saturn, as well as the brightest "hairy stars" or comets. With the invention of the telescope the number of wanderers multiplied beyond counting: new planets, from Uranus to Pluto; the myriad smaller rocks of the asteroid belt; comets by the thousand that never reached naked-eye brightness. The tally of bits and pieces of rock and snow that swing through space as part of the Sun's gravitational domain grew so huge that professional astronomers hardly bothered to count them anymore, much less give them names . . . until it became a matter of urgency to find the one faint dot among the anonymous millions that was neither asteroid nor comet, but something quite different, and far more worrying.

—*The New Yorker*

The computers did the bulk of the work. They were quite good at taking one image of a quarter-degree square section of, say, the constellation Virgo and manipulating it to an exact match with another plate that included most, but not all, of the same stars. The computers were also quite able to identify a point of light in one that didn't exist in the other. The computers were even then able to sort through the infrared and radio images of the same area, if any existed, to see if there were spectrograms or other data that could identify its composition well enough to reject it as normal or flag it for further investigation.

But then it took a human being to decide about that identification, or to order new observations by some available telescope to clarify the point, and to try to figure out an orbit.

All this effort was bearing fruit—of a sort. Previously unidentified comets were being discovered every few minutes. So were new asteroids, if you could call some of those pebbly car-sized things real asteroids . . . but the Scarecrow scout ship remained elusive.

Pat Adcock did her best to wake early in the morning. The advantage of that was that you got the chance to jump right into the shower without waiting in line. Time was when one real bathroom and a closet-sized half bath for guests seemed perfectly adequate in the apartment, but that was before the new Pats and the Ukrainian visitor had come to share it.

On the third morning of the regime she missed her turn. Rosaleen had wakened earlier still, and was first in the shower—and the old lady did like to take long, long showers. While Pat Five had already preempted the half bath and showed no sign of coming out of it, either.

Grumpily Pat joined Patrice in the kitchen, putting together coffee and some sort of breakfast. Patrice inclined her head toward the half bath where Pat Five remained closeted. "Morning sickness again, I guess," she said. "Poor baby."

"Yeah, poor baby," Pat said, pouring herself a cup of coffee and taking it into the living room to drink in solitude.

But that was denied her, too, because there was a knock on the door. It was the Bureau guard who had remained outside all night long, and he was letting in a pair of uniformed people Pat couldn't identify. "They're from the United Nations. They claim they have official business with all of you," he said, but keeping one hand on his gun anyway.

The taller of the two pulled out a sheaf of blue folders. "Subpoenas from the United Nations," he said.

Pat giggled. "We already have them," she informed the man, but he shook his head.

"Not these. There's going to be a special committee-of-the-whole session of the General Assembly to look into the Starlab mission, and you're all ordered to testify."

Patrice looked incredulous. "All of us?"

"All of you and about twenty others," the UN man said. "They're even subpoenaing the space people. So brace yourselves for a long day."

25

Hilda did her best to argue, so did the deputy director, but the director herself was adamant. "Forget the legal crap," she ordered. "It doesn't matter if they aren't human beings. It doesn't matter if you think you can get a tame judge to void the subpoenas. The General Assembly wants those freaks there to testify, so they will. Or the one that talks will, anyway. We don't want to piss the UN off any more than they already are."

"But—" Hilda began, and didn't finish. The director firmly overruled her.

"That's what the President says, and that's what we're going to do."

Outside, Hilda complained to Marcus Pell, "This screws everything up. We've been keeping the ETs closed up and ignorant. Dopey doesn't even know anything about the Scarecrow message yet. So how are we going to keep it that way if he's up in New York and the damn General Assembly people start asking him questions?"

"You can't," the deputy director said flatly, and held up a hand to preempt argument. "Go get the damn things and take them up there. I'll order a plane for you. Get."

She got, seething. They had gone to a lot of trouble to isolate Dopey and the Docs. There had been plenty of argument about that, too. That doctor from Walter Reed, Marsha Evergood, had been bitter in opposition to Hilda's decree. She wanted the medical Doc to keep up with his faith healing or laying on of hands or whatever it was that he did, and wasn't content that she was to be allowed to bring a few of the transportable cases to Camp Smolley for his ministrations. But Hilda had the authority, and what she said was what happened. The technical Doc kept on pouring out his meticulous scale drawings and Dopey continued to complain, and everything was going fine. Until now.

Colonel Makalanos wasn't pleased, either, but he didn't have the rank to complain. "Yes, Brigadier," he said, "I can get them ready in ten minutes. But that means—"

"Yes," she said, "that means we're going to have to tell Dopey some of the things we've kept from him. I'll do that now. You get the van ready."

Although the Bureau had provided Hilda Morrisey with a plane to get her parade of freaks up to the UN hearings, it wasn't one of the Bureau's deluxe jets. It was a damn courier aircraft. It had few amenities, not even coffee, and it wasn't big enough for the sixteen of them.

The problem wasn't the human passengers—Hilda herself, Pat One, and her semiattached Dannerman, along with Colonel Makalanos and Hilda's new aide, Merla Tepp. It was the aliens—Dopey and the two Docs—and the eight, count 'em, eight guards the Bureau had deemed necessary to keep them in order. And the aircraft really stank, because just after takeoff one of the Docs had had to move his bowels. The creature wouldn't fit in the tiny airplane toilets so he had blandly relieved himself on the box of shredded paper included for his use.

Hilda averted her gaze. She wondered absently where the shredded paper had come from. Some Bureau big shot, somewhere, who was addicted to making hard copies of things he shouldn't? And was it possible that those unnecessary documents, or something like them, had fallen into the wrong hands, so that half the crazies in the world seemed to be able to find out everything that was going on in the Bureau? The Ukrainians had known about Dannerman's mission. Most of the wilder religious groups seemed to have detailed information about the whereabouts of the aliens—there had been a knot of men and women and even little children, all carrying the usual placards and shouting the usual demands, where they boarded the courier plane. Which no one should have known; and the pilot had warned her that there were more of the same waiting for them in New York. Bureau security had definitely gone to hell.

But, Hilda decided, the notion that someone was smuggling hard copies of Bureau plans out of the headquarters wouldn't really fly. The logistics were too tough. There had to be another explanation.

She turned around to peer at Dopey. The little turkey had taken the news that he was summoned to appear before the United Nations with equanimity—"It is about time, Brigadier Morrisey, that I had the opportunity to speak to the people of your world entirely, not just one department of one of your 'nations.' " And then when she told him the other bit of news he took it without surprise. “That is good to hear, yes, but who knows when the Beloved Leaders can get here in person? And meanwhile there is the problem of our food—”

What had crossed her mind at the time was that maybe the security leak had a different explanation. Maybe this damn freak had been in communication with the Scarecrows all along. But that didn’t make sense. She couldn’t believe that Dopey had somehow listened in on every conversation in the Bureau, and passed them on to the Scarecrows, who in turn had relayed them to all Earth’s terrorist nut groups. And anyway, he certainly had not known where they would meet this plane.

No. The leak couldn’t come from Dopey. It was almost as if—

“Oh, *shit,*” Hilda said out loud, causing Dannerman to look up from Pat One’s head as it was nestling cozily on his shoulder.

“Is something wrong?” he asked.

“No. Yes. Stay out of it,” she ordered, and crooked a finger to Colonel Makalanos. When he had left his charges to come up beside her she pulled his head down and whispered: “I just had a bad thought. It may be possible that some Bureau personnel have bugs in their heads. Go up and use the pilot’s radio, secure channel: I want every son of a bitch in Arlington X-rayed, and I want it right away.”

He didn’t answer, only nodded and headed for the pilot’s cubicle.

But, she thought dismally, even if that were the explanation, her idea might not solve the problem. It wasn’t just the headquarters staff that needed to be checked for some damn Scarecrow thing. It was everybody. It could be someone on this plane. It could be—that was the worst thought—it could be Hilda herself who had somehow been bugged. And, as with the Dannerman and the Pats, she would never know it had happened.

When the VTOL landed it was at a helipad along the East River. Then they were all hustled into two armored vans—happily enough in two shifts, with the two Docs and their guards filling one of the vans by themselves so that Hilda was spared their aroma for a while. They headed north to the UN Building at high speed, with four motorbike outriders to clear the way and a half-track chewing up First Avenue’s already potholed pavement behind them.

Along the way they passed a dozen knots of protesters of one kind or another, most of them apparently religious. “Damn them,” Makalanos remarked to Hilda. “What do you suppose they want?”

Hilda nodded to her aide, busily making notes about the protesters as they drove. "You're our expert, Tepp."

Merla Tepp looked up. "I've identified three groups so far. The Inerrants—that was my own old bunch—and the Radical Southern Methodists are two of them, plus the Christian League Against Blasphemy. They think the aliens are the Antichrist, or at least agents of the Devil, and they want them to be fired back into space right away. But there's another bunch, too. All I know about them is what I see on their posters, but they look like charismatics to me."

"They want to get rid of the aliens, too?"

"Oh, no. Quite the contrary, if I understand their posters. They think they're angels direct from God. All they want is to be allowed to worship them."

Makalanos laughed out loud. "I know how we can straighten them out on that. Just let them get close enough to get a good smell."

26

Traffic was unbelievable. Dannerman's taxi inchwormed along Forty-sixth Street, lunging forward a meter or two and then stopping dead, with the driver angrily slapping the wheel and muttering obscenities to himself. When at last they reached Second Avenue there was a solid line of cops to keep everybody from entering the last block. "Street's closed," the nearest one bawled, waving her stunstick. "Move it on!"

Dannerman had to walk the rest of the way. At the United Nations Plaza there wasn't any traffic moving at all, not vehicular at least. The whole street in front of the UN Building was choked with thousands of human beings, chanting, shouting, milling around in defiance of the police squadrons trying to move them along. And when he had zig-zagged his way through the pack he found a long line waiting at the gate to the UN complex. Most of them appeared to be would-be spectators hoping to get in for the show. Most of them weren't succeeding.

Tolerantly Dannerman took his place at the end of it. He was in no particular hurry, and a few thousand brawling religious fanatics weren't going to spoil his day. Dannerman considered that his world was definitely improving itself. He had accomplished his mission in Ukraine without bloodshed. He no longer had a guard tailing him every moment. . . .

And then there was Anita Berman, who had been the biggest improvement of all.

Anita had always been a sweet and forgiving woman, with plenty to forgive: any number of broken dates and long absences when he could not tell her what was going on because it was Bureau business. Now that she knew he was a Bureau agent all the lapses were explained. No, better than just explained. Anita was thrilled. She had been as swept up in the Scarecrow turmoil as anyone else on Earth, and here he was, her lover, astonishingly at the very heart of it! "I was always pretty crazy about you, Dan," she had whispered in his ear the night before, "but, wow, now it's really *special!*"

He was grinning reminiscently to himself, when someone tapped his shoulder. It was a cop, pointing at the beginning of the line. There a woman inside the gate was beckoning peremptorily to Dannerman. He recognized her as Senator Alicia Piombero, and she was gesturing for him to come in.

Even at the UN, a United States senator could smooth all ways. When he had run the gauntlet of catcalls from the waiting line and was at the gate, she looked him over, and said, "You're Dannerman, right? You were summoned to appear at this thing?" And, when he nodded: "That's what I told the guard. Just show him the summons and he'll let you in."

The guard did. As they walked toward the actual doorway he thanked the woman, and she said, "You're welcome. Maybe we can do each other a favor."

"What's that?" he asked, but she shook her head, pointing at the other guard post just inside the door. When they had finished with the metal detectors and the patdowns and the sniffers she took him aside.

"Listen," she said, "I only have a minute because I have to get up to the Security Council, but you've been having trouble collecting your pay, haven't you? I mean, because now there are two of you?"

It was a sore point. "The damn payroll people are taking forever to figure out what to do, yes," he said.

"Well, Representative Collerton—I don't know if you know her? She's willing to get a special members' bill through to pay both you Dannermans in full. You're entitled, after all, and that would cut right through the red tape."

Dannerman perked up, then his guard went up. "That would be good," he said cautiously, waiting for it.

"Glad to do it, Dannerman, but you can do something for me, too, if you want to. You know Marcus is a little annoyed with me?"

"I know about Senator Wintczak's stories that he thinks came from you, yes."

She clearly didn't want to discuss the stories. She just said, "So he's doing a lot of stuff that I'm not kept informed on. I can't let that happen. You can understand that. We aren't going to go back to those old CIA days, with you spooks going off on all sorts of tear-ass mystery missions and the Senate kept fat, dumb and ignorant."

Mr. L. Koga: "Whatever may or may not be going on in the Security Council at this time, it is our undoubted duty to learn the facts in this matter to the satisfaction of each and every delegate, not just those who represent the so-called Great Powers, so that we may take appropriate action."

Mr. V. Puunamunda: "Will the gentleman from Kenya please yield?"

Mr. L. Koga: "I will yield to the gentleman from the Marshall Islands for thirty seconds."

Mr. V. Puunamunda: "I thank the gentleman. I wish only to call to the attention of this body that our islands may be endangered, owing to the severe tropical storms of recent years, but they are still voting members of this General Assembly, and we, too, should be allowed to participate in the questioning of the witnesses."

—*Proceedings of the General Assembly*

"No, ma'am," Dannerman said, because she seemed to expect it.

"So we can do each other some good. If you could just keep me posted on what's happening that isn't talked about in the team meetings—"

Dannerman did his best not to laugh; the woman wanted him to spy on the spymaster!

"I'm not asking you for anything I don't have a right to know," she went on persuasively. "Give me a call when you can, and I'll get Susie Collerton started on the bill. Right now I've got to get up to the Council."

That made him frown. "You're going to the Security Council? But I thought it was the General Assembly that was meeting."

She looked at him with faint pity. "That's where the circus is. The Council is where the work will be done. Think about it. We'll talk later."

Once inside the building a uniformed woman in a blue UN beret escorted Dannerman to a waiting room. Dannerman, still mulling over his conversation with the senator, paid little attention to where they were going until she stopped at a doorway, saluted smartly, and said, with an accent Dannerman couldn't identify, "In here, please, until you are called."

The place was marked "VISITORS' LOUNGE" on the door, in all five of the official languages of the UN, but the only visitors in it that day were the ones with subpoenas from the General Assembly. Some of them were there already. Dannerman saw Rosaleen Artzybachova and Pat Adcock sitting near the door and, at the far end of the large room and not sitting at all, four people in the uniform of the People's Republic of China. Dannerman recognized one of them—no, Dannerman corrected himself, he recognized *two* of them, and they both were the pilot who had taken them to Starlab in the first place, Commander James Peng-tsu Lin. He nodded toward the Lins, but, standing stony-faced and silent, they didn't meet his eye. He shrugged and turned to the others. "Morning," he said. "You look like you're all recovered from our trip."

Rosaleen corrected him. "This one wasn't in Ukraine. She's Patrice. Pat's in the ladies' with Pat Five, but, yes, we're fully recovered. How did things go in Arlington?"

"Oh," he said, recollecting himself, "no problem. The D.D. ate me out a little, but then they sent me right home, because they had other things on their minds. They did have orders for me, so you'll be seeing a lot of me for a while. They've put me in charge of your guard details at the Observatory."

The door opened again. When Dannerman turned he saw the two Pats, returned from the washroom, but they didn't enter right away. They were peering curiously down the hall, and so was their escort.

Dannerman had no trouble recognizing which was Pat Five. In just the few days since he had seen her last she seemed to have become much more pregnant. She was definitely heavier than the Pat beside her, and a lot of the gained weight appeared to be in her face, which looked almost bloated. Dannerman had had very little experience of pregnant women, but he remembered hearing that they were supposed to be at their prettiest when pregnant. It hadn't worked that way for Pat Five. The guard in the blue beret spoke to them, and they hastily got out of the way to make room for the next arrivals.

Of which there were a lot. First came Hilda Morrisey and her new aide, along with a uniformed Bureau lieutenant colonel Dannerman didn't recognize; then a couple of Bureau guards, curiously lugging large, flat boxes of torn-up paper. Then there was another clutch of guards surrounding the aliens: the two huge, pale Docs, one of them carrying the little turkey thing, Dopey. Finally the other Dannerman and his Pat One strolled in, keeping their distance from the space freaks; and suddenly the large room didn't seem very large anymore.

Hilda Morrisey glanced around, then nodded to the lieutenant colonel, who began issuing orders. The two guards with the paper boxes set them down near a window, while the others shepherded the aliens to the same area, Dopey looking on interestedly but silent.

The Chinese officers looked up, first startled and uneasy as they found themselves in the presence of the weird beings from space, then in revulsion as they caught the scent of them. The senior officer spoke sharply. They began to move farther away, but the two Jimmy Lins didn't follow. They were speaking agitatedly to each other, then one of them hurried across the room to Pat Five, wearing a broad and suspiciously fake smile. "How nice to see you, my dear!" he cried. "And my unborn child, how is he doing?"

Pat Five gave him nothing but a hostile look, but Patrice answered for her. "He isn't yours, he's ours, and he isn't him. He's them. Three of them. She's having triplets."

"Triplets! How very wonderful!"

"Oh, cut it out," Patrice said in disgust. "Really, Jimmy, you don't want these kids, do you?"

He glanced over his shoulder at the PRC officers. "Certainly I want my children! And I want them brought up in their homeland!"

The senior PRC officer snapped a command as Patrice was saying, "Come off it, Jimmy."

He looked at her, then turned to obey his keeper's order. But as he left he whispered, "I can't."

Hilda Morrisey, standing by the door, watched curiously for a moment, then turned and rapped on the door. When the UN guard opened they spoke briefly, then Hilda conferred for a moment with her lieutenant colonel before waving Dan over. "I don't think you've met. Dan, this is Priam Makalanos, who's helping me with the freaks; Priam, Dan Dannerman. You'll take orders from Colonel Makalanos while I'm up at the Security Council chamber, Dan," she finished, and rapped again on the door.

Warily Dannerman shook the lieutenant colonel's hand, expecting, but wincing from, the punishing grip. "What orders are those, Colonel?" he asked.

"None, I hope. These guys aren't giving us any trouble now, for a change."

He was gesturing at the aliens. They not only weren't causing trouble, they weren't doing anything at all. The two Docs stood silent and impassive while Dopey, curled in the arm of one of them, appeared to be asleep, his great fantail overspreading his body.

Dannerman had expected that as soon as they arrived they'd be conducted into the General Assembly auditorium, but that wasn't the way it was. Colonel Makalanos explained to him that the reason Hilda had left was that some sort of procedural fight was going on. The Security Council was meeting independently of the General Assembly in its own wing of the building, and a fierce battle was going on in the General Assembly itself over who was to be summoned before them for questioning, and who was to be allowed to ask the questions.

Meanwhile, they waited. Dannerman restlessly prowled the lounge, taking note of the pictures on the wall (Trygve Lie, Boutros Boutros-Ghali, half a dozen other figures prominent in the history of the UN), the little barlike cubicle, which contained a coffee machine (unfortunately not in use), the rack of ancient magazines. He became aware of the eyes of the other Dannerman on him, and gave his twin a guardedly friendly hello—another personal problem that he couldn't see a good way of dealing with. The other Dannerman returned it in the same tone.

He was spared the necessity of making conversation when two men in the uniforms of the Free State of Florida entered. One of them was General Martín Delasquez, who had been one of the pilots Pat Adcock persuaded to fly them to Starlab in the first place.

Rosaleen caught sight of General Delasquez coming in and hurried over to him. "Martín!" she cried affectionately. "I thought you were dead! It's so wonderful to see you again—"

And then, when the general gave her a frosty look, her expression clouded. "Oh, hell, you're the *other* one, aren't you?" Shaking her head, she went over to sit before a low table and began tearing up bits of paper. "Anyone for a game of chess?" she asked.

When at last they were brought into the General Assembly Hall Dannerman blinked at the size of the audience.

Dannerman had had the experience of being debriefed, or made to testify, often enough before. At least the Bureau's interrogations had been more or less private. Even in the Pit of Pain there had seldom been more than a few dozen watchers, but this was on a whole other scale. The General Assembly Hall was packed, all 194 nations fully represented in their individual stations, and the visitors' gallery solidly filled as well. There were easily two thousand people in the auditorium, muttering and whispering to each other as the thirteen "witnesses" trudged to the raised dais and took their seats on spindly-legged gilt chairs. Dannerman counted heads: there were four Patrice Adcocks, two Dan Dannermans, two Jimmy Lins, one each of Rosaleen Artzybachova, Martín Delasquez and Dopey, now alert and looking curiously around the room. That wasn't even counting the guards in dress uniform and riot guns, standing behind each chair to "protect" them. The guards wore UN blue helmets, but their uniforms were of the U.S. Marines.

And then, to complete the roster, the pair of Docs, their moss-bearded faces impassive, their half dozen arms moving placidly. Those things weren't real witnesses, of course. They couldn't be, in any practical sense, since they never spoke. Nor, also of course, were they seated on the frail gilt chairs. They weren't seated at all. They stood remote and still at one end of the row of witnesses, and each one of the Docs had not one but three Marine guards standing tensely over it.

Dannerman did not think the Marines were there to protect the Docs. They weren't watching the audience at all. They were all precisely focused on the immense, multiarmed creatures from space, and that was the way their weapons were pointing.

Still, Dannerman thought, maybe the Docs did need protection after all. The word was that some of the demonstrators had briefly broken through the massed police battalions around the UN Building complex, before reinforcements managed to get to that point to drive them back. He had seen half a dozen people turned away as they failed the screening for unchecked weapons. Whether the weapons were on their persons from absentmindedness or malicious intent wasn't stated. It didn't matter. Either way, those people would be watching the televised proceedings, if at all, from their cells in one of New York's city jails.

The delegates to the General Assembly were still earnestly wrangling—in several languages, few of which Dannerman understood. Though Dopey, with his total command of nearly all Earthly tongues, was alertly following it all.

But then the presiding delegate gaveled everyone to silence. "Gentlemen and ladies," he said—in English—"let us begin the questioning. Ask the witness known as 'Dopey' to take the stand."

When the little alien hopped onto the witness stand two thousand people sighed in unison. The interrogator rapped for order, looking pleased as he motioned to the clerk to swear the witness in.

Federal Reserve Inflation Bulletin

The morning recommended price adjustment for inflation is set at 1.06%. Federal Reserve Chairman Walter C. Boettger declined to set an annualized rate, stating, "This unprecedented increase in the rate of inflation is a purely temporary phenomenon which cannot be tolerated. If it continues, a third increase in interest rates must be considered, but I have confidence that the good sense of the American people will assert itself."

When the clerk approached with the Bible he got a curious look from Dopey. The look got curiouser as the clerk rattled off his formula: "Please put your hand on the Bible. Do you promise to tell the truth, the whole truth and nothing but the truth, so help you God?"

"I beg your pardon," Dopey said. "Which God are you referring to?"

So naturally there was another ten minutes of off-mike whispering before one of the interrogator's aides had the intelligence to have his principal ask Dopey just what it was he did believe in. Dopey considered that for a moment, then said doubtfully that one could say, yes, he believed in the Beloved Leaders. Then it took another five minutes before he was allowed to swear himself in in their name, without the Bible; and then the interrogator made the mistake of courteously asking him if he were being well cared for.

When she managed to turn off Dopey's lengthy and even more than usually repetitious reply, things went better. Yes, he had occupied Starlab for the purpose of eavesdropping on Earth for the Beloved Leaders. And, the interrogator asked, what was the information to be used for? Was Mr. Dopey preparing the way for an invasion?

Mr. Dopey took offense. "Invasion? Certainly not! They merely wished to protect you from the tyrannical rule of the Horch—not only now, but in the eternity of the eschaton to come."

"Ah, the eschaton," the interrogator repeated, smiling. "Would you tell us, please, about this 'eschaton' of yours?"

Dopey would. He did. He kept on doing so until a restive delegate, on a point of order, reminded the presiding officer that, after all, what they were here to do was to discuss the *benefits* the world might hope to gain from these extraterrestrials and their technology, not some philosophical question of an afterlife.

Which, of course, produced another free-for-all. Dannerman

wasn't listening. He was watching one of the Docs, who was showing signs of being restive. The creature wasn't going to hold out forever, Dannerman thought. . . .

He didn't. The inevitable happened. A titter and gasp from the audience turned everyone's eyes to the Doc, who had blandly relieved himself, with his paper boxes still left in the lounge room.

Startled, then amused—and a little belatedly—the president declared a recess; and all the witnesses trooped back to their holding room.

To Dannerman's surprise, he saw the deputy director just leaving the room as they arrived. Hilda Morrisey was inside, looking strangely thoughtful.

"Is something wrong?" Dannerman asked.

She considered the question. "Wrong? No. The Security Council has taken a vote, though, so what you guys were doing in the G.A. doesn't matter much anymore. They've okayed the Eurospace launch, only it's a UN thing now and one American and one Chinese is going along. So I'll be seeing you people at your Observatory."

"Why?" Pat demanded, suddenly suspicious.

"Why? So you can give me a crash course on what Starlab is like. See, I'm going to be the American."

27

While Pat was trying to get dressed for work the next morning the atmosphere in the apartment was grouchy. Patrice was complaining about the wasted hours at the UN and Pat Five was grousing about, well, everything: she hadn't slept well, she didn't feel well, she wished the damn kids would get themselves born and get it over with . . . and, she added, the smell of the damn bowl of chili Rosaleen was placidly spooning into herself in the kitchen was making her physically ill. Rosaleen was apologetic. "I'm afraid I got a taste for the stuff while we were captives. Do you know, there isn't a decent bowl of chili to be had anywhere in Ukraine. I won't do it again."

"Oh, it's not just that," Pat Five said, cross but repentant. "It was the smell of the Docs yesterday that started me off, probably. Or just being so damn pregnant and miserable." She looked it, too; Pat and Patrice exchanged glances. "Anyway, I think I'm going to stay home today, if it's all right with everybody."

"I'll stay with you for a while," Patrice decided. "You two go on ahead; I can work from my screen here."

On the way downtown Pat and Rosaleen took a cab—paid for by their Bureau guards, because they didn't want to risk their charges in the subway. For that much Pat was grateful; money was an increasingly urgent problem, with four Pat Adcocks to share what really hadn't been quite enough capital for one. Something was going to have to be done about that.

Then, as they arrived at the midtown office building that housed the Dannerman Astrophysical Observatory, she saw Dan Dannerman strolling toward them, arm in arm with a tall, redheaded woman, and inspiration struck. Abruptly Pat knew what that "something" might be.

Suddenly more cheerful, she sent Rosaleen up ahead of her and waited for them at the door.

Dannerman saw her, nodded amiably and paused to whisper to the woman. She giggled, kissed him, waved to Pat and turned away. Dannerman joined Pat. "Am I late again, boss lady?" he asked cheerfully.

Full of her new idea, she shrugged the remark off. "Dan, you know a lot of lawyers, don't you?"

His expresson sobered. "Have you got a problem, Pat?"

"You bet I have. A lot of them, but the one I'm thinking about is money. Starlab belongs to us! Well, to the Observatory, but that's close enough. We should have some claim to whatever the UN flight finds there, shouldn't we? So I need to talk to a lawyer. I don't want to use Dixler—"

"Right," Dannerman said immediately; they both knew the old family lawyer who had handled Uncle Cubby's estate.

"—and the Observatory's lawyer is real good on leases and employment contracts, but I think I need somebody with a little more shark blood in his veins for this."

Dannerman pondered for a moment. "Let me see what I can do," he said at last. "I'll make a couple of calls."

Upstairs, Brigadier Hilda Morrisey was already closeted with Rosaleen Artzybachova, studying the blueprints of the Starlab orbiter. She wasn't in sight, but her mere presence had made a change in the climate of the Observatory. The Bureau agents were sitting up straighter and moving faster, and they had infected everyone else. Pete Schneyman was demanding Pat's attention to the previous day's harvest of observations, Janice DuPage, sulky because she had had to cancel out on the vacation cruise she had planned, was snapping at Dan Dannerman for preempting a corner of the waiting room as his command post. Even mild old Christo Papathanassiou waylaid Pat on her way in, bristling. "I do not protest sharing my office with the policewoman, Merla Tepp. I understand the urgency of the situation. But must she use my terminal so very much of the time?"

By the time Pat had run that gauntlet she was glad to retire to her own office and close the door.

In a physical sense, the only thing that had changed in Pat Adcock's office was the pictures on her wall. In the old days, before the Scarecrows and the Horch, what the wall pictures usually displayed was the familiar Horsehead Nebula, or Saturn's rings or even the looming shape of Starlab. She kept such pictures on the wall because they were pretty to look at, and even for a more practical reason. They were a reminder of the glamour of astronomy. When prospective donors visited the Observatory the pictures helped get them in the right mood to endow some particular search, or even to kick in with a handsome gift or legacy that would help pay the Observatory's bills.

Those bills still had to be paid, no matter what. Figuring out how to do it was still part of the director's job—the boring part, but what could you do? She settled down to it but, as she worked over the numbers on her desk screen she couldn't help looking up from time to time at the wall display. The pretty pictures were gone; what the wall showed now was all alphanumeric, the constantly changing, always growing, list of new discoveries from the world's telescopes. Each time a new dot was discovered—they were coming less than a minute apart now—its coordinates flashed on the screen. As one of the great telescopes accepted the task of checking it out, the name of the instrument appeared. When the same dot was found nearby in that instrument's search, the coordinates changed color. If there was a third sighting the computers took over; and then, with luck, the first approximation of its orbital elements were displayed in their turn.

Then the object went on the waiting list for instruments operating in other frequencies: gamma rays, infrared, ultraviolet, radio telescopes—even the ancient pair of orbital X-ray telescopes that were still, sometimes, creakily operational. What all those instruments were looking for was the chemical and physical composition of that point of light. The ones that showed a coma of gases, however tenuous, were dropped from the screen. They were nothing but ordinary comets. Their elements went into the cometary databank for any future astronomer who might take an interest, but they were of no importance in the present search. . . .

And, for that matter, dawdling over the search wasn't getting the bills paid. She gritted her teeth and worked doggedly away until hunger reminded her she hadn't had any breakfast.

On her way to an early lunch Dannerman stopped her. He looked amused. "I think I've got a lawyer for you," he said. "He's a shark, all right. He worked for the Carpezzios—they were big druggers; I was working on them before, uh—"

"Before you decided to come and spy on us," Pat said helpfully.

"Well, yes. The only thing is, he's expensive. First thing he said was that he wanted a fifty-thousand-current-dollar retainer before he'd even talk to you."

"I haven't got fifty thousand—" Pat began, but Dannerman was shaking his head.

"Wait a minute. When I told him what it was all about he said he'd waive the retainer, only he wanted half of whatever he collected for you."

Pat was scandalized. "That might be millions!"

"More than that. So we went round and round for a while, and he finally came down to twenty-five percent. You're not going to do any better, Pat."

"I'm not?" She thought for a moment, then sighed. "He's really good?" she asked.

"He's really *bad.* He got the Carpezzios off with two years in a country-club jail, when I figured they'd be away for life. And he's handled big suits against the government before. Anyway, he'll be here this afternoon."

At the elevator Rosaleen Artzybachova came hurrying out of her office. "Take me along," she pleaded. "I have to get away from that truly exhausting woman for a while."

In the elevator Rosaleen described her morning with the Bureau brigadier. Hilda Morrisey had all but sucked Rosaleen's brains out to get the data she wanted, which amounted to a complete plan of the Starlab orbiter as it had been abandoned, with every bit of equipment marked and identified, and then the whole thing compared with the sketches the instrument-Doc had been ceaselessly turning out at Camp Smolley. "I left her transmitting the plans to the Doc back at the biowar plant, so he could mark the positions of all the Beloved Leaders material—oh, sorry. I mean the Scarecrow material, of course; it's just that we called them Beloved Leaders for so long, I got in the habit. But, Pat, do you have any idea how much stuff is there? God knows what it will do to our lives when we get it sorted out. If indeed we ever can do that. It's like—it's like giving some Renaissance genius like Leonardo da Vinci a brand-new pocket screen to play with. Or a fusion bomb. Or like all of current technology, all at once, to see what he could make of it. And we're not Leonardos."

In the restaurant Pat toyed with her Caesar salad while the old lady devoured a huge platter of fajitas, washing it down with a bottle of Mexican beer, talking the whole time. It had been an active morning for Rosaleen, with Brigadier Morrisey setting an unflagging pace—"She's trying to get it all in today because she's leaving for the Eurospace base at Kourou tomorrow morning. And I don't think she'd had any sleep last night, either." She chewed in faintly envious silence for a moment. "Makes me wish I was fifty again."

But those labors had been productive. From the Doc's sketches they had identified four separate power generators of different types—though without a clue as to how any of them worked—plus the gadget that transported people across galactic distances faster than light—plus several dozen other bits of equipment which did God knew what, and God knew how.

Pat glanced at their Bureau guard, alertly nursing a cup of coffee two tables away, and wondered if she would try to stop Rosaleen's chatter if she knew what the woman was saying in this very public place. But of course there wasn't any real hope of secrecy anymore, anyway. Once the UN mission came back with whatever samples of Scarecrow technology they could carry the whole world would be looking on and it would all be common property. . . .

But not if she and this lawyer could prevent it. "Come on," she said, signaling for the check. "Let's get back to work."

As soon as she was at her desk she turned on the screen and instituted a search for all the morning's transmissions from Rosaleen Artzybachova's terminal. Most of what she found was gibberish—the damn woman had encoded all the traffic to Camp Smolley—but among the remaining messages there were the twenty or thirty of the Doc's admirably precise sketches that could be salvaged.

What the sketches might represent, Pat could not say, but they certainly looked potentially valuable. When the lawyer arrived she had a display of them ready for him. He glanced at it, then frowned and said, "Turn off that machine, please. Let's just talk for a bit."

His name was T. Lawrence Hecksher, and he didn't look like Pat's idea of a mob mouthpiece. Hecksher didn't look like a hotshot, jury-befuddling lawyer from some video serial, either. What he looked like more than anything else was somebody's grandfather—white, muttonchop whiskers, twinkly sky-blue eyes under feather white eyebrows, apple red cheeks. He would have made a fine department-store Santa Claus, Pat thought, if his talents hadn't been more in demand for helping tax evaders and mob assassins stay out of jail.

He acted grandfatherly, too. When he had settled himself across from the desk the first thing he said was, "If you have recording systems going, my dear, please turn them off." He had no recorders of his own, either. As Pat began to describe what she hoped he could do for her he made notes. With a *pen.* On *paper.*

"Why can't we use the screens?" Pat asked suspiciously.

He waggled his head at her. "Records we don't have can't be subpoenaed. I don't want to have anything on the record that can be construed as any sort of admission, or anything that represents privileged information we aren't supposed to have. That's why I didn't want to look at your screen. Don't forget, this is not a small matter. In order to protect your interests we will need to prevail against some of the best lawyers in the world. All *over* the world."

Pat gave him a dismayed look, but he smiled reassuringly. "Don't worry. I have dealt with government attorneys for many years. I'll eat them alive. And I'll get all the information we need in disclosures, but I'll do it legally. Now. The first thing I'm going to want from you is documents. . . ."

And so, documents he got: documents, documents and more documents. By the time T. Lawrence Heckshher left the office he had the registry numbers of every document that could have any bearing on the case: Uncle Cubby's will and the probate records; the instrument creating the trust for the T. Cuthbert Dannerman Astrophysical Observatory; the records of the building of Starlab and all the disbursements made from Uncle Cubby's estate to pay for it; Pat's own contract of employment, to show that she had authority to institute a suit on the Observatory's behalf—"We'll need all your, ah, sisters to sign the complaint as well, of course." When Pat suggested that most of this could be obtained with less trouble from Dixler, the lawyer for Uncle Cubby's estate, or from the Observatory's own attorney, he gave her a forgiving smile. "I don't think we'll trouble them, my dear. I find I work best when I don't involve any other attorneys if I can help it. I'll have the complaints and summonses ready to sign and serve by tomorrow morning. Serve on whom? Why, on everybody, Dr. Adcock: the President of the United States, the secretary general of the United Nations, the director of the National Bureau of Intelligence—that's because they have custody of the aliens. For that matter, on the aliens themselves, but I'll have to do a little research on that. Trial? My dear Dr. Adcock, there won't be any *trial.* All we want is money, and they'll throw that at us to get rid of us. What you have to do is decide how much you want. I'm thinking of, let's see, giving them a quit claim for whatever the cost of manufacturing, outfitting and launching Starlab was when it was built, adjusted for inflation, with interest, and perhaps a one hundred percent penalty . . . yes, quite a large sum, I think. But we can discuss all those details later. Good afternoon."

When he was gone Pat spent a few dizzying minutes calculating just how many hundreds of millions of inflation-adjusted dollars all that might come to. It would definitely be a *lot.* It was certainly enough to relieve all four Pats from financial worries forever, and for Pat Five's unborn triplets and all their descendants as well.

She leaned back, studying the numbers on the wall to take her mind off these giddy visions of prosperity. A flash of color showed that another object had been identified and an orbit plotted, but the flashing red showed that this one was special. The funny thing about it was that it seemed to be heading in the general direction of the Earth.

That explained the flashing signal. It also caused Pat a moment's shock, but when she checked its orbital elements she relaxed a bit; its trajectory seemed to bring it within a couple hundred thousand kilometers of the planet, but that was not particularly worrisome. Every few years an object was detected at ranges like that, some of them coming closer than Earth's Moon. It would bear watching, of course. But—

Her phone rang. Annoyed, Pat touched the screen control. "What is it?" she demanded, expecting to see Janice DuPage with some new urgency to make demands on her time.

But the face wasn't Janice's. It was her own face—well, Patrice's face, at least—and she looked scared. "Pat? It's Pat Five. She's hemorrhaging. I've got the medics here and they're taking her to the hospital. You'd better come."

28

Hilda Morrisey got a few hours sleep on the plane to Guyana, needing it. The night with Wilbur Carmichael had been really pleasant, but it might have been a mistake. Was she getting too fond of the man? Should she have promised to see him again as soon as she got back? It had certainly cost her sleep that she could have used. But it was a mistake she would have been glad to repeat, because Wilbur had been *fine.*

She woke at dawn, just as the aircraft was circling the town of Kourou. All she could see from the air was the giant new Holiday Inn between the lights of the Pizza Hut and the all-night casino, but with the dark solid green of the jungle just outside the town limits. The plane swooped out to sea to come in for a landing from the east, and there, a kilometer or so from the town itself, was the starkly floodlighted launch area, ancient gantries still standing in spite of rust and time, the liquid fuel plants steaming away, the hideous barracks blocks where most of the base's personnel lived.

When she got out of the aircraft the heat hit her. Kourou was hot and wet, and there were bugs. The zappers electrocuted a few thousand of them every hour, but there were always thousands more coming up out of the rain forest, thirsty for Hilda Morrisey's blood.

It was not, it seemed, going to be a comfortable assignment. Hilda wondered if it was going to be a safe one; she had never signed on to be an astronaut. It wasn't just that people got killed in space. She had long come to terms with the possibility of early death, because in Hilda's line of work people got killed from time to time just about everywhere she'd ever been. The hard part was the thought that in a few days she would be climbing into that ancient and ugly-looking LuftBuran space vehicle that was squatting on its hardstand at the end of the runway and then she would be departing in it from the planet she belonged on. When was the last time the damn Europeans had fired one of the things? Would it still work? Her skin crawled in ways she had never experienced before as she thought about all the questions.

On the other hand, Kourou had one very great advantage for Hilda Morrisey. It wasn't the Bureau's hated Arlington madhouse.

Here in Kourou she was the senior American officer present, at least until the deputy director got there for the actual launch. So she had no boss at all. She certainly didn't take orders from Colonel duValier—although, in spite of the fact that she clearly outranked him, he did his best to give them.

If Hilda put up with the colonel at all it wasn't because he was chief pilot and commander of the expedition to Starlab. He had something more interesting going for him. He was not only a well-built man but a *French*man, and something in Hilda's brain was telling her that, satisfactory though Wilbur was, it was about time to change her luck. Although Hilda's few experiments with French males had not been very encouraging, there was that old rumor that they were the ultimate in lovers. Well, sure, they went to a lot of trouble to foster the rumor themselves. But still.

As a matter of fact, it was apparent that the personnel roster at Kourou was heavily weighted with rather good-looking men. Not only that, but men who were either single or—just as good—married to someone who was thousands of kilometers away. There were the Belgian, Bulgarian and Danish astronauts, for instance. They weren't in a very good mood, because they'd been bounced from the launch to make room for Hilda, the Chinese commander Lin and most of all that great, silent, smelly creature, the Doc. Hilda sympathized with the rejects. They might well need a little consolation, and, if things happened to go that way, Hilda had an open mind about supplying it for them.

She had plenty of time to think about such matters, because the preflight "training" she was supposed to be going through was a clear waste of time. They were not going to have to wear spacesuits. She wasn't going to be allowed anywhere near the controls of the giant LuftBuran spaceship that would carry them into orbit. All Hilda was really going to have to do was make sure American interests were protected when at last they did dock with Starlab, and when it came to the protection of American interests Brigadier Hilda Morrisey had received all the training she needed long before.

* * *

Hilda's first day was spent listening to briefings she didn't really care about. The launch controller, a dour Welshman who hated Kourou's jungly heat, kept talking about launch windows and trip times; pointless, in Hilda's view. Starlab sailed around the Earth in its Low Earth Orbit every eighty-eight minutes; it hugged Earth's equator, and so the windows that were best for rendezvousing with it, allowing for the Earth's own rotation, occurred just about every eighty-eight minutes as well. When that boring lecture was done the Portuguese who was their combat instructor went over and over the weaponry they were to take along against the outside chance that some Scarecrow troops had somehow managed to sneak back in. But what had some Portuguese to tell Brigadier Hilda Morrisey of the National Bureau of Investigation about weaponry?

More interesting were her colleagues. It was the first time the entire crew of the LuftBuran had been in one place. Hilda looked around and chose to sit between the two most interesting of them. One was Jimmy Lin—the formerly captive Jimmy Lin, along because he had firsthand knowledge of what the Scarecrow matériel on Starlab looked like; the other was the Floridian General Delasquez, along because he knew it from its unaltered state. Both had been recently debugged for the purpose of the launch, but if Hilda had hoped for any interesting tidbits from either of them she was disappointed. When she tried to strike up a conversation with the Chinese astronaut, he shot an agonized glance at his PRC guard, standing stiffly at the back of the room, and shrank away. The Floridian merely ignored her.

Stop the Spaceflight!

Save our planet! Save our country! Every launch produces tons of hydrochloric acid which destroys living things! We, the people of Guyana, well remember the effects of the poisonous Ariane 5 rocket which killed or damaged plants and animals as far as ten kilometers from Kourou. We will not tolerate a resumption of these deadly launches. Our priceless natural resources must be protected! This project must be abandoned!

(Signed) Pou d'Agouti

Besides themselves and, of course, the Doc—stolidly waiting in his little holding cage on the outskirts of the base, and not invited to the briefings—there were four others: the two Germans, the female French lieutenant whose main duty was to be to remain in the shuttle in case of disaster and Colonel duValier, who listened irritably to the briefings, grumpy because he knew it all and because the briefings were being given in English.

It took the Portuguese weapons man nearly half an hour to explain why the handguns they would be issued were to carry a reduced charge—"Because there is much danger of ricochet if fired"—while the carbines would be loaded with armor-penetrating rounds in case of dire necessity. Judging by the expressions on her crewmates' faces, none of them was learning anything more than Hilda herself. She cast a sidelong glance at General Delasquez, who appeared unaware of her existence, and another at Commander Lin on her right. Hilda was not unaware of Lin's reputation. According to gossip of the Pats he had harped incessantly on the sexual wisdom of his great ancient ancestor, some two-thousand-year-old sage named Peng-tsu, though none of them would admit to having experienced any of Lin's expertise for themselves. There might be an additional possibility there, she thought, and allowed her forearm to slip onto his side of the armrest between them.

That produced nothing but a sudden jerk away from her, the man's attention doggedly fixed on the speaker. She sighed and did her best to pay attention to the lecture on the sheath knife and crowbar.

All things ended in time; even this lecture. When they got up to go Hilda's fleeting notion of trying to get Lin aside for a little chat evaporated when the Chinese officer whisked him firmly away. Evidently Commander Lin was not in the good graces of his government.

Her second choice was General Delasquez, but the chance of that diminished when Hilda saw that her aide was waiting for her outside the briefing room. Tepp saluted smartly. "Three messages from headquarters, ma'am. First, Colonel Makalanos reports that the X-ray screening is complete and no bugs were found. Second, Agent Dannerman thought you might want to know that Dr. Adcock—the pregnant one, ma'am—is having some sort of emergency. She's in the hospital, but they give her condition as fair, not critical. Third, Vice Deputy Fennell advises that the deputy director is making arrangements to come here in person as soon as your mission is on its way back from the orbiter."

To oversee the distribution of the spoils, of course, Hilda thought. "Thank you. How's our Doc?"

Tepp's expression didn't change, but there was a touch of strain in her voice. "Apparently doing just fine, ma'am. Do you want me to look in on him?"

"No," Hilda decided; no reason to push the woman to do something she hated. "I've got time before lunch to do it myself. What I'd like you to do is make friends among the permanent-party junior officers here, see what sort of gossip you can pick up. And meet me again after the afternoon briefing."

"Ma'am," Merla Tepp acknowledged as she saluted. She looked relieved. As Hilda turned toward the Doc's pen she wondered if she were being too indulgent. Not really, she thought. For now, at least, Tepp could be more useful functioning as an extra ear than making herself sick in the presence of the space freak. Whether that meant she might need to be replaced sometime in the future was another question. *Maybe not,* Hilda thought. Maybe things would go so well on the mission to Starlab that they might once and for all be relieved of the burden of caring for the aliens.

She glanced up at the tall, rusting shape of an old Ariane 5 rocket, memento of Kourou's early pioneering days, and then caught sight of the man who was studying it.

General Martín Delasquez. Sometimes your luck was good, Hilda thought, and turned to join him. "How did you like the briefing, General?" she asked chattily.

He gave her an unwelcoming look. "It was certainly a complete waste of time for me. I was stationed here at Kourou for months, and there is nothing they can tell me that they haven't already told many times."

She gave him an apologetic chuckle. "Our fault, I'm afraid; they want to make sure we new guys get all the dope. I know being stuck with us is an inconvenience, but I hope you won't hold it against me personally. . . . General? Since you have actually been on Starlab and I haven't, I was hoping you could tell me something about what to expect when we get there."

"And how could I do that, when those creatures tampered with my memory?" he demanded.

It seemed like a good time to offer sympathy. "That must be awful for you," she said.

He glared at her, then shrugged. "What I remember is an abandoned astronomical observatory. There was no gravity, so it was difficult to move about, and the air smelled stale—because, I thought, it had been unused for so long, but perhaps it was the natural aroma of these creatures from space. But I didn't see any sign of them."

"Haven't you seen the Doc?"

He looked at her with what might have been amusement—at last, a human sign! "This one, no. I did see quite a bit of its—brother?—

when it removed that device from my brain. But I was not in a position to study it carefully."

"Well, General," she said sunnily, "I'm on my way there now. It isn't time for lunch yet, so you have the opportunity if you want it. Would you care to look in on the damn thing?"

Hilda's interest in the Floridian was not particularly sexual. She certainly did not exclude that possibility. However, General Delasquez represented a force in the world with which she had little personal experience, that is, the kind of semipatriotism which marked the people of the breakaway State of Florida: adamant on running their own state as though it were a sovereign nation, yet unwilling to, or perhaps too sensible to, provoke the military retaliation that would come with any attempt at outright secession. The Floridians were not ignorant of history, and they were well aware of the outcome of the War Between the States.

Outside the Doc's shed an armed guard was crouched over a news screen, but he was alert enough to forbid them to enter. "What's so interesting?" Hilda asked the man in a friendly way. He shrugged.

"There's an object coming pretty close to the Earth. For a while they thought it might hit, but it's going to miss us by about fifty thousand klicks." Then, more obligingly: "I can't let you go in, but you can look at the damn beast through the door if you want to. It won't disturb him."

The Doc looked as though nothing at all would disturb him, as a matter of fact. The creature was standing motionless, half-turned away from them, not bothering to look around to see who had come to look at him. Delasquez looked at the Doc in silence for a moment, then said wonderingly, "Excuse me, but is this the one that made the pictures of the interior of Starlab?"

"The very one."

"It doesn't look capable of that kind of work."

"I know," Hilda agreed. "The story is that they come from a very high type of civilization, but the Scarecrows conquered them and planted some sort of controls in their brains. It doesn't affect their intelligence, but now they can't make any decisions on their own—especially to rebel against the Scarecrows."

He gave her a sardonic look. "How useful that would be for your country, for dealing with people like myself."

"Oh, but we would never do anything like that, General," Hilda protested—as a matter of form; knowing that that wasn't true, knowing that the General was well aware it wasn't.

"Of course not," he agreed, as duplicitous as herself. "Shall we go to lunch now, Brigadier? I've seen all I need, and the creature does smell unpleasant."

"Of course," Hilda said, cozily slipping her arm into his as they turned away; thinking about how the general was going to feel when they were stuck in the confined space of the LuftBuran with the Doc. "You know," she said, "I've always thought of Florida as a good experiment in cooperation: you have all the advantages of being part of the United States, but the freedom to follow your own principles."

He looked at her in amusement, but without removing her arm. "Yes, that is true. I wonder, though, how well the experiment would work if we Floridians did not have our own National Guard and Air Force."

Brigadier Morrisey would have preferred a quiet table for two, but there weren't any tables like that in the Kourou officers' mess. They wound up at a table for six, sharing it with Colonel duValier and some people on the launch controller's staff. They seemed to be old friends of General Delasquez, though there was something in their gently mocking tone that Hilda did not quite understand. Then Colonel duValier explained: "When our friend Martín was here before it was under something of a cloud, Brigadier. We borrowed him from the Floridians to brief us on what we could expect when we visited your Starlab, since he had been there himself. Of course, then we discovered that there was not much truth in what he told us."

Delasquez said stiffly, "I told you what I thought was so. I did not know that my mind had been tampered with."

"But of a certainty," the colonel agreed. "We did not know that you were transmitting information to our enemies, either. We did not even know that we had enemies! Or else we would have put you in a cage like the one this malodorous Doc we are taking with us is in."

"Dr. Artzybachova says the only way to be sure the Docs aren't transmitting information is to make sure they don't get any," Hilda put in. "Of course, that policy got blown when they were at the UN."

General Delasquez sniffed. "Dr. Artzybachova," he said in a dismissing tone.

"You don't like her?"

"I have no opinion at all about the woman. I saw her briefly on the launch, and then she died."

"That one died, right," Hilda said, nodding. "But the one that's here now, she says you—the other you—and she were great friends as captives of the Scarecrows."

Delasquez looked uneasy. "I have thought about that," he admitted. "But since that other copy of myself is not here, I am not bound by any relationships he may have assumed. She is a type of woman I do not care for."

"What type is that?" Hilda asked. He shrugged without answering, but she didn't really need an answer. She had already diagnosed General Delasquez's own type: authoritarian male, which meant sexist pig. It was a type that she had always enjoyed encountering, on official business or in the boudoir.

The woman from the controller's staff diplomatically changed the subject. "So, Brigadier Morrisey, are you ready to explore outer space?"

"Of course," Hilda said, politely enough. "In fact, I wish it would happen. How long are we going to have to wait here?"

"That's not my decision. The LuftBuran is nearly fueled, and all the supplies are already stowed. As soon as the crew is ready we can go."

Interoffice Memo:
The Eurospace rocket.
Classified.

The "LuftBuran" was built from a German design with German money, but using Russian facilities and labor. The French didn't like the name. They wanted to call it the "Ariane 9," but when that was turned down they settled for naming a French astronaut as chief pilot.

"I'm ready now," Hilda declared, digging into the fish course that one of the waiters had placed before her. She didn't recognize the fish. There were two of them, quite tiny, but delicious; evidently Colonel duValier had made his wishes known to the kitchen staff.

They had reached the cheese course when carryphones began beeping all over the mess hall. "What is happening?" Delasquez asked irritably.

The woman from the controller's staff was already answering hers, and when she turned to look at them her face was pale. "That object that was approaching Earth? It is a spacecraft. It has been observed to make a burn, and its new course will impact the Earth."

The cheese boards sat abandoned on every table, rounds of perfect Camembert, slabs of *bleu* and Brie. There was no one left in the room to eat them. Everyone had flown to the briefing room, where Colonel duValier had a phone to his ear and an eye on the wall screen.

Hilda stared at the pictures. After all the searching, not one of Earth's giant telescopes had had its instruments bearing on the incoming object. That was left to the smaller ones, and so they had been the ones that were dazzled when the object emitted a stream of fire. Beside her Martín Delasquez muttered something in Spanish, but when she asked he said it in English for her benefit. "It is a braking burn," he said. "They are preparing for reentry."

"But what *is* it?" someone asked. No one tried to answer. Everyone was thinking the same thoughts, though, for they had all heard the stories the captives brought back of Scarecrow vengeance that dropped KT-type asteroids on the planets of their enemies, wiping them out as thoroughly as the sixty-five-million-year-old impact not far from where they were standing had wiped out the dinosaurs.

Hilda could not help a small shudder. Then someone cried, "Look at the other screen!"

It was displaying a series of numbers—orbital elements, Hilda supposed, though the digits meant nothing to her. Then the screen provided a graphic, a globe of the Earth, with a great oval of pink light overspreading a west-to-east area from Baja California almost to the African coast.

"That is its landing footprint," Delasquez said tautly. "When it makes final course corrections it can strike anywhere in that area. If you notice, we are inside it here in Kourou."

Everyone in the room had noticed that. Colonel duValier was gabbling with the controllers. Then, grim-faced, he seized the microphone.

"It is my belief," he said, his voice taut and his accent thickening, "that these Scarecrows are aiming this missile directly at us in order to keep us from accomplishing our launch to the Starlab orbiter. I do not intend to let them do that. Our next launch window is in eighteen minutes; we can't make that one, but we can make the one after that. I order refueling topped off and the alien creature to be brought aboard. It is now a little after thirteen hundred hours local time; the remainder of the crew will board the spacecraft by fourteen ten, for possible liftoff at fourteen fifty-seven."

29

Even a Bureau agent was entitled to an afternoon off now and then. Once Dannerman had supervised the changing of shifts for the guards at the Observatory and the apartment, and the other guard at the hospital where poor Pat Five was flat on her back in the ob-gyn wing, he was free for personal business.

Which, of course, was Anita Berman. He met her for a pleasant, if inexpensive, lunch not far from his room in Rita Gammidge's condo, and when he suggested they go up to his place afterward she was not surprised.

The landlady popped out of her own room to see who was coming into her condo in the middle of the day, but when she saw Anita she smiled and closed the door. Then Dannerman and Anita did what they had come there to do; and that went well, too. Then, satisfied, they lay spooned in the bed, Dannerman's arm over her, his face in the sweet, red hair at the nape of her neck. He was quite content. When she spoke he didn't hear her at first, she spoke so softly. "I said," she repeated, "what happens next?"

"Oh," he said. He stretched, yawned and tried to collect his thoughts. "Well, I guess I kind of get back to my life. I'm still waiting for the damn payroll people to clear my status, now that there are two of me. The big problem is—"

But it wasn't Dannerman's file and pension account she wanted to talk about. She said, "That isn't what I meant. I meant, what happens next with us?"

"Oh," he said again, suddenly thoughtful. He readjusted his mind. He had been asked that "what about us?" question more than once before, by more than one other young woman. When you decoded it, it usually turned out to mean, "Are we going to get married?"

All the other times he had been asked that question the answer had been pretty much out of his control, often enough because the woman who asked it happened to be a suspect in his ongoing mission. But now . . .

She wasn't waiting for his answer. She had something else on her mind. "Listen," she said tentatively, "there's something I didn't tell you."

Oh, hell, he thought, because he could decode that one, too; it meant a lot of things, and one of them might be that another man had suddenly appeared in her life.

But not this time. "Dan," she said, "have you ever thought of leaving the Bureau?"

He propped himself up to look at her, honestly puzzled. "And do what?"

"Well, I always had the idea that you really wanted to be an actor. Am I wrong?"

That came right out of left field. Be an actor? He'd certainly thought about it, especially while he was taking all those drama courses in college. It had been a sort of dream-time thought, the way he'd also now and then thought about how nice it would be to win the Olympic decathlon or run for President. It was a daydream and not at all realistic. . . .

> Uncle Cubby financed Dan Dannerman's education right through graduate school, whence he emerged with a doctorate in theater arts—just in time to be called up for active duty from the Police Reserve Officers Training Corps he had ill-advisedly joined as an undergraduate. Working for the Bureau didn't end his interest in theater, it just made it hard to do anything about it . . . until he was assigned to a drug case in New York City, and found the Off-Off-Off Broadway Theater Aristophanes Two, and the girl named Anita Berman who acted in it.

No, that wasn't true anymore. It hadn't been realistic before because of his job. The Bureau wouldn't let him go public as an actor. By definition actors were there to be seen, while a Bureau agent's chief asset was his invisibility.

But he wasn't invisible anymore. That had been taken care of by the Scarecrows.

"If I quit," he said thoughtfully, "I'd be able to collect all my back pay. I guess I'd have to split with the other guy, but there should be enough there to live on, maybe."

"What are you talking about?"

"Well, they don't pay much at Theater Aristophanes Two—"

"Oh, Dan! Who said anything about Theater Aristophanes Two? Do you know who Ron Zigler is?"

"The producer?"

"Yes, the producer. He came backstage at the theater the other night and he wanted to talk to me. Did you ever hear of *Star Trek*?"

"Star Trek?" Dannerman tracked down an old memory. "Oh, sure. Back in—what was it, the 1980s? Uncle Cubby was a Trekkie when he was a kid; that's what got him into the astronomy business."

Anita frowned. "Trekkie? What's that? Never mind; the thing is, Zigler wants to do a remake of *Star Trek.* He's got a script, with the Scarecrows in it and everything, and he's casting. The thing is," she said, clearing her throat, "Zigler's been trying to get in touch with you, either of you, but the Bureau won't pass his messages on. He wants you for Captain Kirk. That's the lead part, in case you didn't know." Dannerman stared at her. She stood up, beginning to dress. "He said there'd be a part in it for me, too, if he could get you for the Kirk role," she finished, sounding embarrassed and defensive, "but that's my problem, not yours. Think about it, will you? Now, which way is that bathroom of yours?"

When Anita was gone Dannerman pulled his own clothes on, thinking.

Too much was happening. Never mind the fact that there were two of him, never mind the Scarecrows, never mind any of those great events that were screwing up the lives of everybody in the world. The things that were happening in his own personal world were already more than he knew how to handle. *Acting?* A starring part?—and with one of Broadway's most famous producers? And what about Anita Berman herself: what a chance this was for her, if only he'd agree to do the thing that any would-be actor in the world would kill to do?

When the hammering began at his door Dannerman was deep in fantasies of stardom, married life with Anita, the stage, the life of a Lunt and Fontanne, fame, riches—

"Here I come, Anita," he called, reaching for the doorknob.

It wasn't Anita, though he saw her standing farther down the hall, looking like a woman in a state of shock. The one doing the hammering was his landlady, and she looked terrified. "Dan!" she cried. "Turn on your screen! Those space people are shooting rockets at us!"

30

Back in New York, Pat dithered for some time before reluctantly leaving Patrice in sole charge at the Observatory. That was where all the excitement was, but sisterly duty was compelling. At the hospital entrance Pat didn't have to go through the weapons search. The Bureau guard spoke to the hospital security man at the door, who listened, then reluctantly waved them through. He didn't even make the Bureau guard check her weapon, though Pat's own little derringer was taken away.

Pat Five was in a private room—really a suite—and paid for, the funny thing was, by the government of the People's Republic of China on behalf of the triplets' putative father. Pat Five's own guard was sitting on a straight-backed chair outside the door; alerted to their coming, she clapped her hands and the door opened.

Pat didn't see her semisister at first, because Pat Five's bed had pull-up sides to keep her from falling out, and they were hung with sheets to keep out drafts. Pat had to step right up to the bed and look down in order to show Pat Five the flowers she'd brought. "How are you doing?" she asked.

Pat Five opened her eyes to peer up at her. She looked like hell. Her face was blotchier than ever, and her auburn hair was sweated into clumps. She was not going to be able to take advantage of the comfortable sitting room next door, with its picture-window view of the city, or even the fully equipped bathroom that came with the suite. One of her arms was strapped down because of the IVs that were taped in place; pulse monitors were mounted on her throat and a respiration microphone on her right side. From under the light blanket that covered the lower half of her body inconspicuous tubes led to plastic waste bags, showing that she was still catheterized. "How am I doing?" she asked. "I'm doing lousy. Do you know they want me to stay flat on my back for the next six weeks?"

"Ah, honey," Pat clucked. The words weren't meant to convey information. It was only what you said when you had nothing better to offer. She thought of reminding Pat that this was all for the benefit of her unborn babies, but the last time she'd tried that Pat had talked fretfully of the attractions of a midterm abortion.

"Anyway," Pat said brightly, "I've got some news. Mr. Hecksher served all the papers, and he has an appointment to talk to the people at the UN this afternoon. He has a new paper for you to sign—something for the Chinese government, to say that you are accepting their financial assistance *ex gratia,* whatever that is, but without admitting any claim to the children. Can you actually sign?"

"Legibly, no. But the nurses help me, so just leave it. What's this about an object approaching the Earth? Is it the goddam Beloved Leaders?"

Pat's strictest order from the doctors was not to excite the patient, so she said reassuringly, "People say it might be, but it's not coming anywhere near the Earth."

"I don't trust the bastards," Pat Five said glumly.

"Well, no one does." Pat cast around for a more cheerful subject. "You wouldn't believe the get-well messages that have been coming for you. From people all over the world. Everybody we've ever known, even our ex-husbands—and relatives we haven't heard from for years."

"Sure, they think we might be coming into a lot of money."

"Oh, not all of them," Pat protested. "There are a lot of people that just like you—us. And—wait a minute."

It was her carryphone. She frowned as she answered it; she wasn't supposed to be called on the private line except in emergency. It was Patrice on the line. She said, "Pat? Get your ass back here. Don't say anything to Pat Five—but the damn thing has changed course, and it looks like it's going to impact the Earth."

When Pat Adcock got back to the Observatory she saw the whole thing, from that first chance-caught burn on, because the news channels kept rerunning every sighting. At twenty-five Earth radii the object—no, damn it, Pat said fretfully to herself; call it a spacecraft, because there wasn't any more doubt that that was what it was—the *spacecraft* produced another great display of fireworks. When the burn was over and they calculated the new orbit—a stretched-out ellipse, with the spacecraft now on the descending leg—there wasn't any doubt. It was definitely going to impact the Earth. "Right on top of us," Patrice groaned as she inspected the oval of the expected footprint, swallowing up half of the western Atlantic and a lot of the bulge of South America. "They know we're all here, and they're after us."

"If it's big enough," Rosaleen offered, "it doesn't much matter where it hits. Remember how the Scarecrows offed their enemies by dumping asteroids on them?"

But it wasn't that big. Pat was sure of that much. *What* it was was another question entirely: supernuclear bomb? Bioweapons? Patrice, thinking along the same lines, said tightly, "I wonder if the government's going to try to evacuate the Eastern Seaboard."

But if they did, where would they evacuate the people to? And how could they move a hundred million men and women out of the way, when they weren't sure just where the way was?

> The Earth is a sitting duck for all the floating bird shot that orbits the Sun. Thousands of meteorites strike its outer atmosphere every day, most of them so tiny that they burn up quickly and are not even noticed by Earth's people. Once in a while a slightly larger one—perhaps the size of a grain of sand—burns brightly enough to be seen as a "shooting star." More rarely one is large enough to reach the ground as a hot lump of pitted rock. Very seldom does one make a crater, and only a few times in a million years will one be large enough to do serious damage. But *never* before has one been seen to change its course by a rocket burn to make sure of hitting its target.
>
> —*Newsweek*

The big telescopes were no use now; the thing was too close and moving too fast for them. But telescopes weren't necessary. Every news camera on Earth was scanning the skies, for there wasn't any other news that mattered at that moment. The lucky ones zoomed in on the Scarecrow spacecraft, and for a few minutes each was able to hold it—sometimes long enough to catch it as the thing plooped out a minor course-correction jet. On the dozen screens in the Observatory's conference room there were sometimes as many as eight or nine different shots of the spacecraft, flickering in and out as the harried operators in the network control rooms tried to keep abreast of the rapidly changing feeds.

Then, abruptly, one screen switched to a wholly different scene: Eurospace's LuftBuran caught in its liftoff from Kourou. "Hell," Dannerman snapped. "They've launched ahead of schedule! Why would they do that?"

No one answered; they were all too full of questions of their own.

And then the spacecraft made a final burn, and turned into a sun-bright meteor as it entered Earth's atmosphere, plunging down.

"It's going to miss us," Patrice breathed.

"It's going to miss the land entirely," Pat corrected, as the footprint on one of the screens wobbled, shrank, finally turned into a point in the ocean.

Then all the ground-based scenes blacked out at once, and one by one each screen came on again, all of them showing a single picture. It came from a traffic-spotter plane belonging to a Puerto Rican TV station, urgently redirected by its control room as the Scarecrow ship's splashdown became predictable. The pilot was quick and the cameraman was good. They caught the fireball of the descending spacecraft from a distance, even saw the immense splash and clouds of steam when it struck. The pilot had piled on the coal, and they were closing in on it before the steam had dissipated, while Pat—and everyone else in the world—held their breath, awaiting the explosion. . . .

It didn't come. When at last the steam blew away a metal object, the size and shape of an old naval torpedo, was floating placidly in the ocean swell, and it wasn't exploding at all.

Within half an hour there were a dozen other planes circling above the floating Scarecrow ship; within an hour, the first surface vessels began to arrive.

There wasn't much to see, but no one in the Dannerman Observatory turned away from the screens. The ships were an oddly assorted lot: fishing vessels, fast cigarette speedboats, even a cruise ship that happened to be nearby and altered course to give its passengers an unanticipated thrill.

When a Navy tug approached, flank speed ahead, a mustache of white foam curling away from its bow, the first thing it did was to put an officer on the loud-hailers and warn everybody else away. Then it slowly approached the floating hulk, circled it suspiciously a time or two, then stopped. A moment later a pair of frogmen went over the side.

Then the tempo of events slowed down to a crawl. One of the frogmen paddled over to the floating object and gingerly touched it with some sort of metallic probe, while the other trod water a few meters away. They jabbered to each other, then one of them waved to the tug. A moment later deckhands flopped an inflatable raft overboard and a couple of others climbed down a rope ladder to get into it. Nothing happened for a moment, then some sort of metallic-gleaming equipment was lowered into the raft and its crew began to row it toward the Scarecrow object.

"They're being pretty damn cautious," Pat grumbled. Rosaleen gave her an amused look.

"Wouldn't you be?" she asked. And yes, Pat admitted to herself, she would. They still didn't know whether the thing was a bomb or not . . . or whether it might suddenly give anyone nearby one of those devastating electrical shocks . . . or even whether it might pop open and a horde of Scarecrows come charging out, weapons blasting.

How the Object Was Found

The "Scarecrow" missile happened to be in Earth's daylight skies when it emitted the burn that changed its course. It was almost directly overhead, as seen from the islands of Hawaii, where a BBC crew was interviewing a group of astronomers at the Canada-France-Hawaii dome. A script girl, glancing up at the sky, saw the flare. When she yelped in surprise the BBC cameraman caught the object in his finder, and that was how the world first saw it.

Within ten minutes every telescope in the world that could bear on the object was searching for it. Cerro Toledo was the first to locate it, once the burn was over. It was moving very rapidly, but the Chileans were able to hold it long enough to project a track, moving east by northeast. Using the Chilean data, telescopes in the little observatory in the hills over Rio de Janeiro picked it up and refined the orbit before it vanished over the Atlantic.

Twenty minutes later telescopes in the Azores, and moments later on the European continent, had it, and since then it has been under constant watch.

—*Sky & Telescope*

But nothing like that happened. Nothing much was happening at all, except that the sailors in the raft were gingerly touching the Scarecrow object with probes, frowning over their instrument readings, talking on their headsets to the command personnel on the tug about what they found . . . who in turn were, no doubt, talking to higher authority somewhere ashore at every step while someone decided what to do next.

Pat grinned to herself. It was actually getting pretty boring, but neither she nor anyone else in the Observatory could tear herself away from the dozen identical displays on the screens. . . .

Until the display on some of them changed. A human face appeared, looking agitated. "A transmission has been received," it began to say, and then it froze; whatever it was saying was no longer heard as the audio portion of that transmission was replaced by the very transmission it had announced.

"Do not be afraid," a mellow, reassuring voice said. "Our intentions are friendly. The lander you are approaching is not dangerous. It simply carried a cargo of food to supply the needs of our loyal associates presently on your planet. As you see, the Beloved Leaders care for those who cooperate with them. We will care for you, too, if you wish it. And most of all, we will help you defend yourselves against the forces of the evil Horch. We suggest that you examine our lander and its contents to reassure yourself we mean no harm, and when you have had an opportunity to do so we will speak to you again. . . ."

"Just *food?"* Pat said incredulously. "They scare the pee out of us just to give Dopey some *food?"*

"Hold it," Dannerman said, listening, because the voice was going on—not quite as mellow, now; almost sounding agitated:

"But we must warn you against your foolish attempt to visit your Starlab! The mechanisms it contains are highly dangerous! Recall your spacecraft at once! Do not enter the Starlab! The consequences will be very grave!"

31

Long before Starlab was in sight the word had come over the LuftBuran's radio that the "missile" was a dud. That did not appear to make Colonel duValier feel any safer. When they came within docking range of Starlab he brought the old rocket to relative rest for half an hour while he studied the exterior of the orbiter centimeter by centimeter. The French female astronaut had unbuckled herself and swum up to confer with him—endlessly; in French, and pitched too low for anyone else to hear.

She was the only one allowed freedom of movement. Everybody else was ordered to remain strapped in their seats in case the colonel decided to get out of there in a hurry. Hilda did her best to be patient, though little twinges in her belly reminded her that a lot of people got spacesick in this kind of microgravity . . . even without the odor of the Doc that filled the vessel.

Then the colonel reached a decision. "Check your weapons, everybody," he ordered. "I am going to dock."

That was a little better, though the odd, slippery-slidey motion of the LuftBuran as duValier twitched it to mate with the Starlab port caused Hilda to swallow nervously. But then he announced the docking secured. Everyone unstrapped and took their places by the door—well, almost everyone. The great pale alien remained lashed to the cradle that had been built for him, of course, and one of the Germans remained by him to release him when Colonel duValier gave the order.

Which the colonel was taking his time about doing. He was obviously mulling something over in his mind—perhaps trying to find the proper historic words to speak before ordering his crew to enter, Hilda thought sourly. But what he said at last was, "You all know your orders.

I will be the first person to board Starlab. You will then follow in the order assigned, except for Capitaine des Esseintes. She will remain in the LuftBuran, in constant radio contact with those of us in the boarding party. This will be done as a precaution. If anything goes wrong, she will undock at once, until the problem is cleared up."

And if the problem weren't cleared up? Hilda tried to imagine what it would be like if the Frenchwoman took it into her head to decide they had all been taken over by the Scarecrows, and then pulled the LuftBuran away for a return to Earth. It was not an attractive prospect. If it were a false alarm, they would all be marooned there for an indefinite period. And if it weren't a false alarm. . . . No, Hilda didn't want to think about that at all.

The colonel was speaking to his controllers on Earth, presumably to announce that he was ready for his historic task. But he suddenly frowned and lost his composure. He spat rapid-fire French into the microphone, too fast for Hilda to follow, listened again, then looked up. "There has been a development. There is a message from these Scarecrows, and they warn that we must not enter Starlab. This is—This causes—" Then he shook his head and was silent.

He was the only one silent. Everybody else was shouting at once—"Warning of what? What do they mean?"—everyone but Hilda. She had a different concern. It wasn't so much what the Scarecrows had said as the fact that they had said anything about entering Starlab at all. For that meant that they weren't thousands of light-years away. They were close enough to see what was going on. And that meant—

That was another thing Hilda didn't want to think about.

Another hour went by while everyone jabbered to everyone else, with many more exchanges between Colonel duValier and the ground controllers. Then the colonel shrugged and pulled the lock door open with a crash. *"Allons!"* he said hollowly; and the troops stormed the citadel.

In Hilda Morrisey's eighteen years with the Bureau she had stormed into enemy territory often enough, guns blazing, people getting killed. This wasn't like that. For one thing, rushing a target when your feet were firmly on the ground and things dropped to the floor when you let go of them was one thing. This microgravity business was something else entirely. They didn't storm the Starlab. They damn well *floated* in through the lock, one after another, as easy a collection of big, slow targets as ever graced any church-carnival shooting gallery. If there had been actual enemies inside, they would have had no problem picking the invaders off, one at a time, as they floundered and soared.

Well, there weren't any waiting sharpshooters. There was nobody in sight at all. Hilda caught a confused glimpse of rows and clusters of odd colors and bizarre objects, looking like some mad interior decorator's going-out-of-business sale; but then Martín Delasquez thumped into her from behind, propelling her into one of Colonel duValier's flying feet; and all her attention was taken up with the job of trying to grab on to something solid. Her interior ear canals were complaining about it, too; her queasiness got worse, to the point where she seriously thought she was going to toss her cookies right into the lap of the Chinese guy, Lin. And it was not helped by the smell of the place: something like spice, something like decay, a lot like a nastily rasping kind of chemical smoke.

The chemical part at least had an explanation. "It's the transporter," Jimmy Lin gasped, hauling himself up Martín Delasquez's leg to clutch a wall bracket. "Dannerman shot it up to keep the Scarecrows from following us. Outside of that, the place is just the way we left it."

Federal Reserve Inflation Bulletin

The morning recommended price adjustment for inflation is set at 3.21%. Acting Federal Reserve Chairman L. Dwight Gorman, replacing the late Walter C. Boettger, issued a prepared statement demanding that all banks immediately adhere to the recent eighth increase in interest rates. "Dr. Boettger's suicide should be a warning to us all," he said in the statement. "If we do not pull together, we can expect financial anarchy, which will cause great harm to our democratic institutions in this time of public unrest."

Maybe so, Hilda thought, but she hadn't forgotten what had happened when this same Jimmy Lin and the others made their first landing on Starlab. It had looked innocent enough then, too; and then, without any foreplay, they'd found themselves captives of the Scarecrows.

The colonel evidently had the same thoughts. He ordered a thorough search of the orbiter, and so the landing party dragged itself through the corridors of the orbiter, looking for—looking for what, exactly? Hilda asked herself. God knew there was a lot to see, for the satellite was full of inexplicable machines and gadgets. The things came in all colors and textures. Some looked like lime Jell-O, some were silver-bright. There was one huge copper-colored thing, like a huge, metal, six-sided pillar, that seemed to be emitting a sullen heat. Some of the objects clicked and whispered to themselves, some glowed, some were silent and dark, and what any of them were for Hilda could not guess.

Still, it could have been worse. The one thing that they feared to find was not there: no living creature, no Docs or Dopeys nor anything else out of the Scarecrows' menagerie of oddities. And when Colonel duValier was quite sure of that, he got on the radio and commanded, "Bring the beast in," and the expedition began to earn its pay.

At that point most of the people aboard Starlab became extraneous, which meant that they were free to follow their private agendas, whatever those were. General Delasquez pulled out a camera and, without a word to anyone else, methodically began to photograph everything in sight. Hilda herself retraced her steps around the Starlab, looking for those particle-beam weapons the Scarecrow troops were supposed to have. There weren't any visible. The Chinese astronaut, Commander Lin, had a priority project of his own; he had stationed himself by the charred wreck of the machine that had brought them there, with his weapon still in his hand. When Hilda came near he pointed the gun at her face. "Back off. Nobody comes near this thing," he announced. "I'm not taking any chances on letting it get fixed."

Hilda looked at him curiously. "How would I know how to fix it?"

"I don't know," he admitted, "and I don't care. Maybe the Scarecrows have some way of making you do it—same as they made us forget all this stuff?"

"Then they could just as well do it to you, Lin," she pointed out.

He scowled. "Stay away. And keep the Doc away from here. I swear, if he tries to touch this thing, I'll blow his damn head off."

The Doc showed no such intention. He, too, had his own program. As soon as he was inside the Starlab he headed down one of the corridors at high speed—startling Hilda; the creature was making faint mewing sounds, the first she had ever heard from him. Clearly he was practiced at getting around in the microgravity environment. Equally clearly he knew just where he wanted to go.

Which wasn't where the colonel wanted him. "Halt!" Colonel duValier commanded, flailing after him with his gun drawn. The alien paid no attention. He didn't stop until he reached a green-glowing panel. He clutched it for support with one huge arm, reached out with a smaller one to touch on its surface. The panel sprang open, revealing a cubicle filled with racks of what looked like plant matter and smelled faintly peppery. Mewing in excitement, the Doc pulled out a clutch of the stuff and thrust it into his great mouth.

General Delasquez was amused. "The creature is hungry, of course," he reminded the colonel. The colonel was not amused at all. He took a moment to scowl blackly at Delasquez, then returned to muttering angrily at the Doc in a mixture of English and French.

If the Doc understood either, he showed no sign. He chewed energetically, cramming new fistfuls of the stuff into his mouth before the last batch was quite processed. He was a messy eater, too, for little sprigs of greenery fell off the clumps he was shoving in; some clung to the froth of white around his mouth.

He seemed to be more than merely hungry. Hilda had never thought she could detect any emotion on the face of either of the Docs, but now there were signs that had to be some kind of strain. He was actually sweating, and the great eyes were darting about as though in distress.

Then he pulled a couple of additional clumps of food from the locker and, clutching them in two of his extra arms, abruptly gathered his stubby legs under him and kicked himself down the hall for a dozen meters.

Colonel duValier was taken by surprise. He barely got out of the Doc's way in time, then clumsily followed after. "Wait!" he ordered. "Come back!" The Doc paid no attention. Munching as he went, he paused in front of a blue-green mirror. Whatever he did Hilda could not quite see, but the mirror vanished, and where it had been was a sort of tool rack. The Doc selected a couple of items, then, still ignoring Colonel duValier, hurried agitatedly back along the corridor until it came to a luminous golden hemisphere. The mewing noises were louder now; they sounded distressed. Agitatedly the Doc slid one of the tools under the edge of the dome. The glow winked out. The dome retracted silently, and a jumble of incomprehensible alien objects appeared behind it.

Alarm bells went off in Hilda's mind. Were these things weapons? DuValier was having the same thoughts, because he was flailing around, trying to get his body in position to aim his gun at the Doc.

If the Doc knew he was in danger he showed no sign. All his attention was concentrated on his task. He thumbed through the gadgets agitatedly, large arms holding him in place, smaller ones sorting feverishly through the array, until he found a length of what looked like woven cloth of gold. Hurriedly he wrapped it around his head, as though in pain.

Colonel duValier slowly lowered his gun and began talking on his radio to the LuftBuran, watching suspiciously as the Doc relaxed.

The eyes closed. The expression on the broad, pale face turned peaceful. He hung there in silence for a moment, then opened his eyes, turned to Colonel duValier and touched him on the shoulder—was it meant as a pat of reassurance? The Doc tugged at the shawl over his head, awkwardly twisting the ends of it to secure them under his chin. Then he found another square of the brassy fabric, tucked it under one of his smaller arms and stepped back.

Joining the Hundred-Mile-High Club?

Private Eye's gaze is on the LuftBuran that's on its way to the Starlab orbiter. Who have we got here? There's the American spook, Hilda ("Hot Pants") Morrisey, who has never explained what she was doing in a makeout bar not long ago. There's the Chinese James ("My-Grandfather-Could-Do-It-Better") Lin, with his little ancestral book of positions and procedures—will he be adding new chapters in zero-G? There are the two French pilots, Il and Elle, and you know the French, not to mention the big zombie from space. Sounds like a first-rate rave to us!

—*Private Eye,* London

He gestured encouragingly at the collection of objects and pantomimed carrying them into the LuftBuran. Hilda began to breathe again; whatever had been on the creature's mind, it seemed he was now finally ready to go to work.

The Doc looked consideringly at a brightly gleaming trapezoid and a pale blue rhombus, but finally began to dissect a purplish pyramid. When he had loosened it from its attachment to the wall he gestured to the colonel to take it away, and immediately began doing the same to a grapefruit-sized blister of orange nearby.

Colonel duValier whispered to himself in words that might have been French or may have been English, but were certainly profane. Then he turned to the others. "The beast is at last doing as he was ordered," he said. "We can start loading these things into the spacecraft."

* * *

Although the machineries of the Scarecrows weighed nothing at all in the orbiting Starlab, they still had mass; it was sweaty work to try to maneuver them down the narrow corridors of the satellite and through the port—careful not to smash them into the walls, the other machines, the fixtures of the LuftBuran.

That kind of grunt labor was primarily reserved to the humans aboard. The Doc was the specialist now, fully occupied in dismantling bits of machinery, pausing only to collect another fistful of the aromatic food. It wasn't light labor, either. Hilda had not done this much physical work in a long time; in her normal existence that sort of thing was what she directed others to do. Even after the machines were inside the lander the work wasn't over. The things had to be stowed with care—with very great care, Hilda thought, imagining one of those bulky objects breaking loose in the shuddery violence of reentry and crashing down on her unprotected head.

The exertion and the well-used air inside Starlab were having their effect on her, too. She wasn't at the point of throwing up, quite. But the queasiness did not go away, and at last she was forced to make her way to the ancient microgravity toilet.

The training she had received at Kourou was not adequate to her present needs. It took her forever to close the lid on her wastes and then manage the stiff levers that noisily disposed of it. And when she came out the Doc had declared a halt. He was demonstrating to Colonel duValier that the other machines of any interest were simply too big to fit through the docking port.

The colonel surrendered. He ordered everyone inside and grouchily sealed the ports. While the French female astronaut checked the stowage of the goods, the colonel himself strapped down the unprotesting Doc, who still had the one scrap of metal cloth bound oddly around his head, the other clutched firmly in one minor arm. Hilda, busy with her own seat fastenings, was paying little attention until a yelp from the colonel made her turn swiftly.

But General Delasquez was laughing. "You should not attempt to take that thing away from him," he said. "Naturally he resisted."

Colonel duValier sucked his wrist, where the Doc had thrust him away—not violently, but enough to hurt. "We will see," he snarled, "if the creature continues to resist when we are back at Kourou." But he left the Doc alone and pulled himself back to the control deck. A moment later he called, "Check your restraints. Are we all secured?"

When the crew, one by one, reported themselves strapped in, he said crisply: "Disengage."

The copilot touched something; there was a gentle lurch. The nausea that Hilda had quelled came back. She inhaled deeply and managed to repress it once again, bracing herself for the thrust that would start them back to Earth.

It didn't come. They weren't moving, except to drift slowly away from Starlab. Craning her neck, Hilda saw that the colonel was speaking into a microphone while the copilot was scanning the interior of the LuftBuran with a handheld camera. He was speaking softly and in French; Hilda could catch only a few words, but it sounded as though he was complaining about the Doc and demanding armed guards to meet them on landing.

Stupid, she thought . . . but then something new caught Hilda's attention. She wrinkled her nose and craned her neck to look back at the Doc.

All that food had had its inevitable result. The Doc had relieved himself again, and the stench was one thing too many for Hilda Morrisey to bear. She barely got the spacesick bag to her face before everything came up at once.

32

When the new orders came in over the command channel Lieutenant Colonel Priam Makalanos saw no particular problem. *Immediately* on off-loading the object will be airlifted to Camp Smolley for study and biological analysis. If suitable, limited amounts of the contents may be included in rations for the extraterrestrials.

Curiously it was signed *D. S. Fennell, Vice Deputy Director,* rather than by the deputy director himself, but that was only a small puzzle that undoubtedly would be clarified in time. Makalanos glanced up at the wall screen, which for some time had been displaying the object in question. The thing from space was lashed to the deck of a Navy tug steaming toward Hampton Roads. Two destroyers, three Coast Guard corvettes and half a dozen smaller vessels were patrolling the perimeter around the tug, keeping the ships of other nationals away from what, after all, was something that had been found in American territorial waters. Makalanos grinned at the thought of all the indignant diplomatic protests that would be storming on the American State Department over this episode, but that wasn't his problem. All Makalanos had to do was to get Camp Smelly ready to receive the cargo.

Actually, he thought, Dr. ben Jayya and his old biowar staff would be glad for something to do that was more along their lines of expertises; but while he was alerting the laboratory chiefs a breathless corporal rapped on his office door. "There's some kind of trouble with the turkey, sir," he panted. "Dr. Adcock thinks you ought to come."

Even before Makalanos got to the isolation room he could hear Dopey's excited yammering. Pat One was waiting for him at the door.

"He's been like this," she managed to get out before the little creature turned to him, great fan almost glowing with passion.

"Lieutenant Colonel Makalanos! What have you done with my bearer? Is he dead?"

Makalanos glanced at Pat One for help, but she only shook her head worriedly. He tried his best. He said, trying to be placating, "If you mean the one at Walter Reed—"

"I do not mean the one at Walter Reed! I mean the one I agreed to let you take to your Starlab for the purpose of obtaining food, which it appears we no longer need, and devices for your study, which I now believe I should never have permitted. What have you allowed to happen to him?"

Puzzled, Makalanos did his best. "As far as I know, nothing has happened to him."

"As far as you know!" Dopey sneered.

"Which is pretty far, actually," Makalanos said levelly, "but it's always possible something has happened I don't know about. If you'll try to calm down, I'll go to my office and check." Turning, he gave Dannerman a curt nod. "You come with me."

In his office, he turned on the agent. "All right. What happened?"

Dannerman shook his head. "Beats the hell out of me, Colonel. We told him about his food package coming—your order, Colonel."

"I know what my order was. What did he do?"

"He seemed pleased, that's all."

"Pleased? Not surprised?"

"Just pleased. Then he complained for a while about the food he's been getting, as usual, and then, all of a sudden, he went ape. He said we'd killed his bearer."

Makalanos scowled. "Just like that?"

"Just like that. There wasn't any warning, just one minute he was pissing and moaning as usual, then all of a sudden he was having fits. I tried to tell him that killing the Doc was the last thing we wanted to do, because we needed him, but he wasn't listening. Shaking all over. Screeching. As close to hysterical as I've ever seen him. We couldn't calm him down, even though we kept telling him the Doc was all right." He paused there, and then asked, "He is all right, isn't he?"

Was the creature all right? The obvious way to find out was to query headquarters. What was wrong with that was that Makalanos felt a little foolish about asking that sort of question on nothing more substantial than the unsubstantiated conjecture—or hunch, or suspicion—

of the bizarre little beast from space. Colonel Makalanos didn't like to feel foolish.

He liked it even less when the Bureau duty officer assured him that of course the Doc was all right, the Starlab party was busily loading Scarecrow matériel into the LuftBuran at that very moment. "Anyway," she added, "when they're through there'll be a report, so why don't you just watch your news screen?"

Nettled, Makalanos sent Dannerman back to give Dopey the word and do his best to keep him quiet. Then he considered what he should do next. Was it worth reporting Dopey's hysterics to the deputy director?

It probably was, he thought—but when he tried to get through he found the D.D. was not taking calls—was getting ready to head for Kourou himself, to be there when the LuftBuran landed with its cargo.

He swore to himself. Colonel Makalanos was as good at following orders as he was at giving them, but what orders was he to give to deal with Dopey? And who was to tell him what to do, with Brigadier Morrisey off somewhere in orbit and the deputy director too busy even to answer his phone?

D. S. Fennell, that was who; the one who had signed his latest orders. Makalanos put in a call to her on the coded line, and found her impatient, harried, annoyed at being bothered—but willing to talk. She listened briefly, then shook her head. "Did you tell him the Bundles for Beasties were on the way? And that didn't cheer him up? Well, just do the best you can, Priam."

"I wish I knew more of what was going on," he complained.

"Don't we all? But what's to tell? There was a Chinese submarine shadowing the tug with the capsule, but be warned them off from territorial waters and now they're headed south. To Kourou, I guess. And there were a couple of Mexican frigates that got too close and had to be chased away—and, naturally, a lot of diplomatic complaints, but screw them. So everything's under control . . . I hope. Now can I get back to dealing with all this crap, please?"

"I guess," Makalanos said reluctantly. "Daisy? What are you doing with this Starlab stuff? I thought you were assigned to head up all the rest of the Bureau's business?"

She gave him a wry look. "What other business? Haven't you been paying attention? There isn't any. It looks like all the subversives are pulling their heads in. Right now this Scarecrow stuff is about the only action around."

Unwarranted Exclusion of Peaceful Shipping

Federal officials in the Costa Rican Naval Department have announced that Costa Rican fishing and pleasure vessels have been driven out of international waters in the vicinity of the recent landing of the spacecraft from the "Scarecrows." Our ambassador in Washington has asked for an appointment with the American State Department in order to file a protest against this high-handed act.

—*Tico Times,* San Juan, Costa Rica

Agent Dannerman knocked and came in while Makalanos was channel-surfing the civilian news. "Dopey wants to talk to you, so Pat's going to bring him along," he reported.

"Talk about what?" Makalanos asked, glancing away from a late-breaking story about the English Prime Minister's hurried visit to Cardiff, in Wales.

"About this idea he has that something's happened to his Doc. He's quieted down some, so it ought to be all right." He was looking past Makalanos, at the news screen. "I guess that's part of this Welsh thing," he offered. And, when Makalanos looked perplexed, he added: "It was scuttlebutt going around in Arlington. The way I heard it, the Welsh nationalists were negotiating with MI5 for a truce, and this Dawid ap Llewellyn guy? He was supposed to be surrendering to the police in Brownsville."

"I hadn't heard," Makalanos admitted.

"It's getting to be an epidemic. The Ukrainians, the Tamils in Sri Lanka, the Shining Path in, where is it, Peru? Even the Cambodian rebels and the Irish. I haven't heard anything like that about our own nut groups, but all over the world there are these revolutionaries packing it in. Makes you wonder—ah, there he is."

Dopey had waddled in, Pat One right behind him, as they were talking. The little alien seemed subdued—worried, Makalanos thought, although he had not learned how to read Dopey's feelings from any expression on the cat face or hues of the great fantail. As Pat One lifted him onto a chair and began to work the controls of the screen, Dopey commented, "It is a common thing."

Makalanos looked at him. "What is?"

"This submerging of differences. Many affiliated races have

behaved so, in that time of fear and confusion before they came to accept the Beloved Leaders."

"Or didn't," Dannerman said sharply.

"Oh, yes, Agent Dannerman, that is true. Some did not. With inevitably tragic results." The thought seemed to cheer him up. He added politely, "One hopes your species will not necessitate extreme measures, but your actions must not give provocation. It is my bearer I am concerned with!"

From her position crouched beside the screen, Pat One interrupted. "Fight later, guys. I've got something."

The news screen she had been working over now showed the face of Colonel Hugues duValier, clutching a bracket to keep himself from floating around, and proudly informing the world that he, Colonel duValier, had successfully completed his mission and they were preparing to return to the Kourou base as soon as they were in position for the reentry.

Then the camera panned around the ship. Makalanos saw Hilda's face, peering into the camera, and the German astronauts, and the baffling bits and pieces of alien technology, and the giant, silent figure of the Doc, curiously wearing a sort of metal babushka, but obviously alive and well.

There was a startled shriek from Dopey.

Makalanos turned to him. "What's the matter? He isn't dead, is he? He's all right—"

The little alien seemed stunned. He mewed to himself for a moment, seeming at a loss for words. Then he said: "He is not at all all right, Lieutenant Colonel Makalanos. It is worse than I feared! Something must be done at once!"

Pat One, perched on the arm of Dopey's chair, tried to soothe him. "Take it easy, will you? Look, they'll be back soon, then you can see him yourself, so if you're worried—"

"I am worried, Dr. Adcock! I am extremely worried! Can't you see, the bearer has cut himself off from contact? It is an extremely dangerous situation, and—and—and there is no alternative. He must be destroyed. Please order him shot at once!"

33

Back on the ground, Hilda Morrisey discovered that Kourou had changed. While she and her shipmates were looting the old Starlab the population of the Eurospace complex had exploded. Planes were landing every hour, bringing in more and more people. The planes weren't just any old commercial jobs, either; these were official government aircraft, from forty or fifty different governments, and every one of them was packed with lawyers and high officials and whatever that government could scare up in the way of scientists and engineers to squabble over the loot as it came off the LuftBuran.

That wasn't Hilda's worry. She had done everything she was supposed to do on the orbiter—had prevented any of the others from pocketing any odd little bits of alien technology, had kept a sharp eye for dirty tricks. She had done her job, and now all she wanted was a bath and some clean clothes and a fast plane back to Arlington . . . but Marcus Pell turned out to have other ideas for her.

The deputy director's plane had deposited him and fifteen others on Kourou's landing strip before the LuftBuran touched down. It seemed to Hilda that he had brought enough manpower with him to do everything that still needed to be done, but Pell didn't agree. "You're one of our best agents, Hilda," he told her benignly. "You've had a chance to get to know some of these people. You can talk to them. So talk. Circulate. Find out whatever you can. Leave the bargaining to us. Rest? You can rest later." He paused, his nose wrinkling. "You'd better clean your teeth first, though."

* * *

So Brigadier Morrisey did clean her teeth—again; and rinsed her mouth four or five more times, too, until she was certain that her breath no longer showed any trace of her unfortunate spacesickness. Then she bathed the rest of her as well.

That, however, she was not able to do in the little room the base housing officer had assigned her during training, because that was now occupied by a pair of high-ranking diplomats from Sierra Leone. At that point Merla Tepp earned her pay. She had made friends among members of the spaceport's permanent party while her brigadier was away and had been able to borrow a key to their barracks. Which had showers.

Cleaner, "So where do I sleep?" Hilda asked her aide, putting on a little of Tepp's makeup before a mirror in the washroom.

Tepp seemed preoccupied with something. "Sleep?" she repeated. "Oh, sleep. On the deputy director's plane. I've staked out a couch in the lounge for you; I'll have to sleep on the floor right next to it, if you don't mind." No surprise there. Kourou had run out of facilities for the influx. Now the LuftBuran's longest landing strip, having served its main purpose when the spacecraft came down, was packed nose to tail with aircraft that had been kept on as emergency housing. The Argentinians were the best off, Tepp explained. They didn't need an aircraft to sleep in. They had the luxury of a battle cruiser steaming in circles offshore, with their people helicoptering back and forth. Other countries had ships on their way to join the bedroom fleet. Some of the more important newcomers had rooms or even suites in the hotels of the old town of Kourou itself, a few kilometers down the coast. They commuted. Most of the influx were less fortunate. They were doubling and tripling up in rooms that didn't have air-conditioning against the steamy equatorial heat, and might not even have windows, because they hadn't ever been intended for sleeping in the first place.

It was nearly dark now, the Sun gone over the hills to the west with a sliver of a Moon following its descent. Out over the ocean there were quick illuminations of lightning, though too far away for the thunder to be heard. Over the spaceport itself there were patches of stars. They were obscured by the lights beating down on the little mounds of goods removed from the lander, but Hilda made out the familiar outline of Orion, queerly lying on his side because of their latitude. There was a constant *bzzt-bzzt* of insects frying themselves on the electrified mesh over the lights. Even so, people were slapping at bugs on their necks and arms.

That didn't stop any of them from doing what they were here to do. The bickering was intense and Marcus Pell was in the thick of it, backing up the President's personal representative. Starlab was American property, the President's man was announcing, and so everything on it was American property as well. Nonsense, said everyone else. The goods were treasure trove, belonging to whoever found them and, besides, the United Nations had declared them the common property of all.

Of course, there was no real chance that the lander's cargo was going to be delivered to the UN Building. It would be divided among the world's powers. The bickering here was over how many pieces it would be divided into, and who would get the pieces. Hilda eavesdropped on a group of Germans and Poles arguing about whether the Slavic countries of Europe were entitled to any consideration at all, but really ought to consider themselves part of Eurospace—"We have had enough experience of being part of your space," one of the Poles was saying in German rudimentary enough for Hilda to follow. A few minutes later some Australians and New Zealanders were complaining that the damn Pommies still thought they were a major power, for God's sake. She wandered past the Canadian delegation, speaking urgently among themselves until they caught a glimpse of her uniform. Then they became freezingly silent—still no doubt pissed off because their country hadn't got anything out of letting the U.S. use their landing strip in the first place.

Then she caught a glimpse of Merla Tepp, standing by herself and gazing somberly at something Hilda couldn't quite see. When she got closer she saw that it was the Doc, placidly silent and still wearing his incongruous, metallic old-lady head shawl, with another like it held in one of its lesser arms—*stolid and stunned, brother to the ox,* some old words came to Hilda's mind. If the Doc was at all aware of the ferocious arguments going on all around, he gave no sign.

Tepp held half a sandwich in one hand, and that reminded Hilda that her recently emptied stomach was ready for refilling. "Where'd you get it, Tepp?" she demanded.

Tepp blinked at her, then came back to alertness. "There's a chow line giving them out, ma'am, but it's only this kind of thing. You're entitled to get a decent meal in the deputy director's aircraft."

"I don't want a decent meal. I want one of those. Where's this chow line?"

"Right outside the general mess. But you've got to queue up."

For a moment Hilda considered requisitioning Tepps's remaining half sandwich away from her, but decided against it—not out of any particular consideration for Tepp, but because a chow line was as good a place as any to listen in on talk.

The trouble with doing that was that some of the people at the end of the line were talking to each other in Japanese, others in what seemed to be Pakistani. Hilda wished for the presence of that ugly, but gifted, little turkey, Dopey, as a translator, then caught sight of Jimmy Lin and his two minders coming along to join the line. "Here!" she called, waving. "I've saved you a place!"

That got them all dirty looks from the Pakistanis just behind her, but they didn't push it any farther than that. The minders paid no attention, since there was an irritated-sounding discussion going on between them—in Chinese. They weren't paying much attention to their charge, either, and, after one searching glance, none at all to Hilda Morrisey.

Low-voiced and with one eye on the minders, Hilda asked Lin cordially, "How's it going?"

Lin looked weary and tired. "How would I know? All I know is I want to go home."

"You'll feel better after you get something to eat."

"Eat this slop? Christ, Morrisey, I used to feed my gardener better than this. We were supposed to have our own meals on a submarine, and sleep there, too, but the damn thing never showed up."

That was interesting. "What submarine are you talking about?" she asked, keeping her voice idly conversational.

But that was more than the minders were willing to put up with. One of them broke off their discussion to say something sharp to Lin, who hung his head. "He says I shouldn't be talking to you, so leave me alone," he told Hilda; and that was the end of conversation on the chow line.

It was pretty nearly the end of arguing, too. Everything that could profitably be said in Kourou had been said already. The next step depended on what happened at the United Nations, and only God knew when there would be any decisions there. Gossip said the General Assembly was pulling an all-nighter. Most of the people in Kourou were drifting away toward whatever beds they had been able to find. And Hilda, she abruptly realized, was bone-tired.

The deputy director's airplane was performing a function it had never been designed for. It was meant as luxury transportation for a privileged few, not as a boardinghouse. The overextended galley stewards did their best. They managed to provide a hot meal for everybody, but it was a long way from epicurean. Sleeping on the plane was no pleasure, either. There just weren't enough blankets to go around. Hilda's rank earned her one for her very own, though it wasn't much of a blanket. The thing had started life as a lap robe and covered very little of Hilda herself. Merla Tepp didn't have that much rank. On the floor beside Hilda's couch she made do with somebody's abandoned trench coat thrown over her.

It didn't keep Tepp awake, though. It didn't even keep her from snoring.

At first Hilda almost enjoyed the sound, which was associated in her mind with enjoyable nights of male bedmates, but it quickly got stale. Tepp wasn't male. They hadn't been making love. The noise was only noise, after all, and it was keeping her awake. She reached over to poke Tepp. The woman muttered something incomprehensible without waking, then turned over on her side. The snoring stopped.

Hilda, however, did not go immediately to sleep. Too much had been happening; her mind was racing with the memories of her first venture into space, and the way her familiar world was being remade, without her consent, by these bizarre creatures from other worlds.

Now that they had actual samples of extraterrestrial machines, and the expertise of the Doc to dissect them, the reverse engineering could start. And what then?

It was one thing to contemplate the possible uses of adding Scarecrow technology to the Bureau's already formidable capacities. That could be very fine. Capturing and bugging terrorists and dopers and turning them loose to be unwitting spies; new weapons; instant transportation anywhere by means of these portals . . . why, the Bureau would have more power than any organization before in the world's history. . . .

Except that the damn UN had forced itself into the act, and those same abilities would be given to their enemies.

That thought made her scowl up at the dimly lit ceiling. There had to be some way of keeping a competitive advantage for the Bureau. Well, and for the rest of the United States, too, but the important thing was to keep the NBI several steps ahead of everybody else in the world. Was old man Krieg, the UN American delegate, skillful enough to make that happen? Probably not. Probably the Bureau would have to protect itself, as it always had. . . .

A new sound from Merla Tepp made her turn her head and look down. It wasn't a snore this time. It was more like a sob. Astonished, she saw that Tepp's face was damp with tears.

Now, what was that all about? Was Tepp, too, worrying about the future? But then Tepp turned restlessly, still asleep, and the snoring started again.

That was insupportable. Hilda was confident there was no way she could ever get to sleep with that racket going on half a meter from her ears . . . but then she did.

What woke her was the deputy director's voice snapping through the aircraft's PA system. "Wake up and get going, everybody! The UN has agreed upon a plan and distribution of the items will start in thirty minutes."

For an old hand like Hilda thirty minutes was all the time in the world. She was down the wheeled steps of the plane in less than twenty, and she had even managed to browbeat the sleepy stewards into coffee and a couple of sweet rolls. Of course, that meant she was still wearing the slept-in clothes of the day before and she hadn't even attempted a turn at the aircraft's inadequate showers, but she was awake and ready. It was still dark in Kourou, though there was a faint early glow on the eastern horizon, and it was not yet unbearably hot.

The UN's decision had been to divide the objects from Starlab into four packets. One would go to the United States, on behalf of the whole Western Hemisphere, one to China for the mainland Asian powers, one to the Europeans, one to Australia to be shared with Japan, New Zealand, the island nations of the South Pacific and the countries of Indochina. Possession did not, however, confer ownership. So the UN's edict said firmly; research would be done under multinational supervision, with the resulting data to be made public as soon as obtained.

It was a tribute to the histrionic abilities of the experts and diplomats on the scene that not one of them was laughing out loud. Data to be made public! Hilda had no doubt that when the Bureau's technicians produced data the part that would be made public would be strictly limited, and the most valuable data would stay within the Bureau forever.

The best part was that the UN resolution clearly said the Doc was to be in charge of any real investigation . . . and, Hilda thought comfortably, she knew who was in charge of the Doc. She made her way to where he was being peacefully led out from the shelter in which he had spent the night by his armed guards. Had anyone bothered to tell him what he was supposed to be doing? That did not seem likely. The creature did not even seem curious as, under everyone's watchful eyes, the lucky nationals began removing the bits they had been awarded. He simply stood immobile in rest mode, still wearing the one coppery babushka with the other still held firmly in his lowest-left hand.

United Nations Security Council
Resolution 4408

Under the powers vested in the Security Council by the Charter of the United Nations, as amended, the Secretary General is ordered to execute the following instructions:

1. The artifacts of alien origin are to be divided into four parts, in a manner to be chosen by the Secretary General, each part to be deposited in an appropriate research facility in one of the four specified regions of the world.

2. All investigations into the nature and functions of these artifacts are to be conducted in the presence of a representative of the United Nations and of each of the nations party to said region.

3. Investigations are to be limited to noninvasive procedures until further notice. It is contemplated that the individual identified as "Doc" is to be present when any dismantling is undertaken, provided the individual is physically able to undertake supervision of said artifacts.

—By Order of the Security Council

But that caused a minor fracas, as one of the Indians announced that the extra babushka was definite Scarecrow technology and, as no one else had claimed it, it should be awarded to China for India to share.

Colonel duValier laughed at that. "You want to try to take it away from him?" he sneered.

"Of course it must be taken from him," the Indian replied indignantly. And, when no one volunteered for the job, she reached for it herself.

Well, Hilda could have told the woman that that was a mistake, but by the time Hilda opened her mouth to warn her it was too late. The Doc's eyes sprang open; one of his great upper limbs pushed the Indian delegate out of the way—not violently, but not gently, either. The woman went flying. The Doc didn't look after her. He turned and plodded away in the direction of the parked American aircraft. His armed guards raised their weapons in bafflement, but someone shouted, "For Christ's sake, don't shoot the thing!" The Doc paid no attention to that threat, either, simply strode along with the one metal scarf on his head and the other still clutched in one arm.

"So," the deputy director said pleasantly, to no one in particular, "I guess that settles that."

It did, of course—though, of course, everyone around began arguing vociferously. Hilda didn't wait to take part in the renewed bickering. She hurried after the Doc, now stolidly climbing the steps into the deputy director's jet.

By the time she got inside the Doc was in the lounge, and he was no longer in standby mode. He had commandeered some of the aircraft's monogrammed notepaper and was busily filling pages of it with his meticulous drawings. The crew was passing them around interestedly until one of them caught sight of Hilda, with the deputy director behind her. Then they passed them over to higher authority.

Hilda puzzled over them. The first sketch showed the two Docs together, both wearing shawls over their heads. The second one showed both Docs in what was recognizably a hospital room, one of them doing something surgical to the head of the other. A human woman, actually a quite good likeness of Dr. Marsha Evergood, was standing by. And in the last drawing the former surgeon Doc was himself being operated on, and Dr. Evergood was doing the surgery.

The deputy director looked up at Hilda. "I think," he said judiciously, "that he's trying to tell us he wants to go back to Walter Reed Hospital."

"Well, yes," she said, suddenly thoughtful. "But what's this one here?"

She was pointing to a drawing that showed a human being next to a very peculiar creature. It wasn't a Scarecrow, nor was it any of the Seven Ugly Space Dwarfs. It looked a little bit like some ancient dinosaur, one of the long-necked, long-tailed ones that they called apatosaurus, but it was standing on two legs, and its rubbery neck was hovering menacingly over the human.

"Yes, well," Marcus Pell said, sounding unhappy, "I was wondering about that myself. The man looks kind of like Dan Dannerman, doesn't he?"

"He does. And that other thing—could it be one of those things Dopey calls a Horch?"

34

All the way down on the early flight to Arlington Dannerman was pondering the question: Should he tell Hilda Morrisey that he and Anita Berman were getting married? Or maybe he should just lay the ultimatum on her: either she got his back pay for him, so he could have some kind of decent life, or he quit the Bureau.

Well, she wasn't at the headquarters. She was off at Walter Reed Hospital, and when he tracked her down there she was standing on the loading dock, giving urgent orders to a flock of serious-looking junior agents, and she wasn't interested in his problems. "Resign? Bullshit, Danno. State of emergency; nobody's quitting; I tried the same thing myself. But as long as you're here you might as well be useful."

So five minutes later Dannerman, borrowed stunstick in hand, was marching with five others down a hospital corridor toward the Doc whom, according to Hilda's orders, he was supposed to "restrain." Although the creature was facing them, he didn't seem aware of their presence. He was simply standing there, pale, ugly and immense, in that next-to-dead trance state the things assumed when they had no orders.

But, damn it, the creature was *big*. The stunstick wasn't much comfort to Dannerman. He would have preferred a riot gun, but they weren't supposed to hurt the Doc, only tackle him if he gave any resistance. Even the stunsticks were to be used only as a last resort, because Hilda had warned them that they didn't know enough about a Doc's metabolism to know if the damn thing might kill him.

Dannerman hadn't been that close to a Doc since the flight home from Calgary. He had almost forgotten the spicy-sour stink of the thing, or how preposterous he looked with his foamy "beard" and six ill-assorted arms. The topmost right arm was the one Hilda had assigned for Dannerman to deal with, and naturally it was one of the big, muscular ones. He was just trying to figure out where to grab it when the other Doc appeared, moving quickly and silently toward his twin from behind. He wore that dumb-looking metal-mesh babushka Dannerman had seen on TV and he wasn't alone; just behind him were Hilda and half a dozen more of the Bureau guards, all trying to be as quiet as they could—

Not quiet enough. Or maybe it was that the immobile Doc had caught the scent of his fellow at the last moment; but just as the one with the babushka was reaching out to wrap another length of the material around the target's head the creature sprang into action. And then it got noisy. It didn't matter where Dannerman tried to grab that gorilla-strong upper arm, either. He didn't get the chance. As he was reaching out for it the flailing arm caught him and slammed him straight across the corridor and into a wall.

A dozen human beings turned out to be no match at all for a fighting Doc; but the one with the babushka was another matter. He had one of those great arms around the throat of his twin from behind, and all of the other arms frantically trying to stretch the metal mesh around his head. It didn't happen right away, because the captive Doc was doing everything he could to avoid it; but when the shawl was in place everything stopped. The attacking Doc mewed, a sharp, high-pitched cat's yowl, to the other, who abruptly let go of the unfortunate guard who had managed to grab him. He stood up, shedding guards, mewing back excitedly to the other, adjusting the shawl for himself.

Linguistics Team report
NBI Eyes Only

The task of providing a translation methodology for the language employed by the "Docs" is without precedent in our discipline. There are of course no loan words or cognates, nor any evident grammatical morphology relevant to any Earthly language or dialect. Lacking linguistic markers, our present line of investigation relies on attempts to identify the "words" (or lexically unitary parts of speech) by analyzing such traits as time depth and sound diversity, and to categorize them in the Bu''hlerian three-modality functional model (expression, arousal and description). So far, however, none have been identified.

That seemed to be it, and wonderfully no one appeared to be seriously hurt.

"Let him go!" Hilda gasped, triumphant. "That does it. Is everybody all right? Fine, now we get them down to the operating room."

The operating room didn't look like an operating room anymore; all the usual equipment had been pushed out of the way and something that looked like a torture rack had been constructed on the floor—ten huge metal manacles of varying sizes, bolted to the cement, looking capable of holding an elephant.

Whether they were capable of holding a Doc was another question, and the two of them, yowling those high-pitched feline sounds at each other, were testing them with all their strength. As Dannerman and the others took their gallery seats Hilda was jubilantly explaining what was going on. "See, as long as they've got those things on their heads they're out of Dopey's control, but they've still got some kind of bugs inside them. So what we do now is we operate, only in order to get them they might have to remove the shields, and then— Well, then see for yourself." She pointed proudly at what was going on in the operating room before them. One of the Docs was lying down, while the other fixed the clamps around arms, legs, neck. "So now we're going to do it," Hilda finished with satisfaction, and then looked at Dannerman in a different way. "Come here a minute while they're getting organized," she said. And, when they had moved out of anybody else's earshot: "Listen. Are there any more of you Dannermans around?"

He looked startled. "Jeez, I hope not. Why are you asking?"

She sighed. "I don't really know. It's just that that other Doc's been drawing pictures again, and one of them showed one of you guys along with what looked like a Horch. Any idea what that means?"

"With a *Horch?* No. I never saw any of those."

She looked pensive for a moment. Then she shrugged, and added in a friendlier tone, "Oh, and by the way, Danno, congratulations. Can I be your best man?"

35

Pat Adcock could have counted on the fingers of her two hands the number of times she'd visited anyone in a hospital. If you left out the visits to Pat Five, she probably could have done it on her thumbs; it was not one of her favorite ways of spending an hour.

Pat Five didn't make it any more appealing, either. She was thoroughly sick of her incarceration, and she let everybody know it. "I want some water," she informed Pat at once. "You'll have to hold it for me; I'm not supposed to lift anything."

Pat did as requested, holding the bottle with the flexible straw while Pat Five sipped. Then, thirst quenched, she spent five minutes explaining how she felt, which was weak and bored and wishing the whole damn business was over. Then she wanted to know how things were going at the Observatory, which was a gratifying change of subject. So Pat told her how hard it was to track the actual Scarecrow ship, and how Rosaleen seemed healthier and stronger than ever, thanks, it seemed, to whatever the medical Doc had done to her metabolism back when they were in the Scarecrow captivity, and how the two Docs seemed to have liberated themselves from Scarecrow control and were now helping with the reverse engineering of the things from Starlab.

"Yes, they're very good at taking things apart," Pat Five said bitterly.

Pat said—humbly, because she hadn't experienced what that taking apart was like for herself—"Well, it's not all their fault. They were under Scarecrow control; now they're not."

"I suppose so," Pat Five said, unconvinced. And then there didn't seem to be anything else to talk about.

When Pat finally got out of the sickroom there was still one other chore to take care of. She tracked Pat Five's doctor down as she stood at the nurses' desk, chatting with somebody who seemed to be a dietician.

When Pat asked after Pat Five's condition the doctor said, "Why don't you come into my office?" She was a slim, Oriental-looking woman, perhaps Bengali, but she spoke without an accent. Her office looked like a smaller, less expensive version of Pat's own. Instead of astronomical pictures the doctor's wall screen was running looped views of some kind of surgery—startlingly, not *human* surgery. The doctor noticed where Pat was looking and, slightly embarrassed, flipped the screen off. "It is the removal of the instrument from the Doc," she apologized. "Not my specialty, of course, but it is simply interesting to see that much of alien anatomy, even if only around the neck and skull. Would you like some tea? No?" Then she got down to business. "As to your—ah, sister," she said, for lack of a better word, "her condition is somewhat improved. The fetal heartbeats are good, but we may have to deliver early. It seems she evidently had some pretty rough-and-ready surgery before she became pregnant, as well as malnutrition and a bad time in general early in the pregnancy."

"That she did," said Pat One.

"Yes. It's a great pity. She's a little older than we usually see for a primapara, but if she'd had decent food and care, she could have a dozen babies without any trouble. She's built for it." Her expression was resentful, as though she were angry at Pat Five for not having taken better care of herself. "Well, as it is, there are some problems. We may have to do a C-section, when it comes to that, but the babies will be better off the longer the pregnancy continues. In any case, the prognosis is reasonably good, but we're watching her carefully. Did you have any specific questions?"

And when Pat couldn't think of any the doctor looked embarrassed again. She pulled a copy of Pat Five's chart out of her desk and displayed it hesitantly. On the margins were two signatures, both in Pat's own hand: *Dr. Pat Adcock (Pat Five)* and *Dr. Pat Adcock (Patrice)*. "If you wouldn't mind—just for a souvenir—do you think I could have your autograph as well?"

In the taxi on the way back to the Observatory, her guard mercifully quiet beside her, Pat meditated on her sudden vicarious fame. Was it going to last? How would it affect her life—would she ever be able to have dates again like any normal human being? For that matter, shouldn't she be getting out more now? And—big question!—what was that the doctor had said about having been built to deliver a dozen babies? And if that was true for Pat Five, after all the things the Scarecrows had done to her, how about Pat herself, who shared the identical physiology?

It was a queer, scary-attractive thought. It made something inside her twitch, and she was glad when the cab ride was over and she had to attend to current reality. At the Observatory's reception desk, Janice DuPage was talking to a woman who looked vaguely familiar, and turned out to be Maureen Capobianco, the cruise companion Janice hadn't had. The cruise, however, hadn't been a total success. Capobianco told her they'd had some sort of accident as the ship approached Rio de Janeiro—engine trouble of some kind; they'd lain dead in the water for most of one night, with the antiroll pumps that shifted ballast around not working and the ship heaving uncomfortably in the Atlantic swell and everybody getting seasick. They finally limped into Rio twelve hours late. "So we had a day in Rio," Maureen told her, "but then they canceled the rest of the cruise and flew us home."

"And they're all getting some kind of a refund," Janice said bitterly, "but I got stuck for the whole thing, and I didn't even get to go. Pat? Is it all right if I go out to lunch a little early?"

Whether it was all right or not, Pat felt, she had to say it was—having made Janice miss her cruise because of the "emergency." Once in her own office it didn't take long to find that that emergency search for the Scarecrow scout ship had still produced nothing. On the other hand, it had pretty well ruled out any new spacecraft heading in toward Earth at any immediately worrisome distance, too.

She flipped on the news screen to see if anything else was happening, but the only fresh items that came up had mostly to do with things like the thousands of religious fanatics at that moment demonstrating before the White House, demanding that the President do something—which particular something they wanted done varying from group to group, who were, as usual, fighting among themselves.

She was checking the latest summaries from the "Scarecrow Search" site when, belatedly, she remembered to make an announcement in everybody's mail about Pat Five's condition. A moment later Rosaleen peered in.

"But she's all right?" she asked.

"Hope so. What've you got there?"

The old lady was carrying a hard-copy printout. "Nothing useful," she said. "I've been going over what's been published about the artifacts from Starlab. The people at Camp Smolley have started disassembling the green object."

"Disassembling? But I thought they weren't supposed to do that yet."

"Yes, of course," Rosaleen said impatiently. "You thought they would wait until observers could be present, or some such thing. You have always been quite naive, dear Pat. In any case, I'm damned if I can figure out what that thing is supposed to be doing, much less how it does it. I'd love to get my hands on it—"

"Talk to Dan. Maybe he can arrange it," Pat suggested. "You're one of the best instrument people in the world."

"I'm one of the best instrument people in the world who unfortunately also happens to be a Ukrainian national," Rosaleen pointed out.

Technology Analysis, NBI
Agency Eyes Only
Subject: Tachyon transfer

The so-called "matter transporter" which is used for communications and travel at speeds faster than light does not transport any matter. The device analyzes whatever is to be transported and transmits a sort of "blueprint" by means of the radiation called "tachyons" by some American scientists. (Until the arrival of the aliens, tachyons were known only in theory; none had ever been detected.) There at the receiving station an exact copy is made. Even living creatures may be transported in this way.

There are two unanswered questions about this device. 1, how is the object or person to be transmitted analyzed and encoded? 2, what is the copy made from? It was at first conjectured that the receiver took all the necessary elements from its surroundings and used them to construct the copy. But that does not seem to be the case. According to statements of the human and extraterrestrial witnesses, there does not appear to be any depletion of matter in the vicinity of the receiver, no matter how much mass is transmitted.

"You could at least ask."

Rosaleen grunted. "Maybe. Listen, I've been thinking about how that transporter works."

Pat looked puzzled. "I thought we knew that. It doesn't transmit anything material, only a kind of blueprint of whatever's involved—people, machines, whatever, and then the thing gets constructed at the receiver."

"Right. Out of what?"

"What do you mean, out of what?"

"I mean," Rosaleen said patiently, "suppose you want to transmit a human being. The raw materials in the human body are carbon, nitrogen, oxygen, hydrogen, calcium and about fifty other elements. What if some of those elements don't exist at the receiving station?"

"Um," Pat said, seeing the difficulty.

"Right. So I was talking to Pete Schneyman about it. Do you know what a virtual particle is?"

"Sure. Well," Pat qualified, "sort of."

"Yes, well, I don't remember that quantum stuff all that well, either, and it's been a lot longer for me than for you. So I asked Pete, and he began talking about the Big Bang. First there was nothing, then particles began to be generated spontaneously—"

"I do know about the Big Bang," Pat said.

"Of course you do. But that spontaneous generation of particles goes on all the time, only they don't last: they appear and disappear in tiny fractions of picoseconds. But sometimes they don't. Sometimes they last for a long time—like our universe."

Pat frowned, trying to remember those long-ago graduate-school classes. "You think that's how the Scarecrows do it? Making things out of virtual particles?"

"Pete does. Well, at least he thinks that's *possibly* how they do it."

"But the virtual particles always come in pairs, particles and antiparticles, and they annihilate each other. What would they do with the antiparticles?"

Rosaleen sighed. "Yes," she admitted, "Pete said that was where the problem was. But Pat—I *wish* I could be there and help them figure it all out."

"Um," Pat said, just as the phone rang. She pushed the phone button. "All right, what is it?"

But what it was was a woman in a nurse's uniform. For one scary second Pat thought it was the hospital she had just left, with something terribly wrong with Pat Five.

But it wasn't. Different nurse, different hospital, and the person she was calling about was Janice DuPage. Who had got herself in the way of a drive-by shooters' car—

"Janice has been *shot?*" Pat asked, uncomprehending.

"No, no. She was hit by the car; it was being chased by police and it seems to have run onto the sidewalk where she was walking." The nurse was peering in bewilderment into her own screen, no doubt catching sight of Pat One in the background, and realizing, for the first time, who she was talking to. "She asked us to call."

"Is she—?"

The nurse shook her head. "She'll be all right. She's got, let me see, a fractured right tibia and a good many lacerations and abrasions. She had head injuries, but the skull is intact and it seems to be only a minor concussion. But the woman she was with"—the nurse consulted her screen—"Maureen Capobianco, that is. She's still in surgery. I'm afraid the prognosis for her isn't as good."

36

By the time the Docs were successfully debugged—and by the longer time it took for Dr. Marsha Evergood to be convinced that they were fit to travel—it was too late for Dannerman to catch the night courier flight home. When he called Anita Berman to tell her he'd be late the tracker found her waiting for him at the Observatory. She sounded excited. She didn't complain when he told her his resignation hadn't been accepted. "No, I guess it wouldn't be, would it? We've been watching the news—I even caught a glimpse of you, hon. I think. Anyway, I talked to Zigler again and he's got a new idea. He's thinking about doing your life story."

Dannerman grunted in surprise. "*My* life story?"

"And with you and me playing our own parts, if the Bureau will let you. And the Pats, too. Which reminds me, Patrice wants to talk to you."

What Patrice wanted to talk about was some papers she needed to get Pat One to sign, and as long as he was staying over, would he mind picking them up from the morning courier plane and taking them out to Camp Smelly? "Just as a favor from one movie star to another," she coaxed. And Dannerman was too dazzled to refuse.

He was still dazzled when he woke the next morning. But the place where he woke was in one of the VIP suites in the deep-down headquarters of the National Bureau of Investigation, where he had cadged a room from the duty officer. A quick breakfast in the canteen sobered him up. Having his life story made into a major production was an intoxicating fantasy. Now he faced reality. The Bureau would never allow it. And besides—

Well, something seemed to have changed between Anita Berman

and himself. He couldn't blame the woman for wanting to be a star, even if it was happening only because she was riding on someone else's coattails. Namely his. It didn't mean that she didn't love him, he told himself. Certainly she'd put up with any number of broken dates and unexplained advances, when there was no advantage at all in it for her except her affection for Dan Dannerman.

But she did seem to be pushing pretty hard for this.

He put it out of his mind and headed for breakfast, where he discovered his luck wasn't all the way out. In the canteen he found an old acquaintance, Sherry Walton, once his contact person when he was with the Scuzzhawks. Over their basically flavorless miso soup and their limp toast Dannerman got a chance to catch up on some of the Bureau gossip. A Chinese submarine had gone lost after being driven off from the Scarecrow landing area, and though it had been found again, the Chinese had shot most of its officers. Activity among the world's terrorist bands seemed to have dwindled to a ten-year low. The deputy director was pressuring the President to denounce the United Nations agreement about sharing the Scarecrow technology. And the Bureau's more sporting staffers were getting up a pool on when the next Scarecrow missile would arrive—a less benign one. "Crap," Dannerman said positively. "If they were going to bomb us, they would have done it already."

"Maybe they didn't have time," Walton offered, pouring herself another cup of weak coffee.

"Of course they had time. They sent the food capsule, and the message with it."

"Ah-ha," she said, nodding, "the message. I was talking to some of the experts about that. Did you notice the second part seemed sort of improvised? Like they'd already sent the capsule and timed the message to arrive when it did, and then they found out we were getting ready to board the Starlab? They could be a really long way away, you know. They can't use that instant-transport gadget of theirs without a terminal, so they probably have to use rockets . . . and what if they've already fired off a rocket, and it just hasn't had time to get here yet?"

There was something new at Camp Smolley. The Bureau guards were still in place, so were the rain-soaked protesters across the road, but now there was also a company of blue-helmeted United Nations troops, fully armed, deployed all around the perimeter, and a detachment of the same at the checkpoints. They were thorough. After they put Dannerman through the electronic search and stripped him of his weapons, *all* his weapons, they had just begun. Two of them opened the little satchel of documents Dannerman had picked up from the courier flight, talking to each other in Spanish—these particular UN troops were Chileans, it seemed. They turned every page, one turning while the other held a lamp that pulsed blue, green, white, orange—looking for some suspicious kind of fluorescence, Dannerman supposed—before they gave them back to him and let him proceed. Two more guards, one Bureau and the other UN, convoyed him to an office and took their posts outside the door.

A Space Future for India

When India signed Part Three of the Non-Proliferation Treaty it carried out all of its obligations, including scrapping all of its missiles and bases and, like most nations around the world, abandoning its fledgling space program. It now seems that was an error. As recent developments have shown, the conquest of space is now urgent. The nations which have retained some sort of rudimentary space capability—the Europeans, the Americans, the Chinese—are now confronted with unparalleled economic opportunities and, very possibly, grave military responsibilities. As the second most populous nation on Earth, we should join them forthwith.

—*Hindustan Times,* New Delhi

Pat One was waiting impatiently inside. She wore a quarantine gown and quarantine gloves, and there was a transparent visor hanging loose under her chin. She looked tired. "All this damn *paper,*" she complained when Dannerman handed her the packet. "Couldn't you get us a lawyer that had ever heard about electronics?"

"I got you a lawyer who's going to make you rich," Dannerman pointed out. And while she was signing he looked around. Half a dozen wall screens were displaying interesting things—a news screen by the door, next to it one that showed one of the Docs disassembling a Scarecrow gadget while half a dozen experts stood by, a third screen that showed the other Doc mewing and gesturing as he drew pictures for another group of experts. Pat One looked up. "Those guys are mostly linguists," she said. "We can't talk to the son of a bitch, you know. They're trying to figure out what they call the deep structure of his language, but all he wants to do is draw pictures."

"Can't they get Dopey to help? He's supposed to be a real hotshot with languages."

Pat One shook her head. "He won't help us. He's not even eating, he's so shook up. He won't even tell us what that thing is they're taking apart, he just says the Beloved Leaders are going to punish us all for this."

Dannerman thought uneasily of his breakfast conversation with Sherry Walton. "Did he say how?"

"Not him. Maybe the Doc's trying to tell us something about that, only we can't figure out what. Maybe—" She thought for a moment, then shrugged. "I don't know if I'm supposed to let you see this stuff, but, what the hell, you're a spook yourself, aren't you? Wait a minute. This is Priam Makalanos's office, and I don't know all the systems, but— Here."

She finished playing with the controls on Makalanos's desk, and the pictures on the wall screens changed. They were drawings, done in the Doc's neat draftsmanship. The first one showed the UN Building in New York, then Beijing's Forbidden City, the Arc de Triomphe in Paris, India's Taj Mahal—one after another, the most celebrated sights on Earth. And in all of them there was something that didn't belong there: Scarecrows. Walking around. The pictures weren't photographs, but they were neat and unmistakable drawings of the pumpkin-headed creatures. They were showing Scarecrows present in all the major cities of Earth.

Dannerman frowned at the pictures and shook his head. "It beats me," he said. "It can't mean what it looks like. If there were that many Scarecrows here, we would have seen some trace of them, wouldn't we?"

"It beats me, too," Pat One said somberly. "But I'm sure of one thing. It isn't good."

37

Lawyer Hecksher got to Pat Adcock's office before Dannerman got there with the signed papers, but he didn't seem to mind waiting. He sat in a corner, carefully rereading his papers and making cryptic pencil-on-pad notes for himself, paying no attention to Pat or his surroundings as she went on with her work.

It wasn't a long wait. Dannerman had made a quick trip from the airport, and as Pat went out to meet him she found him standing at the reception desk, his Anita Berman on his arm, chatting with Janice DuPage, who was standing uncomfortably on her crutches.

Pat frowned. She hadn't expected to see Janice there. Then she remembered why. "I thought you were going to your friend's funeral."

Janice looked put-upon. "It's been postponed. Don't ask me why. Some damn kind of red tape."

"Too bad," Pat said absently, taking the clutch of documents from Dannerman and leaving him there.

Mr. Hecksher took the papers from her courteously and spent a good five minutes checking them over. Then he gave her a cheerful smile. "Looks all right. Signed in all the right places. Now, if you'll excuse me, I'll start getting them served."

"Does that mean somebody will have to fly to China and all?"

"China, no. We'll serve that one on their ambassador here, that's what ambassadors are for. But I think we'd better serve the Europeans in person—oh, I see what's on your mind," he added, beaming at her. "You're worried about the costs. Don't worry. It'll all be on the bill when we settle."

"And if we don't settle?" Pat asked.

He looked surprised. "But we will. Did you read the texts you signed? Part of the court submission is a request for an estoppal, ordering them to make no changes in the artifacts already on hand because of the risk of damaging the Observatory's property."

Pat frowned. "They're not going to do that, are they?"

"Exactly, my dear! They're going to want this little problem to go away, and the easiest way to do it is to throw money at us. Oh, I think we'll have an offer to settle within a week; the only question is how much we're willing to take. We should discuss that, of course. I was originally thinking of a hundred million dollars, adjusted for current inflation, with an additional royalty on all commercial devices based on the discovered technology, but—" He paused, listening. "What's that?"

Pat had heard it too, raised voices from outside. She went to the door and looked out. Pete Schneyman was standing there, looking thunderstruck. "We're invaded," he announced. "It's the Feds. They've taken Janice away, and now they want to question all of us."

As soon as Lawyer Hecksher saw what was going on he patted the nearest Pat on the shoulder, and said benevolently, "I'll take care of this."

But he didn't. He went away with the agent in charge and didn't come back. There were at least a dozen new Bureau agents, tough ones. They were full of questions, though what they were questioning everybody about, exactly, they would not say. The first thing they did was to shuttle everybody in the Observatory up to its top floor, with Bureau agents making sure they stayed there. Phones rang unanswered, computer screens beeped impatiently for inputs that didn't come. The Observatory staff milled in the top-floor file rooms and hallways while they were taken, half a dozen at a time, down to the middle floor for interviews.

When it came Pat's turn she was conducted to her own office, where a middle-aged woman had preempted her desk. Now, that was too much! Scowling, she asserted herself: "I protest this unwarranted—"

"Yes, yes," the agent said without patience. "Have a seat. What I want to know is what Janice DuPage has been doing in the last three weeks."

"What happened three weeks ago?" Pat demanded.

"That's when the three weeks I'm asking about began. Just answer the questions, Ms. Adcock. Have you noticed anything unusual about the subject's behavior in that period?"

Pat thought. "You mean, outside of getting run over by a car?"

"Yes."

"Not really. Of course, she was in the hospital for some of that time, and I was away sometimes, too. What do you mean by unusual, anyway?"

"By unusual I mean anything that isn't usual," the agent explained. "Start with Tuesday, the twenty-fourth—"

"Oh, right!" Pat said, enlightenment coming. "That was the day that Scarecrow spacecraft scared us all half to death."

"That day, yes. Well?"

And so it went, day by day. The questions were thorough, but Pat was pretty sure that the agent wasn't getting anything useful—wasn't getting anything from her that she hadn't already heard from the previous interviewees.

When she was released she was told she could go home. She didn't, though. She went down to the lower floor, where the people the agents had finished with were congregating in the conference room.

Then Dannerman came in, looking worried. "I came as soon as I got your call," he told Pat One. "And I talked to Jilly Hohman—she's the agent in charge here."

"So what's it all about?" Pat One demanded.

He looked even more worried. "It's that friend of Janice's. They did a routine autopsy on her . . . and they found a bug."

"A bug? In Janice's friend? But—but she was never out in space," said Pat, and Dannerman nodded somberly.

"That's the problem," he said. "She never was."

38

The news about the bug in the cruise passenger's head caught Hilda Morrisey on the wing. She was halfway to Arlington. For a moment she thought of pulling rank, ordering the pilot to take her back to the scene of this unwelcome new glitch in New York. Reason prevailed. The New York Bureau people were dealing with it, and most of them had recently been her own people. She could leave that to them. Anyway, she could get a better picture at headquarters.

The picture refused to come clear. When all the questioning was done, nobody at the Dannerman Astrophysical Observatory had any useful information about the late Maureen Capobianco. Neither did any of her friends and family once the Bureau had tracked them down. Nor did the X rays find a bug in any of them. It wasn't until they got a passenger list from the operators of her cruise ship that the Bureau struck pay dirt.

That was a break. A checker recognized two of the names on the list as his own neighbors. When the Bureau's people descended on them they were startled but cooperative . . . and the X rays told the story. They, too, were bugged. Both of them. So, when they were tracked down, were the members of a bridge club from Baltimore who had treated themselves to the cruise, all twenty-six of them. So was a barman from the cruise ship, furloughed to his mother's home in the District itself.

So was every last one they could find of the ship's 826 passengers and 651 crew members.

That wasn't all. Hilda Morrisey got the news first and brought it to the deputy director. "There were these six Ecuadorians from a fishing boat that had been near the splash site. They had it, too."

"Shit," Marcus Pell said dismally. "It's an epidemic. We should have anticipated this, Hilda; it's what the Doc was trying to tell us, with those pictures."

"I guess we thought he meant actual Scarecrows were coming."

"I guess we did." He sighed. "All right. Take off for Camp Smelly, Hilda. See if you can get anything out of that damn Dopey."

She stood up to go, then turned. Pell had not seemed all that surprised to hear about the Ecuadorians. "Is there anything else?"

He hesitated, then shrugged. "Keep it under your hat, but yes. We got a report from an asset in Vietnam. The Chinese are rounding up the whole crew of that submarine that went missing. The one where they executed the captain and the engineering officer?" He grimaced. "You know how they execute criminals, one bullet in the back of the neck—so the organs won't be spoiled for transplant. Well, the shot hit a bug."

"Jesus." A thought struck her. "I thought we had our own asset in the Chinese Navy, how come we had to get this from the Viets?"

"They shot our asset, too."

In the back of Brigadier Hilda Morrisey's mind she had been thinking of this as a good time for another recreational evening—a long soak, a light meal, the new dress with the skirt slits that made the best of her still very good legs, the address of a new bar that was highly recommended for good-looking men. It wasn't much to ask. She was fully entitled to it because, for God's sake, she was *human.*

But here she was at Camp Smolley again, and what was in the back of Brigadier Morrisey's mind stayed where it was. The camp was in an uproar. Daisy Fennell was there, giving Colonel Makalanos a hard time for imagined failings at getting more information out of the Docs. All three of the freaks were back at the biowar station, and security precautions were doubled. There was an armed guard at the door of the interrogation room, where the two Docs were vociferously mewing at Dopey. Whatever they were saying, they seemed to think it was urgent, but the little turkey was adamantly refusing to respond, his cat eyes squeezed shut, his little paws thrust firmly into that coppery belly bag. In a corner of the room Dannerman was having an agitated, low-voiced conversation with a woman; it wasn't until Hilda recognized the woman as Anita Berman that she knew which Dannerman it was. The linguistics team was on hand, doing their best to get a clue as to the Docs' language, but if they were making any progress at all, Hilda couldn't see how. It didn't seem that way to her.

Her first target was Dannerman. As she approached, Anita Berman was in the process of jumping up and delivering a final, scathing remark: “I don’t care about the money, I don’t care about the part, what I care about is getting you out of this crazy life you’re leading!” She flounced away, leaving Dannerman peering after her. The funny thing was, he was actually looking pleased.

“What’s that all about?” Hilda asked.

He shook his head. “Something I was worried about, that’s all. Listen, is it true about all these bugs being found?”

“Damn straight it’s true, but that isn’t what I wanted to ask you. Have you had a chance to talk to Dopey about that drawing the Doc made?”

The fond smile evaporated from his face. “Uh, yes,” he said reluctantly. “He said—well, he didn’t say anything for *sure,* only maybe—”

“Damn you! Maybe what?”

He swallowed. “He said he didn’t know anything really, but, after all, the Horch captured everything the Scarecrows had on that planet. Including the transit machine—the one that made copies of us? So if they wanted more copies of me, or anything else, there wouldn’t be anything in the world that could stop them.”

There was a goddam *limit,* Hilda Morrisey told herself, to the number of things she should have to worry about at one time. How many crazinesses were going to be thrown at her? She sat down, trying to collect her thoughts. Merla Tepp appeared from nowhere, silently bearing a cup of coffee, and when Hilda looked at the woman’s face there was one more annoyance staring at her. The woman had the expression of someone more put-upon than was bearable—even more put-upon than Hilda herself, though perhaps for different reasons. (What was it with Tepp? It couldn’t be just the fact that she loathed the aliens. Was there some personal problem? And if there was, who cared?) Hilda put her aide’s problems out of her mind and concentrated on what was going on.

Hilda Morrisey had presided at plenty of interrogations in her career, but never one like this. This time the subjects were doing their best to spill every last thing they knew. In fact, they were doing it nonstop, their mewing voices sometimes plaintive, sometimes yowling mad, but what they were carrying on about no one could say.

It was the translator who was the problem. Dopey was not cooperating. Occasionally he mewed irritably back at the Docs, mostly he merely sat huddled silently on his perch, eyes closed in suffering, tail plume dull and dejected. From where the observers sat on the other side of the one-way glass they could see Patrice, in the interrogation room with the subjects, where she had been for the last hour. She was expostulating with Dopey, but he was ignoring her as well.

Patrice sighed and came out. "I need a break," she said, looking at the linguistics team as they hovered over their frequency analyzers and screens. "You guys getting anything?" she asked.

The head of the team shook her head. "Can't tell." *Well,* Hilda thought, *theirs was a pretty forlorn hope to begin with.* A language was not like a cipher, and all the computers in the world were not likely to solve the translation problem.

While, infuriatingly, the finest translation system the world had ever known was sulking on his perch not a dozen meters away, and refusing to help. "If we could just get a few sentences that were in both languages to match up, we might make a start," the woman said pensively. "Like the Rosetta Stone, you know."

"Damn the Rosetta Stone and damn that goddam freak," Daisy Fennell said. "Don't we have any way to make the little bastard cooperate?"

Patrice Adcock looked almost amused. "What would you suggest? Threaten his life, maybe? But he isn't worrying about dying. He thinks he'd get brownie points with the Scarecrows if he died doing something in their service—like refusing to translate for the Docs."

"Who said anything about dying? He can feel pain, can't he?"

"Oh, no," Patrice said, shaking her head. "Put that idea right out of your mind. I've told you. He's too fragile for us to beat it out of him. You know we actually killed a Dopey, back when we were captives. Didn't take much, either. Martín Delasquez fell on him, and he died." She thought for a moment, then added, "That time it seemed not to have mattered particularly, because another Dopey popped up right away. But now—"

Hilda knew the answer to that. Now they had only the one Dopey, with no magical mystery transporter box to create another if they wasted this one. Hilda appreciated the difficulties of the situation. She appreciated, too, the fact that Vice Deputy Director Daisy Fennell was here to carry the can. That was a break. If anyone was going to be associated with a failed enterprise, she didn't want it to be herself.

She became aware that her aide was clutching the back of her chair. "What is it, Tepp?"

The woman looked even more haggard than usual, her face strained, her demeanor peculiar—in fact, Hilda thought, Tepp had been acting even more than ordinarily strange ever since they got there. “Nothing, ma’am,” she said thickly.

Hilda glared at her. “Nothing, my ass. Are you going to puke again?”

Technology Analysis, NBI
Agency Eyes Only
Subject: “Virtual energy” and tachyon transport

According to quantum theory there is no such thing as a “vacuum” anywhere in the universe. Everywhere—at the heart of a star, on a planet like the Earth, even in the great “voids” between clusters of galaxies—every volume of space, however tiny, is constantly seething with a boil of “virtual” subatomic particles, particles which appear spontaneously, interact with others, are mutually destroyed by canceling each other’s charges out and disappear—so rapidly that they are impossible to detect.

But—theory suggests—they don’t always disappear. In fact, the birth of the universe in the “Big Bang” can be best understood as a sudden explosion of such particles which somehow are not annihilated, but survive, and increase—and, indeed, become everything we see in the vast universe around us.

Is it possible to reproduce this process artificially? If so, can the generated particles be the ones needed to create particular atoms? And, if this is also so, can this be the way the Scarecrows’ tachyon transporter builds the raw materials to make its copies?

Tepp seemed frightened. “Oh, no, ma’am, I don’t think so. But that smell—”

Hilda sighed, resigned. The time had come. She said crisply, “You’re relieved. Get out of here. Go back to Arlington for reassignment.”

“Ma’am!”

“Go!” Hilda ordered, and turned her back on her former aide. Not for long. When she heard a pathetic throat-clearing from behind her, she turned back, now angry. “You still here?”

Tepp held her ground. “Yes, ma’am. I’m going, ma’am, but there’s one thing—”

"For Christ's sake, what now?"

"It's my aunt. I promised I'd come and see her tonight, and I didn't get a chance to call her before we left the headquarters. She's sick. If I could just have permission to use a phone for a minute—"

Hilda shrugged. It wasn't exactly giving permission, but it wasn't a flat rejection, either. As Tepp hurriedly left the little viewing room Hilda didn't even look after her. Merla Tepp was now a dead issue.

She turned to Patrice Adcock. "Didn't Dopey say anything at all when you told him about all the bugs?"

"He was delighted to hear about it," Patrice said sourly. "He asked me half a dozen times if we were sure it was the same kind of bug I had. The Docs were doing their best to ask him what was going on. He mewed something at them, but then he paid no attention to them at all. Then he said to me, 'You'll see,' and went back to not talking. I took that as a threat. I think—"

"Wait a minute," Makalanos said suddenly. He turned to the linguistics crew. "Did you get that? See if you can check what he said to the Docs right then, the first thing after Dr. Adcock told him about the bug."

"Hey," said the linguist, coming alive. "Good point! It might help."

And indeed it might have, but not right then. That was when the interrogation came to an abrupt halt, and it was Merla Tepp who halted it.

39

Outside the zoo cage Merla Tepp took a deep breath, forcing herself to be calm. She wasn't surprised at what had happened. The brigadier had been on the point of firing her often enough before, but she couldn't help wishing it had happened just a little later. She was going to miss the job. She would even miss Hilda Morrisey herself, a wicked woman, certainly, but in some ways an admirable one—

There was no use thinking that way. She knew what she had to do.

She turned her back on the armed guard, who had been looking at her with some concern, and marched to the office of Lieutenant Colonel Makalanos. His assistant, transmitting copies of the Doc's latest drawings to headquarters, looked up in surprise. "Out," Merla ordered. "I have to make a secure call."

The man got up to leave, looking baffled but obedient, and Merla sat before his screen. When she had terminated the assistant's transmission she sat for a moment, moving her lips in silent prayer.

Then she dialed the number in Roanoke, Virginia, and spoke to the placid, gray-haired lady whose face appeared on the screen. "Aunt Billie? I'm really upset. Brigadier Morrisey has fired me as her aide, and I don't know what to do."

The woman looked concerned, though not particularly surprised. She tsk-tsked sympathetically. "That's too bad, dear. I know how you must feel. Is there any chance that she'll change her mind?"

"I don't think so."

"What a pity," the woman said vaguely. She paused, shaking her head in regret. Then she came to a decision. She said, "I'm sorry if I sound a little upset. It's one of my bad days, you see. The left knee and both elbows again—I'm afraid I'll have to have the surgery very soon now."

Tepp caught her breath. "The knee and the two elbows? When?"

"Oh, very soon. As soon as possible, in fact. I wish it weren't necessary, but there's no sense in putting it off any longer, is there?" She was silent for a moment, then, briskly, "I'm afraid I must go now, dear. I'll pray for you."

Tepp terminated the connection and sat for a moment, breathing deeply. Then she stood up and left the office. "Thanks," she said to the assistant, and headed back for the cage. The outside guard had gone back to his daydreaming but he woke up quickly when Tepp ordered: "Give me your weapon."

"Do what? But I can't—"

"It's Brigadier Morrisey's order," she said, taking it from him and checking the safety. "Here, you can ask her yourself." And she pushed the door open.

Inside Hilda Morrisey turned to glare at her. "Now what the hell do you want, Tepp?" she demanded, and then saw the gun.

The guard, suddenly alert, reached for the weapon. Merla Tepp was faster than he was. She stepped back and put a quick round into his right thigh; the man screeched like an owl and collapsed as she set the weapon to full automatic and, sobbing aloud at last, sprayed Hilda and those devil-inspired alien monsters from Hell. She got off half a hundred rounds before she realized that Lieutenant Colonel Makalanos had a gun of his own and he had drawn it.

Too late she turned toward him. When his first shot hit her right in the breastbone it was like being struck with a leaden baseball bat, and that was the last Merla Tepp knew of anything at all in this life.

40

For Daisy Fennell it was the worst night of her long career with the Bureau, and it went on forever. Dr. ben Jayya dithered uselessly over the casualties, protesting that he was a *research* M.D., not a caregiver, but someone had already called the paramedics.

They were there in five minutes, three cars of them, screeching past the startled UN guards with their siren going. It took them a lot longer than that, though, to figure out what to do once they got there. The leg of the wounded guard was all in a day's work for them. So was the lobe of Dannerman's ear, which he had nearly lost to Tepp's spray of fire. For Hilda Morrisey the big problem was stopping the bleeding from her throat, and getting her into one of the ambulances on the very faint chance that she would still be alive when she got to the emergency room.

And there was nothing at all to be done for either Tepp herself or for the one of the Docs who now lay doubled-over on the floor and exuding great amounts of a pinkish fluid, beyond doubt well and truly dead.

It was the other two extraterrestrials that were the problem. Tepp's shot had caught Dopey in his great, colorful fantail. And, though he was complaining bitterly about the agony he was suffering, he had allowed Camp Smolley's medics to dress the wound as best they could. The surviving Doc was another matter. He had taken three of Tepp's rounds. Two were in his left major arm and, though whatever he had for a tibia had been shattered, those wounds didn't seem immediately life-threatening. It was the one that had struck his chest that worried the medics. The bullet was still in there, and he was mewing softly in pain as he lay flat on his back on the floor, with Pat Adcock—Pat One—comfortingly holding one of his lesser paws.

The head medic looked up from where he was bent over the golem's torso, his face grayish. "That bullet has to come out," he informed Daisy Fennell. "Do you authorize us to do it?"

Fennell hesitated, wishing she could buck that question to somebody higher up, like the deputy director. She couldn't. She temporized. "Do you know what you're doing?"

Pat Adcock spoke up. "Of course they don't know what they're doing," she said scornfully. "Why don't you get that Walter Reed doctor out here? She's the only one who knows anything at all about Doc Anatomy."

"Dr. Evergood? But all she did was take a bug out—"

"Do you have any better ideas?"

And, of course, she didn't. When they got Dr. Marsha Evergood she looked tousled and sleepy and pretty damn mad. "Have you stopped the bleeding?" she demanded. "Applied broad-spectrum antibiotics? All right, then get him over to Walter Reed right away; I'll meet you there."

"We thought maybe you might want to come out here," Daisy offered, aware she was sounding uncharacteristically humble.

"Think that one over again, lady. Bring the dead one along, too; I'll use the cadaver for a quick anatomy course. *Now.*"

No matter how much Daisy Fennell tried to hurry him along, Dr. ben Jayya was being a pain in the ass. No laboratory specimen, he was insisting firmly, should ever be transported anywhere until it was stabilized, preferably by soaking it in formaldehyde first, Fennell overfirmed him. "Shut up," she said, and turned her back on the biologist to beckon to Colonel Makalanos.

"Get some ice," she ordered. "Pack him up and let's get the two of them the hell out of here."

The trouble with that was that the medevac chopper was barely able to cope with the weight of the two extraterrestrials, one in his plastic body bag filled with ice cubes, the other with the head medic standing by with spare compresses if needed on the way. Daisy and the Dopey had to wait for another helicopter to be summoned.

When she finally got to Walter Reed the two Docs lay side by side in the operating room. Evergood had already slashed the corpse's torso open and an assistant was severing ribs—what looked like ribs, anyway—with a power bone saw.

It was more than Daisy Fennell wanted to endure. She fled. In the nearest ladies' room she locked herself in a cubicle and sat. She was breathing hard, and most of her thoughts were not about the surgery going on a few dozen meters away.

Reverend Portman Denies Responsibility

At the headquarters of the Christian League Against Blasphemy, their spokesman, the Reverend Alec Portman, declined to be interviewed but issued this prepared statement:

"We deplore the actions at Camp Smolley. If it is true, as has been alleged, that the woman who committed these vile crimes was associated with some members of our organization, she has done our cause no good. It is our belief that these alleged creatures from space are indeed evil, and may be incarnations of the Devil. However, we are nonviolent. We accept no responsibility for these alleged acts. If these creatures had been returned to the Hell they came from, as has been in our prayers ever since they arrived, none of this need have happened."

—*The New York Times*

The subject uppermost in Vice Deputy Fennell's mind was her career, and whether she was still going to have one by this time the next day.

Of course, the whole damn screwup was Hilda Morrisey's fault. Hilda was the one who had taken this Merla Tepp on as her aide and thus given the woman access to biowar.

But Hilda was not in a condition to be put on trial, at least for now, and neither was the Tepp woman. Permanently. That wasn't Fennell's doing; she wasn't the one who shot Tepp dead.

But she was the senior officer present, and so she knew who the responsibility would belong to. She shuddered.

It was bad, but it would get a lot worse if the deputy director arrived and caught her screwing off in the crapper. She stood up, marched to the washstand, splashed water on her face, looked at herself in the mirror, shuddered again and resolutely went back to the operating room.

To her surprise, she was allowed inside, but not before one of the other doctors stopped her with orders to scrub up and put on a surgical mask.

When Daisy protested he snapped, "Right, the Docs didn't bother with asepsis, but we're going to do it Dr. Evergood's way. Use that washstand, and plenty of soap."

The Docs hadn't bothered with anesthesia, either, and there wasn't anything Dr. Evergood could do about that; she didn't dare try putting her patient out, or even numbing the immediate vicinity of the wound. The patient seemed to accept that. The mewing stopped. He lay immobile, eyes closed, and the only sign that he might be feeling pain was the trembling of his lesser arms while Evergood cautiously widened the entrance wound and probed for the bullet. It took her a while to navigate through the unfamiliar architecture of the Doc's muscles and blood vessels, but when she finally extracted the round she breathed a sigh of relief. She doused the whole area with broad-spectrum antibiotics and stood up wearily, regarding her patient.

Who opened his eyes and gazed at her for a moment, then turned to Pat One, miming writing something with his lesser arms.

"He wants to draw some more pictures," Pat guessed. "Can I let him?"

Evergood shrugged. "Why not? Make sure you give him clean paper and a clean pen, and don't let him touch the dressing. Fennell? Let's go talk."

Daisy Fennell was glad enough to get out of there; she hadn't been willing to leave while the operation was going on, but the smell of the Doc was getting to her. They found the deputy director outside, snapping orders to his portable screen in Colonel Makalanos's office, but he switched it off when he saw them.

Evergood got right to the point. "The bullet's out, I've stopped the bleeding and now we have to watch for infection. I'm hoping there won't be any. If there are any disease organisms around, they're probably terrestrial ones, and the antibiotics should deal with them. Of course, we'll have to do something about that arm."

"Thanks," he said, and remembered to add, "A fine job, Dr. Evergood."

It was a dismissal, and the surgeon took it that way. Then he turned to Daisy Fennell.

"Jesus, Daisy," he remarked. "You let things go pretty sour, didn't you? Tepp dead, Morrisey close to it. The Dopey and one of the Docs wounded—and we can't get the other one to care for them, because he's dead, too. Well. Let's get the facts. We'll have to have a court of inquiry, but for now, start talking."

41

The bodies had been removed and the blood mopped up—carefully sponged up with sterile plastic pads, actually, at least the thin, pink stuff that had come out of the Docs, because Dr. ben Jayya demanded every atom of it for his endless lab work. Dan Dannerman, on his second wakeup pill, finally got a chance to reassure Anita Berman. When she saw his bandaged head she gasped in shock. He did his best to reassure her. "No, no, I'm fine. It's nothing. Just my ear." And had to explain that it was just a little piece that was missing. Reattach it? Well, the Bureau surgeon had talked about that when he got there, he admitted, except that by then they couldn't find enough of it to bother with. Which produced another yelp of horror. "Honestly, it doesn't even hurt," he said, and tried to change the subject. "Have you talked to the people at the Observatory? How are things?"

Things at the Observatory were crazy. Rosaleen Artzybachova was upset; did Dannerman know that the Doc that got killed was the one that had saved her life? And was he sure that Patrice and Pat One were all right? And when—pleadingly—were they going to get out of this lousy place?

"As soon as I can," he promised. "Maybe tomorrow. I don't know. There's going to be a court of inquiry and they want me to stick around for that. Trouble? No. I'm not in trouble. Nobody thinks I'm to blame; it's Daisy Fennell that's in trouble here. But I have to testify." He cast about for something more cheerful to say, and found it. He grinned at her. "Listen, one good thing. You wanted to know how you could tell us apart? That won't be a problem anymore. I'm Lop-Ear Dannerman now."

She was silent for a moment, thinking about that. Then she sighed. "All right, hon. Tell me one thing. Have they found out why she did it?"

That was what the whole Bureau was working on at that moment, and their investigation had begun to bear fruit. Tepp's phone call was easily traced, and, since it had been made from a Bureau secure phone, it had been recorded. The receiving party was Mrs. Willa Tepp Borglund, widow lady living by herself in a little house near Roanoke, Virginia; and when the recording was played the conversation was brief and agitated. The actual words between Tepp and her Aunt Billie were trivial enough, but the tones were not. There was an undercurrent of strain and excitement that didn't match the words actually spoken. Well, it was obvious enough to Daisy Fennell. They were talking in code, and the old lady had given her niece the order.

Obvious enough—but too late to be much use.

When the Bureau raided the house of Mrs. Willa Tepp Borglund they found an armory of weapons and an iron-haired, iron-willed old lady who spoke not to them but to her God, praying in whispers every waking moment.

They checked her phones, of course, and found calls to places all over the country. Bureau agents in Wichita and Brooklyn and St. Petersburg and Spokane were pulled away from their smugglers and tax evaders and assembled into raiding parties—two dozen of them in all. It was a massive effort, typical of the wonders the Bureau could accomplish when it put its collective mind to a task.

Of course, it, too, came a little late.

When Dannerman got to see the deputy director, Pell flicked his screen on and fiddled with the pad until it displayed a picture of a dark-skinned man in a fringed leather jacket, stubbornly silent while he was being questioned by Bureau agents. "I thought you'd like to see," he said grimly. "This guy is one of Willa Borglund's phone chums, runs a souvenir shop in Navajo country. According to his phone records he has been making calls to a Chinese trade commission member at his home. Faxes, mostly, and they're all naturally encoded. But what it looks like to me," he said, sounding somber, "is that the damn nuts are all in touch with each other."

"So there really was a leak in the Bureau," Fennell breathed.

"Right. And her name was Merla Tepp."

The keys to deciding whether the universe would ever slow down and recollapse were the Hubble constant—the rate at which the universe was presently expanding—and the associated value called "q-zero," or the rate at which that expansion was slowing down.

The best way to measure the Hubble constant was by studying the most distant observable type 1a supernovae, which, like the Cepheids formerly studied in the same way, could all be assumed to have the same intrinsic brightness, so the dimmer they seemed, the farther they were. The big advantage the supernovae had over the Cepheids was that they were about a million times as bright. Which meant they could be seen, and measured, about a million times as far away; and once you used that fact to estimate their intrinsic brightness and thus their distance, and contrasted that distance with what *should* be their distance as indicated by the redshift of their light, why then you could tell what the q-zero function said about whether the universe's expansion was slowing down.

There were other things you could measure as well, but they all seemed to give the same answer. The universe was not going to recollapse at all. . . .

So what was it that the Horch and the Scarecrows knew that Earthly astronomers hadn't even guessed?

If it was true that Merla Tepp was blatting out Bureau secrets to half the world, it explained a lot—the way the Ukrainian nut cult knew exactly what the plans were for Rosaleen Artzybachova, for instance; the way the protesters always knew where to go. But it also meant that almost everything the Bureau had done since Merla Tepp arrived for duty, or at least everything that Hilda Morrisey might have known about and let her aide in on, was now compromised. And that meant—

That meant some long, hard weeks or months of cleanup and damage control. All of the Bureau's encryption programs would have to be changed. Every field operation would have to double-check personnel and contacts to see how far the leak had spread. Some good, hard administrative work was called for—the very thing that Vice Deputy Director Daisy Fennell was good at. As she went looking for Marcus

Pell she was planning in her mind the series of orders and directives that would have to go out, this minute. . . .

The deputy director didn't seem to want to hear. He was leaning over an assortment of scraps of paper littering Colonel Makalanos's desk, Adcock and Dannerman by his side. Even Dopey was in the room, waddling triumphantly around with the great bandage on his tail hardly hiding its blazing colors. Pell raised a hand to cut off what Daisy Fennell had to say. "Look at this," he said heavily.

There were a dozen of the sheets of paper, arranged in some sort of order. The first showed a recognizable drawing of the food ship. The second showed the ship again, but this time it was attached to a larger metal capsule. The third showed the capsule detaching itself, underwater, while the food container floated on the surface. The fourth showed that larger capsule with five or six others just like it all around it. The fifth showed one of the larger capsules drawn tiny in one corner, with a balloon encircling a host of aliens—a Dopey, several Docs, but three or four other species Fennell had never seen before.

She looked up, puzzled. "I *thought* there should have been more to that food ship!" Dannerman was grumbling, while Pat Adcock explained:

"Those other creatures are other races that work for the Scarecrows. The ones that look a little bit like Bashful? I think they're warriors."

"Warriors?" Fennell rocked back on her heels, regarding the deputy director. "Does all this mean what I think it means?"

"What I think it means," Pell said heavily, "is that some of their terminals came to Earth along with the food, and now they're making more of them—underwater, where we're going to have a hard time finding them." He shook his head. "We didn't understand those other drawings he made for us, did we? He wasn't thinking about the bugs in those people from the ships. He was trying to tell us that the Scarecrows had their people on Earth already, all around us."

THE FAR SHORE OF TIME

For Betty Anne,
as always

ONE

Before

1

We were actually on our way home when it happened. We didn't have any doubt that that was where we were going, and we were, boy, *ready*. We had been months and months in the captivity of a weird alien creature from another world, the one we called Dopey. He was alien, all right. He looked sort of like a large chicken with a kitten's face and a peacock's tail, and he had kidnapped the lot of us—snatched us right out of the old Starlab astronomical satellite and thrown us into some kind of space-traveling machine that whisked us from *here* to some unbelievably distant *there* in no time at all. And *there* was where Dopey kept us, in one damn miserably uncomfortable prison or another, on this unpleasant planet we had never heard of before.

That was a truly nasty experience, but, the way it looked to us at the time, it was *over!* Against the odds, we had escaped! Our chance to get away came when some rival gang of nonhumans, these ones called the "Horch," invaded our prison planet. In the confusion we fought our way to the matter-transmitter thing, and jumped in, and were on our way home. I was the last to climb into the machine. . . .

And I saw the pale lavender flash that meant it was working. . . .

And I came out again. . . .

But I wasn't home at all. The place I was in didn't look at all like Starlab. A pair of those silvery-spidery Horch wheeled fighting machines that had been trying to kill us were standing there, not half a dozen meters away. This time they weren't shooting at me, though. If they had been, I couldn't have shot back, because something I couldn't see grabbed me from behind—no, *enveloped* me, in an all-points hug that didn't let me move a muscle—as I heard the machine's door open again.

Dopey spilled out on top of me, plume all ruffled, little cat eyes glaring around in terror. He took one look at the machines and began to shake. Something hard and painful was pressing behind my right ear. I managed to yell a question at Dopey; and just before the lights went out he sobbed an answer: "Agent Dannerman, we are in the hands of the Horch."

And that was the nastiest, the very nastiest, moment of all.

TWO

Interrogation

2

When I woke up I was lying on a hard, glassy floor. My head felt as though someone had taken a baseball bat to it.

I kept my eyes prudently closed for a moment. I listened, trying to figure out where I was and what I was doing there. All I heard was an occasional skritchy-tinkly sound, like an incomplete set of cheap wind chimes, and now and then a faint whir that sounded a little like skate wheels on a hard floor.

That told me nothing useful, so I took the plunge. I opened my eyes and scrambled to my feet. That made my headache worse, but was the least of my immediate worries. I was in serious trouble.

The room I found myself in was smallish and square, with shiny walls that looked as though they were made of some sort of pale yellow porcelain. There was nothing on the walls—no windows, no decorations—only a couple of doors, both securely closed.

I was not alone in the room.

Two bizarre machines were hovering over a small chest, made out of the same primrose chinaware as the walls. They weren't the spidery Horch fighting machines I'd seen before. What they looked like, more than anything else, was a pair of squat, crystalline Christmas trees. They had spiky glass branches coming off a central trunk, and twigs off the branches, and needles off the twigs—yes, and littler needles coming off the needles, too. For all I knew there were still littler needles than those as well, but I didn't see them. Each of the machines was topped off by a sort of glassy globe, where the angel should have been on a proper Christmas tree, and these were faceted and glittery, like the rotating mirror spheres people rent to cast little spangles of light around a dance floor. One of the things was a pale green, the other a rosy pink. It seemed to me—that was hope speaking, not wisdom—that they looked pretty fragile. Whatever they were up to, I thought, I would have something to say about, because one swift kick would shatter a quorum of their glassy needles.

I was quite wrong about that, of course.

They evidently took notice of the fact that I was awake. The green one did something queer with some of its needles. Clusters of them rearranged themselves, fusing into colorless, faintly glowing lenses pointing in my direction, while the other extended a branch toward something I couldn't see inside the porcelain box.

I must have made a sudden move, because there was a quick, new pang from my head. I reached up to touch the part that hurt and made an unpleasant discovery. Something that didn't belong there was just behind my ear. It was ribbed and hard-surfaced, and faintly warm to the touch, like my own flesh. It seemed to be embedded in my skin. It hadn't been there before, and I didn't like it.

That was when the littler one—its needles were like slivers of shell-pink glass—rolled up close to my face, waving its nearest sprig of needles under my nose.

Then it really surprised me. It spoke to me. It said, "You will be asked questions. Answer them quickly and accurately."

That put a different face on things.

I know it sounds peculiar, but when the machine said that to me it actually made me feel a bit better. Interrogation was something I understood, having done plenty of it myself. I spoke right up. I said, "My name is James Daniel Dannerman. I am a citizen of the United States of America and a senior agent of the American National Bureau of Investigation. I have been a captive of the Beloved Leaders, who are your enemies as well as my own—"

That was as far as I got.

The Christmas tree unhurriedly stuffed a fist of needles into my mouth to shut me up, and the needles weren't fragile at all. They were curiously warm. They didn't hurt, but it was like being gagged with a mouthful of steel wool. It said, "You have not been asked those questions. Answer only the questions you have been asked."

I'm not sure what I tried to say in response. With that glassy bird's nest stuffed in my mouth it only came out as *"wumf,"* but it made the thing remove the needles from my mouth and speak again.

"You will now supply information," the machine said, "concerning the conspecific persons you identify as 'Scuzzhawks.' Did their poor personal hygiene and use of psychoactive materials adversely affect their mortality and reproduction rates?"

3

Of all the things I could have expected to be interrogated about by a Horch machine, that one was about at the bottom of the list.

I did know all about the Scuzzhawks, of course. They were an ultralight plane gang that roamed the American Southwest, scandalizing law-abiding citizens. The Scuzz were more or less based in Orange County, California, but they rallied anywhere from Bakersfield to Tijuana. They didn't bathe much. They didn't wear much, either—there was a limit to how much load their frail little craft could lift, and they reserved most of their carrying capacity for beer and shotgun shells. They painted the wings of their ultralights with obscene slogans; they relieved themselves wherever they felt a need, which was frequently—even while they were airborne, and often enough over the clean, well-kept patios of respectable homeowners. The Scuzzhawks were not nice people. They earned their fuel and food and beer and dope by drug-dealing and petty crime, and sometimes crimes that were not so petty; and early in my career with the Bureau I had been assigned to infiltrate them. That mission hadn't been my choice. When it was over I felt lucky to get out of it alive and generally disease-free.

Why this pink-glassy Christmas tree was asking about them, I could not guess, but the reason didn't matter. The important thing was that it did want to know about them.

That gave me bargaining room. Information is a valuable commodity, worth trading for. I said, "Let's be reasonable here. I'll tell you all you want to know about the Scuzzhawks, but first I have a couple of questions of my own. What's this thing behind my ear?"

The rose-pink one didn't answer that. It simply rolled away on its little wheels to the chinaware chest, where it extruded enough twiglets to open the chest and take something out, while Greenie rolled forward and grabbed me again.

It was strong, too. It held me tightly, but not painfully. I would have guessed that some of those glassy needles would have punctured my skin where they touched. They didn't. Retracted, I supposed, like a playful kitten's claws.

Then I saw what the pink one was carrying toward me, and I felt better right away.

The thing it had taken out of the chest was a helmet of a kind I had seen before. Dopey had given us one when he was our jailer, and it was a truly wonderful little gadget. When I wore it I could tap into the mind of that other Dan Dannerman, the copy of me who had been sent back to Earth, in a marvelous kind of virtual reality. (I'm not talking about the Dan Dannerman who escaped with the others. This was a different one. I'm sorry about that. I know all these copies are confusing . . . especially to me.) With the helmet on I could see what that other Dan was seeing, feel what he was feeling, hear everything he heard. To all intents and purposes I was *there*—not counting that I couldn't *do* anything, just observe.

It had not occurred to me that the same kind of helmet could be used to give me a sort of briefing lecture instead, but if that was what Pinkie had in mind, I was all for it. I said chattily, "That's better. There's no reason for us to argue, is there? We're both on the same side. You work for the Horch. I was taken prisoner by the Beloved Leaders. And the enemy of my enemy is my friend, right?"

Pinkie wasn't listening. It was fitting the helmet over my head, and I didn't resist. I waited complacently until it had flipped the earflaps into position, expecting some sort of lecture with diagrams, or—well, I didn't know exactly what to expect, but I was pretty sure it was going to be helpful in some way.

It wasn't.

It not only wasn't helpful at all, it was bloody awful.

As soon as everything was snapped down I found myself indeed in another place, but it was not any place I would have chosen. I was lying flat on my back, and I was looking up at a couple of the Christmas trees. And I was yelling. The one standing over me was an unfamiliar golden color, and it was methodically ripping my clothes off. I was struggling to stop it, but there wasn't any use to that. I was tightly fettered to a kind of operating table. I couldn't move a muscle.

Not even when Gold-glass began to operate.

It started by pulling out my toenails, one by one.

Then, as my yells of protest turned to agonized screams of pain, it did even worse. With one set of its twiglets it grasped me by my private parts, and with others it began to hack away.

See, the virtual reality those helmets provided didn't feel at all virtual. It felt bloody damn *real*. The pain was real. My screaming was real. I was fully aware that I was, for no reason I could understand, being slowly and painfully tortured to death, and I was bellowing with agony accordingly.

Gold-glass didn't seem to care about my screaming one way or another. It went right on with what it was doing. And then, as it gouged a slit in the skin of my belly from breastbone to the beginnings of my pubic hair, and then began methodically flaying the skin off my body, the pain passed the point of being endurable.

I endured it, though. I kept on enduring it, for much longer than I would have thought possible, until the machine's rummagings in my belly seemed to hit something crucial. Then, I think, I died.

And then the other Christmas tree, the real, pink-colored one, lifted the helmet off my head, and I was once again cowering on that chinaware floor, still screaming, but intact.

I had my clothes on again. I was alive again, and—not counting the headache that still persisted—as far as I could tell, in as good shape as I had ever been, toenails, balls, bowels and all.

That is, *physically* I was all right, though the memory of the pain was nearly as bad as the pain itself. And Pinkie said, "Now you will answer our questions about those conspecific persons called 'Scuzzhawks.' "

4

From then on I answered all its questions, all right. I had learned that that was a good idea. When I hesitated, all it had to do was gesture toward the box with the helmet. Then I stopped hesitating right away.

See, no matter what you've heard, nobody ever holds out against serious, protracted physical torture. The body doesn't allow it. When real agony starts, the body cuts the volitional part of the brain right out of the circuit. It doesn't matter what your intentions are. First you suffer, then you scream, then you do whatever the person inflicting the pain wants you to do, including giving away every secret you ever knew.

Bureau doctrine told us there were things we could sometimes do about it, provided you had a chance to do them—including, as a last resort, biting down on a capsule of one of the Bureau drugs that turn off all physical sensations, so the guy who's interrogating you can do any horrible thing he likes and you just don't feel a thing. Provided, that is, that you've had a chance to get the capsule into your mouth ahead of time. Even that doesn't really solve the problem. You know exactly what is happening when the guy starts inflicting major and irreversible damage on the only body you own. Then you almost certainly talk anyway.

I didn't have to go the way of irreparable body damage. The pain was enough. I talked, and kept on talking, for a very long while.

I don't know how long, exactly. The only way I had of measuring time was by the internal clocks of my belly, bladder and bowels. By their count, that first round of questioning went on forever. I told the glass machines everything there was to tell about the Scuzzhawks, Green-glass taking it all down with his microphones and lenses. That wasn't the end of it. Then Pinkie switched without a pause to questions about the precise nature of their smuggling operation, and what "smuggling" meant in the context of Earth's more or less independent political entities called "nations," each with its own laws about what was forbidden or taxed. And then it wanted a detailed catalogue of all the sorts of things that were smuggled—dope, money for laundering, weapons—and then what the weapons were used for. Which led to many more questions on some large subjects. Crime. Terrorism. Why such aberrations were permitted to continue when they obviously interfered with the orderly workings of government and commerce.

Then, without warning, the lights went out in the camera lenses. The green-glass machine that had been operating them turned to the wall and a door opened. And the pink one said, "Go through there and attend to your biological needs. We will resume when you have finished."

I hesitated. Perhaps I hesitated a moment too long, because my headache was still slowing my reflexes, but the machine wasn't patient. It reached out toward me in a way I didn't like. I turned and hurried to the doorway.

5

The biological-needs room was a twin of the one I'd just left: bare walls of the same yellow chinaware, no windows, no pictures. The big difference was that there were three doors instead of two—all securely locked against my immediate attempts to open them—and in addition to the chinaware chest against the wall (also unopenable by me), there was a pile of food on a low chinaware table.

The food at least was familiar. I had seen it all before. In fact, I had seen a lot of it. We had been living on identically that same grub for months, me and Pat, in all her copies, and Rosaleen Artzybachova and Jimmy Lin and Martín Delasquez. Apart from a few unfamiliar and unappetizing ropy twists of something smelly and purplish, it was the food Dopey had copied for us when we were his prisoners, duplicated from the stores on the Starlab orbiter we had been snatched from. Apples. Corn chips. Heaps of dried or irradiated meals in cans and jars and cartons, every one of which I was totally sick of. When I first saw that pile of rations it made me suddenly aware that I was, as a matter of fact, pretty hungry. When I realized it was the same boring stuff I'd eaten much too much of already, a lot less so.

There were a couple of jugs of water beside the stack of rations. I took a swig out of one of them—it tasted flat, as though it had been distilled—but while that relieved one biological need, it just made another one worse.

I had to pee.

I looked doubtfully at the floor. When we were captives of Dopey and his Beloved Leaders, our cell had this trick floor that doubled as a sewage-removal system. Any waste that hit the floor was absorbed and carried away without leaving even a stain. Even human waste.

This canary-yellow porcelain stuff was something else again. It didn't look promising. However, nature was not to be denied. I selected a corner of the room and let fly; and when I was through I watched, without much optimism, to see if the urine would seep away.

It didn't.

I said, "Shit." All right, that's a trivial thing. But it was one more damn blow, on top of a lot of others. You have to remember that, just hours before, my future had seemed really bright: home, safe, with the dear Pat Adcock I had just discovered I loved.

But I wasn't home. I wasn't safe. Pat was God knew where, and I was worse off than ever. Literally, now I didn't even have a pot to piss in.

So I did the only thing I could do. I fell back on my Bureau training.

I took a deep breath. I crammed some corn chips into my mouth, popped open a random jar (chicken à la king, it was, and really unpleasant in its cold and slimy state). I looked around the room to see if any curious eyes were observing me—didn't matter if they were, of course—and I began to tap systematically at the walls and chest and doors.

Now, why did I do that?

It wasn't out of any real hope. I didn't see that I had an ice cube's chance in Hell of ever getting back to NBI headquarters in Arlington with whatever odd bits of information I might learn through all this poking and prying. I did it anyway, because it was my job.

Back in basic training, the meanest of my drill instructors had explained that to us, while we were lined up, as sweating and stinking and sodden as we were, right after the obstacle course and just before the five-kilometer run. DIs rarely show sympathy. This one had none at all. "What are you, tired? You don't know what tired is yet. You assholes are gonna be a lot worse off than this before you've put your twenty years in! Times you're gonna be exhausted and shitting your pants, but that don't let you off *nothing*. Whatever happens, whatever the bad guys do to you, you do your job. If they beat the piss out of you, if they cut off your balls and gouge out your fuckin' eyes, you don't forget what I'm saying. You ain't paid to give up. You're paid to keep on doing what you're missioned to do, so, if there's a miracle and you get out alive, you can report on every goddam thing you see and hear. Any questions?"

I was stupider in those days. I said, "Sir! How are we going to see anything if they've gouged out our eyes?"

She had an answer for that. She said, "You! Fall down and gimme thirty!"

So—having nothing promising to do—I did what I *could* do.

I knew what I wanted to do. I wanted to get out of this place, and find some way to get back to the transit machine, and zap myself back home. I didn't quite see how I was going to arrange that, but the first step was to gather information.

So I tapped the walls and tried the doors every way I could think of. The doors stayed locked. They were perfectly ordinary doors that swung open on hinges the way a door should do—nothing exotic or super high-tech, except that they didn't seem to have any handles. However I pushed or kicked them, they didn't move. Neither did the lid of the chest, when I went back to that. I didn't give up. I rummaged through the pile of food to see if there was anything hidden under it, and I even took one fairly nauseating taste of the purplish stuff, and I pulled and tugged at the unknown object behind my right ear, trying to figure out what that was all about. I could tell a few things about it. It was about the size of a pigeon's egg. It was smooth-surfaced, either metal or ceramic—when I tapped my fingernail against it, it sounded more ceramic than metal, but I couldn't be sure. It was ribbed, and the skin of my scalp seemed to have grown right around it as though it belonged there, the way your gums surround your teeth.

But that was all I could tell about the thing. So I went back to my tapping and probing, because, even if there wasn't any drill sergeant around to make me do push-ups if I didn't, that was my job. And while I was hard at it, nibbling at some kind of dried fruit bar while I did, one of the doors opened. It let in another couple of those glassy robots—one bronze, one cherry red; I didn't think I had seen either of them before—along with my former captor and present traveling companion, the little alien creature with a body like a peacock and a face like a nasty-minded cat, Dopey.

The robots stood silently communing for a moment, but I didn't see what they were up to. I was looking at Dopey. It was clear that the ugly little creature had been having at least as hard a time as I. His decorous little muumuu was stained and, where it opened for his peacock plume, it was shredded. The plume itself was muddily dark, with none of its usual shifting iridescent colors. Dopey's fur had stains of its own, his belly bag was missing and he was wearing a decoration I hadn't seen before. It was ribbed like my patch and gold in color, which my own might well have been since I couldn't see the thing. The only difference was that his patch was on top of his head instead of behind one ear. He gazed at me blearily out of those kitten eyes and groaned.

"We are in terrible trouble, Agent Dannerman," he informed me. Then he waddled over to the food and began attacking the purplish stuff without another word.

I didn't need to be told that we were in trouble, but there was a good side to it. Now I had someone I could talk to without penalty.

What stopped me was the presence of the Christmas trees. I eyed them warily, but they were ignoring me. They had busied themselves with domestic chores. The cherry-colored one was mopping my little pool of urine from the floor, while the other did something to the porcelain chest that opened it up. Inside the chest was a heap of something that looked like oatmeal. The bronze one tapped the side of the chest with a thrust of branches and pointed another cluster at me. "This is to contain your excrements," it said. "Do not continue to soil the floor." And then the two of them left.

I had been a captive before, but this was the first time I had been given a litter box, like some old lady's pet cat. The place was full of humbling experiences.

But we were alone, and it was my chance to talk to Dopey. I followed him to the food stacks and said, "All right, as you say, we're in trouble. But *where* are we in trouble? And how did we get here?"

He chewed greedily for a moment before he answered. Or didn't answer, actually. He said, still chewing, "If you have eaten all you wish, Agent Dannerman, you would be well advised to sleep now. You may not get many opportunities."

Well, I knew that, but what he said sounded odd to me. I couldn't quite think why. Then I realized that Dopey had spoken to me in English.

That was when I became aware that I hadn't been speaking English with the Christmas-tree machines. I had been talking to them in their own chirpy language, of which, I could have sworn, I had never known a single word.

6

Well, I was exhausted and I still had the residual headache, but I figured out the explanation for that fast enough. It had to be the thing they'd stuck on my head that accounted for my sudden fluency in Horch. The important thing was that, in whatever language, I now had someone who might answer some questions for me.

"Just tell me what happened," I coaxed.

He looked at me, and then at the remainder of his meal. Then he made the body-wriggle that was his version of a shrug. "Very well, but you should have deduced it for yourself, Agent Dannerman. When we entered the transit machine we were transmitted to your Starlab, you and I along with the others. But, of course, once a pattern has been constructed in the machine for transmission, it remains available, so that from that pattern copies may be made at any time. As, you will recall, I had previously made copies of your Dr. Adcock for you."

I didn't have to be reminded of that. I remembered everything there was to remember about Pat Adcock.

"Therefore it should not surprise you that the Horch made copies of us so that we could be questioned."

"But where are we? I certainly don't recognize this place—is it some kind of Horch base?"

"It is now," he said sourly. "Nevertheless it is the same base, on the same planet in the same globular cluster that we were in before. I do not know by what treachery the Horch were able to break into our transmission channels, but it enabled them to surprise and occupy this base—at great cost in lives and matériel, of course, but the Horch do not care about such things. Of course, the Horch have obviously made some changes in the structures to suit their own purposes. I assume from the changes that some time has elapsed since we were transmitted."

"How much time?" I demanded. He just did that body-twitching shrug again. I tried another tack. "About the questioning, Dopey. They're asking some pretty funny questions. Wouldn't you think they'd want to know the important stuff about Earth, like our technology, what kind of weapons we have, like that?"

"But they surely know all those things already, Agent Dannerman," he said, looking surprised. "They are simply filling in gaps in the knowledge obtained from the others of us whom they have already copied and questioned. Did you think we were the first?"

As a matter of fact, that was exactly what I had thought. I wished I could go on thinking it, because if they had questioned other copies of Dopey and of me, it was unpleasantly likely that they had also done the same thing, with the same brutal tactics, to Rosaleen and Jimmy and Martín . . . and to Pat.

To my own Pat.

My own Pat, whom I knew to be a pretty self-willed person when she chose to be. She wouldn't have taken any more guff from the Christmas trees than I had, at first. And then they would have done to her what they did to me.

That was not something I could bear thinking about. While I was thinking about it anyway, because I couldn't help myself, Dopey was going about his own business. He didn't speak to me again. He finished his meal, decorously relieved himself in the litter box, then selected a spot on the floor and crouched down, tucking his head under his plume for a nap.

I couldn't let that happen, because I needed to get the image of Pat being ripped open by a robot out of my mind. I said, "Wait a minute, Dopey."

He pulled his head back out again and regarded me crossly. "You are willful, Agent Dannerman," he complained. "Did you not understand what I said about sleeping when we could?"

"I did, but I wanted to ask you something. Why do they have to torture us?"

That made him wrinkle up his little cat mouth in annoyance. "Because they want truthful answers, of course."

"But can't they just *make* us do whatever they want?" I touched the ribbed thing behind my ear. "By putting some kind of controller in with this language thing?"

He blinked the cat eyes at me. "Controller?"

"Like the one the Beloved Leaders implanted in you," I explained. "So you would have to do whatever they wanted."

He made an indignant noise and stood up straight on his tiny legs, glaring at me. "You are so stupid, Agent Dannerman! Why do you think I have a controller implanted in me by the Beloved Leaders?"

I looked at him in surprise. "Don't you?"

"Of course not! There is no need for that! I am a rational being, as are all of my people, and so we know where our interests lie." His pursy little mouth was twitching and his plume was an angry red, but then he calmed down enough to explain. "The bearers which you call Docs do require such devices to be of value to the Beloved Leaders, because they are very willful beings. The warriors also need to be controlled. The reason for this is that in the course of their duties many of them must inevitably be dispatched to the Eschaton. Although they have been informed that this 'death' is actually a boon, not a tragedy, their natures prevail. They are not able to rid themselves of their instinct for self-preservation which would interfere with their duties. For the rest of us servants of the Beloved Leaders, my people included, self-interest takes a different form. We are glad to obey the Beloved Leaders, because we know what they can do to us if we fail them."

He didn't seem sleepy anymore, just scared. His plume faded to a bilious green as he said, "You do not know the Beloved Leaders, Agent Dannerman. You have never even seen one. I have been more fortunate—not once, but three times. One even spoke to me, though not in person, of course. It was while I was monitoring your planet from the orbiter Starlab, and a Beloved Leader addressed me on a screen to give me an order. I was very frightened, Agent Dannerman. If you are not also frightened, it is because you do not understand the immensity of their power, or the consequences of their wrath. Do you really think your pitiful little planet can withstand the Beloved Leaders? It cannot. As I have told you, you are a fool. Their scout vessels found your Earth once. They will find it again, if indeed they have not already done so.

"It is true that these evil Horch and their machines are also extremely powerful. I do not think they will prevail against the Beloved Leaders, though. When the Eschaton comes, I believe it is the Beloved Leaders who will rule. Rule all of us. For eternity. And oh, Agent Dannerman, I have failed them, and so I am very, very frightened of what that eternity will be."

7

That was the end of Dopey's conversation. He put his head under his plume again and kept it there. I thought I heard him sobbing for a few moments, but then he was quiet.

I fell asleep then, too, not because I wanted to but because I couldn't help it. When the green-glass machine woke me up Dopey was still in his corner, making the faint, muffled snickering sound that did him for snoring, and an idea was forming in my mind.

I didn't have much time to think it out, because Greenie was already snaking one branch of its twiglets under my right arm to get me up, then hustling me back to the interrogation room. But on the way I remembered doctrine.

Basic Bureau tradecraft said that if you couldn't get your interrogators to give you the information you wanted, perhaps you could at least lead the questioning in such a way that even the questions were informative. In practice sessions, back in my training days, it had seemed like something that might work. I'd never tried it in the field, but it was worth a shot. It was something to do, when the only alternative was simply to give up.

It seemed that the machines had heard all they wanted to hear about the Scuzzhawks. Now the topic of the day was sex. What did sexual intercourse feel like? If it was pleasurable, why did some human beings deprive themselves of it? How often had I had sexual intercourse, and under what circumstances, and with what persons, and why? Why was sexual intercourse with another person preferable to masturbation? What forms of sexual experience other than direct stimulation existed, and what did I mean by "fetishism" and "masochism"? How was it possible that some of my conspecifics could achieve sexual gratification just by inflicting pain on others?

I did what I could. I answered every question, and tacked on a little question to each answer. Masturbation: didn't the Horch masturbate? Hugging and kissing: I supposed the Horch had their equivalents. And didn't some Horch get a charge out of hurting other Horch? Without exception, none of my questions got an answer. Mostly they were ignored. Sometimes Greenie cautioned me to stick to straight responses. Twice it gestured toward the porcelain box that held the helmet, which was enough.

And the questioning went on and on. When it stopped at last it was only long enough for me to relieve myself and cram down a few bites of food, and then it started again.

8

I don't know how long the interrogation sessions went on. I tried to keep count of them, but there wasn't much point to that. The number didn't tell me much, because I had no good measure of how many hours each lasted, or how long I was allowed to sleep when I did. I didn't know, either, whether it really mattered for me to keep on sounding the walls, trying to peer past the doors when they were opened, even, once, deliberately falling against one of the Christmas trees to see how they felt. (They didn't feel like anything I had expected. No needle stabs, no feeling of chill glass spikes against my skin; the thing caught me and cradled me as though in an instantly created form-fitting basket of its twigs and set me back on my feet, and I had learned nothing at all.)

I wished for Dopey's presence so I could ask him more questions. That didn't happen often. We seemed to be on different schedules; once when Green-glass woke me up I caught a glimpse of him, sound asleep. But when I was allowed back in the biological-needs room he was gone.

And the questions didn't stop. Sports: how were players selected for football teams, and why would any sentient being risk life and limb in so violent an activity? Currency: What determined how many Japanese yen were given for one American dollar? What caused "inflation"? Why did humans play board games? How was "ownership" of land areas determined? What was the role of the stock market?

And I was reaching the ragged edge of fatigue.

I wasn't getting very far with trying to slip questions in, either. I was pretty sure that the robots were very familiar with that little stratagem, and I thought I knew why: they had dealt with Dan Dannermans before, and they knew our tricks.

Then I thought I saw an opening.

The questioning turned to religion. What was the nature of the religious experience? What evidence did the priests and preachers have for the existence of a "God" or a "Heaven"? Or, for that matter, of a "Hell," or some other form of postlife reward or punishment for transgressions?

And all of a sudden, I saw what I had been waiting for. I had something to tell them that I was pretty sure would dislodge some data for me. "Excuse me," I wheedled, the very model of a prisoner beaten down past the point of resistance, trying to curry favor with his captors, "but if you permit, I can tell you a story from my personal experience that might illuminate some of these questions for you."

Green-glass paused, its needles stirring in silence, apparently thinking that over. Then it spoke.

"Do so," it said.

What I wanted to tell the machine about was a memory of my grandmother, from when I was six or seven years old. That was when my parents began to make me spend a few weeks each summer at Uncle Cubby's place on the Jersey shore.

Uncle Cubby was J. Cuthbert Dannerman, the one with the money. I didn't specially want to be spending summers in his house. Uncle Cubby wanted it, because he liked having kids around now and then, possessing none of his own. And my father, who hadn't done nearly as well with his career as his older brother, wanted me to be there, too, because he was well aware that when Uncle Cubby died there would be a considerable estate for someone to inherit.

Well, that part didn't work out for me, for one reason or another, but those summers in New Jersey turned out not to be so bad. After I had cried myself to sleep for a week or so I began to enjoy myself. My cousin Pat came along most summers, for the same reasons. Unfortunately she was a girl, but at least she was someone to play with, and after a while her gender turned out to be an asset. That was when we discovered some interesting new games, like I'll Show You Mine If You Show Me Yours.

The bad part of the summers was that Grandmother Dannerman was there, too.

Grandmother Dannerman was a dying old woman, but she was taking her time about it. She was bedridden, feeble and incontinent. There was always a faint smell of old-lady pee in her bedroom, although the big windows that looked down to the river were generally open wide. After her fifth or sixth major operation she had got religion, and she wanted me and Pat to have it, too. She explained that when she died she was going to go to Heaven, because she had been a good Christian woman. She fully intended to see us there with her, so once a day, after our naps and before we were allowed to go swim in the river, she taught us Bible stories in her tiny, wheezy voice.

That was a drag. It did make playing Doctor under the boat deck half an hour later a little more exciting, but it never had the effect on us that Grandmother Dannerman intended. She didn't make us want to go to Heaven. She told us there was no sin there, and what was the fun of someplace where you weren't allowed to sin a little?

That was then. This was now, and I thought I had finally found a good use for Grandmother Dannerman's sermons. I told them to the green-glass Christmas tree and, obedient to my training, I did my best to put a little spin on them. The angels in the old lady's Heaven: Were they sort of like the way the Horch would be at the Eschaton? Did the bright, angelic swords of fire correspond to the weapons of the Horch? When we all got there, would we spend our time singing and playing music and never, ever doing anything the Horch might consider a sin?

That's what I tried.

It didn't work very well. Green-glass didn't want questions from me. Green-glass wanted only facts. The first couple of times I tried throwing in a question it simply ignored what I asked. Then it instructed me to stop doing that. And then it got worse.

See, I couldn't stop. I was convinced that I had no other way of gaining information, and I kept on doing it, and so the Christmas tree took its inevitable next step.

That was the second time I got the helmet. It was just as agonizing as before; but it had a surprising result.

I expect I screamed a lot. When Green-glass at last took the helmet off my head and I lay there, shaken and miserable, I saw that something had changed. One of the room's doors had opened. Something I had never seen before was looking in at us.

It was a pretty hideous specimen.

What it looked like, more than anything else, was a scaled-down model of one of the dinosaurs I'd seen in the museums when I was a kid—an apatosaurus, they called that kind—only this one was standing on its hind legs and wearing a kind of lavishly embroidered jogging suit. Its arms weren't like a dinosaur's, though. They were lightly furred and as sinuous as an elephant's trunk, and so was its long, long neck, with a little snaky head at the end of it that darted around inquisitively. It had a round little belly that was covered by a circular patch of embroidered gold—it almost looked like a particularly fancy maternity dress—and I recognized it at once from the pictures Dopey had shown us when we were his captives.

It was the Enemy. I guess my screaming had attracted it, and so I was in the presence of a living, breathing Horch.

When the Horch entered the room the Christmas trees stopped what they were doing, their twiglets turning deferentially toward it. It did not speak to them. It came toward me, arms and neck swaying, and it darted its little head at my face, sniffing and staring into my eyes. Then the long neck whipped the head away and the creature turned toward the door to the biological-needs room. The door opened at once and the Horch passed through, followed by the rosy-pink robot.

What they were doing there, I could not see, though I could hear sounds from inside the room. The Horch and the Christmas tree were twittering to each other, though I couldn't make out the words. There was something else going on, too: squeaking, gasping noises I couldn't identify. Then the Horch came back into the interrogation room, didn't speak, simply left it again through one of the other doors, with that long neck curved back and the snaky little eyes peering at me.

Rosy-pink buzzed back on its little roller-skate wheels to where I lay. It didn't comment on the visit from the living Horch. It didn't resume the questioning, either. "Attend now to your biological needs," it said, and that was the end of that session.

The mystery sounds had come from Dopey. He wasn't alone, either. A bronze-colored Christmas tree was holding him down while a pale yellow one was doing some obviously painful things to him.

It looked like a torture session to me, and that was both surprising and *wrong*. I mean sinfully wrong, a violation of order and propriety. Interrogations didn't take place in the biological-needs room! No prisoner likes to see changes in the rules, because changes are almost always bad, so I squawked a feeble sort of protest. It didn't go any further than that. The pale yellow one extended a clutch of branches menacingly in my direction, and I took the hint. I shut up. I couldn't help watching, though. Every time the machine touched Dopey he twitched and squeaked in pain, though they weren't asking him any questions. Then, abruptly, they released him and rolled out of the room.

As soon as they were gone I knelt beside Dopey. He was breathing hoarsely, obviously hurting. "Are you all right?" I asked.

He turned the kitten eyes on me. "No, Agent Dannerman, I am not all right," he gasped. "Leave me alone."

I couldn't do that. "Did you see that thing? It was a living Horch, wasn't it?"

Dopey gave me a look of disdain. "Of course," he said, pulling himself together. He stood up uncertainly, then limped toward the water jug.

I followed. "You weren't surprised to see him?"

He took his time about answering, drinking from his little cupped hands. It seemed to revive him. "The Horch rule here," he said, licking his lips. "What is surprising if one looks in on our interrogation? Did you expect it to be kinder than its machines?"

As a matter of fact, I had, sort of. "He looked like he was inspecting the way we were treated," I said, unwilling to give up what little hope I could find. "I thought he might do something to help us, maybe."

He gave me a look of contempt and said his favorite thing: "You are a fool, Agent Dannerman. Kindness from a *Horch!*"

"Not kindness," I said stubbornly. "Common sense. If we get sick, we won't be any good to them."

"In which case," he said, "they will simply scrap us and make new copies. Now I wish to sleep."

He looked as though he needed it. "All right," I said reluctantly. "I forgot they'd been torturing you."

He gazed at me with an expression of blended contempt and woe. "Torturing me? No, Agent Dannerman, they were not torturing me. They were doing worse. They were giving me medical treatment to keep me alive. Now let me sleep!"

9

Day followed day, and the pointless, endless questioning went on, on the robots' capricious choice of subjects. Childhood games: How many players were necessary for hide-and-seek? Were Little League baseball players paid like their adult colleagues? Theater: What had Christopher Marlowe written besides *Dr. Faustus* and *The Jew of Malta*? What was the function of the chorus in Greek drama?

Those questions puzzled me at first. I certainly knew a lot about theater, because that's what I had majored in in college, but why did they ask me about the parts I didn't know instead of the early-twentieth-century playwrights I had studied?

It took me several days to figure it out, and when I did the answer gave me no pleasure. The robots had asked all the obvious questions already, but they had asked them of some other Dan Dannerman. As Dopey had said, now they were simply filling in the gaps that remained.

Along about then that living Horch dropped in again on my interrogation. This time he didn't come alone.

The Horch who came with him was female. There was no doubt about that. The evidence was clear, because she was suckling an infant Horch with one pendulous breast, though otherwise the two adults were hard to tell apart. They both wore the colorful jerkins, with soft, flexible half-sleeves over their snaky arms. The only difference in their costumes was that her belly was covered not by embroidered fabric but by a shiny metal dome, almost like a medieval knight's helmet if it hadn't been on the wrong part of her anatomy. When the infant released her breast it dangled over the metal dome until she tucked the breast away and slung the infant under one ropy arm, the baby's little neck swinging foolishly around.

The interrogation had stopped, the robots standing silent and immobile. The two adult Horch paid them no attention. They conferred for a moment, snaky necks almost intertwined and the little rattlesnake heads so close together that I couldn't hear anything. Then the female darted her head in my face. "The least grandson of the Two Eights, Djabeertapritch," she said—I thought that was the name she used, as close as I could make it out—"is of the opinion that your physical state is deteriorating. Is that the case?"

I goggled at her. The last thing I had expected was that a Horch would concern itself with my physical state. While I was puzzling over that, the other Horch took a hand. "It is to your advantage to answer her, Bureau Agent James Daniel Dannerman," he said. "Please respond."

The most startling part of that was the "please," but the other thing that struck me was that, although there was no doubt they were speaking the same language, the male's accent was markedly different. The female's was identical with that of the robots. His was throatier and more drawn out.

I managed to answer. "Yes. They're really giving me a hard time."

"Djabeertapritch is also of the opinion that if you were allowed to rest, however, you might survive indefinitely," the female stated.

I didn't much care for the way that was put, but I managed to answer. "I hope so," I said cautiously, and that was the end of the interview. The two of them marched out without another word, the baby flailing about under its mother's arm, and at once my interrogators returned to life.

"Tell us," Green-glass said, as though there had been no interruption, "why you consider craps a game of skill while roulette is merely chance." And we went right on with the interrogation.

I decided that what the female Horch had said was a good thing, however unattractively it had been put. I almost believed that the Horch were beginning to take an interest in my future. That was encouraging; it suggested that I might actually have one.

But when I saw Dopey again he cackled humorlessly at me. "Do not attribute kindness to the Horch, Agent Dannerman," he advised. "Their motives are their own."

I could see that he hadn't been receiving much kindness from them. His breathing was fast and shallow, and he was clearly in pain. I don't think of myself as a person without compassion. Treacherous little freak that he was, Dopey was still the closest thing I had to a friend anywhere within some distance measured in light-years, and I didn't really want to cause him more suffering.

On the other hand, the thought that I might somehow survive all this had revived my desire to learn whatever might be advantageous to the human race. I said, doing my best to sound sympathetic, "I guess they're forcing you to tell them all kinds of things, Dopey."

"That is a correct assumption, Agent Dannerman."

"Including the things that you wouldn't tell us when we were your prisoners?"

"Including everything. Why do you ask?"

"Because," I said, "if you've been spilling your guts to the Horch robots already, what's the point in keeping secrets from me anymore?"

He considered that grayly for a moment, then gave his wriggly sort of shrug. "Very well, Agent Dannerman. What is it you wish to know?"

I said, "Everything."

"Everything" turned out to include more information than I could grasp in a single session. Since those sessions occurred only at the convenience of the robots, they didn't come very often, either, and they didn't last long when they did. Worse than that, a lot of what Dopey admitted to having told the Christmas trees did nothing for me. I had no particular interest in the dietary needs of the other species who worked for the Beloved Leaders—Docs, fighters, half a dozen other serving races—and when I asked him what part those other weirdos played in the grand Beloved Leaders scheme, his answers made little sense to me.

But the Christmas trees had also asked him in detail about the way he had come to Earth, and that might be worth knowing. It was radio that had done us in. One of the random scouting ships of the Beloved Leaders had detected some early terrestrial broadcasts, and that was the signal they had been looking for. At once the ship changed course, homing in on the radio signals, and we had become targets.

All that took time. How much time, Dopey couldn't tell me with any precision, but from the nature of those first broadcasts—sports events, political speeches, random news programs, and all in AM sound radio only—I figured out that the scout ship had had to be more than a hundred light-years away at the time of detection. Which meant something over a hundred years of travel time for the ship. And sometime along the way, as the ship sniffed its way down the electronic scent trail of humanity, Dopey was dispatched to the ship to begin the task of deciphering what those broadcasts were all about.

"Not just one of me," Dopey clarified. "It is what I am trained for, but the volume of data was too great for a single person to handle. Many broadcasts, from many parts of your planet, and ultimately with vision as well as sound. We eavesdropped on every scrap of voice and picture. Altogether there were seven copies of me, to share the work of deciphering your preposterous number of languages. I do not know what happened to the other six. But I was the one who was tasked to remain on your Starlab orbiter, until you and your party came to investigate."

That was as far as we got in that session, and I was burning with impatience to learn more. When the next chance came, Dopey was looking frailer and closer to his Eschaton than ever. He didn't really want to go on talking to me, but I wasn't willing to let him stop. He told me how the scouting ship had dropped off the pod that attached itself to Starlab, and how they had filled the old satellite with recording and transmission devices. He described the scout ship itself to me—a vessel much larger than Starlab, with a crew of dozens of beings of several different races. And then he became obstinate. "This is all foolishness, Agent Dannerman," he complained. "What is the use of telling you all this, when there is no chance that you can pass it on to your conspecifics?"

I said staunchly, "I'm still alive, Dopey. So there is always a chance."

"But," he said reasonably, "you do not know if your planet still exists. We have no way of knowing how long it has been before these copies of us were made."

I had an answer for that. "It can't be very long," I told him. "If it was all over on Earth, they wouldn't still be asking me all those questions."

He looked at me in surprise. "That is not so. You are forgetting, Agent Dannerman, that the Horch and the Beloved Leaders wish to know everything possible about all intelligent species. Even the extinct ones. It will make them easier to rule at the Eschaton."

10

I wasn't willing to believe that. I couldn't afford to. But it stayed in my mind.

I stripped down and used my wretched underwear for a washcloth, while Dopey watched me with lackluster curiosity. While I was wringing out my shorts and draping them on the edge of the table to dry, I said, "If I only had some clean clothes, I'd almost feel human."

That wasn't entirely true, but I was trying to cheer Dopey up. It didn't work very well. He didn't respond. He just sat there, perched on the far edge of the table, with his eyes half closed and his great peacock fan the color of mud. He had been taking punishment, all right. There were rips in the periphery of his fan that hadn't been there before, and new stains on the jumper he wore. I tried again, encouragingly. "We don't have to give up, you know. There's always a chance to escape."

He didn't answer that, either, just sat there, breathing raggedly. He wasn't asleep. His eyes were more or less open, and he hadn't pulled his fan over his head to shut me out, but he wasn't listening.

I gave up. I spooned some water out of the drinking jug into one of the cups of dehydrated stew, and ate one of the apples while the stew was soaking. I tugged at the lid to the litter box, thinking it might be some kind of weapon if I could get it off. I couldn't.

Then I saw that Dopey had begun to move. He levered himself painfully off the table and waddled slowly over to the water jugs. He drank some, then splashed some over himself.

I took him by his frail little arm and said clearly, "I intend to escape. I need you to help me make a plan."

He grunted without actually answering. I squeezed harder on the arm. "Talk to me!" I demanded.

He wrenched himself free. "If you make a plan," he said, "you are telling the Horch what to expect. Are you an even greater fool than I thought?"

"But—but that was why I asked in English!"

He sighed. "They listen in, no matter what language we speak. Whether we see them or not, they are observing us at all times."

I said, "Hell." Of course it was only an illusion, but I had believed we had at least that much privacy. I shouldn't have. That was a Bureau trick, too. I'd done it myself: after you've interrogated a couple of suspects for a while, you put them together and listen to what they say to each other.

He was talking again. "In any case," he said gloomily, "there is no hope of escape. We will die here, Agent Dannerman, and the next time I see you we will be at the Eschaton."

His certainty was bringing out all the stubbornness in me. "If there's really going to be an Eschaton," I said.

"But of course there will!"

I shook my head at him. "Pat didn't think so, and she's an expert in that subject—"

"An Earth-human expert!" he sneered.

"All the same. Pat said it had been conclusively shown that there wasn't enough mass in the universe to make it contract again. It will go on expanding forever and never shrink down again to the Big Crunch. So no Eschaton. She said there was no doubt about that at all."

Dopey made the gagging rattle in his throat that was his version of a contemptuous laugh. "Your primitive beliefs! Both the Beloved Leaders and the Horch are far, far wiser than Dr. Pat Adcock. There is no question."

He turned his back on me and limped over to gaze without much interest at his purple food. "You don't seem real happy about it," I offered.

He put a small chunk of the stuff in his mouth, chewing unenthusiastically—and sloppily; crumbs were falling to the floor. Then, with his mouth full, he said, "You do not understand, Agent Dannerman. I have betrayed the Beloved Leaders. Their judgment will be sure."

"Oh, maybe not," I said. "It might go the other way, you know. Maybe the Horch will win, and then you won't have to face your Beloved Leaders."

He turned the cat eyes on me mournfully. "Do you think that would be better for me? Or for you, either?" He swallowed the rest of what was in his mouth, then put the remainder of the stuff down. "In any case, Agent Dannerman," he said, "I think I will find out which it is quite soon."

Well, he was right about that.

A few sessions later, when the Christmas trees released me for my pee-and-chow break, I discovered Dopey lying next to the table. His plume dragged limply on the floor. One of his kitten eyes was closed to a slit, and the other queerly distended. Neither was looking at me. And his body was cold.

I shouted, but no one came. When one of the crystal robots did eventually appear, it paid no attention to my dead companion. It only hustled me off to my next interrogation, and when I came back to the room his body was gone.

11

Never mind about the next while. The easy way to describe it is that it was more of the same, but that's not accurate. It was worse. Not only was I now alone, more alone than I had ever been in my life, but too little sleep for too long was doing me in. My thinking was getting fuzzy. Every time I got to the biological-needs room I fell asleep at once, without bothering to eat, and that was not improving my state.

I can't say that I was giving up hope, because I hadn't had all that much hope to begin with, but I was getting too bleary even to think about a future.

And then something did come along.

The Christmas trees' questions had been getting sillier and more erratic than ever. Sometimes both machines stood silent for a few moments, apparently deep in thought, before coming up with some new asininity.

Then, after a particularly lengthy period of cogitation, Pinkie rolled away from me and stood silently beside Green-glass, whose lenses began to disappear. Both machines seemed to shrink into themselves, retracting whole hordes of their finer needles.

Remember, I was staggeringly weary. By the time it registered with me that the robots were in some sort of standby state, and thus in good condition to be attacked, it was too late to do anything about it. The door opened. Three living Horch came in—the one with the funny accent, the female I had seen before and an unfamiliar male, who wore the same gleaming metal belly helmet as the female.

The female darted her head toward Green-glass, I suppose giving it an order I couldn't hear. I didn't have any trouble seeing the results, though. Both Christmas trees sprang into action. They advanced on me and grabbed me, but not as they had done before. This time not all their needles were retracted. They pricked me in a hundred places, and they hurt. I yelped in pain and surprise. That didn't stop them. They investigated most of the parts of my body with their sharp little spikes. Then, without a word, they dropped me to the floor and rolled back to the Horch at the door. There was a low-toned conversation while I was picking myself up, and then the two Horch with the metal belly plates left, the Christmas trees went into standby mode and the one with the embroidered fabric stomacher came toward me. "Bureau Agent James Daniel Dannerman," he said, "the interrogation is terminated. You have been given to me for disposal."

It was the first time I had ever been close enough to a live Horch to touch, so I summoned all the energy I had and grabbed him by the throat. "Tell those robots not to interfere! You're going to take me out of here," I croaked, as menacingly as I could make it.

He didn't seem worried. He didn't need to be. He was a lot stronger than I was. Both of the Christmas trees snapped out of their down mode and sprang forward, but he waved them away. Those ropy arms of his pulled my fingers from his throat without effort.

"Yes, of course," he said. "Transportation has been arranged."

He turned and left through the open door; and, carrying me, the green-glass Christmas tree rolled after him.

THREE

The Compound

12

Outside the interrogation room the Christmas tree waited for a moment while the Horch climbed onto a funny-looking kind of three-wheeled velocipede. He flopped onto it on his back, belly up, with his long neck twisting around so he could see where he was going. Then he whizzed away and we followed.

As before, it wasn't a sight-seeing trip. The machine carried me hugged to its bristly needles, my face pressed so that I could get only gimpses of the scenery, but I recognized it. Dopey was right. The last time I'd seen any of this, it had been shattered and smoking junk, but it was definitely the old Beloved Leaders base, the fires out now and here and there a Christmas tree diligently taking the ruined machinery apart.

The Horch made better time on his tricycle than we did. He was waiting beside it when we arrived and the Christmas tree set me down.

We were at the edge of the built-up base, with that vast, empty, ocher-colored desert in front of us. A different kind of vehicle was parked there, with an alien standing next to it. I recognized the creature as one of the huge, pale, multiarmed ones we called "Docs," but there was something odd about it. It took me a moment to realize what it was; all the Docs I had seen before wore nothing but a kind of jockstrap, while this one was fully clothed.

I turned as I heard a skitter of wheels on pavement behind me—the Christmas tree was skating away, its work here evidently finished—and when I turned back the Horch was looking me over. He sniffed at me with the little nostril slits in his pointy snake nose, then drew his head back to stare into my eyes. "You will be all right, I think," he said. "This medical sapient will take you to a safe place and care for you."

He signaled to the Doc, who picked me up, more gently than the machine, and held me as the Horch came over for a last word. I could feel the breath from its mouth as his head stretched toward me. "Perhaps you will want a name for me. You can call me Beert—" trilling the *r,* clipping the final *t.* "It is the short form of my name, as yours is Dan. Another one called me that before he died."

I was practicing saying the name for myself when he got to the last part. Then I opened my mouth to ask about this "other one," but Beert wasn't listening. "Yes, you say my name quite well. No questions now, please. I have duties to attend to, but I will come to you when I can. In any case, everything will be explained to you, if you survive."

If you survive. These creatures from other planets were great at dropping conversation-stoppers on me.

Helping me to survive appeared to be the Doc's job. He didn't speak, but he laid me down on a bench in the vehicle and began to palp my throat, belly, groin, skull. I didn't see him do anything to make the vehicle start, but while he was poking at me the door closed, the car lurched and, evidently on autopilot, we began to glide away on its air cushion.

The Doc rolled me over and began doing something radical to the small of my back. It didn't hurt, but it felt unwelcome. Then it began to feel a little better.

If I had been a little less bone-weary-frazzled, I might have tried to see where we were going. I didn't. There were no windows operating in the car, and besides, the Doc's ministrations were making me feel a little bit relaxed, for the first time in quite a while.

So I suppose I fell asleep. At least I was surprised when the door opened and I realized the car had stopped.

Another Doc peered in. The two of them, my medic and the new one, mewed at each other in a high-pitched language I had never heard before. Then they helped me out of the car.

I was standing in bright sunshine, with half a dozen of the Docs gathered around to stare at me. The new one spoke. "You are Dannerman," he informed me—well, more accurately, she informed me; it wasn't until a little later that I got the genders straight. "My name is . . ."

Was something I had a lot of trouble pronouncing, much less writing down; it started with a kind of baritone purring sound, then something like clearing the throat, and at the end finishing with a deep-toned hiss; the closest I can come is “Pirraghiz.” “You are safe here,” she went on. “Do you know what this place is?”

I frowned at her. She was rapidly making my pleasant languor evaporate, and that struck me as a stupid question. How would I know what it was?

Then I looked around more carefully, and I did.

There were a couple of strange-looking buildings that I knew I had never seen before. Shiny. Yellow, like the chinaware walls of the interrogation room. Five or six meters high and sort of elliptical in plan, with sides that tapered up from the ground. What they reminded me of mostly was pictures I had seen of the ancient Civil War ironclad, the *Merrimac,* and they were not in the least familiar.

However, that wasn’t all that was in sight. There was a little stream not far away, crossed by stepping-stones. There were trees in the distance. There was something that looked like a primitive stone fireplace. And there was a tepeelike thing that wasn’t exactly a tepee. The last time I’d seen any of those, Jimmy Lin had given them a name. He called them “yurts.”

“Oh, my God,” I said, because, yes, it was a very familiar place. “I lived in those yurts when I was a captive of the Beloved Leaders.”

“That is correct,” Pirraghiz told me gently. “You lived here before. Now you will stay here again while we feed you and try to make you well.”

13

I spent most of the next few days sleeping. As far as I could tell, Pirraghiz never slept at all. Every time I woke up she was there, carrying me to a toilet, spoon-feeding me more of the foods I had been eating for so long, rubbing the small of my back with that special little touch of hers that seemed to be meant to put me back to sleep, and always did.

So for the next forty-eight hours at least, it could have been more, I was pretty much out of it. I was hazily aware that sometimes she was doing other things to me—massaging, poking, cupping my head in her two largest hands—but I didn't know why, except that it felt good. Now and then I know others came into the room to look at me, mostly other Docs, but once or twice, I think, the Horch. Those fuzzy periods of nearly waking didn't last. When Pirraghiz saw that I was wakeful she touched me with one gentle talon and I was gone again.

When the time came that I was very nearly wide-awake, for very nearly an hour or so at a time, I took a closer look at my surroundings.

The bed I was in was comfortable enough, except for being maybe a little firmer than I would have preferred. However, it was built to Doc dimensions, nearly four meters long and more than half that in width. The room was in the same statuesque scale. On the walls there were a couple of mural-like paintings—or still photographs, I couldn't decide which. One was a group of Doc infants at play, the other a misty, idealized scene of a seashore with gentle waves breaking on a pink-sand beach. Elsewhere along the walls were shelves that contained clothes and things—Pirraghiz's, I supposed—and others with spools of a glassy sort of ribbon (the Horch equivalent of books, I found out later). A squat cylindrical thing by the window blew air at me, I supposed for comfort. In recesses in the walls there was a thing like a chromium soup bowl a meter across that was standing on one edge—for what purpose, I did not know—and a couple of smaller bowls of a different kind that were filled with a kind of peat moss. Unfamiliar blue-green buds poked out of the moss. The whole place had a lived-in look. Naturally enough. It was Pirraghiz's own room. She had given it up for me.

When she came to check up on me she was astonished to find me standing up. Before she said anything she carefully felt me all over. Then, more or less satisfied, she allowed me to walk to the toilet on my own.

I haven't said what the toilet was like. There were three of them lined up, huge, Doc-sized things that looked like Chic Sale outhouses on pilings. They were built right over the flowing stream and you got to them by a small bridge. I must have said something that Pirraghiz hadn't expected, because she looked at me curiously. "Are you dissatisfied with the sanitary arrangements?"

"No, of course not. Well, a little surprised, anyway. It's just that the sanitary arrangements don't seem very sanitary. On Earth a lot of people get very upset if they find anyone using the streams for toilets, because of the risk of spreading infection."

That stopped her cold. The snowy, mossy eyebrows went up in astonishment. "Are you telling me," she asked, sounding scandalized, "that your excrement may contain live pathogens?"

"Doesn't everybody's?"

The great bland face was wearing an expression of revulsion. "That is a disgusting concept, Dannerman. No. We will have to provide you with other facilities, for the protection of other species who are downstream from us . . . and you must not excrete into the river anymore."

By the time Pirraghiz was finally letting me feed myself, and did not immediately put me back to sleep as soon as I was finished, I was remembering the lessons my old DI had beaten into me. I had a duty. It was time for me to start scoping this place out, so I insisted on being allowed to go outside.

Physically I was feeling pretty good—no, more than that; I was feeling better than I had in a long time. I was still weak, though. When we came to a short flight of stairs I wasn't really ready for—tall, Doc-sized stairs, they were—Pirraghiz didn't stop to ask permission. She just picked me up and carried me to the outside door, and I was glad she had.

I had not expected it to be night outside.

If I had had any uncertainty about where we were, the sight of that night sky removed it. My dearly beloved astronomy expert, Pat, had suspected that the prison planet we were on was in the middle of a globular cluster which, she said, was a collection of maybe thousands of stars crowded so close together that the whole clutter of them was bound by each other's gravity, sailing around in complex orbits and all very, very near all the rest. There were certainly hundreds in that overhead night sky that were very near to us: giant brilliant lightbulbs hanging in the heavens, blue and red and yellow and white and all the shades in between. At least a dozen of them were as bright as the Moon from Earth, and a couple so incredibly bright that I squinted when I looked at them. In one corner of the sky there was a cobwebby film of white, brighter than the Milky Way. It wasn't anything like the Milky Way, though, according to Pat. The Milky Way was made up of millions and billions of individual stars, so distant that their light smeared together into a luminous blur. This stuff, she thought, was masses of gas and plasma that some of the stars were stealing from each other.

Pat had had something else to say about this display. According to her, in a globular cluster novas and supernovas might be relatively common, and when a star exploded in one of those ways it was likely to release floods of seriously damaging radiation, with very bad results for any living thing nearby.

When I said something about that to Pirraghiz, she said, "Of course that is so, Dannerman. Showers of deadly radiation are quite frequent. That is why the Horch restored the protective shield over this planet as soon as they finished occupying the base. It was down for only a few days, but in that time many persons of many species died from it." Then she touched my throat with one of her lesser arms and frowned. "You are being too active for your first time out. Come back. You can eat, and then you should rest some more. There will be plenty of time to explore."

I didn't actually need to do a lot of exploring. I already knew this place very well.

Before we escaped back to Earth—I mean, before the ones of us that did successfully escape did—we had spent a lot of time here. It was a prison, or zoo, where the Beloved Leaders kept a few samples of the sentient races they had met—and, often, exterminated. We lived in the yurts, but we didn't build them. Some others had lived here before us and, we guessed, died here too, because all that remained of them was their works.

Now the compound belonged to the liberated Docs, or at least to the thirty or so surviving ones that had managed to escape being killed in the fighting. The Docs looked a lot different now. The ones I had been used to seeing were silent; they obeyed orders, and when no orders were given they stood frozen, waiting for the next command. These present Docs were never still, as they worked around the compound, chattering back and forth in their high, chirpy voices. And they were fully clothed. They wore decorous trousers over their lower parts, and above the waist a sort of loose, gaily colored blouse, with sleeves for all six of their arms. Each wore a huge, floppy hat to keep the sun away.

As I peered inside the surviving yurt—it looked like the one we had kept our food in, but it was empty now—I felt that gentle touch on my neck. I turned. It was Pirraghiz, of course, once more taking my pulse or whatever it was she did when she touched me there. "Are you getting tired?" she asked anxiously.

I assured her I wasn't, though I was pretty certain she knew my condition better than I did. I pointed to the yurt. "How come you left this one standing?"

She looked faintly embarrassed, or as much so as a creature with a great, moss-covered moon of a face could look. "It did not seem right to remove them all. The people who built them are gone, and there was no other way to remember them. I know this is not a sensible thing, Dannerman." Then she patted my shoulder with a lesser hand. It wasn't a medicinal touch, this one, or even a particularly affectionate one. It was the way your mother might put her hand on your shoulder when she wants your full attention. "I have a question for you, Dannerman. You have been all over this area, looking at everything. Yet you have seen almost everything here before, so what is it that you are looking for?"

The truthful answer was, a way to get out of here and go home. I was pretty sure she suspected as much. But I didn't want to confirm it for her, and anyway there was something else I'd been hoping to find.

So I told her the other thing: "A grave. A friend of mine died here. Her name was Patsy, and she was killed by some electric amphibians. We buried her around here."

She bought it without question. She patted me again, consolingly this time, and said, "I will lead you to it."

The plot was farther away from the yurts than I'd remembered, but

I recognized it at once. The ground had settled a little—which suggested to me that some time had elapsed before the Horch whipped up this present copy of me—but you could see where it was. Touchingly, someone—I was willing to bet it had been Pirraghiz—had put one of those flower bowls on it.

However, it wasn't alone. There was another plot beside it, a little less sunken, with its own little bowl of pale buds.

When I asked Pirraghiz she looked at me mournfully. "He was another copy of you, Dannerman. Djabeertapritch begged for him when the machines decided it was better to abandon him and make a fresh one. They let Djabeertapritch have him, but he was too far gone for us to make well. He died; and we buried him next to your friend."

Pirraghiz was about as tactful a nonhuman as I'd ever met. Well, that doesn't say much, considering who the other nonhumans were, but she was a good scout. She ambled away, leaving me to mourn for my dead other self.

I don't think that is exactly what I was doing, though. I was thinking about funerals of Bureau agents.

When an agent is buried he's entitled to a military ceremony, complete with the rifle volley from the honor guard and the bugler playing Taps and all. He usually gets it, too, except when they haven't found enough of him to bury.

I couldn't provide any of that for this other me, but Taps kept running through my mind. There are words to the melody, a fact that most people don't seem to know, and the last line of the song says, "All is well. Safely rest. God is nigh."

I guess a little of Grandmother Dannerman's Bible lessons had rubbed off on me after all, because I was certainly hoping that was true.

14

As my strength began to come back I got serious about my duties as an agent of the NBI. I would need to be in the best possible physical shape if an opportunity to escape ever turned up, so I began systematic exercises. That worried Pirraghiz a little at first because she wasn't sure doing jump-squats was good for me, but she finally stopped objecting. And I got more diligent about spying again.

Pirraghiz had the right of it when she said I'd seen about as much of the compound grounds as there was to see. The inside of their two-story longhouses was a different matter. There might well be some kinds of technology there that were worth knowing about, so I spent some time pondering over them.

I figured out what some of the domestic appliances were for easily enough. The desk was a desk—probably. Its surface was a mosaic of squares the size of my palm, but it had nothing on it except some stacks of my food rations, and no drawers to open. The bowl-shaped object that stood on its rim in the wall turned out to be a kind of TV, though I didn't know how to turn it on. The stubby, purring cylinder on the floor was, as I had guessed, a kind of air conditioner. It had some unfamiliar features: It not only wafted warm air into the room when the night grew chilly, and cool air in the heat of the day, but the scents that came out of it varied with the temperature of the air. They smelled meaty and almost sweaty at night and like fresh-cut greenery during daylight.

That was interesting, but not the kind of thing the Bureau would be wild to hear about—assuming I ever got the chance to see Arlington again. The real puzzle about all this machinery was where the power came from. There weren't any wall outlets, or cables going to them; but they kept on going anyway.

I found Pirraghiz outside and asked her about it. She didn't seem to object to my curiosity, but she wasn't much help, either. She seemed preoccupied, gazing toward the stream where two other Docs were standing. "I am only biomedical, Dannerman," she explained. "I know nothing of mechanical things. Mrrranthoghrow might know."

"And who is Mrr—Mrrran—"

"Mrrranthoghrow, Dannerman. He is a friend. He comes here sometimes, and you can ask him if you like. For now, would you like me to show how the picture bowl works?"

She was still gazing toward the creek. "Yes, please," I said, and then I saw what she and the other Docs were looking at. I thought at first that it was one of the flat rocks that were used as stepping-stones across the water, though this one was of an odd greenish color.

Then the rock moved. It erected stalked eyes to peer at the nearby Docs. Then it raised itself on short, splayed legs and walked away.

I turned to Pirraghiz. "What the hell was *that?*"

"Ah," she said, understanding. "You have never met a Shelled Person before, have you?" And when I asked what a Shelled Person was doing here among the Docs, she was amused. "Is that hard to understand, Dannerman? All we species were enslaved one way or another by the Others. Why should we not talk to one another now and then?"

That sounded interesting. "Can I talk with them, too?"

"Not in this case, no. She has no language you could understand. Some of the other species do, and if one comes here, I will tell you. Now I will show you how to work the picture bowl."

Turning the picture bowl on was easy, once you knew how. I had been looking for controls on the bowl itself, but there weren't any. They were in the desk. You moved a section of the top aside in the right way, and it uncovered a sort of clockface, tiny holes arranged in a circle with what might have been numbers inscribed over each. The numbers were meaningless to me. The little holes weren't much help at first, either. Pirraghiz showed me how they worked by delicately extruding a claw to poke into them, but I didn't have a claw.

The first thing Pirraghiz showed me in the bowl was the planet we were on. It appeared like a globe, in three dimensions, in the bowl, and she showed that it could be rotated or zoomed in. "This is where we are," she announced, pointing with a lesser arm.

It looked like a park, seen from above. I recognized the familiar hexagonal patterns that had been enforced by the Beloved Leaders' energy walls, imprisoning each group of us in our own little space. Now those walls were vanished, but lines of abrupt discontinuities in the kinds of vegetation showed where they had stood.

Some of the plants looked to be in bad shape, and when I said as much to Pirraghiz, she said, "Of course, Dannerman. When the shield was down the radiation killed many things, and not simply plants." There had been nine captive species in the zoo of the Beloved Leaders. Some of them had come from worlds with a higher concentration of oxygen than this place, and so extra allotments had been routinely pumped into their enclaves. When everything broke down the oxygen stopped, and one whole species—Pirraghiz called them Tree-Livers—had gasped and died. Two others had needed extra humidity for their health, which had been supplied in the same way. Most of those species had survived. "But they are not comfortable away from their own areas," Pirraghiz informed me. "So you will not see them here."

I stared at the picture of the planet. Outside of the enclaves everything around was the rust-colored, arid rock and sand. It was not an attractive planet. "Why do you suppose the Horch bothered to take this place over?" I asked.

Pirraghiz sighed. "I do not know. The Horch do not tell us everything. Simply because the Others had it, perhaps."

"And why did the Beloved Leaders have it in the first place?" I asked, covering a yawn.

"Perhaps because it is so hostile to living things. Apart from their preserves, there was no place on it for the captive species to escape to," she said, but she hadn't missed the yawn. "Are you overtired again?" she asked fretfully. And then, "Hold still."

She pinched a fold of my belly flesh in her surprisingly gentle paws, the claws considerately retracted. The results made her give a disapproving lip-smack. "You must gain more body fat, Dannerman. You must eat more."

"I'm getting pretty tired of corn chips and spaghetti bolognese," I complained.

She said defensively, "I added water and heated it, precisely following the instructions on the container." I shrugged. She looked thoughtful for a moment, then turned off the picture bowl. She opened some of the food containers that had come from the Starlab store and, one by one, fished out a tiny crumb from each. She tasted them experimentally.

"I see," she said at last. "Wait for a moment, Dannerman."

She was gone for a lot more than a moment, and when she came back all six arms were carrying packets and clumps of strange-looking vegetable things. "Taste this," she ordered, holding out an object that looked like a small, sky-blue corncob with the kernels removed.

I looked at it with skepticism. "How do I know it won't poison me?" I demanded.

She gave me a surprised stare. "But did you not see me analyzing your food? These are quite compatible with your dietary needs. Also I am right here, in case there is any unexpected adverse effect."

Actually, it wasn't bad, tasting a little like a very mild onion. She opened up a pot of thick stuff the consistency of honey and advised me to dip the cob into it; it was peppery and rather good. Becoming adventurous, I reached for a fruit she had split open, spiky on the outside, round and reddish within, but she snatched it out of my hands. "One moment, Dannerman. Wait."

Then I saw another way in which those little retractable talons were useful. The fruit was full of tiny greenish seeds. She quickly coaxed them out with her claws, one after another. Then she handed the fruit to me. It was moist and cool, and it tasted vaguely of roasted chestnuts. Pirraghiz looked approving. "Now it is safe, Dannerman, but you must never eat the seeds. The other one of you did, by accident. Perhaps he would have lived if he had not. Now try this—" handing me a sort of lemon-colored potato. "it will make you sleepy, and so you will rest."

The new food was an improvement, and so was the picture bowl. That looked like a spy's dream of a bonanza: I figured I could roam around the channels and learn everything there was to know about the Horch. That was borrowing a page from Dopey's book; it was just what he had done about the Earth when he was monitoring all of our broadcasts from Starlab.

That had worked out for Dopey. It didn't for me. I managed to work the controls with a toothpick-sized scrap of ceramic Pirraghiz found for me. I picked channels more or less at random, not knowing any other way to do it. Most of them were incomprehensible to me. There were a lot of what I supposed were the entertainments of the Horch, something like choir singing, something like No plays. They didn't entertain me. There were scenes of what probably were a number of different planets, or different parts of the same planet. Those had voice-over commentaries, all right, and those might have given me a lot of information if I could have understood them. I couldn't. They were in the high-pitched and totally incomprehensible language of the Docs.

There was certainly data to be got from the bowl. I just didn't know how to go about getting it. And then, while I was scowling at a particularly uninformative view—a pair of Horch were silently playing some sort of board game—the picture bowl beeped at me. The game-players disappeared, and another Horch was staring out of the bowl at me. "Hello, Dan," he said, and I realized it was my friend—or my captor—or, actually, my savior—the one named Djabeertapritch.

Evidently the picture bowl doubled as some kind of communications device. I said guardedly, "Hello, Beert."

If he detected anything in my tone, he didn't show it. He said, "I am sorry I have not been able to visit you in person, Dan. There is much I am trying to learn from our Horch cousins, so I must spend much time with them. Also with some projects of my own. We will have more time together when you come to our nest."

It was the first I had heard that he planned to move me again. "When will that be?"

"When you are fully recovered. Are you feeling better now, Dan?"

"Quite a lot," I admitted.

"That is good," he said, sounding as though his mind was elsewhere. "Now there is someone I wish you to meet," he added more briskly, getting to the point. "I have a reason for this. Go outside now. Pirraghiz is waiting to take you to him. Good-by."

That was the end of the conversation. Beert disappeared, and I was looking at the Horch game-players again.

When I had turned off the picture bowl and climbed down the stairs, Pirraghiz was hurrying toward me. "It is a Wet One, Dannerman," she told me, taking my arm to speed me along. "He has language, so you can speak to him. Come, he is in the creek."

Perhaps that should have warned me. It didn't. We were almost to the stream when I saw that someone was half submerged in the water.

Only it wasn't a someone. It was a slate-gray creature the size of a hippopotamus. It had a writhing Medusa mustache of tentacles around its mouth, and it wore a collar. I knew it well. I tugged myself free of Pirraghiz's arm and walked away, shaking. I couldn't help it.

Pirraghiz came after me, put one hand worriedly on my throat, bent to peer into my face. The great pale face was puzzled. "You are upset, Dannerman. What is wrong?"

I pointed to the amphibian. "That's wrong. Those things murdered a friend of mine. Her name was Patsy, and she's the one who is buried next to the other one of me. She was bathing. She didn't even know there were any of those things in the water, but there was a scuffle and they electrocuted her."

She stood for a moment, looking from me to the amphibian. "So you won't even talk to this Wet One?"

"I won't."

"Djabeertapritch wishes it," she wheedled.

"No."

She sighed. "This episode was certainly unfortunate," she said reasonably, "but it is an event in the past. It is true that the Wet Ones use an electric charge for defense, but only when they feel threatened. This one will not attack you, Dannerman."

"I won't give it the chance."

She stood there, looking down at me. "You cannot forgive that incident?"

I shook my head. "Forget it, never. Forgive it—maybe later. But not now."

She was silent for a moment. Then she said sadly, "Then can you forgive me, Dannerman?"

I stared at her. "For what?"

She seemed reluctant to speak, but she sighed again and went on. "You know that there were other copies of yourself and your comrades, and that they were examined physically?"

I did know. I knew what those physical examinations were like, too, because Pat Five had gone through them and she told me. I felt a flush of remembered rage. "You mean they were vivisected," I said.

"Yes, that is true," she said, her tone mournful. "What is also true is that I was one of the ones who did the vivisection, Dannerman."

15

Was I angry at Pirraghiz? You bet I was. In fact, "angry" wasn't a strong enough word; I was seething with rage. My nursemaid and pal was one of the torturers who had cut up the helpless bodies of my living, screaming friends. The first thing I thought of doing was to find the nearest rock and pound her head bloody with it.

I didn't exactly do that. I did pick up a rock, but I didn't attack Pirraghiz with it. I threw it as hard as I could at the nearest tree, and then I stalked away, leaving her gazing unhappily at my back.

I didn't look back. I kept right on walking, right out of the compound along one of the ancient trails that wound through the woods. It had rained during the night, and the footing was still a little slippery. I suspected Pirraghiz was trailing after me, but I didn't turn around. I didn't want to talk to one of the creatures who had carved up my friends—and me!—bit by bit, while they were wide-awake and screaming, just to see what made them tick. As you might do with an unfamiliar machine, and with no more regard for the machine's feelings. What I had gone through with the Christmas trees' helmet didn't compare to their ordeal. It didn't bear thinking about.

So I did my best not to think about it. It didn't matter. What mattered was getting out of there, and there was only one way to do that. The transit machine was obviously still working—the Horch machines had used it to make me. My job was to get back to it, and away.

But I couldn't do it without help. And the only help around was the person who was silently following along the trail, no more than eight or ten meters behind.

So I turned around and beckoned to Pirraghiz. "I'm sorry," I told her as she approached. "I overreacted. It was a shock to me, that's all. I understand that you couldn't help yourself."

She looked at me warily. "Do you understand, Dannerman?" she asked.

I patted her great upper arm. "I do, Pirraghiz. You had a control implanted in your brain, and you had to do whatever the Beloved Leaders wanted."

"Yes, but do you *understand?* Do you know what it is like to be *owned?*"

There was an expression on Pirraghiz's face that I had never seen there before; I couldn't tell whether it was sorrow or implacable anger. "Well—maybe not, exactly."

"But you should know, Dannerman," she told me sternly. "What happened to us may happen to your own people, in exactly the same way. We were not always slaves of the Beloved Leaders. We had our own lives, on our own planet—that was many eights of eights of generations ago, and we have only stories to remind us of what it was like. But it was a good life—I think—and then the Beloved Leaders came, and they saw a use for us. We were a clever people. We still are."

She paused to give me a challenging look. I said, "Of course you are. I know that."

"But do you also know what it is like to be clever, and to be *owned?* Under the Beloved Leaders we could do almost nothing they did not order us to do. Most of the time we could not even speak to each other, only when we were very young, or when we were permitted to breed."

That surprised me. "Breed? I didn't know—"

"No, Dannerman, you didn't know. I did once bear a litter of three after I was bred to the male, Perjowlsti, but I was allowed to keep them with me only until they were half grown. Then I watched while another Doc implanted them with controllers. They were very young and frightened. I had to lie to them. I said it would do them no harm. No harm! Do you hear me, Dannerman? I told them it would do them no harm! And I do not know what became of them. Since the Horch came I have not seen them, or Perjowlsti. Perhaps they were killed in the fighting."

She turned away from me and was silent for a moment. I thought she might be weeping, if Docs ever wept. I reached up and touched her shoulder. I hadn't forgotten about the vivisection, but I couldn't help feeling compassion. I said, "I'm sorry, Pirraghiz."

She said, "Yes," her voice muffled. When she turned around, the great cow eyes were dry, and her expression was less angry. "I too am sorry," she said, "for what will happen to your own species."

I straightened up. "My own species?"

She nodded with the great head, her hat flopping ludicrously. "You will serve them too, if they wish it."

Something was tasting very bad in the back of my throat. I did my best to repress it. "What would they want us for?"

"I do not know, Dannerman, but—" She thought for a moment, then sighed. "Have you ever seen the warriors of the Others?"

I remembered a half-dissolved corpse of a Bashful I'd seen in our escape. "No. Yes. I mean, I've seen a dead body, but—Wait a minute! Are you trying to tell me they'd make Bashfuls out of us?"

"I do not know what a 'Bashful' is"—I had used the English word—"but to use you to fight their battles for them when there is occasion for fighting, yes. I think so. It is known that your species is good at wars and violence. Was that not the reason for your own work before you were captured?"

I was aghast. "No! We won't let that happen! If we're going to fight, we'll fight them!"

"Of course you will, Dannerman," she agreed somberly. "As I suppose we did, all those years ago. Even now, sometimes—you see, the control channels are very effective, but they are not perfect. If one of us finds himself surrounded by a kind of wall of metal mesh—I do not know the name for it—"

I guessed, "A Faraday cage?"

She shrugged. "Perhaps. In such a situation the controls are weakened. Then we have enough volition, sometimes, to try to fight back. But we do not succeed. As soon as that happens the others of our own kind who still belong to the Beloved Leaders come at once, and recapture us. Or kill us. They have no choice, just as I had none when the Beloved Leaders caused me to cut the flesh of your conspecifics."

She gazed down at me searchingly. "It is not only persons of your own species that have been vivisected in that way by us. You are only the most recent. The same has been done to members of every captive species—the Wet Ones, the Shelled Persons, the Tree-Livers, even the captive Horch. Even to my own people. And in every case—" She broke off, looking at me in a different way. "What is it, Dannerman?"

She had puzzled me. "What do you mean, 'captive Horch'?"

She looked at me with surprise. "But I thought you knew. What did you think Djabeertapritch was?"

I blinked at her. "A Horch, of course."

She sounded impatient. "Certainly he is a Horch, but until the other Horch captured this base, he was a prisoner, too. He and all his nest, Dannerman. Look, you can almost see the farms they cultivated, just past these trees. They were kept here since their ancestors were captured, long ago, for study and, yes, to be experimented on, just as your people were."

That was unexpected news. I had thought of the Horch simply as Horch. They were conquerors. I had not imagined that Beert himself had once been a conquered.

I stared through the tangled vegetation toward where Pirraghiz had said Beert's people still lived. I couldn't see anything that looked like farms, but I knew what I had to do. I had to try my best to avert that horrible prospect of a subjugated Earth, and the place to do it was not here.

I turned to Pirraghiz. "You said Beert's village was out there?"

"The nest of the formerly captive Horch is, yes."

"All right. I'm as well as I need to be, and I want to see Beert. I'm going there now."

She did not seem surprised, only thoughtful. "I do not know if he will be at the nest. He may have called from the base."

"I'll wait for him."

"You do not know the way, Dannerman. You have never been there."

"I'll find it."

"It is a long walk. I am not sure you are yet strong enough for that—"

I didn't let her finish. "That's my problem," I said, but she finished anyway.

"—so I will carry you there myself." And she did. Hoisted me up into the crook of one of her great arms, and trotted away.

FOUR

The Nest

16

Dopey had always preferred being carried by a Doc to walking. I could see why. Pirraghiz held me comfortable and secure, and the ride, despite those elephant legs of hers, was rapid and just about jolt-free.

As we left the beaten path to cross over into Horch territory, she had to push her way through wet brush. Considerately she pushed the soggy branches away from me with one or another of her spare arms. Then, as we passed that invisible dividing line where weedy trees gave way to shrubs, we were in Horchland.

The difference between the two compounds was the difference between wilderness and civilization. Behind us was jungle. Ahead, neatly cultivated cropland. We came out onto a dirt road that bordered a couple of hectares of green stalks of grain, shoulder-high—I don't mean Pirraghiz's shoulder, of course. Between the rows two snaky heads popped up to stare at us in astonishment. Pirraghiz paid them no attention, but turned left on the road and loped along.

Although the road was dirt, it was smooth and almost rutless, even after the rain. Obviously the Horch were careful about keeping their place tidy. A kilometer or two ahead I could see something that looked like a huge, six-sided barn, but before we got there I heard a whirring noise from behind us. Pirraghiz didn't bother to look behind. She just moved courteously over to one side, allowing a vehicle to shoot past us. It was a three-wheeled cart, a little like the one Beert had used when he rescued me from the interrogation chambers. That one had had a motor, though; this one was pedal-driven by its occupant—one of the Horch who had gawked at us from the cropland, I supposed. He lay flat on his back, feet pumping at the pedals as fast as he could, while his neck swayed back and forth between staring at us and watching the road ahead.

As we got closer to the barnlike structure I could see that it was a kind of wickerwork tenement, four or five stories tall, with porches jutting out at every level. Some of the porches were enclosed in coarse screens, others open to the sky. I could see figures on some of them, perhaps taking the air. The whole thing looked like something some tribe of aborigines might have built for themselves out of willow withes and bamboo, in the days before the European colonizers came along with their whiskey, guns, row houses and syphilis.

It was the biggest structure in sight, but it wasn't the only one. I began to see sheds nearby, and a couple of peculiar trees, all circled by little clusters of flowering bushes for decoration. The trees were branchless until near the top, where they spread out in a crown like royal palms. The most peculiar thing about the trees was that they were all bent at a sharp angle from the ground up, and all at the same angle. There was something that looked like a wicker band shell—people were moving around it—and, as we moved toward one side, behind the main building a smaller structure appeared of a wholly other kind. This one wasn't wicker. It was made of the same glossy ceramic stuff as my former cell, though this was pinkish in color. A pair of the Horch Christmas trees were industriously unloading some sort of equipment to take inside it.

I wasn't pleased to see them there, but Pirraghiz paid them no attention. She set me down carefully. "Wait, Dannerman. I will see if Djabeertapritch is here."

She left me standing in a plot of damp, spiky grass, I suppose the Horch equivalent of a front lawn. There were low wicker benches scattered around—unoccupied—and a few smaller trees with buttercup-yellow blossoms. Although the robots weren't paying any attention to me, I was uncomfortable in their presence. I walked a little way around the great house to get out of their sight. When I looked up the woven-sapling side of the building, I discovered that someone was looking back at me. Three or four of those snaky heads were peering over the side of one of the porches. I waved, but the only response I got from them was to pull hastily back, some completely out of sight, one still staring at me with just the nose and eyes showing.

As long as I was here, I told myself, I should be keeping my eyes open for the kind of information the Bureau would want to hear when (I didn't let myself say "if") I got back. The trouble was, there didn't seem to be very much sensitive information lying around.

So I made do with what was available. To start, I heard shrill soprano singing coming from nearby. It was that band-shell thing, and it seemed to be functioning as a kind of Horch kindergarten. Eight or ten tiny Horch infants danced around as they sang, waving their sinuous arms and necks more or less gracefully. The two littlest ones weren't dancing. They lay on their backs in tiny wicker baskets, looking like some kind of musical calamari as they waved their limbs and piped along with the others. There was one adult with them to conduct the performance. By the swellings under her jumpsuit I judged she was female.

She moved quickly to interpose herself between me and her charges, thrusting her head toward me suspiciously. "What are you?" she demanded.

That wasn't an easy question to answer. Before I had figured out how to describe myself, she gave the neck-twist that was like a human nod. "Yes, now I remember. You are Djabeertapritch's new pet."

I didn't respond to that. I was digesting the implications of that word, "pet," and anyway, she was still talking. "Please go away. You are distracting the children and they must prepare to sing for the Greatmother." Her tone was commanding, and she gestured accordingly.

She was right. All the children had stopped what they were doing to goggle at me. I apologized. "I'm sorry if I interrupted you. I'm just waiting for Beert—for Djabeertapritch, I mean."

"You should not wait here," she said crossly. I might have argued, but then I saw two Horch ambling around the perimeter of the building toward us. They seemed in no hurry. They weren't looking in our direction at all; they were in animated conversation with each other, their necks winding close together except when they paused to examine some detail of the building's structure.

There was something about them that was different. It took me a moment to figure it out, and then I had it. It was the way they were dressed. All Horch seemed to like to ornament their round little bellies, but not all in the same way. Beert, as well as this teacher-Horch and the little ones in her class, sported a circle of colorfully embroidered fabric there. These two were dressed like the female I had seen with Beert in the interrogation room; their belly bowls were shallow domes of bright metal, as shiny as chrome.

I didn't have good feelings about the metal-wearing brand of Horch. The strollers didn't seem to have noticed me, and I preferred to keep it that way. I nodded politely to the teacher and left, as inconspicuously as I could.

When Pirraghiz found me I was in the middle of a sort of car park of those three-wheeled velocipedes; they were ingeniously put together out of four or five different kinds of wood, wheels, bearings and all. "There you are! You should have stayed where I left you," she scolded. "Now come. The Greatmother has summoned Beert. I will take you to a room that is available, where you can wait for him. And I will go back home to get food for you, and to pick up some of my own things so that I can stay with you here."

The wicker building was wicker all the way through, wicker walls, wicker floors, wicker stairs—and a lot of them—to take us to the upper levels. I marveled at the kind of engineering skills it had taken to create a five-story building out of withes woven together. "They must be pretty good designers," I offered to Pirraghiz, breathing hard.

She looked down at me with concern. "Of course. They are Horch. But are you all right? Should I carry you again?"

I shook my head. I wasn't willing to let her know how quickly I tired, not to mention that the steps sagged and protested Pirraghiz's weight with soft, squeaking sounds. I didn't think it was a good idea to add my weight to hers.

The stairs we were climbing circled an interior courtyard, like the atrium in a five-story Roman villa—if any Roman villa ever got five stories high. Balconies ran all around the inside of the structure at every level, and a few Horch paused in whatever they were doing on them to peer at us. We went up three flights, and I was panting in earnest by the time Pirraghiz reached the right level. She took me to a door—rather like a thick woven curtain—and flung it open. "This is where you will stay," she announced.

The room wasn't anything like the sterile chambers where the Horch machines had questioned me. It wasn't like any place I had ever been in before. I said politely, "It looks fine. I'm glad they had a spare room for me."

"They have very many spare rooms," she said somberly. "There are very few of this Greatmother's nest left. Will you be all right if I leave you alone for a while? It will only be for a little bit, then Djabeertapritch will be here. There is a place to sleep; perhaps you should do that. It will not be long until he arrives, I think," she said again, to reassure me. "You will be quite safe. If you need anything, you can call and someone will come, but do not eat anything until I return with proper food for you."

It had been a long time since anyone had fussed over me in that way. I couldn't help laughing. "Thank you, Mother," I said. "You can go. Honestly. Go!"

She went. But actually I had barely begun to investigate my new room when I felt the wicker floor vibrate again with her heavy tread. When I turned to the door, there she was again, carrying a large pottery bowl. "This is in case you need to relieve yourself while I am away, Dannerman," she said. "Now I will leave again." And she did.

The room the Horch had given me was a good size, maybe three meters by four. The walls were unadorned, except that on the interior ones the wickerwork had been woven together in strands of several varieties of withes, of different colors. The result was rather pretty, almost like an abstract tapestry. The outside walls were made of darker, more robust basketwork, and something like clay had been plastered into the wicker to seal the walls against the weather outside. The door to the balcony outside was made of accordion folds of the same material, and they were ajar. When I stepped out to look around I had a view of farm fields beyond the outbuildings and the curiously bent trees. A stream cut through them—the same stream that went through the old compound, I supposed. There were little rainbow-shaped Japanese-garden bridges over the stream here and there. Oddly, not all the fields appeared to be under cultivation. Some seemed to have been farmed once, but now bore only a scraggle of weeds.

That was all I saw from the balcony, because I didn't stay there long. Adult Horch weighed about as much as I did, and I suppose the builders had allowed some margin of safety. But it sagged disturbingly under my weight, so I stepped back inside. As I did I noticed something I hadn't seen before. Both the doorframe and the outer edges of the accordion doors were thick with some kind of pale purplish mildew.

It was the kind of thing any Earthly housekeeper would scrub away as soon as detected. Were the Horch as sloppy as that? I didn't think so. The stuff seemed to be there for a purpose. There were heavy cloth drapes attached to the lintel and doors. They were rolled back, but it looked as though they could be pulled out to cover the moldy purple stuff.

I put that aside for later thought. Inside the room were the chamber pot and the bed. Their purposes were unmistakable. I used them in turn.

Thankfully, this bed was a lot softer than Pirraghiz's. It was basically a sort of round mattress on the floor, maybe a hundred and fifty centimeters across—just about long enough for me to stretch out. The mattress was covered with something that felt like flannel, and stuffed with little round lumps like bolls of cotton. When I sprawled out on it

I meant only to rest and think about what I was going to say to Beert when he arrived, but I think I dozed off.

What roused me was a sound from outside.

It was an airplane. When I got to the balcony to look out it was just landing in one of those untended fields, coming down slow and nearly vertically, like one of the Bureau's VTOLs. It rolled only a few meters, and as soon as it stopped a Horch got out, met by a couple of others who had been standing by.

Was the one who had just arrived Beert? I couldn't tell, but he was wearing the cloth belly patch, while the abdomens of the two who were meeting him glittered metallically in the sunlight. The three of them were having an animated conversation, snaky arms and necks swirling around. I couldn't hear, of course, but I wished I could; some of the flailing arms were pointing toward the building—in fact, to the balcony I was standing on.

I hastily stepped back, more or less out of sight, but it was too late to matter. The three had finished their conversation. One of the shiny-bellied ones climbed into the plane, still yammering at the other. And the one who had just arrived entered the building.

17

The newcomer was Beert, all right. When I went to the door of my room and peered down the circular stairway, I saw him coming up, the ropy neck pointed straight at me. He called, "I did not think you would come here without authorization, Dan."

He sounded aggrieved. I didn't want him angry at me, but I stood my ground. I said, "I'm well now, Beert. I didn't see any reason to wait."

He came up and stood beside me, his pointy little face only centimeters from my own. "You do not know all the reasons for what I do, Dan," he said glumly, and waved me into the room. He closed the door behind us and sat on the edge of the bed, regarding me. "The Greatmother did not expect you yet," he sighed. "I will have to apologize to her."

Greatmother? That was the second or third time I'd heard her mentioned, and she sounded important. "I'm sorry if I got you in trouble," I apologized.

He waved the apology away with both sinuous arms. "I am not in trouble, Dan, but it is not appropriate for things to happen in the nest that the Greatmother doesn't know about. Where is Pirraghiz?"

"She went back to get some stuff. It isn't her fault, Beert. It was all my idea."

"Yes, I had supposed so," he said moodily. "It has been observed that your species is often unruly." He thought for a moment, long neck swaying, and then said, "You see, Dan, I am engaged in a number of discussions with the cousins. I had to leave them to come here, and I cannot stay very long. Perhaps we can spend a little time together, but first I must speak with the Greatmother about your presence here. Can you remain in this chamber while I make arrangements for you?"

"Sure I can, but I'd rather—"

He was waving both arms and the neck at me again. "Please, Dan. Do not be still unruly. It will not take me long. Stay here."

When he came back he looked less fussed. "The Greatmother extends you the courtesy of the nest," he told me, sounding pleased about it. "When she has time she wishes to meet you in person, but when that may be, I cannot say. Do you need to eat?"

Actually I had been beginning to think of food, but I shook my head. "Pirraghiz doesn't want me eating anything until she comes back to check it out."

"Yes, that's wise. Very well. I'm afraid everyone is quite busy, since we are so shorthanded now, but I think I have something that will occupy you until Pirraghiz shows up. Come, first I will show you the parts of the nest."

He did, too. From where we stood on the landing he showed me the door to something he called the Repository of the Nest—a sort of library, I gathered. We looked in on the children's dormitory, where a dozen or so little ones were taking their naps—the same ones I had seen at the band shell, I thought, because the female who was standing guard over them was familiar. Beert told me her name. He told me the names of all the five or six Horch we met along the way, but I didn't retain any of them. They all greeted Beert with friendly respect, sometimes intertwining necks. Even the teacher-guard. They seemed to be an affectionate bunch.

When we were on the ground floor Beert paused at the entrance. He slapped the accordion door with one arm and said, like any suburbanite with a new split-ranch, "What do you think of our nest then, Dan?" When I told him, as politely as I could, that it was very nice, but it struck me that wicker was a peculiar choice of materials for building a multistory habitat, he said in surprise, "But we could work only with what we had, Dan. The Others gave us nothing."

"The Others?"

"The ones you call the Beloved Leaders. When they dumped our ancestors here we had no tools, no machines, only our bare arms and teeth. Do you not think we did well? Every section of the nest reinforces every other. It has stood for many generations like this, and will for generations more."

"Unless there's a fire," I said.

That amused him. "But there is no fire in the nest, ever," he said, and led me to the shed that was used for cooking and eating. This one was made of clay bricks like adobe—and as likely to wash away in the first rain, I thought, but he showed me how the clay was covered with some sort of vegetable sap to protect it from the weather. A meal was being prepared. Though the smells were unfamiliar, they were definitely food, and I was beginning to wish that Pirraghiz would get back. The two Horch doing the cooking were friendly but busier than any two persons needed to be, chopping up vegetables, grinding tubers in a mortar, tending their cooking fires. When I asked Beert if everyone always worked so hard around here, the question seemed to disturb him.

"Not always," he said moodily. Then he sighed. "We do not have enough people for all the work," he admitted. "The farms to be tended, the children to be cared for, the nest to be kept in repair. Before we were—" He hesitated over the next words. "Before we were *set free*, it was different. Then there were enough of us to do all that needed to be done, and to have time enough to rest, and to study, and to do all the other things we enjoy. But now many of us have left the nest."

"To go where?"

His head darted around uneasily. "When the cousin Horch freed us they offered to take us out of here. Many nest-siblings went to the planets of the cousins. They wanted to see what a life of leisure was like, with machines to tend to all the drudgery. This was natural enough, Dan. They had every right to do so, and the Greatmother did not object."

"But you didn't go?"

"It is my nest," he said simply, and then glanced at the shadow cast by one of those bent-over trees. "But look at the time! I must hurry."

The penny dropped. Of course. The trees had been coaxed to grow in that direction so that they could function as gnomons in vast sundials, the eight bushes planted around them marking the Horch equivalent of the hours of the day. I was so struck by the ingenuity of the system that I hardly heard the rest of what Beert said. Which was: "I have something to give you before I leave."

He wrapped one of those arms around my shoulders—it was warmer than I had expected—and led me to the pink structure. The two Christmas trees I had seen before were standing immobile not far away, but Beert ignored them. He seemed in good spirits, if rushed. "This is my personal laboratory," he said with pride.

I looked at it, and at him. "Does that mean you're some kind of a scientist?"

"Scientist? No, Dan. I am a student. All I hope to learn is what the cousins already know, and this is where I try to learn it. The thing I wish to give you is in the laboratory, but there are delicate machines here; it is better if you don't come inside until you know enough about them to take care. Wait just a moment."

He unlocked the door—at least, I guess that was what he did; he pressed both arms against the door in a complicated, sine-wavey pattern, something like an identification signature, I suppose; anyway, the door opened. Lights sprang up inside, and he went in.

I peered after him.

Beert had been right about the machines. The place was full of them, in all stages of completion. It looked like the way he had been learning his cousins' science was by taking some of their gadgets apart and rebuilding them.

More important, it also looked like this was the place I had been looking for. If there were secrets of Horch technology for me to steal and take back to the Bureau, there was a whole treasure trove of them right here.

And he had implied that, sooner or later, I would be allowed to examine them more closely.

It was the most hopeful thing that had happened to me since Beert rescued me from the torturers. The only sour note was those two Horch robots. Most of their twigs were retracted, but I knew they could spring into action at any moment.

When Beert came back, carrying something in a wicker basket, he saw me watching them uneasily. "Do not worry about the robots, Dan," he reassured me. "You are here with the permission of the cousins, and there will be no problem. The cousins have been very kind. This laboratory could not have been built without their help. Now let us go back to your chamber."

18

I never learned Beert's age, but there was something boyish about him. All the way up the steps he was hissing softly to himself—it was almost a chuckle—and darting his head, almost teasingly, toward mine. But he didn't speak until we were in my room and the door was closed. I was feeling pretty cheerful myself, partly contagion from Beert, partly the thought of all those Horch secrets waiting for me in his lab.

Then he lifted the lid of the wicker basket. "This is something you may use while Pirraghiz and I are gone," he said happily.

He took something out of the basket. I recognized it at once and suddenly was not happy at all. It was one of those Beloved Leader helmets. I jumped back, snarling, *"No!"*

That blew Beert's own cheerful mood. He darted his head at me incredulously. "You do not wish this? Oh, wait. Perhaps I understand. Are you thinking of the way the interrogation machines used this device? No, I am not giving you this for that purpose. I do not intend to cause you pain. Indeed, you can operate it for yourself. See, here are the selectors."

He flipped up the little tab on the side of the helmet, exposing its nest of colored grooves, as though he were revealing a great secret. It wasn't news to me, though. "I've seen this already," I told him. "Rosaleen Artzybachova was tinkering with one like it while we were captives."

That surprised him. "Did she so? I was not aware of this. Was she able to operate the helmet satisfactorily?"

"Well, no. Not very."

He wagged his long neck at me. "Indeed I think she would have had great trouble doing so. The selectors are designed for tinier digits than yours—the talons of your Dopey, or of one of Pirraghiz's people. Let me see if I can find some implement you can use—"

While he was scrabbling in the basket I took the little ceramic toothpick Pirraghiz had given me out of my pocket. "Like this, you mean?"

He swooped his head down almost to touch it, then peered up at me. "You astonish me sometimes, Dan. Yes, that will do." He took the little splinter out of my hand with the end of one arm—it split, like an elephant's trunk, to pick it up securely.

I said, "Isn't this a Beloved Leader device?"

"No longer," he said absently, tweaking the colored lines. "It is now ours." He had pressed the helmet against his belly, and seemed to be staring at nothing. Then, sounding satisfied, he said, "Yes, here it is. See, Dan—" holding up the helmet for me to look at. "I have accessed some of their records for you. You can change from one to another if you wish, but activate only the green selector, otherwise you will be in other files and it will be difficult for you to return to the ones of interest. Do you remember how to put the helmet on?"

I did. I held the thing warily, unable to forget what it had done to me with the Christmas trees.

But was Beert likely to be playing unpleasant tricks? I hoped not. I swallowed. I pulled it over my head, snapped the eyeshades in place—

And, just as before, I was instantly in another place.

I was on a familiar street in New York City. Vendors lined the sidewalk. I had stopped at one of the stalls. I was picking up bits and pieces of the kitschy merchandise this one had to offer, and I felt strange. I felt *female*. My body was not the one I had been born with; it was tightly bound at the breasts, and when I saw my hands the nails were bright orange and one finger bore a ring like a dragon, with wings outspread. Female hands, all right. Certainly not my own. I—*she*—seemed to be interested in an old-fashioned wristwatch with the hands of Mickey Mouse pointing out the time, but when the vendor spoke to her she put it back and turned away.

As always with the helmet, I was *there*. I saw everything this body looked at, I felt everything she touched. I smelled a faint wisp of roasting lamb from a pita joint on the corner, and heard the scream of sirens from somewhere nearby—fire, ambulance, police car, I could not tell which, and the body I was occupying was not interested enough to look.

I pulled the helmet off my head, confused. "What am I looking at?" I demanded.

"Keep looking," Beert advised. "You will see someone you know well, so the other Dan said. These events are not happening now," he added. "These are recordings of transmissions which were received some time ago. See it for yourself."

Hesitantly I put the helmet back on. The body I was wearing glanced at her own watch and, now hurrying, crossed the street and turned a corner.

I recognized the entranceway. It belonged to the midtown office building that held the Dannerman Astrophysical Observatory, my grandfather's legacy to immortalize his name, where I had once gone to work for (and spy on!) my cousin Pat. The body announced herself—the name meant nothing to me—to the floor guard—new since my time—and while she waited for him to call her escort, she was covertly eyeing the man.

I realized that I was looking at a *man* through the eyes of a *woman,* and it was instructive to see where her eyes went: face, shoulders (he was pretty solidly built), with special attention to the region of the crotch, both front and back.

Then some other man I didn't recognize came down, passed her through the turnstiles, into the elevator, up into Pat's waiting room, and there I saw people I knew quite well.

As I entered the room, Pat's receptionist, Janice DuPage, got up from her desk and greeted me with a quick hug. "Sorry I'm late," I—"I"—apologized, and Janice said:

"That's all right. Just let me sign out and then we can go."

Out of the corner of my eye I caught a glimpse of Pete Schneyman, just glancing at us as he passed through the reception room. And while Janice was picking up her purse and checking her makeup, the elevator door opened again. The person who came out was someone I knew very well indeed.

It was Dr. Patrice Adcock. My cousin. My Pat. The Pat I loved. The Pat I had lost.

My hostess's eyes were studying her, too, in her own way, while Janice said, "You remember my friend from the cruise? The one I didn't take?"

There was an edge to her voice, as of some remembered grievance, but Pat only said, "Of course." She shook hands. *I* shook her hand. I was actually touching the warm, firm hand of the woman I loved. And then she turned away and went into her own office and I tore the helmet off my head.

"What is this?" I demanded. "Whose body was I in? Was it Patrice?"

"It was not any one of your party," Beert said heavily, his neck hanging low. "Other humans were implanted with the transmitters."

I scowled at him. "How could that be?" Then a particularly nasty thought crossed my mind, and I said, "Unless—"

Beert's little snake head swung toward mine, looking into my eyes. "Yes, Dan," he said. "The Others have reached your planet now."

19

I don't know when Beert left my room. I was under the helmet, obsessively eavesdropping on the many, many unwitting—or sometimes witting—human beings who were wearing the bugs implanted by the Others.

I knew of only six persons who had been bugged and returned to Earth, the five of us in the original batch from Starlab, plus Patrice from the ones who had been in captivity. Now there seemed to be hundreds of them.

So there was no question about it. I had to believe that what Beert said was true. The Others were on Earth—somehow—and going right ahead with their plans. And if I were ever to hope to get back and—somehow—help fight them off, it had to be done quickly.

All the same, I couldn't help peering out at my planet through the eyes of the bugged ones. They came in all varieties. There was a young woman in what I supposed was China, wearing the tracking collar of a house-arrest prisoner, sullenly trampling seedlings into mud with her bare toes, and seeing nothing but the other young women in the paddy and the old man who was dumping more baskets of seedlings at its rim. There was a store clerk in some hot and Spanish-speaking place; a blackjack dealer on what seemed to be a cruise ship, from the gentle rolling of the floor; a dozen or so in prisons. A *lot* of the bugged ones were in prisons, and a lot of those I took to be Chinese, from the uniforms they wore and the totally incomprehensible language they spoke.

I didn't spend much time with the ones who spoke languages I couldn't understand. There were a fair number of English-speaking ones, and a sizeable number of those were also in some kind of detention. Some, like that first Chinese girl, wore tracking collars as they went glumly about their business. Most were in a cell. Some were being interrogated, and the questioners were getting little joy from the answers they got. Uniformly the bugged ones claimed to have no knowledge of how the little gadgets had been implanted in their skulls.

Once, just once, I saw a face I recognized.

The face belonged to Nat Baumgartner, an NBI agent I had worked with once on the Michigan militia. What Nat was doing was standing in a hospital operating room, looking more worried than any Bureau agent should let himself look in the presence of a prisoner. I was his prisoner. I lay on my back, staring up at the operating-theater lights while someone I couldn't see was doing something with an IV in my arm. I supposed my host was about to undergo surgery, most likely to remove the bug from his brain, but I never found out for sure. Shortly after that, my carrier went unconscious, and that transmission stopped for good.

And all the time that I was looking through the eyes of other people, one part of my mind was scheming what to do about this situation. Make Pirraghiz take me to the transit machine and *go*. No, first take a quick snatch-and-grab run through Beert's laboratory and collect all the Horch technology I could carry to take back. No, before that, pump him for what he might know about the Horch plans for Earth, if any, and for any guidance he can give about what to do to resist the Beloved Leaders. No—

No, there were too many things to think out, and I couldn't think clearly about them while I was hunting frantically through the files of all those bugged humans. But I couldn't stop doing it, either. The person I was really looking for was Pat.

I was convinced there had to be other files in which she would appear. I picked frantically at the green line in the selectors, but I couldn't find them. Apart from that one glimpse in the Observatory office, she never turned up for me again. By dumb luck I did finally connect again with the woman who had gone to the Observatory to meet Janice DuPage, and watched it all over again for the sake of that one brief glimpse of Pat.

That brief glimpse was all there was. When I watched the file all the way through, all that happened was that the woman went to lunch with Janice DuPage. The good part was that I could taste the Caesar salad the woman ordered, but there was nothing else. What they talked about was the cruise Janet had missed, and how it had come to an end when something went wrong with the ship's engines. And after they had left the restaurant and were crossing a street, abruptly and strangely, the transmission ended. I mean, it just *stopped.* At one moment I was laughing and clutching Janice's arm as we dodged past a stopped truck; I heard Janice scream, and that was it. The next moment I was in total darkness, with no sight or sound or smell at all.

I took the helmet off to puzzle over that for a bit. Something like that had happened before, when the man in the operating room went to sleep. That was anesthesia, I had no doubt. But what kind of person went to sleep in the middle of crossing a New York street?

I had the helmet back on when I felt a touch on my shoulder—my *real* shoulder. When I took the helmet off it was Pirraghiz. She wasn't alone. Standing next to her was a male Doc, reaching out one of his arms in hospitable fashion to shake my hand. "This is my friend Mrrranthoghrow," she told me—as close as I can come to his name, which sounded like a voiceless purr, a coughing sneeze and a yowl at the end. "He came along to help me carry what I needed for you, but he cannot stay this time."

"I hope to see more of you soon," Mrrranthoghrow said politely. I mumbled something back. My mind was still full of what I had seen under the helmet; I hardly noticed when he left again.

Pirraghiz was looking at me curiously. "Are you all right, Dannerman?" she asked. "Are you hungry?"

Once reminded, I was. In fact, I was ravenous. I don't know how long I had been under the helmet, but while I was devouring the food Pirraghiz set before me, I discovered it was dark outside my window. Not inside the room, though; the whole chamber was illuminated with a soft glow, which, I saw, came from the mossy stuff around the doorframe.

I paid it only minimal attention, still thinking—worrying—about what the Others might be doing to my world. Pirraghiz watched in silence. It wasn't until I had swallowed the last of the berry-flavored tomatoish thing that was my dessert that she removed the dishes and said, "It is sleeping time. I will show you how to cover the light, Dannerman. Simply pull these drapes out, so, and cover the light like this, do you see?"

She left one little section uncovered, leaving the room dim. But there was enough light for me to see that she was regarding me with concern. "I will be in the next room, if needed," she said. "The Greatmother has given it to me for as long as you want me here." I grunted. Then she reached down and touched the helmet I had left on the table.

"Did Djabeertapritch give you this so you could see what is happening in your home?"

"Oh, yes," I said, sitting on the edge of the bed. "He certainly did."

She sighed. "It is a sad thing, I know. All of you from your planet found it most unpleasant."

That got my attention. "You mean the copies you made of me?"

"Yes, often copies of yourself, Dannerman, but also of the others. Some copies of all of you were shown this material at the beginning of their interrogations."

"Copies of *Pat*?"

"Of course. But it was you who were most useful, since you had a broader experience of the world." She paused, looking down at me in the dimness. "This upsets you. But information was wanted, and so what happened was inevitable."

"Inevitable! Making a copy of Pat and killing her was *inevitable*?"

She looked defensive. "I am sorry. I know this troubles you. The fact that so many bad things are happening to your people troubles me, too." She stopped to consider for a moment, then sighed. "But honestly, Dannerman, it does not trouble me very much. You are not alone. How many sixty-fours of sixty-fours of sixty-fours of sixty-fours of persons have been sent early to the Eschaton in this struggle? And many of them died far more painfully than your Rosaleens and Pats. Here in this nest we have made ourselves look away from such horrors, Dannerman. We could not survive otherwise."

20

Those scenes in the helmet had put the fear of God into me—well, fear of the Others, anyway. They were definitely taking over my planet. Every last person I cared about—even Pat, even my other self!—was threatened with becoming a zombie servant of the Others, just like the Docs.

It was about the worst news I had ever had to face. I didn't see how I would be able to sleep with that haunting me. I was wrong about that, though. I dropped off as soon as Pirraghiz left the room, and I didn't even dream.

Maybe that was my own way of turning away, like Pirraghiz, from what was too hard to face. It didn't last. The minute I woke up, there it was. I didn't have any choice. I had to face it.

I stumbled across the dimly lit room to the balcony, my mind full of what I had seen. When I threw the accordion slides open it was bright daylight outside, and three or four Horch were getting into their tricycles to go to work in the fields. I stared at them without seeing them, thinking hard. What I wanted to do more than anything else was to escape from this place, back to Earth, to face whatever was happening there.

What I had to do first, though, was something different. One additional warm body wouldn't be much help to the human race. To be of any use at all, I had to bring something useful back with me. What's more, I had to do it *now* . . . always assuming, that was to say, that what I had seen was what was still happening, and not ancient history.

When Pirraghiz heard me moving around she came in, bringing food. As soon as she was in the room she glanced at the drapes, shook that big head reprovingly and began to fuss with them without waiting to hear anything I might have to say. She scolded, "You mustn't cover the lights during the day, Dannerman. They have to charge up with sunlight so that you can use them after dark."

I wasn't in a mood to be instructed about housekeeping. I said to her back, "How long have I been here?"

She left off fussing with the drapes and turned around, peering at me. "What?"

"I want to know," I insisted. "Those scenes in the helmet, they come from all different times—some winter, some not. I can't tell anything from them, and I need to know how much time has passed."

"Do you mean since the Horch liberated this planet? Let me see." She stroked the mossy beard on her chin, counting to herself. "About four sixty-fours of days, I think. A little more."

I did the arithmetic in my head. Allowing for the fact that this planet's days were shorter than Earth's, it came out to about six months. A long time, and a lot could have happened. But it wasn't ancient history.

"All right," I said. "Now I want to know everything there is to know about the Horch and the Belov—I mean, the Others. Let's get started."

Pirraghiz was obliging, but she was puzzled, too, and she had a lot of questions. What exactly was it that I wanted to know? When all my answers kept adding up to that same single word—"everything"—she sighed. "I must have advice on this," she told me. "Wait for me. Eat. I will be back very soon."

She was, too. I was sipping from a ceramic bowl the last of something that tasted salty and faintly sour when she appeared at the door. She looked pleased. "Much of what you want to learn may be in the Repository of the Nest," she announced. "The Greatmother has given permission to take you there—as soon," she said, tidily beginning to pick up the dishes from my breakfast, "as I put these in my room."

I didn't want to wait for that, or for anything, but Pirraghiz was firm. Her room was about the same size as mine—pretty small, for a Doc—and she had fitted it with enough belongings to make me think she planned to stay for a while. Among the tiny potted flowers and the bric-a-brac I saw one of those great, cubical cookers Dopey had used. I thought of how much heat those things could produce, and wondered if Beert knew she had it in his fire-free nest. Pirraghiz caught my stare and asked, "Is something wrong?"

I didn't want to get into a discussion, so I lied. "I was wondering why the Horch have so many empty rooms like this," I said.

"Why," she said, closing the door and leading me down the steps, "the reason is simple. When the Horch liberated this planet, all of the captive Horch who wished it were returned home—well, taken to Horch planets, anyway; it has been so long since they were brought here that none of them really has a home anywhere else anymore."

That much I knew, more or less, but I kept her talking. "But not Djabeertapritch and these others."

She gave me one of those massive arms-and-shoulders shrugs. "The ones who stayed in this nest do not always agree with all the things about the cousin Horch."

That got my interest. If Beert and the "cousins" disagreed, there might be a place to drive a useful wedge between them. "What kind of things?"

But Pirraghiz was not willing to be drawn out on that. "You must ask Djabeertapritch himself," she said. "Now here is the Repository of the Nest."

The Repository of the Nest was a library, and it looked like one. It was a suite of three or four rooms, all lined with ceiling-high shelves. In two rooms an assortment of wooden boxes were shelved, most of them looking ancient and worn. In the third some of the wooden boxes had been replaced with bright yellow cubes made of the Horch ceramic. In that room a young Horch female was working at a high table, a spread of documents in front of her. She gave us an unwelcoming glance, but Pirraghiz paid no attention. Pirraghiz knew what she was looking for. She went at once to a great, double-fronted chest of drawers that sat in the middle of the room, and began pulling out an assortment of those silvery spools I had seen in her own room, back in the compound. As she picked each one out she scanned the legend on its label before putting it back, frowning.

I took one of the rejects from her hand to look it over. She didn't resist. She only whispered, "Be careful with it." But it wasn't helpful. Its label bore a string of curlicues and jagged lines—identifying its contents, I supposed.

But the writing meant nothing to me. The gadget behind my ear had its limitations. The Horch had given me their spoken language, but hadn't bothered to make me literate.

I wasn't one of the Bureau's language wonks. Outside of English, the only one I knew well was German. But being unable to read any language I could speak at all was new to me, and depressing. I left Pirraghiz and wandered over to where the young female was at work. She had one of the antique wooden boxes open, carefully transferring its contents to a ceramic one. On the floor next to her was a kind of balloon, almost a meter across, with its valve gently hissing. She elevated her head warningly as I came close.

"Do not breathe moisture on the records," she ordered. "These are very old and very delicate."

I moved back a step, turning my head sharply away from her as though about to be inspected for a hernia. Mollified, she explained what she was doing. The documents were the total records of the captive Horch colony, from their earliest beginnings. Her job was to transfer them from their original containers to the new ones given by the Horch cousins. When she finished the box she would seal it and then purge the air out of it with an inert gas from the balloon at her feet. She was obviously proud of the responsibility the Greatmother had given her. She even pulled a few sheets out of their boxes for me to see. The earliest ones were very old, scratched on tough leaves; later the sheets were paper, somehow or other made by the colonists. But when the librarian read me a few lines, there was nothing there worth trying to remember; after their capture, the colonists had had a tough time, and their hardships were what they wrote about. Interesting. Even touching. But useless.

And so, it seemed, were the book spools Pirraghiz was sorting through. "I am sorry, Dannerman," she told me. "I do not think there is much here that will tell you what you want to know. These are gifts of the cousins to this nest, and they are all music and drama and such things."

"Nothing about the Others? Or technology?"

"No, Dannerman. Djabeertapritch may have some of that sort, but they are not in the Repository of the Nest." She hesitated. "There is one story which is very old and famous. It is about Horch who lived long ago, if you would like to see it? Yes? Very well, but let us do it in my room, so we will not disturb this female in her work."

So I viewed the thing, all the way through. It lasted for a couple of hours. In the first ten minutes I realized there was nothing useful here, but I stayed with it anyway—remember, I got my doctorate in drama and, in spite of everything, I was hooked.

The story took place in a Horch city, time not specified, and the plot was easy enough to follow. It was a kind of a love story. A female Horch and a male Horch wanted to mate, but since they were from the same gens, though not blood relatives, they couldn't. The various threads of the plot struck me as pretty universal; it was *Romeo and Juliet* combined with *Oedipus Rex* and a few snatches of Arthur Miller's *A View from the Bridge*. The male was a space pilot, the female some kind of a farmer. That didn't mean she dug seedlings into the mud with her toes. None of these Horch, however ancient in time, had to do much purely physical work. For that sort of thing they had machines. Those were pretty primitive compared to the latest Christmas-tree models, but they were good enough to free the Horch for more intellectual pursuits. Some of the characters in the play were artists, some philosophers, some teachers, some, as far as I could tell, engineers.

I can't say I followed every detail of the story. There were a lot of references that went right past me, but there are plenty of those in Shakespeare, too. The basic story was clear enough . . . except that I kept thinking what a pity it was that I hadn't had this experience while I was in graduate school. What a hell of a doctoral dissertation I could have written—maybe even one that somebody might actually have wanted to read.

Pirraghiz had gone about her own business while I was watching the bowl. She timed her return perfectly, coming back in just as the story finished, and she wasn't alone. The male named Mrrranthoghrow was with her. After the two of them had greeted me, she looked at me apologetically. "Was any of that what you wanted to know?"

I came alive. "Not exactly. I was more interested in your field, technology, weapons, that sort of thing."

"Not weapons," he protested. "I have no experience with weapons. That is what the warriors and the Horch fighting machines are for."

"All right then." I pointed to the viewing bowl. "What makes that thing run?"

He scratched his beard. "Do you mean where the power comes from? There is a small unit in the base which provides that. It is called a—" I heard the word he said, but it meant nothing to me.

"Something like a battery?" I guessed. I used the English word, because I didn't have one in Horch, but when I explained, "A device in which power from another source is stored, and released as needed," he shook his great head.

"I have never seen the *(incomprehensible)* charged up, Dannerman. I know nothing of such matters; I am a mechanic, trained in that alone. The power in each machine comes from—" he searched for a term I might understand, and came up with—"an accumulator, but what it accumulates, and what it accumulates it from, I do not know. Perhaps Djabeertapritch can tell you, if he wants to, but the Others had no reason to instruct me in such matters. When I disassembled and rebuilt the transit machine for the Horch, I knew what components needed to be connected in certain fashions, but I do not understand how it works."

Suddenly there was a rush of hot blood to my brain. I stared at him. "You worked on the transit machine?"

"With others, yes."

"And it is in working order?"

"Certainly. The cousin Horch use it all the time—for making copies, such as yourself, and also for tracing channels to other installations of the Others."

I swallowed, my throat tight. "Strictly as a theoretical question," I said—I didn't want to scare him off too soon—"would it be possible for me to use that machine to, say, transmit me back to my planet?"

He looked startled, and so did Pirraghiz. "Oh, Dannerman," she said sorrowfully, understanding at once what I was getting at.

So did Mrrranthoghrow. His voice was sympathetic as he said, "I am sorry, Dannerman. It is impossible."

I wasn't giving up, although my pulse was racing. "Why impossible? The Horch wouldn't have to know! You could just smuggle me in—"

He was shaking that great, moon-faced head. "I could not do that without their consent, Dannerman," he said gently. "But that is not the reason. It simply cannot be done. Nothing can be transmitted to any locus unless there is a receiver there, and the receiver in your Starlab has been destroyed."

FIVE

Marooned

21

There was another little period of time there that I'd just as soon forget. The next days passed, but they took a long time doing it. Pirraghiz clucked over me and tried to cheer me up. She proposed entertainments, promised that Beert would soon come back with good news, produced tasty new meals—she did everything she could to cheer me, but I didn't cheer. I was trying to adjust to the fact that I was marooned in this place for the rest of my life, while my world was going to hell . . . and there was nothing I could do about it.

I think I was a big frustration to Pirraghiz. She deserved better. She was my maid, valet, cook, washerwoman and all-day-long companion. Life with her around was like living in a five-star luxury hotel, with my personal Jeeves to care for all my needs. If she had a life of her own, she didn't let it interfere with her total attendance on me. She washed and mended my ragged clothes. She tended my chamber pot, whisking it away to be sterilized and cleaned before I had to use it again. She fed me about as well as I had ever been fed in my life—found new ways to improve the preserved swill from Starlab and added to it actual fresh vegetables, salads, soups, little cakes dripping with something like fruit-flavored honey. There was even milk. It didn't come from an actual cow, of course, because there weren't any of those within many light-years, but it was a sweetish, butterscotch-colored fluid that came, Pirraghiz said, from the females of one of the other captive species.

That startled me. "Don't they object when you take their milk away from them?"

She wagged her great head reprovingly. "Don't be foolish, Dannerman. It is not 'taken.' It is bartered. They give us things we do not have, and we give them things of ours in return. These females are well repaid for what they have in plenty to spare."

I looked again at what was in my cup. But it still tasted good, and while I was checking it out Pirraghiz saw an opportunity. "I am glad that you are taking an interest in this, Dannerman. Would you like to know more about the other captive species?"

I considered that for a moment, then shrugged. "Why not?" I said, meaning, since I was going to be stuck here for the rest of my life, why not find out what that life was going to be like?

Pirraghiz beamed. "That is good, Dannerman. I thought you might feel so, and so I have prepared something for you. Wait one moment." She disappeared into her own room, and when she came back she was carrying the familiar helmet.

It wasn't what I had expected. I protested, "I've already seen all I need to see of what's happening back home."

"Oh, Dannerman," she sighed. "Do you think it was only your people who were bugged? That is not so. Sentient beings of many, many different species have worn the transmitters, species you have never seen, of kinds you cannot imagine, including some of those who shared captivity with you. I could not find all of those in the records," she said apologetically, "but I have selected a single individual from eight different species. Some of the species are here, some are not. Later on I can add others if you wish."

She waited for me to make up my mind. I hefted the helmet for a moment, indecisively. Curiosity won. Gingerly I put it on and pulled down the flaps. I heard Pirraghiz's voice giving last-minute instructions—"Simply say 'next' when you want to go to another subject, Dannerman, and I will make the change for you." And then the helmet took over.

I was no longer myself. I wasn't in my chamber in the Horch nest.

I was surrounded by total blackness. There was nothing to be seen, smelled or felt, except that there before me, not two meters away, was an image of a creature that looked like a frog with the mouth of an alligator. Its skin was as fuzzy as a peach, and more or less the same color. On one bony arm it wore a thing like a wristwatch, but that was glowing with a pale blue light, and there were three golden bracelets on the other. It was dressed in tunic and leggings of a shimmery, silky material. It had four large ears on each side of its elongated head, and a cluster of bright pink feathers topping it off—probably a hat or a decoration, I thought, since the feathers didn't seem to be growing out of the creature's skull.

It wasn't moving at all. I figured that out easily enough; what I was looking at was just a picture, showing me what the first species Pirraghiz had selected for my viewing pleasure looked like; and in a moment the blackness winked away.

Now I wasn't looking at the creature anymore. Now I *was* that creature. What I was looking at—and smelling and hearing and feeling—was a warm, sunny seaside. Gentle ocean waves were breaking on a pebbly beach, where two or three ungainly-looking catamarans were drawn up. I was sitting—squatting, actually—on the side of another catamaran, eating something that crunched in my jaws and tasted richly of blood. I was not alone. There were two other alligator-frogs just below me on the beach, doing something or other with large nets—repairing them, I supposed. I was looking particularly at one of them, and it was giving me occasional sidelong glances in return. I was conscious of a kind of warm stirring that felt like sexual tension as I looked at—I guess, at her. Unless, of course, that one was male and the body I was inhabiting was female, but I could think of no good way of checking that.

People talk wistfully about wanting a change in their lives, generally meaning something like a better job, a new boyfriend, a week on some island resort—anything at all, as long as it is different. I know the sovereign recipe for that. Just slip one of the helmets on your head and tap into the mind of a truly alien being, and you'll never find anything more *different* as long as you live. It wasn't just the sights and smells that were different. My borrowed body interpreted them in ways that were completely foreign to me. There was a pervading stink of rotten fish in the air, powerful enough to make me hold my nose if I'd had one to hold. But I wasn't disliking it. It was actually making me hungry. My hearing was far better than ever before. Not only could I hear the distant sounds of insects and the lapping of the waves on the shore, I could hear precisely *where* they were; the frog's multiple ears were as directional as sonar. I could hear the other alligator-frogs calling to each other—deep baritone hissing, like a dragon's voice—but that was where the helmet's capacities ran out. I couldn't understand a word they said.

Then, *flick,* the scene changed. I was still in the creature's body, or in the body of one just like him, but I was in a series of different places, doing a variety of different things. Once my host was teamed with another frog, both of them wearing a kind of harness and pulling something that was heavy—but I couldn't see what it was—along a marshy dirt road between stands of head-high rushes. Once he and a couple of others were making a lot of noise—singing together or making threats, I couldn't tell which. Once he was asleep. None of it was very intelligible.

So I called, "Next!"

Frog gone away, blackness all around me. I was looking at another picture. This one was a fat, tentacle-nosed thing the general shape of a hippopotamus, and I knew what it was at once.

I was looking at a Wet One, one of the amphibians that had killed Patrice.

Perhaps, in the interests of scientific curiosity, I should have made the effort to understand what life was like for a Wet One. I didn't. I wasn't ready for going into that particular mind. As soon as I saw it I yelled, "Next!"

It took a moment for Pirraghiz to react—surprised, I guess, that I wanted to cut that one so short. But then I felt the faint scrabbling of her talons as she poked at the controller on the side of the helmet, and I had a new bizarre creature to look at.

I kept going through the roster of diverse, but all nonhuman, beings that Pirraghiz had accessed for me. There was a Shelled Person, like the one I had seen in the compound. Very strange, that experience was, because the Shelled Person seemed to see other living things, like the Docs, as luminous, and it had two distinct ranges of odor-detecting senses, one for in the water and one for on land. I tried a thing that looked like a feathered gorilla, with batlike membranes that joined its arms to its body and let it leap and glide for short distances—on, I guess, a planet with a lesser gravity, because I did not think that would work on Earth. Number Five was a four-legged furry thing that made its home in a cave, with its mate and half a dozen young; why the Beloved Leaders had bothered to bug it, I didn't know, because it certainly didn't look very civilized to me. Number Six—

Number Six I knew very well.

Bewildered, I took the helmet off my head. It was unexpectedly dark in the room—evidently the sun had set while I was in the helmet—but I could see Pirraghiz. She wasn't hovering nearby, as I expected; she was over by the window, pulling the drapes back from the light-givers. She turned around questioningly. "I've just seen Dopey!" I told her. "The one who died."

She said comfortably, "Yes, of course. The talker. Did you simply see his image, Dannerman, or did you go on to experience him?"

"Seeing the image was plenty! He was just the way I saw him last, all tattered and beaten up, with that big turkey-gobbler thing of his drooping and all the colors gone. He's about to *die,* Pirraghiz, and I don't want to 'experience' any of that!"

"Dannerman, I would not ask you to. I chose that view of the talker on purpose so that it would be easy for you to recognize him. The tapes, however, are from other parts of his life."

I scowled at her. "What parts?"

"Oh, Dannerman. They are parts that I think will interest you. Why do you not put the helmet on and see?"

So there I was in Dopey's body. I knew it was so, because his head, the little cat head, was bent to look at the familiar, golden-mesh belly bag he wore. I could feel his little fingers, inside the muff, fiddling with what might have been a kind of keypad.

I wasn't comfortable in Dopey's body. His range of vision must have been different from mine, because the colors were odd. I felt odd, too. There was a sort of slow, rhythmic, muscle-flexing sensation at the base of my spine, but in my own body I don't have any muscles there. Perhaps it had something to do with that scaly peacock plume he carried, I thought, and then he looked up.

I caught my breath. What he was looking at was a screen, and on it were four or five figures—human figures—and the nearest of them was me.

It was something from my own life that I was seeing. There were the five of us—Pat and Rosaleen Artzybachova, Jimmy Lin, General Delasquez and myself, when we had first arrived in Starlab. We had come there—God, it seemed a century ago—in the hope of finding some kind of extraterrestrial technology that would make us rich, and what we were doing was squabbling over the division of the Beloved Leaders stuff we saw all around us. I remembered it well. I saw us yelling at each other, and I saw Jimmy Lin get hit on the head.

And then I felt Dopey's little hands scrabbling in his belly bag. There was a bluish flash on the screen. At once, all five of us stopped cold in the middle of the argument. We didn't fall down. We couldn't, being in Starlab's microgravity. But we went limp. We didn't speak anymore. We began to drift around the space in the orbiter.

Dopey had, somehow, put us all to sleep.

Then he got to work. He glanced back over his shoulder. For the first time I saw that there were two Docs standing immobile behind him, in a cramped little space I had never seen before. They began to move at once.

One of them pushed at a section of wall, which opened before him. The other picked Dopey up and carried him through that hidden door. Dopey's body felt pleased with itself; I could feel the warmth and sensual pleasure that emanated from the great peacock fan that my own body didn't have, but Dopey's did. As we glided down a passage, one mystery was solved. I caught a glimpse of the stenciled sign on the wall we had just come through. It was supposed to be a fuel tank. Dopey had emptied it out and made it into a hidey-hole so he could watch us without being seen.

I think I was in a kind of shock again. What happened next wasn't entirely comprehensible, but I couldn't stop watching. Dopey's Docs methodically lifted all five of us, one by one, and put us into the transit machine. Then, each time, without pause, they lifted us out again and went on to the next one. When we had all been transmitted—and copied!—they went to work on the next stage. One of the Docs held Rosaleen's unconscious form while the other opened a cupboard on the wall. He took out a coppery object the size and shape of an almond, while the first Doc, talons extended, slashed a little gash in the back of Rosaleen's neck.

I had never seen an implant put in before.

I saw it happen to Rosaleen. I saw it happen to Delasquez and Jimmy Lin, and I saw it happen to me.

And I saw it happen to Pat Adcock, the woman I loved. I could see her, unconscious and limp. I could almost touch her. I yearned for her. And when it was all over I took the helmet off my head and stared blindly at the room around me.

Pirraghiz said something to me, but I wasn't listening. I got up and walked over to the balcony door, slid it open and stepped outside.

It was full night now, and overhead was that spectacular, star-swarming sky. I wasn't looking at that, either. All I was seeing was Pat, once abandoned to Dopey and his Docs on the orbiter, now abandoned, with the rest of the human race, to whatever the Beloved Leaders chose to do with them.

I had never felt more helpless—and hopeless and useless—in my life.

A moment later I felt the wicker floor move in protest, and Pirraghiz stepped out beside me. I wondered for a moment if it would hold her great weight. Then I wondered whether that mattered at all. She said tentatively, "Dannerman? Was I wrong to show you what Dopey did to you on your Starlab?"

I thought that over for a moment, then I shook my head. "It isn't you who are wrong, Pirraghiz. What's wrong is that everything is going to hell and I can't do anything about it."

She said softly, "Yes. I know what you are going through."

That made me turn and stare at her. "Do you? Do you know what it feels like to see everyone I love about to be turned into robots, and to be able to do nothing about it?"

"Of course I do, Dannerman! I knew that for a very long time, for all the time I wore the Others' controller. I was even more helpless than you are now. I did their bidding! I had no hope at all—but then, you see, suddenly the Horch cousins came and I was free!"

"Oh? And do you think there's any chance that somebody will come charging along to help me?"

She looked at me for a long moment. I could see the struggle going on in her mind over what answer to give me.

Honesty won out over compassion. She said somberly, "No. In truth, Dannerman, I do not."

22

It wasn't easy for me to reconcile myself to spending the rest of my life—what might be a very long life—marooned with the Horch in this place. I tried to think of things I might usefully do. I couldn't think of any. Then I began to think of things that might make it more bearable for me. I'm not too proud of some of those, but—hell! For the first time in my life, I was *defeated*. I could see no way of helping anyone else, so my ideas began to get pretty selfish.

When Beert finally showed up, bubbling with good news, I made up my mind to try one of those selfish ideas out on him. All excitement, he told me the Greatmother would see me at last, and I put it to him. "That's great, Beert," I said, "but I've been thinking about something."

I don't know what Pirraghiz had told him about my state of funk. Everything, I guess, and he didn't seem patient with it. "About what?" he demanded.

"About a favor you could do me if you wanted to. If those other Horch let you have me as a, well, a pet . . . do you think they'd allow you to have another one?"

The snaky neck twisted around so that his eyes could peer into mine. I think I had hurt his feelings. "I do not like to ask my cousins to 'allow' me things, Dan. I do not understand what you mean."

"I mean Pat Adcock."

"Ah," he said. Well, it wasn't "ah," exactly, but it was the same sort of exhalation of breath, indicating that he comprehended. The breath was warm on my face. "You wish me to have a copy of your sexual partner made for you, is that it?"

His tone sounded disappointed in me. It made me defensive. "Is that too much to ask?"

He paused, the sinuous neck curling and straightening thoughtfully. "I don't know if it is too much. Tell me why you want this."

Now he was making me angry. "Why do you think? Because I'm frustrated and lonely and hopeless, that's why!"

"And you think it would make you happier to copy someone you care about, who then would herself become frustrated and lonely and hopeless?"

Well, it sounded all different when he put it like that, but he didn't give me a chance to try to defend myself. He took me firmly by the arm with one of those sinewy tentacles of his and said, "We will speak of this later, Dan, but now we must go. We must not keep the Greatmother waiting."

The Greatmother kept us waiting, though. We trudged to the topmost level of the nest, where a subadult Horch let us into a room, far larger than my own and with many more furnishings. There an ancient female Horch lay sprawled on an immense bed. She had an ungainly thing like a huge metallic corset wrapped around her midsection. It could not have been comfortable to sleep in, but she wasn't sleeping. Her long neck dangled limply off the side of the bed, her eyes half open but unseeing.

I whispered to Beert, "Is she all right?"

"Shh! Of course she is all right. She is simply accessing certain files. Her belly viewer is a thing like your helmet, do you understand?"

I did—after the moment it took me to figure out that the belly was where Horch kept their brains, since of course their heads were too small. I kept looking at Beert to see if he seemed to be getting receptive to my request, but his head was down low, staring at the floor. I couldn't tell what he was thinking; and just as I was making up my mind to ask him again, the Greatmother stirred. Her limbs straightened. Her head lifted to gaze at me, while her arms snaked down to the latches of her viewer.

That was the cue for Beert to spring forward to help her. When she had the thing unlatched he carefully stowed it away in its wicker container, turned his head toward me and said proudly, "The Greatmother will speak to you now."

The first thing she did was to direct Beert to lay out some food and drink for us. While I was munching on the only part that looked familiar she explained to me that she had been viewing some of the scenes of our life as captives of the Others. It was all like a silent film for her, since she couldn't understand any of our talk, but Djabeertapritch had filled her in and she was full of questions. Did the Old Female Rosaleen Artzybachova possess among us the rightful dignity and authority that she herself had in her nest? Had I in fact bred with the young female Pat Adcock—that is, with one of the three young female Pat Adcocks—and if so, what had led me to choose that one over the identical other two? And if breeding was desirable, why had the Old Female not assigned a Pat to each of the other two males in our party so that all three might become pregnant?

When I told her there would be no young coming from our quick idyll, the idea of contraceptives startled her. "But why would this Pat not wish to gestate?" she asked incredulously.

I ran through all the reasons in my mind and settled on one that she might view sympathetically. "We did not wish to bear a child to suffer captivity in a place far from home," I said, and saw Beert's head swerve toward me thoughtfully.

She wriggled her neck at me in gentle reproof. "If our ancestors had thought that way when our planet was overrun, you and I would not be having this conversation. Life is worth saving, Dannerman. Offspring are worth having. Always." She flipped her neck in a complicated curve, and then asked politely, "Has Djabeertapritch told you all you want to know about our nest?"

"Not everything," I said, and then I hesitated for a moment. Maybe I was a little annoyed with Beert for not promising to make me a Pat, but I didn't feel like being tactful. I said, right out, "I know this is a sensitive matter, but is it true that you don't get along with your cousins in the Beloved Leader base?"

Beert gave me a shocked, warning hiss, but the Greatmother answered at once. "We are all one folk, Dannerman. It is, however, true that some of the ways of our cousin Horch have changed greatly in the long, long time we have been separated from them, while this nest has kept to the old ways."

"The ways of your home planet?"

"Of our *particular* home planet, the Two Eights. There were many planets inhabited by our species when we were taken, Dannerman, and each had its own customs. Now there are even more. The Two Eights was one of the newest and smallest at the time, with only eight sixty-fours of sixty-fours of sixty-fours of sixty-fours of inhabitants." I calculated quickly: something less than 150 million. "Most of the other Horch planets were much larger. When the Others came—But perhaps Djabeertapritch has told you all this?"

"Not all, I think."

She gave Beert that quick, reproving neck-twist. He said hastily, "I have been busy with the cousins, Greatmother, as you know."

She patted his arm affectionately. "Of course. Well, you know, Dannerman, that all through our star-going history we Horch had met many strange species, a few of them nearly sentients. Those we always treated with kindness—as, you have seen, we in this nest have treated you yourself, Dannerman. When the Others' scoutship came to our world it was the first time another species had come through space to us. The ones who came to us were not the Others themselves. The Others were too frail to come to the surface of our planet, but they sent their subject species, and those were welcomed. All that they asked was given to them. They did tell us of the Eschaton; that was one gift of the Others. It was the only one."

She looked inquiringly at Beert, who was twitching restively. "They also gave us death," he growled.

She sighed. "Yes, that is so. It is what the Others often give, and they have many ways of giving it. They alter the reaction of a star, so that it goes nova, or change the orbit of a small planetoid so that it collides with the planet they would destroy. They can bring about an emission of poisonous gases from a planet's oceans if they choose. Or they can do what they did to our Two Eights. In their laboratories the Others developed a terrible new disease made out of the proteins of our own bodies, and they spread it secretly among us, and we began to die. Many, many of the people of our planet died. Nearly all. On the Two Eights fewer than sixty-four sixty-fours survived. Those were the ones who were brought here, and we are their descendants. Or," she corrected herself somberly, "the descendants of those who survived what happened here. The Others interrogated our first generations without mercy. Many of us died here as well, usually in great pain. Even when we no longer had any information to give, we were still valuable to the Others, because we were still genetically Horch. So from time to time they seized numbers of us and carried them away, to test new diseases and weapons on them; and that is what our lives were like, Dannerman, for eights of generations—until our cousins of the Eight Plus Three came and set us free."

Abruptly the Greatmother sat straighter on her bed. Her head sprang up to mine, until her pointy, hard-skinned nose was almost touching my own.

"Now I will give a more complete answer to your question, Dannerman. The Eight Plus Threes have treated us very well; they shared everything they have with us, and they offered to take anyone who wished to a Horch planet to live. Most of my nest did go, willingly. A few of us did not. Our cousins have had a long history of struggle and warfare, which we did not share. It has changed them, as our lifetimes of captivity have changed us. We in this nest wish to make a different life for ourselves, though we do not know how.

"But we intend to try.

"What you must remember is that we are all still Horch, Dannerman. We will never do anything to harm our cousins. Djabeertapritch understands this well. You must understand it, too."

23

When we left the Greatmother, Beert's bubbly mood was restored. "She likes you, Dan," he said on the way down the staircase, his neck dancing with pleasure. "Now we can act. Do you remember our earlier conversation?"

My heart leaped. "The one about Pat?"

"No, not the one about Pat," he said crossly. "We have had other conversations, have we not? I am speaking about the one in which I told you that you could help another person in a great matter."

As we walked out into the open air, I tried to remember. "Oh, that," I said, disappointed. "You mean the one where you didn't tell me what it was, or what I was supposed to do. How could I forget all that?"

Irony was wasted on him. "Yes, that conversation, exactly," he said abstractedly, glancing at that bent-tree sundial. He frowned. "The person who needs your help will be here shortly, but first we must go to my laboratory, if you don't mind."

I didn't mind. Didn't have much chance to object, either, because Beert was leading me rapidly toward his pink shed. I looked around apprehensively while he was opening the door, but the Christmas trees were absent. When he touched something just inside the doorway, bright lights sprang up, and he said with pride, "This is my personal workspace."

It was certainly something special. There weren't any luminous fungi here. The lights Beert had turned on came from the glowing walls themselves, with additional spotlights that were fixed on specific items, one a workbench, with several gadgets and tools on it, a couple of larger gadgets on the floor—and one other thing.

I swallowed. The other thing stood motionless against one wall, the light sparkling from its million little needles. It was a Christmas tree.

I must have made a sound, because Beert twisted his neck around from where he was taking objects out of a cabinet and tossing them into a basket. When he saw where I was looking, he reassured me. "I have told you that you need not fear the robots. This one in particular; I have taken it apart and rebuilt it, and now it does not even have a channel to the central controls."

"Um," I said, studying the thing. But it didn't move, so I decided to take him at his word. "Why do you bother?" I asked.

He seemed a little embarrassed, his face held low and not meeting my eyes. "I want to learn all that our cousin Horch know, Dan. It is the only way this nest can ever hope to stand on its own. And," he added, pride returning and his head lifting, "I have even been able to build some instruments for my own use. Like this."

He lifted one of the gadgets from the workbench and held it high. It was a sort of fish-shaped, flattened oval, looking rather like a metallically glittering flounder or sole. "It is a scrambler, Dan. It generates static which interferes with the communications channels of the Others. Instruments of this sort were very valuable to the cousins when they attacked this base."

I looked at it with more respect. "Valuable" was a conservative word for it; something like it would have come in very useful when we were captives. It wasn't the only thing around, either. Beert's lab was full of high-tech alien gadgets of all kind. It was exactly what I'd been looking for to take back to the Bureau's technicians, when I'd still had hope of that.

But I didn't have that hope anymore.

Beert was still talking. "This particular device is not exactly like theirs; I built it in a different shape, to serve the purposes it is planned for, and had to waterproof it to protect its power."

That reminded me. "And it's self-powered?"

He stared at me. "Of course. Why would it not be?"

"Well," I said, "I've been wondering about that. I've looked at some of your other gadgets, and I don't see any wires."

He made a hissing noise of exasperation. "There are no wires. Each device draws its energy from—"

That wasn't the end of his sentence, it was just the point at which it turned into gibberish and I couldn't understand it anymore. I asked, "What?"

"I said it draws its energy from the *garble* of the *garble garble* which is present in the *garblegarblegarble*."

That was no improvement. I shook my head apologetically. "I guess this translator thing doesn't work as well as I thought," I said, touching the thing behind my ear. "I didn't understand any of that."

He sighed, wriggling his neck regretfully. I said, "If you could just try to explain a little—"

"I did try," he said testily. "You simply do not have the background to understand the words, and I do not have time to teach you just now. The person I wish to help will be waiting for us." He put the scrambler in the basket with the other things and closed the lid, gesturing for us to leave the lab.

Outside, Beert slammed the door behind us and grabbed my arm. I let him lead me toward the stream that went through the grounds of the nest, and there, standing by one of those round little bridges, I saw the person Beert wanted me to help.

It was no friend of mine. The thing was a Wet One, one of the amphibians who had killed Patrice.

I didn't say anything to Beert. Well, maybe that's not true. I think I probably did say something like, "Screw this," under my breath, but I doubt that Beert heard me. I wrenched my arm free from his grip, turned around and walked away, not looking back . . . for no more than three or four meters.

Then I stopped.

Beert was a funny-looking little dinosaur, and his unpredictably fluctuating moods—his often *childish* moods—sometimes made that particular little dinosaur difficult to live with. But he had done his best to befriend me. Had, in fact, saved my life, just for starters. And if he was now asking me to help him, even to help him do something for a species I hated—didn't I owe him something?

"Oh, hell," I said, this time out loud, and turned around. Beert was peering after me.

I retraced my steps to the stream bank. "Exactly what is it that you want me to do?" I asked.

24

I don't know if Beert had any idea of why I had walked away. He didn't comment. Maybe he figured it was just another bit of Earth-human queerness. He simply said, as though nothing had happened, "I will show you," and began pulling things out of his little basket and carefully setting them on the ground next to the Wet One.

Who was studying me intently with those bulging hippopotamus eyes that were set on the top of his head. I didn't speak. Neither did he. I did see that the tentacular electric organs that sprouted from his face were writhing restlessly. That didn't seem to be a friendly sign. It crossed my mind that Beert might have misjudged the situation, and I instinctively began looking around for something that might work as a weapon if the thing suddenly jumped me.

Beert's tap on my shoulder distracted me and I looked around. "Are you paying attention?" he asked crossly. "See, this is how the scrambler fits on the Wet One's body." He had it in his other hand, and began carefully to place it on the amphibian's gross belly, just behind its tiny mid-arms. I wondered what he was going to use for glue to make it stick to the Wet One's hide, but he didn't have to do that. He had something more effective than glue. A metal socket was actually embedded in the amphibian's flesh; the creature had evidently allowed someone to fasten the socket to his body surgically, right through the skin. There were two similar sockets flanking the one with the scrambler, and the next thing Beert did was to attach a couple of stout leather pouches to them.

Then he pulled the last of the basket's contents out.

It was a pair of handguns. *My* handguns. Two of the twenty-shot, Bureau-issued guns that had been my basic carry weapon ever since I became an agent.

I nearly lost it one more time, as the anger I had managed to push back out of sight boiled over again. If anybody was going to have my guns, it damn well ought to be me. I made a grab for them, snarling, "Hey! Those are *mine*!"

The amphibian slithered a half step away toward the stream, grunting a protest, but it didn't try to stop me. It didn't have to. Beert was fast as well as strong; he dropped the weapons, and his two rubbery arms clamped quick and hard around my wrists. He didn't raise his voice. "Actually," he said, "these two projectile weapons are for the Wet One. If you have a requirement for one, it can be copied for you, but I do not see any such necessity."

I wrenched free of his grip. He let me go, but his arms stayed near mine and his face danced before me. "They belong to me!" I complained. "That thing is a killer. How do I know he isn't going to shoot me with them?"

Beert said patiently, "He has no such intention."

That was when the amphibian spoke up, surprising me. He wasn't easy to understand. He spoke that same Horch language—naturally enough; I could see that he was wearing an implant of his own, tucked under his jaw. But he didn't have the same sort of vocal cords as I did, or even as the Horch did. The sounds he made were more like a hoarse, unpleasant kind of roaring than conversation, and I had to strain to make them out: "That is true. Shall I now speak of unfortunate past events?"

I guess the question was rhetorical, because the Wet One went right on talking. "The lethal pulsing of your female person should not have happened," he stated. "The sharp-object stabbing of our persons by yours should not have happened as well. The reason for these wrong happenings may be that my party was in Other Water, where we did not know its tastes. In Home Water," he explained, "where our females stay and the pups are reared, we know which tastes are persons and which are prey and which do not matter. In Other Water we may not know all the tastes. Yours were strange to us, and then your persons attacked us, so they were wrongly pulsed." He regarded me for a second with those knobbed eyes, then finished. "There is nothing else to speak on this matter."

I listened to his little speech impatiently, and turned to Beert. "What's he talking about?"

"He is telling you that the death of your friend was an accident," Beert said irritably. "As obviously it was. It is time you put this anger out of your mind."

I considered that for a moment, but damn him, Beert was right. I didn't much like being taught right from wrong by a snaky-headed monster from outer space, but I gave in. "But what the hell does he need my guns for?"

Beert gave me his approving neck-twist. "That is better, Dan. The reason to arm this person is that the Greatmothers have given permission to return him to his home planet, where he is going to resist the rule of the Others."

Resist the rule of the Others? That changed things.

It didn't necessarily make us friends. The first feeling that flooded my mind was simple, burning *envy.* This creature was going to go *home,* while I was stuck helplessly *here*. I was suddenly more jealous than I have ever felt in my life.

But the facts were plain. If I couldn't do anything to help my own human race, at least I might be able to do something to harm the damn Others. It was only revenge. But it was better than nothing.

Beert was picking one of the guns off the ground. He held it out to me gingerly. "It is for these that we need your help, Dan. The Wet One will be in grave danger when he arrives at his home planet. He needs a weapon. His ability to stun or kill other organisms with electrical shocks works only underwater and at close range. That is not good enough."

"Sure," I said, perplexed, "but why do you need one of my guns? Seems to me those Horch fighting machines had plenty of firepower."

Beert gave me that negative neck-wave. "He cannot use the energy weapons of our cousins. They would interfere with his electrical senses. These projectile things of yours might work, but we are not well sure of how to use them. Look, I have made these containers for them." He pulled one of those flexible sacks off its clamp, and I realized they were intended to be holsters for the guns. "Unfortunately," he said sadly, "the containers do not work well. Can you help?"

That put me right in familiar territory, so I grinned at him. "If there's one thing I'm good at," I said, "it's guns. Show me the problem."

He did. Actually, there wasn't a single problem, there were a lot of them. The first one was that Beert had put the holsters in on the wrong sides. I had heard that the flashier cowboy gunmen of the Old West—their TV versions, anyway—wore their guns like that, performing a lightning cross-draw when they had to kill some bad guy. That wouldn't work for the Wet One, because his anatomy wasn't up to the job. His short, skinny mid-arms were as conspicuously inadequate as the arms of a Tyrannosaur. They wouldn't stretch that far. When Beert reversed the holsters, we put the guns into them—after I made sure the safeties were well and truly on—and had the amphibian practice draws.

That was an improvement, but it suggested something else to me. "When he actually shoots a gun, he should fire with his arm straight out, otherwise he may get a broken bone. These twenty-shots don't have much recoil, but he doesn't have much arm." The Wet One, who was listening intently, immediately began trying that out. I sighed as I watched him. "Practice as much as you can before you go," I advised. "Another thing. Where do you think you might be doing this shooting, in the water or out of it?"

Beert swirled his head at me in alarm. "Will immersion in water harm the weapon?"

"Oh, no, they're waterproof, all right. What about it?"

I was looking at the amphibian, who answered for himself. "In most cases, I think, in air."

"That's good. I'm worried about shooting the gun underwater. It's not made for that, and with the resistance of the water, it might blow up in your hand. Try not to do that. Now"—I crossed my fingers—"let's see how good a shot you are."

Unsurprisingly, he wasn't good at all.

The Horch had nothing like a firing range, but Beert produced a wad of some kind of packing material out of the basket; I wadded up some of it and tossed it in the stream for a target. When the amphibian reared up on his front flippers he had just enough clearance to draw the guns and fire them, his tentacles nervously elevated out of the line of fire.

Beert was taking notes, skipping nimbly out of the way when the amphibian's shots went wildest. Then, when the Wet One reached the point of being maybe able to hit the side of a barn if he were locked inside, I decided he was about as good as he was going to get. I told Beert, "The holster clasp is too tight; you'll have to ease it up a little. He'll need reloads, too. Have you got more ammunition?"

It took a moment to make Beert understand that the weapon did not produce its own endless supply of bullets, but then he gave me the head-twist. "We can copy as much as needed."

"Copy a lot; there isn't going to be a gun shop where he's going. And you'll have to make something for him to carry them in." I thought for a moment, then, with some reluctance, told the Wet One, "I think you'd better keep the safety off; you might have trouble handling it if you need to shoot in a hurry. Just don't touch that trigger until you want to fire. Now, let's see how good you are at reloading."

He wasn't good at that, either, but he eventually got the idea, after a fashion. That was as far as we got, because Beert was fidgeting. "I must go back to my laboratory to make these changes in the equipment," he told the Wet One. Who made no response, except to turn and head for the stream. Just as he was entering the water, he paused, turned ponderously around and spoke to me, in that horrible roaring voice:

"Your metal killing device may be valuable to me, also your instruction in its use. For this I owe you the debt of thanks. If I can repay it, I will."

Then he slipped into the stream and was gone. A couple of those electric-shock appendages appeared briefly above the water, fluttering in the air almost as though he were saying good-by. Then nothing showed but those two knobby eye sockets and a pair of V-shaped ripples in the water, leaving Beert and me looking after him.

Beert made that hissing sort of sigh. "He is a brave person," he informed me. I just nodded. I had formed that opinion of the Wet One myself—along with a fair amount of residual envy—and anyway, I had something else on my mind.

Beert wasn't giving me much chance to bring it up. "As soon as I am finished in the laboratory," he said happily, "I must go to my cousins to talk to the Greatmother of the Eight Plus Threes, so that we may schedule a time when Mrrranthoghrow may operate the transit machine for him. I will send Pirraghiz to you, Dan."

I swallowed and took the plunge. "There's one other thing," I said.

"Yes?"

"I've been thinking about what you said. You were right. So let's just forget about making that copy of Pat for me," I told him.

Horch can't smile, don't have the facial muscles for it, but I could have sworn he was looking at me in an affectionate way. "It is forgotten, Dan. I am glad." And he gave my arm a gentle pat before he turned and hurried away.

Listen, I'm only human. Get me depressed enough and you might see a person selfisher than you would have believed. But I didn't have to *stay* selfish all the time.

SIX

Fighting Back

25

There was another lesson that old drill instructor of mine had taught us, in between the pushups and the ten-kilometer runs. What she said was, "Listen, ass-holes. It's always better to do *something* than *nothing,* you hear me? If it don't do nothing else, it'll make you feel better."

She was right. It did. My situation hadn't improved a hair in any tangible way, but I felt different. I felt for the first time that I was playing some part, however insignificant, in an action that might cause the Beloved Leaders some aggravation, even if only a little. Morale-wise, that was a big plus. It almost made me feel as though this interminable lonely life that stretched ahead of me might be worth living after all.

So I decided to start looking for other ways to do the Others harm. I don't know exactly what I was thinking of. Maybe leading a charge of Horch fighting machines into some Beloved Leader stronghold, the way they had taken over the prison-planet base. But whatever I was going to do to the Others, the first step was to get to where the action was.

Beert was the logical person to talk to on that subject, but he wasn't available. When he wasn't over in the Horch base to negotiate with the cousins, he was locked up in his workshop, making the changes in the Wet One's armament. I decided to pester Pirraghiz about it. She was in her room, sterilizing my chamber pot for me, and Mrrranthoghrow was with her.

I hesitated in the doorway. Pirraghiz's room was no bigger than mine, but she had somehow found time to put in homey touches of her own: some of those tiny flowers in a planter, clothing neatly hung, her own much larger bed. She had turned the room into a very personal habitation and, belatedly, it crossed my mind that they might have preferred being alone in it.

Apparently not. As soon as Pirraghiz saw me she waved me in with a spare arm. "Are you hungry?" she asked at once, but I shook my head. I wasn't looking for food.

"I want to know about the Wet One," I said.

She looked surprised, but recited: "He is being sent back to his own planet, so that—"

"I know that. Tell me how he's getting there."

She looked at Mrrranthoghrow, who answered for her. "He will be transmitted on the captured transit machine of the Others, of course."

"And how does he know how to get there?"

"Ah," the Doc said, enlightened. "You want to know how the Wet One will find his way to his home. The Horch have been working on such problems ever since they occupied this base. Capturing a transit machine of the Others is very useful to them. Once we had it disassembled, the robots began tracing its channels."

"That is the one great advantage the Horch have over the Others," Pirraghiz added. "The Others are very strong, but the Horch have in some cases been able to enter the Others' channels, while the Others have never been able to enter theirs."

I mulled that over. I could see the strategic importance of that. "Does that mean there's a channel direct to the Wet One's planet?"

"Of course not, Dannerman," Mrrranthoghrow said. "Not from this outpost. But there are channels to a nexus, which has many channels. One will take the Wet One to his destination."

He was annoying me. "What is a 'nexus'?"

"It is a sort of center where many channels come together," he said patiently. "In this case it is a large installation which also was captured from the Others. Now it belongs to the Horch. There was great damage in the fighting, but much of its equipment is intact—just as is the case here."

"What kind of installation?"

He gave me one of those massive shrugs. "I had no reason to ask such a question, Dannerman. I only know that it is much larger than this installation here."

Pirraghiz had been silent, watching me, but then she spoke up. "Dannerman, I think you are jealous of the Wet One. Do you want to go with him?"

I started to shake my head, then decided to admit it. "I think I could help him fight against the Others. I'm a lot better with those guns than he is."

She made a clucking sound with those thin lips. "You would be discovered at once, Dannerman, and then you would die."

"It's my risk to take!"

"And his as well. His only hope is secrecy, Dannerman, and even so, he has very little chance to survive there. In company with someone as conspicuous as you, he would have no chance at all."

I said stubbornly, "I'm going to ask Beert if I can go along anyway. When will I see him?"

She waved that off impatiently. "Soon. This afternoon, I think, but what is the use of that? He will simply say no."

"And then I will ask him again, and keep on asking him, until he says yes. This is something I have to do. You don't understand what it's like not to be able to do anything for my friends."

She sighed. "Do I not? I am jealous of the Wet One, too."

I hadn't expected to hear that from her. "Because you'd like to try to rescue your own planet?" I guessed.

"Rescue it? But we have no planet anymore, Dannerman. It is long destroyed. Our people no longer exist except as slaves of the Others, countless numbers of them, all over the universe." She sighed. "No. I am jealous because he has a home to return to." She paused, fingering her little amulet, and then added somberly, "Even though it is certain that he will see it only long enough to die there."

I didn't want to accept what Pirraghiz said, but I couldn't get rid of the sneaking suspicion that she was right. Did it make any sense for me simply to get myself killed on some planet not even my own? Would it even inconvenience the Beloved Leaders at all?

Logically I had to agree that it would not. But did I have any other way to strike a blow at them? I couldn't think of any.

I told Pirraghiz to call me when Beert was available and went back to my room, and what I did there was to put on that helmet again. Mrrranthoghrow had selected another set of tapes on the bugged people on Earth for me, and I wanted to see them. I think maybe what I had in mind was to remind myself of what the Beloved Leaders were doing to my own people.

It didn't work that way. The first person I saw was me, and what I was doing was flying out of a transit machine. And when the person whose eyes I was looking through turned, I saw Jimmy Lin and Dopey and a pair of Docs, and Rosaleen Artzybachova and Martin Delasquez and Pat. My Pat. Looking scared and worn and generally shook up, but looking mostly very good indeed to me.

It didn't take me long to figure out where I was. I was in Starlab, and the bunch of us had just made our escape from the prison planet. It was Patrice who I was eavesdropping on—had to be, because she was the only one of us who was bugged at that time. But it was Pat I wanted to see and touch, and be with.

I didn't switch to any other file. I stayed with that one. I listened to us congratulating ourselves on having got away from the damn Beloved Leaders, I watched myself destroy the transit machine so we couldn't be followed, I listened as I—that other I—called the Bureau on Starlab's ancient radio and painfully worked out a way of communicating with them that the rest of the world, and especially the Beloved Leaders, might not hear. With all the rest of the gang I got into the rickety old crew-rescue vehicle that had been berthed at Starlab since the last time any astronomer visited it. I stayed with them as its engines fired up and we started the long, bouncing, bucketing drop toward Earth, and I would have stayed a lot longer if I could, in spite of the fact that a suspicion was dawning in my mind.

What stopped me in the end wasn't that I got tired of seeing Pat, or that that new thought needed to be pursued. It was Pirraghiz. "Dannerman? I have brought you some food. And Beert is here now, if you want to see him."

I took the helmet off and blinked at her. She was taking little fruits and biscuits out of a coppery mesh bag and laying them before it. I ignored them. "Didn't you tell me that the transit machine on Starlab wasn't working anymore?"

She blinked back at me. "Why, yes, Dannerman. That is so."

"That's what I thought," I said—the other possibility having been that that other Dannerman hadn't done as thorough a job of destruction as he thought. "All right, let's go. I want to see Beert right away."

"To ask him if you can throw your life away with the Wet One? At least take the meal with you," she said, scooping it all back into the bag. As she handed it to me she said, "It is a foolish idea, and he will surely say no."

"You might be right," I agreed. "But maybe I have a better idea now."

26

When I knocked on the laboratory door Beert let me in at once. "Look here," he said, neck and arms awriggle. "I have taken your advice. Give me one of the ammunition carriers."

That last part was aimed at his Christmas tree, not me. The thing was hovering over a workbench, littered with the usual cryptic array of gadgets. The robot immediately picked one up and brought it over to hand to Beert. Who handed it happily to me. It was heavy. It was also streamlined and curved, like the other things Beert was attaching to the Wet One, and it had the same clamp arrangement to hold it in place. Which meant, I thought, that the Wet One would have had more sockets carved into his flesh. I admired his dedication. "See," Beert was saying proudly, reaching to touch the thing in my hand, "this release will fit the Wet One's digits. It is this button here; he needs only to touch it and it flies open." Beert did. It did, revealing half a dozen gleaming clips for the twenty-shot. "Also there are eight sixteens of additional clips and several others of the projectile weapons in those containers there—" gesturing at a pair of oblong boxes of that same rubbery material—"but those he will not be able to carry with him. Perhaps he can hide them somewhere, and come back to them when they are needed."

His little head was close to mine, the curly eyelashes fluttering excitedly. He was waiting for a compliment, I thought, so I obliged. "That's fine," I said, and glanced at the hovering robot. "Can you turn that thing off?" I asked.

Beert pulled his head away to regard me. "But I have told you, Dan, there is nothing to fear from this machine—"

I reached out and caught his neck, pulling his head toward me so that I could whisper. "I want to ask you about something I don't want the cousins to hear. I don't want that thing listening."

Beert went suddenly tense. He didn't pull away, as he easily could have, and I felt his warm breath on my face as he thought that over. "This robot does not interface with the others, as I have told you."

"Please, Beert."

He sighed. "Go into inactive mode," he ordered the Christmas tree. Then to me, warningly, "Dan, you recall what the Greatmother said to us. We do not agree with the cousins in all things, but they are still Horch."

"I don't want to harm the cousins. I just want a favor from you, and I think it is better if they don't know about it." I hesitated, looking at the Christmas tree, needles retracted, immobile—but could it still hear? I had to hope not. So I began. "Check me out on this, Beert. When the Wet One goes he won't be heading for his home planet; he'll be going to something they call a 'nexus,' where there are all sorts of channels that belong to the Others."

"Yes?"

"That's true, then? And another thing. When I was using the helmet I saw something funny," I went on. "I was in Patrice's mind, and we were in Starlab. I saw myself destroy the transit machine there. But I didn't lose contact even after it was destroyed. I think that means that there's another transit machine somewhere nearby that's still working—I don't know where. Maybe in the scout ship that found Earth in the first place? But still working, anyway, and somehow or other you're still tapping into that channel, I guess from this nexus."

"Yes, yes," Beert said testily. "I suppose all that is so, but I still do not know what favor you want of me."

And then he took a deep breath, because Beert was not a stupid being. By then he did know.

27

It took a lot of persuasion, and he fought me all the way. "Transmit you to this scout ship? But you do not know for sure even that it exists! The one that visited your planet's system may be long gone on some other errand."

"Or," I said doggedly, "it may not. At least there's some sort of contact, and what else could it be?"

"Oh, Dan," he said, sorrowful though sympathetic, "do you know what you ask? I do not believe the cousins would permit it."

"That's why I don't want them to know about it. But I give you my word, I mean no harm at all to the cousins."

"What about harm to yourself? A ship of the Others is not like your tiny Starlab orbiter. Such ships are quite large, and they are well guarded. There will be fighters of the Others standing by at the transit machine, watchful that they may be invaded by the cousins as this base was."

"I know. Pirraghiz told me all about the Others' ships."

"Then you also know that they will kill you as soon as you appear."

I shrugged. "Maybe I can kill them first."

"More likely you cannot, Dan," he scoffed. "You? Alone against well-armed fighters?"

"Oh," I said, "we Earth people have a pretty good combat record. Pirraghiz said so herself."

He waggled his neck at me reprovingly, then tried a different tack. "And even if they do not kill you, what can you accomplish? Do you think you can simply leap through space from the scout ship to your planet?"

"Whatever I can do, it will be more than I can do sitting here in your jail."

That silenced him for a moment. "I do not think of myself as your jailer, Dan," he said sorrowfully.

"Then set me free!"

He was silent again for quite a while, his head swerving indecisively about—darting toward the immobile robot as though about to start it up again, returning to search my face at close range.

While I—

I was estimating the distance to the nearest workbench.

I could see that there were all sorts of things there that I thought the Bureau's techs would have liked to play with. More immediately important, I saw a sort of chisel, a pink ceramic blade with a handle shaped for Beert's grip, not mine. But I thought I could hold it well enough in a pinch. What's more, I was pretty sure that the blade could cut right through that sinewy neck of his.

Well, let me make that clear. I certainly wasn't intending to kill Beert. I was merely hoping that he would believe I would, once I put the knife to his throat. The real question was whether threatening his life would force him to help me.

I wasn't proud of myself for thinking of taking a knife to a being who had befriended me. I wasn't even sure that I could bring myself to do it. But then I thought of what awaited my whole world—including Pat—and I inched a bit closer to the workbench.

Finally Beert gave one of his whispery sighs. "I do not see that this would directly threaten the interests of the cousins," he said reluctantly, "though perhaps it is better if they are not consulted. But even if I were willing to do what you wish, I do not know how to do it."

Well, I did. Or hoped I did, anyway. "When you transmit the Wet One to this nexus, transmit me too." I had been thinking it all out, as far as I could, and I laid it all out for Beert. The Horch in this nexus probably could find a channel to the scout ship for me. If not, at least to whatever Beloved Leaders relay station was passing on the data from the bugged humans. If they could find the channel, presumably they could use it to send me there. And then I would take my chances.

Beert listened in brooding silence, then finally raised his serpentine arms to stop me. He said somberly, "Do you know, Dan, I was sure that, if I helped you at all, sooner or later you would ask me to do something that the cousins had not approved."

"Then why did you help me?"

Reflectively he rubbed his chin against the edge of the workbench. "I am not sure. Probably because I had seen so many of you die. Perhaps because you and I had both been captives of the Others. In any case, I thought it harmless to keep you alive, even to let you learn all you wished of our ways, since there was no possibility you could use that knowledge against us."

"I haven't really learned very much," I said, wheedling.

He lifted his head to gaze closely at me again. "You have learned enough to lie to me, haven't you? But very well. If I were you, I would fear the cousin Horch as much as I did the Others. Perhaps I do already. Let me find Mrrranthoghrow and tell him what he is to do."

SEVEN

The Nexus

28

The air-cushion van that took us to the old Beloved Leader base was big, but the eleven or twelve hundred kilograms of us, of one species or another, crowded it pretty tight. Beert's Christmas tree stood at the central control pedestal. Pirraghiz and Mrrranthoghrow sat one on each side of the vehicle, I guess for balance. The Wet One had the rear seat all to himself, while Beert and I were in front. Beert wasn't talking, his neck glumly waving from side to side, and I didn't press him. I took a piece of the stuff Pirraghiz had given me out of my pocket and began to eat it—it looked like a carrot, and crunched like one, but it had a sort of lemonade flavor.

Beert suddenly darted his head toward the copper-mesh bag between my feet and then up to confront me in my face. "What have you got there?" he asked suspiciously.

"Extra food," I said—untruthfully. I don't think I convinced him. To take his mind off it I jerked a thumb at the Christmas tree. "Do we have to have that thing with us?" I asked.

"It will carry the gear for the Wet One," he said grumpily, "and it will go with him to the nexus in case there are any problems." But he let it go at that, and then we were arriving.

We climbed a rise in that rust-red rock desert that seemed to be the prison planet's natural state, and the dilapidated buildings of the base were right in front of us. They looked naked. The Horch hadn't bothered to replace the silvery energy dome of the Beloved Leaders. The place looked like, and was, not much more than a junkyard of damaged Beloved Leaders machines.

As soon as we stopped, the Christmas tree silently gathered all the Wet One's possessions, guns and scrambler and ammunition boxes, and led the way outside. "Pick him up," Beert ordered, and Mrrranthoghrow obeyed. The Wet One was a lot of mass, and ungainly to handle, but the Doc lifted him and carried him out of the car, puffing slightly with the effort as Pirraghiz followed. Beert and I got out just behind them. Then, as the two Docs moved out of the way, I saw what was standing just inside the building line.

I froze. A silvery Horch fighting machine was poised there between a wrecked, man-high purple cylinder and a heap of coppery junk that might once have been anything at all. I knew all about those fighting machines. Two of them had done their best to kill me and all the others as we tried to escape the first time, and they had come pretty close. The good part was that they had turned out very vulnerable to a gunshot, having been designed to expect more sophisticated weapons, but that was not of immediate importance since I didn't have a gun. My adrenaline surged.

But the machine wasn't paying any attention to us. It stood like a statue on its spidery, wheeled legs, evidently abandoned there when the fighting was over. I breathed again, but I kept my eye on it as I sidled past, and that was what kept me from seeing the other Christmas tree, the one that was barring our path.

The first I knew of it was the sound of its little roller-skate wheels, but as I looked around it spoke. "Stop there," it ordered.

It didn't look hostile. Its needles were mostly retracted, but it didn't look as though it wanted to get out of our way, either. Beert shouldered his way past our own Christmas tree to confront it. "This Wet One is to be transmitted to his own world, for which the Greatmother of the Eight Plus Threes has given permission," he told it. "It cannot walk well on land, so these persons are here to carry it."

There was another noise of wheels coming from somewhere nearby, deeper and louder than a Christmas tree's skates, but the robot paid no attention. It extended a branch of needles toward me. "What is the reason for this other organism being here?" it asked.

If the question was meant for me, I didn't answer it. I was squinting down the passage, where a pair of those Horch three-wheeled velocipedes were rolling toward us. Each cart carried a single cousin Horch, their belly plates gleaming and their necks extended in curiosity toward us. I was wondering if my whole plan was going to collapse right there.

Beert answered for everyone. "This other organism is my project, for which the Greatmother has also given permission. I am investigating whether such a primitive person could learn to use advanced technology, or whether he is at too low a level to be a possible ally against the Others."

Whether the Christmas tree was buying that, I couldn't tell, but it didn't matter. One of the cousin Horch spoke up. "We have been called for nothing. It is only Djabeertapritch's puppy."

Well, he didn't say "puppy," exactly. What he said was more like "immature lower-form creature possessed for entertainment," and he sounded amused as he said it. But he went on to the Christmas tree: "He is harmless. Let them pass. Escort them to the transit machine in case they need help."

And the other cousin Horch said to Beert, equally amused, "You are still not used to the blessings of technology yourself, are you, Djabeertapritch? Imagine using organisms to carry another organism! You should have summoned a vehicle." And, with the Horch equivalent of chuckles, the two of them rolled away.

For the benefit of the glass robot, I did my best to look harmless, while, for Beert and the Docs, doing my best to prove the cousin Horch's estimate of me wrong. I hadn't cared for being called a puppy.

What I cared about was that the guard Christmas tree had been instructed to accompany us. It did. It rolled along in silence, apart from the occasional faint jingle of its needles. It paused when we paused, so that Mrrranthoghrow, panting, could turn the burden of the Wet One over to Pirraghiz for a while. It didn't seem to be paying any attention to us, other than that, though the sparkly ball at its top was flickering rapidly. It was just *there,* and it stayed there until we reached the space where the great green transit machine stood.

Two other Christmas trees stood there, apparently waiting for us. Worse still, one of the spider-legged fighting machines stood immobile against a wall. It seemed to be in standby mode, but I was pretty sure that it would come to life very quickly if needed. The only plus factor among those unwelcome negatives was that there were no living Horch cousins on the scene, but I wished their machines would go away. And they had no apparent intention of that.

When Pirraghiz had set the amphibian down, Beert looked around at the machines. "We have come to transmit this Wet One on his mission," he announced, in case they were interested. They didn't seem to be. I know of no way of telling what a Christmas tree is looking at—one configuration of needles is pretty much like another—but I didn't think they were even watching as Mrrranthoghrow opened a flap on the side of the transit machine and began rearranging its little rainbows of color. Beert's own Christmas tree was busy, too. It was expertly fitting all the Wet One's paraphernalia into its receptacles on the amphibian's body.

There was something I wanted there, so I walked over to where that was going on. The amphibian raised himself up, staring at me with those hippopotamus eyes. I patted his thick body encouragingly. "Good luck," I said, loudly enough so that everyone could hear, at the same time relieving him of one of his guns. That wasn't hard to do, since the holsters were made for quick release. I didn't think anyone had seen me.

Whether the amphibian had, I didn't know. Those electric Medusa snakes around his broad mouth were waving wildly, but not coming close to me. "I wish the same to you," he said thickly, and waddled over to the transit machine.

There was no ceremony. Mrrranthoghrow held the door open. The amphibian climbed in. Beert's personal Christmas tree followed, lugging the ammunition cases. Mrrranthoghrow slammed the door shut and touched one of the colored lights.

And a moment later he opened the door again, and the chamber was empty. The Wet One was on his way.

That was when we came to the hard part.

I picked up my little copper-mesh bag of goodies and strolled to where Mrrranthoghrow was holding the door for me. "We will now transmit this other organism," Beert announced, and everything went bad at once.

All three of the robots spoke up. "No," said the violet one. "We have no instructions for more than one transmission."

"Why did this organism take the weapon from the Wet One?" the greenish one asked.

And the third one, the pale orange jobber that had stopped us in the first place, moved toward me. "What has the organism got in that bag? Has he been stealing from you, Djabeertapritch?"

The whole scheme was falling apart before my eyes. I could not let that happen, not when I was so close. "Wait!" Beert ordered, but the robots weren't waiting, and neither was I. I had the gun in my hand. I got the pale orange robot right in the globe at its top, first shot. I was drawing a bead on the second one when Pirraghiz grabbed me. She leaped into the machine, me and my bag in her arms, mewing at Mrrranthoghrow. Who put his hands on the controls. Beert bellowed in surprise and anger, but he was looking at the fighting machine, which had come to life and was advancing toward us.

I don't suppose Beert was thinking very clearly. What he did was jump into the transit machine with Pirraghiz and me, and the door closed.

I was on my way. To a place very far from Earth, as it happened. But on my way.

29

Travel in these alien go-machines was no trouble at all. You got in at one place, you came out at a different one. That was all there was to it.

This time the other place was really different. The first thing I noticed about it was that it was a microgravity environment, like Starlab's, where I weighed nothing at all.

No, that's wrong. The *first* thing I noticed about this "nexus" was that three ugly Horch fighting machines were standing there, looking ready to blow my head off. That's wrong, too, though, because they weren't standing. They were clinging to a network of cables that spanned the bare-metal-walled room we were in, and they hung there in three different orientations—heads up, tails up, every which way up—because the microgravity gave them no place to stand on. Beert, flailing around for something to grab on to, squawked, "Don't shoot!"

Mercifully, they didn't. I still had my twenty-shot in my hand, but I don't think I could have fired it to any effect if they had. Pirraghiz was holding me tight, but Pirraghiz was floating herself until she managed to catch on to a couple of the cables. Then things stopped whirling around for me; such were the advantages of a few extra arms.

By a doorway a couple of the glass robots were tugging the great bulk of the Wet One away. They stopped as we got there. One of them, an unfamiliar Prussian blue, shot out a crystalline tendril in our direction and spoke. "We were not informed of a second transmission. What is your purpose here?"

I didn't have a good answer for that, so I was glad that the question seemed to be aimed at Beert. He didn't look as though he had a good answer, either. He had caught one of the lines to moor himself—upside down relative to me, as it happened—and his neck was darting this way and that worriedly. That had me worried, too. Could he forgive me for shooting up one of his cousins' machines? And if he couldn't, what then?

The only thing I was sure of was that whatever might come after that would not be good news for me.

As inconspicuously as possible, I jammed the gun in my pocket to get it out of sight, but I kept that hand near it, just in case. I was well aware that if Beert said the wrong word, one of those fighting machines would start shooting, and that would be the end of this particular Dan Dannerman. Of course, I would certainly be shooting back. But it wouldn't do any good in the long run, because I wasn't fool enough to think I could defeat the whole Horch race single-handed.

Which would not have kept me from giving it a try.

The machine apologetically repeated its question, and Beert finally bestirred himself. "I am Djabeertapritch of the Two Eights," he said, sounding wretched but determined. "I was a captive of the Others. My ancestors were caught there when the Two Eights planet was invaded, and I am one of their descendants."

The Christmas tree silently processed that information for a moment, then extended one branch toward Pirraghiz and me. "And what are these organisms?"

"They are my servants. Since I am from a lost colony, we have not had machine servers for many generations. I am used to using living species to work for me. The larger of the two was carrying the Wet One; the other is—a volunteer like the Wet One," Beert said miserably, not looking at me. "He is to be transmitted to his own planet to resist the Others."

The machine processed some more, and evidently did some unheard communicating. After a bit it said, "You are welcome here, Djabeertapritch of the Two Eights. The Greatmother of this nest instructs me to provide you with quarters and whatever else you need until she can come to welcome you in person."

Since Beert hadn't blown the whistle on me, at least not yet, my chances of making it back to Earth began to look a little better. That was when I remembered that I didn't want to come back empty-handed. The little copper-mesh bag of goodies I had swiped from Beert's lab was a good start, but I wanted more.

There wasn't much more to be seen. The corridors we were scudding through were starkly bare. I remembered being told that this place, like the prison planet, had fairly recently been captured from the

Others; no doubt there had been a lot of wreckage, but no doubt, too, that had been some time ago and the resident Horch had had time to clean up. Nestled in one of Pirraghiz's arms, I had every chance to look around, but there wasn't much to look at.

We, on the other hand, must have been an interesting spectacle for the locals. The two Christmas trees were making easy work of tugging the Wet One along, though the amphibian himself was emitting snuffling noises of discomfort and complaint. Pirraghiz had no trouble carrying me hand over hand along the cables, even though behind us Beert had glumly wrapped both his rubbery arms around one of her huge feet to be towed as well. The corridors weren't entirely empty. Along the way we passed half a dozen of the Christmas-tree robots, who simply got out of the way but showed no sign of interest in us, and one or two living Horch, who did. But, although the Horch goggled at us as we passed, they didn't interfere.

There was a mix-up when we got to our destination. It was in a better neighborhood—some of the rooms were occupied here, and a couple of infant Horch stuck their heads out of the doorways to see the sight—but the room the Christmas tree offered Beert was small. Heaven knows what cattle pen the robot had had in mind for us lesser breeds, but Beert was having none of it. "They must all stay with me," he declared, in a tone that accepted no arguments. The robot didn't offer any, actually. It communed with itself for a moment or two—probably really was communicating with higher authority—and then led us to a larger suite.

It wasn't just large, it was handsomely furnished. It had a central reception area with those Horch bowl-shaped TVs and racks of the Horch glittery-tape books strapped in place so they wouldn't float away, and webbing to hold an occupant in place while he watched or read, and lighting that could be brightened or dimmed with switches that looked like mushroom caps. A couple of short passages led to other rooms, also nicely arranged. Evidently nothing was too good for a Horch who had suffered captivity under the Others.

Our robot guide indicated that the largest of the sleeping rooms was to be Beert's, so we underlings checked out the others. Each had sets of sleep-webbings attached to the walls, a good size for me but nowhere near adequate for Pirraghiz or the Wet One. Pirraghiz didn't complain. The amphibian did. "It is very dry here," it roared. "Is there no water anywhere? And why am I not already on my way to my home?"

I left Pirraghiz to try to placate him. I could hear Beert in his own room, talking to the robot, but I didn't want to see Beert just then, so I explored. What I was really looking for was some small additional bits of Horch technology to add to the store in my bag, but there wasn't much of that. I did find a nifty zero-G toilet—luckily, because the need was getting acute. Whether the technology was Horch or Beloved Leader, I couldn't tell, but it was kilometers better than anything on Starlab. I would have been glad to take that along if I could. Since I couldn't, I made do with another couple of the glitter-tape books.

When I got back to my room, Beert's Christmas tree was relieving the Wet One of his weapons and gadgets to stow away. Then it came to me, a branch extended meaningfully. I hesitated, but Pirraghiz commanded, "Give the weapon to it," and I passed over my twenty-shot. When it had put the gun away I marked the place, but it was as well there as in my pocket, for the time being.

Then the Christmas tree ordered us into Beert's room. I found him nervously rubbing at a stain on his tunic, his long, supple neck dancing all around his body as he checked his outfit—like a debutante about to be presented to the queen, I thought, and found out how close I was. "It is the Greatmother of this nest," he told me. "She is actually coming here herself to see us! Be very respectful to her, Dan—and when she has gone, you and I have much to talk about."

30

The Greatmother did not travel alone. First came a couple of new Christmas trees, dexterously scrambling along the cables and bearing gifts. One had a variety of capsules and clumps of what appeared to be the food Beert had requested, the other a rubbery ovoid the size of a pig. That contained water, and when the Wet One found that out, he begged to have some of it sprayed on him. There wasn't time for that, for the next to enter was the Greatmother herself.

This one was even fatter than the Greatmother of Beert's nest, and a lot more fashionably dressed. She wore silvery body armor that covered not only her belly but nearly her whole torso. It struck me that that had to be uncomfortably heavy. Garments and all, the creature had to mass at least a quarter of a ton.

But not, of course, here. She came floating weightlessly into the reception chamber, towed by a pair of glass robots to save her the bother of swarming along the cables herself. Her long neck was covered with bangles like a Ubangi's, and it was dancing a hula of greeting. The Greatmother gave the most cursory of glances at the clutch of us lesser species, and addressed herself directly to Beert. "I welcome you, Djabeertapritch of the Two Eights," she declared, touching her nose almost to his. "We are glad to have you in our nest, but how does it happen that you come?"

It was clear that Beert was the one she was welcoming. I was sure that if Pirraghiz and I had turned up without a live Horch as company, our reception would have been a lot less hospitable. For Beert, she was different. The Greatmother was thrilled to meet a conspecific who had endured the vile captivity of the Others. She wasn't disposed to question Beert's stumbling explanation of his nest's history and the rapidly invented mix-up that had brought him here, either. Actually his rather creative description of the blunders that had made it happen amused her. She had a superior kind of tolerance of one planet in the Horch federation for another, reminding me of the way Canadians talked about New Zealanders in the British Commonwealth. "Well, what do you expect of a bunch of Eight Plus Threes?" she asked jovially. She cast a mildly disapproving eye at the amphibian and me. "It is odd, however," she added, "that Horch should concern themselves with the problems of lesser species."

"They are more worthy than they seem, Greatmother," Beert said humbly. "Permit me to introduce them—"

She shrugged that idea away impatiently, neck and arms all twisting at once. "My least of grandsons is interested in such other organisms. I am not. But tell me of your captivity, Djabeertapritch. You were allowed no machines at all? But how did you live?"

I am sure Beert had more urgent things to talk to her about than his nest's tribulations, but he was not capable of denying the request of a Greatmother. "We were Horch," he said simply. "We used what we had or could make. For building materials we took clay from the ground and long, thin shoots from the local vegetation—"

I didn't want to hear it all again, so I took a chance. "Excuse me," I said deferentially, addressing Beert. "The Wet One needs water, so if we may withdraw—?"

The Greatmother answered for him; it was the first time she had spoken to me directly. "Go, go," she said irritably. "But leave food for Djabeertapritch; the poor thing must be hungry."

We all crowded into one of the other rooms, or all but Beert and his personal robot, which remained behind to serve him his meal. I had two things on my mind. For one, I knew I was going to have that little talk with Beert before long, and I wasn't looking forward to it. I was definitely looking forward to the other, though. However much I tried to warn myself that there were many hurdles still to get across, I could almost taste the nearness of my escape to Earth. While Pirraghiz was taking charge of the food we had carried away with us, sniffing and tasting each item, I looked around the room for things that might be useful when I got back. By the time she had approved a few things for my meal, I decided there weren't any. But there might be information worth having.

Pirraghiz handed me a collection of fruits and spoke doubtfully to the amphibian. "I do not know if any of this is suitable for you, Wet One."

The Wet One waved a flipper at her. The robot with the sack of water was carefully spraying his rubbery skin, a squirt at a time, like Spanish peasants taking wine from a goatskin, while a second robot was busy mopping up the droplets that splashed away. The Wet One was wriggling with pleasure as his skin welcomed the damp, but it did not distract him from his purpose. "I do not need to eat now," he grumbled, in that thick, muddy voice. "I will eat well when I have been transmitted to my own planet. When will that happen?"

His bath boy-robot answered him. "The channels are being prepared. The Greatmother will give the order to transmit you when she wishes."

I thought that was a good opportunity to try to get some information, so I interrupted. "Can you tell us what kind of a place we're in?"

The spraying robot did not respond, but the one on mop-up detail stopped what it was doing and extruded a glittering branch of twiglets in my direction. "This is a nest of the Four and Ones, formerly occupied by the Others," it said.

That wasn't informative. I said, "I mean, what *is* it?" That was no better. The robot stood silent and impassive, only the glittering ball at its top flickering unhelpfully. Pirraghiz sighed, put down the loaf of something she was breaking into pieces for me and issued an order.

"Display the appearance of this artifact we are in," she commanded the Christmas tree.

It worked. The thing immediately went to the video bowl, fussed with the controls for a moment and did as commanded. An image sprang up in the bowl. It was obviously a space station of some kind, but what it looked like was a child's impromptu building-block construction, all jagged angles and bits and pieces tacked on. It gleamed of metal, though not very brightly. At first I thought it was a kind of engineering drawing, since it was displayed against a background of solid black, like the images I'd seen of other species in the helmet.

But then Pirraghiz said, "What are those things?" and I saw that the blackness was not quite complete. It was a sky, and not a kind of sky I had ever seen before. It was certainly nothing like the brilliant globular-cluster display of the prison planet. It wasn't even like a starry night on Earth. There were no stars at all. Instead there was a scattering of fuzzily glowing little scraps of light, hard to make out. Most were white, some bluish, one or two a ruddy orange in color. And apart from them there was nothing but blackness—total, unrelieved, unfriendly blackness.

I had not been in love with an astronomer for nothing. "My God," I said, "those are galaxies!"

Ever since the five of us found ourselves on the prison planet, I had been aware that we were far from home. Not *this* far, though. Not in intergalactic space! Even the globular cluster of stars that surrounded us could have been somewhere within that fuzzy whirlpool of stars that was our own galaxy, but now—

No. We weren't even that close anymore.

I know it's silly. If we had been close enough to see Earth as a star in the sky, say marooned on the surface of Mars, I still would have had no way of getting to it other than one of these alien transit machines. And with the machines, no distance was really far. Wherever I was, I was as close to home as a single step, no matter how many millions of light-years I had to cross to get there.

All the same, it *felt* different. It felt frightening.

It wasn't until Pirraghiz touched me on the shoulder that I realized I was still staring at that picture in the bowl. "Are you all right, Dannerman?" she asked anxiously. "You aren't eating."

I looked down at the crinkly pale fruit in my hand, then gave it back to her. "I'm not hungry," I said.

"You should eat," she said, "but if that is not what you want to do just now, perhaps you should go to Beert. Have you forgotten that he wanted to talk to you?"

Well, actually I had, at least for the moment. But it was something that needed to be done, so I headed for the reception room.

I was surprised to find that Beert was still talking; he had just got to the beginnings of the building of the nest and their invention of a kind of paper. And the Greatmother was absorbedly listening still, but when I came in she glanced at me, with the absent look a visitor might give the family cat as it slunk into a room, then shook herself. "I am being selfish, Djabeertapritch," she sighed. "All the nest will want to hear your story. We must have a banquet and sing so that you can teach them what Horch can do, however wretched their circumstances."

"I am honored by your visit, Greatmother," he said, lowering his head respectfully.

"Yes," she agreed. And as her personal Christmas tree began to bear her away she twisted her neck teasingly and added, "You will enjoy the banquet, Djabeertapritch. We will show you someone you have never seen before."

31

The talk with Beert didn't get off to a good start. What was on my mind was why we were so far from anything at all; what was on his was wonder about who this previously unknown "someone" might be. It turned out quickly that he couldn't answer my question, and naturally I hadn't a clue about his. So we got serious. I said, "I'm sorry if I got you in trouble, Beert."

He gave me one of those nose-to-nose looks for a moment, then pulled away. "You should not have destroyed one of the cousins' machines," he said, sorrowfully judicious. "The rest is my fault. Now show me what you have in that bag."

He caught me by surprise that time, but I sighed and retrieved the bag. There are times when you just have to throw in your hand and take what's coming to you.

When I loosened the drawstring and shook it gently, its contents spilled out: all the little odds and ends of Horchware that I had surreptitiously filled it with, tools stolen from Beert's laboratory, a batch of Pirraghiz's tapes and the ones I had taken from the room here. I had been careful when I opened it, but the things began to fly around the room. I caught as many as I could, and Beert reached out for others. He stared at the first one that came his way, a black oblong with rows of dimples along its side. "This is mine!" he said. I didn't answer, and he darted his head toward me. "You took it from my workshop!" I didn't say anything to that, either. I was busy cramming the loose items back in the bag. Beert didn't stop me. He even handed a couple of them back to me, but he wasn't meeting my eyes anymore. When I had everything stowed away again I cleared my throat.

"I didn't want to tell you about these things," I said.

"No, you would not," he agreed. "These are Horch technology! They came from the cousins. I did not think you would try to take such things with you. I do not think my Greatmother would approve."

I said miserably, "I didn't like doing it, Beert, but what choice did I have? Do you remember what you said? That in my place you would fear the cousin Horch as much as the Others? Well, I do!"

Beert gave me a look I couldn't read, then turned away. Well, "twisted away" is a better way to put it. He corkscrewed his neck around itself until it came to rest with his chin on his shoulder, or what would have been his shoulder if he'd had one, looking away from me. "I need to think," he said. "Leave me, Dan."

And I did.

Pirraghiz insisted that I eat, so I did. Then she urged me to sleep, because there was no knowing when I might get the chance again, so I tried to do that, too. Sleep didn't come quickly, though. What made it difficult was my conscience.

The difficulty was that although this Beert was a weird-looking creature with a snaky neck and the face of a rattlesnake—not to mention that he was also a member of that race who had just finished murdering a whole bunch of my fellow humans, one of whom (or several of whom) had been me—in spite of all that, he was something else. He was one of the only two friends I had left, anywhere in this part of the universe. And I had put him in the deep shit, and had every prospect of getting him in deeper still.

You might ask how I could do something like that to a friend.

I guess the only proper answer would be "practice," because actually I had had plenty of experience along those lines. Betraying friends was basically the job description of what I did for the National Bureau of Investigation. We called it "infiltration." In order to get the goods on some gang of criminals or terrorists—or whatever—my first step was to make some new friends, who would remain my friends just as long as it took me to get the evidence that would put them in prison for most of their adult lives.

I had never had much of a problem with my conscience in those days, because those "friends" weren't friends at all. They were bad guys, and they needed to be put away. But Beert wasn't a bad guy. Neither was my other new friend, Pirraghiz. And I was definitely screwing up her life, too.

So I didn't get much sleep, hanging on to the webbing in my alien room in this alien thing called a "nexus." Neither did anyone else, because it wasn't long until one of the Christmas trees poked in on me and announced, "The channels for the Wet One have been accessed. It may proceed now to its transmission."

32

I don't know if Beert had slept, either. When I got to where the Wet One was, Beert was there, too, painstakingly reattaching all the amphibian's gear to his body, but he didn't speak to me.

He didn't speak on the way back to the transit-machine chamber, either. The trip seemed shorter than it had coming the other way, maybe because my mind wasn't on what we were doing. What my mind was occupied with was wondering what Beert's mind was. I knew he was feeling guilty. I didn't know what he would do about it. If duty overcame friendship, he only had to speak a couple of words and my hopes of ever getting back to Earth would be right down the tube. Or if he dithered indecisively for very long, that would be nearly as bad. What I wanted was to be on my way before it occurred to anybody to put in a call to the Eight Plus Threes.

A couple of the Christmas trees were waiting for us at the transit machine. So was a living Horch—a very young Horch, I thought, because he was no more than half Beert's size, but handsomely decked out in a scaled-down version of his Greatmother's body armor. "I am Kofeeshtetch," he said—or something like that. He was talking to Beert, but his neck was swaying toward me and the Wet One. "I am the Greatmother's least grandson. Can these organisms talk?"

Kofeeshtetch turned out to be pretty nearly the best thing that had happened to me in a while. He was a pampered, and fairly well spoiled, youngster, and that was very good for us lower organisms. He wasn't just interested in us, he was *fascinated.* He was even more fascinated—no, the right word is "thrilled," thrilled enough to be peeing his pants if he'd had any—at what we two aborigines were planning to do. Invade strongholds of the Others! Do it single-handed! "When I myself am grown," he boasted breathlessly, "I too will command forces to capture stations and worlds from the Others, just as my parents did in this installation! But I will not, of course, be foolish enough to attempt it alone. Do you imagine that you have any hope of succeeding at all?"

I wasn't sure whether he was asking the Wet One or me, but I wanted to be the one who answered. "With the generous help of you Horch, yes!" I said.

Beert gave me a disapproving look, translated as *Shut up, you've made enough trouble.* "It is kind of you to take an interest, Kofeeshtetch," he said, doing his best to be polite to a grandson of a Greatmother, "but we have urgent business. This Wet One is most uncomfortable in this dry and weightless environment. He should begin his mission without delay."

The youth shrugged impatiently. "Of course, but first I wish to hear his plans in detail. Speak to me if you can, Wet One."

The amphibian's little electric whiskers were twisting about. For a moment I thought the Greatmother's least grandson was going to get a cattle-prod shock to hurry him along, but courtesy, and prudence, won out. The Wet One began telling his plans in his thick, slobbery voice.

Kofeeshtetch listened with a lot less courtesy, his neck drawn back from the Wet One in repugnance. "I can hardly understand this one," he remarked to Beert. "He speaks very poorly, as do you. I am disappointed." He turned to the nearest Christmas tree. "At least display for me what his planet looks like, also"—shooting one arm in my direction—"the planet of this one."

"We have not yet identified the other organism's home," the machine apologized.

"Do so! Meanwhile, the display!"

There was no doubt that Kofeeshtetch was used to having his orders obeyed. They were. Another of the Christmas trees, the one hovering by the transit machine, quickly swung itself to a TV bowl in the wall and made adjustments.

As a picture sprang up in the bowl, the amphibian caught his breath in a sort of loud, abbreviated snore. To me, the picture was just a planet, and not a particularly interesting one. None of its few land masses looked anything like Earth, but it meant something to the amphibian. He croaked, "That is it! I believe that is my true Home Water!"

One of his shocking tendrils was resting on the image, touching a wide bay that looked like any other wide bay to me. It didn't seem to mean much to Kofeeshtetch, either. As he pulled himself closer, one of those mean-looking fighting machines got in his way, but he shoved it rudely aside. Then he made a sound of disgust. "This is a very tedious object, Wet One," he told the amphibian. "There is too much water. But if you wish to go there, then do so."

And he waved to the Christmas tree, who opened the door of the transit machine.

The amphibian crawled in, attachments and all, and the other robot tossed his ammunition boxes after him.

The door closed.

Kofeeshtetch made a gesture of dismissal. "I do not think that Wet One will survive for long," he remarked, and that was all there was to it.

After a moment Beert sighed. "I would have liked to wish him well on his venture," he said meditatively. "In any case, thank you for your help, Kofeeshtetch, but now I am quite tired. I think I will go to my chamber and rest before the banquet. Are you coming, Dan?"

I looked at the young Horch. He seemed poutily disappointed in the entertainment, but he hadn't left.

"You go ahead, Beert," I said. "I think Kofeeshtetch still has some questions for me, so I'll stay a bit."

It took me about thirty seconds to get the kid juiced up again—he was, after all, a kid. All I had to do was to ask him if he would please grant me the favor of telling me how his ancestors had captured this installation. That did it. He was off, and then all I had to do was make the appropriate thrilled noises from time to time.

His story was full of Horch names that I didn't retain, and matters of who took precedence over whom that I didn't understand in the first place. Most of it, though, was blow-by-blow descriptions of how his parents' technicians had managed to insert their fighting forces into the Others' channel. And how the first wave of Horch fighting machines had been destroyed in a few moments. And how the Horch had sneaked a second wave in through a different transit machine while the defenders were distracted by what was happening at the first one. And—

And on and on. Kofeeshtetch loved the subject. He acted it out, with limbs and neck flying in all dirctions. It was interesting to me, too, as an insight into how the Horch did their fighting . . . but, at that moment, not very. I wanted to get on to my own problem, but I didn't want to interrupt.

When Kofeeshtetch got to the point where their Horch robots were mopping up the rags and tags of flesh that was all there was left of the Others' warriors, I began to hope for an ending. "The Greatmother has told me," he was saying proudly, "of how vile the stench of those decomposing corpses was, so that for a time it was difficult to breathe, even more difficult to eat without vomiting. To carry on the work of this installation was very hard."

Carry on? I did interrupt him then. "But this was an Others' installation. Why would you want to carry on their work?"

He gave me a scornful hiss, thrusting his head in my face. His breath was not nearly as inoffensive as Beert's. "Of course it had been operated by the Others. What of it? The Others are filthy vermin, but there are some few objectives we share in common. Do you want to hear the story of my parents or do you not?"

I wanted to hear what those common objectives were, but I wanted even more to get to my own desires. "Your parents were very, very brave," I said with admiration. "I only hope that I can be as brave, and as successful, when I too fight against the Others."

Kofeeshtetch swayed his neck indecisively back and forth for a moment. I could see that he was reluctant to give up his favorite subject, but he was torn.

I understood his dilemma. When my uncle Max Adcock, the not-very-successful buccaneer capitalist, told me about the next great stock raid or franchise operation that was going to make him rich at last, if only Uncle Cubby would help him out with a little seed capital, I always listened. To the ten-year-old I was at the time, it was exciting. I don't mean that I liked Uncle Max. Apart from the fact that he was my cousin Pat's father, I didn't have much use for the man. Kofeeshtetch didn't have a lot of use for lower organisms like me, either, but he had the same yearning to hear about exciting adventures. "Tell me your plan," he said sulkily.

Actually, the word "plan" was a lot more dignified than my hazy notions deserved, but I did my best. I said, "A scout ship of the Others is somewhere near my home planet. With your Greatmother's gracious permission, and assuming the proper channels can be accessed, I am going to invade it and kill everyone aboard."

"Hum," he said—actually, it was more like an approving growl. But he looked puzzled. "What do you mean by a 'scout ship'?"

It was my turn to be puzzled. Neither Beert nor Pirraghiz had had any difficulty knowing what I was talking about, so why did he? I floundered. "In order to discover civilizations like mine, the Others send out exploring vessels which travel slower than light speed. When they find one—"

"Yes, yes," he said, sounding impatient. "But such vessels come in many varieties, both for us Horch and the Others. Which kind do you mean?"

I winced. It had never occurred to me that there might be different kinds. But I said staunchly, "Whatever kind is there. It doesn't matter. I will slip aboard and start shooting. Only," I added, "there is a problem. I won't be able to do any of that unless I have weapons and a scrambler to disrupt their communications, like those the Wet One had. Now those are gone—"

Kofeeshtetch was waving his arms reprovingly. "You are so ignorant," he complained. "All such patterns are stored in the transit machine. It would be quite simple to make copies if there were any point to it, but is there? I am not satisfied that your plan is good."

He meditated for a moment, then gave a decisive neck-swirl. "I wish to see this scout ship for myself." He turned his head to the nearest Christmas tree and barked, "I am waiting! Haven't you found that planet for me yet?"

You wouldn't think a Christmas tree could look embarrassed, but this one's branches and twiglets hung low. "We have not yet made a positive identification."

That bugged me. "Of course you can do it! You've been relaying data from it for months!"

The robot didn't extend even one tiny spring in my direction. To Kofeeshtetch it said, "Relays occur automatically. We have traced all such, but there are two eights of planets transmitting this sort of data. Can this organism say whether his people use radio?"

I resisted an impulse to laugh. "Oh, yes. All the time," I said.

Still to the Horch: "That eliminates some. Then how many moons does this planet have?"

"One big one."

"Then, Kofeeshtetch," the robot said, shooting out a sprig of needles to touch the controls of the screen, "it is likely that this is the planet you seek."

And when the picture had formed in the bowl, it was.

I could see the dagger of India stabbing down into the Indian Ocean, with the little island of Sri Lanka dripping off its tip. As the planet slowly spun I could see Africa emerge, and the beginnings of Europe. There was something strange about the image, though. Tiny dots of reddish light that I had never seen before were sprinkled around the globe. But there was no doubt what I was looking at. I swallowed. "That's the Earth," I said, suddenly homesick.

Kofeeshtetch was not sentimental. "Not the planet!" he snapped at the robot. "Isn't there a survey vessel of the Others nearby?"

"We have identified one, yes. Here is a plot of its transit machines—"

Three or four of those reddish lights appeared, close together, against a background of stars. It was the stars, more than those little lights, that made me catch my breath. This was none of that awful intergalactic black, nor all those multicolored headlights of the globular cluster. These were my own stars, the very constellations you can see from Earth. I recognized at least one of them, the seven stars in a cup-and-handle pattern that every child knows as the Big Dipper.

Kofeeshtetch wasn't interested in stargazing. "So many transit machines," he muttered. "Can we see the ship itself?"

At once stars and ruddy lights vanished and we were looking at another set of children's Tinkertoys. "We have no view of the specific craft, but it is probable that it is this model," the robot said.

It looked to be smaller than the nexus itself, or at least a little less complicated, but it impressed Kofeeshtetch. "But this is no mere robot scout! It must be in fact a major vessel of the Others." He swung his head to face mine. "You could not possibly succeed in attacking it single-handed! It will be staffed with many, many warriors of the Others, all better armed than you. Such a venture would require a full-scale assault, almost as large as the one with which our nest stormed this place."

That was not at all what I wanted to hear. I think I'm more or less brave, but I'm not stupid. A one-man suicide venture against impossible odds didn't sound attractive—at least, unless there was nothing better on offer. I took a chance. "I don't suppose you could interest your Greatmother in, well, in launching such an attack?"

Kofeeshtetch laughed in my face, little raucous puffs of bad breath. He didn't say anything. He didn't have to. His laughter made it quite clear that the Horch were not going to launch a major battle to please a lower organism like me, especially over a pissant little planet like Earth.

What he did say was, "Your plan is not worth pursuing. Perhaps you should return to the Eight Plus Threes. I will leave you now to prepare for the feast the Greatmother is providing for Djabeertapritch."

He looked like he was getting ready to do it, too. I could feel my dreams collapsing around me, but one faint hope of an idea was percolating through my mind.

"Wait a minute," I begged. "Can I see the planet Earth again?"

I had nearly lost him. He was just a child, after all. If I wasn't about to pursue the feats of derring-do that fired up his kid imagination, he had no further use for me. He hung indecisively from his cable for a moment, then said petulantly, "Oh, very well, but do it quickly."

Quickly was how the robot did it. The planet had revolved a little more. Now we were looking at the Atlantic Ocean, South America bulging out into it and the East Coast of the United States just visible on the periphery. I peered at that unfamiliar scattering of red spots, clustered mostly along the shorelines. I pointed. "What are those?"

Kofeeshtetch gestured, and then the robot answered me. "We have no definite identification. They appear to be satellite installations, but we do not know their purpose."

"But they're smaller, and they're right on the surface of the Earth."

"That is not precisely accurate," the machine corrected me. "If you will observe, they are all in the water regions of the planet, close to the land masses but not on them."

"But still—" I began to argue.

I didn't finish. Kofeeshtetch waved me to silence. He was beginning to catch the spirit. "That might be a workable plan," he said thoughtfully. "A smaller installation. Only one transit machine each. Perhaps only operated by machines, certainly with a much smaller complement than the ship in space—yes! This may be worth considering. I will think on this, and perhaps seek advice from the Greatmother."

When I got back to my room, as jubilant as I dared be, Pirraghiz was waiting for me. She listened, but didn't comment, as I told her what had happened. "Where's Beert?" I asked. "I must tell him!"

"Djabeertapritch is sleeping, Dannerman. This has been exhausting for him."

She didn't sound excited at all, and she was bringing me down with her. "But he will want to hear all this!" I insisted.

She gave me one of those six-limbed shrugs. "You can speak to him when he wakes, Dannerman," she said firmly. "He has some important decisions to make, and he has ordered me to let him rest. It is better if you rest, also. Would you like to eat first?"

33

I didn't get a chance to talk to Beert after his sleep. I didn't get much sleep for myself, either, because Pirraghiz woke me up to tell me that the Greatmother's banquet was just about to happen and we'd better get a move on.

I could have wished for a little more warning. I really needed to talk to Beert, but when I tried to grab him he simply waggled his neck at me. "Later, Dan," he said, sounding distracted and not really all that interested. "We can't keep this Greatmother waiting." I was also conscious of really beginning to need a bath, and there wasn't anything of that sort in the chambers they'd given us. So, unwashed, I followed Beert and the Christmas tree along the roped passages, hoping that the Horch sense of smell was not acute. Because I was sure I was a lot less than fragrant just then.

I could hear the noise from the feast long before the banquet hall was in sight.

The hall was shaped like a pyramid—well, like a tetrahedron, with four triangular sides, none of which was either a floor or a ceiling—and it was big. It had to be. There were at least forty Horch present. They weren't sitting. They weren't even doing what Horch do instead of sitting down like a human being. They just hung there, clipped to one or another of the brightly glowing cords that were stretched across the volume of space, like strands of a 3-D spiderweb. And they were very loudly singing.

It is hard to say what a Horch group sing sounded like. It was a little like the howling of a pack of constipated wolves, a little like hogs grunting ferociously as they battled for tidbits in a pen. The big difference was that the Horch were doing all that in unison, and that there were lyrics to the tune they sang. They sang of the Greatest of Greatmothers, and of the undying delights—or of the later-on undying delights, that is, after they'd finished whatever other dying they had to get there—of living forever, cherished in the Greatest of Greatmother's love. Does that sound awful? Sure it does. It was.

They hadn't waited for us to arrive. They were eating as they sang. A squad of the glassy robots were busily slithering along the cords, hand over hand—well, branch over twig—to serve the diners with great gobs of something that looked like pink mashed potatoes, only gluey enough to hold together in a ball; clusters of figlike fruits that probably weren't fruits at all, because they were squirming; hinged food dishes containing stuff that I couldn't see, but could smell when the nearest Horch opened theirs; mesh bags of what might have been nuts or vegetables or—well, anything at all. All I could see through the mesh was varicolored lumps of God knew what. The other thing the Horch were doing was drinking, out of bagpipe-looking bladders with spouts on one end. The Horch took the spouts in their triangular little mouths when they wanted a drink, and then some of them pointed the spouts at friends nearby and squeezed. For fun, I guess. The thin streams of yellowish liquid, looking unpleasantly like urine, splashed when they hit another Horch and kept on going when they missed. It didn't matter which they did, though. The Christmas trees were diligently sucking the spilled liquid out of the air as they passed. These masters of the universe were having their fun at a kind of college fraternity brawl. I guess the overworked robots weren't enjoying it, but probably they weren't programmed to enjoy anything anyway.

Our personal robot first escorted Beert to the heart of the web. The Greatmother was there and eating industriously, pausing in her own consumption only, now and then, to stuff some particular delicacy into the mouth of her least grandson, Kofeeshtetch. Having their mouths full didn't keep them from singing along, welcomingly waving Beert to join in.

Pirraghiz and I weren't included in the invitation. We weren't given the good seats, either. A pair of serving robots dropped their waitering duties long enough to tug us to webs at one vertex of the tetrahedron. Then they scuttled away to fetch fresh delicacies for the Horch.

We weren't alone there. There were three or four Horch nearby, singing along lustily with the others though they couldn't have been very high ranking—our place was the exact equivalent of a table by the kitchen door in a human restaurant, even to the procession of serving robots that streamed back and forth past us. Our neighbors didn't stop singing. They darted their heads to glance at us as we arrived—not cordially. I could almost hear them asking each other what cretin had invited these nasty-looking lower orders to the feast. Especially ones who smelled as strange as Pirraghiz and, no doubt, me.

We weren't totally neglected. After a few moments the robots began dropping tidbits off for us, too. First there were a couple of net bags containing some of those things like green plums I remembered from my interrogation days, then a wine sack, then two lumps of that pink dough. They didn't hand them to us. They attached them, somehow, to the cables we were clinging to. I didn't see how, exactly, because I was trying to figure out what was going on up in the high-rent district.

The Greatmother's party wasn't singing anymore. The least grandson seemed to have left the group, but I could see Beert and the Greatmother talking to each other, necks intertwined in deep conversation. I was pretty sure what they were talking about. It was me. Every once in a while one or both of them would dart their heads in my direction, but what was being said, I couldn't guess. I could only hope that it had nothing to do with my destruction of valuable Horch machinery at the Eight Plus Threes.

Pirraghiz interrupted my fairly apprehensive thoughts about that by poking my shoulder. "Eat," she said.

That was easier said than done; I didn't see how I could hang on to the cable and eat at the same time. Pirraghiz solved the problem for me. She had linked herself to the cable with one of her lesser arms. Now she took a firm hold of my leg with another, thus safely mooring me, while she finished picking over the goodies the robots had left us with a couple more. Having six arms certainly had its points.

She drew me close enough to hear her over the noise of the singing, which was getting even more boisterous. "You can eat this," she said, offering me a lump of the pink dough. "Some of the fruits, too, after I pick the seeds out. Not the liquid. Not anything else."

The pink stuff was warm and soft and smelled a little like garlic. I nibbled at it to be polite. Although I was hungry, I still had the hope in my heart, now dwindlingly faint, that before long I would be where I could get a thick steak, with french fries and a few slices of red, ripe tomatoes, and maybe even a bottle of beer. . . .

"Look," Pirraghiz said, sounding surprised.

What she was pointing at was the least grandson, rapidly swinging himself in our direction, looking as though he had something to talk to us about.

He did. As soon as he was near he announced importantly, "I have solved the problem of the order of battle—theoretically, provided it is allowed to occur. Listen attentively."

He didn't have to say that. I was doing it already. He settled himself in, close to my head, and stared into my eyes.

"There are three eights and two of the vessels on your planet," he informed me. "One is considerably larger than the others, so we will not attack that one. To one of the smaller ones, first we will send in two waves of fighting machines, two at a time. I had thought," he said meditatively, "of perhaps using a pair of the warriors of the Others as a deception tactic for the first wave."

He surprised me. "You have some of their warriors?"

"Of course. Quite a few were still alive, though wounded, when this place was taken. Most did not survive, but some did, even after questioning. Later, when they had been removed from the control of the Others, the Greatmother gave them to me as pets. I possess a number of such creatures," he told me proudly. "I study them to learn what lesser organisms are like, so as to be prepared for dealing with them at the Eschaton. Perhaps sometime I will show some of them to you."

This particular lesser organism was getting impatient. I coughed to get him back on track. "That would be nice, but about your plan—?"

"Yes, the order of battle. I decided against using the organic warriors. Since they are no longer controlled, they have become quite cowardly and I do not trust their fighting skills. So we will use our machines in the first two waves. Then you and your—uh—associate"—he was looking at Pirraghiz—"will go in the third transmission, also armed with copies of your projectile weapons. By then the fighting machines should have neutralized whatever forces the Others have in place. Not many, I think. The Others will not expect us to bother them in a place like that. Then you will be free to act as you wish." I was rapturously hanging on every word. Then he brought me down. "Assuming, of course, that the Greatmother gives such orders. I believe she and Djabeertapritch of the Two Eights are discussing it now."

He twisted his neck to look in her direction. Then he said in sudden alarm, "I believe she is getting ready to speak! I must go! I will talk to you further later on. That is, I will if the project still seems feasible."

* * *

I could have wished for fewers ifs and maybes, but I could feel my heart speeding up. Pirraghiz was looking at me curiously. She had certainly heard every word, but if she wanted to say something about the exchange, she didn't have a chance, because just then the singing stopped at some signal I hadn't caught. Everyone was silent. Even the robots paused in their rounds for a moment, as the Greatmother began to speak.

"Nestmates and honored guest," she began—I noticed the "honored guest" was in the singular; Pirraghiz and I were not included. "We rejoice at this time at the reunion of a lost nest with the grand consortium of the Horch. We are greatly, and most pleasantly, surprised to have Djabeertapritch, descendant of our people of the Two Eights, with us. I have made him a promise, which I will keep at this celebration." She darted a coquettish look in Beert's direction. "What I have not decided," she went on, sounding like a teasing Santa Claus with a young child on his lap, "is whether it is better to prolong his suspense a bit longer or to reveal the surprise to him now." That brought on murmurs from the audience. I could hear that some of them were saying, "Now!" while others said, "No, make him wait," and a fair number were speaking what I took to be jocular obscenities. But they were all laughing about it, even the Greatmother. ("I believe they have had a great deal of the intoxicating liquid," Pirraghiz whispered in my ear.)

The Greatmother bent her neck to her least grandson, who was tugging at her arm. I noticed that Kofeeshtetch was hanging upside down relative to her, but she didn't seem to care—well, that didn't matter as much for the Horch as it would for us, since their heads could go every which way.

Then she lifted her head, giggling. "My least grandson asks to have the surprise now," she announced. "Djabeertapritch? Do you agree?"

Beert wasn't doing any of the laughing, seemed to have something serious on his mind, but he rose to the occasion. "I will be pleased with whatever pleases the Greatmother," he said diplomatically.

"Yes, of course. Very well. This surprise is a very great fool, Djabeertapritch. She was unwise enough to come to this place after the fighting had begun, and we did not allow her to leave." The Greatmother paused for dramatic effect, then issued an order to the robots. "Bring the prisoner in!"

34

Every Horch head in the banquet hall turned toward one of the vertices of the tetrahedron, where the diners were scrambling to get out of the way. They needed to, for what entered was a procession.

First came a fighting machine in full combat alert, backing into the room with its weapons trained on what followed. That was a couple: a Christmas tree chained to a creature with spindly legs and arms and a head like a jack-o'-lantern. Another fighting machine brought up the rear, also with dead aim on the captive.

I knew what she was at once.

I was in the presence of one of the Others. One of Dopey's Beloved Leaders. A member of the species that, at this very moment, was casually deciding whether it would be more advantageous to annihilate everyone I knew and loved, or turn them into abject slaves.

When Pirraghiz put one worried arm on me I realized I was shaking. I gave her a nod to reassure her, but I couldn't stop.

I wasn't the only one affected. For most of the Horch this poor captive was old news, but not for Beert. His neck and both arms were stretched out toward her, frozen motionless, and his little snake mouth was open in shock.

The Greatmother made that choking, staccato sound that was a Horch laugh. "Well, Djabeertapritch," she said, delighted with her effect. "How do you like your surprise? Would you like to speak to her? Ask her some questions about how it feels to be a captive, as you were to her people?"

He managed to make a slow, negative shake of his head, but that was it. The female Beloved Leader was not so reluctant. She turned that great, round, scarecrow head toward Beert and spoke through her huge teeth. "I excrete into the mouth of your Greatmother," she said in a shrill, piping, venomous voice. "I will do the same to all of you when the Eschaton comes and you organisms are all shrieking in pain as we trample you under our feet."

She was speaking perfect Horch, far better than Beert's farm-boy drawl. I saw the reason: one of those ribbed, golden scabs tucked under the swell of the pumpkin where it joined the skinny neck. When she leaned forward to hiss at Beert, I saw, too, that the last link of the chain that held her to the Christmas tree had actually been grafted into her flesh. They were taking no chances with this representative of the ultimate enemy.

The Greatmother was switching her head about ominously. I thought for a moment there was going to be a major hissing match between the two of them, if not something more physical. Beert prevented it. He spoke up.

"Prisoner," he said, "the Greatmother called you a fool, but you are an even bigger fool than you know. You will not win. We Horch are stronger and braver and wiser than you, and even the lower species are going to rise against you." He turned to the Greatmother. "Have I permission to speak now?"

She graciously waved her neck in assent, and he began to talk. I hung there in suspense, almost dreading to hear what he was going to say.

He began, "I speak to you from the belly, revered Greatmother, and to all you Horch of the Four and Ones. I am Djabeertapritch of the Two Eights, which is no more."

That was a letdown for me, right there. Beert wasn't delivering any casual talk, it was an oration! I was willing to bet that the son of a bitch had been rehearsing it to himself all along. Discouraged, I slumped back, waiting for him to get to a point, but I was the only one in the room who felt that way. Every one of the Horch had stopped their foolery and were listening with their little mouths wide-open.

Beert seemed to intend to give the whole history of his nest: "When the Horch came to the Two Eights they slew us by the sixteens of sixteens of sixteens, most cruelly and treacherously. . . ." Well, I had heard all of that. And about how the survivors had been taken to the prison planet, and what happened to them there. However, the Four and Ones were eating it up. They hissed and moaned when he spoke of how people from their nest had been studied and used for experimental purposes, and when he came to their rescue by the Eight Plus Threes there were scattered cheers.

I might have cheered myself, because that was when he got to what I wanted to hear. "Then our little nest was free at last. As were the members of those other species whom the Others had imprisoned there. And it is of those other species that I would speak, revered Greatmother."

Now he had my full attention, all right. "Some of you have seen the Wet One, whom we have helped return to his own planet to do battle with the Others who have enslaved it. His species was fortunate—a little fortunate—because their planet still exists. Not all were that lucky.

"You all know the species of the large one with many limbs"—his neck was outthrust toward Pirraghiz—"because some of them were here when you bravely captured this place. Their fate may be the worst of all. Not only were they compelled for a long, long time to be the servants of the Others, but their planet is long lost.

"The planet of the four-limbed one, whose name is Dan, is yet free, but perhaps not for long. The Others have already begun to infiltrate it. Dan wishes to be returned there so that he can help fight them off."

He hesitated, eyeing me with a look I couldn't interpret. Then he said, "Dan's are a simple people, Greatmother. Their machines are crude. They have little wisdom. And they are not a peaceful race. I say only of them that their people are divided among themselves, with many 'nations' which make their own customs and laws, and sometimes actually go to war with each other." Shocked stir among the Horch; Beert went bravely on, overriding the mutterings. "Nevertheless, they do not deserve to be made slaves of the Others. It is not their fault that their limbs are stiff and their brains are imprisoned in a box of bone on their necks. They are not animals. Their brains are in some ways almost the equal of our own. So I ask you to help him in this cause, revered Greatmother, and"—he hesitated, then got it out—"I ask you for more than that. I wish to go with him myself, to do what I can to prevent what happened to my planet from happening to his. Greatmother, will you grant me this wish?"

When Beert finished speaking there was a stir among the assembled Horch. Our nearest neighbors craned their necks to study Pirraghiz and me curiously, silently at first. Then not so silent. One of them abruptly clapped his hinged feeding dish against his belly armor. Then another did. Then they were all doing it, rhythmically, like the kind of we-want-a-touchdown thing that people do at football games. And then they began to sing again, first one or two, then the whole damn collection of them at once.

I don't think it was the same song I had heard before, but I wasn't paying attention to the words. I was staring at Beert.

The guy had taken me by surprise. Not only had he chosen not to denounce me as a capricious destroyer of Horch machines, but what was this about coming to Earth with us? That had never been part of the plan.

I realized Pirraghiz was shaking my leg. I blinked at her. "The Greatmother is beckoning us," she whispered. "I think she wants us to come to her."

They were all looking at us, as a matter of fact, even the Greatmother. As soon as I was close she darted her head at mine, inspecting me at close range far more thoroughly than before. But I was looking at the female Other. At close range I could see that the creature had not had an easy life lately. Her clothing was smudged and torn, and there were recent scars on the bulbous pumpkin face. As Pirraghiz set me down, not two meters away, the Other rattled her chains and hissed venomously at me. The Greatmother didn't even look at her. "I tire of this filth's presence," she said to the air. "Remove her!"

As the crystal robots were dragging the Other away, the Greatmother twisted her neck to look at Beert. "You are determined to do this?" she asked. "To risk your life for the sake of some lower organisms?"

He didn't look at me. "I am determined," he said.

Then she sighed. "It will be done. My least grandson has prepared a plan which we will follow." And added, "You are very brave, Djabeertapritch."

And so he was, in more ways than the Greatmother knew.

EIGHT

Going Home

35

When the Greatmother said "Do it" she didn't mean do it on Tuesday. She didn't even mean do it when the feast was over. Kofeeshtetch disappeared at once, promising to meet us at the transit machine, and then it was maybe five minutes before a pair of Christmas trees came charging along the cords to drag me and Beert away, Pirraghiz following. Cheers broke out as we left, and then another burst of raucous song. I was glad enough not to have to stay for that.

We stopped by the rooms to collect Beert's personal glass robot. That was useful, since it gave me a chance to pick up my little mesh bag of Horch goodies. Beert gave me a dark look but didn't say anything, and we were at the transit machine long before Kofeeshtetch and the troops.

Our Christmas trees deserted us then to fiddle with the machine, and I finally got the chance to ask Beert the question on my mind. "Why, Beert? Why are you coming with us?"

He swung his face partly toward mine, then away. To the air he said, "I want to be able to go back to my own nest."

That didn't make sense. "Why not just jump in that thing and go home?"

This time he did look at me. "And if I did that, what would I tell my Greatmother? That I turned loose somebody who had destroyed a Horch machine, with a bag of Horch material, and no way to know what you do with it? No, Dan. I can't go home yet, though I wish with all my belly I could."

"But—" I began, trying to be reasonable, but then I ran out of time for being reasonable as Kofeeshtetch made his entrance.

The kid had an entourage with him, not only the four deadly

Horch fighting machines but a large, ugly alien which had four or five tiny, different aliens clinging to his fur. I had seen them in pictures before, but never alive: the Bashfuls and the Happies, as the comics had named them on Earth.

"I promised to show you my other species," Kofeeshtetch said proudly. "This large being is a warrior of the Others; the little ones are used for delicate work by them. Do not fear the warrior," he added kindly. "He has been freed of his bondage and will do you no harm." Kofeeshtetch allowed us a moment to admire his menagerie, then waved them off and gave one of the robots his orders.

Then he turned to us and got down to business. He extended one arm toward the TV, which the robot had made to display the globe of Earth again, and said: "Of the three eights and two vessels of the Others which are on your planet, I have chosen this one for your mission."

I looked where he was pointing. The thing was down in the Gulf of 'Aqaba, of all places. I demanded, "Why?"

He looked almost embarrassed. "It is not near any of the others. Also I liked the look of that funny-looking land mass."

"No," I said strongly, and then remembered to add, "Please. Do you remember what Djabeertapritch said about our many independent countries? Well, that one's in the wrong country." I stabbed at the map, in the vague direction of the East Coast of the United States. "Over here would be better. Can you enlarge this part of the globe?"

The Christmas tree did, and I saw the Eastern Seaboard swell up before me. There were four or five of those ruddy dots between Florida and Newfoundland. The best-looking one was not far from the alligator shape of Long Island, as close to the Bureau headquarters in Virginia as I could get. I pointed at it. "That one . . . please."

"Oh, very well," Kofeeshtetch said sulkily, and gave an order to the Christmas tree by the machine, which began to fiddle with the controls. "Anyway," he said, brightening, "now it is time! Remember the order of battle! These two fighters first; they have their orders. Then two more to mop up. Then you, Djabeertapritch, with—ah—the 'Dan.' I wish you all good luck."

Pirraghiz stirred. "Wait a minute," she said. "I'm going too. Also Djabeertapritch will want his own personal robot with him."

Kofeeshtetch gave her an angry look. "It is very foolish to make trivial changes in a battle plan just before the engagement," he complained.

"But it would be better that way," Beert said, his tone placating.

"Perhaps my robot could go with the second wave of fighting machines, then us, then—"

"No, Djabeertapritch," Pirraghiz said firmly. "I will go before you. We do not know what the conditions will be when we arrive."

Kofeeshtetch looked at Beert, who nodded agreement then gave up. "All right," he said. "Now, if you're ready? First wave! Go!"

It was the quietest beginning of a battle I can imagine. The first two fighters entered the machine, the door closed; it opened again; the second wave entered with Beert's Christmas tree. It closed.

As Pirraghiz was going into the machine I checked my twenty-shots, one in each hand. Then I remembered something. "Oh, Kofeeshtetch! You were going to tell me what this installation was for."

He blinked his little snake eyes at me, his mind clearly changing gears. He threw a look at the transit machine, already yawning open for Beert and me. "You are upsetting the timetable," he said pettishly. "Why, the installation is for the Eschaton, of course. Now go!"

36

It was peaceful when we got into the transit machine. It wasn't when we got out. Whatever we had arrived in—a chamber the size of an eighteen-wheeler truck, metal walls filled with displays and gadgets—it stank. Partly it smelled of scorched protein, like an ancient fish-and-chips store after a long, busy winter night, when nobody had cared to open a window. Partly it smelled of seared metal and destruction. It looked that way, too. The fighting seemed to be over, though most of our first-wave fighting machines had already become sizzling junk. In the first quick glance I saw an unfamiliar Doc, with a copper blanket over his head—I recognized my goodies bag—a distraught Dopey perched at one end of the chamber and a couple of dead Beloved Leader warrior-Bashfuls. The place was suffocatingly hot. And it was noisier than I would have believed.

Most of the noise didn't come from the crackling metal or the whimpering Dopey perched at one end of the compartment as he gazed with horror at the Horch, Beert. The deafening part came from my friend Pirraghiz. Bafflingly, she was shrieking at the top of her lungs, a long, meowing garble in her own impenetrable language. She sounded either terrified or in pain. I swore to myself in alarm and staggered toward her in the sudden Earth gravity, looking for the wound that was causing her such agony. There didn't seem to be any. Still screaming, she shook me off, at the same time gesturing to the strange Doc with the copper blanket over his head. I had no idea what she wanted from him, but after a moment he did. Wounded as he was—one of his lesser arms was terribly burned—he limped over to the control boards and quickly played his clawed hands over the colored dots.

When the Doc said something to Pirraghiz she stopped screaming at once and gave him a quick hug of greeting. Then she bent to examine his burned arm and tsk-tsked over it—in her case it was actually a sort of *bup-bup* sound—before she turned to me. "Wrahrrgherfoozh"—I think that's what she said the Doc's name was—"needs attention! I fear he may lose that arm! I must try to help him!"

"Well, sure," I said, "but what was all the screaming about?"

Pirraghiz was already delicately probing the skin around the Doc's—well, shoulder; at least, around the little bony bump where his burned lesser arm joined his torso. Her full attention was on his injuries, and she didn't look up. "I didn't want the Others to know what was happening," she said, still gently working away on him. "So as soon as the machines and I got him neutralized with the mesh, I turned off the scrambler and began to scream—yelling that there were explosions, water was coming in, all that sort of thing. My intention was to make the Others believe we had some kind of a terrible accident," she explained. "Then, as you saw, we turned off the communicator and the transit machine. Is that all right?"

It was a hell of a lot better than all right. I wished I had thought of it myself. What I said was an inadequate, "Thank you."

She spared me a quick glance. "Yes. But, Dannerman, what do we do now?"

That was what I needed to figure out. It was great to be back on Earth again, but I was still a long way from Arlington.

I took a moment to get a better idea of what I had to work with. The Horch fighting machines had been surgically efficient in their assault. As far as I could tell, none of the fittings of the sub had been damaged, but I didn't see much that was helpful. There had been two Beloved Leader warriors on the sub, both now dead. There had been four Horch fighting machines, three of which were now scrap; the Bashfuls had put up a pretty good fight before they died. Beert's personal robot seemed unharmed. So did the Dopey, who had stopped his terrified whining and was staring from one to the other of us as Pirraghiz and I talked.

There was something I needed to know about that Dopey. So, watching him, what I said to Pirraghiz was, "The first thing we do is kill the Dopey, so he can't make any trouble."

Pirraghiz stiffened in surprise. The Dopey didn't. He just kept looking back and forth at the two of us, with an occasional frightened glance at Beert. Even his tail plume didn't change color. So either he was a wonderful actor, or he didn't understand the Horch language we were speaking.

As Pirraghiz began to object I said, "Cancel that." I pointed to the wounded Doc. "Can he drive this thing?"

She gave me a strange look, but then she mewed at the Doc and he mewed back. "Yes, he can. Wrahrrgherfoozh is engineer for this vessel. He can operate any part of it, but he wants to know where to drive to."

Another good question. If I can see some kind of a map, I'll tell him.

More mewing. Then, "The locators are turned off, Dannerman," she reported. "They are part of the communication system." While I was absorbing the notion that we were somewhere in the Atlantic Ocean, and blind, she added, "However, Wrahrrgherfoozh says it is possible for him to alter the system to receive only and not to transmit. But that will take some time."

That lifted a huge weight from my soul. "Tell him to do it, then!"

"He is badly hurt, Dannerman. I do not think we can save that arm."

That was when Beert spoke up. He had been quietly talking to his Christmas tree, and he said, "Dan. I have used my machine to work on many devices of the Others. Perhaps it can help."

I looked at Pirraghiz. "Can it?" And when she nodded, "Then tell them to get on with it! I mean, please."

The Christmas tree scuttled over to the board, Pirraghiz explained to the Doc what was going on, and I had my first chance to say anything to Beert. He was standing silent, his head darting this way and that, his arms slumped by his side. He looked dejected.

I said, "Beert? Listen, I'm sorry that I got you into this."

He turned the head toward me, but all he said was, "Yes."

There was nothing to be done for the dead warriors. The one surviving fighting machine was poking at the ruins of the other three, but it didn't look like they were going to be repairable for a good long time. If ever.

By then the Dopey had managed to collect himself. He fixed his little kitten eyes on me and spoke up. *"Sprechen-sie Deutsch?"* he asked. He was looking at me. *"Panamayoo Paruski? Parlez-vous—"*

I cut him off, "Try English."

He switched at once, gazing at me intently. "I must ask, why are you here? Do you have any understanding of what fate awaits you for daring to bring a filthy Horch into a vessel of the Beloved Leaders?"

"They have to catch us first," I said. It was oddly pleasing to be speaking my own language again, even with this creature.

"But they surely will," he said reasonably. "Then it will be terrible for you. You have only one chance to avoid the worst of the punishment, and that is to destroy the Horch and his machine with that projectile weapon of yours. At once. And then—"

"Forget it," I said.

"But—"

I put it more strongly. "What I mean is, shut up. I'll talk to you later, but if you don't keep quiet now, I will turn you over to the filthy Horch."

That didn't stop him, either. I turned my back on his arguments and spoke in his own language to Beert: "Do you think you could get your fighter to scare him? Not kill him. Just make him be quiet."

Beert's head lifted to gaze at me. "Then you don't really want him killed?"

"Of course I don't, Beert. What use is he dead? I want him alive to be interrogated. Do you think I would actually murder an unarmed person?"

He gazed at me in silence for a moment. Then he said, "I was not sure."

37

It didn't take the Doc and the Christmas tree as long as I feared to get some of the systems running, and then the wall over the controls blossomed into a display. A golden dot marked our position. There weren't any other dots nearby, which I thought was good, and at the top of the picture was an irregular mass which I took to be the coast.

I grunted at him as I tried to figure out what to do. Back in those New Jersey summers with Uncle Cubby, my parents had sometimes taken me out for a fishing trip in Uncle Cubby's seldom-used cabin cruiser. I wished I had paid more attention to the charts. What I saw looked nothing like any coastline I remembered.

Then I saw one of the problems. I was accustomed to maps in which up was always north. Evidently the Beloved Leaders had no such prejudice. I guessed the land had to be east, and—once I craned my neck to peer at it sidewise and got the Doc to widen the view—it made sense. Island that forked at one end, like an alligator's opened jaws, narrow body of water behind it and then the mainland—"Long Island," I announced. "Great! That water over on the left has to be New York Bay. That's where we want to go! Tell the Doc, Pirraghiz!"

She didn't move right away. She was looking at me puzzledly again. So was Beert, and I realized I had used the English names for what I saw, since the Horch language didn't have any. When I explained to them that "New York Bay" was one of the busiest harbors on Earth, and we would have no trouble making contact there, Beert swung his neck around closer to me. "First answer a question for me, Dan. What will you do when you get there?"

"Call the Bureau," I said promptly. "See if they can get this sub under wraps before the Others can see what we're doing—"

I stopped there; what I had just said didn't sound right to me. Before I could figure out what it was, Beert went on. "And then?"

To tell the truth, I hadn't thought much about that "then." Especially about what *then* would mean for him and Pirraghiz. "Why," I said, "I guess we'll let the Bureau figure out what to do next."

"What you mean," he said meditatively, "is that you will turn this vehicle, and us, over to your human spy organization. Who will question us, and no doubt do their best to copy its technology, both Others and Horch."

"I guess that's about the size of it," I admitted.

He sighed—that shrill Horch whistle of released breath that meant resignation. He didn't say anything. He just nodded to Pirraghiz, who spoke to Wrahrrgherfoozh.

The Doc touched only a few dots on the board, but I felt the results at once. The submarine was turning and beginning to accelerate. The picture on the wall whirled to a new orientation, and we were beginning to go home.

That felt good. It felt like things were going to work out after all. It even felt as though I were going to get that steak before long, and sleep that night in a real bed . . . and maybe even see Pat . . .

But we weren't there yet.

The air fresheners had removed a certain amount of the stench from the sub, and things were quieting down. Cowed by the Horch fighting machine looming over him, the Dopey was still muttering—but softly, and to himself. Pirraghiz and the other Doc were in close conversation with each other. It looked as though they had left the navigation to Beert's Christmas tree. Beert himself was standing by the control board, gazing at the changing display that showed where we were moving. I didn't think he was seeing it, though. His neck was waving a slow sine, as though he were deep in thought.

When he saw me looking at him he turned his head toward me. "I have reasoned out," he announced, "that your order to kill the little one was a ruse of some kind, not an actual intention."

"That's right, Beert. It was a trick," I admitted. "We Bureau agents are full of tricks, but listen, Beert, I don't mean to trick you. When we get to the Bureau they will know how much we all owe to you and Pirraghiz, because I'll damn sure make sure they understand."

"I will be grateful for that," he said sadly.

And made me feel like a rat. Or, more accurately, made me feel that he was feeling the way I had when the Horch machines were working me over. Alone. Depressed. Pretty near hopeless. And all of it my fault.

There wasn't anything I could do about it, though. I tried to take his mind off it by changing the subject. "Listen, Beert, I've been meaning to ask you. What did Kofeeshtetch mean about the nexus thing helping the Eschaton?"

It didn't cheer him up. He gave me a three-snake shrug. "Perhaps it is something to be used when the Eschaton comes."

"Yeah, but," I said, "nothing physical is going to survive to the Eschaton, is it? Isn't everything supposed to go back into a kind of a point at the Big Crunch? So how would they get it there without its turning into a mess of quarks or something?"

He shrugged again. "I do not know. The cousins have not yet shared that kind of knowledge with me."

Pirraghiz didn't know, either. Neither did the wounded Doc. If the Dopey knew, he wasn't telling. I added that to the lengthening list of questions I was not likely to get answers to any time soon.

Anyway, other things were beginning to jostle for attention in my mind.

Like Pat. Very much like Pat. I was deeply, excitingly aware that every minute that passed was getting me closer and closer to the minute when I could actually see and touch her again.

And although that was fine, it wasn't all fine. Another itchy little needle of reality was beginning to force itself upon me.

Pat already had a Dan Dannerman. What was she going to do with me?

As we approached New York's Lower Bay I got one more of those nasty little stabs of reality.

Pirraghiz assured me that the other Doc had assured her that, yes, it would be possible to bring the sub close enough to the surface to be awash, and yes, there was a hatch that I could use to get out of, and then—

Well, then what should I do? Wave to a passing Staten Island ferry and hitch a ride to shore? Use a flashlight—if I could find anything like a flashlight—to send a message in Morse code—if I could remember the Morse code—to—

Well, to whom?

And what about security?

The sub's display was really great stuff. I could see the wide-open mouth of the bay, Coney Island on one side, Sandy Hook on the other; I could see little splotches that had to be Ellis Island and Liberty Island; I could even see the long old piers that stuck out into the Hudson from every side. And I could also see objects moving around that I supposed were tankers and cruise liners and excursion boats, and what was I going to be doing about them? Not to mention any U.S. Coast Guard stuff that might be patrolling against just such a Horch sub as ourselves; no doubt the human race had figured out that the Beloved Leaders had sneaked in underwater vessels that had given them the opportunity to kidnap and bug a lot of mariners.

According to Wrahrrgherfoozh, the Horch stealth capabilities were a lot more effective than any primitive human sonars. But I didn't want to take the chance of being depth-bombed by some jumpy lieutenant in a Coast Guard corvette.

I studied the display. "Change of plan," I said.

Both Beert and Pirraghiz turned to me, Pirraghiz's expression wondering, Beert's merely resigned.

"I don't think we'd better get into all that traffic," I told them. "Better if we can find some quiet bay somewhere along the shore. Show me what's down—here."

I put my finger on the barrier island that began around the Highlands and went south. Why did I pick there? I don't know. Maybe I thought we might just pull in at Uncle Cubby's old boat dock and knock on his door.

I didn't think it long. Uncle Cubby was long dead. I had no idea who owned his house, and didn't want to investigate. "There's a bay," I said, pointing between the Sea Bright barrier island and the shore. "Let's take a look."

38

It wasn't a bay. It was the mouth of a river that I had forgotten about, but that was just as good.

Slowly and carefully the Christmas tree piloted us upstream on this nice, wide river with no boats visible anywhere on its surface. I never took my eyes off the display. Not far ahead I saw something that stretched clear across the river, which worried me for a moment. A dam? So we'd have to go back and try again?

But it was a bridge. And off to one side of it was a system of docks with small objects moored to them: a boat basin.

"That'll do," I said, hoping I was right.

In fact, it did very well. The Christmas tree brought us to the surface, the robot opened the hatch and I climbed out into a cold, wet—but Earthly!—drizzle.

I saw lights up on the road. I found a little driveway that led up to them, and when I was at street level, there, right across the road, was a large and lighted seafood restaurant.

When I was inside the cashier gave me a thoroughly funny look—reasonably enough; I was tattered, unwashed and long unshaven—but she pointed me to a telephone anyway. There was a scattering of diners in the place; curiously, most of them in uniform. They were staring at me, too. I turned my back on them.

Naturally I had no encryption facilities. I didn't even have a payment card, and the restaurant's smells of good, hot human food were driving me crazy. But I managed to get a collect call through to the Bureau in Arlington.

The duty officer must have thought I was crazy, too, but she listened as I talked: "This is Senior Agent James Daniel Dannerman calling. I'm the one that—ah"—I tried to figure out how to put it—"the one you haven't seen for quite a while because I've been away. A long way away. Relay this information immediately to Colonel Hilda Morrisey or Deputy Director Marcus Pell. I require immediate pickup and a full squad to take charge of important assets."

There was a moment's silence while she thought that over. "I thought Brigadier Morrisey was dead," she said doubtfully.

I don't know which shook me up more, Hilda dead or Hilda a brigadier. But I didn't have time to think about it. "Tell *somebody* in authority at once," I ordered, and got the restaurant cashier to tell me where I was so I could pass it along. "And most of all," I finished, "tell them *no shooting.*"

I guess she did pass the word along, because in about twenty minutes half the helicopters in the world seemed to be jockeying to land in the restaurant parking lot, and I could hear sirens coming toward us from the highway.

It's amazing what the Bureau can do when it puts its mind to it. Although the gaggle of Bureau people who popped out of the first two choppers claimed to be from the New York office, I didn't know a soul among them. But they knew me. "Jesus, Dannerman, how the hell many of you guys are there, anyway?" one of them asked wonderingly, and didn't wait for an answer. "Never mind. Let's get some damage control going here."

They did. Faster than I would have believed possible, the next few choppers of federal police and the co-opted local cops had the place sealed off. They blocked the bridge at both ends, with roadblocks on our side to keep anybody from getting near the boat basin. A couple of uniformed noncoms were going from table to table in the restaurant to tell the late diners that everything was all right, they just couldn't leave just yet because (showing a lot of imagination) there was a boat down there with a leaky fuel tank and they didn't want anybody hurt in a possible explosion. They were erecting screens around the sub itself, and a Bureau colonel named Makalanos, this one by then already up from Arlington, was on the phone to arrange for a Navy submarine to tow the Horch ship to a secure place, underwater.

It was this Colonel Makalanos who got back into the sub with me.

I don't know what he had expected to find, but his eyes popped when he saw the Dopey, the Docs, the Horch machines . . . and Beert. "Mother of God," he whispered, and then pulled himself together. "Tell the Meows and those other things what's going on, Dannerman," he ordered. "They'll all go with the sub, and I'll put a couple of guards on board, too. You? No, not you, Dannerman. I'm taking you straight to Arlington so you can explain all this to the deputy director."

I don't know what Beert had expected, either. He didn't say. He just listened while I told him what the colonel wanted, his neck down around his midsection, his head tipped upward to regard me sorrowfully. "I'll come back to you as soon as I can," I promised. "Just don't let the machines do anything, all right?"

He didn't answer that. He had stopped looking at me and was staring at the four husky Bureau people who were climbing in, their weapons at the ready.

"Ah, Beert," I said. "Listen, everybody's going to be really grateful to you for your help against the Others. It'll be all right."

He twisted his neck to look at me again. "I hope that is so," he said.

NINE

Home at Last

39

Twenty-four hours later I wasn't so enthusiastic about the Bureau's efficiency, because they had spent those hours very efficiently questioning me. They did it in relays, three or four of them at a time, and they questioned me *hard.* They didn't give up a thing in return, either, no matter how much I begged to be told what was happening here on Earth. Or what they were doing with Beert and Pirraghiz or the sub. Or anything.

It took me right back to those good old days with the Christmas trees and the helmet. This time my interrogators weren't causing me any actual physical pain, true. But, you know, interrogation is interrogation whoever does it. If the interrogators are really serious about it, it's no fun at all for the party being interrogated.

The place I was in was what we called "the Pit of Pain," one of the Bureau's interrogation chambers. They had me and the interrogators down in the bare little working space where the action took place: a table and a few straight-backed chairs and nothing else. I knew there were people observing us in the gallery seats that surrounded the pit, but I couldn't see them. They were hidden behind the one-way mirror walls.

The first question the Bureau's goons asked me was, "What's that thing on your neck?" They didn't like the look of it, and they didn't like my answer, either. When I said it was just so I could understand Horch, not a bit like those Beloved Leader spy bugs, they weren't believing a word of it. They suspended questioning for a moment, just left me with the interrogators glowering at me in silence until someone came back with a couple of strips of coppery mesh which they wound around my head and neck. Then they wanted to know everything, and I mean *everything,* starting with when the Dopey and I popped out of the transit machine.

The questioning was pretty much nonstop. They did let me pee a couple of times—not giving me any decent privacy while I did it, of course; a Bureau goon stood alertly behind me every minute, in case I had some kind of evil trick to play with the urinal. They even let me eat once or twice, dry ham sandwiches that looked as though they'd been salvaged from somebody's lunch meeting and black coffee out of the same urn the interrogators used. It was not the homecoming meal I had been dreaming about. What they wouldn't let me do at all was sleep. When I began getting woozy they handed me a glass of tepid water and a couple of those Bureau-issue wake-up pills. The things woke me right up, but I would rather have got horizontal. Even the Christmas trees had been kinder than that.

I thought I'd seen the woman who handed me the wake-up pills around the headquarters before. I pressed my luck. While I was still swallowing, I asked her, "What about my friends in the sub, are they all right?"

She might have answered. She opened her mouth as though she intended to, but one of the other interrogators shouldered her aside. He took the glass from my hand and said, "Don't worry about your buddies, we're taking care of them. Now, tell us about these Horch that you say are good guys." So I told them about the Two Eights and their nest, and why they were different from the cousin Horch.

It kept going until, along about the third or fourth wake-up pill, there was a change. My interrogators all stopped talking at once, turning toward the mirror wall. I knew why: they'd all heard something on their little earphones. At once a little door in the wall opened. Someone I knew walked in, looking both irritated and grim. It was the way Deputy Director Marcus Pell usually looked.

I stood up and offered him a hand to shake. "I'm Agent Dannerman," I told him.

The deputy director didn't answer at first. He ignored the hand and took one of the straight-backed chairs—its previous occupant getting up and out of the way fast—and regarded me for a moment. "That remains to be seen," he said. "How do we know you're who you say you are?"

I guessed, "Fingerprints? Retinal scan?" I think I was getting a little light-headed by then, regardless of the pills.

"Not good enough," he said judiciously. "I understand the Scarecrows can make an exact copy of anybody or anything they like. You could be a Scarecrow brain wearing a human body, for all I know."

"I'm not," I said wearily, and couldn't help adding, "For that matter, so could you."

He didn't take offense. He just nodded and said, "I think we need confirmation of your identity. Brigadier Morrisey! Come in, please."

The door that opened this time wasn't to the auditorium seats; it was the one that allowed suspects and interrogators to get in and out from the corridors outside. In a moment a clumsy-looking thing like a white-enameled kitchen refrigerator on wheels rolled in. I frowned at it, puzzled about what the deputy director was bringing this big metal thing in for, annoyed because it was blocking my view; I couldn't see my old boss, Hilda Morrisey, at all. Even when the thing rolled up close to me and I could see the door behind it closing again, there was no sign of Hilda.

Then a voice that I knew came out of the box. "Tell me, Danno, what was the name of the Kraut broad from the Mad King Ludwigs you were shacking up with?"

"Oh, my God," I said. "Hilda! They told me you were dead! What the hell are you doing in that thing?"

It—she—came to a full stop right across the table from me. There was nothing that looked human about the box. It had no face, only a rectangle of mirror glass at head height; I could not see what was behind it. But the voice was Hilda's, all right—a little fainter than I was used to, a little breathier, but definitely Hilda. "I'm not quite dead, Danno. I got shot up a little, is all, and the reason I'm still alive is that I've got this box to keep me going. Answer the question."

Evidently we wouldn't be catching up on each other's news for a while. "You mean Ilse?" I asked.

"Last name too," she ordered.

I cudgeled my memory. "Keinwasser? Something like that. I never heard her real name until somebody, I think it was you, told me about it after she was arrested, and I wasn't paying a lot of attention. If you remember, I was in Intensive Care at the time."

She didn't comment, just rapped out: "The name of my sergeant when you were working on the dope ring in New York."

"Uh. McEvoy? He was a master sergeant, but I don't know his first name."

"Your mother's birthday?" And when I told her that, she wanted the names of all my fellow lodgers in Rita Gummidge's rooming house, and the date of my promotion to senior agent, and the address of the little theater in Coney Island where my then girlfriend, Anita Berman, worked as ticket clerk when she didn't have a part in whatever play they were doing at the time. Hilda was thorough—maybe a little more thorough than the deputy director enjoyed, because he was drumming his fingers on the table before she was through.

Then she turned the big box to face him. "Looks all right as far as I can tell, Marcus," she said cautiously. "We'll get a better fix when the other witness gets here. I suggest we let him get some sleep."

She caught the deputy director in the middle of a yawn of his own. He suppressed it and said, "Very well. Put him in a cell."

That didn't sound good to me. Or to Hilda. "We can do better than that, Marcus," she said. "If he's him, he's entitled to a little something. I've reserved one of the VIP suites downstairs for him."

I think because he was too sleepy to object, Pell only shrugged. "Put a double guard on it. Now take him away."

The VIP suites were what they sounded like, plush little accommodations for high-ranking or otherwise important visitors who might need to be put up temporarily by the Bureau. They had comfortable beds and private baths and all the fixings. I didn't pay much attention to the niceties, though. I fell into the sack and, wake-up pills or none, in two minutes I was gone.

When I woke up there was an orderly standing by my bed, a coffee tray in his hand. "They want you to be ready to leave for another destination shortly, Agent Dannerman. There are clean clothes hanging behind the bathroom door."

Of course I asked him what this other destination I was supposed to be leaving for was, but the door was already closing behind him by the time I got the question out. I swallowed one whole cup of the coffee, scalding as it was, and headed for the shower. While I was dressing I got my first good look at myself in a human mirror. I looked skinny, and the beard I'd grown in captivity needed either trimming or shaving off entirely, I wasn't sure which. I was a good many months behind a haircut, too. I came out of the bathroom, wondering absently if the Bureau was going to have a barber wherever I was going. . . .

A woman was standing by my unmade bed. Not just any woman; this one had the face and form of the one I had been dreaming about. I gaped at her unbelievingly. "Pat?" I croaked.

That seemed to annoy her. "Actually I'm Patrice," she said. "The Pat you're talking about is over at Camp Smolley, and by the way, you might be interested to know that she's married now. Married to you, as a matter of fact." She didn't give me time to absorb that, but went right on. "Listen, I'm starved. Put your babushka back on and let's get some breakfast while we talk."

40

I hadn't had anywhere near enough sleep, and the question of what the Bureau was doing with Beert and Pirraghiz and the sub hung heavy in my mind. But right then, not *very* heavy, because I had more personal things to distract me. Partly it was the presence of Patrice Adcock. She was a lot cleaner and better-dressed than the last time I'd seen her, with her more or less reddish hair curled around her pretty face and looking so *exactly* like Pat that I had to remind myself that she wasn't *really* Pat. That was confusing, and I had too many other things on my mind to want to be confused about the woman I loved.

The other part of it was food. I didn't hear any order given, but almost immediately two Bureau noncoms appeared at the door, rolling in breakfast tables that were covered with hot plates and cold. I think the meal must have been prepared in the deputy director's private kitchen, because it was *fine*. There were eggs, four of them, lightly fried with their perfect golden yolks staring up at me. Hash browns, crisp and oniony. A liter or so of orange juice that had obviously been squeezed within the hour. Crisp bacon. Crackly-crusted sausages. Pancakes with melted butter and hot syrup dribbling down their sides. More coffee—more of everything, in fact.

It was the precise kind of meal I had been dreaming about for a long time.

The metal-mesh babushka kept getting in the way of my mouth, but I didn't let that slow me down. I managed to get down a good share of everything in sight as we talked, while Patrice contented herself with picking at some toast and half a papaya. "The reason I'm here," she told me, "is they wanted somebody who knew you to check you out, and who better than me? So let's get down to it. What was the name of Uncle Cubby's cat?"

That made me grin, with my mouth full of sausage. "Starting right out with trick questions, are we, Patrice? Uncle Cubby didn't have a cat. Grandma Dannerman was allergic to them. The cook had a little yellow dog, but it wasn't ever allowed out of the servants' quarters. I think its name was Molly."

She made a face at me. "Was it? I don't remember. So tell me how old you were when we first met, and what rooms we had in Uncle Cubby's house."

So I told her that and, when she went on to ask, told her what it was like to swim in the muddy-bottomed river below the house, and the names of Uncle Cubby's servants, or as many of them as either of us could remember, and what games we used to play. Except that when I started to mention the games she and I had played under Uncle Cubby's big front porch she cleared her throat and changed the subject. Well, I knew why that was. I had no doubt that every word we spoke and every expression on our faces was monitored so that the Bureau's gumshoes watching us wouldn't miss a thing, and there were things Patrice didn't choose to discuss in front of strangers.

By the time I had reached the point where I couldn't eat any more, she had run out of questions. "All right," she said, and looked away. She spoke to the air. "Hilda? If he's a fake, he's a damn good one. Come on in."

The door opened at once, and Hilda's mobile life support rolled in. The big white box stopped right in front of me, so she could take another good look at my face, but when she spoke it was to Patrice. "You're sure about him?"

Patrice shrugged. "As sure as I can be in twenty minutes. I think it's him, all right."

Hilda meditated for a moment, then sighed. "All right, Patrice, but you'd better come along with us to double-check. The chopper's waiting."

Patrice frowned as if she might be about to object to the idea. I didn't give her a chance. All this talk about good times in the old days had put more urgent matters out of my mind, but they came flooding back. "Hold it," I said. "What's happening with my friends and the sub? And where are we going?"

"We're going to Camp Smolley," Hilda informed me. "Ever been there? The old biowar research plant? That's where the action is on trying to reverse-engineer Scarecrow artifacts these days."

"My friends—"

Her voice got harsh. "I said the chopper's waiting, Danno. We'll see your pals when we get there. The Navy towed the sub to Hampton Roads for security reasons, and now they're flying it to Smolley."

I stared at her. That huge thing? Flying it? But when I tried to ask her about it she wasn't patient anymore. "You'll see when we get there. Now get your ass in gear."

41

Outside it was still dark and there were a few stars in the sky—unusually, for foggy, cloudy northern Virginia. I didn't think it was going to stay dark for long. I didn't have any good idea of the time, but a full moon was down near the western horizon and daybreak couldn't be far away.

Getting into the helicopter took a little longer than I would have guessed. The problem was Hilda's life-support system; we had to wait while they brought up the kind of lift they use to bring meals into passenger jets. She rolled her white box onto the lift, it elevated her, she rolled onto the chopper, two attendants guiding her. Then Patrice and I were allowed to board. The rotors began to turn before they'd finished strapping Hilda down, and we were airborne.

I had about a million more serious questions—*really* serious ones—on my mind, but I couldn't help it. First I had to clear up what she had said. "Patrice? You said Pat was married?"

As she was buckling herself in she paused to give me what struck me as an unsympathetic look, I could not guess why. "Pat One, you're talking about. Yes, she's definitely married. To Dan M.—M for mustache, see? That's what we call that particular Dan because he's got a mustache. He's the one who was with us on the prison planet. And Dan S.—the clean-shaved one, the one that never got there—he's married, too, to that little girl you were romancing from the theater. I guess all your other Dans have been taking all your old girlfriends out of circulation while you were away." She gave me a considering look. I wasn't sure what was in her mind, but what she said was, "Maybe you should tidy up that beard a little and keep it for a while, Dan. So we can tell you apart. We could call you Dan B., for beard."

She went on to explain some of the other problems of nomenclature for all us identical copies. She was still Patrice, just as Rosaleen had named her back on the prison planet. The Pat I had been thinking of as my own particular Pat was now called Pat One. The one who had been pregnant was still Pat Five (and no, she wasn't pregnant anymore; she had given birth to triplets, three little girls). And the Pat who had been returned to Earth with a bug in her head and never got to the prison planet with the rest of us had flatly refused to be given any number, so she was called P. J.

While she was telling me how to tell the Pats apart by sight—it had to do with the colors they wore—I remembered the important stuff. I broke in on her explanations with, "What about the Beloved Leaders?"

She looked startled, then relaxed. "I haven't heard them called that for a while. The Scarecrows, we call them now. What about them?"

"Jesus, Patrice! Nobody's said a word about them, but you must know they're planning to kill off a lot of people. Whatever you call them, why aren't you worried?"

She considered that for a moment. "Well, I do worry, a little bit, sometimes," she admitted, "but not much. The situation is under control, Dan. Honest. The Scarecrows call in every once in a while—lots of bluster, warnings, demands we let them come down to talk to us—but it's just talk. They sneaked in those damn submarines that caught a lot of people and bugged them a while ago—the same way I was, remember? So they could use the people as spies? But we've located most of those people and debugged them. The Scarecrows haven't done anything aggressive since then, not even their submarines."

I frowned. "How did you know they had subs on Earth?"

"Figured it out, Dan. All the bugged people turned out to have been at sea. The only Scarecrow object from the scout ship landed in the sea. Had to be. Only," she said without pleasure, "the damn things aren't easy to find. Every navy in the world's been looking. No luck. There was this one Turkish destroyer that thought it had one and depth-bombed it, only it turned out to be an Italian submarine. But nobody ever actually saw one—well, until you brought us yours, I mean. We don't even know how many of the things there are—probably at least a dozen—"

"Twenty-six," I said. "Twenty-five besides the one I brought in."

"Oh," she said, dampened. "Well, if you've got some way of locating them, probably they could be depth-bombed for real."

I stared at her. "Are you crazy? The subs aren't the problem. The Belov—The *Scarecrow* are the problem! They can wipe us out any time they like!"

She gave me a strangely indulgent look. "Not really, Dan. We know what they're capable of. Dopey told us. What he said," she went on, sounding a lot like a mother telling her two-year-old that there aren't really any monsters under the bed, "was that the Scarecrows could tweak a big near-Earth-passing asteroid out of its orbit and dump it on the Earth and kill us all that way. You know. Like the old KT event that killed the dinosaurs. Well, that's what Threat Watch is all about, Dan. You don't know what Threat Watch is, though, do you? It's what's been keeping us busy at the Observatory; I was working there, keeping track of all the findings, when they called me about you. Every decent telescope in the world is searching for objects with orbits that can come anywhere near us. We've mapped just about everything bigger than a panel truck for ten or twelve AU in every direction, whether they're asteroids or comets or can't-tell-which. I promise there's absolutely nothing big that's in an orbit that can come anywhere near hitting us for a minimum of two years. And there isn't any tweaking going on, either. Threat Watch hasn't found a single object that shows any signs of interference with its ballistic orbit."

I wasn't willing to be convinced. "All right, but that isn't the only weapon they've got, Patrice. They've turned some suns into novas—"

She was smiling tolerantly at me. "*Our* sun, Dan? You're not much of an astrophysicist, are you? Can't happen. Our sun isn't that kind of star."

She seemed so confident. I stared at her. "You're sure?"

"As sure as I can be. No, the asteroid impact is the only scenario that makes sense, and trust me, we've definitely got at least two years grace on that one, Dan. Every observatory's computer models agree on that."

Two years. I thought about two years for a bit. It was a lot better than no margin at all, but I couldn't help asking, "And then?"

She gave my hand a reassuring pat. "Ah, by then we'll be ready for them, Dan. There are big new spaceships building all over the world. Fighters. High-mass ships with plenty of delta-V. And weapons!"

I frowned. "So if the Scarecrows nudge an asteroid, we'll nudge it back?"

"Better than that, Dan. We're going to go after the poppa. I said 'fighters'; we've located the Scarecrows' scout ship, and when we're ready we'll go out and blow the damn thing up. *Then* we'll nudge any asteroid that looks like trouble out of the way." She gave my arm a friendly squeeze. "It's okay, Dan. Honest. We haven't just been sitting still and waiting for the bomb to hit. We'll be ready when the time comes."

So that was good news, right? If Patrice was correct, and she sounded really sure of herself, the human race wasn't just going to let itself be taken over or wiped out without a fight—exactly as I had boasted to Pirraghiz and Beert.

But the funny thing was that it didn't feel as good as it ought to. I mean, to me personally. What it felt like was that I'd been filling myself full of magnolious notions of coming back a hero to save the world, and it wasn't looking that way at all. The damn situation seemed to be saving itself just fine without me.

While all that was soaking in I felt the chopper change course. A minute later the pilot got on the horn. "Folks," he said, his voice sounding peculiarly amused, "we're only a couple of minutes from the Camp Smolley landing pad, but they've told us we have to orbit for a while. There seems to be some tricky traffic ahead of us. Matter of fact, if you look out of your left-hand windows, you can probably see it as we turn."

We did look, and boy, we saw it, all right. I'd never seen anything like it in my life. It was a giant blimp-copter, shaped like an immense fat sausage, its red and green lights blinking, and it was settling down toward the earth.

I don't mean I'd never seen blimp-copters before. Actually I'd even been in one, years earlier, when we were retrieving some wreckage for evidence from a bombed-out survivalist compound. This one was a whole lot bigger. In the early dawn light it looked like an airborne ocean liner, and the funniest part was that slung under it was some other large thing that was shrouded in tarpaulins. It took me a moment to figure it out, but then I sucked in my breath. "My God," I whispered. "That's my submarine!"

Up ahead Hilda was complaining furiously to the pilot because the way her life-support box was strapped down, she couldn't turn and look out. I didn't blame her. It was something to see.

The blimp-copter pilot seemed to be pretty good at his job. Slowly his whirly blades pulled the big bag down, jockeying this way and that, a meter or two at a time, until his load was resting on a wheeled metal cradle between two low buildings. Then the aircraft sat there without moving for two or three minutes. Nothing seemed to be happening, except that the envelope of the big sausage wrinkled and shrank a little, almost invisibly.

If I hadn't seen a blimp-copter in action before, I wouldn't have known what was going on, but I was able to explain it to Patrice, who had loosened her seat belt and leaned over me to get a better look. "He's pumping some of the helium back into the high-pressure tanks to cut the lift," I said into her ear. "Otherwise he wouldn't have neutral buoyancy when he lets go of the load, and the rotors couldn't handle it."

"Wow," she said, craning her neck. She was practically in my lap. It had been a long time since I had had so much woman so close, so warm and smelling so good. I put my hand on her shoulder—to steady her—and she turned her head to look quizzically up at me.

I thought—no, I still think—that what had crossed her mind just then was something about kissing. It certainly crossed mine. Kissing Pat Adcock had been a dream, yearned for most thoroughly for a long time, and now our lips were not much more than twenty centimeters apart.

They didn't get any closer. She didn't move any nearer and neither did I. She was Pat Adcock, all right, but she was a different Pat Adcock, and I couldn't sort that out.

Then the moment passed. The pilot was already on the horn again. "Okay, people, they say we can come in to land now. Make sure your seat belts are fastened, will you?" And Patrice straightened up and did as ordered. So did I, and that particular conundrum had to be set aside again.

The blimp-copter pilot had eased his big ship down another meter or two, until the cables that held his load went slack. Workmen on the ground had quickly released them, and the blimp-copter lifted and went sailing away into the sunrise. I lost sight of it as our own pilot was setting us down on the pad a few dozen meters away.

While we were waiting for somebody to bring up a forklift to get Hilda's box to the ground, I could see that the handlers had already hooked a little tractor to the cradle the sub was on. They weren't wasting any time. The machine was pulling the whole thing, sub and all, into a cavernous loading dock the size of a hotel ballroom.

As soon as we were off the chopper a couple of Bureau guards were waving us inside. Next to me Patrice stumbled and frowned; she was looking curiously toward the perimeter of Camp Smolley. Some sort of argument was going on there, Bureau guards and a couple of soldiers in unfamiliar blue berets yelling at each other. But what the squabble was about, I could not see.

The Bureau people weren't just beckoning us inside, they were *rushing* us inside. As soon as the sub and we were in the loading dock, its big steel door folded itself down to shut us off from the outside world, and the workmen began pulling the tarps off the submarine.

42

Even in that moment I noticed something funny. The workmen weren't the usual uniformed grunts the Bureau used for heavy lifting. They were high-ranking officers. I recognized some of them as upper brass from the Arlington headquarters, and they didn't seem to like being used as manual labor.

I didn't spend much time thinking about that; there was something more important. It was the first time I'd seen the whole Scarecrow submarine exposed. It didn't look a bit like any vessel I'd seen before.

When the tarps came off at one end of the sub they revealed a squared-off stern with three great openings, making a triangle, looking like exhaust nozzles on a huge rocket. There was neither propeller nor rudder. At the bow end was a group of tightly nested jointed rods, for what purpose, I could not say. A whitely gleaming squarish thing was between them; it looked vaguely familiar, but I couldn't quite place it. The rest of the hull was featureless metal, marked only by the hatch on the upper deck.

I heard my name called and turned around. It was Deputy Director Marcus Pell, looking recently slept and freshly bathed. From behind me Hilda's voice said, "He wants you at the sub. Go!"

I went. The brigadiers and department subheads were rolling a wheeled ladder up to the sub's side and Pell was standing impatiently beside it. "Up you go, Dannerman," he snapped. "See if you can keep those freaks of yours from making any more trouble."

I did as ordered, somewhat confused because I had no idea what kind of trouble Pell was talking about. Then the people on the desk opened the hatch and it got a lot more confusing than that.

* * *

The first thing that came out of the sub was the stink, worse than ever and with some unpleasant new ingredients added. The second thing was a uniformed police lieutenant, looking as if he'd had a hard ride. He glowered at me. "Who the hell are you?" he demanded, and didn't wait for an answer. He turned to the deputy director, who had followed me up. "Is there somebody who can talk to those freaks? They wouldn't let us touch the machinery at all. Then kept getting in Dr. Evergood's way when she was trying to take care of the Doc with the burned arm and . . . and Sergeant Coughlan was airsick all the way here," he finished bitterly.

That explained the new aroma. It didn't explain the fact that the second person out of the sub was a portly black woman in a stained white smock, whom I'd never seen before. The deputy director didn't give me a chance to ask questions. "You heard what the lieutenant said, Dannerman," he snapped. "Get in there and straighten the freaks out!"

As soon as I lowered myself inside, Beert and Pirraghiz came clamoring around me for news and explanations. "Give me a minute," I begged—in Horch, of course—while I looked around. Part of the stink came from three Bureau-issue body bags stacked one on top of the other—four body bags, actually; two bags had been put together to hold a larger carcass. That would be the dead Doc; the other bags would be holding the bodies of the two dead Scarecrow warriors. Another component of the stench was a couple of drying puddles of vomit on the floor, just under the perch where the ship's Dopey was fastidiously shielding his face with his fan and squawking his own raucous complaints at me—in English, this time. The sergeant who had been airsick gave me an aggrieved look and said faintly, "He's been going on like that the whole time. They all have."

They all still were. The surviving Doc was holding up his ruined arm, now neatly bandaged and a lot shorter than it had been, and mewing earnestly to Pirraghiz. The only things capable of speech or action that weren't demanding attention at once were the two machines, Beert's Christmas tree and the surviving robot fighter. They stood totally silent and unmoving in a corner of the sub's cabin. I appreciated that.

I raised a hand and said loudly, in English: "Shut up." Then in Horch, "I'm sorry if you had a rough trip, but it's over now. Pirraghiz? What happened to your friend?"

She was standing next to him, with one big hand on his shoulder for comforting. "At the other nest—the first place they took us to, I don't know where it was—the human female amputated most of his stump," she told me. "She did an excellent job, I think."

I blinked at that. "You let her operate on him?"

"I had no choice, Dannerman. It was clear that she knew what she was doing, and the medical attention was urgently needed. Then she came with us to care for him on the trip."

"But I thought you were the medical one—"

"Only for dealing with your species, Dannerman. I have been given no skills for my own."

Beert had been standing behind me, listening. Now his neck snaked over my shoulder and his little head twisted to peer sidewise into mine. "May I speak now, Dan?" he asked, sounding sorrowful but resigned. "I do not complain, but can you tell me what place we have arrived at? And for what purpose?"

It was a tall order, but I did my best to pass on to him—adding apologies every few sentences—what Hilda and Patrice had explained to me: We were at a research facility devoted to analyzing the technology of the Others, where he and the Docs would be—I took a moment over the choice of words—would be cared for, I said. I didn't want to say "imprisoned."

The hard part of answering his question was when it came to purpose. I didn't know what the Bureau had in mind for him, and didn't much like my suspicions. While I was stumbling over that, the deputy director stuck his nose down the hatch. "What's going on?" he demanded suspiciously. "Come on out of there! Bring those—things—out with you."

That sounded like a good idea. The stink was getting to me. Beert and the Docs followed me up the ladder agilely enough and in a moment we were all standing uneasily on the slippery, rounded deck of the sub, which had not been intended for anybody to stand on. I could see Patrice standing down below, a few feet from the big wheeled dolly the sub was resting on. The plump black woman was beside her, and Patrice's mouth was open in wonder as she saw Beert. Pell nudged me, pointing to the exterior ladder. "Get them down there!" he ordered. And when I added a few sentences to the Horch translation of his order, trying to reassure them, Pell demanded, even more suspiciously than before: "What are you saying to them?"

"I'm telling them what you said," I informed him.

"All right," he grumbled, "but I want you to translate every damn word both ways, do you hear me? Now move it, all of you."

* * *

When we were all on the ground he hadn't finished giving orders. "You!" he barked at me. "Go see the doctor."

He was pointing to the black woman standing with Patrice. Pell did not choose to mention what I was supposed to see her about. Before I could ask, he was already stalking away, barking orders at everyone in sight. When I got there, Beert and the Docs trailing after, Patrice's eyes were all on Beert, but she hadn't forgotten her manners. "This is Colonel Marsha Evergood, Dan. She's a neurosurgeon."

I shook her hand. "I hear you have a side specialty in amputating Doc limbs," I said.

She acknowledged the remark with a grin. "It happens I'm the world's greatest expert on Doc anatomy, Agent Dannerman. I didn't plan it that way, but I've debugged one and autopsied another. Now will you hold still for a minute?"

She didn't wait for an answer. She reached under my babushka to run her fingers over the thing behind my right ear. Marcus Pell came up behind me as she felt and peered and poked. "Well?" he demanded testily.

The doctor withdrew her hand and gave me a friendly pat on the shoulder. She pursed her lips, considering. "I can't say for sure without X rays and an ultrasound and maybe a little exploratory surgery, but I'd say it's architecturally similar to the Scarecrow bugs. If so, it has probably invaded a lot of tissue. I doubt I could remove it without risking serious brain damage."

"Hey," I squawked, pulling away. Pell didn't even look at me.

"So you think he's transmitting everything he sees?" he asked.

Marsha Evergood shrugged, so I answered for her. "No! I'm not transmitting anything! It's nothing like that. It isn't a spy bug! It's made by the Horch, not the, uh, Scarecrows, and all it does is give me their language."

He gave me a glance that time, but didn't respond. The doctor patted my hand reassuringly. I thought what she was trying to tell me was that she wasn't going to turn me into a slobbering idiot with her scalpels, no matter what Marcus Pell wanted. At least I hoped so.

Anyway, whatever decision he might have wanted to make got deferred by another call on his attention. The duty crew had been carrying bits and pieces of loose equipment—including my sack of Horch goodies—out of the sub. They were stacking it all on the floor next to a Bureau van, but they came to a stop. The officer in charge hurried over, looking worried. "Deputy Director? I don't think we can lift the big cadaver without more men, and we'd better get it into refrigeration pretty fast."

For a moment it occurred to me to volunteer the Docs for the job, which they could have handled easily, but Pell was already gone to sort this new problem out. Anyway, I wasn't in a mood to do him any favors, and I had something else I wanted to do. I beckoned Pirraghiz and Beert to come forward. "Patrice," I said, "I'd like you to meet my two best friends."

She stumbled over their names, but gamely stuck her hand out. Being a considerate person, Pirraghiz barely touched Patrice's hand with her enormous, taloned fist, but Beert wrapped one snaky arm around it. He kept his eyes on her but slid his head up close to mine, whispering. When I answered Patrice spoke up. "What were you saying?" she demanded.

"Oh, well," I said, trying to think of a lie, deciding to tell her the truth, "he, uh, wanted to know if you were the human female I was talking about back in his nest."

"And you said?"

I shrugged and stuck with the truth. "I said, more or less."

"Ah," she said, nodding. "More or less." Then she added, in a tone of friendly curiosity, "Tell me something, Dan. Why do you wriggle your arms and neck that way when you talk to your friends?"

She caught me by surprise. "Do I? I never noticed it. Maybe I'm just sort of copying the way Beert talks."

"You ought to try to stop it. It looks pretty dumb." And the look she was giving me that time had no suggestion of kissing in it.

By then the cleanup crew had loaded the casualties onto a couple of waiting gurneys—and a hand truck for the dead Doc—and Marcus Pell was peremptorily calling my name again. "Those robot machine things in the sub," he said, sounding harried. "The crew's afraid to touch them. Can you make them come out?"

I shook my head. "No, but Beert can. Give me a minute."

Beert and I climbed back onto the deck, and he called his orders down through the hatch. Both the robots immediately came to life. I wasn't sure how the Christmas tree was going to manage the two ladders, up and down, but it simply extruded four or five more branches and whisked itself along, the fighter robot following briskly.

"Tell them to get in the van," Pell ordered when they were down. I opened my mouth to ask why, but he didn't give me a chance. "Do it!" he barked. And while they were doing it, impassive as ever, he climbed onto a crate. "Listen up, all of you!" he called. Those high-ranking workmen stopped what they were doing and turned toward him. "You will not, repeat not, ever under any circumstances mention to anyone at all the fact that you have seen any of this Horch technology. The Scarecrow stuff is different; that's covered by the treaty, and in a minute we'll let the UN people and everybody else in this project in to see it. Nothing about the Horch! Understand me? This is a national security matter, and violation carries a death penalty. Plus," he added savagely, "I will make you pray for the firing squad long before the sentence is carried out." He met the eyes of everybody in the loading area, then jumped down and turned to me. "Tell your Horch friend to get in the van, too," he ordered.

That was pushing it a step too far. I didn't know what Pell was up to, but I didn't feel like going along with it. I said, "No."

Pell looked as astonished as though a waiter had turned down his request for a clean spoon. "What the hell do you mean, no? That's an order!"

"No," I said again. "Beert stays with me. I promised him."

The deputy director's expression changed. He didn't look angrier; he looked as though he had suddenly turned to ice. "I don't give a shit what you promised that thing, Dannerman! I want him out of here before anybody else sees him. Do you want me to put you under arrest right now?"

Out of the corner of my eye I saw Hilda's life-support box rolling toward me dangerously, but I ignored her. I said, "Well, Deputy Director, if that's what you want to do, I guess I can't stop you. I ought to remind you, though, that I'm the only one who can speak to these people. I don't see how I could do that for you if you put me in a detention cell." He stood silent for a moment, swallowing what I had said to him. It looked as though it might choke him. I went on, "Anyway, what's the point? Why do you want this stuff taken away?"

He glanced at Hilda, standing silently by, but didn't say anything until he had finished processing the situation in his head. When he had made up his mind all he said was, "The Horch can stay. Just keep your mouth shut about the equipment."

I could feel Hilda's warning eyes on me in spite of her one-way glass. I persisted anyway, "Yes, but why?"

"Security," he snapped.

That puzzled me. "I don't see the problem. Isn't this place secure from the Scarecrows?"

Pell had regained his composure. When he answered it was as though our little head-to-head had never happened. "It's secure from the Scarecrows, sure—I hope. That's not the problem. Camp Smolley is full of UN personnel and I don't want them nosing around the Horch matériel. It's bad enough we have to share the Scarecrow technology with them."

That was even more of a puzzle. "Why are you worrying about the UN? I thought the Scarecrows were the enemy."

Pell gave me the kind of look a kindergarten teacher might give to a child who hadn't covered his coughs and sneezes. "They're the *present* enemy, Dannerman. Who knows who our friends are going to be when this is over? Remember what country pays your salary, and keep your priorities straight!"

That was the end of the discussion. Pell turned away and gestured to the van driver, who started up and drove away through a smaller door to the outside.

Then, paying no further attention to me, Pell called to the guard at the inside door: "Open up! Let's let the rest of the team come in and see what we've got!"

43

I don't know how many people had been waiting impatiently on the other side of those doors, maybe a hundred or more. They came pouring in, full of indignation at being kept outside, even more full of astonishment when they saw what was waiting for them. The ones in front stopped short, goggling, until the ones behind pushed them forward. There was a curious sort of collective sigh. Then some rushed toward the sub and a dozen or so zeroed in on Marcus Pell, full of complaints and accusations. A tall woman in a sari got to him first. "I must protest this unnecessary delay, Deputy Director Pell!" she snapped sternly. "Under the terms of the UN covenant we are entitled to immediate access to every item of Scarecrow technology, without delay!" And a man, in the uniform of some army I didn't recognize but wearing a blue United Nations beret, backed her up: "I have already filed a protest because your people did not allow UN observers to be present when this submarine was landed!"

Pell wasn't fazed. He'd had plenty of practice in dealing with indignant foreigners who were pissed off at something the Bureau had done. He spread his hands benignly. "I understand your concerns, Major Korman, Doctor Tal, but these are exceptional circumstances. The Scarecrows don't know we have captured this sub, and they mustn't find out. So we have had to take unusual security precautions—"

He didn't stop there, but I stopped listening. I had a nearer problem. Several dozen of the new people had circled my little group, staring in fascination at their first sight of a real, live Horch. A couple of them were cameramen, shooting from every angle, and when Beert saw the lenses pointing at him he couldn't help flinching away. Pirraghiz and the wounded Doc, Wrahrrgherfoozh, saw what was happening and moved to surround Beert protectively, but the audience was all raucously shouting questions: Did they speak English? What happened to the big one's arm? How come the other Doc was wearing *clothes*? Were they dangerous?

I tried to reassure Beert and Pirraghiz and at the same time keep the more adventurous of the spectators from reaching out to touch Beert, but it was Hilda, the expert in crowd control, who rescued us. She produced four Bureau police to surround us and then—she must have turned up the gain on her internal microphone—she thundered at the people:

"Don't come too close! There's a risk of communicable diseases." With the help of the police, that made them fall back a little. She added, more civilly, "When they've been examined you will have your proper access to them, and before that we'll arrange for Agent Dannerman to meet with you in the auditorium to tell his story."

She didn't give me a chance to react to that. While the police were moving the spectators away she came up close to me and said softly, "I'd go easy on telling Marcus to go screw himself if I were you, Danno. You're not making any friends for yourself that way."

She was telling me what I knew already. I shrugged. "I already have all the friends I need."

She was silent for a moment. Then she said, "Maybe you do. It's a good thing for you that I'm one of them." And then, with a change of tone, "Anyway, here comes our transportation."

The transportation was one of those electric-motored people carriers you see in airports. It was big enough to hold all of us—including the Docs, though just barely. With a couple of Bureau uniformed police ahead of us to clear the way we moved pretty fast out of the loading area, through the halls of Camp Smolley. Hilda wasn't on the vehicle and didn't need to be; her box's wheels kept up easily as she rolled along behind us. Behind her still half a dozen more guards were following, half-trotting to keep up; most of them wore the blue UN berets. All the way the two Docs were mewing to each other, taking a lively interest in the rooms they passed, the fire extinguishers on the walls, the water fountains, the ceiling-mounted TV screens at every intersection that were all displaying the scene in the loading dock, though no human beings were present in the halls to watch them because everybody who could get there was there already. Beert was darting his head in every direction, too, and full of questions. I couldn't tell him much. I'd never been in Camp Smolley before either.

I knew right away when we got to the rooms they had reserved for my friends, though, because two people were standing in front of one of the doors. One was a blue-beret guard, looking uneasy, and the huge figure next to him was unmistakably a Doc. I was astonished to see him there, but Pirraghiz saw him at the same moment I did and her reaction was a lot more violent. She screamed something and leaped off the carrier—I thought she was going to overturn the thing—and flung herself into the other one's arms, the two of them mewing at high volume at each other. I got off, too, turning to Hilda. "Oh, right," I said, memory returning at last. "There were a couple of Docs with the bunch that escaped from the prison planet, the escape party, weren't there?"

"Two of them. The other one's dead," she said shortly. "This one we call Meow; he's been helping out figuring how the Scarecrow stuff works—can't talk so anybody can understand him, but he's good at drawing pictures. Tell your Horch friend this is where he's going to live for a while."

For a while. When I looked inside I hoped that "for a while" would be really brief, because the room they wanted him in was not attractive. It was a damn jail cell, is what it was. It had bars on its one window, and a lidless open toilet, and a washstand, and a narrow cot. That was all.

Hilda was watching my face. "Tell him it's only temporary," she suggested.

I looked at her. "Yeah, sure," I said. I did tell Beert that. What I didn't tell him was how long "only temporary" was likely to be in government practice. I glossed it over as fast as I could, and tried to explain to him how the toilet worked, and offered to get more blankets for his cot if he wanted them, and promised I would see him as often as I could—I didn't then realize how intensive the questioning was that lay ahead of us, and therefore how often that would be.

Beert listened in silence, head hung low, ropy arms wrapped around his belly for protection. All he said, his voice low-pitched and somber, was, "What about food, Dan?"

That took me aback. "Oh, hell," I said. "Right. Food." I hadn't given that little problem any thought at all.

So I asked Hilda for help. She wasn't, much. "There's plenty for the Docs and the Dopeys," she told me. "The Scarecrows sent some food down for them—that's how they sneaked their subs along. I don't know about the Horch. What does he eat?"

I turned to Pirraghiz for help. That took a little doing, because all three of the Docs were still excitedly mewing to each other. Wrahrrgherfoozh and the one they called Meow were hugging each other at that moment—by no means with the same passion as Pirraghiz had shown, but you can do a lot of hugging with six arms apiece, even if one of them is only a stump. When I got Pirraghiz's attention and explained the problem, she looked remorseful. "I did not think, Dannerman," she said sadly. "Let me ask the others." They chattered back and forth for a moment, then she shook her massive head at me. "I am not sure," she said. "Perhaps I can do for Djabeertapritch what I did for you in the nest of the Two Eights—get samples of all the foods your species eats, and see what among them resembles the foods of the Horch."

"I understand Meow has food of his own," I said, pointing at the other Doc. "Maybe some of that can be used, or the food for the Dopeys."

She looked puzzled. "Perhaps," she said, "but why do you call him that? It is Mrrranthoghrow."

I stared at her, slack-jawed. "Mrrranthoghrow?"

"Exactly he," she said happily. You would not think that a six-armed creature with a face like a bearded full moon could look coquettish, but she managed it. "He is a copy of the one we knew in the Two Eights, of course, but it is Mrrranthoghrow whom the Others copied for this mission and he remembers me well from earlier times. But you surprise me, Dannerman. Did you think I would be so affectionate with a total stranger?"

Next stop for me was my press conference—well, there was certainly no press there, but that was what it felt like to the person in the hot seat. I climbed up onto the platform, before the hundreds of staring eyes, and gave them a sketchy outline of my adventures with the Horch. Then I opened the floor for questions. That was a mistake. There were about a million of them, and all the time I was searching the hundred or more faces in the room for Patrice.

When I found her, squeezed into almost the last row, I managed an inconspicuous wave. She waved back, all right, but there was something about her that seemed wrong.

I took me a moment to figure that out. It was the clothes and the hairdo. Patrice had been wearing a pretty pants suit; this one was in Bureau coveralls. All right, she could have changed her clothes—not very likely, but possible—but she hadn't had time to let her hair grow into a long ponytail.

There was only one possible explanation. The woman I was looking at wasn't Patrice. She had to be Pat! The *real* Pat. And sitting beside her was a man who looked a lot like me, except that he wore a mustache, and I realized I was looking at the other me, Danny M., the man who was married to Pat.

That did not help my concentration.

When the deputy director, sitting behind me on the platform, saw that I was stumbling through the next couple of questions, he took pity on me—or, more likely, was afraid that I was getting tired enough to say something he didn't want said. He got up and preempted the mike. "No more questions, please," he said. "Agent Dannerman has had a very exhausting time. We must see that he is fed, and allowed to rest. As he is debriefed over the next few days the records and transcripts will be made available to all of you, under the terms of the UN agreement. Please leave now."

There was a rumble of discontent from the audience at that, but they left—or I guess they did; Pell had me by the arm and escorted me backstage before I could see. Hilda was waiting there amid the tangle of ropes and discarded pieces of sets. "Nice job, Danno," she informed me. "The way you duck the questions you don't want to answer, you'll make a good administrator someday."

The deputy director gave her an opaque look, but all he said was, "Have you got a schedule for Dannerman yet?"

"Working on it, Marcus. He's got to eat first, though."

He looked surprised, as though that sort of pampering had never crossed his mind. Then he looked resigned. "Take care of it," he ordered, and left without another word—to catch up on his harassing of somebody else, no doubt.

I looked at Hilda. I hadn't realized I was hungry until she put it in my mind, but I was. "You mentioned food?"

"Right next door," she said, rolling away. I followed her down a steep ramp, through a doorway, and came out in a little room—I suppose a dressing room at one time, now set up with a table and four chairs. Three of the chairs were occupied already: the Pat in the Bureau coveralls, that other Dannerman and old Rosaleen Artzybachova. "I thought you'd like company while you ate," Hilda said indulgently. Then, less indulgent: "You've got forty-five minutes."

As she left us I fixed my gaze on the Pat. "Patrice?" I guessed, very unsure of myself in more ways than one. She shook her head.

"No, Patrice went back to the Observatory to work on the Threat Watch," she said. "I'm Pat—Pat One—but won't I do for now?"

The food was typical Bureau on-duty fare: platters of sandwich materials, a big bowl of salad, coffee, fruit for dessert. I was hungry again and I ate, but I wasn't paying much attention to it. I had never had the experience of sitting down at a table with myself before.

They began at once to tell me all the news that I hadn't heard from Patrice, what a commotion they'd made when they got back, how this Dan and this Pat had been put in charge of their Dopey and Meow—"His name is actually Mrrranthoghrow," I told them, and they practiced that for a while without a lot of success—and thus assigned to Camp Smolley. And all the while I kept looking at the two of them, and trying to figure out just what I was feeling.

Odd. That was how I was feeling. Not uncomfortable, exactly. Just odd. I guess it showed, because the other Dan grinned at me, then looked serious and said, "Weird, right? But you'll get used to it."

And Pat said sympathetically, "We all did."

"Except in my case," Rosaleen put in, "because I didn't have anything of that sort to get used to. When I returned I learned that the other of me had died while we were away. That was more than simply a bizarre feeling, Dan. It was quite distressing. But as Dan says—as Dan M. says—one gets used to it."

Then Pat—Pat One—began to show me pictures of Pat Five's triplets; they looked like rather ordinary little girls to me, somewhat Asian-looking. As was to be expected, considering that what got Pat Five pregnant was some of the Beloved Leaders' experimentation with sperm from their copy of Jimmy Lin. Who had managed to secure visitation rights, after a lot of high-level and acrimonious diplomatic discussion between the United States and the People's Republic, and was surprisingly turning out to be a fondly besotted new father. And Pat Five was doing fine, too, except that the drugs she was taking to enhance her milk flow—three babies sucking away six times a day each!—had made her breasts so sensitive that she complained of being horny all the time. And how busy Patrice and P. J. were at the Observatory, with the Threat Watch using up so much of their resources, and the Observatory's scientific staff constantly pissing and moaning because they weren't getting enough observing time to do any real science since the world's telescopes were kept busy hunting comets that might be a threat.

All the time, out of the corner of my eye, I was watching Pat, my true love whom I had been missing so urgently, for so long. And what I was thinking was how much she looked like Patrice, with all of Patrice's mannerisms and every bit of Patrice's looks. I cleared my throat. "Will she be coming back soon, do you think?"

That made them all look at each other. "I don't know," Dan M. said at last.

And Pat bit her lip, and then leaned toward me confidentially. "I guess you know," she said, "back in the prison planet Patrice, well, had a kind of crush on you—that is, *you,* I mean"—pointing a forefinger at each of us Dan Dannermans.

I blinked at that. "She did?"

Rosaleen was laughing, a dry old chuckle. "Of course she did, Dan, as did we all," she said kindly. "Do not let it make you conceited. You were simply the only worthwhile man for many light-years in any direction. What did you expect?" She gave me a demure look. "Perhaps I should confess that I even had some sorts of foolish old-woman thoughts about you myself."

"You did?" That was astonishing, too, but in a different way.

"Patrice didn't exactly get over it, either," Pat went on. "So when she heard you were here—well, look, I'm telling tales out of school, but we're all kind of family here, aren't we? And now you've just kind of hurt her feelings, you know."

That baffled me. "What did I do?"

"Something you said, I'm not sure what. Did you say she was just a copy of me? Because we're all a little bit sensitive about that."

Well, I hadn't done that. Not exactly, anyway. What I had done was to admit to her that I'd told Pirraghiz she was "more or less" the woman in my dreams, but what was so bad about that? It was true, wasn't it?

They all kept talking, mostly Dan M. telling me about the religious nut who had wormed her way into Hilda's confidence and repaid it by shooting her and three or four other people. I listened and responded. But I was still mulling over the Patrice problem when Hilda herself rolled in.

"Finished, Danno?" she asked. "You better be. Wipe the crumbs off your face, because family time is over and the debriefers are waiting to get at you."

TEN

The Most Important Man in the World

44

There were half a dozen people impatiently waiting for me in the debriefing room, some male, some female, some wearing the blue UN beret and some in Bureau tans. They didn't waste time. They started in right away—"Describe in more detail the robots you called 'Christmas trees,' " one of them commanded, and we were off.

It didn't stop, either. It didn't even slow down. After I told them how the robots had acted I had to tell them what their needles felt like when I touched them, and what they had done to me with their damned helmet, and what they had been doing to the Dopey. The questioning didn't even pause for breath—my breath, I mean; the debriefers had plenty of breathing space because they took turns with the questions—until Hilda's great white refrigerator box rolled back into the room. "Time's up for this segment," she said. "You go to the sub now, Danno."

"Slow down a little, Hilda," I begged. "I have to go to the bathroom."

"Sure you do, Danno. I've got you down for a pee break right after the next session. You can hold it until then, can't you?"

And rolled away, leaving me to follow her, without waiting to hear whether I could or couldn't.

There were more questions at the submarine, but this time they weren't for me. They were for the two Docs who waited there, Pirraghiz and the recent amputee, Wrahrrgherfoozh, and all I had to do was translate. The head debriefer seemed to be a middle-aged, red-haired woman I sort of knew—Daisy Fennell, her name was, one of the Bureau higher-ups. She started with the questions before I was all the way inside.

They'd had the sense to leave the hatch open, and so the sub smelled a little better. Someone had also cleaned up the airsick guard's puke, but outside of that nothing much had been touched. There was one woman in there as we climbed down, operating three or four cameras that were methodically scanning around. "Watch where she's shooting," Fennel ordered. "We want to know the function of every piece of equipment in this vehicle, also as much as these, ah, persons can tell us about how it works. Understand? Start with this one."

She was pointing where one of the cameras was pointing, to a sort of Chinese lantern, twelve or fifteen centimeters high, that was fixed to one wall. It glowed with a pale green light and was softly humming to itself. I passed the question on to Pirraghiz, who mewed to Wrahrrgherfoozh, who spoke at some length. When Pirraghiz translated for me, it came out as, "Wrahrrgherfoozh says it monitors the lighting system. I don't know why that's necessary, do you?" And while I was putting that into English for the debriefers, she kept on going. "He also told me what systems are inside it, but I did not understand the terms he used."

"One moment, please," one of the debriefers said, while I was adding that. He looked unhappy. "Will you please make sure you give us exact wording in every case? Also ask Pir—Pirr—the one with the purry name to do the same when she translates for you."

I opened my mouth to ask why, but Daisy Fennell was already talking. "Do as she says, Dannerman," she commanded. "Dr. Hausman and Dr. Tiempe are linguists; the deputy director has given them permission to record your translations so they can work on learning these languages."

"Like a sort of Rosetta stone; do you know what that is?" Dr. Hausman said eagerly. "That's why verbatim translations are so important. Once we can match up individual words, we can build a vocabulary, and then we can start trying to identify a grammar. We've been trying to do that with Meow, but it's been very slow."

Fennel flagged her down. "Another time, Dr. Hausman. We've got business here. Dannerman! I thought there was supposed to be some kind of chart here that showed where all the other subs were, but I don't see it."

I looked around and spotted the place where it had been, but now it was only a sort of glassy oval that displayed nothing at all. "There. I guess it's turned off for some reason."

"*Why* is it turned off?"

I put the question to Pirraghiz and got the answer from Wrahrrgherfoozh. "He says it's because the way the systems are hooked up—"

"Please!" the linguist begged. "Exact words! Also the Doc's when he speaks to Pirraghiz, if you don't mind."

I didn't, particularly. Pirraghiz was less obliging when I told her about it. "It is very tedious this way," she sniffed. "If these other persons wish to speak the Horch language, why do you not implant them with language modules of their own?"

When I translated that, there was an amused titter all around, though she hadn't sounded to me as though she were joking. But Fennell wasn't amused. "Get the hell on with it, Dannerman," she ordered. "Cut the comedy!"

So I did, as best I could. Trying to translate word for word made the job about twice as tedious, and it was tedious enough already. Still, we finally got that message cleared up. Wrahrrgherfoozh had cut the sub's communications out completely when we took over. That was good, since the Scarecrows stopped receiving data from us, and thus wouldn't know what had happened, but it was also bad because we stopped receiving anything from them at the same time. Nothing was incoming. No talk on the circuits between subs, no data to locate the other subs on the screen. No nothing at all.

But when I asked, Pirraghiz conferred with Wrahrrgherfoozh and reported that, yes, he'd never done it before but he thought he could maybe rejigger the sub's communications systems so that we could receive without transmitting. It wasn't an easy job, but if he could get Mrrranthoghrow to help him, maybe, in a day or two.

Fennell didn't enjoy that news. "Meow's needed elsewhere," she said.

I shrugged. "If you think so. If you want my opinion, I'd say he's needed here. We don't know what the Scarecrows are doing, do we? If Pirraghiz could listen in, we might be able to find out whether they've really bought the idea of an accident, and the sooner the better."

I guess my tone wasn't very deferential, because she gave me a hard look. "I'll take it up with the deputy director," she said. "Get back to work."

So I did, and we had named and more or less described about half the visible gadgets on the sub when Hilda called in to say that it was time for me to go to my next appointment. As I came down the ladder, Pirraghiz and the linguistics team following, Hilda studied me for a minute. "Are you deliberately trying to piss Daisy Fennell off?" she demanded.

I shrugged. "Not deliberately."

"Well, you're doing a good job of it," she said, and then she made a little sound that must have been a chuckle. "On the other hand, I guess it doesn't matter much, since she can't get along without you. Hey, I guess none of us can really, can we, Danno? How does it feel to be the most important man in the world?"

The most important man in the world. It had a nice sound. I pondered over it between pauses for translations at the next stop, which was in a kind of laboratory.

I'd seen the Bureau's forensic lab at the headquarters in Arlington. The one at Camp Smolley was a lot bigger. It was a twenty-four-hour operation, and it was bustling with all kinds of activity. In one room technicians were doing mass spectroscopy, its door closed but the nasty, dentist's-drill sound leaking through as they sputtered ions off samples of Scarecrow metals. In another the chemists had other samples bubbling and fizzing under glass hoods. The place Hilda took us to was a larger room, filled with rows of workbenches. Each of them held its own piece of Scarecrow gimmickry being investigated, with a handful of techs poking and prodding at its innards.

We stopped where Mrrranthoghrow was waiting with two or three techs, one of them wearing the UN blue beret. While Pirraghiz was hugging her long-lost friend in greeting, I got a look at what was on the bench. It was a huge thing, the size of Hilda's mobile box, but it wasn't on wheels, and instead of being refrigerator white, it was iridescently greenish. When Mrranthoghrow finished hugging Pirraghiz he picked up a sheaf of carefully executed drawings and thrust them at me, mewing earnestly.

"This is a part of a transit machine of the Others," Pirraghiz translated. "It comes from the human astronomical orbiter called Starlab and Mrrranthoghrow has made these sketches of its parts, which these people wish to discuss when one more person arrives."

By the time I had translated that, the one more person was arriving, speeding along in her wheelchair with an apologetic expression on her face. It was Rosaleen Artzybachova. "Sorry if I've kept you waiting," she said. "I didn't expect you to be on time, I'm afraid. Hello, Meow."

She was speaking to Mrrranthoghrow, and the surprising part was that he replied with "Hello, Rosaleen" in English. Well, almost in English. It came out, "Uh-woh, Wozzaweeeen," but close enough.

Hilda, of course, was having none of that. "We are seven minutes behind schedule, Dr. Artzybachova," she said crisply. "Please do not delay us any more."

"Of course," Rosaleen said. "Here, Dan." She plucked a couple of the carefully executed drawings out of my hand and pointed to the sketch of a round object with a partly serrated edge. "Ask him if this thing is meant to fit in with this other one—" pointing to another sheet with a detail of something that looked like a clamshell.

And on and on. Well, there's no sense describing every last thing I did around then, because there were many too many things to be done.

See, I was the only one who could talk to Beert or Pirraghiz, and through her to the other Docs. There was a lot of talking to be done, and every bit of it required my participation.

It wasn't much of a stretch for Hilda to call me the most important man in the world. The busiest, anyway. So it isn't really surprising that some really important matters just sort of slipped my mind.

45

I don't know if you've ever found yourself in a situation like mine. By that I mean finding yourself back on your home planet when you'd pretty much given up hope of ever seeing it again. And meeting once more the girl of your dreams . . . more or less. And worrying about what your human associates were going to do to your best friend, who happened to be a Horch. And trying to catch up on food, sleep and news, the accumulated news of a world I hadn't seen for many months. And all day long answering questions and asking them—of Pirraghiz and Beert—and always, every minute, hustled from one interrogation place to another with little time to eat and barely enough for sleeping.

The worst part was the constant interruptions. We would go from trying to figure out whether Mrrranthoghrow was talking about magnetism or electricity or something entirely different to an emergency trip to the sub, where Daisy Fennell was having hysterics because the Doc had begun ripping one whole panel out of the sub's wall. By the time we finished convincing her that he was just doing what he was told to do up the chain of communication (Wrahrrgherfoozh, Pirraghiz, me, Fennell) and she finished demanding that he let Bureau mechanics observe and record every move (back down the same chain—four or five times each way), Hilda was already getting calls from the reverse-engineering people to complain that their allotted time was being frittered away. And when we got back to the hunk of Scarecrow transit machine, Mrrranthoghrow was in the middle of trying to explain the way the thing's laserlike weaponry was generated and Rosaleen Artzybachova was begging to be told where the power came from. And while we were trying to deal with that, the head of the UN detachment showed up to protest that some of the semiorganic Scarecrow matériel was making fizzing noises and seemed to be rotting away, and why were we wasting time with hardware when valuable stuff was being lost because they didn't know how to preserve it?

It was pretty hectic. Trust me on that. The only ones who were enjoying it all were the linguists, and they were in heaven. After months of effort, they'd picked up only a few words of Doc; now they had their Rosetta stone, me, and a completely different new language, Horch. Two new languages! Not just "new" in the sense that some newly discovered African hill tribe's language was "new" to, at least, Western linguists, but wholly new in provenance, languages that had developed with no ancestors in common with any language any human being had ever heard before, all the way back to the earliest presentient screeches and grunts. I could almost smell their ecstatic daydreaming about the papers they would someday contribute to the linguistics journals.

I was glad they were having fun. Nobody else was. Definitely I was not, and least happy of all was my friend, Beert. When they brought me in to question him he was belly-down on his army cot, head held dejectedly low.

The way I looked at it, he had a lot to be dejected about. The room he was in was Spartan and not at all private; two wall-mounted cameras followed him wherever he went. Which was never very far, since the cell was only about two meters by three altogether. When we all piled in, there was hardly room to move at all.

"They want me to ask you some questions, Beert," I told him.

His neck had swerved to the two armed guards in UN blue helmets. "Yes, I supposed that they would," he said absently, and then asked, "Those persons with the blue metal on their heads, are they your cousins?"

"Something like that," I said, but that was all the chitchat we were allowed. And before we could get down to business the translators were on my case again for verbatim translations of everything we had said.

When the debriefers' questions began he stayed dejected, but answered civilly enough. It wasn't a very useful interview, though. The first things the debriefers wanted to know about were weaponry, and Beert complained that he had had no experience in that area. "My robot may have more of that data," he said, "but I think not much." And then when I translated that, Hilda cleared her throat.

"Since we don't have one of his robots to ask," she said warningly, "let's go on to some other subject."

I took the hint. When, disappointed, the interrogators switched to questions about other kinds of Horch technology, Beert complained several times that his robot was the one to be asked of such matters, but I simply didn't translate. Technology wasn't a productive area anyway; even when Beert had answers, the terms he used meant nothing to me. Or to the debriefers.

That didn't stop them from asking, though. They were entitled to a full hour, they said. They claimed every minute of it, although the need for sleep was catching up with me and I was yawning long before Hilda announced time was up and hustled me out of the room.

For once the linguists didn't follow. That puzzled me, but when I asked Hilda she said, "You don't need to take them to bed with you, do you?"

"Bed?" I had almost given up on the hope of being allowed to go to bed.

"Bed, Danno," she confirmed. "You'll need your rest. You've got a long day ahead of you tomorrow." Then she added approvingly, "You did good in there, Danno. Just remember: Scarecrow stuff, tell them everything. What you saw and did, tell them everything. The Horch stuff at Arlington, you don't tell them anything about it at all."

"Um," I said, meaning, you've told me all this before and I'm too tired to hear it again. Then I said, "Can't you do better for Beert than that dump? Remember, we owe him—"

"I do remember," she said crossly. "We'll do the best we can. Give it a rest."

I stopped, turned and peered into her one-way glass, which made her recoil a little. "What the hell are you up to now, Danno?" she demanded.

"I'm trying to see if you still have a heart."

"As much as I ever did," she snapped. "Back off, Danno. You have to get over this nasty little curiosity about what I look like inside this box. I can see out, but you can't see in, and that's the way I want it. Now go to bed. You're going to have a full day tomorrow."

When the door closed behind me, I looked around. My room wasn't much better than Beert's, except that it did have a TV set and washstand, and there was a lid on the toilet. I thought about turning on the TV to catch a little news before I went to sleep, but I lay down to think about it, and then I didn't want to get up again. I wondered what Pat was doing just then. Then I wondered what Patrice was doing. Then I wondered what it was that was niggling for attention at the edges of my mind. Then I fell asleep, and when I woke up I had forgotten that there was anything like that at all.

46

I knew my new life with the Bureau was not going to be any bed of roses. I found out just how tough it was going to be as soon as I was awake. I was eating the breakfast an orderly had delivered—a lot less pleasing than the last human breakfast I had had, with its room-temperature eggs and not-quite-crisp bacon—when my TV screen beeped at me and displayed my schedule for the day:

0700	Reveille
0800–0915	Debriefing, solo
0915–1000	Break and medical
1000–1130	Debriefing with Horch
1130–1430	Lunch
1430–1500	Debriefing, submarine, with Docs
1500–1715	Translation, technical, with Docs
1715–1730	Break and medical
1730–1930	Debriefing, solo
1930–2100	Dinner
2100–2200	Debriefing, submarine, with Docs
2200–2230	Administrative conference
2230	Medical, and retire for night

It looked pretty formidable, apart from that one surprising exception. When Hilda came to hustle me over to *Debriefing, solo* I said gratefully, "I guess you do have a heart, Hilda. Thanks for that long lunch hour."

"Oh, that," she said, turning slightly to see if we were alone. We weren't. She was silent for a moment, then said in a lowered tone, "Yes. Well, I'll explain about that part when we come to it."

That was the Hilda I knew. There was going to be a catch to her generosity. And, of course, there was.

We got through *Debriefing, solo,* with its million questions about Beert's lab and Horch technology in general, and *Break and Medical*—five minutes for me to go to the bathroom, ten more for a couple of medics to peer down my throat and squirt something nasty-tasting into it so I wouldn't lose my voice—and *Debriefing with Horch,* where they asked the same sort of questions of Beert, with me translating. And, of course, wherever we went, our entourage trailed along.

The linguists did their best to stay out of the way, but we now had an additional group keeping us company, mostly United Nations MPs. They didn't wear blue berets like the technicians, they wore blue helmets, and they were everywhere, watching everything, muttering reports into their pocket screens, acting suspicious of everything that was done with the Scarecrow stuff. (Suspicious of the Bureau! How very strange. I couldn't think why.)

But they didn't stay with us when the questioning of Beert was over. Hilda shooed them off. "Agent Dannerman must have his time for relaxation," she said firmly, and they went. As soon as they were out of sight she turned to me. "We're going," she said briefly. "Bring your Horch friend along."

"What—" I started to ask, but didn't bother finishing. Hilda wasn't answering questions just then. I sighed and told Beert to come along, and when he asked what I would have asked, I just shook my head. A couple of Bureau cops were waiting for us, and they led the way to an outside door. A van was waiting for us there; and when it had taken us to the chopper pad, a helicopter was waiting for the van.

Then I guessed.

"We're going to Arlington, aren't we?" I asked Hilda.

And all she said was, "Where else?"

Well, we did get lunch there, such as it was. It amounted to no more than the trademark Bureau sandwiches and coffee for me, and a few scraps of what looked like stewed rhubarb for Beert, all that Pirraghiz had been able to sort out in the time available. We weren't given much time to enjoy it, either.

The Bureau's forensic laboratory was built to do whatever might be needed in any Bureau operation—everything from dissecting a spray bomb full of radionuclides in its containment ovens to analyzing the toxins in an assassin's needle-tipped umbrella or picking apart the linings in a smuggler's suitcase. The place they gave us to eat in smelled of ancient ashes and acids, but nothing was going on there at the moment but our lunch. Nor was much happening in most of the lab chambers we passed on the way in, but when Hilda informed us lunchtime was over and escorted us to a locked wing of the lab, there was plenty. At three or four work stations technicians—all Bureau people, not a single blue UN beret in sight—were delicately prizing apart pieces of the wrecked Scarecrow fighters. At a couple of other benches the objects being examined were the bits and pieces I had stolen from Beert and Pirraghiz—her books, his instruments. Beert snorted sadly as he saw them, but Hilda didn't let us linger. "Keep moving," she ordered. "We're going to see the live ones."

The Bureau wasn't taking any chances with the live ones. The room the fighting machine and the Christmas tree were in was steel-walled. A couple of senior Bureau technicians were waiting for us, gathered around a monitor screen that let them see inside. There a pair of Bureau sharpshooters were covering the machines from separate angles in case either of them made some sudden hostile move. They weren't making any, apart from an occasional twitch.

That made Hilda ask why they were doing that, and when I asked Beert he said somberly, "They are simply running routine systems checks, to be sure everything is functioning in case of need. There is nothing to fear."

She mulled that over for a moment, then sighed. All she said was, "Let's get on with it."

When we were inside the chamber the sharpshooters came to attention. "You have to stay out of our line of fire, Brigadier," one of them warned.

"Yes, yes," she said testily, but she obediently rolled to one corner of the room and let the technicians take over.

They knew what they wanted. Evidently they had studied everything I had said in debriefing about what the Christmas trees were capable of, and one by one they asked to have the machine put through its paces: extend branches down to the tiniest twiglets, display its recording lenses, speak. One of the techs was recording every move while the other gave me orders. Which I passed on to Beert to repeat, until he got tired of that and sulkily told the Christmas tree, "Do as Dan orders." Then it went a little faster . . . but still interminable.

When they had seen everything the Christmas tree could do—at least twice—they turned to the fighting machine. That made the sharpshooters more nervous, but the machine obediently turned, moved and displayed its weaponry for a good twenty minutes. Then the technicians paused, looking at each other. "We'd like to see it fire its weapons," one of them said. "Do you think we could take it out to the range?"

"You damn well could *not,*" Hilda barked from her corner. "Neither of these things is leaving this room."

The tech sighed. "All right, but we need to know its effective killing distance, firing rate, all that sort of thing."

But when I asked Beert those questions all I got from him was some violent neck-twisting. "Do not forget, Dan," he said obstinately, "I came late to this world of high technology. I know nothing of weapons."

I wasn't sure I believed him. I didn't want to call my old friend a liar, though, so I simply translated his words with a straight face. The way I looked at it, Beert was entitled to an occasional lie when his conscience didn't want him to tell the truth. After all, he had given me pretty much the same kind of slack when I was in his nest.

When it was time to leave I was surprised to see that we'd had an audience. Marcus Pell was standing outside the cell, watching the machines on the monitor. He gave me a quick look. "I remind you, Agent Dannerman, that none of this is to be spoken of to anyone, especially those UN people. This is a Bureau matter. The only person outside the Bureau who knows anything about it is the President of the United States."

"Yes, sir," I said, a little surprised that he had bothered to take the President into his confidence.

Inside the cell the machines were twitching slightly again, and he jerked a thumb at them. "Do they have to be doing that?"

"Beert says it's just systems checks," I told him, though I knew he had been told that before.

"Well, I don't like it," the deputy director said. "Can't he turn them off?"

When I put the question to Beert it seemed to bother him. He studied my face at close range for a moment before he said glumly, "Yes, Dan, I could do that. Why should I?"

"Because they scare the hell out of some of the people here."

"I do not mind that that is so, Dan. Do you remember that I am alone on this planet? These machines are the only security I have."

"It isn't much, Beert," I told him. "First suspicious move either of them makes, the guards will destroy it."

"Even so," he said flatly, closing the discussion. So I told the deputy director:

"He can't do it."

He didn't believe me. "So what was all that palaver about?" he demanded.

"He was telling me all the reasons he couldn't do it. I didn't understand most of it."

He gave me one of those deputy director looks. "Do you know what I think, Dannerman?" he asked. "I think your pal isn't being entirely frank with us. Maybe he needs a little encouragement."

I didn't like the way his mind was going. "If you're talking about beating the piss out of him, that's against Bureau policy, isn't it?"

"Only against human beings, Dannerman. Nobody ever said anything about space freaks."

It was impossible for me to tell how serious he was. So I reminded him that not only was Beert a good friend to whom we owed a debt, but we knew so little of his anatomy that torture might kill him. He sniffed, meaning I did not know what. "Time's up," he said. "You're needed back at Camp Smolley." And that was all he said.

On the way back we had to wait for the dolly to lift Hilda into the chopper. I took advantage of the moment of privacy to try to get back on the sort of fellowship I owed Beert. I tried to tell him I knew how he must be feeling, but he didn't let me get very far.

"Do you indeed, Dan?" he asked angrily, but then collected himself. "I suppose you do. Do not concern yourself about it. This is my personal worry, not yours."

"What worry do you mean?"

He waved both arms and neck unhappily. "It is simply that I feel I may have made a mistake. I think I will never see my Greatmother again . . . and that may be as well, for I think she would not approve."

47

Between the 1730–1930 *Debriefing, solo* and the 2100–2200 *Debriefing, submarine, with Docs* there was an hour and a half marked for dinner. This time it was real. Hilda not only gave me all that time for a leisurely meal, she let me have it in the little apartment belonging to Pat and Dan M., and she left us alone for it.

It wasn't exactly a home-cooked meal. It seemed they didn't do much cooking, because both of them worked for a living. Dan—*that* Dan—was in charge of Camp Smolley's resident aliens, their Dopey and Mrrranthoghrow; he told me that right now the job mostly amounted to monitoring all the Dopey's contacts to keep him from learning anything about the captured sub and Beert. It wasn't a demanding job. The Dopey's contacts were few; he had been well and truly interrogated long since, and there weren't many questions left to ask him.

Dan M. was waiting for me when I got to the apartment. He offered me a drink, and I took it gladly—it was the first I'd been allowed since I got back. "Pat'll be along in a minute," he told me, as he poured the Canadian and ginger ale—naturally he didn't have to ask what I preferred. As I was holding the copper-mesh babushka out of the way with one hand in order to lift the glass to my lips, he gave me a disapproving look. "Why don't you take that thing off?" he asked. "We aren't going to be talking any military secrets here, are we?"

"Well, Hilda said—" I began, and then reconsidered. Hilda, after all, wasn't there, and the thing certainly was a damned nuisance. I slipped it off and set it down on the floor next to my chair.

"Better?" he asked. "Fine. Now you can look over the menu and see what you like." He scrolled the screen for me, offering comments.

The gazpacho was more or less all right, but they made it with canned tomatoes; the soup of the day, though generally canned, was better. He didn't recommend any of the fish, but the steaks were pretty good. So I studied the menu with care, not so much because I was having trouble making up my mind as because I was feeling a little uneasy. It was the first time the other Dan and I had been alone together.

It didn't seem to be bothering him much—well, he'd had the practice. He freshened my drink without being asked, and politely offered to show me around the apartment. I said no. I could see the workroom and bathroom from where I sat; the kitchen was only a little appendage off the main room, and I had no interest in visiting the bedroom he and Pat shared. I don't mean that I was consumed with jealousy, exactly. I just didn't choose to look at their bed.

While he was placing our orders with the kitchen Pat came in, looking exactly as I expected her to look. "Sorry," she said. "Pell is such a pain in the ass sometimes." She took a quick look at the screen, made her choices and then sat down next to me, explaining what Marcus Pell had done to make her late. It was her job to take the Threat Watch synoptics as they came in from the Observatory and dumb them down enough for Marcus Pell to understand. That was a tricky tightrope for her to walk. If she didn't make them simple enough for him to grasp at the first hearing, he complained she was wasting his time. If she simplified them too much—as tonight—he got suspicious and demanded to know what she was leaving out.

I listened to her story, but not attentively. What was mostly on my mind was less what she was saying than the mere presence of Pat herself beside me. This was the precise Pat I loved, the Pat I had made love to back on the prison planet; this was the exact, specific, identical physical body that I had undressed and explored, and had yearned to do the same to again for all that long time I spent with the Horch.

Of course, so had this other Dan Dannerman with the mustache.

I wondered if he felt any jealousy, with me sitting right there in the room with them. For that matter, I wondered if I did. I definitely felt *something*. When Pat passed me the salt and our fingers touched, I was aware that that was the hand that had caressed me. . . .

And, of course, the same hand that had caressed him as well.

That was a jolting thought. On the other hand, Dan M. was definitely me, wasn't he? And was it possible for me to be jealous of myself?

I didn't know the answer. This whole question of living in a world that contained more than one of me took a lot of getting used to, and I was nowhere near that point.

* * *

I don't know what Dan M. made of my absentmindedness, but he surely noticed it. What he said after a moment, kindly, was, "I guess you'd like Patrice to come back, wouldn't you?"

I thought for a moment, then came to a conclusion. I did want her to come back, if only to sort out what, if anything, I felt for the carbon copy of the woman I loved. I said, "Yes."

"She didn't really want to leave, Dan," Pat said reassuringly. "She didn't have any choice about getting back to the Observatory. We're all working for the Bureau now, Patrice, too; she has to keep me posted on Threat Watch so I can pass the data along."

I mulled that over. "Aren't there a couple of you Pats there already?"

She gave me a forgiving smile. "Pat Five has her hands pretty full with the triplets, and it needs both Patrice and P. J. to handle the job at the Observatory, Dan. They work in shifts. There's all the administrative work to do, the stuff I used to hate—signing payroll checks, travel vouchers have to be approved, somebody has to keep the interns in line—especially keep them from flirting with the Bureau spooks these days. And then there's the regular staff, Kip Papathanassiou and Pete Schneyman and all. Some ways, they're the hardest part of the job. Patrice says they keep barging in on her at all hours, all of them, because they're not getting the observing time to keep up with their Cepheid counts or gravitational-lensing studies or whatever. Observing time! They know perfectly well that every big telescope is fully committed on Threat Watch. . . . And then there's Threat Watch itself. Patrice and P. J. have the synoptics to prepare every six hours and send me so I can tell the deputy director what's going on. Now and then, when there's something special, I even get to brief the President." She nodded her head approvingly. "That's the good part of the job. The President isn't a bad guy, for a politician. And he always treats me as though I were a human being—not like Marcus Pell."

I chewed away on my steak, listening. Something had crossed my mind about this Threat Watch thing, but there was something else on my mind that drove it out. "About Patrice," I said when Pat paused for a moment, getting the subject back to what interested me. "You said I hurt her feelings."

"Well, you did. You shouldn't have said she was 'more or less' me, Dan," Pat informed me. "Patrice isn't more or less anybody. She's herself. And also me, of course, but none of us like to be told we're part of a matched set. Even if we are. It's better if we just think of ourselves as family, isn't it? Saves a lot of confusion."

But it didn't. Not for me, anyway. Thinking of us as family didn't make it easier to handle for me, because I had had no experience in that area. I had never had a family to get used to. No siblings, parents long dead, no one to call a relative but Cousin Pat . . . and that was in the days when there was only one Cousin Pat.

The fact was that I didn't have much time to be part of a family, anyway. I didn't have much time for anything at all. Hilda made sure of that. She came to collect me right on the dot, hurrying me to my last session of the day, this one at the submarine.

I guess the talk had made me a little absentminded. We got through the session at the sub without my noticing anything was wrong—work coming along well, Wrahrrgherfoozh promising the sub's incoming comm systems would be back on line in a day or so—and it wasn't until we were in the final talk session between Hilda and me that I put up my hand to scratch my head and said, "Oh, shit."

Hilda interrupted herself in the middle of telling me that I really had to press Beert and the Docs harder for information to ask, "Now what, Danno?" Then she saw for herself. "Oh, Christ! Where's your damn Faraday shawl?"

I said apologetically, "I guess I forgot to put it back on when I was having dinner. I'm sorry."

"Sorry!"

"Well, hell, Hilda, I didn't do it on purpose. But look, if I really was transmitting data to somebody, I've done it, haven't I? So why don't we just forget about the damn babushka?"

And after a certain amount of chewing me out, she sighed and said, "Oh, what the hell. Maybe we could."

48

Naturally, the deputy director blew a fuse. But in the long run he had to admit that if there was any damage to be done by letting me off wearing the babushka, it was done already. And that was the way my life went. Debriefing, translation, more debriefing, more translation . . . and bed. Apart from the fact that my head was babushkaless now—and that Hilda squeezed twenty minutes in the next day for me to get a haircut and a beard trim—every day the same.

It wasn't all that unlike the days when the Christmas trees were pumping me for everything I knew about the human race.

I did now have better food and a more comfortable bed, and even a little entertainment. There wasn't much variety to the entertainment, though. Every morning I turned on the news channels, and every morning the news was the same. There were stories about plane crashes and stock-market gyrations; there were senators denouncing the opposition party for not responding to the Scarecrow threat vigorously enough, and opposition leaders denouncing those senators for recklessly damaging national unity in this time of crisis. There were sports scores and weather forecasts and about a million other kinds of news items that the media thought worth passing on, but there was not ever a single word of any kind about the captured submarine, the Horch or the unexpected arrival of another Dan Dannerman.

So security was holding. Whatever the faults of the National Bureau of Investigation, it was still outstanding at keeping its secrets buried.

There was something else that wasn't there, and when I had a free moment with Hilda I asked her about it. "Don't they have traffic advisories anymore? I didn't see anything at all about terrorists on the news."

"Oh," she said offhandedly, "those are last year's worries. The nuts've all calmed down, now that they've got something else to worry about. We haven't had a terrorist scare in weeks. Now get a move on, they want us at the submarine."

That stopped me in midthought. "The schedule says we're supposed to be doing solo debriefing," I protested, not liking the sound of a break in the routine.

Hilda wasn't patient. "Let me worry about scheduling, will you, Danno? It's the submarine now. They've got the stuff working."

When we got there Hilda waited outside as I climbed up to the sub's hatch, the linguists trailing as always. As always, the congestion inside the vessel was acute: all three Docs, the linguists, the technicians and me.

But it was worth the crowding. Wrahrrgherfoozh and Mrrranthoghrow had finally finished the job of rebuilding the sub's communications for receiving only—would have had it done a lot faster, Mrrranthoghrow said, sounding aggrieved, if all those Bureau and UN techs hadn't kept getting in the way. Well, I couldn't blame the techs for that. It was their best chance ever to watch people who knew what they were doing in the actual process of repairing a piece of Scarecrow machinery.

The two Docs had done a good job. The display screen was alight again, with all its red dots showing the location of every Scarecrow sub. The pattern wasn't the same as before, as far as I could remember—I hadn't had time for careful scrutiny in the excitement of invading the sub—and Wrahrrgherfoozh confirmed that some of them had changed stations, for what reason he could not say. More important, the two of them had restored the message circuits, so that now we could listen in on communications between the ships. There weren't many of those, though; Wrahrrgherfoozh informed us that crews were discouraged from talking to each other except in emergencies. What did come in were occasional bursts of gibberish which, Wrahrrgherfoozh said, were instrumentation reports that were in a machine code unreadable for any of us, even himself.

"I think they are sensor readings," he said, and explained. "Now and then we would get orders from the scout ship to go to a certain point on the sea bottom, always near a land mass and at shallow depth, and deploy sensors through the forward hatch. Then the sensor readings are automatically transmitted to the scout ship. What do the sensors sense? I do not know that, Dannerman. We simply did as ordered."

That stirred the technicians right up. They demanded to be shown how these "sensors" were extended and controlled, and when Wrahrrgherfoozh had done that they demanded that he extend them. "But not right away," they ordered. "Wait till we get a camera outside so we can see what's happening."

So the techs split up. A couple of them went out for a camera while others handed a portable screen down through the hatch, and all the time they were giving me orders to pass on to Wrahrrgherfoozh about what they wanted him to do, and he was telling them why he couldn't do some of it, and they kept me busy translating back and forth. Then, when camera and screen were in place, it got even worse. The part they most wanted to see was the sensor, but in order to reveal that, Wrahrrgherfoozh had to deploy four or five of the nested handling rods to get them out of the way.

I'd seen it before, but I couldn't help sneaking looks at the screen as the rods moved. They looked a lot like the tentacles of a squid. I wondered what they were intended for—"to handle objects," Wrahrrgherfoozh had said, but what objects were to be handled, he didn't know; that hadn't come up yet in his orders from the scout ship. That didn't stop the techs from asking him all over again—about the handling tentacles, about the sensor that looked a little like Beert's snaky head and mouth—about everything; and trying to keep up with questions and answers and explanations.

Halfway through, Pirraghiz looked at me curiously. "Tell me something, Dannerman. This is very difficult for you. Why do you not do as I have suggested and implant a translation module in some of these others?"

I glanced at the linguists to see if they were about to become annoyed at a little untranslated chatter. It didn't look that way; they were murmuring to each other and letting the recorders handle our talk. I said cautiously, "I've been thinking about that, but the trouble is that I don't have one to implant. Will you ask Wrahrrgherfoozh something for me? Ask him if it would be possible to build one out of whatever materials are available here."

She looked surprised but obediently mewed at Wrahrrgherfoozh. The conversation between the two of them went on for some time before she reported, "He says, yes, he thinks it may be possible, but quite difficult. Certain metals and other substances may not exist at all here, so they would have to be synthesized, or perhaps cannibalized from other pieces of equipment."

Actually, that wasn't any worse than I had expected. "How long does he think it would take?"

"Oh, very long, Dannerman. Some sixteens of days at least. But why do you wish to make it out of local materials?"

Perhaps the lack of sleep was getting to me, but I was having trouble understanding her questions. "What else, then?"

She waggled her beard at me. "You could use the transit machine, of course."

That made no sense. "You mean send to the Horch and ask them to give us a few dozen of the things? Do you really think they would do that?"

"Certainly they would not, Dannerman, but there is no need. I am not sure," she went on meditatively, "if either Wrahrrgherfoozh or Mrrranthoghrow is skilled enough to simply make a copy of the implant without making a copy of you as well, but that is not necessary. We can simply remove the module from your head—I can do that quite easily and without harm to you. Then we put the device in the transit machine and make as many copies as we like. Then, if you wish, I will put one back on you so that you can continue to talk to us yourself."

I blinked at her. "Make copies?"

"Of course. You have seen that the transit machines have made a number of copies of you, have they not? This one can make copies of the device as well."

That was when the linguists woke up to the fact that there was a lot that I hadn't been putting into English and demanded to know what was going on.

I lied to them. I said, knowing it was going to screw up their recorded comparisons, that she had been telling me at length that Beert had to, absolutely had to, have better food. And then I told Pirraghiz that we would have to continue that discussion at some later time, because right then they wanted us to get on with our work.

I didn't forget about what she said. I just put it aside to ripen at the back of my mind, because it definitely sounded like something I would like to do, sometime. Some other time than now.

Rosaleen hadn't been around the last couple of times I'd been translating Mrrranthoghrow's explanations of his drawings. I had wondered if at last she was following doctor's orders to take a little time off for rest.

She wasn't. Next time I went to the research lab the Docs were late in arriving, but Rosaleen was there already, sitting straight and perky in her wheelchair as she studied some fragment of a Scarecrow gadget under a crystal hood. She looked up and smiled at me. "Oh," she said when I asked about her absence, "it is just some personal business of my own. I've been visiting the Observatory to ask some questions. And oh, yes, Dan, before I forget, just as I was leaving Patrice gave me something to give you."

To my surprise, she reached up and pulled my head down to plant a kiss on my cheek. It was more grandmotherly than sensual, but I found that I appreciated the thought. "Hum," I said, pleased and a little embarrassed. "Thanks." Then I cleared my throat and got back to the subject. "What kind of questions?" I asked.

She looked a little embarrassed, too. "It is simply a notion of mine. Perhaps it is no more than an old woman's foolishness, but still—" She paused to look around for the Docs. They still weren't in sight. "If you are interested, Dan, since we have a moment, let me show you something."

She spun her chair around and rolled briskly to another workbench. Under a different sort of crystal hood were two objects, one the shape and almost the size of a doughnut, the other looking like a miniature dark brown peppercorn. "The big one," Rosaleen said, "we took from the wreckage of Starlab's matter transporter, the other from a bug. Look here."

She leaned forward and lifted the hood, taking out the bigger gadget. At the same time she rummaged in her pockets and found a magnifying glass, and handed them both to me.

The doughnut was faintly warm, and it made my fingertips tingle. Without the glass it looked faintly spongy, with pits on its surface. Magnified a little, the pits turned out also to be pitted. "It is a fractal object," Rosaleen told me. "Do you know what that is? It means that no matter how much we magnify it, we see the same surface structure repeated, over and over. As far as we can do so, that is."

I hefted it for a moment, then put it back on the bench. I didn't like the feel of the thing. "And you don't know what it's for?"

Rosaleen looked surprised. "Oh, did I not tell you? They are the power source for their Scarecrow machines."

"Like batteries?"

She sighed. "I thought that at first, but Meow—Mrrranthoghrow—says they are not. Or if they are, they are batteries of a kind which never needs to be recharged. Then I thought they might be receivers for some sort of broadcast power, but that means there would have to be some sort of transmitter somewhere. Mrrranthoghrow says—if I understand him—there is not."

"Then what?"

She shook her head moodily. "That is what I have been asking the quantum people at the Observatory. You see, there is this thing called 'vacuum energy,' about which I know little more than the name. When I ask Kit Papathanassiou he tells me that, yes, it is all about us, everywhere, all the time. Virtual particles spring into being and disappear, vast quantities of them. We cannot detect them, but quantum theory says they are there. They are gone almost as soon as they occur—usually—but some scientists think they do not always disappear. They even think that it is such a 'vacuum fluctuation' that caused the Big Bang long ago, and thus created our whole universe."

"I never heard of any of that," I admitted.

"No. I had heard not much more. But when I ask Papathanassiou he says certainly this vacuum energy exists, the theory is quite complete in this respect, but it cannot be tapped for any useful purpose. He is very positive about that. Yet these little things do tap into something, and I wish I knew what that was."

Thoughtfully she replaced the cover over the objects, then looked up. "Ah, here come our Docs."

So we got started late, but we made up for lost time: questions pouring out of the techs, Pirraghiz struggling valiantly to make sense of the answers from Mrrranthoghrow and Wrahrrgherfoozh, me translating both ways. I didn't have much time to think about Rosaleen's worries.

But they did stick in my mind, and there was something else that was bothering me, too. When we had finished the session and I saw Hilda's great white box rolling toward us to take me to my next date, I asked Rosaleen about it. "Isn't that sort of, well, low priority?"

"My interest in how the Scarecrows get their power? But it is of great potential, Dan."

I waved a hand at her. "In the future, sure. But right now the Scarecrows are maybe going to kill us all, and shouldn't we be concentrating on doing something about that? I don't just mean you, Rosaleen. It's everybody. They don't seem to be worried."

She looked a touch offended, but then she put her hand on my arm and smiled. "You are right, Dan. Have you ever read the story by Mr. Edgar Allan Poe called 'The Masque of the Red Death'? It is about the time of one of the great old plagues. All over the city people are dying, but in this one place there is a ball and the people there are dancing and drinking and pretending nothing is amiss—although it is only a matter of time before the plague will come to them and they, too, will die. It is denial, Dan. What you cannot face, you deny. Perhaps it is better to do that than simply to dissipate your energies in useless worrying."

"Well," I said obstinately, "I do worry."

And Hilda, rolling up just in time to catch the end of the conversation, said irritably, "You sure as hell do, Danno, and you make me nervous. How about if you quit worrying and get on with your job?"

Well, she was right, too. But that didn't stop me from worrying. The human race was experiencing some sort of reprieve, sure, but I didn't think it could last.

And, of course, it didn't.

49

Actually, it was that same night that things began to go sour.

When I got through with the 1730–1930 debriefing Hilda was waiting for me as usual, but she didn't hustle me off at once. "Listen, Danno," she said, sounding either embarrassed or annoyed, I couldn't tell which. "Do you think you can take yourself to dinner without me?"

"Well, sure," I said, startled. "Does that mean you trust me to go off on my own?"

"It means I'm a little tired tonight, Danno," she said, sounding irritable. "No argument, just go do it. And listen, I might be going to bed early tonight, so I'll see you in the morning."

I guess I was in my prisoner state of mind again, and any break in the routine made me uneasy. But when I got to their apartment Pat and Dan M. were unsurprised. "Actually," Dan M. said, "she called me a while ago, asked me to escort you to the rest of your dates if she wasn't up to it."

"She's about ready for dialysis again," Pat told me.

It was the first I'd heard of dialysis; Hilda had never said a word. "So she's sick?" I asked, trying to imagine Hilda Morrisey allowing herself to be sick.

Pat looked reproving. "She's always sick, Dan. That Tepp woman did a good job on her. Do you have any idea what she has to go through every night?"

I didn't, so Pat explained it to me while we were waiting for our dinners to arrive. It pretty nearly spoiled my appetite.

I knew that this religious fanatic named Tepp had killed a Doc and shot Hilda before she offed herself as well. I didn't know quite how shot up Hilda actually was. There wasn't much left of some of her organs—thus the dialysis every couple of weeks—and even less of her whole autonomous metabolism. Every night, Dan said, when she rolled herself into her private little clinic, the medics extracted what was left of her body from the life-support box—as gently as they could, but never without pain. Then they did all the undignified things that had to be done for a body that had lost the skills of doing them for itself. Check the Foley catheter, empty the urine bags. Roll her over for the daily high colonic. Patiently massage every last muscle and tendon, kneading hard to keep them from wasting away entirely. Bathe her. Feed her the extra nutrients that weren't included in her permanent glucose drip. Lift her onto the air-cushion bed that hissed and grumbled at her all night long, but saved her vulnerably fragile skin from bedsores, and, yes, brush her teeth for her, too.

It sounded like a hell of a life.

"But," Dan said, "better than no life at all. At least she can work." Then he grinned at me. Let's talk about something else. Pat, did you tell him the news?"

Pat looked coy. "Oh," she said, "well, it's just that Pat Five is going stir-crazy, stuck in the house with the three babies. She wants to get back to work in the Observatory. So they're setting up a little nursery there—had to kick Pete Schneyman out of his office to make the space, and he's really mad about it, too."

"Yes?" I said, with only moderate interest.

But then she said, "So that means Patrice might have a little free time. She's talking about coming down here again for a visit."

I stopped eating, with a forkful of lukewarm Bureau mashed potatoes on the way to my mouth. "That—would be nice," I said.

Pat was grinning at me. "Just nice? Who do you think she's coming to see, Dan?"

"And listen," Dan M. said sternly, "don't blow it this time. Take my word for it, this is what you want. When a Dan Dannerman and a Pat Adcock get together, it's a match made in Heaven."

Well, I didn't doubt that. I didn't even mind this other me telling me so, either.

I don't mean that there were not some residual male-primate flashes of jealousy still floating around in my head. How could there not be? Jealousy is in the genes. No previous male primate had ever had to deal with this particular sort of situation before. My genes weren't up to the subtleties. They were still loudly complaining that this man had taken this woman away from me, and what was I going to do about it? Settle, for instance, for second best?

It was an unworthy thought. Patrice wasn't second-best anything. I knew that, but my genes weren't sure, and I was too busy refereeing the debate between reason and instinct that was going on in my mind to be very good company at the rest of the meal. And then the news came that took my mind off the pointless interior debate.

Dan M. stretched and yawned, pushed aside the rest of his uneaten soggy apple pie, glanced at his watch and said, "Well, about time to hit the road for your nineteen-thirty, Dan." But as we were standing up there was a call for him on his private screen. He took it in the other room, and when he came back he wasn't cheerful anymore. "Shit," he said. "There's been a leak. Let's see if I can call it up."

Pat said, "What do you mean, a leak?" But he waved her off while he tinkered with the wall screen. It took him only a moment before he got a bare frame with the legend:

National Bureau of Investigation
Excerpt from "Maxwell at Night" program
Recorded at 1850 local time

The legend disappeared and we were looking at the face of the TV newscaster known as Robin Maxwell. I knew who the man was. Everybody in the Bureau did. Maxwell had been on the Bureau's watch list for a long time because he seemed to have contacts in some dubious places.

It looked like he had found himself a new contact now. "The spooks are at it again," he was telling his audience. "You know what they've got at the NBI now? They've squirreled away a Scarecrow submarine and a live Horch, would you believe it? Take a look." The face disappeared and we saw a picture of the sub, with Beert standing on top of it. "They don't want you to know about it, but hey, that's what Maxwell's for, telling you the things the big guys don't want told . . ."

He kept on talking, but there wasn't any point in listening anymore. The thing that mattered had been said, and said on broadcast television which the Scarecrows were no doubt monitoring. So the secret was out.

50

I never did get to my 1930. All Camp Smolley's schedules were disrupted for sure, because inside of an hour there were a hundred reporters battering at the gates of Camp Smolley, demanding to know everything there was to know about this Scarecrow submarine and actual living Horch that we were hiding from them, and why hadn't they been told about them before?

The reporters didn't get in, of course. They didn't even get any answers. What they got was Daisy Fennell, sent out to face them down and tell them that: a, there was no truth at all to the rumor; b, those alleged pictures were obviously morphed fakes; and c, if any of Maxwell's story had been true, it would be an act of treason to the human race to report it, because the Scarecrows would hear. While inside the camp the deputy director was raging through the hallways, demanding that every living soul in the installation take a PET lie-detector test to find the criminal who had broken security.

Whether any of the reporters believed Fennell, I couldn't guess. The funny thing was that part of what she said was true. The photos Maxwell showed weren't photos, they were morphs, probably made from descriptions he got from someone who had seen Beert and the sub but hadn't taken their pictures. Beert looked more like the hideous cartoon of a Horch the Scarecrows had showed us than his living self, and the alleged photo of the submarine got the handling machinery at its bow all wrong.

It made a nice little no-win situation for the Bureau; they could easily prove Maxwell's pictures were fakes, but only by admitting that the sense of his story was true.

So the media carried Daisy Fennell's denials, but that didn't solve the problem. Wrong as it was in detail, Maxwell's pictures clearly showed what the Scarecrows would instantly recognize as their missing sub.

The question on everybody's mind was: what were they going to do about it?

As far as anybody could tell, nothing. At least, not right away. Pirraghiz reported no special traffic to or among the Scarecrow submarine fleet.

All the same, there was a lot of worrying going on around Camp Smelly. Even Hilda was snappish, and the deputy director was hemorrhaging wrath, blame and worry all over the installation. He had his own way of dealing with worry, and it took the form of starting a one hundred percent interrogation of everybody in sight, thirsty for the blood of the despicable traitor who had broken security. By "interrogation" I don't just mean questioning; he had four PET-scan machines flown in from Arlington for lie-detector tests.

I didn't expect much from that. Position emission tomography is pretty good at sorting out facts from fantasy, because those two files seem to be stored in different parts of the brain, but it takes three or four hours to test a single subject. Marcus had not only the couple hundred people at Camp Smolley to test but all the ones at Hampton Roads as well. The good part of that was that it kept him out of my hair.

And then even Hilda left me alone. When I finished my breakfast it was Dan M. who was waiting for me outside my room. "I'm your new shepherd, Dan," he told me wryly. "Hope that's all right with you. Hilda couldn't put her dialysis off any longer, so she's out of commission for the rest of the day."

"Fine," I said, more or less meaning it. I still wasn't entirely easy in the company of this other myself, but as the day went on it got better. He wasn't just someone to talk to, he was that nearly ideal person for a conversation who was nearly ideal because he had the advantage of thinking exactly the way I did. As we moved from one appointment to another we chatted about what was going on around us, and if nothing new came out of any of the chat, at least it was useful to be able to talk, but then the world obtruded itself on us.

We were just entering the chamber where the techs waited when every screen in the area turned itself on at once, and when we saw what was on all those screens it took our minds right off the planned questions.

The Scarecrows were talking to us again.

51

At least the Scarecrows were no longer going to the trouble of faking the face of a human being to deliver their little homilies. The creature displayed on the screen was unquestionably a Dopey. He was squatting comfortably on a gold-colored cushion, his little hands busy in his belly bag. Behind his head was a pretty background landscape, distant hills and fleecy white clouds in a blue, blue and very Earthly sky. All faked, no doubt. The Dopey was doing his best to look amiable and trustworthy, not an easy job for a Dopey. When he spoke his voice had the cajoling quality of a late-night, golden-oldie disk jockey.

"You know who I am," he said, the little cat eyes gleaming, his fan spread in glorious iridescence. "I have spoken to you before, bearing the generous messages of our Beloved Leaders, who know what is best for all of us and whose patience is great—but not without limit."

His plume darkened and his voice became sorrowful. "But you are a willful species," he scolded. "You have betrayed the trust of the Beloved Leaders. You have wickedly stolen a vehicle which is their property. You have begun the construction of armed spacecraft. And you have done even worse. You have brought to your planet a representative of the despicable Horch.

"The Beloved Leaders cannot permit this to go on.

"Therefore they command you to take two steps. Within the next four days you must broadcast an invitation for representatives of the Beloved Leaders to come to your planet. And, as a token of good faith, you must rid yourself of this evil monster, the Horch. Kill him. Do so in a public place. Broadcast his execution. And when he is dead amputate all of his limbs and head. Let it be seen that this is done, so there can be no question of the sort of trickery you have shown yourself capable of."

He raised himself on his little legs and peered sternly into the camera. "Four days!" he said sternly. "If you have not complied by that time, at that hour you and your entire race will die."

He stood silent for a moment, then sank back on his cushion. The colors of his peacock tail brightened into soft pastels and his tone became wheedling.

"You must understand," he said, "that the Beloved Leaders seek no personal gain from you. It is for your own good—indeed, if you force them to put an end to your lives, even that is for your good, since it will speed your way to the Eschaton.

"The Beloved Leaders know that, in your present primitive state, this is frightening to you, for it is what you call 'death.' But death is only an incident. It will come sooner or later to each of you—the temporary death which all organisms experience. It is not to be feared. It is only the way which we must all pass, in order to reach that great eternity of the Eschaton.

"Yet the Beloved Leaders do not wish to take this step unless you force them to it. It would be tragic if your entire species went prematurely to the Eschaton. You are a young race. You have not attained full development. You cannot ever achieve that on your own. That can only happen to you under the wise and benevolent guidance of the Beloved Leaders. That generous proposal is still open to you, but you must act now. Destroy that vile Horch. Invite our people to come to you. Accept the great gift that is offered you.

"Remember, four days! And if you have not done as instructed, at the very moment of the end of that time you and all your species will immediately perish."

And the Dopey curled his lipless little mouth into what he might have thought of as a friendly smile, and his image faded from the screen.

Next to me Dan M. was wearing the strangest expression I'd ever seen on his face, part anger, a lot confusion; mostly he looked as though he were either going to laugh or cry. "But, Dan," he complained, "*how?* The Pats guarantee that there's absolutely nothing in orbit that can get here in four days! Do you think he's bluffing?"

I was staring at the blank screen, hardly hearing him. "No," I said, "I think it's worse than that. I think maybe we've been worrying about the wrong thing. I'd better talk to Hilda right away."

52

When I got to Hilda's room she was there, all right, but the medics didn't want to let me in. "She was sleeping," the doctor in charge told me. "We woke her up after we saw the message from the Scarecrows. She's watching a replay now, but she doesn't want any visitors while she's undergoing dialysis . . ."

I didn't argue with the man. I just pushed him out of the way. As I opened her door I called, "Hilda? Sorry to break in on you, but—"

And then I stopped, because I saw why Hilda Morrisey didn't want any visitors.

I had never seen Hilda like that before. It was bad enough trying to get used to her white-enameled box. This was worse. She was out of her steel-enamel shell, but she still didn't look anything like the Hilda I used to know. She was lying flat on an airbed, with tubes going into her in a dozen places and a sort of steel corset surrounding her upper body. The thing pulsed rhythmically, because it was doing Hilda's breathing for her. Apart from that, all she was wearing was one of those inadequate hospital shifts, and she looked smaller, older and more defenseless than I had ever imagined her before. The sheet that had been thrown over her didn't hide the fact that there wasn't much left of Hilda Morrisey.

But she spoke right up as soon as she saw me. "It isn't going to be a comet, is it, Danno?" she demanded. "It's something to do with the subs, isn't it?"

She had put her finger right on it; it was what I had picked up on as soon as I heard the Dopey speak.

The fact that Hilda was ahead of me again didn't surprise me; she often was, which was what made her bearable as a boss. Her voice did surprise me, though. It was the voice of the authentic Hilda Morrisey. I guess most of the toxins must have been dialyzed out of her blood by then. She still looked terrible, but not pathetic anymore. I said, "I think so, yes. But I want to get something settled first." I hesitated, then got to the point. "We aren't going to kill Beert for them, Hilda. No matter what. I won't let that happen, and that's definite."

She gave me a Hilda Morrisey stare. "Are you giving me orders, Danno?"

"I'm telling you that we can't afford to. He can help us figure out just what the Scarecrows are up to. And," I added, "we'll need that robot of his; it has a lot of information Beert doesn't. So get it flown in from Arlington right away, will you?"

She made a face. "Christ. Marcus will have a fit. All right. I'll give that order, and then I'll tell Marcus about it."

I didn't want to let it go at that, so I insisted. "And you'll tell him not to get any ideas about stalling the Scarecrows by wasting Beert in front of the cameras."

She gave me an opaque look. "Not right away, anyway. Now get the hell out of here so they can take all this crap off me."

Then it got crazy.

While Hilda was getting a team together I took a quick run to the sub. There was only one Doc on listening duty, and it was Foozh. He was jabbering at the duty guard as I came through the hatch, and mewed and whined at me twice as fast as soon as he saw me. Of course I couldn't understand a word, but I could hear the meows and growls that were coming from the speaker. Lots of them. They were busy out there, and when Pirraghiz and Mrranthoghrow got there she began translating at once.

The subs were doing something, all right. They weren't traveling very far; they were pausing at discrete points along the various continental shelves, then moving no more than a kilometer or two and pausing again. Pirraghiz said it sounded like they were depositing things on the sea bottom. What things? She had no idea; the orders from the scout ship never said. For what purpose? She didn't know that, either.

But I had no doubt that it was bad news.

An hour later we had a kind of a task force gathered—me and Beert and his Christmas tree, plus eight or nine Bureau specialists. Hilda was there, back in her box, and so was the deputy director; he had taken time out from his witch hunt to bring the robot in person—

and also to let me know that this was all my fault, because if I had let him hide Beert away in Arlington, the way he wanted to, nobody would have known he was there.

He was wrong about that, of course—whoever leaked the story would have known about the sub, anyway, with or without Beert. I didn't argue. I spoke to Beert, ignoring everybody else. "Something the Greatmother said has been nagging at me, something about the Others killing off rebellious races by poison gas. Do you remember what it was?"

"Of course, Dan," he said promptly. "It is part of our history. What do you wish to know?"

"What kind of gas? How do they get it to the planet?"

He waggled his neck at me. "It isn't necessary to do that, Dan. On most planets like your own, such poisons are already there in the oceans. They need only to be released."

And when I translated all that, the yelling began. There was no poison gas in the oceans, the experts insisted. There certainly was, Beert said stoutly, because the Greatmother of the Greatmother had said so. All right, snapped the experts, what poison are you talking about?

Naturally, Beert's words meant nothing when he answered. Nor did the robot's, when asked, but the robot had a better way of communicating. It drew pictures for us. A big dot with a little dot near it. A cluster of a dozen big dots, some filled in, some just circles, with six little dots near it.

It was the Bureau's chemical-warfare specialist who figured it out: "They're diagrams of elements! Hydrogen and carbon!" And when the robot said there were four of the second diagram for every one of the first in this poison, the chemist blinked and smote her forehead with her hand and said, "Of course!"

It was the first time I had heard the word "methane."

ELEVEN

Methane

53

All right, I admit it. I should have thought of it before. Call it fatigue, call it too much going on—no, just call it that I screwed up. That's certainly what Hilda told me. It was what the deputy director told me, too, but he didn't waste any time. Two hours later he and Hilda and I, pumped up with the Bureau's wake-up pills, were watching the sun rise on the landing pad, where an oceanologist was tumbling off a VTOL from New Jersey. His name was Samuel Schiel, and he came from the Lamont-Doherty Institute—well, actually he came from his bed, because the deputy director's summons had come in the middle of the night—and he barely had time to catch his breath before Marcus Pell had whisked him into a conference room and the questioning had begun.

Pell didn't even sit down. He stood behind the big chair at the head of the table and turned on the man. "You, what's your name, Schiel? Is this methane thing possible?"

Schiel was unfazed. He took a seat halfway down the long table, next to me, across from Hilda, looking around the room with interest. "Possible?" he repeated ruminatively. "Yes, in principle, Mr. Pell. Methane is a very common compound. It's the first member of the alkane hydrocarbons, a very simple molecule, and there's a great deal of it around in the form of clathrates, at least ten to the fifteenth cubic meters—Pardon? Oh." He moved his lips for a moment, doing arithmetic. "At least ten thousand million million cubic meters of the stuff, that is. Probably more. Much of it's locked up in permafrost in Asia and North America, but there's a tremendous amount on the sea bottoms. If you'd care to look—I asked my staff to transmit a map of the main deposits to me on the plane—"

He did something to the control for the screens at each place. While we were looking at them he investigated the coffee jug at his place, found it was full, poured himself a cup and waited for us to see what he was talking about.

I swallowed when I saw where the main deposits were: some of the biggest along the Atlantic Coast of the Americas, along the Pacific shore of Panama, the Bering Strait—I knew those areas well. "That's exactly where the subs are concentrating," I said.

Pell gave me a shut-up look; he had obviously figured that out for himself. "How come you know all this?" he demanded, looking at Schiel.

Schiel put down his coffee cup. "Why, the methane beds have been investigated quite thoroughly; there was some hope of tapping them as a replacement for petroleum resources. Methane is a very good, clean-burning fuel, but some of the best deposits are a kilometer deep or more, and they're not easy to exploit. Perhaps I should explain their physical nature?"

Pell sighed, reconciling himself to being lectured at by an expert but seeing no way out of it. "Perhaps you goddam should," he grumbled.

Schiel nodded briskly and went on. "The methane content of the clathrates is hydrated," he said. "That means that each methane molecule is surrounded by a sort of cage of water molecules, in the form of ice under pressure. If the temperature rises or the pressure decreases, the clathrate disintegrates. When samples are trawled up from the sea bottom they begin to bubble and sizzle and fall apart even before they reach the surface, often quite explosively. Worse, there is some evidence that any attempt to exploit these resources for fuel may be quite dangerous. You see, under the clathrate beds there are trapped bodies of gaseous methane. When the crust is broken through, the methane gas can escape. In great volume, Mr. Pell. In which case it appears capable of turning the ocean itself into a sort of froth which is no longer dense enough to float a vessel. A Soviet drilling ship which was mysteriously lost many years ago is thought to have sunk when that happened, and there have been conjectures that such events, off the coast of the Carolinas, may have been responsible for some of the alleged disappearances in the so-called Bermuda Triangle." He looked around the room. "Is that what you wanted to know, Mr. Pell?"

The deputy director was frowning at the map. He stabbed at the Carolina coast. "Those submarines," he said. "Could they be used to blow a hole in this clathrate cap thing?"

Schiel shrugged. "I know nothing of the Scarecrow submarines," he said, "but if they could plant some very large mines, yes, I think so. That might not be necessary, though. If they simply disturbed the clathrates sufficiently, they could start a release, which might then sufficiently lower the pressure to cause a greater release, entraining more and more clathrates as they rise to the surface. Once started, it could be a runaway effect, increasing exponentially as long as the methane held out."

Pell thought that over. "That would be a pain in the ass," he said at last, "but it doesn't sound fatal. All right, they can turn some coastal waters into club soda for a while. We might lose some shipping, but so what? It wouldn't destroy the world."

"Oh, Mr. Pell," Schiel said forgivingly, "but it quite well might. Once a large-scale release began—Well, similar events have already happened here on Earth, you know. For example, it is believed that one such might have ended the Ice Age."

The deputy director blinked at him. "What?"

Schiel nodded. "That was twenty-two thousand years ago," he said. "Geologists have determined that there was a huge landslip in the western Mediterranean at that time. That was when the Ice Age was in full force; worldwide ocean levels were the lowest ever, the amount of ice the highest. This caused some sea bottom to be exposed in the Mediterranean basin around Sardinia. There were deposits of icy methane-containing hydrates there, as there are in many shallow seas. When the sea level dropped, the pressure on them fell, as I discussed. They began to release their methane; the methane lubricated the slide; the slide released more methane—we think about half a billion tons altogether, nearly doubling the amount of methane in the atmosphere at the time. And the world warmed up and the Ice Age ended. Methane is dangerous stuff, you see. And that was just one local release. Actually," he said, sounding almost pleased to be able to tell us about it, "there is some evidence that one of the great extinctions of the geologic past took place as the result of a larger event. It was when all the present continents were joined together in one great land mass, called Gondwanaland—"

"Screw Gondwanaland," Pell snarled. "What happened?"

"Why, as you may know, methane is a very powerful greenhouse gas. There would have been wide-scale warming—"

"Warming?" Pell looked almost reassured. "We could stand some warming, couldn't we?"

But Schiel was shaking his head. "We wouldn't live long enough to see it. I don't think I've made clear just how much methane we're talking about, Mr. Pell. Released, it could form a layer of gas thirty meters deep, covering the entire world. Because it is denser than either oxygen or nitrogen, it would tend to concentrate near the surface. We can't breathe methane."

Pell's expression was icy now. "And the Scarecrow subs could make this happen?"

Schiel looked stubborn. "Given the application of enough heat or physical intervention on a wide enough scale, given the likelihood that it could become a self-sustaining reaction—"

"Yes or no, damn it!"

"Well, yes," the scientist said.

The word hung there for a while. Then the deputy director stirred himself. "Will you excuse us for a moment, Mr. Schiel? If you'll just wait outside . . ."

He drummed his finger until the scientist was gone, taking his coffee with him. "All right," he said then. "What are our options? Hilda?"

She spoke right up. "We only have one immediate option, Marcus. It's out of our hands now. We have to tell the President."

"Negative," he said crisply. "You don't seem to understand. We've screwed up. We're the ones who're supposed to provide intelligence ahead of time, and we didn't do it. I'm not telling the President anything until I can tell him what we can do to fix it! We're going to sit right here until we have a plan." He gave me a look. "You, Dannerman; you know what the subs are like. What's wrong with sending out antisubmarine ships with depth charges to take every one of them out?"

He took me by surprise, and I gave him a knee-jerk response. "No! Those things are full of innocent people! It's the Scarecrows on the scout ship that *make* them run the subs!"

He overrode me. "Screw the innocent freaks! I'm not going to jeopardize the world's safety for a bunch of space weirdos! Hilda! Get me the Combined Chiefs right now, conference call. Wake them up if you have to."

"Hey," I said. "Wait a minute."

Marcus Pell was as tired as I was, and probably even more frazzled. It was not a good time to be getting in his hair. Staring at me in a way that promised no kindness, he took a deep breath before he spoke. "I understand your concern for these animals on the subs. I don't want to hear about it again."

"Then listen to some common sense," I said. "It can't be done. You can't locate the subs except in general terms, from what the board in our sub shows, and there are twenty-five of them. If you're lucky enough to hit one, what do you think the other twenty-four will be doing?"

"Ah," he said. "I see." He thought for a moment. Then, "You successfully invaded one sub. Could we use that transit machine thing to do the same with the others?"

Hilda answered for me. "Same problem, Marcus. There are twenty-five of them. If we were real lucky, we might get two or three before the others fired off their whatever it is they fire. No, Marcus. We can't take them out one at a time. We have to go after the scout ship."

The deputy director suddenly came to life. "Hell, yes!" he cried, excited for the first time. "That could work! A couple of those armed spacecraft are pretty close to ready. We send them off to the scout ship, blow it out of space—"

"Marcus," Hilda said, "when the Scarecrows see those ships coming at them, what do you think they would do?"

"Oh," he said. "Hell. Then we send a commando through that transit machine, same as you did for the sub. Tough men, heavily armed, they come out of that thing shooting. When you strike at the snake's head you don't have to worry about the rest of the animal. Right, Dannerman?"

I hated to pour cold water on him, but I didn't have a choice. "I don't think it would work," I said. "When we hit the one sub we had four Horch fighting machines, and we were only up against two Scarecrow warriors and a couple of Docs—and even so, they put up a hell of a fight. I'd guess there'd be more in the scout ship, and they'd probably be watching the transit machines pretty closely."

"Expecting us to attack?"

"More likely expecting the Horch, but it'd come out to the same thing."

Hilda spoke up then. "There is one alternative," she said. "Instead of sending them a raiding party, what would happen if we send a bomb?"

The deputy director was frowning. "But that leaves all the subs still in place. Wouldn't they just push their buttons and start the methane release?"

He was looking at me. "Maybe not," I said cautiously. "If the scout ship was destroyed, the crews wouldn't be controlled anymore—except for the Dopeys. But we could get Pirraghiz on the horn to talk to them all, and they'd deal with their Dopeys. The others all hate the Scarecrows too, you know."

"So that's it," Hilda said. "We bomb the scout ship."

I found myself instinctively arguing against that one, too. "I don't think so, Hilda. We don't know how big the scout ship is, or how well bulkheaded. And there's a limit to the amount of mass the transit machine can handle at one time. A few hundred kilograms, maybe. And—"

I stopped. Hilda wasn't listening to me. As far as I could tell, her eyes were on the deputy director.

Who was looking at her with a considering expression I hadn't seen before. "You aren't thinking of chemical explosives, are you, Brigadier Morrisey?" he said.

That startled me. "Come on, Hilda," I said, "what're you talking about? Nukes? But they've been outlawed all over the world, ever since some of the terrorists got their hands on a couple."

She said reasonably, "Shut up, Danno." She waited for a moment to see if the deputy director was going to say anything else. When he didn't, she went on. "I've been hearing these rumors for years, Marcus. Latrine gossip. About how some nations have been cheating on the nuclear disarmament treaties, maybe stashed away a few little backpack-sized ones, just in case. Have you heard those stories, too?"

He stared at her tight-faced. Then he sighed. "Shit," he said. "You don't have any idea how much trouble this is going to make."

"More trouble than being exterminated, Marcus?" she asked politely.

He passed a hand over his face. "All right," he said. "Let me go talk to the President."

54

Things went fast then. I don't know who the President gave orders to, or what the orders were, but by the time I was back in the sub, telling Pirraghiz what she would have to do about talking to the other sub crews, the word came. A special jet from some installation in Amarillo, Texas, would be arriving in two hours with "the matériel that was requisitioned." Nothing more specific than that, but I knew what that matériel was going to be.

While the Docs were left to rerig the sub's comm systems so Pirraghiz would be able to talk to the crews when the time came, Hilda and I went into Beert's room. He was making himself as comfortable as possible on the cot that had never been designed for Horch anatomy. He lifted his head languidly toward me. "Hello, Dan," he said, his voice mournful. "I was sleeping. When I came back here I found myself thinking about our friend, the Wet One whom we sent to try to liberate his people—or, more likely, to his death. Do you suppose they have killed him yet?"

It was a good question. It reminded me, a little guiltily, that I hadn't given the amphibian a thought since we got back to Earth, had never even learned his name. But when I was translating what Beert had said for Hilda, she broke in. "Screw your noble hippopotamus friend, Danno. Tell the Horch what we're going to do."

So I did. "We need your help," I finished. "Also your robot, to operate the transit machine and find the right channels."

He waved his neck around thoughtfully for a moment. "Do I have a choice about helping you?" he asked.

I shrugged. "Do you want one?"

He considered that. Then he said, "Oh, perhaps not. Of all the things I have done for you that the Greatmother might not approve, I think blowing up a ship of the Others would be about the least. Very well. Let us get the robot, and I will instruct him in what you want done."

The little Scarecrow submarine was more crowded than it had ever been intended to be, and it still stank. I had forgotten about the persistent scorched-fish smell of the sub. For the two surprisingly elderly men from Amarillo, sweating in their white laboratory coats, it was something they had never experienced before. They didn't like it. They muttered to each other as they took the hatch plates off the "requisitioned matériel" and began to set their fuses. There were four of the chrome-plated beachballs, and I only hoped that the stink wasn't making the men careless in their settings.

Marcus Pell insisted on being present, though he stayed by my side, as far away from the nukes as we could get. It wasn't very far, and of course that kind of distance wouldn't have helped a bit if they had accidentally triggered one of the damn things. At the transit machine Beert's Christmas tree was methodically sorting out channels to the scout ship, with Foozh talking to it and Pirraghiz translating. "What are they saying?" Pell demanded. His collar was loose, and he looked nervous.

"The robot says there are evidently five transit machines on the scout ship."

"Hell!" Pell groaned. "We only have four bombs."

I didn't respond to that. If four nukes couldn't do the job, we were out of luck anyway. Beert drifted over, his neck pointed toward the bomb technicians. "Why are those persons so old?" he asked.

I told him, "I've been wondering the same thing. I guess there haven't been any additions to the nuclear weapons staff in a while." Which made the deputy director demand a translation of that, too.

Then the older of the techs stood up. "We're ready. Give us the word when you want to start the operation."

"You're sure these things will still work?" Pell barked.

The man shrugged. "Sure as we can be," he said. "Everything checks optimal. How about you, Deputy Director? Are you sure this machine will get them out of here right away? Because we've got sixty-second timers on them. It'll take about half that to activate the fuse, pop the hatch back and set the first bomb in the machine. If they're still here thirty seconds later, we aren't going to know it."

Pell swallowed and turned inquiringly to me. "Ask that thing," he ordered, pointing to Beert.

There wasn't any point in asking Beert again what he had already told us ten times, so I just observed to him that it was crowded in here, and when he agreed I reported to Pell: "He guarantees it."

The man from Amarillo sighed. He glanced at his partner, then said: "All right. We'll start arming the first device."

In the event, the men from Amarillo didn't take any thirty seconds. I guess they were worried about the time pressure; anyway, they closed up the first beachball pretty quickly and the two of them together rolled it on its little wheeled pallet over to the transit machine. By the time the door was closed and the Doc activated the transmission, less than twenty seconds had passed.

And when the Doc opened the door again, the chamber was empty.

So far, so good. "Reset for the second machine," I ordered the robot. It didn't move. All it did was extend a couple of twiglets questioningly toward Beert.

Who sighed. "You will obey this person," he ordered, and it did. When it reported the setting was complete I told the technicians to ready the second bomb; which went as expeditiously as the first.

But when it came to getting ready for the third, the Christmas tree fiddled for a while, then spoke up. "No additional transit machines are in operation at the target. It appears destruction is complete."

"Thank you," I said absently, thinking. Beert could not have known what I was thinking about, but it was clear that he knew something was going on in my head.

"What is it, Dan?" he asked worriedly, just as Pell ran out of patience: "What the hell, Dannerman? Are we going to send the third bomb or not?"

I gave Pell a shake of the head and turned to Pirraghiz. "Get on the horn to the subs!" I ordered. "Tell them to take their Dopeys into custody!"

And then, as she excitedly began meowing into the microphone, I faced Beert. "Do you want to go home?" I asked.

That shook him up. His head darted to within centimeters of my face, his jaw dropped. "Dan," he whispered pleadingly, "what are you saying?"

I couldn't meet his eyes. "Just answer the question," I said.

His long neck was trembling with excitement. "Go home, Dan? My belly yearns for it! Would you allow this?"

Marcus Pell was turning from Pirraghiz to me, his expression angry. "What's she jabbering about? What's going on?" he demanded.

I ignored Pell, speaking to the Christmas tree. "Can you transmit Djabeertapritch to the machines in the nest of the Eight Plus Threes?" And when it confirmed that it could, I ordered, "Set the machine up for transmission." And then at last I turned to the nearly apoplectic deputy director.

"I just wanted to make absolutely sure," I said apologetically. "The job's done. The survey ship is destroyed; there's nothing left to transmit to."

He made me repeat it two or three times, alternately blinking at me and at Pirraghiz as she meowed urgently into the ship-to-ship microphone. I jerked a thumb at the two remaining bombs. "Don't you think you should get the hoists back so we can get these things out of here?" I suggested.

That took him by surprise. "Right," he said, as glad as I thought he would be of the excuse to get away from them. And when he was out of the hatch to find the hoist operators, I said, "Good-by, Beert. Don't linger. If he comes back, he'll try to stop you."

Horch don't cry, but Beert's hard little nose was running as he wrapped those reptilian arms around me for a moment, then leaped into the chamber. The men from Amarillo were goggling at what was going on, but they didn't have any authority to prevent it.

I had one other thing to say to Beert. I held the door from closing for a moment, making him dart his head at me inquiringly. "Tell them for me, Beert," I said. "Tell them we will fight the Others in every way we can. We won't let them conquer us. But if we have to, we will fight the Horch as well. Tell them that."

"I will tell them, Dan," he said as I closed the door. And when it opened again the chamber was empty.

TWELVE

Victory

55

By the time Beert was gone the deputy director was already scrambling back down the ladder, shouting my name in a very unfriendly way. I didn't look at him. For that matter, I didn't stop to rejoice, or even take a deep breath; I had more important things to take care of.

First priority was giving Pirraghiz the orders to pass on to the sub crews: "Tell them all to turn off their transit machines and *keep them off.* Make sure they do that! Then," I added as an afterthought, "tell them all to head out to deep water and stay there." I didn't want any of them where somebody could try a depth bomb.

When I was sure she was passing the word on I turned back to the deputy director, interrupting his tirade. "I'm sorry, Marcus," I said, reasonably politely, "but I'm too busy to talk to you now."

That was nowhere near the kind of deference he was used to, and it made him yell even louder. "The hell you say! You've got a lot of explaining to do, Dannerman!"

I sighed, and put it less politely. "Shut the hell up," I ordered.

Amazingly, he did. Or else had a heart attack. He turned a peculiar color and sat down heavily on the nearest flat surface. Whatever he was doing, I let him do it and went back to Pirraghiz. "Have they all done what I said?" I demanded. She raised one of her lesser arms to fend the question off while she was meowing into the microphone and listening to the yowls that came back.

Then at last she turned that great pale face toward me and said, "They are doing it, Dannerman, but not without much trouble and fighting."

"Doing it isn't good enough! Make sure it really gets done, by every last one!"

"Yes, Dannerman," she sighed, and began polling the subs one by one. When it occurred to me to turn around again, Pell wasn't there anymore. He had evidently gone out of the sub again—probably, I thought, to line up a firing squad for me.

At that moment I didn't take much interest in what Pell might be up to. I was tired and cranky and not all that sure in my mind that I had done the right thing by letting Beert go. But it was done. Whatever the consequences might be, I had no way to deflect them.

Of those consequences there turned out to be plenty, though it took me a while to find out what they all were.

The deputy director didn't come back that day, but Lieutenant Colonel Makalanos did. He gave me another of those unfriendly looks, but he didn't say anything. He just sat down, silently watching my every move and occasionally stealing glances at the news screen he had brought with him. I wasn't ready to talk to him, so I did my best to pretend he wasn't there. It wasn't that hard. There was plenty of back-and-forth talk with the subs to keep me busy.

They had followed my orders. Every one of them had turned off its transit machine, and they were all slipping quietly away from the shallow coastal waters. None reported any human attempt to bother them.

It was time to start asking them questions. I did—at length—and the answers came back the same way. After nearly an hour of that I sighed and turned around to face Makalanos. "All right," I said. "I'd better tell you what they say the subs were doing so you can pass it on to the deputy director."

He leaned back and scratched his chin. "I was hoping you might," he said.

I let that go. "The freed crews, the Docs and the warriors, are all in control now. There was a lot of fighting. In the Sixteen Plus Eight and One—I mean in sub twenty-five—their Dopey tried to activate the methane release manually. They had to kill him. Four or five of the other Dopeys got killed too, but only one warrior died—his Dopey happened to have a weapon at the wrong time, so that was a close one. And," I added, "we were right about the methane, I think, although none of the controlled crews were ever told what was going on and the Dopeys, the ones that survived, aren't talking. Starting a couple of days ago the crews began receiving objects through their transit machines. They were tapered metal cylinders that they'd never seen before, and their orders were to push the things out through the disposal hatch. The crews weren't told what the objects were supposed to do. Dr. Schiel's idea was that they might use incendiaries, or maybe just high explosives, to blow up and release the trapped methane. It looks like he was right. I would guess," I said, striking off on my own, "that the bombs were meant to be triggered from the scout ship, but I don't think they were all in place yet. The sub crews were still busy emplacing the things when we blew the main ship up."

I stopped there. Makalanos was staring at me. "Jesus," he said. "And they're still out there, those live bombs?"

It was a dumb question, but it was one I hadn't thought of. "Shit," I said. "I guess somebody's going to have to pick them up and disarm them before we're through. Anyway, get the word out. The D. D.'s going to want to know all this."

"Oh," he said, gesturing to one of the cameras, "the word's out, all right, though whether anyone is paying attention right now, I don't know. They've got other things on their minds." And he turned his news screen around so I could see what was on it.

56

Things weren't going exactly the way I had expected. I had always understood that when you won a war it was a big event, so big that you stopped everything else to celebrate it. *Extensively,* with dancing in the streets, bands playing, maybe a ticker-tape parade down Broadway for the returning heroes with everybody laughing and drinking and hugging the handiest stranger.

There was no trace of any of that. When I looked at the screen what I saw was a free-for-all scramble for loot. The President had had nearly two hundred ambassadors all trying to make urgent diplomatic representations at once—plus every major executive in his own administration, plus Congress, plus every news medium and just about every single individual in the world who happened to know the telephone number of the White House. That was bad news for the deputy director's probable desire to have me shot. He would need the President's permission for that, and the President looked to be a lot too busy to give my personal future much of a thought.

See, that was the other thing that was different about winning this war.

As I understand it, the way it was usually done was that the victors took what they wanted that had formerly belonged to the losers—it was what they called the "spoils of war"—and everybody was happy (well, everybody except the losers).

This time it couldn't work out that way. The victors were everybody in the human race. But there were spoils of war, all right, mostly comprising those twenty-five free-ranging Scarecrow submarines. Each one of those subs was packed with so much priceless Scarecrow technology that every last nation on Earth was demanding to have one for its very own, and there just weren't anywhere near enough of the things to go around.

It was Pirraghiz who shook me loose from the news screen. "Are you all right, Dannerman?" she asked worriedly, touching my forehead with one lesser arm, like any human mother. "You appear to be near clinical exhaustion."

"I'm fine," I said, although it wasn't true. She peered incuriously at the screen, but didn't ask me what was going on and I didn't volunteer. "What's happening with the subs?"

She was looking worried. "The submarines are quite intact, but there is a problem," she said. "The crews no longer have functioning transit machines."

I was too tired to take her meaning right away. "Damn straight they don't! They're going to keep them that way, too."

She gave me one of those six-armed shrugs. "That is the problem," she said. "The crews will be getting hungry."

Well, I couldn't have thought of *everything*. It simply had not occurred to me that the transit machines were what kept the sub crews supplied with food and water. I swore a little bit, and then said reluctantly, "I guess we could make more food for them with the machine here, but maybe we're going to have to let them surrender themselves so we can get it to them."

"Perhaps not, Dannerman," she offered. "Mrranthoghrow says it is possible for the crews to rework the machines so that there can be no incoming, but they can be used to make copies from stored data. Is that all right?"

"If he's sure," I said reluctantly.

She looked at me with reproof. "Of course he is sure. I will tell him to give the order." And all the time she was talking she had begun touching me all over in the way I had become used to while I was recovering in the compound. "You require much more rest," she informed me, motherly and stern. "You cannot continue with this work without sleep indefinitely. Is it now an appropriate time to copy your translation module so that one may be inserted in some of your conspecifics?"

I blinked at her. I hadn't been thinking about that possibility. When she brought it back to my mind it seemed like the best idea I'd ever heard. Sharing the translation work with two or three of the linguists would delight them, and let me get a little time off—not to mention a little time to think about such personal matters as what I wanted to do about Patrice. On the other hand—

On the other hand, I had got pretty used to being the most important man in the world. I temporized. "We'll see about that when we get all this straightened out. How long will it take the crews to rejigger their machines?"

When she told me it seemed a reasonable time, so we began checking the subs, one by one, to make sure they could handle the job. And while we were doing that I felt Colonel Makalanos tap me on the shoulder. "It's Brigadier Morrisey," he said. "She's outside the sub and she wants to talk to you right away."

I thought about telling Hilda what I had told the deputy director. Still, getting out of the sub for a few minutes sounded pretty good to me, and besides, Hilda wasn't the deputy director. She was always thorny and sometimes she was just damned brutal, but she was my friend.

So I climbed the ladder up to the hatch and clambered down the one on the other side, breathing deeply of the cleaner air. Hilda was waiting for me at the foot of the ladder. "Well, Hilda," I said, "what's it going to be? Are you going to discipline me?"

Her box stirred slightly on its wheels. She said, "Not me, no. The President might, though. He wants to see you."

That wasn't good news. I stared at her vision plate that didn't look back. "Have a heart, Hilda! I can't leave here to go traipsing off to the White House."

"Who said White House? The President's got the idea that you're a VIP, Danno. Important enough for him to come to you. Right now his plane should be about touching down on the landing strip. Pop another wake-up pill and get over there. He'll be waiting for you."

57

The President hadn't tried to bring his big Air Force One to Camp Smolley. He had come in his VTOL, which was still an incongruously big ship to be perched on the camp's little landing strip. It was snow white with the lettering *THE UNITED STATES OF AMERICA* luminously emblazoned on its side.

At the plane's ramp an army of American Marines were guarding the VTOL under the eyes of an army of blue-beret United Nations troops. That was as far as Hilda was going to go. She stood motionless at the foot of the ramp while a couple of Marine officers body-searched me, their hands in all my pockets, their sniffers all over my body, poking into every fold of my clothes. At least they didn't bother with body cavities before they allowed me to enter. "Hurry up," the female colonel ordered me as she led the way to the President's cabin. "The President doesn't have much time."

Apparently he didn't. He didn't keep me waiting. When the colonel shoved me into his office the President was sitting at his desk, looking up from his array of miniscreens to regard me. There was no one else in the room, just the President and me, though I had no doubt there were eyes and recording gadgets in the walls—and maybe even, behind some panel, a Marine sharp-shooter with his weapon aimed at my heart, just in case. When the President had finished looking me over, he said, "Sit down. Talk to me."

So I did.

I had never been alone with the President before. He looked a lot older than his pictures: suntanned face, mop of curly white hair, the powerful shoulders of the Harvard oarsman he had once been. He was a lot better listener than I had expected. He didn't interrupt. He didn't speak at all. A couple of times, when he wasn't quite catching everything I had to say, he cocked one of those bushy white eyebrows at me. Which I interpreted as a request to clarify, so I clarified. When I got to the part about letting Beert go home he didn't start throwing the book at me. He looked, if anything, amused. He didn't speak then, either, or even push any buttons that I saw, but a moment later the office door opened and a pair of good-looking girls in Marine uniform pushed in a dolly with white linen, a silver coffeepot and two cups. "Help yourself, Agent Dannerman," the President said, speaking at last. "So you took it upon yourself to order the Scarecrow subs away from the coast.

There didn't seem to be any point in trying to explain my reasons, so I just said, "Yes, sir."

He nodded. "Maybe that was the smart thing to do. Or," he corrected himself, "the wise thing, anyway. It's not hard to be smart in politics. It's a lot tougher to be wise. Of course, that doesn't solve the long-range problem of what to do with the aliens on board."

"No, sir."

The President sipped his coffee meditatively for a moment, and then he sighed and began to talk. "Ever since you got here, Agent James Daniel Dannerman Number Three," he said, "your friend Marcus Pell has been on my ass. He likes you even less now. He says letting a known enemy of America go free—he's talking about your Horch friend—is something pretty close to, his word, treason."

That made me start to open my mouth, but he gave me the kind of look that made me close it again. "See," he said, "I don't agree with him. I'll tell you what I think. I think you were protecting a friend, and you've way exceeded your authority to do it. Don't say yes or no to that, Dannerman. It's not an accusation. It's what I might be doing myself, if I were in your shoes, and anyway it's done, so we just have to live with it. But it does make a problem."

He paused long enough to refill his coffee cup, motioning me to do the same to mine. He didn't seem to be in nearly as much of a hurry as I had thought, and then he began to get reminiscent.

I don't know if you paid any attention to my election," he said. "Sixty-seven percent of the voters evidently didn't, because they didn't bother to go to the polls at all. I won with fifty-four percent of the thirty-three percent who voted. That wasn't much of a mandate, actually—though that's not what I say to the Congress. I campaigned on two main issues: Stop inflation, stop terrorism. So I'm batting five hundred right about now. I haven't been able to do a thing about the inflation rate, but terrorism is down all over the world. Did I do that? No. It happened on my watch, so I take the credit, but what did it was the Scarecrows. It has now become pretty clear to most people that someday we're all going to find ourselves in a shooting war worse than any we've ever known before, and if we don't hang together, like the fellow says, we're sure to hang separately.

"So, for the first time in the history of the world, the human race is starting to act as though there are more important things than what some part of us wants to do to some other part.

"I'm not talking about the various nations. They've all got their own superpatriots—I won't name any names, but you can probably think of a couple right here—and they're all getting grabby. But we can deal with that, as long as the terrorists don't screw everything up. They aren't doing that, Dannerman. The IRA, the Tamil Tigers, the militants in our own country, the Sons of Palestine, even the Lenni-Lenape Ghost Dancers—they've all been turning in their weapons caches, and even the ones that haven't gone that far are mostly laying low. For that matter, the Floridians are beginning to talk as though they were part of the United States again. I can see it happening myself—do you know that nobody's tried to assassinate me for nearly three months? And it's not just here. Why, a couple of Sundays ago the President of the Russian Republic took his grandchildren for a walk in Gorky Park without a single bodyguard, and nobody roughed them up.

"I like that. It makes my job a lot easier. And I don't want it to stop."

He finished his coffee, looking into space for a moment, as though he were coming to an important decision.

As a matter of fact, he was. "So, two things," he said. "As long as you're exceeding your authority, exceed it one more time. Don't let any of those subs contact any human forces until, and how, I tell you. I don't want them landing anywhere until we've sorted this out a little better. All right?"

I said, "Yes, sir." At that point I would have said, "Yes, sir," to just about anything the man said.

"Good," he said. "The other thing doesn't affect you directly, but I think you ought to know. Today I'm going to push all the chips into the middle of the table. I've asked our UN ambassador to call an emergency session of the General Assembly, and I'm heading up there as soon as I've finished with you. I'm going to admit that to attack the Scarecrow ship we used a few nukes that we'd stashed away—well, I don't have much choice about admitting that. Pell wanted me to claim we'd used only conventional chemical bombs, but the astronomers have already detected gamma radiation from where the Scarecrow ship used to be, so that's that. And I'm going to tell the General Assembly exactly how many nukes we still have, and exactly where they're hidden, and I'm going to invite UN troops to come in to safeguard them. And I'm going to release every last bit of data we have on the Scarecrows and the Horch, including all your translations and all the secret work we've done at the NBI place in Arlington. And I'm going to tell them that, using my powers as President, I am pledging to accept whatever decisions the UN makes as to where the submarines at sea should go, and what should be done with them.

"And then I'm going to come back here and face up to the Congress. God knows what they'll do to me.

"But that's not your problem, is it? So you go back to work, Agent Dannerman Number Three, and—Now what? Is something bothering you?"

I said, "Sort of. I mean yes, definitely. I was hoping to get out of this job pretty soon."

The President looked surprised. He opened his mouth to speak to me, but someone somewhere cleared his throat. So instead the President said testily to the air, "What is it, Hewitt?"

The air sounded apologetic. "It's your appointment with the ambassador, sir. If you want to meet with him before you go to the General Assembly, we're cutting it pretty close."

"We'll cut it a little closer. Call him to say we'll be late." Then, to me, "What did you have in mind?"

So I told him about my hope of fitting some others with language implants, and what Pirraghiz had said about my needing more rest, not to mention my wanting to get on with some of my personal concerns. And then—because he seemed to own the most sympathetic ear I was likely to have for a while—I went on to tell him what some of those personal concerns were, such as Patrice Adcock.

When I ran down he took another meditative sip of coffee, and then he looked up at me and grinned.

"I love solving other people's problems," he said, "because they're always so easy. You've got yourself tangled up in a problem that doesn't exist, Agent Dannerman. I've met your Patrice, you know, briefing me on Threat Watch now and then. Seems like a very nice woman to me. Why do you think she isn't the real one?"

I frowned. "Because she's a copy, naturally."

"Naturally she is," he agreed, "but so are you, aren't you? And how 'real' do you think you are? Shit, man! Marry the girl, if she'll have you. Only," he said apologetically, "don't count on any long honeymoons, because I've got to say no to making any more translators just now. See, you're all I've got."

I can't say I didn't hear the last part of what he said. It was on a sort of delay circuit, though, shunted aside while I considered what he had said about me and Patrice. As the man said, other people's problems were the easiest to solve, especially when—as he said—the problem didn't exist, but was only something I had put into my own head.

Then I woke up to his last remarks. I said. "What?"

He was patient with me. "The thing is, as long as you're the one and only person who can talk to these, ah, persons from other planets, everybody has to be reasonable. I'll make damn sure this job is made as easy as possible for you, Dannerman, I give you my word. But until further notice, I'm afraid you're stuck. If that's all right with you?" he added, just as though I had a choice.

I said glumly, "I guess."

He grinned and stood up, shaking my hand to show that the interview was over. He didn't let go of it right away, though. He said, "I know what you're thinking, Dannerman. You're saying to yourself, 'Cripes, I just got these guys out of the worst trouble they've ever been in, so doesn't that settle it?' Only it doesn't, Dan. It never does. You solve one problem and another one comes up and starts biting you on the ass before you have a chance to catch your breath. Welcome to the real world, where the only final solutions come when you die. And," he added, dexterously turning me toward the door as he let go of my hand, "if these people are right, maybe not even then."

Author's Note

One of the questions that confront a science-fiction reader is to decide how much of the "science" in a story is real—i.e., is at the time of writing consensually agreed by a significant number of actual scientists—and how much is made up by the author. I don't personally make up much in my writing. I do, however, quite often make use of scientific ideas that have been put forth by some actual scientist but fall a long way short of being consensual. For example, I did not make up the faster-than-light "tachyons" I have used in this story (and in others) in order to provide a mechanism for getting my characters around this very large universe in reasonable travel times. They were originally proposed by Dr. Gerry Feinberg and others thirty or more years ago. Tachyons may or may not exist. There is no direct evidence that they do. Feinberg was able to show that they are not excluded by relativity theory; but they have never been detected. So the question remains open for scientists—but, in my view, such concepts are perfectly legitimate for writers like myself to borrow.

Which, I think, is also true of the concept which provides the central thesis of this story, the "Omega Point" or eschaton at which every person who has ever lived will, it is said, live again, and then go on doing so forever.

Much of what I know about the stranger scientific ideas that are floating around comes from the kindness of friends, who know what sort of thing interests me and are often good enough to send me copies of obscure papers from unlikely sources. The stimulus which led to the present story came from a paper by Dr. Frank Tipler, sent to me some years ago by Dr. Hans Moravec of the Robotics Institute at Carnegie-Mellon University. Tipler's paper, originally published in a journal devoted to religious questions, was quite tentative in tone. However, it appears that, having started thinking on the subject, Tipler began to feel that he was onto something really important. So in 1994 he published a book, *The Physics of Immortality,* expanding on the original notion and buttressing it with what he says are formal, scientific proofs that it is true. There are some differences between the arguments in the original paper and those in the book, however, and I should mention that in this novel I have preferred to follow those of the original paper.

Tipler's claimed scientific proofs take the form of quite abstruse arugments that are dense with equations and occupy 223 pages in his book. I am not qualified to pass judgment on the accuracy of his science, and the reviews of the book that I have seen in various scientific publications have been, to put it as impartially as possible, pretty uniformly unconvinced. Still, Tipler is a heavyweight scientist in his own right, and we all know that the history of science is full of pioneers who were at first scorned—but were ultimately shown to be correct.

So the question remains: Are we indeed all going to be reborn at some remote time eons in the future?

I don't know. If I had to bet, I must confess that I would be inclined to bet quite heavily against it . . . but it is certainly pretty to think so.

FREDERIK POHL

Palatine, Illinois
March 1995

About the Author

A multiple Hugo and Nebula Award–winning author, Frederik Pohl has done just about everything one can do in the science fiction field. His most famous work is undoubtedly the novel *Gateway,* which won the Hugo, Nebula, and John W. Campbell Memorial awards for Best SF novel. *Man Plus* won the Nebula Award. His mature work is marked by a serious intellectual agenda and strongly held sociopolitical beliefs, without sacrificing narrative drive. In addition to his successful solo fiction, Pohl has collaborated successfully with a variety of writers, including C. M. Kornbluth and Jack Williamson. The Pohl/Kornbluth collaboration, *The Space Merchants,* is a longtime classic of satiric science fiction. *The Starchild Trilogy* with Williamson is one of the more notable collaborations in the field. Pohl has been a magazine editor in the field since he was very young, piloting *Worlds of If* to three successive Hugos for Best Magazine. He also has edited original-story anthologies, including the early and notable *Star* series of the early 1950s. He has at various times been a literary agent, an editor of lines of science fiction books, and a president of the Science Fiction Writers of America. For a number of years he has been active in the World SF movement. He and his wife, Elizabeth Anne Hull, a prominent academic active in the Science Fiction Research Association, live outside Chicago, Illinois.